THE COLOR ALCHEMIST

THE COMPLETE SERIES

NINA WALKER

ADDISON & GRAY PRESS
WWW.NINAWALKERBOOKS.COM

Published by Addison & Gray Press, LLC.

ISBN: 978-1-950093-14-4

For the dreamers and romantics

PRISM

THE COLOR ALCHEMIST BOOK ONE

ONE

JESSA

I didn't collect secrets. I only had one. One little, messy mistake I'd kept buried in the back of my mind for months. Now, I felt the danger of its existence as I stared into the eyes of the person whose job it was to dig up those secrets. She would inch around it, gentle at first, before she'd rip it out by the roots. Then the intruder would take it away, and I would go with it.

"Do you know why we're here?" the royal officer asked. Her glare locked me in. I shook my head, knowing the lie had to be seamless.

The officers had come with their questions on the worst possible morning. Every minute of this day should have been spent preparing for the most anticipated ballet performance of my life. Not this. Anything but this.

I wanted nothing to do with magic.

I glanced at my parents and little sister. The four of us sat side by side on the sleek couch. Our bodies stuck together as the summer heat pressed its way through the family room. Lately, our luxuries, like air conditioning, were faltering. We didn't ask why. We just waited, letting the sweat permeate our lives.

My sister Lacey nervously held our dad's arm with one hand and grasped mine with the other. Aged six, she couldn't know what was at stake, but she could sense the danger all the same.

"Lacey, I have some questions for you," the royal officer in charge said, showing a tight-lipped smile. She was a pale woman, with severe cheekbones and a glossy, tight blond bun.

Her subordinates lined the walls of our living room. They stood at attention, stony expressions etched into their features. They wore white uniforms, the royal family insignia was stitched on the left shoulder of each. I'd never actually seen a royal officer of the court before, and I'd hoped I never would. They were the highest level, the protectors of the monarchs and alchemists. They didn't belong in my living room.

The lead officer reached into her pocket and pulled out a small vial. It was deep crimson, filled to the brim. She held it up between her long fingers, showing us the blood inside. She reached into her other pocket and pulled out a second vial. The lifeless, gray fluid seemed unrelated, but from the way her eyes leered at Lacey, something wasn't right.

"Do you know what this is?"

But Lacey's face only registered the same confusion as before. How was a child supposed to understand what it was, especially when everyone else was clueless? Well, not everyone. Not me.

"What about you, Jessa?" She arched an eyebrow in my direction. "Any ideas?"

"I don't know." The lie burned my throat but came out smooth.

"This is a sample of Lacey's blood."

My father sprang from the couch. He grabbed Lacey. She wrapped her thin arms around him and began to cry. The room grew unimaginably hotter. Gray blood? That had to be linked to alchemy. And anywhere there was alchemy was not a place Lacey should be.

My mother shook her head, apparently refusing to understand. "What's wrong? Is Lacey sick?"

"Lacey is lucky. She'll be fine. Our mission is to find out who did this to your daughter. Of course, it's likely she did it to herself."

Mom's hand flew to her mouth. Dad tightened his grip on Lacey.

I sat still on the couch, lost as to how to fix this. I tried to keep my breathing in check, fighting the suffocation pressing down on my body. How could this be happening? I'd kept Lacey's run in with alchemy hidden for months. Never uttering a word, I protected my family. But despite all that, our life was about to unravel anyway.

"Did you see anything you didn't understand? Did anyone hurt you?"

The woman's voice drew us back to the truth. Something was happening to Lacey and this woman didn't care how that might affect the rest of us.

Everyone quickly settled back into the couch.

"No," Lacey replied. She looked at Dad as her lower lip trembled. He wiped at her tear-stained cheeks. "Am I in trouble?" she asked.

"No, you're not in trouble," the woman continued with fake tenderness in her voice. She wasn't fooling me. "But it's important you tell the truth so that you won't be in trouble later." The threat lingered.

Lacey nodded, her eyes glued to the woman.

It was finally clear that she was speaking of color alchemy. She had to be probing for something, hoping that Lacey would slip up on an important detail. Then they would take her away to some guarded place color alchemists go, to train her as their own. The problem with that? She wouldn't come back.

No matter how much I wanted to stay in denial, I knew it was true. Something *had* happened to Lacey on that cold day six months ago. I wanted to believe it was just a playground accident gone awry. But I'd known. Of course I'd known. It was color alchemy; the strange ability, that mysterious magic that allowed color to be used as a tool. Sure, it was mostly an unknown to a regular girl like me. But what else could it have been? It was the only explanation.

An explanation that I hated accepting.

Color alchemists were sent away from home as soon as they were discovered, no matter their age. And they didn't return. I'd seen it twice myself.

The first time, it happened to the neighbors, three houses down. Their boy seemed normal enough. He was the instigator, the ringleader of the boys our age. On those warm summer nights, I sometimes watched as they ran wild through the quiet streets. Even though I was also seven, they always said girls weren't allowed to play. I didn't mind so much, I wanted to be a ballerina anyway.

And then one day, that boy, his name long forgotten now, was simply gone. When I asked Mom and Dad, they'd briefly explained what a color alchemist was, then asked me to drop the issue. No one talked about it. His parents moved a few months later and that was the end of it. It wasn't until the next spring, when the same thing happened to a girl in the classroom across the hall, that I started to ask more questions.

Between the hushed whispers and rumors, I knew little, but enough. The younger the alchemist was when discovered, the better. They were trained, day in and day out, to harness the magic in color and use it to society's advantage. No one I knew really understood the details about color alchemy and those who wielded its supernatural power. They, and their strange magic, were kept out of the public eye. We did know that it kept our electricity strong, our medical facilities advanced, food on our tables, and most importantly, alchemy kept the rest of the world out of our prosperous kingdom. Our neighboring enemies hadn't maneuvered a successful attack in decades.

We also knew to keep a lookout for anything out of the ordinary, anything unexplainable. The law mandated us to report possible color alchemy immediately.

Again, I wasn't entirely sure what "possible alchemy" was, or how I'd recognize it. I guessed the idea was that I'd be a good citizen, going about my business, and if something magical happened, I'd report it.

Instead, I kept the secret hidden. When Lacey's blood had changed before my very eyes, I didn't report a thing. I couldn't risk the outcome!

One thing everyone knew about color alchemists: they became members of the most elite and secretive branch in the kingdom, the Guardians of Color. "GC" for short.

The Royals assured us that we needed the GC. They said the guardians assisted our society economically. Their magic provided us with extra power, aided industry in advancement, and even sustained crops. Otherwise, there wouldn't be enough food to go around. While most of the world suffered, the people of New Colony, our home, thrived. We had everything we needed in our kingdom. More, actually. And it was all because of alchemy and the royal family's guidance.

But having this mysterious ability ruined people's lives. Freedom wasn't a possibility for alchemists. Not really. Their mission was too important. I was grateful I wasn't one of them. I couldn't imagine having such valuable abilities discovered as a small child, being trained to forget about my family just to learn how to do a job. A job so important that there was absolutely no other choice but to do it, and do it well.

The royal officer droned on but I couldn't quiet my mind about the day that started all of this. The day, six months ago, when Lacey had injured herself on the playground and the unimaginable happened.

My heart ached to think Lacey was an alchemist, but I didn't have any other explanation. After all, it was little children who developed color alchemy. She was six. It made sense.

I wanted to protect her. Whether on the playground or in my own living room, I couldn't.

With the gray vial now gripped in this royal officer's hand, I was sure Lacey had used alchemy on her own blood. What had that done to her? The magic only lasted a moment.

I peered at the royal officer as she ordered her underlings to begin searching our home. They wanted answers. Too bad there was no way I was going to let Lacey slip away. Valuable to society or not, she was my little sister, my only sibling. She wasn't going anywhere.

I peered out the window and wondered if any of our neighbors were aware of what was happening in their seemingly safe neighborhood. Did they have any idea that we were harboring a potential color alchemist?

"Jessa Loxley." The royal officer turned her gaze on me. "We have reason to believe that either you or your sister may have performed unauthorized color alchemy. One of you, or someone you know, tampered with Lacey's blood and failed to report the incident to the proper authorities."

So it *was* true…

Lacey was a color alchemist. Her own blood betrayed her.

Lacey was still confused. I was grateful she didn't remember the accident. She had likely been so traumatized that she'd blocked the whole memory. Lacey needed to stay here, with us. Her family. The truth would only get in the way of that. I had to come up with a plausible story and cover for Lacey, to convince this woman that there wasn't an alchemist here.

"Why is her blood gray?" I prodded. "What does that mean for Lacey?"

"That information is classified."

"Okay," I said. "And who are you again?"

I had to be bold. I had to do something to get the attention away from Lacey.

"As I already told your parents, I'm Royal Officer Faulk, I preside over the Guardians of Color."

Her official-sounding title wouldn't stop me.

Dad reached out, resting his hand on my knee. "Jessa, please behave yourself." His tone didn't scold, but it was stern. Could he know I was lying? And if he did, would he want me to continue?

Mom and Dad were accustomed to me being on my best behavior around "important" people. I was walking a thin line.

"Are you an alchemist, then?" I asked.

"No. Royal officers are never alchemists. I'm here as part of our Illegal Color Alchemy Task Force," Faulk spoke slowly.

"Yes, I get that," I said. "Which is why it makes no sense that you're here."

"Jessa!" My mother's sharp elbow jutted against my arm. I caught her wide eyes, but quickly looked the other way. She might've disliked my attitude now, but she'd thank me later.

"We've been alerted about unusual properties in Lacey's blood work." Faulk narrowed her eyes. "You are aware that she recently underwent a physical examination?"

I stared at her dead on. *Bring it, lady, let's see what you've got.*

Dad was the first to respond. "Lacey had a bad accident about six months ago on the playground. She went to the hospital recently for a follow-up. But what does any of this have to do with Jessa?" His brow furrowed as he exchanged a quick look with Mom.

"You were the only one with Lacey during her accident." Faulk watched me as she spoke. "There were no other reported witnesses, except the person who heard the cry and called the police. After going to the hospital, Lacey was stitched up and sent home. If it hadn't have been for the follow-up, no one would have known that she had a small amount of gray blood flowing through her system. The doctor immediately extracted it. She's lucky there wasn't more of it…very lucky."

"I didn't see anything unusual during her accident," I said pointing to the vial still in Faulk's grip. "How was I supposed to know she had gray blood? Was I supposed to be watching out for something specific? No one told me."

Once again, Faulk ignored my question.

She held my gaze. "As you know, any unauthorized color alchemy is illegal. If you or someone you know has failed to report their abilities, now is your chance to speak up before we start a full-scale investigation. This is a very serious offense that could result in jail time and many citizen privileges revoked."

"Citizen privileges?" my mother asked.

"Surely, Mrs. Loxley, you already know what I am speaking of." Royal Officer Faulk peered closely at my mother.

I frowned. What did they know that I didn't?

The room was silent as I considered my next move. If I lied to cover for her, I risked getting caught. I didn't care about what would happen to me as much as I cared about how it would damage my family. What would this woman do to my parents if she knew I was hiding alchemy? I had heard rumors of people losing their jobs and homes, being forced to relocate to undesirable locations and work long hours in factories or other menial jobs outside the capital city. Was it true?

Surely, the consequences couldn't be that harsh? Surely, it was understandable why a sixteen-year-old girl wouldn't want her little sister to be taken away?

Surely, New Colony didn't care?

I didn't think my parents knew about Lacey, but if they did, what would they do? If I told the truth right now, then Lacey would be taken from our home. There was no way they'd be okay with that.

Her color alchemy had been an accident. No one had meant to break any laws. From the looks on the officials' faces, they wouldn't take pity on us either way. Maybe Faulk could help Lacey, but that was a risk I couldn't take.

And of course, there was ballet to think about. Ballet was my life. My passion. I'd worked so hard to become a dancer with New Colony's Royal Ballet Company. Last season I was signed as a novice, and had attended classes nonstop for months. I had pushed myself through vigorous training and worked through the pain of bruised feet and sore muscles—not to mention the mental and emotional stresses that were normal in the world of competitive dance.

I've worked too hard to let anything get in my way.

Tonight, in fact, was one of the deciding moments of my life. I had landed a solo. And, as small as it was, it was a significant step forward for my professional career. I finally had a chance to dance on the most coveted stage, in front of a truly respectable audience. The royal family, many members of the court, high-ranking citizens, and government officials, were all scheduled to attend. It would be the chance of a lifetime. My problem? The opening performance was tonight. If I told the truth now, I would certainly lose the opportunity. I'd no doubt be sent away for more questioning.

Even if that didn't happen, if word got out about Lacey, the Royal Ballet Company wouldn't want me anymore. They were incredibly cautious about their reputation—any opportunities they afforded us dancers came with the expectation that we were unblemished model citizens. I had no doubt that hiding a color alchemist would make me unsavory. I might never be allowed to put on another pointe shoe.

That thought alone terrified me far beyond Faulk's threats.

"I honestly don't know what you're talking about," I told Faulk. "I've never even seen color alchemy in person. Most people never do. And it's not like I would know what it was if I saw it."

Faulk shook her head. "I've been doing my job a long time, Jessa. I know that the most probable scenario here is that someone in this family or Lacey herself caused the abnormality in her blood. And you all also have the biggest motive to keep any involvement with color alchemy hidden. Illegally, I might add. So if you choose to keep lying to me, where do you think I will go from here?"

This can't be happening. How am I going to fix this? If I don't figure out how to get these people out of here, Faulk will take Lacey away for sure.

The idea came quickly, like an unexpected gift.

"Didn't they give Lacey a blood transfusion? Have you questioned everyone at the hospital? Maybe there was an accident."

Faulk paused, and from the frustration lining her face, I knew I had backed her into a corner.

She stood up, barking orders at the other royal officers to get ready to head back to headquarters. From the way she took control over everyone, I figured she was a general or something. Didn't matter. A wave of triumph swept through my body. She wouldn't be gone forever, but at least I'd bought us some time.

My parents, each visibly relieved, stood to see the officers out. I smiled slightly, happy that I'd managed to save the day.

When she got to our front door, Faulk turned around and gave her final warning. "Color alchemy is an extremely rare and dangerous talent. There are reasons we've created strict laws policing it. Those who don't know how to use it properly aren't just hurting themselves. They are ticking time bombs waiting to explode."

She slowly looked us each over as she waited for someone to break. When a confession didn't come, she nodded at one of her remaining royal officers. He was the oldest man in the room, and I could tell he didn't buy my story either.

"Let's go, Thomas. I've got a busy day. I don't have time to deal with people who won't talk."

The man began rallying the final few officers out the door. They were eerily quiet for such large creatures.

"You had your chance," Faulk added as she moved out into the morning light. The door shook when she slammed it behind her.

We sat there for a moment, frozen, before Lacey broke the silence.

"Am I in trouble?" She rubbed her red-rimmed eyes.

"Don't worry, honey," I said, reaching for her hand again. "Everything is going to be okay. Let's just get back to our day and forget about all of this."

"What's going on here, Jessa?" My mother turned to me, her voice shaking. "Did you lie to that royal officer? If something happened with alchemy, you need to tell us right now. We can help but we need to know what we are dealing with here."

Everything in me wanted to tell them the truth. But I just couldn't put them in such a terrible position.

"I told you. I have no idea what that was about. That woman is jumping to conclusions. Lacey is fine. I mean, look at her."

My parents exchanged a guarded glance. Mom held her hand to her hip, head cocked, as she studied me before taking in Lacey. There was no question that she appeared the same as always. After a tense moment, Dad let out a long sigh.

"We'd better get you something to eat," he said as he reached for Lacey.

I immediately went upstairs to my bedroom. Finally alone, I let out a deep breath, willing the stress to fall away. It didn't work. Not with what I now knew. Not with the truth burning its way into my every thought.

Lacey was an alchemist, and I'd just committed a crime.

■

The accident flashed through my memory.

Babysitting Lacey for a few hours between ballet rehearsal and Mom and Dad getting home from work was part of my daily agenda. On that day, just like most days, I took Lacey to our neighborhood playground. On that brisk January afternoon, the cool air was refreshing on my sore dancer muscles.

Lacey immediately ran to the swings. She jumped in the seat and rocked herself higher and higher with each motion. Giggling as she swung, she leaned forward as if she were about to sprout wings.

"Slow down, Lace!" I yelled, and a twinge of worry cracked my voice.

Beyond her, the bare trees held onto the last fragments of fall.

I sat down on the bench and began running through the highlights from this afternoon's rehearsal. Ballet had been tough lately, but I smiled knowing that I'd done well. Better than yesterday, which was always my goal.

Abruptly, Lacey's hands slipped and her little body catapulted from the seat. For the brief moment, she was in flight.

Stunned, I watched my little sister crash into the waiting earth. Mounds of frozen gravel pummeled her face.

What followed was blood. A lot of blood.

It poured from her knees, her wrists, and her palms. And the worst of it streamed from her mouth.

I sprinted to her in a dizzying frenzy. I held her close, fumbling to assess the damage. The mix of confusion and anguish cut into her features as she let out a sharp cry. There was so much blood. I didn't know how to fix her. I frantically looked around for help. The area was deserted.

I looked back at Lacey, and something strange and peaceful grew inside. An overwhelming feeling of love passed through me. The world stilled as a gentle calm ran through my body. I looked at my beautiful little sister, battered and hurt, and a fierce urgency to help her took over my senses.

"It's okay. I'll take care of you. It will be as if this never even happened. You'll see."

Lacey wailed, oblivious as I tried to soothe her. Tears rolled down her face as she gasped for breath. I needed her to calm down, to hold still so I could help.

"Stop crying."

She immediately relaxed, her cries fading. We sat there, covered in her blood and stared at the stream of life pouring from her. All logical thought disintegrated as I realized what I was seeing.

The deep red of her blood had turned pale pink. And just as strange, it continued to change as it faded to ashy gray. I sat motionless.

Her red blood had actually *changed*, physically altered its color. How was that even possible?

It still poured out of her in waves, but the blood was no longer its normal color.

Even stranger was the air that wrapped around us, a cloud of luminous red energy, seemingly not of this world. I almost didn't notice when Lacey lost consciousness.

It all happened so fast. Too fast.

Later, when she came to, I questioned Lacey. She didn't understand what I was talking about. The whole incident was wiped from her vulnerable mind. How was that possible?

It took the medics a while to arrive at the scene and cart Lacey off to be stitched up. Thankfully, a neighbor had heard the cries and called an ambulance. Maybe Lacey had become so weak that her mind blocked the memory. I could only pray it was all a big mistake.

I still didn't want to admit how one second her blood could be gray, and the next, return to vibrant red. It had to be alchemy.

It all happened so fast. The next thing I knew, the medics were shaking me, calmly asking their standard questions. They took my pulse and gave me some water as they assessed Lacey and the wide pool of red blood around us. The gray was nowhere to be seen. She was small enough that the wounds on her knees, palms, face, and tongue warranted her going to the hospital for stitches and painkillers. She even ended up needing a blood transfusion.

They drove away with Lacey, actually leaving me in that empty playground. I couldn't believe it. At least someone had contacted our parents, who were already on their way to meet the ambulance.

I sat in a daze. The worn black crescent seat of the swing still swayed.

The next six months were spent in anguish over what really happened. I had nightmares about it, tortured by the idea of speaking up. Whatever had happened to us, it seemed no one knew. I doubted Lacey would understand it. When it turned out she didn't remember, I tried to push the memories away, hoping my suspicions were all wrong.

Either way, I was grateful no one else was on the playground that day. And thank goodness that a neighbor had alerted the authorities. That someone was able to find us, and help her.

Because, apparently, I couldn't.

■

I walked to the bedroom window and peered between the curtains. Outside, the flashing lights from the officers' vehicles were gone, but I was sure this wasn't over. It appeared to be a quiet, lazy morning in our typical capital city suburb. The tall trees in our neighbor's yard cast long shadows in the early sunrise. Something shifted beyond them.

I stopped, not daring to move as I waited to see what, or who, was there. Several minutes passed before a royal officer emerged. He was dressed in the same white uniform. He stood motionless, his eyes scanning our house.

General Faulk might be gone for now, but that didn't mean we were in the clear. She'd left someone to watch us.

Why would she do that?

The answer hit me like an arrow to the heart.

To make sure we don't take Lacey and run.

TWO

LUCAS

"It's time to put that away, son." My father's dark tone failed to match his charming smile. The smile said, *There are people watching us, so you better behave.* A warning more than a piece of advice. I ignored him and continued swiping the glass surface of my state-of-the-art slatebook. It was the only thing that entertained me during these dull evenings. Well, that and the beautiful women.

If my parents were going to insist on my attendance at these ridiculous social events, they ought to be impressed that I was busying myself and not doing anything to embarrass them. Like flirting, or drinking, or flat-out leaving.

It was true that I liked to ruffle their feathers every now and again. But normally, I played along with their games. Yesterday, it was a political dinner; today, it would be the ballet.

Because where else would an eighteen-year-old guy want to spend his Friday nights?

My whole life I'd been told how lucky I was to be the only child of the New Colony royal family. I was the only heir to the throne of the world's leading nation. But the envy bothered me more than I let on. People only saw the façade, the smoke and mirrors of politics.

I knew the truth.

My mother softly touched my arm. Her pleasant smile contradicted the look in her eyes. "Please respect your father's wishes."

I sighed and slipped the thin device into my pocket. I'd give her this small victory. It was hard to see her this way, so meek and agreeable…a wisp of the woman she once was. She'd changed so dramatically over the years. I preferred to remember her as she had been during my childhood.

She never laughed anymore.

Lately, my mother had become "Natasha" to me. My father himself had always preferred being called "Richard" instead of "Dad." But being on a first-name basis with my parents didn't make me feel like an equal—it made me a stranger. At least she had been attending more functions with us in the past few months. I was accustomed to my mother spending most of her time in her darkened bedroom, fighting her chronic headaches. Headaches that even the most gifted color alchemists couldn't seem to cure. Now that she was out again, I was grateful not to be alone with Richard. He was easier to deal with, during the constant barrage of events, when she was there. My mother had a way of getting me to behave.

Tonight would be different.

I relaxed into the red padded theatre chair and stared blankly at the people in the auditorium below. They were always watching us. They wanted nothing more than to impress my father. *Well, good luck.*

On the surface, he was the perfect king. He was handsome, charming, and well-spoken. He was easy to believe in, easy to follow. Everyone trusted him. I, however, knew that he wasn't as he appeared.

But no one ever asked my opinion.

A few of our palace servants were strewn across the balcony with us tonight. Like my mother and our security team, they all carefully watched Richard. He was the sun and we were the planets, moving in sequence around him year after year. But lately, I had started to think of myself as something else: an asteroid. Cutting through the blackness. Making my own path.

My father motioned to Thomas. He was one of our top royal officers, our oldest. He'd known me my whole life.

The ruddy man scurried over, then straightened the white jacket of his uniform. He was a royal officer, not to be confused with a guardian. Alchemists didn't get to come to public venues like the ballet. Ever. And they didn't wear white. They wore black.

"Why is there someone else in a theatre box?" Richard asked, stiff in his over-sized chair.

I knew better than to trust the calmness in his voice.

Across the auditorium, a plump man sat with his two young boys. They were all dressed in matching tuxedos. The children were comically endearing in their formal attire. They bobbed up and down in their seats, obviously excited. I wondered how long they would last before they fell asleep from boredom.

"Sir, I wasn't aware you had a problem with them, but I am sure the family is no threat," Thomas replied.

Thomas had always had a kinder heart than most royal officers. That was probably because he'd been around for so long. He'd been my grandfather's number one advisor before my grandfather passed away. Richard, however, wasn't as impressed with Thomas's soft spot. The two kings, my father and late grandfather, took different approaches to leadership. Still, Thomas stayed on. He was almost part of the family by now. *Almost.*

"No civilians should be sitting up in the balconies," my father slowly responded.

My mother's face paled, before turning away.

"You're our royal officer in charge of security. Do I need to explain our safety procedures to you?"

"I understand, Your Highness. It was an oversight and I take complete responsibility. Where would you like us to relocate the family to?" He'd been with us so long, I was sure groveling was something he'd learned many years ago. I almost felt bad for the guy.

My father waved his hand to point below him. "I'm sorry I was so short with you, Thomas. But you know the rules. Seeing as there are no seats left in the auditorium, what am I supposed to do?"

Actually, there were plenty of open seats. But judging from the swarms of people mingling in the aisles, those seats wouldn't stay empty for long. Did it really matter if someone other than royalty sat up there?

"They will just have to leave," Richard said.

"That's ridiculous!" I jumped up. Maybe Thomas was going to back down, but I wasn't. "Don't do that. They're no threat to us."

My frustration with the man never ceased to amaze me.

"You're the expert on security now?" He raised an eyebrow sarcastically.

I couldn't stand it anymore. Just because Richard was the king, just because he was my father, it didn't mean he had the right to walk all over people.

But as I opened my mouth to reply, I made the mistake of looking to my mother for support. Her teary expression nearly startled me. Her auburn hair fell in waves around her pale face as she rubbed her temples. I realized she was warding off another headache. The last thing she needed was for Richard and me to get into it.

I closed my mouth and sat back down, ending the argument before it could really begin. As I waited for the show to start, I stared at the disappointed looks on those little boys' faces as they were escorted from the theatre. I deserved to see their pain and feel the guilt creep through my body. I had let it happen.

The lights dimmed.

And it's my cue to leave.

I jumped up and muttered something about the bathroom as I hurried out of the back door. Two of our security guards peeled off the wall to follow me. Of course, I was expecting that. But I had years of experience dealing with these guys. All I needed was one moment of distraction and I could slip away.

As soon as I was out in the hallway, I realized my mistake. The whole area was completely empty.

I should have realized this during Richard's outburst. Cursing myself, I had only seconds to try something else or I probably wouldn't get another chance.

I decided to take a different tactic.

"Chill out," I stopped and allowed the guards to catch up.

The men studied me for a minute, then relaxed. I was the prince, and we'd been through this many times before. Just let me use the bathroom in peace!

I walked away, rounding a sharp corner. I passed by the men's bathroom and headed toward an unmarked door. I hoped this was the right one. I quietly slipped inside, locking myself in.

The woman waiting was younger than I expected, probably nineteen. She was also much prettier than I would have imagined. I guess I'd wrongly assumed spies weren't beautiful.

The black dress she wore hugged her small, curvy body. Her smooth hair was long and blond. Her dark blue eyes sparked impatiently.

Wait, did she just say something? Well, I did always have a thing for blondes. No surprise here.

"Uh, what?" I stammered, bothered that the small janitorial closet was so brightly lit. I was probably blushing. Not a good look on me.

"Shhh! Seriously? Do you have it or not?"

She put her hands on her hips and raised an eyebrow. I noticed the way her red lipstick perfectly stained her full mouth and momentarily felt off balance. Was I too frightened to talk to a beautiful girl? I needed to get a grip.

I gave her my best grin and shrugged. "Maybe I do."

She sighed and moved toward the door. "I don't have time for your games."

"Wait, I'm sorry. I was just kidding—I have it."

She paused when I handed her the slatebook I had tucked in my suit jacket. I studied her carefully. Was she relieved or suspicious?

"You're doing the right thing." She smirked at the screen and swiped it with her index finger, turning it on.

"What do you want with it, anyway?" I asked, though I was pretty sure I could make an educated guess.

"To spy on him." She peered at me like I was dense.

"Okay, yes, I get that. But what are you looking for?"

Her expression grew unreadable. "Why would New Colony's only prince turn on his own father?"

All the times my father had nagged me to be a better prince flashed through my mind. The weeks my mother had locked herself in their dark bedroom with another headache. Or the way he always appeared kind and trustworthy to the public. The way he talked to his advisors about the country, as if the citizens weren't real people with real feelings and real problems—just people to be manipulated and used as he saw fit.

Surprisingly, none of those things would've caused me to turn on him. I wasn't just some child crying for attention, as this girl seemed to be suggesting.

There was something much bigger going on here. And my anger toward my father had gone beyond the merely personal. This wasn't about me.

"I've seen some of the things he's done. I know about the tests he runs." Fleeting images of the shadow lands came to mind, even though I hated to think of it. The way he'd been using alchemy in the rural areas was devastating to the people there. Many were left with nothing, or worse, dead. And it was all kept hidden from the rest of the citizens, brushed under the rug. It'd made me sick when I found out. But honestly, I couldn't say I was surprised. Richard was all about more power, more money, more control. If we were ahead of West

America, keeping our borders secure from their democratic influence, then it was worth it.

"I want to change things, and your people can help me."

Her guarded expression relaxed into one of pity.

Great, she's sorry for me. Just what I need.

But I could understand the sympathy. My own father was a corrupt man. I was supposed to follow in his footsteps. It wasn't an ideal situation.

Still, I didn't want her pity.

I looked down at the slatebook in her hands. The device glowed as she maneuvered through the programs. She smiled knowingly. An icon appeared, indicating that a new program was downloading —although I couldn't quite make out what it was. Within seconds, the download was complete and she passed the slatebook back to me.

"All done. Make sure he doesn't figure out it was ever gone. Do you think you can handle that?"

I slipped it into my pocket. "Where's your faith in me?"

"Right. You'd better get to it, then," she said, the slightest crescent of a smile unmistakable as she moved for the door. I wasn't ready to let her leave.

"What's your name?" I slid in front of her and blocked the exit.

The heat between us was sudden and thick.

I expected her to do what other girls did. Right about now she'd either freeze up or lean into me. Instead, she held her ground. It was the kind of unexpected reaction I thoroughly enjoyed.

"How did you *really* get involved in all of this, Lucas?" she asked.

I considered how much to reveal. Ultimately, we were part of the same cause, right? Stopping the corruption that was happening within the Guardians of Color. The corruption of color alchemy that was slowly creeping across our country without the citizens being any the wiser.

"Your people approached me first. Turns out being a prince makes me someone of interest."

I never expected to end up here, but maybe I never had a choice. The memory of my first contact with the Resistance flashed through my mind.

The woman had approached me while I was alone.

I was running along one of the paths, working out. I stopped to catch my breath when a middle-aged lady practically materialized from out of the shrubbery. She was dressed like any other palace gardener. I figured she was just doing her job. But then she walked over and asked if I had done any new traveling lately.

As the only child of two distant parents, I tended to make friends with people around the palace quite often. Our conversation was no different. Every day for some time, she stopped me on my run to talk. I didn't mind it so much. It was always toward the end of the run, anyway. And she seemed kind, curious, essentially harmless.

But after a few weeks, she told me who she was.

She said she had been watching me for a reason. She'd studied my reactions to see where my loyalties lay and whether she could trust me. And after enough time, she felt comfortable asking me to join her cause.

Normally, I would have refused. Who was she kidding? This kind of thing wasn't okay. I would have called for a palace guard under normal circumstances. But there was something different about her. Trustworthy. And I was still livid at the way Richard had destroyed whole communities. On a short trip weeks before, my father had brought me to the shadow lands. It was just a "little experiment."

"You've seen things you wish you could forget, haven't you?" she'd asked. And then she told me what she knew about my father. About what the alchemists were really doing. She knew what I knew.

And she wanted to help me.

I needed more proof than that. Could I really align myself with these people so easily? It wasn't that simple.

The bodies. That's what did it.

She sent me a file of classified information, straight from the email server of Royal Officer Faulk. Faulk was my father's most trusted officer. How these people had an inside line into Faulk's computer, I didn't know. In the file were photos of the dead: adults and children. The color drained right out of many of them. Also attached were memos explaining what happened to these people. Essentially, they were murdered. They were test subjects. Failed experiments. The result of alchemy pushed to its brutal limits. And why? What was so important it mattered more than human lives?

My father, Faulk, they'd both ordered these tests. And then ordered more.

Before that experience, I didn't even know that the Resistance existed, or that anyone cared what the GC did. Sure, my father had enemies—lots of them, in fact. And our country had enemies, too. We'd been on the brink of war with West America for decades. But this was different. This was about magic, about an evil that was consuming the palace from within. Not the other way around.

So when this woman told me that the Resistance was a nonviolent group, I wanted to believe her. If they were violent, wouldn't I have heard of them before? She said they were people committed to making change happen quietly and without bloodshed. They wanted to do this the right way. For everyone involved.

Was that still the case?

Looking at this girl now, I couldn't help but wonder. How had she became a part of all this? Had someone approached her, too? Did she know the woman who'd disguised herself as a gardener?

"But why would they trust you? You're the last person I would trust. No offense."

"I already told you. I know what's going on. I know what my father is doing. It needs to be stopped civilly. I've been promised that assassination isn't something your group supports. That better be the truth, or I'm dead, too."

Yes, I was a traitor. I could admit that now. But it was for the right reasons. I wasn't turning on the people. I was turning on my father. And it wasn't like I wanted Richard dead. But there was murder on his hands. I hated that truth.

And knowing that I likely had decades before Richard would step down, allowing me to rule, I needed to find another way to stop him.

The girl stared back at me. "I guess you have more on the line than me, after all."

She ran her hand through her hair and brushed it away from her face. The motion sent a waft of sweet perfume into the air. Was that citrus or vanilla? "Anyway, thank you. You did a good thing today."

"You still haven't told me your name," I reminded her. We were still just inches apart.

She smirked and kissed my cheek. I felt the thick mark of her lipstick stain my skin. One small movement and I could have my mouth on hers.

"Play along, little prince," she whispered. Abruptly, she laughed aloud and pushed past me, opening the door and stumbling out in the hallway. I followed behind, amused but somewhat irked by her "little prince" comment.

What did she mean, "play along?"

"There he is," a voice called from down the corridor. The two security guards appeared, their blue uniforms now uncomfortably rumpled. "Some bathroom break, huh?"

The girl continued to laugh. "Oh, Lucas, you're trouble!"

She grabbed my tie, pulled me in, and kissed me hard on the lips.

Before I could get control of myself and kiss her back, it was over. Not that I exactly minded the surprise. I still didn't know her name.

Giggling, she skirted down the hallway, stumbling as she went. This girl, whoever she was, could seriously put on a show. I'd given her exactly what she wanted. And what did I get in return? Nothing.

The guards seemed embarrassed but not at all suspicious. For all they knew, I had been hooking up with some girl who'd had a little too much to drink. Not really my style. I preferred my women sober. But they didn't have to know that. *Nature calls, right boys?*

I winked at the pair of guards and coolly shrugged before heading back down the hallway to my parents.

■

My father didn't even bother to look in my direction as I sat in the plush seat beside him. I assumed he was angry with me for taking off. What he would do if he knew where I had been?

I was justified in my actions. This was my first assignment, and I'd done it without hesitation. I had to.

You crossed a line, a small voice rang in my head.

No. Richard crossed a line. I can't let myself feel sorry for him.

I peered over at my mother, who had gone from gently massaging her temples when I'd left, to furiously rubbing her forehead. It was always hard to watch her unsuccessfully fight off a headache. She noticed me and shot a glare in my direction. *Ah, finally, some fire out of the woman!*

But I'd done it. I'd actually pulled it off.

Normally Richard banned me from using my slatebook at events. But he failed to notice when I'd so easily made the switch and stolen his own identical device tonight.

I guessed correctly that he wouldn't pay attention to it. Richard always made a point of *not* using his slatebook while he was in the public eye. He wanted everyone to love him, feel that he was one with the masses. To an extent, anyway. It wasn't like having the whole upper level of the auditorium to ourselves could be perceived as normal.

Most people didn't have access to luxuries like our family. Even though this was the wealthiest country on the planet, our people didn't live like royalty. They had slatebooks, sure. But not like the technology we carried.

He doesn't suspect a thing, does he?

When I was sure no one was watching, I discreetly slipped his slatebook back into the pocket of his suit jacket. It was simply lying over the back of his chair, exposed. It was almost too easy and that made me uncomfortable.

I had made a bet. My family would never suspect anything out of the ordinary. Not from their own son. So far, it turned out I was right.

And just like that, the stakes got higher.

■

I spent most of the ballet nodding off. Sure, it was nice, but it was the same orchestral music and sweeping jumps across the stage, times ten, which got boring fast. At the very least, I was grateful for the dark auditorium.

Maybe I could sneak in a nap?

I tried to focus on the ballet, hoping it would get better soon. The dancers were talented. I'm sure they were the best of the best, or something like that. After a long piece involving a lot of identically costumed women running around, the lights dimmed and a girl dressed in violet stepped out onto the empty stage.

As she began to move to the piano's melody, I leaned forward in my seat.

Of course, she was technically trained but she also had something else. Something about her motions couldn't be taught. This girl was born to be a ballerina, even an unappreciative guy like myself could admit that much.

I was momentarily surprised by my reaction. Who knew a dancer could have such a magnetic effect on me?

Just as I was about to come to my senses, the tempo increased and I was pulled back into her dance. I joined the rest of the audience, mesmerized.

She began to twist into a series of spins. Her delight flew off her as if it was contagious. As her moves accelerated, she was transformed into a blur of purple.

And then all at once, the colors changed.

Is that what I think it is?

She just kept going. Apparently oblivious to the swirling cloud of purple that was lifting out of her costume. She continued to dance.

So did the color.

She was free, alive, the hues exploding around her like wildfire.

The audience was stirring now, something pulsed like a collective heartbeat. Fear? Of course I had seen color alchemy countless times, and I certainly knew quite a bit about the magic behind it, but most of the audience didn't.

Color alchemy had taken our country to the top. The wealth, the prosperity, the magnificent advances in technology. I'd spent much of my education studying alchemy. I knew all about its powerful uses. And its negative side effects.

Which is how I knew that the sheer amount of power coming off this girl was staggering. It was bright, moving above and around her, dancing with her. Her costume was completely gray at this point, which meant she had taken it all, removed all the color. In only a few seconds. And from an artificial item no less. Remarkable. I wondered if she knew how to harness that power and actually do something useful with it.

Then something strange began to transpire. The purple colors slowly separated. Shifted. Together, spinning with lavender, were shades of blue...and red. The two colors that combined to make purple had actually separated. And there it was. Red.

How is she doing that?

This girl was about to change *everything*. Her level of talent was absolutely unprecedented. To separate the colors down to the primary sources like that? It was rare enough to find someone who had the ability to harness color at all, but this display of skill was unfathomable.

My father erupted from his seat, shouting instructions to his operatives. The audience snapped out of their trance. Calls of confusion pummeled like a tidal wave. Most people hurried to exit the theatre, practically crawling over each other. Others stayed frozen in their seats. And a reckless few actually pushed their way toward the stage.

The girl finally stopped moving. She stared wide-eyed at the spectrum still whirling around her body. I could see her features better now. She was young despite her height. Wispy, tall, and uncommonly beautiful. Her pale skin contrasted nicely against her dark hair and large eyes.

I studied her expression and looked for any indication that she knew what was happening. Would she take control over her alchemy? But she was utterly stunned. Just as the curtain began to descend, her knees buckled and she dropped to the floor.

THREE

JESSA

I woke lost to the world. Floating in a foggy void.

I was lying on a hard surface in a nearly pitch-black room, my eyes focusing in and out on a sliver of light coming from under a door. Was someone there? I tried not to come undone as the images of my most recent memory flooded me.

Oh yes, I'd been dancing. And I had felt so good. Alive. Free.

And then, in an instant, it had all shattered to pieces.

What have I done?

I tried to sit up, but a ring of pain enveloped my wrists. I was tightly handcuffed to a hard surface. I laid flat again and waited for someone to notice I was awake.

No one came.

I tried not to drift back into sleep, but I didn't know how much longer I could keep my eyes open. If it wasn't for the small red light, I'd question if I was awake at all. Despite the disorientation, I didn't mind the darkness. As uncomfortable as this featureless room was, I was more afraid of what would happen when the lights came on. Then I'd have to face the truth.

As if my very thought triggered the action, the room exploded in a burst of fluorescent light. The walls, the ceiling, the floor, everything was chalky gray. The door opened, and a man in a matching gray lab coat walked in. His face was mostly covered by a doctor's mask. Two pale blue eyes, and that was it.

"Where am I?" I asked, trying to keep my voice calm.

He walked right to me, peering down.

"Relax, this doesn't have to hurt."

Before I had a chance to respond, the needle pierced my arm, and a burning ache shot deep through my bicep. He stepped back.

"What did you..." I blinked, stunned, as the words were lost.

■

The color behind my eyelids was a warm, inky red. I couldn't open them.

I pushed and pushed, willing them to part, but they didn't move. Wasn't I supposed to be somewhere? The heaviness of sleep was too strong for me to finish the thought as I drifted. Just before it overtook me, a man's voice spoke.

"Let me see her."

■

The echo of a door slamming bounced through my memory.

You've been drugged. Wake up!

I'm trying. I don't know if I can.

But no matter how hard I fought, the darkness pulled back even harder. I was just too tired.

There was a clatter of footsteps.

Again, I tried to open my eyes, but I gave up easily. The voices began to speak near me. It took all my energy to comprehend what they were saying.

"What do you intend to do with her?" The voice of a younger man asked.

"It's none of your concern," the deeper voice responded.

"You wanted me to get more involved. Well, here I am."

There was a pause before a woman's voice jutted into the conversation. Something about the sharp lilt in her words rang familiar to me.

Did I know her?

"Not only has Jessa broken several laws—she lied about her alchemy. I advise you to keep her here. I don't trust this girl."

"That would be a bad move," the young man interjected. "She could be a huge asset to the Guardians of Color. She has abilities we've never seen before. And that's without proper training. Just think about it. What could a few months with the GC do for someone with that kind of aptitude for color alchemy?"

"You don't know anything about her. She is a liability. She's dangerous and too old to start training. It's too late. The best thing would be to keep her under lock and key."

"She's incredibly talented. It's as simple as that. And it's not your decision, anyway."

"Nor is it yours. I will not be lectured by some boy about the intricacies of color alchemy. You don't know what it takes to properly train an effective alchemist. Years of hard work and dedication are required to hone the magic. This girl is already a teenager. She's too volatile. She's had time to come forward with this. Where was she ten years ago?"

"I'm hardly a boy. And I know enough about color alchemy to know that she deserves a chance."

"Enough," scoffed the deeper baritone voice. I tried to recall how I knew him. Was he the one from earlier in the conversation?

"I have final say over what happens to this girl. Not either of you. And my son is right. She accessed red. And that means we need her. *I need her*." Nobody bothered to contradict him.

Everything inside was screaming that this was too important to miss, to hold onto this conversation. Instead, I fell closer to the darkness.

■

I opened my eyes. The room was dark again. Bits and pieces from the earlier events floated into my drug-induced sleep.

I knew something important had happened, but I couldn't remember exactly what. A conversation between three people about color alchemy. About me.

The door swung open and two armed guards, dressed in blue uniforms, entered the room. Dread tumbled down my spine. They turned on the lights and I was reminded that the room had no color. It was a cube of gray. No windows. One door. One light.

They released my handcuffs from the metal bed and roughly pulled me up, barely giving me a chance to catch my balance. Before I could console my aching wrists, I was handcuffed again. They yanked me from the room.

"Where are you taking me?"

They didn't answer. I started to repeat my question, louder this time, but stopped when I got a better look at the men.

They were clearly in control here. But despite their dominance, there was a bit of stray emotion pulling at their faces. Fear.

What did men like these have to be afraid of?

I caught the shifting eyes of one, and then I knew. *Me*. He was afraid of me. A very large, heavily armed New Colony guard was afraid of me. A ballerina. I would have laughed if I hadn't been so bewildered. I looked around for a way to escape. I needed to get away from them. I just wanted to go home! But it was no use; the men had a firm hold on me.

■

We walked through a maze of gray hallways lined with closed doors. The handcuffs still in place, one of the guards pulled out a thick blindfold and wrapped it around my eyes. They were treating me like a violent criminal!

I'd thought Lacey was the alchemist. But I'd been so wrong. And the fact that I had to find this out about myself in front of hundreds of people? What luck! My eyes returned to the darkness under the blindfold and that's when I understood the reason for the gray room. I didn't realize it before. I hadn't been around color since passing out at the ballet. If I somehow wanted to use alchemy as a weapon, I didn't have any ammunition.

This is not necessary!

I bit my tongue to prevent myself from yelling the string of obscenities that was running through my mind.

If someone would just talk to me, they would know that I was not a threat.

21

What happened was a mistake. I was just a teenager. I wanted nothing to do with color alchemy. All this time, I thought it was Lacey who was the alchemist. No. It was me. *How could I have been so stupid?*

At least Lacey wasn't in my place right now. I would never want this for her. I hoped she was home safe with Mom and Dad.

It wasn't long until the air around me shifted and I was guided up a staircase and into a cool room. The blindfold stayed snugly in place, keeping me in darkness.

"Where am I?" Again, silence. "Please don't hurt me. It was an accident. I swear. I'll never do it again!"

Still nothing.

"I promise. Just please say something. Anything! What is going on?" We continued to move. The men pulled me by my elbow, much faster now. Still no one uttered a word.

I thrashed out, resisting the rough hands that pulled me forward. I still couldn't see anything, what did they expect?

I tried to move away, but my strength was nothing compared to theirs. The men simply lifted me up and continued forward. Jerks!

"Stop it!" A door slammed and we abruptly stopped.

"Let her go!" Someone boomed from behind.

They dropped me and I slammed to the ground. Pain erupted across my jaw and the taste of metal warmed my mouth. Blood.

Footsteps rushed forward. Someone gently removed my blindfold.

"Idiots," a male voice mumbled.

I took in the boy kneeling before me. Stormy gray eyes stared back, framed by disheveled dark hair.

For a moment, neither of us made a move. No one said a word. I just stared at him, trying to figure out why *this* guy was staring me down like I was a wanted criminal. I knew him.

Prince Lucas.

Is this really happening right now?

He was barely a breath away. His height, lean athletic build, unruly hair, and striking charcoal eyes made him almost too perfect. Painfully gorgeous, actually. All the girls—and women—of New Colony were basically obsessed with him. Did he know that? Yes, of course he did. From the way his mouth turned, he probably knew what I was thinking.

How embarrassing.

He stood up. My hands were still restrained behind me. He carefully helped me stand. His closeness bothered me. I didn't want to think of how disheveled I must look after all that time drugged and confined. Mortified, I looked away, willing him to do the same.

"Take off the handcuffs and don't treat her like that again." I was surprised by his kindness and thick anger toward the guards. Both looked chastened. Ashamed, even. *Good!*

"What were you thinking? You could have set her off. Don't forget, she's deadly."

Well, so much for chivalry!

Once my wrists were free, I gingerly rubbed at the tender bruises. I nearly jumped when Prince Lucas reached toward them. He stopped short, his expression unreadable.

"We'll have someone take care of that," he said, eyes still studying me, drinking me in.

Unsure of what to do or say, I stood motionless. He had just warned armed guards that I was dangerous, but he didn't seem to fear me himself. At the same time, he seemed uncomfortable.

"Why am I here?"

"Excellent question. You and I need to have a discussion." He nodded to the guards and added: "In private."

■

Moments later, he took me to a nearby parlor room and motioned for me to sit down. From the ornate décor, I immediately knew we were in the palace.

I can't believe this is happening!

Prince Lucas wasn't someone I ever thought I'd set eyes on in the flesh. Certainly not so close. I could touch him if I wanted. Not that I would! But still, I could. Weird.

New Colony's palace was more than just a royal residence. It was a huge set of connected buildings that housed the most exclusive government agencies, including the headquarters of the Guardians of Color.

Even though the elegant room had large oil paintings, plush rugs, and mahogany trimmings, it still managed to exude coziness. A fire crackled in the large fireplace.

Does he want me to remain calm?

Well, I was anything but calm. The hard sheath of material didn't help the matter. I was still wearing the lavender ballet outfit from that night in the theatre. I looked ridiculous wearing a costume in here. At least it was back to its original color.

I frowned down at myself. The spattering of crystals across the bodice had rubbed at the soft insides of my arms. *Did no one care enough to let me change out of this?*

"I know who you are," I said. I attempted to betray no emotion and ignored the nerves that bubbled inside.

He laughed. "And I know who you are, Jessa."

So he knew my name. I could only conclude that Faulk, or one of the other officials, had told him all about me. Had they studied me? Followed me?

"Jessa, are you okay?"

I didn't respond. Instead, I stared at the floor, breaking his eye contact. I didn't know what to think of him. Was he also afraid of me? Did he think I was star-struck to meet him? Impressed because he was the crown prince?

I could feel him give me the classic guy once-over. I was slender, yes. But that shouldn't be mistaken for weakness. I was strong and healthy. My long brown curls had come loose from my ballerina bun, returning it to its natural bird's nest. I doubted that I looked very threatening.

"Jessa, are you hungry? Do you want some water?"

"Why do you care? But since you're asking, yes, I'm hungry. I haven't had much to eat in a while." Placing a small hand across my stomach, I glared at him, as if this was all his doing.

Whoever was assigned to guard me obviously didn't care about my stomach. Anger churned in my belly as I tried to figure out how long it had been since I'd had a meal.

He pulled out a very thin, very expensive slatebook and dialed a number. Within seconds, he ordered someone to bring in food and water. I continued to glare at him. He wasn't going to bribe his way into my good graces.

"Send in a healer while you're at it, please," he added. We both stared uncomfortably at my chafed wrists. Somehow the bruises looked even worse now. "And some women's clothing too, please."

Finally, I can change from this ridiculous costume!

I still didn't trust him. Why should I?

"Listen, we need to talk about a few things. I am not going to hurt you. Actually, I want to help you."

"Am I supposed to thank you?"

"I—I don't need any thanks," he replied, faltering.

"Look, I know you're the prince. What on earth would a prince want with me?"

He didn't respond.

"No one will tell me what's going on!" I jumped out of my seat. "Why are you even talking to me? I thought I was a prisoner. Since when do princes talk to prisoners? I just need someone to tell me the truth. Why am I here?"

He sighed and stood.

"Fine. If you want to do this now, then we can do this now. But you should be thanking me. Stop being so defensive. If it weren't for me, you would still be stuck in that prison cell, probably for the rest of your life. First of all, you broke the law. Second, you put a whole building full of people at risk when you pulled that stunt at the ballet two nights ago. You could have gotten yourself killed."

"It was an accident."

Two nights ago? So I've been drugged for two whole days...

"It doesn't matter. You don't know how to control your abilities, and that's dangerous. I don't care what your reasons are for hiding the truth. You're in a lot of trouble!"

I tried to stay calm but how could I? He didn't get it!

"I didn't know...it was an accident." I tried to steady my voice. I frowned and sat back down. I was about to cry and felt sick at the thought. That was the last thing I needed right now.

Don't cry. Come on, Jessa, get it together.

Lucas sat down next to me, putting his hand on my arm. I stiffened as a wave of heat rolled across my flesh before I pulled away. He was too attractive for his own good. I hated it.

Now is not the time to be acting like such a girl.

"I'm dangerous?" I asked, holding back the tears.

"Yes, but we can change that. That's why I got you out of prison as quickly as I could. I want to help you."

"Why?" I asked.

"I've been studying alchemy my whole life. I know dozens of alchemists and have worked with many on different projects. I've seen remarkable things, but none of their talent has even come close to what I saw the other night. Yes, you're dangerous, but only because you're untrained. With the right direction, you could become a huge asset. You could help a lot of people."

I studied him and waited for a flicker of deception to cross his face. We sat in silence as I considered his words. Why did he care so much? What was in it for him? He was charming but I wasn't sure I could trust him.

Then I asked the question I was pretty sure I already knew the answer to. The one that scared me the most. "Will I have to join the GC?"

The Guardians of Color were the only alchemists legally permitted to use their abilities. Those who didn't qualify for the GC were usually incarcerated, and apparently some were drugged and strapped to tables. I could testify to that.

I didn't know a lot about color alchemy. I did, however, understand that it was a delicate art that could quickly become deadly if it wasn't controlled. Being a member of the GC was an honor. Only the best of the best were able to reach the level of skill necessary to join. And the ones that weren't up to par? I wasn't sure what happened to them.

I was heartbroken to think about my prospects. Guardians were forbidden from having other careers. They didn't live in normal society. They lived apart from their families. Did they even have children? Get married? I had never known an alchemist, so I knew they didn't lead public lives. The GC had always been a foreign group. In my sixteen years, I had yet to meet a guardian. Alchemists were so rare.

"You're not going home," Lucas said. "We need you here."

"And do I have a choice?"

His silence told me all I needed to know.

I didn't know why he was here. Or what it was like to be a guardian. But I knew for sure that nothing would be the same. No more dinners with my family. No more sleeping in my bed or retreating to my room to be alone with my thoughts. I wouldn't get to talk to Mom and Dad about my day or have arguments with them about normal things like homework and curfews.

I would be absent as my little sister grew up. I wouldn't be there for the milestones, broken hearts, fits of laughter, conversations about school and which teachers to avoid. When the moments came that Lacey needed to confide in someone, just needed someone to listen to her fears and secrets, to console her through her first heartbreak, I wouldn't be there.

25

Long ago, I promised myself I would never give up on my ballet dreams, but now I would never dance on stage again. Why would New Colony care to have a ballerina when they could have an alchemist?

My friends, my family, ballet, *my life*. They would all become memories.

"Just tell me. Do I have to become a guardian? Do I have to live here now?"

"It's not so bad. It's the highest civilian honor."

A pain unlike any I'd felt before dropped into my chest.

How could this be?

My vision blurred.

Oh no, I can't breathe. This can't be happening to me. No!

Lucas was speaking, but I couldn't hear him. I couldn't process anything outside of my body. My fears were taking over, amplified.

Am I having a heart attack?

Did I even care? What would be the point of living now, anyway? Maybe it would be nice to die, to be free from all of this. If there were such a thing as an afterlife, would I get to visit my family? Maybe I would get to watch Lacey grow up, after all. I relaxed into the thought, allowing the darkness to spread through my vision, pulling me under.

Don't give up! This is not the end!

I stood and staggered through the room, desperate to get away. But then I tripped. *I never trip!* And I fell in the worst possible direction. The flames of the fireplace seemed to reach out as I let my palms take the impact.

White heat caught my hands. I screamed and pulled myself away from the crippling pain. In the same moment, a burst of brilliant energy shot from the fireplace. The room was illuminated in a bright yellow glow. The fire exploded with an ear-piercing shriek before becoming nothing but dark billowing waves of smoke. I clutched at my blistered hands. After a moment of intense agony, I realized what had just happened. Lucas reached for me, but I shoved him hard, screaming in agony.

Unbelievable. I used color alchemy. Again.

This time it must have come from the color of the fire. After a second to calm my nerves, I looked around for Lucas, hoping he'd know what to do to take away the pain ripping through my hands. But Lucas Heart, the beloved prince of New Colony, the only heir to the throne, was lying on the floor, limbs awkwardly twisted.

He was completely unconscious.

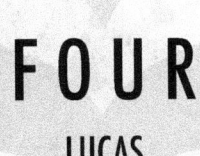

FOUR

LUCAS

I was only out for a minute. Okay, maybe two.

I opened my eyes to green energy swirling around my vision and weaving through the air. Bright, fluid, and filled with sparkling neon light. It wasn't a typical green. It was vibrant. Alive.

I sat up and rubbed my head. *Well, that was unexpected.*

A calming warmth of the green energy filled my body. It tingled every sense within me and tasted faintly of sugar. A tinkering sound danced inside my head, like far away wind chimes. An overwhelming feeling of peace expanded across my chest.

Everything is going to be okay.

My whole body relaxed as my mind cleared. The green energy that was once so bright, so powerful, so real, was gone. The pain that would have racked my body for days had dissipated, just like the green. Carried away in a moment.

I took quick stock of my surroundings and breathed in deeply.

An older woman kneeled in front of me. She had twinkling brown eyes and long gray hair that was braided down her back. An eclectic collection of long necklaces draped over her loose clothing. I noticed she'd brought one of the potted plants closer. She must have pulled the green from it to use for her alchemy.

I was surprised to find that she was not dressed in the typical guardian attire. They usually wore black from head to toe. Her skin was tanned and wrinkled, like worn leather. Despite her wizened appearance, I liked her. *I knew her.* She turned to Jessa, who was just next to her, also leaning over me.

"You're both okay now," the woman said, laughing at Jessa's expression. "You had a panic attack, dear, plus burned yourself and he passed out. What did he say to you?"

Neither of us responded. She studied the fire, which still crackled as if someone had tossed water over the embers. She could probably guess the answer.

Yes, lady, that's right. I was just knocked out by an untrained color alchemist.

"It's okay," she said to Jessa. "You'll adjust. We all do." Her smile was magnetic. Maybe this woman was the perfect person to get through to Jessa. *Should I keep her around to help me?*

"I'm a color alchemist. Primarily, a healer," the old woman continued. "I used the green color of this plant to heal your wounds, as well as calm your panic attack. Not to mention, wake up Prince Charming here." She laughed at her lame joke. "You'll be fine, but if you need anything else, you're welcome to ask for me. My name is Jasmine." She held out her hand and shook Jessa's.

"Thank you," Jessa replied.

"By the way," I added as I brushed off my suit and stood. "Jessa is not getting into trouble for that, because we aren't going to tell anyone."

I peered at Jessa. "But please, try not to do it again."

"Everything is going to be just fine now," Jasmine said. "Do you need anything else, Prince Lucas?"

"That's all, thank you." I was grateful for her perfect timing, of course, despite the embarrassment. Jasmine curtsied to me before leaving the room. I reminded myself to have a conversation with her later.

As soon as we were alone, Jessa and I were immediately transported back to our earlier tension.

"What just happened?" she asked as I sat next to her. "One moment, I was sure I was having a heart attack. I tripped. I *never* trip. And I burned myself. Then the next moment, you're on the ground knocked out. That lady comes in here and makes it all go away as if it was nothing. Using color. Green color, from a plant right? I didn't even catch the whole thing—I was too shocked."

"That was only a little bit of healing. Jasmine used green color alchemy. It healed you and woke me from whatever you'd done to me with that fire. I have to admit, you're the first alchemist I've met who's actually touched fire like that."

I meant it as a joke, but she wasn't laughing. She sat speechless, staring at her healed wrists and hands. She probably never suspected alchemy existed on this kind of level. Maybe she'd heard of other alchemists, but if she'd seen one before, she certainly didn't look it.

"It's just a glimpse of what's to come, Jessa," I continued. "Before long, you'll be able to do that, too. And more. Welcome to your future."

At that, she was ready to listen. *What can I say? It's a good line.*

I couldn't admit that what had just happened with the fire had bothered me. I'd never seen anyone react the way she had. I certainly hadn't been expecting her to fall into the fire, let alone pull the orange energy out. Again, I was reminded of how lucky we were that Jasmine had already been on her way in. I had called for a healer, and apparently they'd sent only the best. Now…where was that food and clothing?

As I racked my brain, I realized that Jasmine's face was familiar. I was pretty sure she'd been a GC staple at the palace for years. But since I typically avoided their area in the palace and really had no purpose for healers, our paths hadn't crossed much. Was she one of the guardians who regularly attended to my mother? There were well over two hundred guardians by now. I didn't know them all.

Despite Jasmine's rescue, Jessa's emotions were still all over the place. *This is the danger with untrained color alchemists,* I reminded myself. I had to keep her calm while I explained the situation.

I momentarily wondered if I should summon the guards back in. But I decided against it. I needed to gain her trust if this was going to work. Given Jessa's unprecedented power, it was clear that my father wanted to use Jessa for his own ends. I needed to get close enough to her to stop that from happening. I didn't just *need* to gain her trust, I *had* to. She was the tipping point. Perhaps she could even help the Resistance. Maybe together we could save New Colony from my father.

"You're struggling with this because you're a little late to the game," I explained, trying not to get too far ahead of myself. "The fact that your abilities weren't discovered earlier is astonishing."

"It really *was* an accident."

"Was that actually the first time?" I asked, pushing thoughts of her beauty from my mind. I didn't need the distraction.

She hesitated, but I didn't want to irritate her and risk another accidental blast of power. She shook her head. "It was the second."

I paused to consider that. The first time it happened, she should have turned herself in. This must be why General Faulk was so bent on keeping Jessa locked up. We had to make examples out of people like Jessa. But I had no intention of punishing this girl. Luckily, Richard had seen my logic for once. He'd even put me in charge of seeing she got the training she needed. That was normally a royal officer's job, but ever since I turned eighteen, Richard had been bringing me in for more and more work. His orders had enabled me to be in this room, talking to this potentially dangerous girl.

"Color alchemists are born, not created. There are different degrees to their power, and some only have abilities as children before they quickly grow out of it."

"They're lucky."

"Yes and no," I replied. "Yes, because they usually are able to integrate back into their families. We keep tabs on them, but in most cases, they seem completely normal. But many who are discovered with this power become strong enough that they must fight to have control. They join the GC because it means they've trained enough to handle their abilities. It means they know what they're doing can make a difference. Those that can't control it—" I paused to consider how to say this. "Let's just say it's not very appealing."

Her gaze held me, a trace of pain buried beneath her eyes. Was she recalling the brief time spent in the isolated prison, with its dull gray surfaces? The first time I'd seen her up close, she had been drugged and asleep. I felt a twinge of empathy, remembering the way she'd been so helpless.

"To be a Guardian of Color is an honor. Most of the alchemy the GC does is kept secret from the public. People don't usually accept what they can't understand. But I can testify that their magic is remarkable and instrumental to our kingdom."

Her brow furrowed skeptically, but she didn't interrupt.

I took that as a good sign and continued. "You already know that New Colony is the only country that takes care of its people. Many have returned to the Dark Ages. Why do you think that is?"

"Standard answer? Because when natural resources dried up, the rest of the world was holding onto their democracies. But no one agreed on anything. They didn't take care of what they had. They were too busy fighting with each other, which meant no one got anything done. So we broke away. Our monarchy created stabilization. The kingdom was named New Colony, and your family became our royal family decades ago, in our last ever election."

Each word sounded like it had been lifted verbatim from a history book. *Richard would be proud.*

"Yes, initially that's how we survived. But what did alchemy have to do with it?" As I suspected, she didn't have an answer. She wouldn't. Regular citizens knew very little about color alchemy or the guardians. They only knew to report anything suspicious. That was it. My father and grandfathers before me had gone to great lengths to keep our secrets well hidden from our enemies. Our biggest weapon? We knew why alchemy worked—*and* how to harness it.

"Did you know that throughout history, color alchemists have been persecuted?"

"There aren't very many of them. Didn't they hide it?"

"Sometimes they did. And sometimes they were murdered, burned alive with accusations of witchcraft. More civilized societies would just throw them in prison. That's only if they were lucky enough not to accidentally kill someone, which ended in execution."

From the horrified expression on her face, I could tell this was new information.

"There's a lot about the past that New Colony has kept from society."

"To keep us safe?"

Typical obedient civilian answer. "To keep the citizens safe, sure. But it's also been for you, to keep the color alchemists safe from the people. You saw the way those people in that auditorium reacted to you. They were the wealthiest, most educated and elite citizens in our nation, and even they were ready to create a mob. Normal people don't understand you, Jessa. They never will."

She flinched at the word "normal."

"So what makes you royals so different? Why is the GC located here at the palace, of all places?"

"Generations ago, our family created the GC to study color alchemy. We housed it here, right in plain sight. Instead of fearing it, we've used it to our advantage. New Colony has not only survived, but we've thrived. What Jasmine did today was only an ounce of what she's capable of. Before the GC, we had scheduled blackouts, poverty, and a lot of unhappy people. And that's what still happens outside of our borders."

Jessa still looked pained. Was she conflicted? If she believed me, then she understood why her power was so important. We needed her. She could never go back to her old life.

"If I join you, what happens to me? What about my family? What about ballet?"

"I wish I had a better answer for you, but I don't."

"Don't pretend to feel sorry for me," she murmured.

Why did I have to do this to her?

"Please, if you know so much about it, can you help me turn it off? I could have my life back." She held off tears. "Please just let me try."

"There's no turning it off. It's impossible." It took everything in me not to go over to her and hold her. I couldn't risk revealing my unwanted feelings. I was angry with myself for even acknowledging them at all. I needed to stay in control.

Guilt threatened to rise to the surface knowing how I'd lied. She'd asked if she could turn off her powers and I said no. Alchemy wasn't exactly impossible to turn off. It was just *nearly* impossible. Sure, she could try. I know it had happened once before. An alchemist was able to do it. Turn it all off.

But I couldn't tell her that. I'd never tell her that.

I kept my face still. She was too valuable. I suspected the Resistance could use her to stop Richard. She wasn't indoctrinated by the alchemists yet. Clearly, Faulk hated her. Maybe we could gain Jessa's trust and get her on our side.

"You can't make me do it. You can't make me do anything. I don't want to be a Guardian of Color."

"You don't have a choice. Besides, we can't just let you go. You'd hurt someone. Would you rather sit in that cell for the rest of your life?"

She scowled at me. "What does any of it matter to you?"

How was I supposed to get through to this girl? Was she hearing a single thing I was telling her? So stubborn, so frustrating!

And that makes you like her more.

Just then, the heavy oak door opened and a woman dressed head-to-toe in a white uniform walked in the room. The white alone meant she was part of the special forces group that governed the Guardians of Color. I recognized her immediately though: Royal Officer Faulk. She was the head of that department, and she loved every controlling minute.

My body contracted. I still hadn't figured out why Faulk cared so much about what happened to Jessa, besides the obvious "make an example of her to the people" argument. There had to be something more.

Faulk was flanked by several palace guards. They were dressed in the standard blue uniforms. I identified another as a guardian, because he was dressed in the typical sleek black GC getup. He was more relaxed than the others, more sure of himself. He was also the youngest in the group. If I had to guess, I would have pegged him for seventeen, not much younger than me.

His arrogance was irritating. Who was this kid? He was staring at Jessa with an appreciative boyish gaze, unlike the regular palace guards, who were obviously afraid of her. He clearly saw her beauty. Her potential.

"Hello, General Faulk," Jessa said, eyes downcast.

If Faulk was the one who'd questioned the Loxley family just a few short days ago, then Faulk was the one Jessa had lied to. Not the smartest choice.

Faulk didn't return the hello. She gave me a slight glare and a small bow before moving into the room. To her, I was insignificant to the conversation. But we both knew this wasn't true. My father wanted me here. Ever since I'd confronted him about the deaths he had caused with alchemy, he'd wanted me to learn more about this world. To understand his reasoning, I supposed, though I would never agree with his tactics. *Never.* But still, I had authority that even Faulk didn't have.

"I've heard some of your conversation," Faulk said. Jessa frowned, confused, and rightly so.

I caught the proud expression on the young guardian's face. He looked a little too pleased with himself.

I recognized him. He had strong abilities in communication, which meant he could intercept conversations. Certain shades of blue could be used to replicate powerful listening and surveillance devices. Blue was a tough magic and highly useful. I looked at the boy with a newfound respect, despite myself.

Jessa was at a loss for words, and just when I was about to intervene, Faulk moved in closer.

"I would have you locked up for your crimes," she said. "But the king has other plans. So you will do what you are told, or I will make sure your family loses everything."

I wondered just how much of our conversation Faulk had heard because of that annoying kid! But I guessed she didn't know about Jessa's earlier accidental alchemy with the orange color from the fire. Otherwise, it would have been the first thing out of her mouth. She wouldn't be the sort to withstand yet another violation of the law.

"Lay off, Faulk. Jessa knows what has to be done. There's no need to threaten her family. You can leave them out of this."

"They're innocent," Jessa said to Faulk. "I swear they had no idea. It was all me."

"So you admit you lied?" Faulk asked.

"I'll do what you ask. But please, leave them out of it." Going after family was a low blow, which of course was why it worked.

"Your family will be fine," I said, shooting a dangerous glance at Faulk. She needed to ease up on the threats before Jessa had another breakdown. "Jessa, you'll be staying here as my guest," I continued, nodding toward the guards. "I'm sure Miss Loxley is tired. Please show her to her room."

Jessa practically gaped at me. Was that gratitude or suspicion reddening her cheeks? I knew she still had a barrage of questions, but she kept them to herself. Now was not the time. Smart girl.

She stood up and quickly followed the guards out of the room.

Faulk watched the whole exchange silently. She turned on me once Jessa and the guards were gone. "How dare you dismiss that girl when I clearly had unfinished business with her!"

I was unfazed. "Jessa has been through a lot. And quite frankly, you're not going to get anything out of her tonight. Just let her get some rest. We can start her training tomorrow."

"It's not your call."

"Actually, if you'll remember correctly, it *is* my call. Your king, my father, put me in charge of overseeing Jessa's training. Not you," I said.

"That may be true," Faulk responded. "But he wants her in the GC. And as the head of that program, I'll also be making sure that this girl stays in line. If she doesn't get through the basic training, there will be no initiation."

I doubted that. If Richard wanted Jessa in the GC, it would happen.

"And how are you planning to keep her in line?"

The younger guardian stepped forward, smirking. I frowned, having forgotten that he was still in the room.

"I'm Reed. I'll be working with you both from here on out."

"He's my eyes and ears." Faulk said. "Your father already approved it."

Great. Faulk's spy kid was going to be following us around. That was the opposite of what I needed right now. If I was going to get Jessa to help me, Reed needed to be out of the picture. But what choice did I have? As much as it bothered me, I knew this wasn't a battle I could win. At least not right now.

"So, Lucas," Reed continued boldly, "when do we start?"

I studied them both before turning on the kid. "You'd be advised to call me Prince Heart. We'll start first thing in the morning. I'll find you."

I turned and strode away before I lost my temper completely. It was only once I was out of the room that I let myself consider the implications of everything that had just happened in there.

There were a few things I knew for sure.

First of all, Jessa was dangerous and talented. She wasn't afraid to put up a fight. She had a fierce spirit and, despite everything, it still wasn't broken.

Second, I wasn't the only one who wanted something from the girl. Faulk, Reed, and my father all had their hooks in her. She was a valuable resource. She had separated purple into primary colors, which was unheard of. Alchemists could access variations of five of the seven colors: purple, blue, green, yellow, and orange. And all the shades in between. White and red remained a mystery. Black, as well. Jessa had accessed red that night at the ballet. This could change everything.

Moreover, it was possible that separating color wasn't the only remarkable talent hidden inside Jessa.

I admired the fight in her. Her vulnerabilities echoed my own. But she had no idea what she had gotten herself into. The last thing was hard to admit, if only to myself. I wanted to protect Jessa Loxley with my life.

Man, what in the world has gotten into you?

I found Jasmine in the now-empty GC dining hall. Realizing that Jessa must still be starving, I quickly ordered some food to be sent directly her room. Jasmine watched me with curiosity as I stood in the doorway.

I slid the slatebook back into my pocket and walked over to the old woman. She picked at her salad, distracted.

"What do you do for the GC?" I asked, sliding into the chair next to her.

"I teach. And I heal. I used to help out with your skinned knees as a child. Boy, did you get those a lot. I even fixed your broken arm once. Do you remember that?"

I laughed. I'd forgotten all about those experiences. But they came back instantly. "Actually, now that you mention it, I do remember."

Jasmine was so different to me now. Back then, her hair had been brown instead of gray. And she'd dressed in the customary GC black, instead of the casual clothing she now wore. I still wondered how she'd managed the trade.

"But you grew out of your clumsiness. So you stopped needing my help."

That was a point we seemed to differ on.

"Why do you want to know what I do here?" she asked.

"I was really impressed with how you handled Jessa just now."

"Thank you. I was just doing my job."

But it was more than that. She cared. She put Jessa at ease in a way that I just hadn't managed yet.

"You teach? Can you tell me about that?"

"I'm a strong healer, so I focus on working with green. Teaching others to heal is a delight. These young children that come here—they don't know what's going on. They're practically babies. Their minds are so open and vulnerable. I always do my best to teach them the difference between right and wrong, to teach them to use their gifts for good." She glanced at me quizzically. "That's what the GC is all about, isn't it?"

"Yes," I said, though I knew differently. I knew it was really about the royals being able to control the kingdom. "That's what it was designed to do—help people. And I was wondering if you would help me."

"What do you need?"

"I'm not an alchemist, but I've been tasked with training Jessa. Yes, I have extensive knowledge on the subject, but I can't possibly do it alone."

"And nor should you. The royal officers governing us guardians aren't alchemists, either. That's why they have people like me teaching. *Someone* needs to know what they're doing."

I thought I heard a hint of something troubled in her voice, but I could have imagined it. "Yes, exactly. We have an alchemist named Reed assigned to help us. But I don't trust him. He's working for Faulk, and I certainly don't trust her."

"Trust is a delicate thing."

"So that's why I want you to join us in Jessa's training. She likes you. I could

34

tell immediately that you would be the perfect mentor for her. Will you do it? Will you help us?"

"What's so important about this girl? She is probably too old to be starting this process."

"Yes, she's about ten years late. But she's special. When she was discovered, it was because she'd accidentally stumbled upon purple alchemy. But what was remarkable about it was that she separated the blue and the red."

"Red? But no one has red alchemy."

"Yes, I know," I said. That was a color that seemed to be untouchable. "She didn't actually do anything with the red, but she accessed it. It was there. Right there. I saw it myself."

"I can imagine your father wants to get to that."

I nodded but didn't say more. I needed to tread carefully.

Jasmine looked down at the plate of barely touched salad, a small smile tilting her mouth upward. When she hovered her open palm just above the green leaves of lettuce and spinach, delicate tendrils of emerald magic danced in the air. It was like watching light take on a physical form. It swirled and played beneath her fingers, haunting and mysterious.

"Yes, Lucas. You really do need my help."

We sat in silence for a long minute.

"How's your mother doing? Another headache today?"

How did she know?

She lifted the green even higher into the air before allowing it to fall back into the leaves below, like raindrops.

"Are you the one who helps her heal?"

"I try," she said. "It appears to be a chronic condition, unfortunately. We haven't found a cure, as you know. But I help with the pain."

"You're probably with her often, then?" I asked, trying to push for more information. I should know this, but hated to admit that I avoided my mother. It was just too hard to see what she'd become.

"Too often. She's a good woman. With a kind heart. Don't ever give up on her, okay?"

Before I could comment, Jasmine stood up and nodded.

"We'll be seeing each other soon."

FIVE

JESSA

After Faulk's threat against my family, I decided to keep my mouth shut. Fuming on the inside, I forced myself to stay calm.

Alone, I was now lying on a large bed, trying to process the many thoughts battling inside my head.

After finishing my conversation with Faulk, I'd been led to a guest suite. When the tray of food arrived a few minutes later, I'd devoured every last bite. Then I took a long shower, wrapped myself in a plush bathrobe, and curled up like a kitten under the heavy white duvet.

I wasn't content, but I could breathe steadily again. Did I have Lucas to thank for that? He confused me. He didn't seem to care about what I wanted, and yet he'd ended the conversation with Faulk for me. Also, he had told me he was the one who'd gotten me out of prison. The memory of the short time spent in the dark room wasn't one I wanted to revisit.

I had to admit that this room was much nicer than anything I expected. Faulk would have put me up in a dank closet somewhere if she'd had a say in the matter. Luckily for me, Lucas was the one who gave the orders. Once again, he'd come to my rescue. A part of me questioned his motives, while another part warmed at the thought that Lucas was on my side.

The suite was large, with dark, polished wood floors and trimmings. The walls were a soft white, and a large four-poster bed sat next to a wide floor-to-ceiling window. The drapery and linens, also white, contrasted nicely with the rich wood.

The bathroom itself was larger than my bedroom. The glass shower was sleek and modern, with an expansive set of buttons on the wall. Most exciting was the claw-foot bathtub, cutting an impressive figure in the center of the white marbled floor. The entire place was calm and luxurious.

But I still couldn't decide how I felt about all this. Part of me felt guilty for enjoying it. The gorgeous amenities were unlike anything I'd experienced. Sure, we were well taken care of in New Colony. We had a nice home. Anything we needed, we had. How could I enjoy this suite when all I longed for was my own lived-in bedroom?

The palace was beautiful, yes, but it was not my home.

I didn't know who I was anymore. Nor did I know what I was capable of. Tomorrow I would start my training. Maybe then I would be able to find answers. With no idea of what to expect, I stared blankly out the window. The bright moon floated in the darkness. It was full tonight, and watching it made me feel extra lonely. The tears came back again, pooling on my pillow. It wasn't until the early hours of the morning, when the black night began to turn blue, that I finally fell asleep.

◼

"Slow down," the sweet voice calls behind me as my child-self runs through the grass. My bare feet press into the lawn and leave small tracks as the blades fold in on themselves, a cool imprint of my movements. Instead, I move faster, my little legs rubbing together.

"To the special place! To the special place," I singsong, calling behind me to the girl following. She catches up quickly and grabs my hand. Instead of stopping me, she runs with me, fueling my excitement. A head taller, her blond hair streams behind her like ribbons of light in the sea of blue sky.

"Okay, Jessa," she says, "let's go to the special place."

She leads me out from the back of the lawn and into a thicket of trees. They stand tall, their trunks papery white with branches that reach out to the sky. The leaves dance together, making a sound like fluttering wind chimes on the afternoon breeze. Once inside the cropping of trees, we are hidden, the shadows our only playmates. But that's okay. These games are played in secret, anyway.

"Show me the magic," I say, whispering.

She always wants me to whisper.

She smiles and picks a dandelion flower peeking through the grass. Its stem separates from the ground with a little pop. Holding it in front of her face, she fixes her shiny blue eyes upon it, concentrating. When she squeezes, the yellow petals stain her fingers.

And then the flower's color begins to fade, as the hues of yellow puff out into a cloud of smoky light. It floats on the air, waiting for her command.

"Can I touch it?" I ask.

She smiles and blows. The color drifts to me as I eagerly reach out to meet it.

◼

I floated through that place between sleep and waking. Exhaustion pulled me down. My body was heavy, my mind dense. Somewhere, the world was going on, moving, without me. I wanted to stay here in this garden, in this happy dream of giggling children, but a stark thought jolted me back into consciousness.

Where am I?

I sat up, my eyes adjusting to the strange surroundings. Then the flood of memory filled me, and I fell back into the sea of pillows with a groan. This had been happening too much lately!

Since when did I start remembering my dreams?

Someone lightly knocked on the door. Before I could respond, a girl dressed in a maid's outfit shyly entered the room. She was young, petite, and carrying a tray of breakfast items. The salty smell of bacon wafted through the air. Bacon, like most meat, was a luxury food that my family didn't often eat. My mouth watered as I imagined the taste. Since I was still wearing the bathrobe from the night before, I considered excusing myself to quickly dress, but my stomach growled in protest.

The maid placed the tray on a small table in the corner of the room, peering at my rumpled appearance. "Excuse me, would you like anything else?"

I gaped at the feast of eggs, potatoes, cheese, pastries, fruit juices, and, of course, crispy bacon.

"It's perfect."

Skipping to the closest chair, I reached out a hand and introduced myself to the young maid. "I'm Jessa. What's your name?"

"It's Eliza, miss."

"Well, Eliza, you don't have to call me that. Just call me Jessa."

She smiled, eyeing the plate of food.

"Would you like some?" I asked her.

She blushed and looked down. "I couldn't."

"Yes, you can. Here." I lifted the basket of pastries. "Take one."

She gingerly took a chocolate-filled croissant and nibbled at the edge. I laughed and grabbed some bacon. When she grinned back, I wondered if she'd be bringing me more meals. *Maybe she could be my friend.* My mood got lighter than it had been since this whole nightmare began.

A heavy knock sounded on the door, and it abruptly swung open. A guardian dressed in black marched into the room. I immediately recognized him as the one who'd come in with Faulk. He was young—probably around my age—with sandy blond hair, dark-brown eyes, and, I had to admit, adorable dimples.

"There *is* such a thing as privacy," I said. I was in my bathrobe, after all.

"I knocked."

Actually, he'd knocked once and then walked right in. But I decided not to belabor the point. Given his inviting smile, maybe he wasn't as bad as Royal Officer Faulk. But still, I knew I couldn't trust him. Or anyone else in the palace, Lucas included. When all was said and done, fancy room notwithstanding, they were my captors and I was their prisoner.

"Whatever. Why are you in here?"

"On behalf of Faulk and the Guardians of Color, I'll be overseeing your training." He smiled even more widely. "I'm Reed."

"Already? You don't waste any time."

"Well, you do need to learn how to control color alchemy, and I happen to be a great teacher," he replied, practically laughing. Was there a joke here? Maybe this was Reed's idea of flirting but I wasn't having it.

"I'm not ready," I said. "I just woke up."

"I've been waiting all morning for you to get ready. I guess you're a stereotypical teenage girl. Sleeping all morning long. You'll probably need two hours just to do your hair?"

I stood from behind the table and folded my arms. *Judge much?* But I immediately regretted the gesture when I felt the cool air on my bare legs. Reed drank me in, stepping back. He scanned my under-dressed body.

On my tall frame, the bathrobe I'd slept in was entirely too short. As a dancer, I was used to people looking at my body. But the way Reed was staring at me with his flustered boyish expression was different. Embarrassing.

"Can I help you?"

"It depends on what you're offering."

Eliza stood off to the side during this whole exchange. She coughed on her croissant and scurried out of the room without a goodbye or an apology.

I eyed Reed, annoyed again at the interruption. I was making a new friend in Eliza until he had shown up and ruined it.

"I'm not offering anything. I was forced to be here. Or did you forget about your little eavesdropping stunt already?"

I hadn't forgotten that he was the guardian with Faulk last night. They had listened in on my conversation with Lucas. I was still not sure how he was able to do it, given the seemingly impervious walls and the fact that I hadn't seen any visible devices that would've clued me into the possibility of spies. As much as I didn't want to care, I was curious.

"Impressed?" He plopped down into the chair across from me. He tried to reach for the last piece of bacon, but I slapped his hand away.

"Hey! Where are your manners?"

"I'm a growing boy. I need my second breakfast."

He grinned, snatching it up, then split the bacon in half and handed me a piece. Somehow, I found myself laughing.

■

I let him eat with me while I questioned him. He was seventeen. He'd lived primarily at the palace for eleven years now, training in color alchemy. Soon he would be sent out on long-term assignments. When I asked him what that meant, he clammed up and changed the subject.

Just as we were finishing up, there was yet another knock. Prince Lucas stepped inside. He was dressed casually in dark jeans and a black t-shirt. The shirt was cotton, and on a body like his, it created the perfect male contrast of soft and hard. As much as I hated to admit it, he looked incredible. The royals always did look great though. Most often they weren't dressed so casually. In newspapers and on the news feeds I'd always seen him in his royal uniform.

"Are you ready?" Lucas asked.

I couldn't read his blank expression. "Wait, are you training me, too?" I looked from Lucas to Reed.

"I'm overseeing your progress," Lucas said. "I've assigned one of our healers, Jasmine, to train you. Reed here will also help."

He spoke of Jasmine as if I hadn't already met her. I guess because of the fact that I'd knocked Lucas out, which was still a secret. Was that even possible with someone like Reed following me around?

I got up and started to stack the plates before realizing I probably didn't have to clean up after myself. I noticed the two boys staring at my bare legs.

Seriously, are there no girls in this palace?

Reed grinned with enjoyment, but Lucas looked bothered.

"What is your problem?" I said. "It's not like I was going to sleep in that costume again."

Lucas shook his head. "You have a closet completely stocked with clothing."

He walked over to the dark-wood wall and pulled on a handle I hadn't noticed before. It slid open to reveal about six feet of wardrobe space. Each hanger had an item. Most of the clothing was black. Was all that for me?

Well, okay then.

Reed doubled over in laughter. "The look on your face right now is priceless."

I glared at him and tilted my head toward Lucas. "And how was I supposed to know that? I heard you called for clothing last night, but it never came. I figured someone forgot."

"Well, you're obviously not ready for training," he said.

"Thank you for pointing out the obvious."

He glanced down at my appearance again, and I pulled the robe, attempting to cover up as much as possible.

"Guardian." Lucas stopped Reed's laughter short. "Please allow Jessa some time alone to prepare herself. We'll meet in an hour to begin our training. It's a nice day, isn't it? Let's spend it out in the royal gardens."

"Your Majesty, we should begin her training somewhere more appropriate. Those gardens are hardly guardian headquarters. If it's greenery you're looking for, we've got plenty in the GC area."

"The royal gardens are exclusively used by the royal family and our guests. I'm sure Jessa would like to get a breath of fresh air. It will be just the three of us and Jasmine. No one else."

I breathed a sigh of relief and nodded.

I loved the outdoors. And something about the idea of being amid the lush gardens and their beautiful flowers reminded me of my childhood.

Didn't I have a dream about a flower?

"Too macho to hang out in the gardens?" I asked Reed.

I bit my tongue before I could say anything more. I didn't want Lucas to think I was flirting with Reed.

Both of these boys were attractive, but I wanted no part in that game.

Instead, I tried to focus on the matter at hand. Namely, how was I going to get myself out of this palace? As exciting as all this was, alchemy wasn't my plan. It wasn't dancing, and it took me away from my family. I had no clue how any of this could work in my favor, but I had to try, at least.

I'd been so lost in my thoughts I hadn't noticed Reed and Lucas were still here. *Hello? What are they waiting for?*

"Hey guys, you can go now."

They mumbled a string of awkward goodbyes and left the room. I wanted to go back to bed but knew it was time to get ready for the day. Hopefully I wouldn't embarrass myself.

■

Reed was waiting for me when I left my room an hour later. We engaged in trivial conversation as we walked down to the gardens together. When we came out onto the palace steps, I stopped short.

I don't know what I was expecting, but this wasn't it.

It wasn't just a garden. It was beautiful greenery that stretched for what looked like half a mile, and beyond that was a towering stone wall. Picturesque rose bushes, symmetrical flowerbeds, perfectly trimmed hedges, marble statues, beautiful fountains, stone paths, and vast lawns sprawled out around me.

We approached a bench where Prince Lucas sat waiting. He gave me a polite smile but didn't bother to acknowledge Reed's small bow. I got the feeling that Reed was only doing it out of obligation and nothing else. I wondered if I was supposed to curtsy, but before I got the chance, Lucas stood and waved at someone behind us.

"Jasmine. I'm glad you could make it."

Again, the older woman wasn't dressed in the black uniform that Reed wore, even though she was GC. Did the Guardians of Color have a little more freedom than I'd originally thought? Or was it just her?

"It's my pleasure," she said.

"I didn't know you were helping out today." Reed frowned.

"I'll be helping every day."

Lucas stood and led our group down one of the paths, a few of his guards following at a distance. Lucas must have been listening, but he didn't join in on the conversation. I could tell the two guys disliked each other. And yet they seemed so alike to me. They could probably be friends if the egos involved weren't so big.

After several minutes of navigating the garden, Lucas stopped at a charming pavilion and sat down at a small table. We were secluded, surrounded by the tall trees. Spindly green vines covered the delicate white structure. The spring air was breezy, and the pleasant scent of freshly cut grass wafted through the area.

"Before we start testing your abilities, it's important that you're educated on the intricacies of alchemy," Lucas said.

He motioned for us to join him at the table. Reed and Jasmine sat across from Lucas, leaving me no other place than right next to him. Strangely, I felt vulnerable there. I still couldn't believe the wild situation I'd found myself in.

"What better way to learn than by practicing?" Reed asked Lucas. "If you're not too afraid."

I wasn't sure if the comment was directed at me or at Lucas. Either way, I was definitely not ready to take another crack at color alchemy.

"Jessa is different," Lucas said to Reed. "She's older, so her magic is strong, but she's also very new to this. She's better off understanding what she's doing before she tries again."

Lucas was right. I was not ready to do any alchemy. The three times I'd done it, I'd had no control. The experiences with Lacey's blood, the ballet, and the fire last night had been terrifying.

I'd rather just talk, even if it meant listening to Lucas and Reed bicker. Sacrifices, right?

"Okay, I like your plan, Lucas. And I do have a lot of questions."

"I'm sure you do, but let's start by explaining the basics. After we're finished, we'll try to answer some of your questions."

I nodded as he pulled out his slatebook, the same high-tech device he'd used the night before. He typed in a quick password, and the screen pulled up a search engine.

"There is a lot of information out there about color alchemy, but most of it is only speculation. You probably believe all sorts of false rumors. We don't like to correct the public, because the less they know, the better for us. New Colony is the only country we know of that uses alchemists as assets. We don't accuse you of witchcraft, and we don't publicly execute you."

Wow, how nice of you.

I didn't like to think about it, but it made sense. After a number of crippling wars and most of the planet's natural resources in scarce supply, the world wasn't thriving anymore. People resorted to desperate measures as they were struggling to survive. Having a scapegoat gave people an outlet for all their rage. Was it misdirected? Yes. But it happened. New Colony wasn't at war anymore, but we knew our government used alchemy to take care of us. I'd heard other countries wanted the information. Why wouldn't they? West America probably wouldn't be able to agree on what to do with alchemy anyway. Still, with such powerful magic at our disposal, I was certain we had ways to keep our secrets.

Lucas typed something into his slatebook. "That's why most of the real information about alchemists and guardians is banned from public access. We don't want our foreign enemies learning our secrets."

Besides West America, who exactly are our foreign enemies?

"But couldn't it help? If people are struggling, wouldn't this be valuable information for them? Maybe they could train their alchemists and live the way we do here."

"And then we'd be back to more world wars," Reed argued. "There are still plenty of people out there who want us to return to the old ways of democracy. What makes you think they wouldn't use alchemy against us?"

Democracy? I didn't know much about it except what I was told. In the old country, called America, people voted for their leaders. But that only led to more disagreement, hatred, and division. We split off, becoming New Colony. Things were better now.

Lucas placed the screen face-up on the table. "That's a discussion for another day. But if I were you, I wouldn't repeat your sentiments to anyone."

He winked, and I realized my mistake. Had I sounded treasonous?

"Anyway, if you have a very high level of security clearance, like I do, then you can access this." He pointed to the screen.

It was an image of a colorful drawing. A man was sitting, his legs crossed, with his palms open on his knees. From the crown of his head to the base of his spine were circles of color. Together they made a rainbow, moving from white at the top to red at the bottom. Although the image was on a modern screen, it still had an ancient quality. Unlike anything I knew.

Reed's eyes glittered. "Whoa! I know what this is, but even I've never seen it before."

"This is a very old document. It comes from a time even before America was established. Possibly from before there were people on this continent. Its teachings are ancient."

I tried to imagine this, but I didn't know what he meant. The history classes I'd taken never went back that far.

"This document gave my family huge clues on how to control color. We've succeeded, while so many others have failed. What we're looking at has many names. Some texts refer to this concept as chakras, others as the wheels of light. We refer to each sphere as an energy center." He nodded at Jasmine to explain.

She put a hand to her head. "White." Then she placed it on her forehead. "Purple." She moved her hand to her throat. "Blue." Her heart. "Green and pink as well." Her upper torso was yellow, her stomach orange.

Jasmine motioned to her pelvis. "Red."

I peered at the drawing. "I don't understand."

"Energy exists in some way or another in all things. Humans have seven main energy centers. You wouldn't know that because you can't see them, but I promise you, they are there."

"We're not sure why, but some humans are born with the ability to tap into their own energy centers and connect them with other energies. That's where color alchemy first begins."

Lucas peered at me. "When you were dancing, what were you feeling?"

It hurt to remember. I'd been full of joy, and that was all gone now. But I needed to understand, so I decided to push my feelings aside and talk about that night. "I felt like I was exactly where I was supposed to be. I felt sure of myself. I was free. I knew what I was doing. I've practiced that a million times, so I just let all my thoughts go, and I danced. It was like breathing."

I held back my tears. I'd allowed myself to cry last night. I couldn't do that anymore if I hoped to gain any respect.

"And that's why you were able to use alchemy so strongly." Reed grinned.

43

"In that moment, you were most connected to your violet or purple energy, the ball of light here," Jasmine said, pointing to the man's forehead. "This has been historically called the third eye. That's because the brow is associated with self-knowledge, intuition, spirituality, and self-reflection. I suspect you were also connected to other energy centers in your body, but I can't know for sure."

Reed stood excitedly. "This is where it started. Do you understand?"

No, I couldn't say that I did.

This was confusing. They may as well have been speaking a different language. What I didn't get was how this so-called energy center in my head caused the show of color alchemy. My dress had become gray, while the air around me sparkled in an electric cloud of purple. Almost like physical light.

"What color was your costume?" Reed asked.

"It was dark purple and lavender. Yes, it was similar to that." I pointed to the sphere of purple around the man's head.

"Exactly," Lucas said. "In that moment you let go, that perfect moment when you were dancing, something happened. One of your energy centers, the one in your forehead, was activated. The energy was so strong that it needed a way to escape. So what did it do? It connected with the object that corresponded to its color. One you just happened to be physically touching. Purple."

"My dress."

"Yes! The energy connected with your dress, and the color released. Do you remember the dress briefly turned gray? That's exactly why. What's even more extraordinary is that your dress isn't exactly a living organism. It's made of manufactured fabrics. Most alchemists can only connect with organic things, like plants. Our strongest are able to connect with nonliving things, but that takes years of training. You went beyond that without even meaning to!"

So physically touching the color was part of the process. I remembered Lacey's blood and how, when I touched it, the red had seeped away from the liquid, turning it gray. According to them, my power had been responsible for the brilliant display of color alchemy that had followed. I shook my head in disbelief.

"So what happened to the color after my dance? I passed out, remember? When I woke up the next day, my costume was normal again."

"Even for a natural like you, it's not easy." Reed smirked. "You have to know what to do with it once it's out. Or else it goes back to where it came from."

"Yes," Lucas said, "but that's complicated. Best to see it for yourself. Since we're not ready for that yet, I think it's best we stop here for today."

I didn't want to stop the conversation. I needed to know more. What did the other colors mean? How were they contained? What did the New Colony want with them? Why did they need me? And was Lacey really okay after what I'd done to her? After all, the blood I'd changed had remained gray, as Faulk had shown us. What had happened to the red? Where did it go? Had we used it somehow? The questions were endless.

"Why don't I get you a copy of this?" Lucas pointed to the screen. "You can study it today and come back with questions tomorrow."

"Can I get a copy, too?" Reed asked.

Lucas paused. Just when I was sure he was going to deny Reed his request, he sighed. "I can grant access for all of you with a temporary copy only. So I suggest you study it well. I'm going out on a limb for you, so please don't break my trust. Do not share this with anyone. And printing it is illegal, so don't even think about it."

We nodded.

"Jessa," he added, "I'll make sure you receive a slatebook today. You'll need it." He powered off his own and stood to lead us from the garden.

At his words, a heavy load of weariness slowly lifted from my chest. Of course our family had a slatebook at home, everyone did. Sure it wasn't nearly as high-tech as the ones here at the palace. So what? It still worked! I knew immediately what my first order of business was. As soon as I got my slatebook, before I studied the energy centers, before I did anything else, I was going to call home. I was going to talk to my parents. They would know what to do.

SIX

LUCAS

Reed immediately wanted his copy of the old chakra drawing, and without a good excuse to keep it from him, I emailed it to his device. It wasn't ten minutes later that Officer Faulk found me in my study. Coincidence? Doubtful. Not bothering with a polite "Your Highness," she stormed in unannounced. "How dare you undermine me!"

I turned from my bookshelf, already wishing she would leave. "I assume this is about Jessa?"

She really had it in for the girl, and something about that made me want to defend her even more. So what if Jessa had lied? It wasn't the first time someone had tried to hide alchemy, and it certainly wouldn't be the last. How was this girl any different from so many others? She deserved a break.

"Giving her a slatebook with outside call access? You may as well just give her complete freedom. And apparently the two guards posted at her door have been ordered to let her come and go from her room as she pleases. Have you lost your mind? She is a prisoner and a criminal! She is not a guest."

I could only guess that Reed must have gone running to tell Faulk about the slatebook and Jessa's housing situation. He'd put up a front of wanting to be Jessa's friend. She probably thought he cared for her. I was stupid to believe he would be anything other than another one of Faulk's golden boys.

"As much as you don't approve of my approach, I'm in charge. If you have a problem, then you can take it up with my father."

We both knew she hated that I had the reins. She was ordered to assist me with what I needed, but to essentially stay out of my way. I also suspected she had been tasked to report the efficacy of my methods to Richard.

"Don't think I won't be telling your father all about this. He knows as well as I do that the Loxley family is trouble."

"What do you mean, her family?" I asked, my heart jumping to my throat.

There was something going on that Faulk wasn't telling me about. Was there more to why she was so strict with Jessa?

But she only stared at me for a minute before briskly turning on her heel and leaving my study. With the slam of the door, my suspicions were confirmed. She was hiding something. And it was highly likely she'd be following my every move, reporting it all back to my father.

I walked over to the door and made sure it was locked this time.

Going back to the bookshelf, I found what I was looking for. Pulling out the non-descript title, I opened the large leather-bound book. The one with the hidden compartment. I'd altered the book years ago, looking for a place to hide the access to my unauthorized research.

This is where I'd hidden my undocumented flash drive. The slatebook attachment held electronic information that couldn't be found on any computer or information cloud. Information I was sure no one expected me to have. I was only eighteen, but I'd been collecting it for years.

Granted, alchemy was a very important part of New Colony's success. My great-grandfather was the one who had created the GC. But over the last few decades, Richard had built an empire based on the extraordinary uses of color alchemy. He'd dived into the project as no one else before him, looking for the most talented alchemists and taking their skills to the limit. I'd seen myself how they'd depleted some of our rural areas of color. What was left could only be described as utter devastation. To keep everything quiet he'd enlisted only the brightest minds to become royal officers...like Faulk. Their job was to make sure things ran smoothly and that no alchemist stepped out of line.

Even if he would never admit it, I suspected my father would have done anything to be an alchemist. Since he wasn't, the next best thing was to control those who were. And just to make sure no one became more powerful than the royals, he'd created strict laws governing the guardians. Appointing non-alchemists to police their activities and oversee training was just one more way to stay on top. People like Faulk only had power because he said they did.

I think it helped that guardians were first brought to the palace at such a young age. Color alchemy was something that developed quickly. Not in infants or toddlers, but in young children. Most of the GC didn't have many memories of their families. The palace was their only home.

But things couldn't be all bad or else guardians would rebel, wouldn't they? So in return for their obedience, they were provided with lavish lifestyles, not too unlike us royals. They mostly resided in the palace, in their own immaculate areas. GC headquarters were off limits. I, of course, could go there. A prince could pretty much go anywhere. Despite that, I had intentionally avoided anything GC outside of special assignments from my father.

I was in a delicate position. I had too much knowledge of deadly repercussions of alchemy, but not enough power to actually change anything.

After a few more minutes browsing through my research, I found what I was looking for. On the sleek screen was the list of names I'd slowly compiled of those alchemists who had been incarcerated. Most of them had been locked up because they weren't able to control their dangerous talents, but some were on this list because they had refused to join the GC. These were the ones who had rebelled. And if there was one thing I knew about my father, rebellion was squashed immediately.

Next to each name, I'd noted what information I'd uncovered, if any. I began searching for something to indicate why Faulk had said the Loxley family was trouble.

Marissa Levi: Lost control of her mind, became increasingly violent with each attempt. Entered training at age 5, was placed in custody at age 11.

I knew that "custody" was the polite way of saying that this Marissa girl was sent to a mental institution. Had she really lost her mind?

Jackson Spears: Repeated refusal to use his abilities. After three attempted suicides, he was placed in isolation, deemed a danger to himself and others. Started his training at age 8, joined the guard at age 15, incarcerated at age 16.

I remembered him. Jackson had been a natural talent, but he'd hated to use his powers and he couldn't control his mind. He had turned out to be deadly. In fact, he'd almost killed another alchemist in the final suicide attempt that had landed him in solitary confinement. I often wondered if coming here at eight years old had been too late for Jackson. If they'd gotten to him sooner, would he have been happier?

The list continued, reaching back through the last fifty years since the formation of the Guardians of Color. I'd added anything I could find about people not being able to control it and what happened to them.

I was looking for something—anything—that would lead back to Jessa.

The public believed that color alchemists popped up at random. That was true sometimes. But most often, color alchemy could be tracked through DNA. The problem was that many people were born with the trait and never developed any powers. But they were marked at birth and then watched closely. All citizens were now required to submit to genetic testing as infants. That was probably my father's idea. I wondered how Jessa had kept herself hidden for so long. Maybe she was telling the truth.

About 30 percent of the population had the genetic trait, but less than 0.1 percent ever needed to be taken into custody by the GC. The trait usually stayed dormant. Like it had with our family. We actually were part of the 30 percent, but not the 0.1 percent. I suspected my father had tried to find a way to somehow activate alchemy in himself, but with no success.

I continued to comb through my research.

Since it ran in families, it was very likely that somewhere along the line, Jessa had a family member who was an alchemist. All I could hope was that we'd known about them. It would provide tremendous insight into her training. Just as regular talents were passed down through families, so were specific color-alchemy abilities. Maybe she had a family member out there who knew more about her alchemy than she did.

Someone who could help us understand how she'd separated the purple into red and blue. As it stood, none of our trainers could do that.

My records included information about people who were trained but never actually initiated as members of the GC. While this information was technically off limits, I'd found ways around that problem. Sure, it took time, but I'd been at this for years.

I continued to scan my notes until I found it.

Francesca Loxley: Training began at age 5, initiation into the GC at age 6, and went missing from guardian custody at age 9. Whereabouts unknown.

Whereabouts unknown?

Whoever this girl was, she was young while she was at the palace. That was not unusual. She would have been trained by the GC, as everyone was given a shot. I wondered why they had initiated her so quickly. Six-year-olds were not ready to be full-blown guardians, at least not that I was aware of.

Unfortunately, I had nothing else on file for Francesca except a few dates. But dates were valuable.

Francesca went missing eleven years ago. If she was still alive, then she would be nineteen. Jessa would have only been three years old when Francesca was taken. Even if they were related, Jessa probably wouldn't remember her—assuming her parents had kept the whole thing a secret, which was possible. I knew there had to be more to the story than Faulk and Richard were telling me.

Could I question Jessa's parents? Find out if they knew Francesca? The easier solution would be to sneak into the royal officer's computers and find the information myself. I'd done it a few times over the years. But with Faulk watching my every move, I wasn't so sure of myself.

Francesca was my clue as to why Faulk was so distrusting of Jessa and her family. I couldn't be sure yet, but I suspected that Francesca was Jessa's older sister. A sister who was also an alchemist.

That begged the question: Where was Francesca now?

Either Jessa was as clueless as she acted or she was hiding something even bigger than I could have imagined.

A long-lost sister.

■

I needed someone in the GC on my side. I'd worked with different guardians on random assignments, but never one-on-one like this. Not how I would be working with Jessa. She would be taught by other guardians, of course, but those guardians weren't allowed to actually oversee the whole process. My father had always put his best non-alchemist royal officers—a mixture of scientists, soldiers, and the government's various "secret weapons"—in charge of those matters. But I still didn't understand why Richard had given me the assignment of working with Jessa. Why not Faulk or someone else with more experience? I had resolved that keeping Jasmine around would be best for me, and I wanted to make sure Richard would stay on board with that.

I found him alone in his large office. This surprised me, as my father typically spent his time in other, less private, areas of the palace. He was leaning over a map on the desk, concentration etched into his brow.

"What do you need, son?" My father motioned me into the room.

I took a seat in one of the large chairs and glanced at the map. There were red pins stuck in clusters around the edges of the country. I recognized the areas to be shadow lands. Places where our overuse of alchemy had destroyed everything. Crops, animals, even people, all gone.

"What are you going to do about that," I said, pointing to the map.

Richard didn't bother to look up at me. We'd already had this argument. He wasn't going to change his mind. He didn't care what sacrifices were made for power. He thought I would see his side soon enough.

"It's nothing we need to talk about right now, Lucas. What do you need?"

I sighed, pushing down my anger, knowing I was doing something.

"I want to know why you assigned me to Jessa Loxley," I said, changing the topic.

He looked up from the map and leaned back in his chair. "You don't want the assignment?"

"I didn't say that. It just seems more important than any of the ones you've given me before."

"And this concerns you?" He laughed. "Well, that's a bad sign."

"Just tell me why."

"Your mother has been wanting me to give you more responsibilities. And since you turned eighteen, I've been looking for something. When you came to the prison in defense of the girl, I figured it would be a good place to start."

Could it really be that simple?

I'd essentially been my father's apprentice since I was a young boy. I'd go on little errands with him or sit in on boring meetings. As I got older, I went on trips with him as well, but nothing exciting ever happened. It wasn't like we were going to fight wars or anything. They were usually just marketing campaigns to sway public opinion.

Most of my time growing up was spent with tutors, reading, playing games with my nannies, or running around outside. Sometimes I'd find the other children in the palace, all guardians in training, and we'd play. But as soon as my parents figured that out, they stopped it. I cried for hours the first time they separated me from my friends.

They told me I was above the alchemists and that I would never fit in with such strange children. I was forbidden to play with them from that day onward.

It had broken my heart, and I'd gone back to being lonely, a child in a world of busy adults.

Mom probably felt guilty about that, because as I grew up, she started bringing in other children for me to spend time with—the offspring of government officials, celebrities, and her society friends.

As a teen, I demanded more. I tried to get permission to go to a public school in the city. But Richard wouldn't allow it. As their only child, I was too valuable to leave the palace. So instead, I had to be content with my personal tutors and the occasional pre-screened play date. But once we started going to parties, I began connecting with other teenagers. Email, phone calls, and video chats kept things going between meetings.

It had worked out okay in the end. By the age of thirteen, I had decided it was better to keep others at a distance, anyway. By fifteen, everything changed when girls started taking notice. Actually, they became obsessed with "winning" the prince. I used it to my advantage when I wanted, and when I didn't, I ignored them.

But then everything in my world changed. I'd started to suspect that maybe Richard wasn't who I thought he was. And recently, I learned about the shadow lands, and then the email came about the deaths. It was what I needed to make a decision. If I was going to change anything, I had to work with the Resistance. And maybe Jessa was our way to change things.

"There are plenty of things you could assign me to. But overseeing the training of Jessa Loxley? I mean, the girl pulled from lavender and then shifted it into primary colors. It's a big job. I can do it. I know I can do it. But…"

"What are you trying to say?"

"Why are you suddenly taking an interest in me?"

There had to be a catch. Only a couple of months ago I'd found out about the extremes my father was doing with his color experiments. I didn't want to believe them, but I think I'd always known, deep down. After making contact with the woman from the Resistance, the one I'd met in the palace gardens, she'd confirmed it. There was no life left in the shadow lands. There was nothing.

"I've always had an interest in you," Richard replied. "But do I need to remind you that you were the one who came out to see her? You defended her."

He was right. The image of her falling to the stage flashed through my mind. So did the way she'd collapsed when those guards had dropped her, handcuffed and blindfolded. I realized that something about Jessa reminded me of myself. Sure, we came from opposite ends of the social spectrum, but we had one thing in common: our lives weren't our own.

"Yes. I did defend her."

"Why did you do that?"

"What do you mean? I told you, she's worth too much to just lock up." It wasn't a lie.

"You've never taken a particular interest in color alchemy before. So why this girl?"

"She's not a regular alchemist. She has something more. I'm just not exactly sure what it is yet." I paused. "I know Mom's condition is chronic, and the doctors have said that we can only treat it, not cure it. But what if…"

"What if Jessa could heal her?" He frowned.

"I've wondered. Maybe there's a way."

"I agree that Jessa's powerful. We've already seen her separate the primary colors from purple. That alone could prove to be invaluable. But your mother's migraines aren't going anywhere. The best doctors have all confirmed this. All we can do is keep Natasha comfortable."

Something about his tone bothered me. It was cold. Final.

"So then what do you want Jessa for?" I suspected I already knew the answer. Even if he wasn't going to tell me, I still had to ask.

He smiled, pressing clasped hands to his lips. "To make this country stronger."

Hope laced his every word, and I had a sinking feeling we had two distinct definitions.

"I need you to be a part of this," Richard said. "As my heir, I need you to fully comprehend why we do things the way we do. I think Jessa is the key to fixing everything."

Except his own wife. I looked away, attempting to ignore the ache. What could he possibly want fixed outside of that? New Colony was already the most powerful nation on Earth.

I glanced at the map and its clusters of red pins. They reminded me of what I was fighting for. Whom I was fighting against. Could I be the only one? I knew of the Resistance, but even they seemed so small. How many people out there knew what I knew? How many would be willing to help us?

Richard caught my eye, caught me staring at the red pins.

"One day, Lucas, you'll understand."

No. I wouldn't. I got up to leave.

"Don't mess this up. You won't get a second chance."

"About that. You know that Faulk assigned a young guardian to help with Jessa's training?"

"Reed is an asset. What's the problem?"

"No problem, except that I don't think he's got enough going for him to help someone like Jessa all on his own. I've asked another alchemist, Jasmine, to also step in and assist."

"I know who she is. She's one of your mother's favorites. Are you asking for my permission?"

"No, actually, I'm not."

I turned the corner and walked down the hallway of our secluded residence, intending to find a distraction. Maybe go for a run?

But there was someone I needed to talk to first. I switched direction and headed instead for my parents' bedroom, knocking gently on the door before entering the darkened room.

"Mother, are you in here?" I whispered. I slowly walked toward the canopied bed and found her lying in a heap, with several pillows propped up behind her. A cool washcloth was draped across her pale forehead. Her auburn hair was fanned around her like a fiery halo.

"Lucas," she smiled. "How are you, sweetheart?"

"I'm good, Mom." Something about that word felt comforting. The last few years, I'd taken to calling her by her name, Natasha. So much about her had changed over time. She used to be spirited, fun, playful, and nurturing. But all of that had disappeared as her illness took over.

"What do you need?" she asked.

"I just wanted to check on you. How do you feel?"

"Oh, you know. It comes and goes. They've been worse lately, but farther apart. So that's good."

"I don't know if I'd call that a good thing."

"Well, at least it allows me to get back out into public when I'm feeling up for it. I'd rather have really good days and really bad ones. Not being stuck in here with the lights off constantly."

"I guess you're right." I stood up from the edge of the bed, not sure what else to say. This conversation was depressing, and I wanted to get out.

"Will you call for Jasmine to come to me?" she asked.

"You know Jasmine well?" I was curious about their relationship now, since my mother had never mentioned her before, but Richard had.

"Oh, yes." She smiled. "I'm afraid I'm not much use around here. Jasmine helps with the pain. We've become friends these last few years."

Friends? I wondered how my father felt about his queen being friends with a color alchemist. I studied her, holed up in this darkened room. My heart sank as I realized that maybe Richard was right. Maybe there was nothing we could do to help. But somehow, I knew I wasn't ready to give up just yet. I needed to get Jessa trained and figure out what powers she actually had. And to do that I needed her to trust me. I knew it was wishful thinking, but I couldn't help myself. Maybe Jessa could not only help the Resistance, maybe she could save my mother.

"Something's wrong." Mother grabbed her head, pushing her palms against her ears.

"What is it? Are you okay?"

"The pain is *on purpose*. Someone is hurting me."

What was she talking about? If someone was hurting her, I needed to know who it was.

"I can't remember. I can never remember anything."

"Who's hurting you?" I asked. Urging her to have a moment of clarity. *Please, Mom, don't go silent on me now.*

But her face cleared again, and she peered up at me. The moment was lost. Those few words clung to me: *on purpose*. They changed everything. This wasn't just about chronic migraines. Was something darker going on? Of course, I had failed to see it all these years. Someone was *causing* her pain, stealing her away. It had to be alchemy. How else could it be done? But the bigger question wasn't what was happening, it was who was doing it, and why? Jasmine was with her often, but so were other healers. My father, Faulk, and a few of the royal officers saw her daily. Plenty of people were around her. She was Queen Natasha after all. So why would someone want to ruin her mind?

I wasn't sure exactly why this was happening, but I was sure someone was hurting her, using her. I would have to be more observant than ever. Just as I left the room, she called out to me in an even voice, "Be careful, Lucas."

SEVEN

JESSA

By the time Eliza delivered the slatebook, I'd learned something new about myself. I was a seriously impatient person. I sat in my room, picking through my dinner halfheartedly, waiting hours until I finally had the brand new device in my hands. It was square and thin, but strong and smooth, made entirely of glass.

I couldn't believe it was mine!

I turned it on, pleased by how easily I could navigate through the options. I found the telephone icon with no problem but decided on the video chat instead. Just as I was about to call home, I paused to reconsider.

What would they think of me, their daughter, the alchemist?

I wrung my hands out, then sat on them to stop myself. Would they even want to see me? I could only imagine their disappointment when they'd learned the truth. I wasn't the person they thought I was.

By now, they'd probably figured out that I'd been the one to tamper with Lacey's blood. Was she still okay? I remembered Officer Faulk's nasty threats against my family. If I didn't follow her rules, they would be the ones to face the consequences. It was possible they could lose their home, be relocated out of the capital city. They could end up in jobs they hated. Lacey might not have a good school anymore. Those thoughts terrified me. Despite my pride, I had to make sure they were safe.

Sitting on the edge of the bed, I took a deep breath and made the call. The device was so advanced it had holographic capabilities, but I was happy to use the traditional video chat option. I studied myself in the shiny reflection of the screen while the phone rang. Even though I felt different, I looked the same. The same pale skin, the same large blue eyes, the same wavy mess of brown hair.

After what felt like ages, the shiny screen changed and my mother's face materialized across the glass. Her equally curly hair was a disaster. Her dark eyes were swollen and red-rimmed.

Guilt swept over me, washed by the pain of utter homesickness. I wanted to cry too, but I resolved to hold it together. For her sake and my own.

"Jessa?" she asked. "Where are you? Are you hurt?"

My body tensed. Did she really have no idea? How could they have left my parents in the dark? It had been days.

"There have been royal officers standing outside our doors, but they won't answer any of our questions. We didn't know what to think."

"I'm okay, Mom," I said, my voice shaking. "I'm in the palace. I'm safe now."

She sighed slightly before calling out, "Christopher! Lacey! It's Jessa!"

My father and Lacey quickly appeared behind her. They peered over her shoulder, getting a better look at me.

"What happened, Jessa?" my Dad asked. "Are you all right?"

"She's in the palace," my mother said.

"Like a princess?" Lacey clapped.

Oh yeah, it's definitely been princess treatment so far.

Lacey's smile was a lifeline for me. It was the only thing keeping me from breaking down in front of my family. She was dressed in her favorite pair of pink pajamas, ready for bed. Her blond hair was dark, wet from the bath. She was tucked comfortably against Dad's chest while he held her with one strong arm. The familiarity of that bedtime embrace nearly broke me.

Who am I kidding? I can't hold this in anymore.

"I'm so sorry. I tried to stop it. I tried, but I wasn't even sure about what was happening. I didn't know what to do."

"So it's true, then?" Mom asked, her hopeful expression deflating.

"Why didn't you tell us, honey?" Dad asked, puzzled.

I wiped at my tears. "I know I should have told you. But I was scared. I didn't want to ruin everything. I didn't want it to be real."

I spent the next few minutes explaining what was going on. When I told them I wouldn't be coming home for a while, my mother started to cry again. I couldn't bring myself to let them in on the truth, that I'd likely never get to spend any significant amount of time with them again. I was lost to them.

"Come home, Jessa," Lacey whimpered. "I miss you."

"I miss you, too. I know it's going to be hard, but somehow I am going to turn this whole thing around. Right now I have to be at the palace, but only so I can find a way to come home later."

Was that true? I wasn't sure. But it was the only plan I could hope for.

"You promise?"

I hesitated. Could I make her that promise? Her eyes, normally full of innocence, were filled with a grown-up sense of knowing.

I looked her straight on. "I promise."

Mom and Dad exchanged a quick, almost imperceptible, glance. I had a feeling they'd already discussed this. I immediately detected doubt.

Do you know something I don't? I bit my tongue. Maybe they just didn't want me around anymore. They probably didn't want to risk having an untrained color alchemist near Lacey. I didn't blame them. As much as I wished it wasn't true, I wasn't safe.

Lacey fought back a sweet yawn as she rubbed her eyes with her small fists. She was too young to understand, but she was smart enough to know that something was wrong. She wanted to be treated like a grown-up, and that stung. All I wanted was for her to stay little and happy, like a six-year-old ought to be.

"We have to go, honey," Dad said. "It's past her bedtime."

With Lacey still in his arms, he waved a quick goodbye and they disappeared. I could hear Lacey's exhausted whine that she *wasn't tired* in the background.

"Goodbye, dear. Always remember, we love you." Mom stared, as if she wanted to say more. "You're there, but we're here. We can't help you right now. You need to help yourself. Please, be smart. We love you more than you know."

The screen went black.

"I love you, too," I said to the empty screen, the empty room.

I'd missed my chance to schedule our next call. They hadn't told me anything about what their lives were like now. Did they still have the same government-assigned jobs? Had Faulk done anything to punish them? Were they afraid for me? Afraid for themselves?

Maybe I was just being overly sensitive, but it felt like they'd already given up, already dismissed me from their lives. How could that be? I was their daughter. They loved me. I loved them.

So why did they act that way? Why did she say those things?

The brief call home wasn't what I was expecting. Family was family. We would always have each other. My parents taught me that. They were my flesh and blood. Perhaps they weren't ready to fight for me, but I was going to fight for them. I didn't know how yet, but I would return home. I would keep my promise to Lacey. I would get my life back.

■

Sleep wouldn't come easily. It was too early for me to be in bed. At home, I was always the last one to go to bed and the first one to wake. Besides, the conversations of the day—earlier in the garden and recently with my parents—had been turning over and over in my mind.

I got up and slid open the door to the huge closet, filled with elegant clothing. I pulled on the simplest jacket I could find and headed for the door.

But when I tried to turn the knob, it didn't budge. I had one of those surreal moments where something that should have been obvious to me became suddenly clear. Of course they had locked me up. Just because it didn't look like the gray room from the prison didn't mean I wasn't a prisoner. The evidence was right in front of me.

Frustrated, I raised my hand to bang on the door, demanding to be let out. But before my fist reached the dark oak, it swung open and I nearly punched Prince Lucas in the face.

"Well, at least you didn't use color alchemy this time to try and knock me out," he said, catching my wrist with a swift hand.

He moved into the room, still holding onto me as he softly closed the door behind us.

"Can I help you?" I asked, flushed with embarrassment.

He laughed, seemingly taking pleasure in my discomfort.

The fact that he was amused only made the heat burn deeper in my cheeks. A large smile filled his face, reaching his steel-gray eyes. They darted from my face to my wrist, which he still held in his grasp. He ever so slightly caressed my skin with his warm thumb before letting go.

Did he mean to do that?

And then he winked.

Yes. Yes, he did.

So the stories were true. Lucas was rumored to be a huge flirt. Maybe he couldn't help acting the part. Maybe he was so used to the effect he had on women that he saw me as just another ordinary girl who would succumb to his charms. But that wasn't me. I needed to get back home to my family. The last thing I needed was some lame fling, even if he did get a rise out of me.

"Why am I locked in here? I thought you said I was a guest."

"You were, and as far as I am concerned, you still are."

"Explain the locked door then."

"Faulk tattled. She got upset about your arrangements and told my father. He wanted us to come up with a compromise. It's stupid. I'm sorry, but for now, you'll only be able to move freely around the palace when you're accompanied."

"So, no alone time anywhere but here?"

"I'm sorry."

"Why are you here, Lucas?" I stood as tall as I could, looking him squarely in the eye. So what if he was famous, royal, and attractive?

"That's a loaded question," he said, holding my gaze.

The heat built between us, and I didn't know how to respond. If I opened my mouth now, who knows what nonsense would come stumbling out? The silence stretched before he laughed again, breaking the tension.

Why is this happening? I don't want to deal with this right now!

"Don't worry, I don't bite," he said, before adding, "usually."

I froze and he laughed again.

"If you're just here to tease me, then you can go."

"Oh, relax, Jessa. I was just coming to check on you. It's been a depressing evening, hasn't it? Were you wanting to go somewhere?"

"Yes, it has. And yes, I was. I have been cooped up in this room all afternoon. I want to go for a walk. Checking out where I am going to be staying wouldn't be so bad. But I guess that's off the table."

"Sorry about that. You should consider yourself a student here. And even the students have rules. They're mostly kept sequestered in their areas, too. In the GC wing."

"Looks like I'm still a prisoner then."

"You can leave your room if you're with someone who is comfortable enough to spend time with you. Or if you don't mind guards following you. Being such a dangerous alchemist, well, it limits your options. However, you're in luck. I don't scare easily."

"Gee, thanks. But I don't need a babysitter."

"It's not like that. Anyway, soon enough, you will become a guardian. You'll be living with them and will have much more freedom to do what you want. But for now…" He turned and opened the door, pausing at the entrance. "Well? Are you coming?"

"You really want to take me for a walk?" Was he willing to spend time with me only because he felt sorry for me? Or because something in him felt the same way I did—drawn to the other despite better intentions? I wasn't sure which answer bothered me more.

"Sure I do. Unless you don't want to be seen with me?"

This huge palace was my home now. And however temporary it would be, I was dying to check it out. Before I could talk myself out of it, I summoned courage and followed him out of the room.

■

We strolled through the labyrinth of hallways as he pointed out different areas. Libraries, ballrooms, guest suites, and government departments were all located here. The palace was by far the largest building I'd ever been in. In fact, it was multiple buildings strung together. Even the theatre where the Royal Ballet was housed couldn't hold a candle to this place.

The main building had three stories that stretched wide across acres of land. It was comprised of a delicate hodgepodge of old and new architecture. The original building was part of the old country's capital building. I think it had been called the White House. But as New Colony grew, the royal family had leveled all of the surrounding buildings and new wings had been added to this property. The rest of those old buildings didn't correspond to the new ways of thinking, so no one had really protested their removal. At least, I didn't think they had. A small part of me was starting to question everything I'd been taught.

Some areas were built to match the old southern style, with tall ceilings, marble pillars, and beautiful oak trimmings. And some were built in the current modern way, with clean lines, white shining surfaces, and walls made entirely of glass.

Despite the clashing styles, none of it felt jarring. Actually, there was a delicate flow to the design that felt both regal and industrial. Somehow, it worked. I had to admit the palace was beautiful.

We approached another hallway. At the end, guards were posted by a padlocked door. A couple of men had their backs to us. They were let in without a fuss. They were dressed in the same black uniform Reed wore.

"Is this the Guardians of Color headquarters?"

"Yes, they have that whole wing." Lucas cleared his throat. "But we're not going in there tonight."

Oh, thank you! I didn't question him. It wasn't a place I was ready to visit yet, anyway. Instead, we turned a few more corners and descended the stairs to the ground floor.

From the look of this palace, I may as well have been transported to a different country. But I knew it wasn't the case. The thought kept popping into my head that we were still in the capital city. Which meant I really wasn't that far from home. Only a twenty-minute ride on the high-speed train would put me a block from my suburban doorstep. It hurt to entertain even a glimmer of hope, but I held on tightly to the thought anyway.

As soon as the scent wafted through my nostrils, I knew.

"Let me guess. This is your favorite spot in the whole palace, right?"

He laughed. "You got me there."

He opened the double doors, revealing a huge kitchen. Correction: kitchens. There were multiples of everything we had at home, plus lots of things we didn't. Between all the diplomats, guardians, advisors, guests, and staff who inhabited the palace, there were probably several hundred people here at any given time.

It was late, so all the cooks had already retired for the day, leaving the entire space quiet.

"Why is this your favorite room in the palace?"

"The area where I live with my parents is pretty nice, no doubt. But I don't like to hang out there too much. I spend my free time in my study, outside, or down here in the kitchen. I appreciate the ordinary things in life, and yes, the unlimited access to food is a nice perk. Besides, I like people. I like the workers. They've always been kind to me. I grew up knowing many of them."

I wondered what that must have been like. I'd never considered that Lucas wasn't close to his parents. But perhaps his life wasn't as good I'd thought it was. Maybe he was lonely.

We went over to a row of large refrigerators. He opened one, with a sly smile on his face, as if he knew the contents would surprise me.

"You're kidding?"

Lucas grinned and grabbed the largest piece of chocolate cake I had ever seen. He used his other hand to pull out a slice of cheesecake. "Aren't you going to help yourself?"

It was amazing. Desserts, sweets, puddings, and delectable items I didn't even recognize filled the fridge. I spotted carrot cake and moved in for a slice. I'd had it once at a ballet banquet, so I already knew how sweet it would taste. The memory of cream cheese frosting wetted my taste buds.

Lucas rummaged through a nearby cupboard and pulled out a handful of salted caramels twisted neatly in waxed paper.

"Oh, wow." Any kind of sweet treat was a rarity in my life…in the lives of all of us beyond the palace gates. We were accustomed to having more than enough, but simplicity was the norm. Caramel was basically sugar, so it wasn't too hard to make when we had some extra rations. But these certainly didn't look like the ones we made at home. These were perfect.

As with everything in the palace, the food was presented very neatly. The plates were in clear containers to keep the desserts fresh and moist, ready to be served tomorrow. I stared down at the cakes in our hands and tried not to squeal with delight.

"It's been a long time since I had anything like this." Something about all this food felt naughty and exciting. And to be honest, an emotional eating session seemed appropriate after everything I'd been through.

"Well, that's good because we're going to share. Come on."

◼

We ended up back in the gardens, and even though I wanted to see the rest of the palace, I took solace in this area. The air was warm, and the sky still clung to the last bit of light. It was the perfect summer night, not too hot and not too cold.

Walking through the near dark, I worried about tripping and knocking the delicate cake from my hands. Somehow, though, we both managed to make it to the empty lawn and sat down on the manicured grass. The light from the palace was behind us, and the last rays of the setting sun were quickly disappearing.

Lucas pulled a couple forks from his back pocket, and together, we dug in. The flavors were incredible, better than anything I ever tasted before. I could only imagine the amount of fat and butter wrapped up in each bite, but I didn't care. This was heaven.

"So, do you always eat this late?"

"Not always, but I like the kitchens, so I end up eating more than I should," he replied, reaching for a caramel.

Following his lead, I took one. I popped the warm silky sugar into my mouth and sank back into the grass. The caramel melted around my tongue.

"Why do you like the kitchens? You don't seem like someone who cooks," I asked.

"No, I don't cook. I've never had a reason to, although it might be one of my undiscovered talents. Maybe I'll take lessons."

I noticed he hadn't answered my question. I was beginning to understand something about Prince Lucas. He liked people, but spent a lot of time alone. "Are you out here often?"

"Yes, quite a lot. I come running out here every morning. I usually eat lunch here, too. It's just my place, I guess. Except for winter, when I hole up in my family's library. Sounds stupid, maybe, but I generally like to distance myself from all the politics."

"But isn't that something you should get used to? I mean, you are going to be the next king."

As soon as the words were out of my mouth, I regretted them. Perhaps I was being insensitive by prying.

"Basically, yes."

He started in on the rest of my carrot cake and dropped all conversation.

I let it go, focusing on enjoying a few more pieces of caramel. Soon, I found I couldn't eat another bite. Lucas, in typical boy-fashion, didn't slow down until every last crumb was gone. I looked at him with strange admiration. From his lean physique, I would never have guessed he could put food away with so much gusto. He must exercise *a lot.*

Lying on the grass, I allowed a gentle peace to sweep over me. It was something I hadn't felt in a long time. Not since before Lacey's accident months ago. I gazed at the first stars peeking through the clear sky, thinking of my family. Were they watching the same ones? Stargazing was a favorite pastime of ours, and I could almost imagine myself with them, enjoying this warm night.

Lucas turned back to me for a few minutes, then moved the plates aside. When he lay down next to me, I bit back a small smile.

He didn't touch me, but he was close enough that I could feel the heat of his body against my arm. The urge to look over at him was so overwhelming that I almost gave in. But I didn't. I was afraid he'd be looking back.

And I was more afraid he wouldn't.

"I'm always being watched." Lucas's voice was calm. "Ever since I was born, I've been the property of New Colony. Everybody wanted something. Everybody thought they knew who I was. They still do."

I could tell he wanted to say more, but he fell silent. I didn't know how to respond. I was more surprised by his openness than anything else. So I just waited, ready to listen.

"I guess that's why I come out here a lot or go downstairs to the kitchens. To be alone, or at least be around people who won't bother me. I'm trying to figure out who I am. I don't like all that other stuff getting in the way."

In that moment, I wanted to say the perfect thing. I wanted to tell him that I understood, but honestly, I wasn't sure I did. I had always known exactly who I was, exactly who I wanted to be and what I wanted to do. And even though people were telling me I couldn't be that person anymore, I couldn't let her go. That girl on the ballet stage was more real to me now than ever.

Maybe Lucas wasn't such a bad guy.

Without stopping to think it through, I reached out and laced his fingers through mine. It was intended to be an act of friendliness, support, solidarity.

But when he stiffened, I shut my eyes tight. I was sure he was going to laugh or push me away. But he didn't. He squeezed my hand tighter and rolled toward me.

My fear of looking at him, and what could happen if I did, was no match for my need to see his face. I had to know if the electric chemistry between us was real. Did he feel it too? My eyes fluttered open and caught myself in his steely gaze. His charcoal eyes held mine, intense, like smoke from a wildfire.

He moved in closer, ever so slightly raising his chin, parting his lips. I knew what was about to happen. I knew he was going to kiss me.

And I was going to let him.

"There he is!" a female voice echoed through the night.

Lucas shot up, letting my hand—and the moment—go.

She was coming from the direction of the palace, her laugh ringing out, sultry and comfortable. I sat up and saw the silhouette of a petite girl flanked on either side by four palace guards.

When my eyes adjusted, insignificance burned through me. Her beauty was obvious. She was perfect in all the ways I wasn't. While I was too thin, she was softly curved. While I had unruly brown hair, hers was long, glossy blond, and neatly styled. Her smile was so infectious that I couldn't help but return it, despite my embarrassment.

She sashayed over to Lucas and practically yanked him to standing. He didn't look at me when she wrapped her fingers through his and spoke in a sweet singsong voice.

"Baby, they wouldn't let me into your room. I thought we had a date. You didn't tell me you were working."

Working? Did Lucas have a girlfriend?

I was so stupid. Obviously, they were together. She was the type of girl he would date. Of course she was!

Why don't I follow the gossip feeds?

"You know I hate it when you work all the time," she continued, pouting.

Was that what I was to him? Work? But something in me didn't believe it. He was going to kiss me before this girl came along. *And so what? That doesn't mean he cares about you.* Apparently, his reputation was justified. He played around. He was a flirt. And he got into girls' hearts.

Well, he wasn't going to get to mine. I wouldn't be so naïve again.

"What are you doing here?" Lucas asked, his voice cracking. I almost laughed. He probably thought he'd been caught cheating on his girlfriend. *Almost* cheating. Strangely, this girl didn't seem to care.

The palace guards stepped forward. "Sir, is this woman bothering you?" one asked, motioning to the girl and shining his flashlight on us.

She looked close to Lucas's eighteen years. Given her casual indifference to the question, I was sure they were dating. That, or something else I didn't want to think about.

"Don't be rude." She playfully slapped Lucas's arm. "Don't you remember inviting me over tonight? Seriously, Lucas, you need to start writing things down."

He paused and then relaxed, still never looking down at me. "I forgot. I'm sorry," he said, pulling her into an intimate hug. "You're right. I was working, but we're done now."

Are you kidding me?

Lucas had his back to me, and the girl smiled over his shoulder and curled herself into his embrace. When she looked down, I was taken aback by her expression. It wasn't angry, accusing, or predatory like I was expecting. Instead, she looked sorry for me.

And that made it even worse.

I jumped up, brushing the grass from my clothes. Politeness took over, and before I knew it, I was gathering up the dirty dishes.

Lucas turned to me, puzzled. "Jessa, you don't have to do that. The guards will call someone to take care of it."

I carefully handed them to the nearest guard before meeting Lucas's gaze. "You two have a wonderful night," I said, before giving them the most sarcastic curtsy I could manage.

Then I turned and walked away.

"Wait, Jessa, let us walk you back," Lucas called.

I refused to stop or turn around. I stumbled across the lawn, eager to make it to my room before anyone could see the tears blurring my vision. Why did I care so much? I just met him! He shouldn't matter to me anyway. All my focus needed to be on getting out of the palace. He would only get in the way of that. I had to find a way to prove to these people that I wasn't the alchemist they wanted. I needed them to give me my old life back. I would not let these stupid tears fall. Enough was enough. I was done with crying.

EIGHT

LUCAS

"Sorry about that," the girl said, letting go of my hand after the guards left. "I guess I never properly introduced myself. I'm Sasha."

The name suited her. It matched her exotic qualities. Her timing. The reason she was here, the Resistance. Yes, she was very mysterious, but I couldn't help my frustration at our situation.

Sasha had just interrupted something I wanted to happen, despite my better instincts. And yet my feelings didn't matter. I should've been relieved that I didn't kiss Jessa, but I wasn't. At the same time, my desire was foolish; kissing her would have made things too complicated.

"Sasha." I shook her hand. "Nice to see you again."

She was the woman from the ballet, the representative that the Resistance had sent to install spy software on my father's slatebook. She carried herself like a woman of society, but she looked almost as young and innocent as Jessa.

"What are you doing here?" I asked. I couldn't imagine how she got access to the palace, let alone, to me.

"Is it safe to speak out here?" She was all business now.

I considered going farther into the gardens, since our voices might carry out here. But then again, anyone could easily hide in them.

"It's not safe to speak to you anywhere." This place was always crawling with people. At least we were alone outside. "Let's just keep it down and hope we'll be fine."

She raised an eyebrow. "Again, I'm sorry about your friend. I told the guards that you are I are dating. It was the only way I could find you. One of them remembered me from the other night and agreed to bring me here."

It made sense. And she was so stunning that nobody would have been surprised. Just a few days ago, I was attracted and intrigued. It's likely that I would have tried to casually date her. But right now, those feelings just weren't there. I suspected that had a lot to do with Jessa and the feelings she brought out in me. Feelings that would be better served to keep to myself. "Honestly, you just did me a favor. And it's actually a good cover. We'll go with it."

"It's the only believable one." She glanced around one last time. "I've been relocated to the palace, to join the guardians here, so it should be easier to communicate."

Relocated? That could only mean she was one of the guardians who'd been assigned to a different location. I would say that it was a convenient coincidence, but more than likely, the Resistance had pulled some strings to land her here.

"You're a color alchemist? You're GC?"

She nodded and then looked around, searching for something. She held up a finger, then skipped off in the direction of the nearest flower bushes. After a moment, she jogged back with a silky flower held snugly between her fingers.

Immediately, she manipulated the color, pulling a bit of the delicate blue out of the flower and into the open air. It danced between us. Even in the darkness, I could discern her talent. After a moment, she released the color into us and placed the flower gently behind her ear. Must mean she had blue alchemy.

"Shhh," she whispered. "It's a secret. Wouldn't want the officers to know about that little trick." She was good. How had the Resistance gotten her on their side? Before I could ask the question, she explained.

"I was sent to the northeastern edge of the kingdom when I was still really young. Too young." She stared off into the night, a mixture of longing and fear etched across her face.

I frowned. I didn't remember her. I'd been involved with the guardians ever since I was a child. It was my father's most important project, and he included me in their work now and again.

But that didn't mean I should know her. There were a few hundred guardians at the palace at any given time. And most of the ones living full-time in the palace were the children, teenagers, and their trainers. Older guardians were sent on assignments all over the kingdom.

"Tell me about the Resistance. Why should I continue to align with them?" I was eager for information. It seemed that the more I worked with them, the less I knew. And I was beginning to worry I'd jumped into bed with them *way* too quickly. If I didn't get some solid ground with them soon, I would have to pull out. What other choice did they leave me?

"There's a lot you probably think you know. But you don't." She returned her gaze to me, her eyes stoic. Maybe there was a lot I didn't know, but I had my secrets too.

"The thing is, Sasha, I can't be led on forever. I need some concrete information about who you people are and what you're planning. It's too risky for me to be in the dark much longer. I need to know I am doing the right thing."

The warm breeze caught her hair. A warm, flowery scent brushed by.

"Oh, you're doing the right thing. I honestly don't know what I can tell you at this point. But I can tell you this. We're the good guys."

"I hope so. So why are you here with me now?" Her vague responses were starting to get to me. Yes, they wanted to stop the deaths happening in the shadow lands. But beyond that, how could I really know what they wanted?

"Listen," she said. "I don't know if I can trust you either. My life is on the line here. But we came to you first, and I've been told that you're the real deal. But seriously, Lucas, you're the crown prince. How do I know you're not going to turn on me? How do I know this isn't just some boyish vendetta against your father, and tomorrow you'll wake up and change your mind?"

Of course, I already knew she was risking her life to be here, talking to me. But when I'd first met her, I'd told her that I'd also been to the shadow lands. I'd seen what was happening up there, too. I saw the death, the destruction. We had that much in common—wasn't it enough for her to trust me? "I'm not changing my mind unless the Resistance gives me a good reason to. I know why I'm here."

I sometimes felt suffocated by my own secrets. There were so many layers to my identity; I was constantly concealing myself. First, I was the New Colony prince, the boy who would one day be king—loyal to his people, forever in service to crown and country. Then there was the supposed playboy—the one the media loved to create, always looking for the smallest flirtation to spin into a full-blown romance. Whose heart would I break today?

I cringed. This was the persona Sasha knew above all else. It was what everyone saw. And Jessa was the most recent person to witness it firsthand.

But under all the layers of masks and secrets and lies, in the dark corners of a beautiful palace, lived the truth. And I would have to spend the rest of my life trying to make up for those empty spaces, hiding the real me.

I couldn't tell Sasha all the reasons I was working with her. The Resistance was an underground organization with a mission to overthrow the monarchy and return the country to the democracy we had once been. And even though that meant I wouldn't be king one day, I supported them. Because what Richard was using alchemy for was wrong. And honestly, I was afraid what being king would do to me, who it would make me become. Would I be like him? No, democracy had to be the better way.

The members of the Resistance were well hidden. If Sasha was telling me the truth, they were nowhere and everywhere at once.

At least we had the same end goal: we wanted to stop Richard from harming more innocent people inside and outside of our borders. And we didn't want civil war or execution to be the means for making that happen.

"I know what my father is capable of. I've been where you've been, remember? I heard the rumors, read the reports. And then I saw parts of it for myself."

"The shadow lands?"

I nodded and she frowned. I was grateful that this was enough to satisfy her. But I didn't want her pity. I was here to do something about the problem. And I was willing to betray my family to do what was best for the people. I couldn't sit back and watch my father take innocent lives, just to get a chance at stronger alchemy. It didn't matter what his reasons were.

"Fair enough," she said, as if to seal the deal. "Let's trust each other."

I sighed, hoping I wouldn't regret letting this mysterious girl in.

"There's something I need help with. It's my mother. I think someone is using alchemy to hurt her."

"Her headaches?"

"How do you know about those? Are you guys doing something to her?"

"No, it's not us, I swear. But, we've had our suspicions. We don't know who's doing it to her, Lucas. Is it getting worse?"

"Yes, they're not as often, but each one is worse now. Can you help me? She's losing her memory...her mind. I can feel it."

"I'll talk to my people, see what more we can do. And I'll keep a look out myself. We'll let you know if we find anything."

I hoped that would be enough. I didn't know how much more of this my mother could take. And I was scared to talk to anyone in the palace about it, clue them in, in case they were the culprits. What if my father was the one behind it? I didn't want to entertain that thought. I needed to find the answer soon. "I need to save my mother."

■

I promised myself that the next time I saw Jessa, I would apologize for leading her on. I never wanted to hurt her. I didn't know if she'd forgive me, but at least I could try to smooth things over. But when I knocked on her door the next morning and let myself in, she wouldn't even look at me.

"Listen, about last night. I never meant for any of that to happen."

"Nothing happened," she quickly cut me off, pretending to be interested in whatever was going on outside her window. Which I knew was just a side view of the lawns.

Neither of us said anything for a while. I didn't know what to do to get through to her. Should I just apologize? An apology would be disingenuous. I had wanted that kiss to happen. This whole mess wasn't her fault.

"I need to take a shower. Can you please leave?"

Of course she didn't want to see me. I didn't deserve anything more from her right now. As I left, I uttered the only apology I could give her. "You can have the day to do as you please."

"Are you serious?" she asked, turning to me with wide eyes.

Was I? I wasn't sure how I'd explain this one to Faulk and Richard. But then again, it was just one day. She'd be happier for it. *And that's better for her training.* "Yes, but stay within the grounds. Obviously." She perked up. "Oh, and tonight you'll be accompanying me to a palace party where you'll officially be introduced to the Guardians of Color and my parents."

Her mouth dropped. "Won't you be taking your girlfriend?"

I blinked at her. I hadn't thought about Sasha being my date when my father had announced the party plans over breakfast. But it was the perfect place to get some real traction for our cover. Sasha was a guardian, after all. But Richard had told me to escort Jessa myself.

"Sasha will be there, yes. But I'm taking you."

"Sorry, but contrary to what you thought of me last night, I am not the other woman type of girl."

Unfortunately for her, when Richard gave an order, he gave an order. Period. For her sake, it was better I forced this issue instead of him.

"I'll pick you up at seven," I replied, quickly leaving the room.

I stood outside her door and inhaled deeply. *How am I going to do this?* I had to escort Jessa tonight and, at the same time let everyone know that Sasha and I were together. It was a totally bad maneuver either way. I needed Jessa to trust me. But I also needed an easy excuse to be seen with Sasha.

I wasn't looking forward to this evening.

■

Faulk's office was at the top entrance of GC headquarters. All the royal officers' offices were here. The area itself was the most modern of the palace, and the most recently constructed. Everything was charcoal gray and stark white, but it also felt lived in. Busy. People spent a lot of time there.

A few guardians came out of a nearby doorway, their voices light as they echoed through the corridor. The younger guardians were still in training, while most of the teens were official initiates. I didn't know these faces well. They barely took notice of me as they disappeared around a corner.

I tended to stay away from most of the guardians. My parents preferred I didn't make friends with alchemists, and personally, I no longer wanted to. They weren't bad people, but they wielded powers that my father worked hard to control. With such small numbers, he could. He treated the few hundred guardians well in return for their obedience. But, no, I didn't fear them. I just chose to stay away.

I walked into the GC headquarters, eyes peeled for my target.

Faulk was essentially in charge of the GC, second only to the king. So I went to her office. Of course, the sleekest, biggest, and nicest one had to be hers. As I walked through the area, the royal officers stopped their work to watch me. This wasn't a place I customarily frequented.

It looked almost like a normal office. Except for the modern glass, which covered most of the surfaces. And the fact that I knew what these people actually did for a living. Royal officers were anything but normal. Their whole existence revolved around controlling the GC, and thus, the kingdom.

I stood there for a minute, still looking for Faulk. An older man got up to greet me with a bow and a smile: Thomas. "Prince Lucas. How can I help you?"

He was my favorite officer. I returned his smile. "Why do you work here Thomas? Aren't you tired of all this?"

"I wouldn't know what else to do. I've been committed to this post for decades now." His tone was kind, unlike most of the other royal officers I knew, who were cold and unemotional—all business. Still, it bothered me because I was sure *he knew the truth*. He had to be involved in the shadow lands project.

"When my grandfather was king, didn't you have Faulk's job?"

He frowned, nodding.

"So what happened? Why did Faulk replace you? No offense to her, but I like you much better."

"Well, I appreciate that. But Richard wanted to make some changes. I guess there are things he and I don't always see eye to eye on. But that's okay, Lucas. I do what I'm told. I'm loyal to your family."

I couldn't be sure what he meant by all that.

"I need to talk to Faulk. Is she here?"

He pointed behind and above me to her office. It was at the top of a set of industrial stairs. It was no surprise to me that she'd set herself at an elevated level; whoever worked up there could watch what everyone was doing. *Royal Officer Isadora Faulk: General* was written in big bold letters across a heavy glass door.

As I moved for the staircase, he quietly added, "Be careful, Lucas. Remember who you're dealing with." He turned and walked away. Was he trying to intimidate me or warn me?

The office was made entirely of opaque and clear glass with wide sweeping views of the back gardens, an area used for guardian training and recreation. This was all exclusive GC territory.

I entered quickly, wondering how Faulk felt about people barging in on her. I didn't care either way. After all, she'd done the same to me yesterday. Faulk was busy typing furiously on a slatebook. She continued for a moment, ignoring me.

"Lucas, please have a seat," she said, still typing.

I sat back in one of the uncomfortable chairs and waited for her to look at me. After a few long minutes, she finished up whatever she was working on. She wanted control. And she hated me for taking some of that away from her. I assumed her indifference was all part of her game.

"What do you want?" she asked, finally breaking the silence.

"I came to inform you about Jessa. She's had a rough couple of days, so I gave her the day off. Except for tonight, of course. Richard is throwing a party in her honor."

Faulk's chair screeched as she stood up. "You did *what*?"

"Do you have a hearing problem?"

"Who do you think you are? We have a schedule for that girl!"

"Who do I think I am? I'm the crown prince of this kingdom. The *only* prince of the most powerful country on the planet. Who do you think you are?"

"I am a royal officer, the First General of the Guardians of Color, *not* you. You have a long wait before you get to be king. And that is only if your father steps down. My guess is that he'll stay on his throne until the bitter end, especially knowing he has you as a successor."

I observed the vein in her temple as it pulsed with every word.

Maybe she was right. Maybe my father would never step down for me to take control of New Colony. But that didn't change the fact that he had charged me with overseeing Jessa's training. Not Faulk.

"Look," I said, standing. "I didn't come here to fight with you. Yes, you are in charge of GC training, but Jessa isn't a guardian yet. She has to be initiated for that. And we both know I'm the one making day-to-day decisions for her right now. I came to tell you what I did out of courtesy, not to get your permission. Anyway, it's done."

I got up. Just as I turned to leave, I was startled by Jessa's blurred figure standing on the other side of the glass door. What was she doing here? I quickly opened it and pulled her inside.

"Do you have a built-in radar?" I asked.

"For what?" Jessa replied, her face flushed.

"For opening doors just as I'm about to walk through them?"

Faulk cleared her throat. "To what do I owe another interruption in your honor, Miss Loxley?"

Jessa glanced at me. "I've been trying to call my parents all morning." Her words were directed at Faulk. "It's their day off, and they're not answering my calls. I was wondering if you knew what's going on. Are they okay?"

"You just spoke to them yesterday," Faulk said. "We have royal officers stationed at their home, you know."

"Yes, I called them. But when I tried again, they didn't answer. That really isn't like them."

Well, this is interesting. I sat back down in the uncomfortable chair and pulled one over for Jessa.

"Yes, Faulk," I said. "What's going on with my trainee's parents?"

Faulk peered at us, tilting her head. "Whatever Lucas says, you should know this Jessa: I am in charge of GC security around here. Do you recall getting permission from me to call home?"

"I didn't know I needed permission to talk to my own family." Jessa's voice rose with each word. "They never did anything wrong. And I'm here, aren't I? Doing exactly what you've asked of me. We had our first training session yesterday."

"Let me be clear, Ms. Loxley. I did *not* want you here. My job is to put threats like you in prison. We need complete loyalty of our guardians. The only reason you are here right now is because the king has taken an interest in your alchemy. I've decided to agree with him and give you a chance. Don't think it means you're off the hook."

"Please," Jessa said, truly sounding apologetic. "I didn't want to lie. I didn't know what else to do. I was afraid. Please, I just want to know if my family is safe. Did they get punished for my crimes?"

"And what makes you think I would know?" Faulk asked.

I scoffed. Of course she had the power to answer Jessa's questions. She just didn't want to.

"I think it's your job to know. You've met them. You've talked to them. And you just said you have royal officers stationed at the house. Just tell me, are they okay?"

I suspected Jessa's parents weren't as innocent as she believed them to be. I was still pretty sure they'd lost a daughter or some kind of family member to the GC years before. I studied Jessa's frustrated face. Did any part of her suspect that her parents had been harboring a giant secret from her? I was sure Faulk knew the truth. Maybe that was why she hated Jessa so much. Who was Francesca Loxley and how did she get away from the GC?

Faulk paused, her hard face softening slightly. "They're fine. It turns out you're a bit of a celebrity after your ballet stunt. We've had their phone number changed for their privacy, as well as yours."

A good reason, but I wasn't sure I could buy that simple of an answer. I mentally added "further inquiry into the Loxley family situation" to my to-do list.

"So I can call them? Do you have the new number?" Jessa asked.

"You cannot call them. You're the property of New Colony now. You're a huge asset and a huge liability. Part of your agreement here is that you will do as we say. Security is my top priority. I am not giving you permission to call home. Lucas never should have given you a line out. It is not safe, and I will not allow it to continue."

"What? You can't do that!"

"What does any of that have to do with security?" I shot back.

"Jessa has been trusted with classified information and will continue to be trusted with State secrets. All guardians must cut off outside relationships. No exceptions." She turned back to the work on her desk, excusing us.

"So that's it?" Jessa asked. "You expect me to give them up, just like that? I won't do it. I won't join your stupid Color Guard. I won't help you."

Why couldn't Faulk see things my way? Jessa wasn't a young child that she could manipulate into forgetting her family. Giving Jessa an easier life here meant she would be easier to train. It was a simple, win-win situation. And besides that, I wouldn't have to watch her struggle so much. I hated to see her upset like this, knowing there wasn't much I could do.

"You don't have a choice," Faulk replied. "It's that or prison. Either way, you're not going home."

Jessa doubled over as if she was about to be sick. Was she just realizing what I had known my whole life? New Colony had all the power. She had none. It didn't add up, since she was the one with the powers they wanted. But that's how things were going to be.

"Fine, I'm not going home. But you're not going to keep me from my family. If you do, I'll make sure you lose your job."

And that's why I like her so much. No one stood up to Faulk. Except me, that was. I had to admit I was impressed.

Faulk laughed. "There's nothing you can do, Jessa. I make the rules and you follow."

"Actually, that's where you're wrong—the king makes the rules," I interjected.

"And what's your point?" Faulk squared her shoulders.

"My point is that my father wants her to help her country. And if he wants her to do that, then I'm pretty sure he needs us to help Jessa."

"Where are you going with this?"

"I'll help you," Jessa said. "I'll work as hard as I can. I'll do whatever you ask of me, but I won't give up my family. And if you take them from me, then you can explain to the king why I refuse to work. I mean it, I'll go to prison instead of staying here if you keep me from them."

Faulk and I both studied her determined face.

"You're bluffing," Faulk said.

"I don't think she is," I mused.

"Try me."

"Fine," Faulk said after a long pause. "After you learn how to control the color red, I'll give you a line out to call them. That is what the king wants most, you know—he wants red. That's all I can offer. Phone calls, twice a month."

"Twice a week," Jessa replied.

"*Once* a week."

Did Faulk just say red? No. No. No. Red? That's what he wants? Of course it is. How could I have been so blind?

My stomach dropped. I knew there had been a reason my father wanted Jessa in his custody. There was a reason he'd taken such a huge interest in her. *Of course* it was red. A memory flashed through my mind of the first time I saw Jessa. She'd used alchemy on the lavender of her ballet costume. And the colors had separated. Blue. And red. How had I not put two and two together?

We still didn't know what red could be used for. It was the only color on the spectrum that none of the guardians had any power over, besides white and black. They weren't even sure white or black were colors that could be used by alchemists. But red? Well, with a color that symbolic—representing everything from bloodshed to passion to *control*—it definitely had to be useful for someone like my father. I had no doubt he could get even more power once he could control Jessa.

Jessa stood and reached her hand toward Faulk's. For her, this was a done deal. I wanted to say something. To scream at her to stop.

Don't agree to this!

But what could I do? My cover would be blown if Faulk knew I had an issue with Jessa helping my father. I was supposed to be on the side of the GC, of the New Colony.

They shook on it. Their grip was tight and unforgettable.

NINE

JESSA

After a quick walk around the palace, I decided to go back to my room. Lucas had tried to delay me, but I barely gave him a second glance. I was still infuriated about his decision to take me to the ball without my consent. Besides, I needed to get to work and figure out how to access red alchemy. Unfortunately, I had no idea how to go about something like that. Even when I'd messed with Lacey's blood, I hadn't known what I was doing, or what it did to her.

I ended up sitting on my bed during the early afternoon hours, pondering how I was going to pull this off. If I helped Faulk, I would at least get to call home. And maybe I could sabotage my alchemy after that, show Faulk that she didn't need me after all. After what felt like an eternity, I realized I needed to distract myself from my own thoughts…thoughts about color alchemy, thoughts about my family and Faulk, and far too many thoughts about Lucas. About his smile. About the way his naturally tanned arms looked in that t-shirt.

No, those thoughts could only get me into trouble.

And then there were my parents to consider. When I called them last night, something wasn't right. I couldn't put my finger on it, exactly. It's not that they were afraid of me, as I had worried. Or even disappointed.

No, they'd been dismissive. Did they believe they'd lost me? Until I got privileges to call home, I'd have to wait to find out why.

An idea hit me with such clarity that I couldn't believe I hadn't thought of it before. There was only one thing that would serve to distract me from all this turmoil and clear my mind. It had always been the one thing in this world that could make me feel better.

I needed to dance.

A light tap sounded on the door, followed by the maid, Eliza. She was holding a tray of afternoon snacks. As appetizing as they were, I hated to dance with anything fresh in my stomach. If I ate now, I would need to wait an hour before dancing.

"Is there an empty ballroom somewhere around here?"

"Sure, which one, miss?"

Perfect. I felt like I could breathe again just thinking about it.

"Whichever one is empty and closest," I said, jumping from the bed and pulling Eliza into a hug. She squeaked in surprise, nearly dropping the tray. I laughed. We weren't exactly on hugging terms, but I didn't care. Right now, Eliza was my ticket to emotional freedom.

Tonight I had to attend a guardian event. I had to meet the king and queen. I had to be introduced to people who'd probably be my colleagues until I made it home. But this afternoon, I would dance.

■

It came back to me as if I hadn't been away at all. Had it really only been five days? Even so, I couldn't remember the last time I'd missed five days in a row of dance. So much had changed for me in such a short time. If I could erase the past week, I would. Then I'd be able to return to the core of what I loved. Of who I was.

As I moved across the marble floor, I felt immense gratitude for the moment. I counted my blessings that no one had dared touch me after my performance at the Royal Ballet. Thanks to that oversight, I'd still been wearing my pointe shoes upon arriving here. I didn't need the costume to dance, of course, but I was happy I at least had some shoes. They wouldn't last long. Pointe shoes never did. But I had them for now. I plopped to the floor to slip them on and lace them up.

The empty ballroom was all hard shiny surfaces. The white floors were polished like ice, but they were not too slippery for dancing. The walls were a beautiful well-oiled mahogany, dripping with antique tapestries. But nothing was as stunning as the gorgeous crystal chandelier that hung from the ceiling.

For some reason, the guards didn't follow Eliza and me in here. I was reluctant to admit that Lucas probably had something to do with that.

As I danced, I imagined a simple melody. Eliza stood at the far end of the room, peering out the back window. Even though I had told her she could leave, she had insisted on staying with me in case I needed anything.

"Are you trying to give me space or something?" I laughed, dancing over to her at the far end of the room. She paled, shaking her head. She was young and petite, like a mouse. *Too young to be working here.* But her smile was sweet, and her innocence reminded me of Lacey.

"It's okay." I laughed. "You can watch. Or not. I don't mind. Like I said, you don't have to stay."

"Do you want me to leave, miss?"

"You can call me Jessa. And no, you're welcome to stay. But I don't know why you would want to sit around and wait for me. Unless you're supposed to?"

75

Eliza blushed.

"Are you supposed to be spying on me or something?"

"I'm sorry, miss." She couldn't even look me in the eye. "I sort of am. But I promise I won't tell them anything that could get you in trouble. I'm supposed to stay with you today. We can do whatever you want. Are you mad?"

Who was she working for? Lucas? Faulk? The king? But given the frightened look on her face, I decided not to push her. I liked Eliza. I didn't think she was out to get me. If she'd been appointed by someone to spy on me, she most likely didn't have a say. And being forced into something doesn't breed loyalty. I should know. "I believe you. And I'm not mad."

She let out a sigh of relief and smiled back.

"How long have you worked here?" I asked, hoping I wasn't prying too much. But I was curious about this young girl who was working her tail off instead of attending school. I didn't know people did that. I always thought all capital citizens lived the same way; taken care of, educated, assigned into the perfect job for their qualifications.

"Two years."

"How old are you?"

"I'm almost sixteen." She'd been working since she was thirteen?

"What about school?" I blanched.

"I home-school in the evenings. They have it all digitized. This way, I can work full-time."

I gaped at her. How was that fair when my teen years had been spent going to normal school and dancing all afternoon?

"I know what you're thinking. But I have to support my mother and little sisters. I'm all they have. My mother…she's very sick. She can't work. And my father…he died three years ago. That's when I applied for work-study."

"I'm so sorry." I didn't know what else to say. I didn't know work-study was a thing.

"It's not so bad. I like this job."

"Well, couldn't an alchemist heal your mother? I mean, I've seen it in action. It's pretty remarkable!"

"I don't know." She paled. "I am forbidden to ask anything of the alchemists that I serve. Please don't say anything."

"Forbidden? That's ridiculous. I'll ask Jasmine for you."

"No!" Eliza nearly jumped. I'd never seen her so anxious before. "I could lose my job. Please just…forget it."

I wanted to argue, but what could I say? I was fuming inside at the thought that she couldn't ask for help. Alchemists were right at her fingertips! If the GC weren't healing people like Eliza's mother, then what were they doing?

"What would you be doing if you weren't with me?"

"Probably cleaning somewhere. Maybe working in the laundry facility." She stared sheepishly at her hands.

"We can't have that! You're not going anywhere," I said, happy I could give her some time off from her duties. She responded with a laugh that was so sweet, it was contagious. It broke the fury that had been building in my chest and I couldn't help but laugh with her.

"Take a seat. I always did like an audience."

I pranced to the center of the room, deciding to start with an old piece from a few years back. I closed my eyes and allowed every note to echo through my mind. The ballet was fun and fanciful, full of quick jumps and turns. I let my mind and body relax. Soon, the dancing slowed, and I began to move in my own way, taking each step as it came to me. I simply allowed my heart to guide my body, which felt incredibly freeing.

A deep sense of peace washed through every inch of me. I couldn't help but feel like everything was going to work out. *There must be a way to find myself again,* I mused. Because right then, I felt like that girl. The one with a life that revolved around ballet and family. The one who had lived with total trust in her world. How could I love something so much and not be meant to do it? It just couldn't be possible. Closing my eyes, the weight of the world lifted from my shoulders, and I was myself again. I wrapped my arms around myself in a soothing embrace. Dance was everything. It was all of me.

I was instantly rocketed back to my reality. The shrill sound filled every inch of the large room. The horrified, ear-splitting, gut-wrenching scream of pain was undeniable. I reached out, looking for the source. And then I saw her, Eliza. And I saw all the blood. Her blood. *Everywhere.*

What have I done? The color shattered my vision, and then it was gone. The blackness took its place.

■

When my eyes popped open, I sat up too quickly, causing a rush to blur my vision. I hurried to look around the room. I was in a hospital bed. Actually, no, this was still the palace. The view from the window was too familiar. It was the palace infirmary.

I lay back in a bed and put my hand to my head. Looking at my reflection in the metallic surface next to me, my face was ghostly white. Aside from a few small cuts, I looked healthy enough. I tried to sit again, but the fog returned when I did. So I relaxed. *Why am I here?*

And then the memory returned to me. It was Eliza. I had hurt her. Maybe even killed her. I hadn't realized the power that had been building inside me during my dance. I thought bitterly of all those years of ballet without incident, and now it seemed that would never be the case again. And Eliza had gotten hurt in the process. Did I use alchemy again? I should have known better. I did know better. What kind of person was I? This had to stop.

Lucas strode into the room, concern drawn all over his face. "How are you feeling?"

I didn't answer.

"It was an accident. You couldn't have known."

I lifted my hand to wipe an angry tear. I didn't want to cry in front of Lucas.

But I couldn't help it. I had done something unthinkable.

"Is Eliza dead?" I feared I already knew the answer. "I don't know what happened. We went to an empty ballroom. I was just dancing. That's all. I wanted to give her a break, so I invited her to stay and watch. Then, suddenly, she was screaming and there was glass everywhere. I saw it all. Then the… the…the…"

Lucas already knew what happened. I had accidentally used alchemy with such force that it caused the chandelier to fall. Somehow, it didn't land on top of me as it should have. No. It flew across the room, right at Eliza. I wouldn't have believed that was possible if I hadn't seen it with my own eyes. I was so lucky she wasn't killed on contact. But there had been so much destruction. And I'd passed out before I could help her.

I looked down at my clothing, looking for the source of color. But I'd been redressed in a gray hospital gown.

"What color were you wearing?" he asked.

"Orange t-shirt. Black leggings," I said. "Can orange do that? Move things? But…but it was so large. How is that even possible?"

"It can, given the strength of the alchemist. Maybe you should start dressing in black like the others. There's plenty in your closet."

"And what about Eliza?"

"They're doing everything they can. So far, it's touch and go. But there's still a chance…"

"Can I do anything to help?" I asked. But the look on his face said there wasn't anything I'd be helpful for. I didn't know how to control my abilities.

"I sent Jasmine. She's one of the best healers we have."

"I didn't mean it. I swear. I would never hurt someone."

Predictably, General Faulk burst into the room, furious.

"You're a danger to yourself and others," she barked at me.

I wish I could disagree with her. But she's right.

Turning on Lucas, she added, "And you should have known better than to let her dance like that."

In his defense, he hadn't known I was going to dance. Why couldn't I have gone to the library instead?

"I'm so sorry. I had no idea this would happen," I said.

"Only time will tell if that girl will survive," Faulk replied, folding her arms. "This is exactly why you should have come forward sooner with your abilities, Jessa. Can you image if this had happened at the Royal Ballet? You could have inadvertently thrown a theatre light at the crowd. Or what if it had happened in your home and your family got in the way? They were in danger for years with you under their roof. I warned you that you were a ticking time bomb."

I didn't try to defend myself. I knew I was broken. I couldn't cry anymore. There was nothing left for me to say. Faulk was right.

"If it were up to me, you would be back in solitary confinement until you got control. But fortunately for you, you're a rare breed. We've never seen anyone develop so much power this quickly. The king wants to keep you around, despite the danger. As you already know, we need you to access red alchemy."

Maybe I should have been relieved, but at the mention of the king, I could only be nervous. I didn't know if I'd be able to access red. And if I did, what if it was dangerous?

"Despite today's unfortunate events, you two are still required to attend the ball together tonight. It's a direct order from the king. Don't be late. And Jessa, for everyone's sake, wear black." She gave us both one glance before leaving the room.

"No," I insisted to Lucas. "I can't go. I could hurt someone."

"I won't let that happen."

"You can't control it any better than I can. I'm better off in solitary confinement. Faulk is right."

"It's not up to you."

"I can't be here. I can't do this. You have to help me."

"Help you do what? Lock yourself up? I can't believe what I'm hearing. I've been around a lot of color alchemists in my time, but no one asks to be put away. Who would want that?"

"I do. Please, talk to your father. Tell him it's the right decision."

I understood something about myself in that moment. I would rather spend the rest of my life alone than harm another human being. What had happened today had been horrifying. I couldn't be that monster.

"It's a noble idea, maybe," Lucas said. "But it's also a waste of talent. And anyway, Richard would never let you go so easily. Jessa, don't you get it? If you don't cooperate, he'll use force. He'll do whatever it takes to get what he wants."

"Then help me stop it. Help me bury the alchemy so deep it never comes back again." Then I could forget this ever happened and go home.

"You know I can't do that."

"You have no idea what it's like to feel the way I feel right now. Your life is perfect, and yet you find little things to complain about. Ways to feel like you don't belong. Well, that's all in your head. This—" I pointed to a larger cut on my hand. "This is real. This is my life. You can either help me or you can get out of my way."

My own words stung. Was this who I was now?

"I'll get out of your way." Without another word, he left the room.

Breathing deeply, I pushed the emotions back down, deep inside. Accident or not, I didn't want to cause another person to get hurt.

I placed my bare feet on the cool floor and stood. I pulled the short cotton gown tightly around myself and tentatively walked out of the small room. I found myself in a hallway lined with pristine beds. Palace guards stood at attention. I needed to get out of here. If I could break out, maybe I could hide. Maybe I wouldn't hurt anyone if I wasn't *forced* to be around alchemy all the time. But I knew it was no use. As I padded down the hallway, the guards followed behind. They didn't say anything, but it was obvious. If I tried to get away from this awful place, they'd lock me back up.

What was I supposed to do now? Without thinking, I instinctively knew where I needed to go.

■

Eliza was barely recognizable. I expected to find blood, but that was mostly cleaned away. It was her face that startled me. It was swollen, bruised purple, yellow, and deep blue. Besides that, she was pale from all the blood loss. Too pale.

I choked back a sob, biting my clenched fist. This was my fault.

"Step back." A nurse appeared.

Suddenly, I became aware of the others in the room. I'd been so narrowed in on Eliza that I'd failed to notice the four people staring at me. One appeared to be the doctor, two nurses, and one I recognized. Jasmine.

"It's okay," Jasmine said. "Nothing will happen again while I'm here."

Are the staff afraid of me, too? I didn't blame them. I was afraid of myself.

"Do you remember that I am a healer?" Jasmine asked.

"Yes," I said, focusing on my teacher. She was a healer. But all the same, I felt helpless.

Jasmine smiled and motioned me closer to Eliza. "We have many ways of connecting with the colors, but the most powerful is through accessing other living things." She held up her hand, in which she was holding a small potted plant. "So I am using my own life force, with the life force of this little plant here to support me. The green energy is healing. It knows where it's needed." She looked back to Eliza and closed her eyes, wrapping her fingers around the green leaves. At first, nothing happened. Was I missing something?

Slowly, little green wisps of light began to float from the small plant. They grew, multiplying by the second, and moved toward Eliza. The moment they reached her skin, it happened. Her complexion began to return to a normal flesh color. The green light washed over her, somehow penetrating her every pore. It was incredible. Unlike anything I could have imagined. Powerful. Beautiful. And somehow, orderly.

Then it stopped and Jasmine smiled at me. "Neat, isn't it?"

I didn't know what to say. The plant, so small and delicate, had almost returned to normal. Only one leaf had turned a milky gray, and Eliza looked exceptionally better than she had only minutes ago. Remarkable.

"How?" I asked.

"Honestly, I don't *exactly* know how. I just know that I have to touch the plant. And then I have to imagine where the color will go." Jasmine stood from her chair and put the plant on the bedside table. Next to the shiny medical instruments, it looked out of place. How could it have more healing power than all those medical instruments? I still couldn't wrap my mind around it.

"But I do know that color alchemy from living things is the only way I have ever been able to heal anyone. Very few alchemists can use man-made items. It doesn't take much. I usually carry a plant of some kind everywhere I go. Have you also noticed them in the palace?" Jasmine asked.

Actually, now that she mentioned it, I had.

"Green is the color of healing, vitality, and longevity. It's the easiest of the colors for me draw upon with my alchemy. The live plants make the green much more powerful. I set my intention. And the color seems to know exactly what to do."

Looking at Eliza, I saw what Jasmine meant. Eliza's eyes were still closed, but her face was her own again. Calm and peaceful. There was no hint of what she'd been through. She was in a content, deep sleep.

"She's going to be okay?" I asked, hopeful.

"Yes. We caught it in time."

In time? So she still could have died. I could have killed her. I almost had.

"Jessa, color alchemy is a gift. There is no need to be afraid. This is who you are. In time, you'll learn to control it. You'll do many amazing things."

I hadn't allowed my thoughts to go that far. To imagine what I could do, who I could be. If I did get to that point, I still wanted it to be on my terms. I wanted my family back. I wanted to dance. Was this possible for me? So far, I'd only seemed to be able to hurt people. Not help them.

Something about that thought reminded of my conversation with Eliza. Maybe there was something I could do for her.

"Eliza's mother is very sick. Could you heal her?" I asked.

"We have to be careful about where and how we use our powers. But yes, I would love to help. Do you know what's wrong?"

"No, just that it's been going on for years." Could I hope that this would make things better between Eliza and me?

Jasmine frowned. "I'm sorry, Jessa, but I can't heal chronic conditions. I can only treat wounds, pain…this kind of thing here. But I can't change something that's been an ongoing problem. Some things are fated, it seems."

"But what you just did—it was so powerful."

"We need to finish cleaning her up," the nurse said, interrupting us. "Time to go."

Jasmine only nodded at the nurse and moved us toward the door. "We'd better get going. You have to get ready for tonight."

"Tonight?"

"You've got a party to prepare for. Tonight is your introduction," Jasmine said with a knowing look.

Oh no! I'd almost forgotten. I couldn't believe it was happening so soon. And I was definitely not ready for that. "Can you do me a favor?"

"What is it, dear?" Jasmine replied as we left the hospital room.

"Lucas is supposed to be escorting me to this party tonight. But I'd rather go by myself. Is that a possibility?"

Jasmine smiled. "I don't know what is going on between the two of you, but I'll do my best to let Lucas know your guards will be dropping you off. I don't know if he'll listen."

After the argument we'd just had, I doubted he would put up a fight.

"It's not going to be so bad," Jasmine said. "Who knows? Maybe you'll enjoy yourself."

Unlikely.

I had so many more questions to ask. I wasn't ready for this conversation to end. "Is there any other way alchemy could have healed her...maybe by using another color?"

"Not that we know of. Why do you ask?"

"Just curious," I lied. If I had manipulated Lacey's blood that day on the playground, and I hadn't healed her, then what had I done? Because Faulk had shown up that morning on our doorstep with a vial filled with gray blood. Gray meant I had used the red for something. But what? And why did the king want it?

TEN

LUCAS

It was always the same people. Sure, the venues changed from time to time, but nothing about these events ever surprised me. That was…until that ballet. I still couldn't get the image of Jessa's dance out of my head. By now, everyone at this party had heard about her, which was probably why the atmosphere in the room was different tonight. It was almost electric.

The ballroom was elaborately decorated with lavender roses and dark purple tablecloths. In honor of Jessa's first alchemy, I assumed. As if on cue, she walked into the room, and I lost myself.

She was stunning. There simply was no other way to describe her. Everyone noticed, especially the men. How could they not? Her light complexion contrasted with her dark hair and full red lips. Her blue eyes were innocent and unassuming. She was fresh and refined.

She wasn't formally announced as she entered the room. That was because I hadn't introduced her, like my parents had requested. Apparently, as I'd been informed by Jasmine, she didn't want to be seen with me. I knew that would bother Richard but he'd just have to deal with it. Then again, he still hadn't shown up.

Unsure of what to do, Jessa stood frozen, wide-eyed and perfect in a form-fitting, floor-length, purple gown. Its open neckline left her neck and shoulders exposed and vulnerable. The dark color of the dress played nicely against her creamy skin. Her long curls hung loose around her face and back.

Seeing her discomfort made me uncomfortable, too. I brushed myself off and headed in her direction, unsure of what I could say to clear the air. I faltered, wondering if she would even talk to me.

But it looked like she wouldn't be alone, after all. Reed appeared at her side, smiling. He leaned in to whisper something in her ear, and when she laughed, her mouth melted into a grin.

I wanted to be the one to make her laugh.

As if she could feel my eyes on her, she turned and looked directly at me. Her expression went flat. Why couldn't I forget this girl?

"Hey there, stranger," Sasha said, appearing beside me. She casually put her arm through mine. I'd been wondering when she would show up.

"Oh, hey," I replied, taking her hand. We'd agreed that tonight we would appear as a couple for the sake of our cover.

Her small, curvy frame fit perfectly into her tight red dress. Normally, I would have been all over a girl like her. But with Jessa watching, I wasn't in the mood for flirtation.

"Want to dance?" I asked, already knowing her answer would be yes.

Taking her hand, I led her to the small group of couples in the middle of the ballroom. It seemed like a good place to start.

As we danced, I tried not to pay any attention to Reed and Jessa, but I couldn't help myself. I really didn't like him. I didn't like that he was working so closely with Faulk. I didn't like that he would be involved in Jessa's training. And I especially didn't like the way he was dancing with Jessa now. He was dominating her time, and I still hadn't gotten a chance to talk to her. I wanted to apologize for our fight, but not with Reed standing right there. It wasn't any of his business.

"What's wrong?" Sasha said.

"Nothing." I really didn't want to talk about this right now. Not with the girl who was supposed to be my girlfriend. The very fact that she knew we weren't *really* together meant she was probably the only one I could talk to. But I didn't know where to begin, because I didn't understand my feelings myself.

Why do I care so much about Jessa? This isn't like me.

"You can't be with her, anyway," Sasha said.

"Is it that obvious?"

"Well, I mean, you could mess around with her, sure. But you can't really *be* with her. A royal and a would-be guardian? It would never work."

"*You're* a guardian. Aren't we supposed to be together?"

She smirked. "Trust me, no one thinks we're that serious. Together, in our case, is a loose term. It's not like you've ever been monogamous for long before."

"Ouch. All right, you have me there."

"Seriously, this pretend relationship we have going on here can't last long. Who would believe that coming from you, given your dating history? And anyway, would your parents *really* let you be with a color alchemist?"

"I haven't thought about it before. But you're right. There is no way my father would let someone with that much power cross the line into royal territory. We're on one side. And you're on the other."

"And that is why you should stop staring at Jessa. Let her go. It can't possibly end well. You and I, on the other hand, understand what is really going on between us." She winked.

"It's work," I agreed.

"Yes. We probably only have a few weeks before our *break up*, right? Better make the most of it." She pulled me close as the music changed to a slower tempo. I folded my arms around her.

"Why did you stay with the GC?" I asked. "Why did you decide to come back here if you knew what they were doing?"

She stiffened, but I continued.

"I've been thinking about this. If you're with the Resistance, you probably know someone who could get you out. There must have been chances to leave New Colony. To go into hiding or something."

"I can't talk about this."

"You knew what I was talking about with the northeast. You said you've been there. The shadow lands. You saw it too, right?" The image of gray skies and dead things leaked into my mind.

"Lucas." Sasha pulled slightly from my embrace. "This is not the time or the place. This conversation isn't our assignment."

"Our assignment?" I asked. "What's that supposed to mean?"

"Our assignment is to establish a reason to be able to see each other often, sometimes during late hours. We have work to do and we don't have much time. But we can't talk about that here, in public. It's not safe."

She was right. And this assignment of ours wasn't so bad. Sasha was beautiful—exactly the type I went for. Blond, curvy, petite. And she had a maturity, a sophistication, that very few of my previous girls had boasted. As if she'd been to more places and seen more things than even I had. She checked off all the right boxes. We could get away with our cover, at least for a little while.

I glanced across the room, not realizing I had been looking for Jessa until I saw her. She was still dancing with Reed. They were chest to chest. His face pressed into the hair at her ear, and her eyes were closed as she giggled.

Oh forget this.

"You're right, we have work to do. We better get started." Then I bent my head down and kissed her, hard.

She reacted the way they always did, returning the heat. I pushed thoughts of Jessa out of my head, enjoying the woman in my arms.

After a few minutes of taking my frustration out, I pulled away and looked around. Had we gotten the attention we needed? From the many eyes that kept darting between the two of us, I'd say the answer was yes.

Sasha was getting glares equivalent to daggers from most of the women in the room, but she didn't care. I liked that about her. She just smirked back and then laughed. It was our secret. According to everyone else, we were clearly a couple. I finally started to relax and actually found myself having a good time.

When the party got its busiest, Sasha pulled me outside onto a terrace. The few people out there scurried inside when they caught sight of us. Giving us privacy, I assumed.

"We've got some news for you," Sasha said softly as she pulled me farther into the shadows. There was no one around us now. "It's about your mother."

"What is it? Do you know who's messing with her?"

"Have you noticed that Jasmine is frequently with your mother when she's ill?"

I had. I couldn't imagine why Jasmine had a reason. But if she was responsible, I had no problem doing whatever was necessary to stop her.

"It's not what you think," Sasha said. "We still don't know who's doing it or why. But we've been watching Jasmine carefully, since she's your mother's main healer."

"And what have you found?"

"It's not Jasmine. She's never so much as raised her voice at your mom, let alone done anything to hurt her."

"So I can rule Jasmine out?"

"We think so."

This was good information. I wasn't completely sure I could trust it, but my gut agreed. Jasmine wasn't the enemy. *If not her, who?*

"Will you keep watching? Let me know if you find anything."

Sasha nodded. "Let's go back inside."

The dance floor was filled to capacity now, and we squeezed our way in with the others. After a few songs, I was aware that we were directly next to Reed and Jessa. Jessa was forcing polite nods as Reed talked. Actually, I was pretty sure he was holding a one-way conversation. Maybe she didn't enjoy his company as much as it appeared earlier. She didn't say a thing. Just stood there as Reed prattled on about his life with the GC.

"What are you thinking?" I heard Reed ask. Maybe the guy had finally realizing that Jessa might have a voice too.

"Can you introduce me to some of the other guardians?" Jessa asked.

Sasha peered up at me, whispering. "Is this the kid that's working for Faulk?"

I nodded and she glared at Reed's back. "What a tool."

I laughed, and together, we turned toward the couple. Jessa crossed her arms, not meeting my gaze. Okay, apparently she was still angry with me. She was right, I had tried to kiss her just last night.

"I'll introduce you to some people," Sasha said, intruding upon their conversation. "But I'll warn you, I haven't been back here myself for a while, so I'm kind of the new girl too. I don't know if I told you my name. I'm Sasha."

Her smile thawed its way right through Jessa's defensives. The two girls smiled at each other and shook hands.

"That would be great," Jessa said.

"I can help with that," Reed said, grabbing her hand and leading her to a group of young people mingling by the buffet table. Sasha shrugged and we followed.

The group appeared to be normal teens. Some wore bookish glasses, and some were more attractive than others. But they all had perfect clothes and hair. They were all dressed in expensive outfits. They oozed wealth and privilege—perks of being a color guardian.

I wondered what Jessa thought of them. She had grown up just outside the capital city. She'd been in the same house, going to the same schools, mingling with the same people her whole life. Her parents had tested well enough to be placed in a middle-class neighborhood and had never fallen below the minimum requirements to hold their jobs.

That's how it worked. Everything was done via testing. An aptitude test would tell a teen what sort of professions they could consider. But we still believed in the power of the human spirit. So once every year, someone had the opportunity to try for a better job. Sometimes they got it. Most of the time, they didn't. As long as they passed the minimum for their current workplace requirements, they would get to keep their job. And those who didn't do so well weren't abandoned, only reassigned into something more suitable. My father prided himself on taking care of the citizens. So he said.

Each job had a certain standard of living attached to it. What their house was like, what type of school their children attended, whether or not they had the luxury of a car, if they had the opportunity for a once-yearly vacation to the capital city or countryside. Did they get the chance to participate in local entertainment? Well, it was all determined by their job placement.

And that placement, of course, was determined by strict government guidelines and the strength of the royal family.

I'd researched Jessa's life that first night. Her family had fallen somewhere in the middle. Just barely high enough that she could choose an activity to participate in after school. And she'd chosen ballet. It had been her ticket to a better life. Some artists were allowed to continue their art as their jobs. With her talents, I was sure Jessa had been on the fast track to professional dancing.

I was sorry Jessa had lost that. But then again, being placed here in the palace was the best anyone could hope for…even if living within the royal precincts was a double-edged sword.

We moved closer to the group of guardian teenagers, and they peeled apart to meet us. Their smooth smiles were almost icy. Forced. And nervous, which was probably because of me. I didn't spend too much time around these kids if I could help it.

Reed introduced everyone, but I barely heard him. I stood back from the group, watching the way they sized Jessa up. Obviously jealous. Every now and then, they looked at me, but I never met their curious gazes.

"Hello," Jessa said, extending her hand to the nearest member.

The girl's jaw jutted upward as she refused to return the offer. "I don't mean to be rude. But I don't think it's fair that you get your own party. We don't even know what you're doing here. You're not a guardian. You're not even training the way we do."

"Brooke," Sasha said. "Don't be like that."

"What?" Brooke looked to the others. "It's not like it's a secret. Everyone knows she doesn't belong. Not yet, anyway."

Jessa turned to Reed. "What is she talking about?"

"It's nothing."

Brooke laughed. "You're not safe. You have no control. No training. This party shouldn't even be happening. This is not how we do things here. It's not even how we do things in New Colony. You have to earn your place. Period."

A few of the group members nodded along. Brooke showed no sign of remorse, adding, "This whole charade is completely unfair. Do you have any idea how long the rest of us have to work before we get any sort of recognition around here? Before we even get initiated as guardians?"

"I'm sorry," Jessa stammered. "What do you mean, initiated?"

Brooke laughed, as if she found the ignorance of Jessa's question offensive.

"Come off it, Brooke," Sasha said. "Jealousy is not a good look on you."

Is this how guardians act, or just teenagers? I hadn't spent tons of time with people my age, but still, I'd never witnessed anyone being so openly rude. If this was the way these people acted at a party—in front of me, no less—then I could only image how ruthless they were in private.

Jessa's face had drained of color.

"Jessa *did* earn this party," I said, stepping into the center of the girls. "I've seen what she can do with my own eyes. You haven't. She has more potential in her than this whole group of alchemists combined."

Brooke and her gaggle of girls immediately hushed. I resisted the urge to laugh. Did they think I couldn't hear them? For a heavy moment, they stared at me, taken aback. But then Brooke curtsied deeply and walked away, followed closely by the rest of the group.

"Don't worry about it." Sasha put her arm around Jessa. "They're just mad because you're already a superstar and not even a guardian yet."

"They all heard about what you did at the theatre," Reed added. "That was some seriously impressive alchemy, separating the colors like that. Uncharted territory for everyone here."

"It's not like I planned any of it."

"We know. That's exactly why they're threatened," I said.

Jessa turned on me, angry. Again. "Why did you have to step in like that? I didn't ask for that. You just made it worse. Now they hate me even more."

"I was trying to help you." I stepped back, hands up.

"Don't you get it? I don't want to be a special case!"

I looked around. But when my eyes found Brooke and her friends, I saw that they had joined another bunch of young guardians. The whole group was whispering and staring right at us.

Jessa watched them, a scarlet blush sweeping across her face. I hated to see her upset. But I had to admit, she was cute like this.

"Okay, maybe you're right. I'm sorry. I'll never understand girls like Brooke. Just try to ignore them."

"Have you eaten?" Sasha turned to the buffet table and grabbed a plate. "There *is* one good thing about these lame parties. The food is amazing."

The four of us filled our plates with piles of pastries, fruit, meats, and cheeses before finding an empty table.

The atmosphere was unexpected. Jessa and Sasha were acting like best friends, which surprised me. I'd assumed the women would become rivals. Reed and I, on the other hand, couldn't even look at each other. I couldn't stand the guy. He kept finding ways to touch Jessa or to inject his opinion into the conversation. He was also trying to be funny. The thing about being funny is that you can't try too hard. *This guy has no game.*

All the while, I could sense that Jessa was still mad at me. I touched her arm. "Can I talk to you in private?" She shrugged as I took her elbow and led her to the least populated corner of the large ballroom. "Listen, I know we've had our differences, but we need to put them behind us." I wanted to sound sympathetic, but even I could admit every word felt forced.

"Fine."

Fine? That was all I was going to get? "Look, about Reed." I glanced over to Reed and Sasha. He was making her laugh, too. How was that possible? The guy wasn't funny!

"What about him?"

"He's working with Faulk, remember? Don't let him get too close. I don't think we can trust him."

She laughed. "Are you serious?"

"Why wouldn't I be?"

"Aren't you supposed to be on the same side as Faulk? Why do you care what I do? Anyway, what I do with my free time is none of your business. I can be *friends* with whomever I want."

"I'm just trying to watch out for you," I said, and then I bit my tongue to keep from screaming out that Faulk and I were definitely *not* on the same side.

"I can take care of myself."

"Really? Because from the looks of it, you can't. Reed has been all over you tonight. You don't even know him. You don't know what his true intentions are. He spied on us just a few nights ago, remember?"

"I know what I'm doing. And anyway, you have no room to talk. You and Sasha were the ones making out in front of everyone. Or have you already forgotten about your girlfriend? You seemed to have forgotten about her last night."

She stepped back, folding her arms and taking me in. She was right. I wasn't being fair. But she didn't know the whole story about who Sasha really was to me. She *couldn't* know.

"Fine. Do what you want. But remember that I am in charge of overseeing your training. Reed is involved with it, too. It's a conflict of interest to get close to him."

"Are you kidding me? You are such a hypocrite! And like I said, Reed and I are just friends. I'm not like you."

"Like me?"

"I don't go from one guy to the next overnight. It's not so easy for me to play games," she said, turning and stalking back to the table.

The image of last night at our garden picnic played through my head. She was right. I was unintentionally playing with her emotions, and it needed to stop. I wasn't going to let Jessa get under my skin anymore. As far as she knew, Sasha and I were together. I had to keep it that way. For her sake, and for mine.

There wasn't any point in following her. There was nothing left to say. I stayed where I was, hiding out in the corner of the room, unsure of what to do with myself. I was beginning to feel annoyed that my parents were no-shows. This morning, Richard had been insistent—so where was he now? Fashionably late? Maybe. Making a point? Likely. I was sure it would come to light soon enough.

I spotted Jasmine and wondered if she had any new insight. She wore a simple black gown. Her gray hair, no longer braided down her back, was brushed out in waves around her shoulders. Her brown-sugar eyes held a knowing glint.

"Good evening, guardian," I said.

She turned to me and smiled. "Good evening to you as well, Prince Lucas."

"I was wondering if you know where my parents are. Should I go look for them? They're not being very gracious hosts, I'm afraid."

Jasmine frowned and stepped in close. "Your mother's headache got a little out of control today," she said confidentially. "It's the worst I've seen her. She won't be coming. I was just with them. Your father should be here soon. Thomas, Faulk, and some of the others are going to stay with her until we're sure she's stable."

"I should go to her."

"No, Lucas, she's sleeping now. There's nothing you can do for her."

I was tired of hearing that. I hated being so useless. I turned, finding myself looking for Jessa before I could catch myself. She'd gone back to the table where Reed and Sasha were bantering in light conversation. Apparently, my mother wasn't the only one who didn't seem to have any use for me.

ELEVEN

JESSA

Oddly enough, I was enjoying the party. Reed and Sasha were entertainment enough as they bantered, explaining the inner workings of guardian training.

It turned out that most of the older guardians were out on assignments. The rest were here for training, which they did often. Guardians started out as novices when they were young children. Each alchemist was trained a little differently, depending on the abilities they had and how quickly they learned to control them. But most trained for several years before they were initiated into the GC and given actual assignments.

Initiation wasn't something I would learn about until later, it seemed. But as it happened sometime during adolescence, I figured it couldn't be too bad. After that point, some left the palace, but most didn't get stationed elsewhere until age eighteen. It was similar to how job placement worked for citizens.

And yet, here I was. The sixteen-year-old newbie alchemist.

"You'd be surprised how seldom guardians actually get to use color alchemy while out on assignment," Reed said. "It's nice to come home and get some real work done. Training is the best."

Home? I couldn't even imagine calling this place home. With its endless hallways and ever-changing guest roster, the palace was anything but homey. Despite my best efforts to ignore him, I couldn't seem to get Lucas out of my thoughts. After our argument, I'd gone back to the table with Sasha and Reed. Apparently, Lucas had decided to make himself scarce. The whole notion that I was supposed to be his date at this party was laughable. He had a girlfriend… who was charming and kind and beautiful. Despite my initial reaction to Sasha, I couldn't help but like her.

Dressed in an exquisite red mini dress, she was physically the complete opposite of me. She was curvy and sultry…in a word, *womanly*. I felt childlike and gawky. No wonder Lucas was dating her. They looked great together. Like they existed in the same world. And I wasn't about to become one of *those girls* who hated another girl just because she had good things in her life.

Focusing on Reed, I allowed myself to feed off his infectious energy. His charisma helped ease my nerves. And of course, he was pretty good-looking. His sandy-blond hair, tanned skin, and brown eyes gave him that wholesome quality. *Oh, did I mention the boy has dimples?* Plus, he was definitely attractive in a suit. I didn't mind his casual flirtation. I knew it wouldn't go anywhere, though. I wouldn't admit it to Lucas, but he was right. Reed wasn't someone I trusted. Not yet.

"Are you having any fun?"

I decided to answer Reed's question honestly. "Some. I mean, I guess I'm okay. This just isn't my idea of fun. I guess I'm a little too introverted. "

"This is your party," Sasha said.

"You might as well have a little fun," Reed added.

"You know what?" I said, looking around at all the people enjoying themselves. "You're absolutely right." And he was. This party was being held in my honor right?

"I know something that could help," Reed said, turning to Sasha. "What do you think? A little orange bubbly for the party girl?"

Sasha laughed. "I guess a little wouldn't hurt."

"What do you mean?" I asked.

"You'll see." Reed smiled. "It just enhances your personality a bit. That's all."

I suspected it had something to do with color alchemy. Couldn't I avoid alchemy for just one evening?

"This party is all white and lavender." Sasha frowned. "Don't they normally have orange accessible at stuff like this?"

Orange! I didn't want to even think about orange right now. Not after my day with Eliza. Sasha got up, flagging down one of the servants laden with a large tray of drinks.

"What are those?" I asked, nervously.

"It's not quite what you think," Reed said. "There's no alcohol in the drinks at guardian events. No need for it."

"I knew they had something." Sasha brought a champagne flute back, holding it up for my inspection. It was filled with a clear, bubbly liquid. A single orange flower petal floated gently on the surface. It looked like it had once belonged to a tiger lily. Fire-bright and full of color.

"On second thought, maybe we shouldn't have her do it," Reed said. "She doesn't have the best track record with alchemy. No offense." He smiled apologetically at me.

"None taken," I replied. Despite my better judgment, I was intrigued.

Sasha placed her hand over the glass, the tip of her finger barely touching the flower. She smirked as the color from the lily seeped into the liquid, turning the whole drink a glowing orange. "Drink it," Sasha handed it to me. "But only half."

"Don't worry," Reed added, "all you're doing is enhancing your own orange energy center by drinking this. It's a little trick alchemists have been using for quite some time. Consuming color right after manipulating it tends to draw out those attributes in ourselves."

"And orange does what?"

"A number of things as it taps into base emotion and passion, but mainly, this is going to allow you to have fun." He took his own drink, now orange as well, and drank it quickly.

This was surreal. Could this work? This was a flower petal. One measly, albeit lovely, flower petal.

I picked up the glass and took a few sips.

It was light, citrus. Just as I'd imagined orange would taste. It tingled as it slid down the back of my throat.

Immediately, my body warmed. Anxiety lifted from me. Something welcoming bubbled up inside. Joy. My eyes began to water. But a smile pulled at my cheeks. I hadn't felt this since the night at the ballet, *before* the disaster.

I was light and effervescent, just like the bubbles in my glass. Looking around, I realized that I just wanted to dance! I jumped up as a loud, upbeat song blasted through the speakers that lined the ballroom.

"This is my song," I yelled to my new friends, pulling them to the dance floor. This wasn't ballet, not that kind of passion. I felt safe giving it a shot.

Ten minutes later, the three of us were dancing in the middle of the room. Most of the party guests had joined us, and the whole atmosphere had lightened up considerably. It was actually starting to feel like a party, not a stuffy palace event.

Sasha was becoming my friend. And Reed was handsome. He knew how to have a good time. He was arguably the best dancer on the floor. Maybe I could have fun with Reed? I could enjoy a fling. Honestly, I had only ever kissed a couple boys before. Nothing exceptional. I'd always been too focused on ballet to care about dating. But ballet was gone, and everything, including me, was changing.

I smiled as the music blared and the crowd danced. I wondered why Lucas had left. He'd been gone for at least an hour now. Where was he? And where were his parents?

I frowned. He could be having fun with us. He could be dancing with his beautiful girlfriend. But he wasn't. He was avoiding me.

Ugh, why do I even care?

There was a hush among the crowd, and the blaring music scratched to a silent thud. The crowd stopped pulsing, and parted, everyone bowing low.

The king had just entered the room.

And he was coming straight toward me. *Oh no! I'm not ready for this.* I joined the others and fell into a low curtsy. My head felt light, and I willed the orange joyous energy to leave my system. I wanted to make a good impression. *This is the king!* Reed had said this was different from alcohol. He must be right. The second I wanted the orange haze of excitement to lift, it did. *Thank goodness.*

"I think it's time we formally introduced ourselves, Jessa." The king stopped in front of me as he spoke to my downturned head. He slowly said each syllable of my name, provoking a chilling sting to run down my spine.

Oh yes, the orange is definitely gone.

His black shoes were so reflective that I caught a glimpse of my startled expression. I imagined how I must look to him, bowed low. A rare bird, now captured and placed in her cage. What tricks could he teach me?

"Your Highness," I said, standing back up. "It is an honor to meet you. Thank you for throwing this party."

With a flick of his wrist, he motioned to the onlookers to go back to dancing. They obeyed, obviously. "Don't mind me. I hope I didn't interrupt too much fun."

I reached for a smile that didn't seem to come. This was the king, the most powerful person in the world. I couldn't help the intimidation burning a hole through me.

I stepped away, hoping to excuse myself. Technically, it was my party, right? I'd be happy to get back to it.

"You and I need to have a discussion," the king said, grabbing my arm before I could slip away. "Why don't we have a dance and talk about…things."

I didn't know how to respond. He wanted me to dance with him? Reed was still standing by my side, but he nodded to the king and disappeared. Sasha was nowhere to be seen. And where was Lucas?

Laughing, the king said, "Don't worry, it will be all business."

The music returned, much more subdued than before.

I noticed Lucas was back, finally. He was standing rigid in the far corner of the room. I caught his eye.

What does your father want with me?

A flash of confusion crossed his face as his eyes narrowed. Sasha appeared next to him then and whispered in his ear. He nodded, and together, they watched us with blank expressions.

"Welcome to the palace, Jessa." The king pulled me into a slow dance. It felt wrong to be touching him, even if we were at least a foot apart. He wasn't just *a* royal, he was *the* royal. The leader of our country. And he was *old*. The father of Lucas, whom I'd been reluctantly crushing on all week.

I didn't want to be near this man. But what choice did I have?

"How are you coming along with your studies here?"

"It's going okay, Your Highness," I replied. "It's all so new. There's a lot to learn. I've just barely scratched the surface. We've only had one lesson."

He considered me, staring down. His gray eyes resembled Lucas's so strongly, and yet…they were different. They lacked something. Kindness?

"No need for formalities. Call me Richard. And that's good to hear. I can only hope we've barely scratched the surface with you."

I gulped, unsure what to say to that.

"You're old for a trainee. Especially for a novice. Normally, someone your age wouldn't be given a chance. Late developers are usually not strong enough to control their abilities. Lost causes. But somehow, you seem to be different, don't you? I think we can help you."

"How am I different from any other alchemist? I don't understand what's so special about me."

"Your power is strong, yes. But we have many strong guardians. We can do more with you. The alchemy you did with that purple the first time you were discovered was very different."

"What do you mean?" I was unsure how I felt about his excited tone. Something about it was unnerving, darkness threatening to surface.

"You used alchemy on purple and separated the blue and the red. How did you do that?"

"I don't know." And that was the truth.

His large hand tightened on mine, squeezing my knuckles together in a painful vice. I bit my lip, holding in the pain.

"You must learn how to control it. We need the red."

"Faulk told me...why red?"

"It's because color alchemists haven't been able to use it yet. You just focus on getting that color. Then we'll see what we can do with you, shall we?"

I thought about Lacey and how I had been able to pull the red from her blood. I could tell him about that, but I'd vowed not to bring her into this. Just the thought of him implicating Lacey made my stomach drop. He wanted red. But I would have to find another way to get to it. There had to be an alternative that didn't involve blood. Something about the very idea gave me the creeps. I hoped separating colors was the way. I'd done it before. I'd just have to figure out how to do it again.

As if reading my thoughts, he continued, "You are the only one in quite some time who has shown any progress in this area. Without even trying, it seems. Lucky girl."

"But *why* do you want red?"

He stopped and stared down at me.

"It's very likely we can use it to help people. To advance this kingdom. We won't know until we try. But we can't try until we figure out how to get to it. Until *you*, Jessa, figure out how to get to it."

"So you need my help?"

"Ah...that, my dear, is where you are wrong. *You* need *my* help." His grin lightened his wrinkled face. It was a truly handsome face. A politician's face. The older, weathered, mature version of Lucas's. "I believe today was an example of just how much you need us," he continued. "It was your maid, was it not?"

The image of young Eliza, lying under the broken chandelier, the shards of crystal and glass everywhere, snapped through my mind. Blood had poured from her head. Her cries had pierced the room before she'd lost consciousness.

How could I let myself forget, even for a moment, what I did to her?

"You're dangerous. You need discipline, focus, and training. Before you kill someone." Impossibly, his grip tightened on my hand.

He was right. I knew he was right.

"The guardians are the only ones who can provide that to you. So, you see, you need us. You need me."

"Okay," I whispered. It was all I could manage. The only word I had.

"You'd be smart to remember who is in charge here. Help me and I will help you."

All I could do was nod.

"I can't help but wonder, why didn't your parents turn you over to us sooner? Surely they are law-obeying citizens."

It was a threat; I knew it the moment the words came out of his mouth. "They didn't know."

"Strange. I think most parents know their children, secrets and all."

"What are you saying?" I couldn't care about pleasantries any longer. I wanted him to spell it out for me.

"Nothing yet. Just that you'd be smart to fall in line here. Get yourself in control of your abilities. Get a handle on the red. Do that, and I think I can overlook your lawless parents."

I gaped, pushing down the urge to spit out a string of angry words.

"Father, may I cut in?" Lucas interjected.

Lucas put his hand on my back, but I skirted away from both of them. My fingers were still locked in the king's tight grip. Up close, the resemblance between Lucas and his father was stronger than ever.

So, how could they be so different? Or were they?

The threats against my family were tearing me apart. No, these men, this family, these people here…they were ripping me in two.

"Actually, I think I am done for the night." I turned my back on Lucas as, thankfully, the king released my hand. "Thank you for the dance, Your Highness."

I quickly curtsied and turned, promptly fleeing the ballroom. I'd had enough politics for one night. Enough guardians. Enough alchemy. Enough royals. Enough.

It wasn't until I was back in my bedroom that I noticed the sharp tingle in my right hand. The pinprick of sensation filled me as blood slowly returned, one by one, to my bruised fingers.

■

The next morning came too quickly, and I was back to work. I woke early and dressed in casual clothing for another day of training. I wondering if we would be returning to the gardens or heading into guardian territory. The very idea of the latter left me shuddering with nervous energy. Lucas picked me up at my door. When he opened his mouth to say something, I shook my head.

"Not today, okay?" I was tired of his apologies.

Thankfully, he only nodded and led me down the hall. From the direction we were headed, my fears were confirmed. Training would be spent at the GC headquarters. A nervous flutter arose in my belly and I willed it to go away. I could do this.

We rounded a hallway and walked through the guarded doors. I knew it was GC not only because of its modern design, but because of the people dressed in black. One by one, they all turned to stare.

Let them stare. I don't care anymore.

We walked down to the ground floor.

There were even more people, which meant more gawkers. Hadn't they seen enough last night? Of course, there were others here who hadn't been at the party. Younger ones. There were a *lot* of small children. Most of them couldn't have been older than Lacey.

They're practically babies. My heart ached for their forgotten parents.

I could tell who the trainees were, because they were dressed in gray. The actual initiated guardians, who were mostly teens, were dressed in black from head to toe. And again, I recognized the royal officers dressed in their white uniforms, the same style Faulk wore.

Didn't they believe in color around here? Apparently, they used it for alchemy but didn't actually wear it. Maybe my emotional experiences yesterday were the reason. I too was wearing black.

Lucas led me through a few of the hallways. It seemed that the farther in we went, the more the rooms were empty. We passed a large gymnasium filled with people working out. It had glass walls, so we could see inside.

They looked beyond fierce. Fighters.

What—are they trained soldiers, too?

"There she is." Reed bounced into step with us. He was dressed in the black uniform that he always seemed to wear with pride.

"Where to, boss?" he asked Lucas sarcastically.

Lucas only glanced at him and continued walking.

"More studying?" I asked, catching up to the prince.

"There's a lot to learn."

"I bet you're tired of reading about energy centers." Reed laughed. It was true. That was the only training I had done since the garden. And quite honestly, I hadn't made it through half of what Lucas had assigned me.

Lucas led us into one of the glass classrooms. It was filled from top to bottom with plants. The humidity was dense, and right away I could tell it was an actual greenhouse. He flipped a switch, and the glass wall facing the hallway turned opaque, giving us privacy. I'd never seen anything like it. I walked over to the switch and flipped it a few times.

"Your mouth is hanging open," Reed observed wryly.

"What was that? Did that have anything to do with alchemy?"

"No," Reed replied, walking over to me and wrapping his heavy arm around my shoulder, "just good old technology."

Something about Reed's touch bothered me. He was too confident.

"Are you two done yet?" Lucas asked.

"Knock knock!" Jasmine opened the door and joined us. She was dressed casually, in a simple cotton dress. *Why does she dress differently?*

"Good, the gang's all here," Reed said sarcastically. I think he liked being the only other alchemist here before Jasmine showed up.

"Before we get started," I said, "I have some questions. We never got to go over them the other day. Can we do that now?"

"Sure," Lucas replied. "We can, but it's already hot in here, so just a few for now."

Where do I even start?

Images of Lacey flashed through my mind. Of gray blood. Of the way she hadn't remembered what I'd done.

"I've seen things lose their color and turn gray. Why is that?"

"The color has to go somewhere, doesn't it?" Jasmine said. "When an alchemist uses their abilities, whatever we're using as the source of color gives itself to us. We can choose where it goes. For example, does it go back to the original plant or does it go somewhere else?"

"Okay, but it wasn't like Eliza turned green when you healed her."

"That's true, but the green just transforms into matter. The colors are also very pliable, living in so many small little cells of light, that they can move into almost any matter easily."

"I don't understand."

"In science class, did you ever learn how cells work? What about atoms?" Reed interjected. "Everything that we think of as matter holds space, as well. Nothing is actually solid."

I thought about that for a second. I actually did remember learning that. The teacher had pointed to his chair and said there were particles small enough to pass through it.

"Okay, so the green went into Eliza—or the empty spaces in her atoms? How did it heal her?"

"All living things have energy centers," Lucas said. "And we can all access them, all the time. It's alchemists who can also access energy centers outside of ourselves. So in the case of Eliza, Jasmine used her own green energy center to draw out the healing properties of the green plant, and then she gave them to Eliza. Eliza then accepted them, drawing those healing properties into her own green energy center. From there, it took over." He placed his hand on his heart.

"And she was healed," Jasmine finished.

My mind was spinning. As much as I hated to admit it, so much of this felt...well, spiritual. We'd never gone to church when I was a kid. Church was allowed in New Colony, but very few families participated in my area. I hadn't ever contemplated anything as esoteric as energy centers. Could it be that there was a whole world beyond the one I could see?

"Okay, I think I'm starting to understand. But the gray—what does that signify? What happened to the plant? I saw part of it change."

"It died. It gave its energy away." Reed stepped forward, pointing to the lush greenery all around us. "But it's just a plant. There's plenty more where that came from."

I'm in trouble. I always thought that maybe I'd done something to help Lacey when I'd changed her blood. But actually, it was the opposite. I could have killed her. If Reed was right, I could have sucked the life right out of her.

I took a step back, processing this information. Should I tell them?

"I think we'd better move on." Jasmine smiled.

"So it seems you showed Jessa what we primarily use green for, then?" Lucas asked Jasmine.

I nodded, remembering again the way the green had flowed from the plant and into Eliza, healing her.

"It's pretty amazing stuff," Reed said.

"Reed will do another demonstration," Lucas replied.

"On what?" Reed scoffed, motioning to the room full of lush plants. "It's not like you took us to the medical ward. There's no one to heal."

Lucas raised an eyebrow, then reached into the back pocket of his jeans and pulled out a small, shiny pocketknife. The blade popped up thin and razor sharp.

"Are you going to cut yourself?" I asked, shocked. Lucas shook his head.

He handed the knife to Reed. "Go ahead, Reed. Cut yourself."

TWELVE

LUCAS

"You're crazy," Reed flared. "I'm not doing that. We can practice on something else. Someone else, if we have to."

I considered how to handle his reaction. Part of me knew I was being childish. I knew we had other options. But after Reed had told Faulk about the slatebook and after the way he'd danced with Jessa, I was more than willing to let my childish tendencies lead our session.

"If you're scared, then I'll do it," I said moving the edge of the blade to the palm of my hand. I would, too. Jessa's training needed to be kept under wraps as much as possible. I didn't want her doing anything that could hurt someone else. And the more people got involved, the more nervous she'd become.

"You wish," Reed said, his pride getting the better of him. "Give me that thing."

I handed it over and he held it to his open palm. He grinned back at Jessa, obviously trying to impress her.

"Don't faint on me," he said to her. Then he cut a deep incision.

It didn't take long for the blood to start gushing. He reached out toward a nearby plant, but Jasmine stopped him just in time. "Just a minute. Let Jessa try."

Jessa shook her head vehemently. "No way."

She stared sheepishly at Reed, who was holding his hand, putting pressure on the wound. His face was pinched, but he nodded. "I can handle it."

I took one of her hands and placed a small green potted plant in her palm.

"Now place your other hand on Reed," Jasmine said. "You don't have to even touch his hand. Anywhere will be fine."

She carefully grabbed his arm.

Reed interjected, "Relax, I'm fine. You can do this. Just picture your own energy connecting with the plant, and then imagine it crossing to me."

She closed her eyes, and after a few seconds of nothing, asked, "Why isn't it working? I don't feel anything."

"Trust yourself," Jasmine said. "The green energy knows what to do. It knows who, and how, to heal. But you're the bridge. You are the power."

After a minute of concentration, she opened her eyes again and looked at Reed's hand. The blood was beginning to splatter on the floor. Its deep color contrasted with the glossy white surface. Reed was looking paler by the second. How deep had he cut? I was beginning to think he'd underestimated just how sharp that knife was.

"Are you okay?" I asked. I hadn't wanted to actually hurt him.

He blinked rapidly. "I think I need to sit down." Just as he bent his knees, his eyes fluttered, rolling into the back of his head. He fell to the floor, out cold.

"You have to do something!" Jessa cried, looking at Jasmine. "Please help!"

Then she kneeled next to Reed, who had completely passed out.

I held my hand to stop Jasmine from stepping in. Jessa could do this. "Jasmine, please step outside. I'll call you in when we need you."

"What?" Jessa gasped.

Jasmine caught my eye. She seemed to understand. Her presence was a handicap to Jessa. She only paused for a moment before leaving us alone with the unconscious, bloody Reed.

"Just try one last time, Jessa," I said. "That's all I ask. Thirty more seconds and I'll bring Jasmine back in."

I knew she was upset, but she had no time to think about it. Just to act. Exactly as I'd planned. She closed her eyes, mind focused.

"Healing," Jessa whispered. "You are healing Reed. You are healing Reed with the green from this plant."

She gripped the plant in one hand and put the other hand on Reed's chest.

Sure enough, a cloud of green formed around the plant, pulsing and rising from the small leaves. It jumped up and connected to Reed. She opened her eyes and watched, dumbfounded. The gushing blood from Reed's hand stopped. The color reddened in his complexion.

Jessa glared up at me. "You are such a jerk! How could you? Jasmine was right there."

"It's my job to teach you. You wouldn't have learned anything if Jasmine did it for you. I assure you, I had it under control."

"You call *this* under control?" She stood up and held out her hands, slick with blood. "You're sick!"

I opened my mouth to argue, but my words got caught on my tongue. I could only stare at what was dripping from her fingertips.

"What? What do you have to say for yourself?"

"Jessa, you did it."

"Okay, thanks, I got that already."

"You're not understanding. You did it. Look at your hands."

She turned them toward her and saw it too. She knew exactly what I meant. The blood that was on her hands wasn't red. It was gray. And hovering just above us, ever so slightly, was a churning mist of deep crimson energy. The red alchemy pulsed, awaiting her instruction.

"What do I do now?"

I wasn't sure what to tell her. She'd done this so fast, and I hadn't expected her to manipulate blood. This was unchartered territory. Reed coughed, waking up.

"What happened?" he asked, rubbing his head and sitting up.

"Jessa healed you. You passed out."

"Oh right, because you made me cut myself!"

"Calm down, Reed," Jessa said. "You're okay, right?"

He took a deep breath, visibly relaxing. "Dang, that knife must have been like a razor." He peered at his hand, examining the now healed wound. By then, any gray blood had returned to red. It looked like nothing had even happened. Gratitude washed over me that Jessa had been able to return the red. Had she used any of it?

"I'm sorry," Jessa said to Reed. "I'm sorry you had to go through that."

"It's okay." He obviously hadn't woken up in time to see the blood on her hands. Nor had he seen how she'd managed to access red alchemy, because he didn't say anything. He just studied his healed cut, shaking his head. He gave out a little laugh.

"You're good! I better get cleaned up. I'll be right back," Reed mused as he looked at his clothes.

As he was about to leave the room, I called after him, "Will you ask Jasmine to give us another minute?"

"Sure thing, Your Highness," he said, the door closing behind him.

"Listen, Jessa," I whispered as quietly as I could. "Don't tell anyone what just happened. I mean, you can tell them about the green, but don't tell them about the other thing."

"Why? What healed him? Green? Or..."

"Shhh," I cut her off. "Green. Don't say anything else. Reed could be listening to us right now, remember?"

"Isn't that why I'm here, though?"

She didn't have to say it. We both knew she was speaking of the red.

"Yes and no. It's why many people want you here. But not everyone. It's complicated. But please, promise me, don't let them know."

She studied her hands, but the blood was all back to normal, drying into a scaly red crust.

"If it had stayed gray," she whispered, "would it have killed him?"

"I don't think so. It wasn't that much. But I'm telling you, gray isn't good. It's the opposite of life."

"This is disgusting," she said, looking at her hands. "I need to wash them."

"You can. But first, promise me you won't say anything."

"What about Reed and Jasmine? Can I tell them?"

"No. Especially not Reed," I say. "He doesn't have your best interests at heart. I know you like him. But don't say anything to him. Or even when he's near.

He can spy, remember? I think he's too out of it right now to spy on us or else this conversation wouldn't be happening. I'm not sure about Jasmine yet. To be safe, just don't say anything. You need to trust me on this."

"I need to trust *you*? I don't even know you. It's been pretty obvious over the last few days that you're not looking out for me."

"What are you talking about? I'm probably the *only* one who's been looking out for you."

She opened her mouth but didn't have anything to say. That alone burned a hole in my chest. I didn't want to be hurt by this girl.

"Please, Jessa," I pleaded one more time. "Promise me you won't tell."

How could I help this girl? I meant every word. She needed to trust me.

"But it's my family, Lucas. They're keeping them from me. I don't have a choice."

"You *do* have a choice. You always have a choice."

"Maybe you're not close with your parents. But my family is everything to me. I can't put them in danger."

"Listen to me Jessa. What you don't get is that by telling anyone about what you can do, you *will* be putting them in danger."

She stared at me. "Why?"

"Because alchemy is more dangerous than you can ever imagine. And I wish I could tell you more, but I'm not even sure it's safe to talk right now. To explain myself with someone like Reed so near. You're just going to have to trust me. I've said too much already."

The door opened, pulling us into silence. Reed and Jasmine walked back into the greenhouse. Reed carried a clean wet washcloth and tossed it to Jessa. He didn't seem any wiser to the conversation he interrupted. "Thought you might want that," he said. "Now, where were we?"

He was all smiles for her, but when he turned to me, his face soured. I wasn't sure if he had been spying on us using his blue alchemy. But with Jasmine in the mix, I hoped he didn't have the chance.

"Your Highness." Reed glared. "Would you like me to cut my other hand? How about my neck? Would that suit your taste?"

Okay. Maybe pushed him a bit too far.

I shook my head. "Let's move on."

"Jessa, are you ready to keep going?" Jasmine asked, watching her. "You did a great job. I just examined the cut myself. All healed."

I waited for Jessa to blurt out the news. One word about the red and everything could come crashing down. Before we knew it, she would be using red to help Richard control others. I was sure of it. Catching her eye, I willed her to trust me. I could tell she was filled with questions. And she was dying to get some answers. But there was something else there, too. A pause. A resolution. Trust.

"Thanks." Jessa smiled. "Actually, can we get some lunch?"

The breath I'd been holding slowly released.

Jasmine and Reed led us outside to the courtyard, where there was a buffet set up under a tent. There were several guardians milling about with plates piled high. Of course they all stared at us, albeit less obvious this time. Reed waved to a few girls his age, raising his eyebrows. His need to flirt made me dislike him even more. But then again, who was I to judge? I used to be the same way.

Jessa shook her head at Reed's antics. "Can we hold off on the rest of the practice for another day? That was a lot to take in back there."

"We should keep going," Reed said. "Are you sure?"

"Give the girl a break," Jasmine said. "I'd like one, too."

I nodded my approval, and Jasmine walked back inside. Looking around at the groups of young guardians around here, I didn't blame her.

Reed reached for Jessa's elbow. "Maybe you and I can go get something to eat?"

My stomach rumbled at the mention of food, but it looked like I'd be eating my lunch alone. Not unusual for me, anyway.

"Now that you mention it, I am pretty hungry." Jessa smiled at Reed.

I wondered if I should go with them. I needed to keep an eye on her. What if she said something to Reed about his blood? I stopped myself. I had to trust she'd keep quiet. For now, anyway.

I noticed Jessa was staring at something behind me. I turned to look. Sasha. I was relieved to see her. Yes, she was fun to flirt with. But beyond that, we had important work to do together.

"What?" Reed asked when Jessa failed to follow him.

"Do you think Sasha would want to eat with us?" Jessa asked.

I decided to stop them right there. I didn't like the way the three of them had been so cozy last night. Sasha and Reed were on opposite sides, even if he didn't know it.

"Actually," I said, "why don't you two go ahead? I've been wanting to have some alone time with Sasha, anyway."

I walked away before they could stop me, before I could let Jessa's startled reaction register in my heart, and went over to Sasha. I steered her away from the nearest group of people. We walked silently until I was positive we were out of earshot. But I decided it would still be best to whisper. I knew Reed wasn't listening in right now, since he was talking with Jessa. But could there be others with his ability? I didn't know.

"Jessa did it," I said.

"This isn't the safest place to talk about Jessa," Sasha replied casually.

"Haven't you ever heard of hiding in plain sight? We're supposed to be dating, correct?"

"Fine," Sasha said, glancing around her. "What happened?"

"Well, I did a little test." We both turned to watch Jessa and Reed. They had plates of food and were headed to sit under a far-off tree. Jessa laughed at something Reed said. I couldn't seem to look away.

"You were saying…" Sasha said.

"What?"

She sighed. "Oh Lucas, it's so obvious you have a crush on her. Why won't you take my advice? Get over it. She's an asset. You can't let your feelings cloud your judgment of her."

"I know that. I'm confused why she's spending so much time with a guy like Reed. Do you think she trusts him?"

"I know why. He's cute and fun. Oh, and he's nice to her. All the other guardians her age have been rude. All of them. They're friends, Lucas. Get over it already."

"But he's working for Faulk,"

"Don't worry about Faulk just yet. Jessa isn't an idiot. You were saying? Jessa did something. Did what?"

I carefully explained to her about our morning in the greenhouse. About what had happened with the knife and how when Jessa had touched Reed's blood, she accidentally used alchemy on the red.

"There's something you need to know about red," Sasha said. "We do know what it does. Red itself is a power color. But red blood? Manipulating that controls people, Lucas. It can literally be used for mind control. No matter what happens, Jessa cannot get into Richard's hands. We may have to get her out of here."

"Why would you not tell me this! How can you be sure?"

"Look, she isn't the first to use red, okay? There have been others."

"Does my father know this?"

Her gaze held mine, unwavering. "Of course he does."

"So what do we do?"

"Do you think she'll listen to you? Keep it secret? I could warn her."

"No. Don't get involved. Just keep being her friend so she has someone else to hang with, besides Reed. We need to see how this plays out. I don't want to jump the gun and alert anyone to what's happened before we figure out what to do with her."

"Maybe. But you need to keep me informed of how this develops so I can report back to my handler."

"Your handler? What, like your boss? I need to talk to them."

"You will. In time," she said, smiling faintly.

"How long am I expected to keep this up? I need more from you guys."

"We know. And you'll get more soon. I promise."

That had to satisfy me for now.

"If you report to your handler and I report to you, does that mean you're my handler?" I asked, unable to keep myself from teasing her.

"Something like that," Sasha played back. Then she put her hand around my neck and pulled me in for a passionate kiss. I didn't know if it was for show or for real, but I didn't care. Suddenly, I felt a whole lot better, even if it only lasted for a minute.

■

The next few weeks, we spent training time concentrating on practicing with the alchemy of green. It was one of the most valuable colors, since healing was such a powerful and useful ability.

I had to report to Richard every few days about Jessa's progress. I could tell he wanted me to push the other colors, but I was able to convince him to train her like everyone else...just in a more accelerated fashion. We'd get to the red when she was ready. That's what he believed. His impatience was becoming obvious, and I didn't know how much longer I could hold off. Eventually, we'd have to try something with the red. For now, we pretended it didn't exist. I was too afraid that she'd reveal herself in front of Reed or Jasmine, and it would all be over.

I kept waiting for Jessa to say something about her experience with Reed's blood. But she didn't. I knew she missed her family desperately. And she probably couldn't last forever with this secret. Every once in a while, I saw it in her eyes. The questions.

■

After an afternoon of practicing with plants, Jessa asked Reed to go ahead without her. That was surprising, considering the amount of time they'd been spending together lately. Everyone wondered if they were dating, myself included. But Sasha didn't think so. She'd become closer to Jessa too.

Reed raised his eyebrow at her request, but didn't ask questions.

"Perfect," Jasmine said. "I need someone to help me categorize some plants in my office. Would you be so kind as to lend me an hour of your time?"

Reed shrugged and followed her out. That left us alone in the greenhouse and away from listening ears. The afternoon heat pressed in, making the large space feel smaller than it was.

"Can we talk?" Jessa asked.

"Not sure what there is to talk about." I picked up the potted plant and headed toward the back of the room.

The heat in here was distracting. That was why we'd been taking frequent breaks from training Jessa with green alchemy. With the heat, we had to dress lightly. She was wearing jean shorts and a tank top. Her hair was pulled back into a messy ponytail. Dark tendrils stuck to her glistening neck and forehead. She looked amazing—casual and effortlessly beautiful.

Carrying the plant, I made my way through the shrubbery to return it to its proper place. Jessa noisily followed before leaning against the edge of the nearest table, her head tilted. "Have you forgotten our conversation from a couple of weeks ago?"

So here it was. This had been a long time coming.

"Oh, that." I turned, pretending to study the plants surrounding us. "There's nothing I can tell you, Jessa, you're just going to have to trust me."

"Why do you have to act like it's nothing?" she asked, frustrated.

The truth was if I told her about her power, about red, I was afraid of how she'd handle it. I was pretty sure she would try to bolt. If she knew just how much danger she was in, how close she was to becoming Richard's pawn, what would she do? I wanted to have a solution for her. A way out. Something before I dropped this bomb on her.

"I wish I had an answer for you."

"Well, me too, because I'd like to talk to my family. You know? The people who raised me? The ones I haven't spoken with in, I don't know, three weeks? You know the deal I made with Faulk."

"I wish I could help you, but I can't. I promise I'm working on it."

"You could talk to Faulk. Or better yet, your father," she said, crossing her arms. She wasn't going to make this easy for me.

"That's not an option."

She obviously didn't understand the nature of my relationship with Richard. He was not the sort of man you could talk to about your problems. Not to mention—what did he care about Jessa's family, anyway? All that mattered was getting what he wanted. He talked, and people listened. He ordered. They obeyed. He wanted to make sure Jessa unlocked the mysteries of red. Once he found out, he would never let her go. She would become his tool, bending to his every will. Now that I knew why exactly he wanted red, I could only assume what he would do with that. The ability to control someone's mind? He would be unstoppable.

"You won't even give me a good explanation."

I held my ground. I needed to find a solution first. If I told her the truth right now, it would scare her too much.

"Fine, then you can forget about me keeping Reed's blood a secret. I'm telling Faulk. She'll believe me, you know. I did that blood thing once before."

She'd used red alchemy on blood before? When? Why hadn't she told me?

"Who else knows about that? What happened?"

"My baby sister, and it was an accident. She's fine. Nothing happened. I think Faulk knows. But I never outright admitted to it."

"Don't say another word to anyone about it," I pleaded.

She shook her head, jumped up, and moved to leave. I went after her. There was no way she was going anywhere. Not now. Not like this.

THIRTEEN

JESSA

He grabbed my arm and pulled me back to him. A heartbeat later, our bodies were pressed together, his eyes two heated gray slits.

"You're not telling anyone. I'll explain when I can. But I can't right now. It's not safe yet."

"Why?" I asked, my voice barely above a whisper. "You can trust me."

"Maybe I can," he said. "But you're too close to Reed. And I know I can't trust him. Please, Jessa, when I can help you, I will."

What did any of this have to do with Reed? I hadn't even been thinking of Reed. He was my friend, and we worked together. But it's not like I was telling Reed all my secrets. Yes, I was pretty sure Reed wanted something more from me romantically. But that wasn't going to happen. There wasn't a spark.

Like there is right now.

Pressed up against Lucas, anticipation welled in my chest. "Why do you care who I spend my time with?"

I never forgot whom he spent his time with. Sasha...his girlfriend. Most days, I didn't see her. But when I did, I couldn't help but like her. She was kind and friendly. She always made a point to say hello and to stop and chat. And that made it even worse, because deep down I hated that she had what I didn't.

"I care because I care about you," he said, his gaze intense.

I stepped away. I couldn't think clearly. The greenhouse humidity made me sweaty and disoriented, his closeness only added to that. "How is keeping me from my family looking out for me? Look, training has been fun and all, but I really miss them. I want those phone calls." His expression tore. Did I have to explain everything I'd been trying to tell him? I wasn't going to be an alchemist who forgot about her family. "Faulk says I can have an exception, remember? If I can learn red alchemy, then I can call them. And guess what? I can change blood. So why not tell someone? Faulk? Your father? Someone!"

Lucas practically growled, shaking his head with frustration. "And turn blood gray again? You know that's probably dangerous, right? Gray means the life is gone. How could that be okay to do to someone? No Jessa... Don't you see they're using you? Faulk? The GC? My father?"

"I thought you worked with them! Aren't you supposed to be a team or something? None of this is making any sense to me. I need you to explain it."

"I can't," he replied, running his hand through his dark, disheveled hair. "Have you not heard what I've been saying to you? I swear, sometimes you are so infuriating. Listen! Your life would be in danger if you did what they asked of you. Don't give red to them. You don't know whom you're dealing with. I do. Now, please stop asking questions and have some trust, will you?"

"All I know is that Faulk can grant me my phone calls with my family and you can't. No matter what I do, you don't give me anything I want."

Heat burned my cheeks when I realized the implication of what I'd just said. Did he read between the lines as I had? His eyes narrowed as he stepped closer, drawing the heat down even harder.

"What do you want me to give you, Jessa?"

"Nothing. I know that you have a girlfriend, even though you were seriously considering kissing me that night on the lawn. And I know that Reed is my friend, even though you are telling me to stay away from him. Why are you so jealous of him?"

"Jessa, Reed is working with Faulk. He's her golden boy and everyone knows it. And no, I am not jealous of Reed."

His eyes flamed as he took another step forward. I realized he was still holding my arm, but his grip wasn't tight anymore. It was soft. Gentle, even.

"Why do you like him, anyway?" he asked.

I had to think about that for a moment. Why *did* I like Reed? Well, I didn't have any romantic feelings for him. But I wasn't about to tell Lucas that. Something about his jealousy, even though he refused to acknowledge it, caused my chest to swell. "He's funny. And he's cute. And he is nice to me. And he's smart. Oh, and talented."

Lucas only glared even more.

"Why do you like Sasha?" I fired back.

"She's funny and cute," he replied, deadpan.

We were only about an inch apart. I ached to touch him. Instead I held still, my chin raised, as I gave him an icy stare. The normal Jessa would've stepped back or turned away. But I couldn't move. I didn't want to.

"Sasha is... Well, it's complicated with her. I wish I could explain what we have. It's not exactly what it looks like."

When he looked at my lips, I couldn't breath.

I waited for Lucas to close the gap. To press his lips against mine so we could finally have a moment of relief. As much as I'd hated to admit it, I'd longed for this moment since I first met him. Just when I couldn't take it any longer, just when I knew the kiss was going to happen, he pulled back.

Breathing heavily, he put his forehead against mine and shook his head. I wanted to tell him to kiss me anyway, but my words got caught on my breath. The heat of the greenhouse had intensified yet again, and the air was too thick between our bodies. A bead of sweat ran down my spine. I trembled.

"We can't do this," he said, stepping back. "Sincerely, I apologize for confusing you. I don't want to play games with you. I really *do* want your trust. But this can't happen."

"Is this how you treat all the girls?" Why couldn't he just figure out who he wanted, what he wanted? An unfamiliar storm of anger gripped me. At any moment, I could say something I'd regret. This sensation of rejection hadn't been tamed the last few weeks. It had only grown into an angry wildfire.

Lucas actually had the nerve to look offended. "You don't know what you're talking about."

"Why should I believe you?"

"This is not how I treat girls. First of all, I don't date color alchemists."

I had to laugh at that one. I mean, really, was he serious?

"That's right, I guess you forgot about Sasha again."

What was he doing, trying to kiss me? And more importantly, why had I been so willing to let him? Whether he considered it monogamous dating or not, Sasha clearly thought of herself as Lucas's girlfriend. And from the looks of it, she was! I hadn't forgotten all the times I'd seen them together. She deserved better. And I deserved more.

"Honestly, it's not what you think," he insisted.

I was tired of the broken record. "Are you kidding me? I've seen you with her. Multiple times! Kissing her. I don't know what's going on between you two. But something is, so don't stand here and try to tell me it isn't."

"You're right. You don't know half of what's really going on."

A surge of courage pulsed through me and I couldn't help myself, "Then why have you almost kissed me? Twice."

"But I *haven't* kissed you. And I won't."

Somehow, that was not the response I was expecting and it certainly wasn't what I wanted. I wanted to ask why not. I wanted to demand an answer. I wanted to make him hurt, as he'd hurt me. But I didn't seem to have the courage. Not when it came to him. I turned away.

"Jessa, being with you would be dangerous."

About a million responses came to mind, but I didn't speak.

"Sure, there's chemistry here. I'll admit that. But we're not meant to be. Let's just leave it alone before someone gets hurt."

Didn't he realize someone had already gotten hurt? The more I tried to push the ache of rejection down, the more painful it was. I wouldn't let him see that. If there was one thing I had learned while being at the palace, it was that I couldn't let anyone see me as weak. Everyone here was strong. Especially Lucas. I knew the truth now. I needed to be strong.

Trying to hold onto the last remnants of my pride, I turned back and reached out my hand in surrender. That small gesture nearly killed me. "Friends?"

His expression was unreadable as he tentatively shook my hand. I hoped I was coming across cool and collected. Lies. All lies.

"Please, Jessa, trust me. We'll talk about it when I can give you more answers. Answers about everything, okay? Be patient with me." He really did look sorry now.

Why should I care about his 'sorry'?

He let go of my hand and raised his own in mock surrender. "I'll keep you at a distance from now on. Just…don't say a word about the red. As soon as I have news to share, you'll be the first to know."

What does he mean?

I realized he was talking about the color alchemy argument we'd been having earlier. Given the abrupt change in conversation, he was already moving on. I wish I could be so cold.

How could he just forget another almost kiss—brush it aside like it had meant nothing? And when had I developed such a huge crush on Prince Lucas? I was living my worst nightmare. I had become an annoying, lovesick teenager. No, it was worse, because I was one of many who dreamed of this prince.

You need to grow up.

Before I could respond to him, before I could get another chance to dig for the answers around red, he was gone. He disappeared behind the lush plants without another word. This time, I didn't follow. I waited, the minutes creeping by. I needed to get a handle on myself but I couldn't take the humidity of the greenhouse anymore, either. I gave up and practically sprinted out the door.

Not making eye contact with a single person the whole way out of the GC wing, I ran up two flights of stairs before collapsing on my cool bed, determined not to cry.

■

Lucas may not have wanted anything to do with me, but Reed certainly had a different opinion of my company. After I showered and changed, Reed knocked on my door and asked if I wanted to study with him. We'd been studying together several times over the last few weeks. I let him in.

Reed was nice to me when most people treated me like an outcast. He introduced me to his friends, dragged me to a few guardian dinners, and generally cared about my feelings. It was really too bad I wasn't attracted to him the way I was to Lucas. Reed would make an excellent boyfriend. Well, if I could put aside the fact that he spied on me that first night. I still wasn't sure how I felt about that. Had he done it again?

Even though I'd be one of them soon, I was not technically a member of the GC. Reed had insisted we study in GC territory but had started coming around my room when I kept telling him I didn't like it over there.

The angry stares bothered me the most. From children, teens, and adults alike—it didn't matter. They all seemed to hate me. Something about my presence upset their balance. I hoped the novelty would wear off soon, so I could learn to enjoy myself in GC headquarters. So far, no such luck.

Other than going there for training, I'd spent a lot of time studying in my bedroom. The historical texts were most interesting. They held a much more detailed account of our past than what I'd been taught in the public school system. In fact, a few things were completely different. I suspected Lucas was sending me more than a few classified documents.

Reed and I sat on the bed, studying. The late afternoon sun warmed the airy room. I leaned over my slatebook, intrigued to find another discrepancy in this text, information that was very different from what I had been taught back home. This had been happening more and more lately. "Reed?" I asked.

He sat up, rubbing his head. His slatebook pinged, the sound of a game. I smirked. Studying, huh?

He shut it off, giving me his attention. "What's wrong, Jessa?"

"It's just that there have been little things in these texts that don't add up. A lot of what I was taught as a citizen is completely different from what they're teaching you here in the GC training."

He frowned. "Well, you're no longer an ordinary citizen. You get to know things that others don't. It's all for the good of the kingdom. Don't stress yourself out over it."

"Something about that doesn't sit well with me. Only a few weeks ago I *was* an ordinary citizen."

He sighed. "Okay, I get your point. And what exactly is bothering you?"

"This says that New Colony was established in 2030, which was ninety years ago. But we've always been taught that the New Colony is younger than that. As far as I always knew, this country was reestablished sixty years ago, in 2060. Right? Because after the War, there was a twenty-year period of unrest in America, which is why New Colony was even created in the first place. Our society decided we valued protection more than democracy. We broke off from West America."

"Well, it's true. New Colony was created because people were fed up with starvation, war, homelessness, and all the other things that democracy had created. So what's the problem?"

"The problem is that these new texts are telling me that for its first thirty years, New Colony wasn't doing much to help anyone. I'm beginning to think that someone decided to change the history books to make our kingdom seem more effective. What happened during those thirty years that they don't want to claim? It's dishonest to do that to people, to lie like that."

"It's just a little fib. It's not hurting anybody. I'm sure it's all meant to protect the people, anyway. Keep things stable. You know history isn't something we deal too much with in school anyway. Focusing on the future, on progress, is what's most important."

It was true. That's what I'd always been taught. To move forward rather than to get stuck in the misdeeds of the past. "But that means that for thirty years, New Colony wasn't doing anything to help anyone. Then, in 2060, when they got things in order, they decided to claim that New Colony was established much later? Why did our grandparents let them lie like that? It's trivial to assume we're not smart enough to handle the truth. If they're willing to lie about something as simple as dates, then what else aren't they telling us?"

"It's New Colony we're talking about. Everything the kingdom does is to protect the citizens. I'm sure there's a good reason those dates were changed."

"I think it's because they don't want people to know that there was ever a time this place wasn't perfect."

And really, what was so wrong with not being perfect? Our people were happy. They'd understand. Right? But maybe not everyone was happy. Maybe not every citizen actually *was* protected. I thought about Eliza. After the accident, she had asked to be transferred to another part of the palace. Her mother was sick. Her father was dead. And she'd been working since she was thirteen. How was that okay?

"See, you figured it out." Reed relaxed into the bed. He picked up his slatebook and started to play his game again. He was satisfied with that kind of explanation?

"I guess just knowing that my own government is lying to me doesn't make me feel very protected."

"Jessa." Reed laughed. "You need to relax. There's going to be more stuff like this when you become a guardian. Trust the system. New Colony has taken care of you so far, hasn't it?"

Has it? If so, then why I am here against my will? Why is the king threatening me, and why is the prince keeping secrets?

Reed put his game away again and grabbed my hands, looking at me with his most earnest smile. I'd seen it before. "Everything is going to be okay. Remember, we're lucky to be here. No other country takes care of color alchemists. In fact, no other country even takes care of their people like we do. We're lucky."

I wondered about that. It's what we were told. Again and again, we were shown footage of the rest of the world. Sometime over the last century, everyone but us had practically returned to the Dark Ages. People were starving, crops wouldn't grow, and water was contaminated. It was a dangerous world for most. And that's why we were so lucky to live where we did. To have what we had. We had our New Colony. We had the royals. And we had alchemy.

Maybe Reed had a point.

Once again, I noticed his boyish good looks. It was no wonder that the GC girl, Brooke, and her friends hated me. I was pretty sure Reed was a highly sought-after guy around here. His buttery blond hair and chocolate-brown eyes would attract any girl.

So why don't I like him back?

Something about what he'd said still bothered me. That this system had taken care of me. But that wasn't exactly true. I was here against my will, wasn't I? And yes, I'd been trying to make the best of it, but that still didn't mean I wanted to be here. I *had* to be here. I'd spent the last few weeks suppressing thoughts of ballet and home, but I could feel it eating away at me.

I turned away from Reed, not wanting him to see me cry. But his strong hand turned me to face him as he wiped at my hot tears. *Are you kidding me right now, Jessa? More tears?*

"Sometimes I forget how new you are to all of this. I'm sorry I've been so brash about it."

"I'm not mad at you, Reed," I said, meaning it. "You're one of the only good things about being here." And it was true. He was my friend. Even if he had some backward views about New Colony, that didn't mean he was a bad guy.

There was a look in his eyes that I recognized. Immediately, I realized he was going to kiss me. Sure, he would be a fun guy to date. But I didn't have those feelings. Given everything I'd been through with Lucas, I knew I couldn't do that to Reed. So I looked away, pretending not to notice his intentions.

"Can we talk about something else?" I asked, scooting away from him.

He sighed and nodded. "So what do you want to talk about?"

"Where are you from? I mean, before coming to the palace."

He frowned. "Why does it matter?"

"Well, I don't know. I'm curious. What are your parents like? Do you have siblings?"

"Well, if you must know, that's not the type of thing we're encouraged to talk about here. So I honestly don't think about it much anymore."

"You don't have to tell me if you don't want to."

"It's okay. I don't remember where I'm from. I remember having an older brother. I think his name was Charlie, but I'm not sure. I don't remember my parents' names or faces. Except, my mother was blond, like me. And that's about it."

"Do you miss them?"

"I've been here since I was five years old, Jessa. You have to understand, that's not me anymore. Those people? They're not even the ones who raised me. I'm happy to be a guardian. I have a lot of respect for the teachers and mentors who taught me to do what I can. I like my life."

It made sense, but I still felt sad for him. It was disturbing. Families were torn apart so the GC could function the way the officials wanted them to.

"So, what is it you can do with alchemy? Any special talents?" I asked, changing the subject.

He grinned. "All sorts of things. I am especially good with listening. Spying, I guess. I have an affinity for blue, the communication center. And luckily, blue is valuable to us. Not many alchemists can do what I do. Listening is one of the main things I use it for. Here, I'll show you."

He pulled a blue stone from his pocket and held it gently in his palm. I'd noticed recently that a lot of alchemists carried colored stones with them. Now

I knew why; it gave them easy access to organic color.

After a few moments, the color started to lift from the rock, leaving the tiniest speck of gray. The blue exploded out. It swirled and shifted around us in a waterfall of light.

And then Reed did something I hadn't seen before. He actually used his other hand to carefully guide the color into a shape. It looked like a cone. Then he pointed it toward the window on the far wall.

"How did you..."

"Everything in time. Put your ear right up to the blue. Hurry, I can't hold this for too long. It's not the easiest alchemy. But it's got to be one of my favorites."

I slowly leaned my ear against the blue cone of floating light, nervous. I felt the color touch my ear; hot and fluid, but dry. Was it going to work on my ear? I didn't want to ruin Reed's plan, so I closed my eyes and concentrated on my hearing. I didn't notice anything at first, but then I started to get something.

Birds chirped, a little girl giggled, and high-heeled shoes clacked across pavement. Then it got louder. The whooshing sound of a car zoomed by. It was so loud now. Like I was standing on a busy street corner myself.

I pulled back, the reminder of normal life stinging. "That's amazing."

Reed nodded, and suddenly what was left of the color flew back into the stone. It was blue like before, but the gray spot was still there. He slipped it back into his pocket.

"All color can be manipulated in different ways to create power. We can use it for just about anything. We're constantly developing new techniques. You'll learn this more and more throughout your training. And once you're GC, you'll get to start helping people."

The idea sent a shiver of excitement through me. Could this be something I wanted? The thought that I could embrace this life startled me. But helping people was definitely a welcomed thought. At the same time, I was doubtful I could pay the price. This place hardened people. I'd yet to see anything that proved to me that the GC actually bettered anyone. Well, except for when Jasmine healed people.

I remembered again that Reed was the one who had helped Faulk listen in on my conversation with Lucas my first night here. But so much had changed between us since then.

And yet, I finally understood something important about Reed. Something I needed to remember. He *lived* to be a guardian. He was as loyal an alchemist as they came. I knew that was why Faulk had assigned him to me. If push came to shove, he'd choose his job, his duty, before our friendship.

"Are you here with me because you want to be here? Or are you here because Faulk wants you to spy on me?"

He shook his head. "We're friends. I want to be here. I really like you."

"But you work for her, don't you?"

"Yes, I do, but that doesn't mean I run and tell her everything you do or say. I thought you knew me better than that."

But there was something about the whole situation that didn't sit well. Sure, he liked me. I knew that he even wanted to date me. But was liking me enough for him to protect me from her?

I peered into him, searching for a genuine emotion, something I could hold onto. He reached out and held my hand. His brown eyes stared into mine, pleading.

I can trust you. I don't know how or why, but I do.

"I'm sorry. I didn't mean to accuse you of anything. You're such a good friend. I trust you, Reed."

"You're right. You can trust me with anything." He paused. "Is there anything you want to tell me?"

As a matter of fact, there *was* something I wanted to tell him. I reached back into my thoughts, trying to remember what it was. I knew it was important. I knew it would help. My mind felt hazy and clouded. I nodded, pulling the tangle of memories to the surface.

Red. That was it. I wanted to tell him about the red. About the blood.

"What is it?"

I opened my mouth, ready…

Lucas's voice flashed through my mind. *Don't tell Reed. Don't tell anyone.*

But why?

It's dangerous.

I shook my mind, trying to clear the confusion. Something was wrong. I needed to figure this out before I lost my line of thought…

Wait, this isn't right. Why are my thoughts so convoluted?

I realized that Reed must be using his alchemy on me. He was trying to get me to speak. Using what? The blue? "Blue is the color of communication," he'd said. Could he communicate his ideas and will to me? Was he doing that now? He must have the ability to become incredibly persuasive when he wants to be. *What a jerk!*

I noticed then that Reed's other hand was in his pocket. I wanted to punch him, to yell and scream and kick him out of my room. Fortunately, my better judgment took over and I decided it was safer to play along. I would pretend he was actually in control.

"I don't know," I said slowly, hoping my voice sounded as airy as it had only moments before. "I don't have any secrets. I just wanted to tell you that I trust you."

"You can tell me what it is. What's your secret?"

"But there's nothing to tell. What's wrong, Reed?"

He cleared his throat, eyeing me. I smiled peacefully, hoping he couldn't sense the wild anger that burned just under the surface. How dare he treat me like this? Had he been manipulating my emotions this whole time?

"I'm sorry. I believe you. I have to go. I'm late for a class. I'll see you later, Jessa." He jumped off the bed and left the room abruptly.

Did he know I'd figured out what he was doing? There was no way to tell.

He had to have figured out something was up to take off so fast. Either way, I was in trouble. Lucas was right. I couldn't trust anyone. Even my closest friend here was using me. If I was ever going to see my family again, I would have to find a way out of here myself. But after that experience, I really didn't want to tell anyone about the red. Not if they could use the blue center to do stuff like that...mess with my thoughts and emotions, and even spy on people. It made me shudder to think what they wanted with red...which was the color that signified ultimate power.

I knew then and there that I wouldn't give in. I wouldn't go to Faulk and tell her about the blood. I wouldn't trust Reed. I would do what Lucas asked until I could figure out a way to get out of this place.

FOURTEEN

LUCAS

My confrontation in the greenhouse with Jessa left me in a tangle of mixed emotions. If I became romantically involved with her, I'd lose myself. She brought out the kind of emotions in me that I wanted to keep buried deep. I couldn't allow it. I did the right thing by stopping that kiss, as hard as it was. I could only hope I didn't get pulled in by her again. There was just something about her that made me feel strong and weak all at the same time.

I found myself avoiding her for the next couple days. A few hours after our heated exchange in the greenhouse, I sent a message to her slatebook. I gave her instructions to spend the weekend reading, with a large attachment of historical texts. When she was finished with that, we'd get back to work with Jasmine and Reed. I knew I'd have to move on from green alchemy soon, and that worried me because I still wanted to stay far away from red. Maybe we could work with orange. That would lighten everyone's moods, at least.

I spent my days running or reading. One late afternoon, when I was at the library, a light knock on the door pulled me out of my most recent Jessa daydream. It was the one I had been having over and over. The one where I kissed her in the greenhouse instead of pulling away.

I jumped out of the desk chair and brushed myself off. *Get a hold of yourself, Lucas.*

I opened the door and found Sasha peering up at me.

"Prince," she said, motioning to the guards standing watch at the door, "can we go somewhere private?"

I looked around, confused. Wasn't the empty library private enough? She moved over to a desk, grabbed a paper and pen, and scribbled: *I don't know who could be listening nearby. Let's go outside.*

I should have seen that coming. Reed always seemed to be lurking nearby these days. I thought back to all I could have possibly said inside these walls that was incriminating. Except for my conversations with Jessa and Sasha, I'd kept everything locked in my head or hidden in my private study. I should be okay.

"Sure, let's get out of here."

∎

As soon as we were out of the palace, we walked into a thicket of trees to conceal ourselves. Sasha pulled a nearby blue flower from its roots. The color quickly left it and she maneuvered it into a shield of sorts around us.

"There, now we can talk."

"How did you learn to do that?" I asked.

"I can't seem to master listening in on people, but I have been working hard on creating privacy for years. Lucky for us, I think I got it down."

"And you think people are trying to listen to us?"

"Not entirely. All I know is what my handler told me. Apparently, they got this information off Richard's slatebook directly. They've been looking for more and more blue alchemists. Listening in on conversations? That has to be one of the reason's why."

"Who's your handler, Sasha?"

"You already know that's not up to me to say."

I wanted to push the issue more. I had to protect myself. But I knew Sasha was protecting herself, too.

"Okay, but tell them to make contact soon, or I'm done with this."

She grimaced and nodded. "An assignment is coming for you. Soon. Right now the important thing is that we have your back."

"I sure hope so."

Her smile faded. "Lucas, this is nothing. Things are going to get a lot more intense. Richard started another round of testing."

Another round? In the past he had pulled so much color from the land, that he had killed it. Stripped it down to nothing but gray. But that wasn't the worst part. The worst part was when his alchemists started turning their powers on people. They pulled color from their bodies or pushed mass amounts on them. Most often, it ended in death. I knew it was happening, but I still wasn't sure *why* Richard was doing it. Only a handful of alchemists were involved, *so far.*

"I have a lot at stake here. If I am caught working with you, I don't know what my father will do. We both know what he's capable of. I'll help you, but please don't put me at risk unless you're willing to bring me in on your plans," I said.

"What have we asked you to do that was so risky?"

As if this entire conversation couldn't have us both killed. I laughed. "Are you serious? Have you forgotten how we met?"

Recognition lit her eyes and she smirked. It wasn't all that long ago that we'd met each other in that dark closet.

"Oh, right. Thank you for that. It's been a world of help to us."

The person who'd informed me about the Resistance had agreed they would help me stop my father. My only condition was that everything must happen nonviolently, to which they had agreed. So far, I still believed them. I'd heard of nothing that would spark my father's suspicion or temper. Which was good news for them, considering that he was the kind of leader who ruthlessly squashed opposition.

"We need to tell Jessa what's really going on."

"We're not sure she's ready."

"She can be trusted." Admittedly, I didn't know if it was the truth, but everything inside me wanted to tell her all my secrets. I was still worried how she would react to the news about red. But if I could tell her who Sasha really was to me, maybe she wouldn't hate me so much. Maybe she'd join our side.

"She can help us," I added.

"Are you sure this isn't about your crush on her?"

"I don't have feelings for her like that." The lie fell flat. "Okay, fine. I don't know what's going to happen there. But I do know we're friends. The point is, she's powerful. It's time we get her on our side."

"Everyone knows she's powerful. The Resistance already knows that. That doesn't mean she could handle the truth yet."

"But what about the red? She used red alchemy again, Sasha. No one's been able to do that before. I can only keep her quiet for so long. What if she gets swayed by Faulk or Reed or someone else?"

"Jessa is not the only one who's ever accessed red."

"Well, I figured as much when you told me what red can do. I'm assuming one of your people figured out how to do it. Or is there something else?"

"One of ours used to. But I came to warn you. We think someone is using red on your mother."

"How can you be sure?"

She bit her lip. "We're *not* sure. But it fits, right? With what you told me."

"You still don't know who it could be?"

She shook her head.

"So you came to tell me that someone is using mind control on my mother, but you have no idea who. And that my father is starting more rounds of testing that will essentially kill innocent people? Great. Anything else?"

Sasha put her hand on mine. "I know it's a lot to take in, Lucas. I'm sorry."

"I feel like I don't even know him. That I never really did."

She sighed. "Well, if it makes you feel any better, I never knew my father, either. Not really."

"How come I don't remember you?" I had thought about it several times, but I couldn't seem to place her anywhere in my childhood, or in the alchemists I encountered.

"I was always really shy. But, anyway, I was moved to another facility when I was still a child. This is the first I've been back here in a very long time."

Another facility for training? I frowned. She must have already been a member of the GC, initiated as a child. That was practically unheard of. Most didn't qualify until their teenage years.

"You're very strong," I said, meaning it.

"So are you."

"I'm sorry you didn't get to have a childhood." We started walking back to the palace, the blue sound-shielding magic now dropped.

"Don't be sorry. It's not your fault. And anyway, I barely remember my birth family. It's all in the past now."

"Like I said, you've become strong." I admired her attitude. But still, I felt sorry for her. There was something underneath her demeanor today, a hidden pain that was just now coming to the surface. It actually made her prettier. More human and less mysterious.

"You want to know what was hard for me?" she asked, stopping. "It was where I was placed as a child. I was sent up north, Lucas. I saw it for myself, what they're doing out there. I participated."

I couldn't understand how my father managed to keep something so big hidden from the people. More alchemy? Just the very fact that it had been kept quiet, that there weren't massive protests and rebellions, was perplexing. That must have had something to do with red. How else could he control that?

"It was you who used the red, wasn't it?" It wasn't an accusation. If she had been up there as a child, there must have been a solid reason.

A single tear rolled down her cheek, a silent answer to my question.

"Lucky for me, that…talent…is gone now. It disappeared when I got older. I think I repressed it somehow. Please, don't say anything. Trust me, I learned my lesson. I can't use red anymore, and I need to make sure that nobody else ever does."

◼

Dinner with my parents was mandatory. It was also incredibly unbearable. Tonight was another one for the books.

For the first ten minutes, my mother and I waited at the table for Richard. She sat silently, picking away at her measly plate of food and rubbing her head. Then Richard joined us and spent the next twenty minutes discussing strategies with his advisors. They stood in the back of the room while he ate a huge plate of roasted lamb, sweet potatoes, and freshly baked bread.

What bothered me was that I was expected to be here, to sit and listen and only speak when spoken to. I was eighteen years old, but they still treated me like an insolent child. It was called "being supportive," or at least that was what my mother had begun to say in recent years. Richard was happy to have me add something to the discussions *only* when asked.

Tonight, the topic of discussion was about lending more resources to the southern region of New Colony. Spring storms had been exceptionally bad this year and had damaged most of the local crops.

"Whom do we have stationed out there?" he asked. "Anyone good?"

"Sir, the only healing alchemists there aren't capable of handling that many crops," Royal Officer Thomas said, scrolling through a slatebook as he looked up the information. "We'll have to rush someone down there right away."

"Should we send Jasmine?" I interjected. "She's the best healer we've got. I've seen her work during our trainings with Jessa. She's impeccable. She could heal those crops. I'd be happy to go with her." I felt excited at the idea of being able to do something useful. I knew it was one of the poorer areas of the kingdom, and they'd need our support.

"That's not a possibility," Richard said, taking a large bite of food and slowly chewing. "We need her here."

Thomas paused. I was sure he was going to agree with me. Maybe he could convince Richard. Thomas had been with us for years, and there was a chance he could get through to my father. Those people needed Jasmine's help. After a moment, Thomas kept scrolling through a list, rattling off other names as possibilities. No one could do what Jasmine could do. We all knew that.

Am I the only one who will stand up to Richard?

"Why is she needed here?" I asked, but he just ignored me. I already knew the answer. He kept Jasmine around as a precaution. She was our own personal insurance policy. Not only had she healed many people—she'd healed the worst of the worst. She had the capacity to fix injuries that there was no coming back from. He didn't want her away, just in case he needed her for himself. He could argue that he kept her around for Natasha, but I was convinced that my mother was hardly a priority.

"Hundreds of people will be without jobs in that area. Thousands will be affected by the food shortage. You know that's not how New Colony operates. We always take care of our people. I'm sure we can spare Jasmine for a few days. She's the only one with enough talent to be able to fix this quickly."

"That's enough," my father bellowed, putting down his fork and wiping his face with his linen napkin. "Don't argue with me, Lucas. It isn't your place." He got up from the table, kissed my mother on her cheek, and left in a flash. The advisors and royal officers scurried out behind him. The room fell silent.

"Why is he like that?" I asked my mother.

"You and your father are so different, Lucas. Don't try to understand him, because you never will. Just support him. That's all we ask."

I laughed. She expected me to sit back and allow his choices to let an entire geographical region of his country go hungry? No way.

"I should support him even when he's wrong?"

"You'll have your turn. He's been giving you a lot of responsibility lately. Be grateful. Don't ruin your chance to make him proud."

"Are you angry at him or me?"

"I'm not angry," she said, her pale face turning blotchy. She rubbed her temples and closed her eyes. Had someone recently gotten to her mind again?

"The old you would *never* have stood for this."

"Please, Lucas. I'm doing the best I can. I'll talk to him, okay? I'll see what I can do."

I nodded, knowing it was all I was going to get. I didn't know where to go from here. I thought about questioning her headaches, but thought better of it. She never seemed to have an answer. So I changed the subject to one I knew she relished; my love life. "You know I've been dating that alchemist Sasha for a few weeks now, right?" I said, plopping a piece of bread into my mouth.

She eyed me warily. "Oh, Lucas, I hope it's not serious. She's hardly the stuff of royalty, being an alchemist and all. Though she is lovely."

There was nothing mean-spirited about the way she said it. In her mind, she was merely stating the facts. I laughed. Apparently, her candor hadn't gone away. "All right, then. What *is* the stuff of royalty?"

She flashed me a genuine smile.

"You surprise me, Lucas. I hardly thought we'd be having this conversation already. Eighteen is old enough, I suppose, but far younger than I thought for you. You've always been so independent."

"What do you mean…having what conversation?" I asked, teasing.

"The one where you are already thinking about your future queen."

I burst out with laughter. "Don't worry, Mother. I'm not planning on getting married anytime soon. Can't a guy date around here?"

"Well, you brought up the alchemist girlfriend. Not me."

"What's so wrong about alchemists marrying royals?"

"The color guardians are not meant for leadership. They're unpredictable and dangerous. Not to mention, what they do is unnatural. We can't give them any more power than they already have."

"*Unnatural?*" I asked. I'd always thought the opposite. Had my mother always felt this way? I had never known her to be cold. Something about her tone bothered me. She sounded like a puppet, mimicking the ideas of my father. Or was it someone else?

"Anyone with that much power needs to be controlled, darling. We can't have them running the country. They're not royals. They couldn't be trusted to do both jobs. I'm sure you agree." She returned to her meal.

I'd been around plenty of alchemists throughout my life. Sure, they could be dangerous. But they weren't the ones abusing power. How could she not see what I saw? It was Richard, her husband, who needed to be kept in check.

We finished our dinner in the usual silence.

"Excuse me," I said, getting up from the dinner table. I needed to find Sasha and convince her to get Jessa on our side immediately. And if she wasn't going to agree, then I would have to do what I thought was best without her support. I strode from the dining room, cool and collected, ignoring the hollow knot in my stomach.

■

Sasha was in one of the guardian training rooms. A small crowd of young recruits were busy practicing with some plants.

"Hello, Boyfriend," Sasha said when she saw me, mockingly batting her eyelashes and fanning her face. A gaggle of preteen girls erupted in laughter at her antics.

The whole training room was crowded, but mainly with young kids. Still, I needed to talk to her privately. The palace had been busy all day, and the gardens were especially teeming with people. They were preparing for some political brunch that would be taking place the next morning. I was sure I'd be expected to attend it, whatever it was.

"We need to talk privately." I pulled her into a hug and whispered in her ear. "The gardens are out of commission right now. Where can we go?"

"You tell me. This is your house, isn't it?"

That gave me an idea. I'd always made it a point to take my girlfriends to other areas of the palace or even out into the city. But I had never taken someone to our private living quarters.

I knew my father. Despite his ruthless tactics, he was proud to a fault. Very few people were allowed to go into our wing of the palace. He liked his privacy. There was no way he'd allow any spies in his own home. It was the one place that was nearly always empty. Because that was what our area of the palace was: our home.

I took Sasha's hand, knowing if we were going back there, for all intents and purposes, it had to look like we were up to something more predictable than plotting against my father.

We headed out of the training room, several watchful eyes following us. A few older girls glared at her and turned to whisper to each other. Sasha didn't care about that. In fact, it was probably better for our cover.

"Where are we going?" Sasha played right along and squeezed my hand. Then she weaved her fingers into mine and giggled, kissing my cheek.

I laughed and raised my voice, "Somewhere we can be alone."

We continued through the GC areas and out into the main corridor of the palace. It took us ten minutes to walk from that side of the palace to the other. All along the way, people stared at our unabashed public display of affection. I was used to nosy stares. I didn't let it bother me.

I could admit to having a reputation with women in the past, but my relationships had always been fleeting. I'd never found any one girl to be interesting enough to actually want to be with her for more than a few dates. And anyway, everyone knew that despite being the most eligible bachelor in New Colony, there were very few women who would ever be permitted to seriously date me. I was "Prince Lucas," and not even I could change that.

I suspected that my parents put up with my antics because they assumed, in the end, that they'd be the one to choose my queen. And even though I didn't want to be forced to marry for Richard's political gain, a big part of me was sure that one day, he'd find a way to make it happen.

When we reached the set of large wrought-iron doors, flanked on either side by palace guards, I caught a glance at Sasha. She was pale, and her hands were shaking. For her, this was probably like walking into enemy territory.

"There aren't listening ears in here," I whispered.

She straightened up and walked through heavy doors and into my home.

There was no modern design here. And it wasn't classically southern like most of the original palace architecture. Our area was still grand, but different. My mother had decorated it with a much cozier feel.

"Wow, so this is home, then?" Sasha was busy eyeing all the closed doors. "Is he here?"

"No, he's rarely here. He spends his time working in other offices."

"What about your mother?"

"Natasha is already in bed." I pointed to the closed door at the end of a long hallway. "She won't come out before morning."

"No one knows we're here?"

"He might spy on my mother and me. But there are some places that even he wouldn't invade. Not here. Not his own house."

I took her hand and led her directly to his private study.

The door was locked, as usual. But it was an old lock and an old door. And there were no palace guards allowed in here. Or alchemists.

"You'll have to open that. Is that going to be a problem?" I knew there were multiple ways alchemy could open a locked door.

"I'm not getting caught breaking in there."

What she didn't know was that although Richard probably kept a few things in this office, there were no documents or anything else centered around national security. I would know. I'd broken in at least a dozen times over the years, looking for information.

I pondered Sasha's presence in the palace. Her small, curvy build and long blond hair were enough to give anyone the illusion that she was just another carefree, beautiful girl. But I knew differently. Why would she be afraid of breaking a lock?

She must've read my expression. "I don't want to risk the mission. Maybe you won't get in trouble for getting caught in there, but I will."

She was right. "Well, since my study hasn't been swept for bugs, that only leaves us one other option for privacy. We'll have to go talk in my bedroom."

She followed me down the hallway and into my most private space.

FIFTEEN

JESSA

I was avoiding everyone, especially staying clear of Lucas and Reed. The best way to manage that was to hide out in my boring room. I couldn't stop thinking about the night before when I'd attempted, unsuccessfully, to fall asleep. A thought kept surfacing in that dramatic "this is really important and you won't sleep all night until you fix this" kind of way.

You're acting suspicious.

And it was the truth. Ever since Reed had tried to manipulate my emotions with blue alchemy, I'd been avoiding him. Why shouldn't I? He pretended to be my friend, spent weeks hanging out with me, all in order to use alchemy on me, against my will, to see if I would reveal my secrets. I was sure now that he was reporting everything back to Faulk. I knew I should have told Lucas and apologized for not having believed him in the first place, but I couldn't bring myself to go looking for him. Not after our second almost-kiss and the feelings of rejection that had left a bitter aftertaste.

So I decided to get over myself and go find Reed. Maybe if I acted normally, he wouldn't worry about me. Or maybe I should just confront him?

"Hey, Reed!" I called out, running to meet him in one of the GC hallways. "What's going on?"

"Hi, Jessa." His voice faltered. "I was just going to spar for a little bit. Do you want to watch?"

He nodded toward the gymnasium, just behind a large sheet of thick glass. There were black mats lining the floor. Most had a pair of guardians on them, fighting. Maybe it was kickboxing, wrestling, or, as Reed had called it, sparring, but all I saw was fighting. Combat.

This was so foreign to me.

"Sure, sounds fun." I smiled, forcing myself to follow his muscled form into the gym.

As we walked in, I immediately noticed there was another area in the space that I hadn't seen through the glass, filled with shiny exercise equipment. Almost every machine had a person utilizing it. Treadmills and weight-lifting machines were lined in neat rows.

The entire space was loud and buzzing with adrenaline.

Sure, it made sense that the royals would want the alchemists to be strong and healthy. But this was something else. These people were beyond athletic— they were machines.

My jaw must have been hanging open as I watched the pairs of people, because Reed reached out and actually pushed my mouth shut, laughing to himself. "Okay, so you can kick butt. Note taken."

"It's part of guardian training. Royal officers, too." He pointed to some of the people in white clothing. "And all the recruits. You'll be in here soon enough."

So they were *all* lethal. I wondered if guardians ever fought with color, but I was too afraid to ask. I think I had a pretty good idea of the answer already.

"You ready?" a girl purred from behind us. I turned and recognized Brooke, the one who'd been rude to me at my introduction party. She smirked when she saw me. "Do you want to play, too?"

"I don't think Jessa came to fight."

"Too bad." She rolled her eyes at me.

I stepped back as Reed pulled her out onto the closest mat. They stood apart for a moment before she dived for him, and they ended up wrestling. Something about the whole exchange didn't feel right. They were definitely fighting. He knocked her head against the floor hard, and she retaliated with a kick to his jaw. But despite the pain, it seemed like they were enjoying themselves way too much. The way they moved was almost sexual, but in a way that made my skin crawl. And when Brooke looked up at me and winked before wrapping her legs around his torso, I had to turn away.

I didn't know what to think. But something about watching them, about this huge gymnasium and the GC headquarters in general, felt wrong. I didn't want to be there anymore, so I left, hoping the short conversation with Reed was enough to keep him satisfied for a while. Maybe just coming down here would throw his suspicions to the back of his mind for now.

As I made my way back toward the sanctuary of my bedroom, I noticed a familiar face and stopped short. "Eliza!"

She slowly turned, before stepping back.

"Miss Loxley, how are you?"

"I'm fine. Eliza, how are you? I've wanted to talk to you ever since the accident. I need you to know how sorry I am."

She just stared at me for a moment and nodded before looking away. She took another step back, and I noticed that her hands were shaking. Guilt plunged through me. "Really, I am sorry. Are you feeling better?"

"I'm fine, miss. Just busy working."

She'd been transferred somewhere else, I guessed, and was no longer working with alchemists. I assumed I had somehow gotten her into trouble, but I realized now that maybe she'd asked to be moved. And that was my fault. "How's your mother doing?"

"Jessa, I really don't want to talk to you about my mother. I already told you I could be in trouble for that. And to be honest, I really don't want anything to do with you."

Of course she hated me. I'd almost killed her.

"Oh, okay," I frowned. "I'll leave you alone, then."

She nodded and scurried off. Another maid joined her as they walked down the hallway, whispering to each other. I didn't recognize the other woman, who turned back to me with a snarky glare.

And then, just like that, they rounded a corner and disappeared.

I continued down the hall, bothered by everything. Why did I have to be here? This wasn't the life I wanted. I was on track to living my dreams before the alchemy surfaced. Wasn't there a way to shut it all off? Lucas had assured me there wasn't, and from what I could tell, no one else was developing anything like that. Maybe I could find a way to do it, but as it stood, I still felt clueless every day I spent in training. I was such a newbie!

And as much as I pretended it didn't bother me, it really hurt to be treated like an outcast. The other alchemists hated me. I wasn't yet in with them, no GC initiation plans to speak of. Not that I even knew what that meant. But I was invading their training rooms daily. Lucas and Jasmine gave me special treatment, Richard had made it clear I was "chosen" and Reed was Faulk's little spy. I clearly didn't belong.

Maybe it wouldn't be so hard if I could just have contact with my family.

Just then, I spotted Faulk stalking around the corner with her royal officer, Thomas. I was pretty sure he was second in command. Could I convince them to let me have a call home? I still hadn't said a word to Faulk about the blood situation, and I wasn't going to. Not yet, anyway. As much as he infuriated me, I felt like Lucas was telling me the truth. I needed to keep my mouth shut.

Just as I was about to catch up to them, I stopped short at the mention of a familiar name: *Lacey.* They had turned the corner now and couldn't see me. But I could hear their every word.

"You've had eyes on the Loxley house?" Faulk asked.

"Yes, constantly. I don't know how it happened."

There was a long pause.

"They were acting normal enough. Going to work, sending the girl to school. Anytime we questioned them, they answered everything," Thomas said.

"But this wasn't the first time. I should have known better than to let them continue on like that. Like they aren't criminals, hiding alchemists from us. It was only a matter of time."

"So you think Lacey is an alchemist then?"

Another long pause.

If they think Lacey is an alchemist, they'll take her. She'll become part of this twisted system. And my parents? They'll be destroyed.

"What do you want us to do?" Thomas asked.

Please don't bring her in.

"Don't you think we're a little late to the party, Thomas?" Faulk spat.

The next thing I knew, they rounded the corner, practically running me over. There was no use in hiding I'd overheard them. "What's going on? Is everything okay with Lacey?"

"Lacey isn't your concern right now," Faulk said.

"She's my little sister. I have every right to be concerned."

"Did you already forget about our little deal? When you produce red alchemy, then you'll have contact with your family."

Thomas stepped back, peering at Faulk as if confused. What did he know that I didn't?

"So," Faulk continued, "do you have red or not?"

I wanted to tell her the truth. I wanted my family and speaking up would do that. But, until I knew what red did, I couldn't risk it. I shook my head.

"That's what I thought. Don't worry about your family. Worry about your job as an alchemist."

She brushed past me, heading for her office. Thomas shuffled after her, only once peering back at me. He shrugged and mouthed, "Sorry." I could tell he felt bad for me, but not bad enough to actually do anything about it. He may be the nicest royal officer around here, but he was still under Faulk's command.

Why did she have to be so horrible? The royal officers would get more done if they didn't treat the guardians like such criminals. Yes, guardians got to do some cool magic. Yes, they got to live in the palace. But at what cost? Was I the only one who saw the flaws with the system?

I couldn't take it anymore. I hurried back to my room to be alone. It was my only sanctuary. What would it feel like when I had officially moved into the GC wing? I didn't want to think about how hard that would be.

After Reed showed me blue alchemy, how he had used it to create a listening device, I'd been trying to do the same thing in private. I had stolen a blue stone from one of the classrooms a few days ago. But so far, I'd had no luck getting blue to do much of anything. I didn't know what I was planning. But I hoped to figure out some way to get in touch with my family. I still wanted to find a way to go home, but for now, communication would be better than nothing.

I originally believed blue to be a harmless color. But the alchemy Reed used it for wasn't innocent, prying into my emotions like that. At least he hadn't tried anything more—that I knew of.

I sat on my bed, holding the stone. Again, I wondered if I could access the blue to speak with my parents. Was that possible? After my run in with Faulk, now more than ever, I needed to talk to them. I looked back at the stone. I didn't want to think too hard. *Just start small.*

I allowed myself to relax and focus on the stone.

Who do you think you are? You can't do this.

Yes, the calm voice within me responded. *Yes, you can.*

And just like that, I did it.

The color exploded around me. Blue swirled through the room in ribbons of brilliant light. Tentatively, I reached out, hoping I could mold it the way Reed had shown me. But when I touched it, it spun away from me, like ink in water.

I tried again. Still, it seeped away from me in chaotic swirls. I didn't understand. Why wouldn't the blue do what I wanted? So far I could access green, orange, and even red. What was so hard about blue?

You will be able to figure it out if you practice.

If there was anything I'd learned from all those years of dancing, it was that practice and hard work paid off.

But for how long? It took you years to master ballet.

I reached again, and the color darted away in a flash. I couldn't even get close. A prickle of frustration bubbled into my chest. *Why am I even here?* My true place wasn't with these people. They only wanted to use me. I was meant to be at home with my family. I was meant to be a ballerina. The anger raged inside as I threw the stone across the room. It hit the wall with a ping and dropped to the floor. Suddenly, the room was normal again.

Maybe I shouldn't be so upset, but I couldn't help it. Jasmine had told me that not every alchemist could manipulate every color. That must be why red wasn't something others could tap into. It seemed so strange to me that Reed could control blue, and I could control red. Maybe we just had different talents.

Fatigue washed over me. I lay down on the bed, realizing that the attempted alchemy had taken an enormous amount of energy. All I could think about was sleep. I started to drift away, my eyes getting heavier by the second. A thought tried to push its way through...something about the red blood and about how I had felt the times I had turned it gray. Was that important? But just before I could formulate a clear thought, sleep swiftly took me away.

■

Their faces are ghosts. I know they are there, but I can't see them beyond the darkness. The hot lights blind me. Floating purple orbs fill the horizon. I blink rapidly, trying to clear my vision. The oxygen moves quickly in and out of my lungs, like a smooth stone skipping violently across water.

It is quiet, and the rush of blood and adrenaline swishes through my ears. A drop of sweat runs down my back, tickling my spine. Instinctively, I straighten a bit more as I take my position. The music chimes to life, and with it, I begin to dance.

I fly effortlessly across the smooth stage, creating a beautiful story with my body while the delicate melody meets me. Each movement is soft yet precise. Calculated. Studied. Natural. From the tips of my loose fingers to the strength of my pointed toes, I am in complete control.

The dance is the best of my career, validating my position as a prima ballerina.

And with every effortless step, I fill with pride. The music builds to a crescendo and I leap high, my legs extended and powerful. Falling into a crouch, I complete the performance as I fall to the floor. I pant with exhilaration.

There is a pause before the audience erupts with applause. I can't help but smile widely. Catching my breath, I stand and curtsy, looking out into the crowd. I want to see their faces. I want to know them. Somewhere in the distance, over the roar of applause, someone is chanting my name: "Jessa! Jessa!"

I search for them, a prick of familiarity burning at my memory. The voice is young.

Lacey appears on the stage. My little sister is wearing a simple white dress. Her dark blond hair curls sweetly around her small face. As she steps forward, the crowd continues applauding, oblivious.

I try to run to her, but my knees buckle, and I slip. Falling at her feet, I look up. I try to speak, but no words come out. All I want to do is hug her. To get to her, somehow. But my body won't move.

Lacey smiles. A drop of crimson falls from the corner of her mouth. She holds out her hands, and I watch, horrified, as rivers of blood flow from her palms. The moment stills as drops hit the floor, thick and heavy.

I reach out, urging my body forward. I will myself to get up. To help her. But it's as if I am moving through quicksand. It's like she is behind a wall of glass. The audience continues their cheering, louder now. Maddening. Don't they see her?

Lacey falls to the floor, and the blood continues to pour from her mouth. Her eyes flutter and roll into the back of her head as her complexion pales. Can't I fix this? Can't I heal her? I'm screaming in my head, desperate to hear myself over the noise.

She starts choking on her own blood then. Straining to get air that just won't come. Dying under the heaviness. Someone needs to help her. I need to help her.

Something shifts in the audience. They are laughing. A chorus of cackling hysterics drowns my senses.

Lacey abruptly sits up. Her thin torso is perfectly straight. "Help me!"

■

"No!" The scream erupted as I flew out of bed.

Where's Lacey? She needs my help.

My heart pounded in my chest. My throat prickled. I shook my head, trying to clear the terror as I realized it was only a nightmare.

I stumbled out around the room to find a water bottle. I walked over to the window and looked at the dark sky outside, chugging the room-temperature water. Then I checked the red numbers on the bedside alarm clock. They blinked glaringly: 02:18. 02:18. 02:18. 02:19.

The alchemy I'd tried before falling asleep pushed through my mind. It seemed like something had happened, but I wasn't sure why I couldn't touch the blue. The amount of energy I'd used knocked me out for part of the night. Why?

I yawned and lay back in the large bed. But my eyes didn't want to close, so instead I stared at the dark ceiling, trying to make out the features of the room. I registered the door to the bathroom and the door to the hallway, where undoubtedly, there were two palace guards. Even if they'd heard me screaming, they hadn't bothered to check on me.

I closed my eyes, but the image of Lacey in the bloody white dress appeared. The fear of the dream rushed back through my body.

This was about the day Lacey had fallen from the swing. It hadn't been as dramatic as my nightmare, but the fall had definitely been impactful. Blood had streamed from her palms and mouth after she landed in the gravel. I must have used red alchemy on her blood when I tried to help her. But that didn't heal her. She'd passed out and ended up in the hospital. So what had I done? Had I used the red for something else without realizing it?

It was maddening to feel like the answer was right in front of me, but I just couldn't wrap my mind around it. Not yet, anyway. What had Lacey said in the dream? *Help me.* Did she really want me to help her? And how could I do that if I was stuck here? The very fact that I had neither heard from nor seen my family in weeks was killing me! I doubted I could trust Faulk. The conversation between Thomas and her made me nervous. Plus, if she was truly trustworthy, Reed wouldn't have manipulated me. I was sure he'd been trying to get me to talk about the red. I'd been ignoring what I knew deep in my gut. I couldn't deny it any longer. Lacey was in trouble. That dream was an omen—I was absolutely sure of it. I knew with every fiber in my being that I couldn't stay here any longer. Especially after hearing Faulk and Thomas earlier today. I had to find Lacey.

I knew what I needed to do.

I stood up and walked to the tall window again. I assumed it was locked from the outside, just like everything else in this room. But what if it wasn't?

I wrapped the tips of my fingers under the rim of the windowsill and lifted. The window slid open easily, and a warm summer wind danced through the room, brushing my tangled hair out of my face. I peered out at the dark night. It waited for me. The lights of the capital city loomed just beyond the palace garden wall, beckoning. Reaching out to me.

I stood peering down from the third floor. Below me in the darkness, the edge of the palace intersected with the hard manicured lawn. Something had been slowly formulating in my mind for weeks now. Something so completely crazy, so reckless, that I'd tucked it away in the back of my mind. *But what if it works?* Before I could talk myself out of it, I lifted myself onto the window frame and jumped.

SIXTEEN

LUCAS

My bedroom was one of the few places I had to myself. Sasha slowly walked around it, taking in everything that was mine. She peered at a row of black and white photographs on one wall before turning back to me. The photos held various stages of my growth. Pictures of my childhood and more recent ones too. Behind her, the darkness waded through the large window. "You're sure it's safe in here?"

"Privacy is everything to my father. And to me. No one is listening."

"I hope you're right. What did you want to talk about?"

I sat on the edge of the bed. Sasha tilted her head and bit her bottom lip, staring at me.

"We need to talk about Jessa."

"Have you really told us everything you know about her?" Sasha asked. "Something is...missing."

Francesca Loxley, I thought, but just shrugged instead.

By "us," I knew she meant the Resistance, but it wasn't like I'd met more than two of its members. The gardener woman had been the one to convince me to join them. But she vanished after Sasha showed up, and I never got so much as a name. What about the rest of them? I wanted to meet someone higher up in the organization.

"You're right, something is missing. It's about time you take me to meet some of your leaders. I can't go down this path with you much longer. You already know that."

"Okay. I'll talk to them. I know you're right. But hey, at least you know we're serious about nonviolence. We haven't hurt anyone yet, have we?"

"But once I'm firmly on your side, how do I know you won't assassinate Richard? Then I'll become king, and you could essentially try to control me."

There it was.

Sasha stared at me for a moment, and then she laughed. "Lucas, I'm sorry to burst your bubble, but it's not like that. First of all, we don't want a king. Period. Not even you. We want democracy back. Second, you would probably become a talking head, but things would continue as they always have. It's the whole organization of the GC that needs change. And worse—the people would turn against us, in retaliation for their beloved king. Richard has enemies, but not enough. No one knows what he's really doing, do they? We're not going to kill your father."

"Okay, fine," I said. "What do you need to know about Jessa?"

"What else do you know about her?" she asked. "Is there anything we should know? Anything she's hiding? Or anything your father is hiding?"

"I know that she's ready for the truth. That's what I know."

Yes, there was more. Maybe Jessa had an older sister who was once a member of the GC. Maybe her parents knew more about color alchemy than we'd suspected. But that was information I wanted to keep to myself for now. I trusted Jessa. I didn't think she knew about any of those things. And I'd already let the Resistance in on the information about her red. That should be the only thing that mattered, anyway.

"All right, well, I've been told we need to get Jessa on our side. So I guess someone agrees with you," Sasha said.

"So what's the plan? How are you going to get her to listen to you?"

"Have you made contact with the Loxley family?"

The realization of my mistake came at me, sharp and sudden. After my last conversation with Jessa a few days ago, I had meant to reach out to her family. I'd wanted to make sure they were okay. Maybe I couldn't give Jessa everything she wanted, but that was something I should have done. She deserved to know about their situation. But I forgot. When she'd come to me about it, I'd pushed her away and had been avoiding her ever since.

How could I have been so careless?

"Did something happen to them?" I asked.

I tried not to picture them in prison, or worse, but the images burned into my mind anyway. Jessa loved her family above all else. How would she handle something like this?

"They're safe."

"The Resistance has them?"

"Yes. We extracted them a couple days ago. New Colony officials have no clue of their whereabouts. Believe me, Faulk isn't happy. It won't be long before Jessa gets questioned again."

"What are you going to do with them?"

"We want to work with the young one, Lacey. To see if she has any alchemy abilities, too. It's very likely that Jessa's powers run in her family. But the parents aren't cooperating. They don't want any of our alchemists near the little girl. They're confused, to say the least."

They asked for the parents' permission?

That would never happen here. People were forced to give their kids up to

134

the GC. They were not asked. That fact alone relaxed me. Maybe the Loxley family was in good hands, after all.

"So you want Jessa to talk to them?" I asked, putting it all together. This must be why they decided to let her in. If the Loxleys weren't open to the idea of Lacey being tested for color alchemy, then maybe Jessa could talk them into it.

"Exactly," Sasha said.

It wasn't such a bad idea. But it was risky. I couldn't even begin to imagine the logistics of getting Jessa in contact with her family without Faulk noticing. Not to mention, now that the Loxley family was MIA, I was certain Faulk was keeping an even closer eye on Jessa. Of course, no one had said a word to me or Jessa about any of this. Faulk must have decided to pretend the Loxleys were still under her control.

"How are you going to pull this off?"

She sat down next to me and frowned. "We need your help. Your father has been communicating in emails that he wants to take Jessa out of the palace for field training. He wants to see what she's capable of."

"Where?" I asked, afraid that I already knew.

"Not north, though I'm sure that's only a matter of time. He won't be patient for much longer."

I hoped we still had time.

"So how does this help us?"

"You're overseeing her training, right? You can ask to take her there. Make it seem like your idea. First thing tomorrow, go to the king. Request that I come with you. We'll be making contact with the Resistance while we're gone."

It sounded reasonable, but I knew there was more to it than just this simple plan. It was too easy. Too convenient.

"Won't Faulk be coming? What about Reed? And Jasmine has been a part of her training too, perhaps the biggest part. She'll want to come but my father seems to want Jasmine here."

Sasha studied me, as if she suspected I was going to say something more. "I'm sure the whole gang can come along. If not, we'll just figure it out. Don't worry, I'll take care of that."

"We can't get caught," I said, stating the obvious.

"You think I don't know that? Don't forget my life is on the line too."

I knew she was right. I still didn't know too much about this mysterious woman. She had revealed that she could use red alchemy as a child, but it seemed that it had disappeared. But then what? Maybe when she grew out of it, the royal officers let it go. It was true that alchemists' powers could change over time. But other than that, Sasha was not exactly an open book.

She put her hand on mine, rubbing her thumb gently along my knuckles. Without meaning to, I became acutely aware of where we were. My bedroom.

What is going on between us, anyway?

"How long do you want to keep this cover of ours going? Because I think it's working."

"Why do you ask?"

"It's been fun. We know there are no real expectations between us, so there's none of the pressure that goes along with actually dating someone."

I knew what she meant. Most girls seemed like they all had the same goal in mind. The same eye-on-the-prize mentality. What would start out as fun would soon turn into hints of marriage. Talks about "our future." So I'd learned to always end things before it ever got further than a few dates. But still, some girls went in with that attitude from the very beginning. And how was that fair to me? I wanted to see what my possibilities were. I wanted to be a normal eighteen-year-old. Everyone assumed I was looking for a princess. I really wasn't.

She understands. There's nothing between us.

"I agree, it has been fun," I replied.

It didn't hurt that Sasha was gorgeous and sophisticated. And she was easy to talk to. That was what I liked about her the most. She had inadvertently become my first true female friend since I'd matured.

"So we agree?" she said. "That's all you want? To have fun?"

When she put it that way, I knew it wasn't all I wanted in a relationship. But it was all I wanted *from her*. I was happy to have her as an ally and a friend. That was all.

My mind shot to Jessa and that electric spark that was building between us. I thought of her sweetness and her innocence, her fire and her endearing uncertainty. Her smile... And the way she'd trusted me when I couldn't tell her what she needed to hear—that felt good. All those things had added up to something more powerful than the show Sasha and I had been putting on over the last month.

"Actually, I want more." With Jessa, I wanted more.

"Me too."

Sasha's mouth crashed against mine, hands encircled my neck. She grabbed my hair and pulled me against her. In another breath, she was sitting on my lap. My thoughts instantly went murky. At that point, I was kissing her back. I ran my hands down the curve of her back. My body tensed as my fingers gripped the warmth of her skin. She sat back for a moment and smiled sheepishly. A curtain of blond hair brushed my face.

And then I remembered what I was going to say to her before we'd started this. I cared about Jessa too much to continue with Sasha. Jessa brought something out in me I couldn't explain. She made me want to be a better man. Actually, she made me want to be a man, to grow up, to be mature for once in my life. I knew that if I continued to kiss Sasha, I'd lose Jessa.

That can't happen.

I gently pushed Sasha off of me. Her cheeks flushed.

"I'm sorry," I said, not wanting to look at her. If I saw that seductive gleam in her eye again, I might lose my cool. She was undeniably beautiful. And the old me would have gladly jumped at the chance. But I'd changed over this last month, without even realizing what was happening. I'd grown up.

"What's wrong?" Sasha said combing her fingers through her thick hair. "If you don't want more, if you just want to have fun, I'm pretty sure we can manage that, too."

"It's not that."

"Well, then if you want to make this relationship something real, you already know how I feel about that too. No hiding it now."

Sasha inched closer and wrapped her arms around my neck, glowing with determination. "I want what you want."

I was pretty sure if she knew what I wanted, or rather, *who* I wanted, she wouldn't be smiling anymore.

"We can't have a relationship. Not even a fake one. And definitely not a real one. Whatever is going on here needs to stop. I'm sorry."

"Why?"

Should I tell her?

"Is this about Jessa?" She guessed.

I shrugged, not ready to admit it to her out loud. I had barely admitted my feelings to myself. I didn't know how to put them into words.

Sasha stepped back and did the last thing I expected. She laughed.

"What's so funny?"

"You're so transparent. Do you know that?"

I didn't know how to answer. Was I that obvious? She'd caught us almost kissing that night in the garden. How could I forget?

"You're not mad?" I asked.

She shook her head and shrugged. "Maybe a little disappointed, but I'll live. I've got plenty of options." She said it with such confidence that I wondered if she was deflecting. I didn't want to question that. I didn't want to hurt her.

"So, what are you going to do about Jessa?" She asked.

"I don't know. Maybe nothing."

There was nothing I *could* do. Jessa was still so young. She was only sixteen and hadn't lost that glow of innocence yet. And I was overseeing her training. If we got close, I knew I would lose my judgment. And if Faulk or my father found out, they wouldn't trust me with her training anymore. They could separate us.

Sasha shook her head. "If you say so."

"Are we okay?"

"We're fine. But let's lay off the kissing for a while, okay? It's getting late. I'm beat. Can you walk me out?"

I thought about that for a minute and wondered if I was ready to let the cover we'd created with our relationship die so early. As much as I wanted Jessa, I wasn't going to pursue her. I couldn't. And as much as I hated to admit it, I needed Sasha's help. Would she be upset if we played our game without any of my feelings getting involved? Without kissing?

"So, are we supposed to break up now?" I asked.

"Well, we could keep the façade going if you want. But I'm seriously not going around kissing a guy who has the hots for someone else. I'm not that pathetic. Sorry."

I felt a twinge of guilt. She was right. She deserved better.

"You could spend the night." My face burned at the implications of those words, especially in the context of what we'd nearly done. "I mean, not to do anything with me," I quickly added. "But to give the impression that we've gotten closer. Maybe we could just hold hands in public, and you could sleep here every once in a while to keep this going. And in here, we're safe to talk about what we need to."

"It's not a bad idea, actually. But don't try anything."

I nodded. But was Sasha really okay with this? On the one hand, she was laughing about our situation. But on the other hand, her ego was obviously bruised. I watched as she took her socks and shoes off and walked over to the bed. She lifted the heavy black comforter and climbed inside.

"Coming, honey?" she asked sarcastically.

Deciding I didn't want to make her any more uncomfortable than I already had, I grabbed one of the pillows and tossed it on the floor. "I'll sleep down here."

She just looked at me for a long moment before rolling onto her side with her back to me. I lay down on the hardwood floor with only the pillow for comfort.

That night, my thoughts spun circles in my head. I stared into the ceiling. I questioned, not for the first time, what I was doing here. Why did I have such a complicated life? Who was hurting my mother and why? It was something I thought about often. When Sasha had explained what red did, I knew that had to be what was happening to my mother. They were controlling her mind and wiping away the memories. Someone had access to red, but they must be hiding it from Richard. *Unless he knows about it.*

Could *he* be the one hurting her? His own wife? I hated to even entertain the thought, but it kept creeping back up. Sure, he was a bad guy, but he wasn't abusing his own wife, was he? I didn't think it was him. I would have seen something. And it's not like he's an alchemist. He would have to be using a guardian. There wouldn't be a good enough reason for all of that. Right?

No, someone else was behind this. Someone lurking in the corners, hiding their access to red. I needed to do a better job of watching out for my mom. I was letting her down every time I allowed myself to forget what was at stake.

But there was so much on my mind these days. Like, how was I going to stop Richard? When was the Resistance going to let me in on their secrets? How were we going to help Jessa and her family? It was all too much to handle. *But I had to handle it.* And, despite the various important things I needed to worry about, I couldn't get Jessa out of my mind. She danced through every moment. Every memory I had of her played itself out, again and again, of the girl with stormy, ocean eyes.

SEVENTEEN

JESSA

The pain seared through me, scorching me from the inside out. I was sure it was going to kill me. I'd jumped out the window, knowing it wasn't high enough to kill me. Instead the fall broke both of my legs.

I gaped at the bones that punctured through my skin, raised up like jagged knives from the surface. My thin pajama bottoms were hiked up to my thighs, exposing the gruesome state of my body. I bit down against my forearm as I screamed, muffling the agony. Everything in me wanted to call out for help, but despite the shocking pain, part of me still knew what I had to do. Part of me remembered why I had made the third-story jump in the first place.

You need to heal yourself Jessa. You must get moving,

Trying to slow my hurried breaths, I lay back against the cool grass. Tears pooled in my ears as I tried to focus. I looked up into the dark sky and found the pinprick of a star. It drifted in and out of focus, but it calmed me just enough to clear my mind. I placed my palms on the cool earth and willed myself to concentrate.

The grass curled around my fingertips as I clawed my anxious hands into it, digging for relief.

I can do this. I have to do this. Now.

I squeezed my eyes tightly shut against the darkness and trusted that the green would make its move. That these weeks of training would pay off. That I could heal myself, and all the pain would fade away. But the more I willed it, the more I knew I needed to relax. I needed to find some balance, to clear my mind, so the healing could happen. I caught a memory and focused.

■

The candles flicker playfully atop the birthday cake, ten winking opportunities for my wish to come true.

"Happy birthday to you!" Mom and Dad finish their booming rendition of "Happy Birthday," holding the "you" just long enough for me to take a deep breath and blow hard.

"What did you wish for?" Mom asks, turning on the kitchen light. The magical atmosphere of anticipation is lost with the sudden brightness. Still, I don't mind.

"Don't tell," Dad says. "Or it might not come true."

So I nod, keeping my mouth shut, but my eyes can't help but move to my mother's swollen belly. The baby's due date isn't for another week, and for months now, I've been worrying it would come on my birthday. I never said anything because I didn't want to sound selfish. But the truth is I am used to being an only child and I am nervous that the baby might hijack my special day. But considering the baby is obviously still in Mom's belly and the day is almost over, I am starting to relax.

"Laura, should we give her the present now?" my father asks over his shoulder as he rummages through one of the drawers. He pulls out a silver spatula and a knife, and winks at me. "Or should we have cake first?"

That is a hard question to answer. Cake is usually reserved for birthdays, and Mom's recipe is the best. She carefully prepared it after coming home from work after her secretarial job, despite the protruding belly that had been getting in her way so often these days.

"Let's do the present first," I decide, wanting to keep the yellow iced cake in one pretty piece just a little while longer.

Mom sits down in the chair across from me and closes her eyes for a moment, a pained expression on her face. But as soon as she sees me looking, she smiles.

"Here you go!" Dad carries in the box wrapped in newspaper and tied with purple ribbons.

I only hesitate for a moment before ripping into the paper, pulling open the box. Inside the box rests the most beautiful pair of pink ballet pointe shoes I've ever seen.

I scream in delight. "I get to start dancing en pointe!"

They laugh and explain how they filed paperwork to receive more money for my activity. Every child in my neighborhood gets to participate in one activity. But since mine started becoming more expensive as my talent grew, we needed the kingdom's help to keep me moving forward.

"Thank you!" I jump up and hug my father. When I move to my mother to give her a hug, I see another look of pain on her face. "Are you okay?"

After a few seconds, she relaxes and opens her eyes.

"You better hurry and eat your cake, sweetie."

Dad jumps up and looks anxiously at my mother. "Is it time?"

Mom nods. "The contractions are three minutes apart now. We need to go to the hospital soon."

■

Her voice rung through my mind as the memory faded away. All at once, a burning heat prickled my body. It rushed through my broken legs and began to numb the area, inch by inch. I exhaled in relief and sat up to watch the magic happening, careful to leave my palms against the grass.

The green mist of energy was hard to see in the darkness. But even the darkest night couldn't hide the alchemy. The energy was so alive that it almost glowed. It threaded its way through my legs, filling every pore.

I watched and felt the healing flow through my body in fascination. It was so intense that it was as if I were in two places at once. The energy was coming from me, and from the life source of the grass. It was as if each individual blade held within it a whole universe, teeming with energy. It burst from the grass to aid me in my healing. Every bit of me was focused on my healing. Within a few minutes, my legs looked and felt as if they'd never been broken at all. The bones fused back together, the ligaments and tendons mended, the swollen skin smoothed, and the pain that was once razor sharp was now barely a dull ache.

I pushed myself from the ground and stood, moving with ease. I looked up at my open window and the dark bedroom beyond. Had I really just jumped from there? Anyone watching would say I was crazy! And maybe I was. But when someone had a strong enough reason to jump into the void, they would do it. I was proof. *Really Jessa, you should have thought of this earlier!*

I surveyed my surroundings. It was the dead of night, but that didn't mean I was alone. There were probably palace guards on patrol. Plus, the wall that surrounded the grounds was meant to keep people out. Could it keep me in? I'd thought jumping from a third-story window would be the hard part, but maybe I was wrong. I'd come too far to turn back now.

Slowly, I walked away from the edge of the palace to get a better look at where I was. There was an open space of about a hundred feet—I had to pass through it before getting into the cover of the gardens. The lawn was well-kept. It would probably be easy to sprint across, *if* I was fast.

I decided I didn't want to push my luck any farther by hesitating. I couldn't see anyone, so I set off. The lawn pounded beneath my feet. I was sure each footstep echoed. At any second, I'd be tackled to the ground and cold, hard handcuffs would be tightening my arms behind my back.

The corner of the hedge was so close now. It was all I could focus on. After a few more deafening strides, I ducked beneath it. Catching my breath, I looked back at the lawn. It was still dark. Still quiet. And still empty.

I took a deep breath and slowly made my way through the gardens. I stayed as close to the insides of the paths as I possibly could. I caught sight of a few guards farther out, closer to the palace. I stilled and watched them until they moved out of my sight. I needed to move carefully. As I walked the acres of gardens it would take to get to the wall, I thought about the memory I'd conjured up after the fall.

My tenth birthday had ended in Lacey's birth. At the time, we didn't know if Mom was having a girl or a boy. The whole pregnancy was a surprise, and Mom liked the idea of keeping the gender a secret. But ultimately, I was used to being an only child. The few times I asked for a little brother or sister, my parents had always agreed they wouldn't have another child. That never made sense to me, but my life was a happy one, so I didn't mind too much.

And then Lacey came, a squishy pink ball. I'd been so mad that I would have to share *my* birthday. But as soon as I held Lacey and looked into her knowing sapphire blue eyes, I completely forgot about why I was so angry before. This baby, this tiny girl, was my sister. My mother had given birth to a girl! The wish I'd blown on those candles had come true.

I still believed that, somehow, Lacey had known all along. She had planned to come on my birthday. She knew how much we'd love each other, how fierce my commitment to her would be. It was only fitting.

Somehow, I didn't cross paths with another human being as I made my way to the garden's edge. I thought of Lacey the whole way. I knew that she needed me, that something was wrong, that my dream had been my wake-up call.

The palace wall was tall and smooth, made from gray stones. Each fit perfectly together, like a jigsaw puzzle. I looked up to the top and guessed the wall had to be at least fifteen feet tall. How was I going to get over it? There were no trees close enough to climb. There were no footholds. My fingers couldn't manage any significant grip on the edges where the stones met. I panted with frustration as I slid against the wall and sat down hard. How could I have been so stupid? I jumped from a third-story building, broke and healed my legs, and had just assumed that would be enough.

I shook my head. *I failed my family. I failed myself.* Angry thoughts coursed through my mind, dark and insistent. The pain of weeks without contact mixed with the fear of what could really be going on with my family. I couldn't hold my anger in any longer. In a rush to let it go, I slammed my fists back against the wall with as much force as I could manage.

So what if you break your hands? The pain of broken limbs can't compare with the pain of losing your family.

Again, my fists slammed into the solid wall, pounding even harder.

Something shifted.

I jumped away from the wall and studied it. There was a dent in the stone. Cracks reached out like a spider web from the imprint of my fist. I held my hand in front of me, sure I had broken it, but it looked and felt fine.

What just happened?

This had to be the effect of color alchemy. There was no way I could have done that on my own. I was strong from my years of dancing, but I wasn't superhuman. And the dent in front of me looked like it had been made with a sledgehammer.

I studied my surroundings, wondering if I could figure out what color I had connected with. But in the darkness, it was hard to tell. What had I called on to help me? Looking down, I realized I was sitting in a rainbow spread of flowers.

I quickly thought about the energy centers. Yellow had to be around here somewhere, right? I remembered reading that yellow connected directly to the ability to heighten the physical. By now, I'd memorized the basic properties of each color. The pounding of my fists had come from the fear and anger I had about my family, and if I had yellow alchemy in me, those punches would have been stronger than ever.

I decided to figure out how to use this new revelation to my advantage. I stayed in the flowerbeds, kneeling in front of the dented wall. I placed my hand against it, conjuring up the same angry feelings as before.

The stone shifted.

This couldn't be safe. What if it fell on me? But the image of Lacey in my dream, calling out for help, flashed through my mind. I pushed against the stone as hard as I could and gritted my teeth, hoping with everything in me that my life didn't end here.

The stone broke apart, crumbling at my fingertips. I smiled when I realized it was only one of the square stones used to build the wall that had actually been affected. I hurriedly pulled at the pieces, clearing out the space. It was probably only about two feet wide and eighteen inches tall. But I knew I could squeeze through the space if I cleaned it out well enough.

The time for second-guessing was over. I had to move forward.

■

My goal was to make it home before sunrise. We lived on the edge of the capital city—so knowing I wasn't far made it easier. The problem was that it took twenty minutes and three train stops to get to my neighborhood. And that was on the high-speed train. It would take a couple hours by bus, or most of the day to walk. What would be the least risky? I had to make a decision.

I didn't know what time it was, but since I woke up around 2 A.M., it had to be at least four. The train station would be opening at five. It would be my quickest route. I would just have to blend in with the early-morning commuters as best as I could, even though I was still wearing pajamas.

Why didn't I think to change my clothes?

I peered around the sleepy unknown neighborhood and made a beeline for the closest train station sign. I would have to take the risk. The most valuable thing I had on my side was time. I figured that no matter where I was, I was going to look suspicious. I needed to move quickly. I could change clothes when I got home, and then my family and I would be high tailing it out of the city.

And I would have to forget all about my alchemy training. There was no way I could return to the palace. Ever.

The urgency of my situation hit me, and I started to run. Even if the train station wasn't open yet, I wanted to be the first one inside that building. Every atom of my body pulsed with the need to be on that train heading away from the palace.

I arrived just as the attendant was opening the doors. She ignored me as she lifted the metal gates with a clatter that echoed down the city street. Like most people I knew, I didn't have any extra money. I couldn't buy a ticket. I would have to sneak through.

My pajama bottoms, which were a delicate heather gray, now had blood and grass stains on them. My sneakers were dirty from the gardens. And I was wearing a light blue cotton t-shirt with no jacket. Luckily, the warm nights of summer had stuck around. I hoped I didn't look too out of place.

The train station was mostly deserted at this early hour. A few morning commuters, dressed for business, began filtering in. I watched the attendant, waiting for her to get distracted. But nothing was changing. She just stared at each passenger that walked through the gates. Finally, someone approached her window. It was now or never. I hurried and jumped the barrier, crossing my fingers that she was too distracted to notice me.

I hurried down to the platform with the other passengers. We all stood in a row, waiting for the train. They all seemed to ignore me, lost in their own routines. I looked around for security guards, royal officers, or even worse, guardians—but I didn't see anyone. As far as I knew, no one had realized I was missing yet. I wasn't scheduled to eat breakfast for another two hours. By the time my new maid arrived with food at 7 A.M., I would have already left home with my parents and Lacey.

The sound of the approaching train pounded through the tunnels. I stepped inside quickly with the rest of the glassy-eyed people, and waited.

Twenty minutes. It was only twenty minutes until my stop. Could I make it? So far, I'd gotten here without being caught. This was the final test. Once I got to my stop, I knew I could exit the station quickly and then weave my way through a few backyards before getting to our house. No one would see me. I would get in, get my family, and get out. We'd find somewhere to hide. We'd find a way to be safe. I had no plan, but I was sure we'd think of something. We had to get away from the alchemists.

We made it through the first stop with no fuss. A few people got off, more got on, and the train kept moving. I tucked myself away in my seat, head ducked. The city beyond the windows flew by in a whirl. The sun still wasn't up yet. But I knew it would be making its appearance soon.

At the second stop, almost all of the passengers got off. I exhaled a breath I hadn't even realized I was holding.

The train started moving again, and I looked up to lock eyes with a young girl. She was staring at me. Panic set in when I realized I recognized her. How? Where from? Then I remembered: the face belonged to one of the girls from my old high school. I didn't know her name, and we'd never talked before. But the spark of recognition lit her eyes, as well. She was trying to place me.

I looked away and stared out the window, hoping she would forget about me. But a few seconds later, she sat down in a seat only two rows from me. At least she couldn't see my blood-stained pants from where she was sitting. I took a careful breath.

"How do I know you?" the girl asked with a friendly lilt in her voice.

"I don't know," I lied. Even though school had been out for the summer, I knew there had to be plenty of gossip about me. It wasn't every day that someone turned out to be a color alchemist. I was definitely visible now.

The girl frowned. Her espresso colored hair was tied in a knot on top of her head, and she was dressed in jeans and a white t-shirt. "What are you doing up so early?"

I didn't know how to get her to leave me alone.

"Just heading home from a friend's house."

"Me too. My parents don't let me sleep at my friends' houses. But I talked them into this one on the condition I would come home really early."

"Yup, same here." She liked to talk, I could tell that already.

"Where do you go to school?"

How was I supposed to answer that? *Oh, you know, the palace.* "I graduated." The girl nodded.

The train started to slow, and I didn't know if I'd ever been so grateful to get off a train car before.

"This is my stop." I would wait to stand until the last possible second, giving her little time to notice my filthy pajama bottoms.

"Oh, okay, I've got one more stop. Have a good day."

"You, too."

"Hey, wait a minute. That doesn't make sense."

"What?" I stammered, sure she had remembered who I was. Maybe she even knew my name. She'd pull the emergency alarm, and I'd be swarmed by those awful royal officers in their staunch uniforms.

"If you already graduated, then why would you have to ask for your parents' permission to stay with a friend?"

"Let's just say they're overly protective."

The train stopped, and I darted off. I glanced back at the girl. She waved. I could only hope that in a few hours, maybe even a few minutes, she'd forget all about me. She'd go back to her world of high-school sleepovers and regular teenage life.

I quickly exited the station. The sun was barely beginning to rise. The sky was turning a lighter shade of night. Or was it a darker shade of morning? I smiled as I slipped through the first backyard unnoticed. I was almost home. I was almost free.

EIGHTEEN

LUCAS

I woke to heavy pounding on the door. The black of night was barely turning blue. The sun would be rising soon. Who was here so early?

Stumbling to the door, I opened it before remembering I wasn't alone. Sasha was sitting up in my bed, running her hands through her sleep-tangled hair.

Faulk stood in the doorway, the hall light casting shadows around her. My father was at her side. He was dressed in powder-blue pajamas, an unusual sight for even me to see. Faulk was clean and professional, dressed in her standard white uniform. My eyes adjusted to the light as I took them in.

"What's going on?" I asked, my voice raspy and dry.

"Do you know where she is?" Faulk spat.

"Who?" I tried not to yawn but couldn't help myself.

Faulk shook her head, frustrated. There was also a tinge of something else in her stance. Was it fear?

My father glared. "Jessa has gone missing."

The fog of my mind immediately cleared at the mention of her name. Jessa was missing? What did he mean by "missing"?

"She could have been kidnapped. But from the looks of it, it's more likely that she ran away."

Richard glanced past me and froze. Sasha was in my bed, staring back at him with a guarded expression. I knew how this must look. But I reminded myself that we wanted people to think we were a couple. It was the only reason she'd slept over, even though nothing happened.

"Guardian!" Faulk gasped, startled to see her. "What on earth are you doing in here? You can't be in this wing. *Ever.*"

Sasha's eyes darted to me. I laughed, pulling on the rakish mask I'd used so many times in the past. "What do you *think* she's been doing in here?"

My father and General Faulk both turned beet red.

"Forget it, Lucas," Richard said. "Let the grown-ups take care of this. Your judgment has obviously gone sour."

"Why do you suddenly care what I do?"

"I never cared much for the girls you've dated, but I didn't interfere, either. I always assumed you knew what was appropriate. It appears, however, that I was grossly mistaken. A color alchemist? You've gone too far this time."

"What's wrong with color alchemists?"

"They don't belong in your bed!" His voice burned. "Our guardians work for us. They are not meant to be *with* us. You're the crown prince. It's high time you acted like it."

He reached past me, grabbed the door, and slammed it in my face.

Cool silence fell over us as I turned to gauge Sasha's reaction. Even in the near darkness, I knew there was anger in her eyes. I could feel it radiating off her in waves.

"I'm sorry. He's always like this around me. I forget that other people rarely see that side of him."

"You're his own son and he doesn't even treat *you* right!"

"Well, so much for the whole sleeping over idea. I don't think that got us anywhere productive."

Stupid!

"We've got bigger fish to fry," she said, getting out of the bed. She fumbled with the light switch on the wall and blasted us into brightness. "Get dressed. We need to get to Jessa. We have to find her before they do."

Jessa had not only crossed the line—she had gone far beyond it. Accidental alchemy was one thing. Even hurting her maid hadn't landed her in prison. But purposely running away from the palace? Fleeing my father and her promises to him? That was something else entirely.

I pulled on a sweatshirt and running shoes from my closet. I hurried to get dressed so I could stop this disaster from getting any worse.

"Where do you think she could be?" Sasha asked as she finished lacing her own shoes.

She didn't even have to ask. We both knew where Jessa would go. Without a doubt, Jessa was looking for her family. I'd never met a person who cared so much about her flesh and blood the way she did. She hadn't been permitted any communication with them for over four weeks. Faulk had assured her they were safe and moving on with their lives. That wasn't good enough for her. And to Jessa's credit, it had turned out Faulk had been lying.

"But they're not home anymore," I said, realizing just how dire this situation was. No wonder Faulk was so angry. She'd lost the *whole* family.

Jessa was going home to an empty house. Sasha had already told me that the Resistance had extricated the Loxley family. They were somewhere in hiding. I wondered how Richard had reacted when he'd found out about this. And why hadn't anyone told *me*?

"It'll be a trap," Sasha said. "The place has to be swarming with Faulk's people by now. Jessa is going to walk right into their hands."

"So what's your plan?"

"Obviously, we have to beat her home and intercept her. Are you ready?"

"And then what are we going to do once we get her? Just bring her back?"

"No." Sasha paused. "We need to get her in communication with her parents so she can convince them to let us see if Lacey is an alchemist."

"And how do you plan to do that?"

"I need to get the go-ahead. But I'm pretty sure the only way is to take her into hiding, as well."

Take her into hiding? Just when I realized how much I cared for Jessa, I was going to lose her. And probably forever.

Can I do that to myself? Can I let her go in order to keep her safe?

I didn't have to think twice about my answer.

"Let's go."

■

Getting out of the royal wing should have been easy. I was sure Richard and Faulk had left immediately. But I hadn't stopped to think about my mother.

Sasha followed close behind as we walked down the hallway and into the large living room. The padlocked door had guards stationed outside, but I knew they wouldn't bother us.

"And who is this?"

I jumped at the sound of my mother's voice. "Good morning, Mother," I said, stepping closer.

She was sitting quietly on a sofa in the darkened room. A cup of tea balanced delicately in her hand and a throw blanket covered her legs.

"Your Highness." Sasha stood next to me and bowed. "I'm Sasha."

"Hello, Sasha. I'm Natasha."

"I was just walking Sasha back to her room."

"In the guardian wing?"

"Yes."

There was a long pause before my mother nodded.

"Would you mind waiting outside, dear?" she asked Sasha. "I'll only keep him a moment."

Sasha nodded, bowed again, and immediately bolted for the door. I hoped she would wait for me. Maybe she could use this time to formulate a plan for how we were supposed to rescue Jessa. How were we supposed to do that without getting caught by my father? If anyone could figure it out, it would be Sasha.

"Come sit by me." There was a softness in her voice that I hadn't heard in a while. "Do you remember much of your childhood?"

I sat down next to her, despite my urge to hurry. She was small and frail, and the thin blanket wrapped around her legs seemed to drown her body.

"Some," I said. The truth was that the very best memories from my childhood included my mother. While my father had always been so strict, Natasha had

148

been kind. She used to take me everywhere with her. We'd play what she called "games of the wild imagination." She was never afraid to crawl through the grass with me or climb trees. I would always cherish those memories of my mother, but it was painful to dredge them up.

"You were such a bright child. Always full of energy."

"Are you okay, Mother?"

"I'm sorry, Lucas."

"About what?" I asked. What had gotten into her?

"I've been so absent lately. Always nursing my headaches. I haven't been here for you. Not like I used to. Not like you deserve."

"It's okay."

"I'm going to do better. I promise."

I didn't know whether or not to believe her, but the little boy inside me jumped at the thought. The very idea of it brought a hope I hadn't felt in a while.

"Me, too. Listen, about Sasha…"

"I'll handle your father." My mother smiled. "If you really love her, we'll find a way to make him understand."

What? Is she coming back to me?

"Thank you, Mother. But actually, I don't love Sasha. We're only going to be friends from now on."

Natasha laughed. "You young men are so fickle."

Unexpectedly, I wanted to tell her about Jessa. I wanted to spill my guts and go into detail about our exchanges with each other. But of course, I would never do something so juvenile. Too much had happened. And I needed to be careful. "I've got to go, Mother."

It took everything in me to stand up. I hadn't experienced this lively version of her in years, but I didn't have time to stick around to enjoy it.

"Wait. I need to tell you something."

Her voice had turned frantic and she reached out for my hand.

"What is it?"

"Something is wrong. I've been living in a fog, Lucas. I'm not myself."

"It's going to be okay."

"No. Something is *wrong*, Lucas. I don't know what is happening. But my thoughts…they're not right."

"What do you mean?"

She shook her head and placed her hand on her forehead. "They won't let me say. They tell me not to say, and I can't."

"Who won't? What are you talking about?"

She bit her lip and looked up at me. Her eyes went from clear and alarmed to cloudy once again.

Who's been hurting her?

"I need to lie down," she said, laying her head against the arm of the large couch. She rubbed her eyes. "I've got a headache."

One second ago, she insisted that she needed to tell me something, and the next, she was complaining about her headache. The same headache that had been plaguing her for years. It was as if she'd forgotten our conversation in the blink of an eye. This had to be the result of color alchemy. It was even clearer to me that someone was controlling her mind. Of course there was another red alchemist somewhere in the palace. But who? What was I going to do about them? As soon as I got Jessa to safety, I would come back here and help my mother.

"Please, Lucas, leave me to rest," she whispered.

Something sinister was happening, and I had to stop it. I left the dark room and hoped it wasn't too late.

■

Sasha was waiting for me just outside the doorway. As soon as I exited the royal apartment, she motioned for me to follow her. She took my hand and spoke loudly so the guards could hear. "Will you walk me back to my room, babe?"

"You got it."

No one followed as we strode quickly toward the front exit of the palace, where the cars were kept. This early, there weren't more than a few guards milling around. And of course, they didn't say a word to me. I could do whatever I wanted while inside the palace. At least, as far as they were concerned.

"Let's get you out of here before someone stops you. Your father made it pretty clear he wants you off Jessa's case."

I considered that for a moment. The truth was, I couldn't go anywhere unnoticed. I never had. We walked out onto the front-entrance steps, just as the sun was rising. I turned to the closest guard and spoke with complete confidence. "We need a car. Can you order us one? Immediately, please."

He looked at me, a little dazed at first, before nodding and repeating my words to someone at the other end of his slatebook.

Sasha grabbed my hand and steered me away from any listening ears. "We're just going to drive away?"

"I'll tell my father that I was trying to help. He doesn't have to know that we actually found her. I'll send you two away and return empty-handed, and claim that you ran off with her."

"Am I expected to leave with you but not come back? No way. That will send too many red flags. My cover would be blown."

"So what's your idea, then?"

She shook her head. "I'm finding another way out of here. I don't want anyone to know I was ever gone. You go ahead and I'll meet you in Jessa's neighborhood."

"How are you getting out?"

"Don't worry about me," she said as a shiny black car pulled up. A driver got out and walked around to open the passenger door. "We're wasting time. I'm going to get Jessa out of the capital. You just get to her before anyone else does."

"Do you have her parents' address?"

"I'll get it to you. Just go find her, Lucas. Go find Jessa."

She shoved me toward the vehicle before turning on her heels and jogging back inside the palace. How was she expecting to get out of here? The Resistance had more pull than I first realized. They had no excuse not to meet with me. This was the last time I was helping them without a proper meeting. But there was no time to speculate. I needed to act quickly.

I jogged over to the driver and plucked the keys from his hands. I closed the passenger door and hurried to jump behind the wheel. "Sorry, buddy. I'm going alone."

The tires peeled out as I sped down the driveway. In my rearview mirror, I watched as a pair of security guards ran out onto the steps. At home, they didn't follow me everywhere. They didn't need to because I never went anywhere, anyway. And no one came inside the palace without going through security first. These poor guards were probably going to get in trouble for this.

I knew Faulk had more than a head start on me. I had no time to spare. The black wrought-iron gates opened wide, and I steered the car out into the early morning of our capital city.

Luckily, my slatebook was with me and I could easily pull up directions to Jessa's childhood home as Sasha had already forwarded the address to me. Man, she worked fast. The time read thirty-nine minutes until arrival at my destination, which made me swear violently under my breath. I hurried to memorize the directions. It was a good thing no one was out this early, because I was about to be driving very fast. I would do everything in my power to make it to Jessa in half the time indicated by the directions if I could. I *had* to get to her before Faulk did.

The phone on my slatebook rang, and I answered it immediately when I saw Sasha's name pop up.

"I'm texting you a map of where we're meeting. Memorize the location."

"You're not meeting me at Jessa's house?"

"No, too obvious."

"How's that?" I asked, turning down a city street with screeching tires as I headed up the ramp to the freeway.

"Oh, you'll see. And Lucas, power down your phone now. Just in case its location is being tracked." She hung up.

I glanced at the directions a few times before shutting down the device and pushed my foot down hard against the gas pedal. I was in a race. A race against Faulk and my father. A race against my memory and the places I was supposed to go today. And right now, a race against the brilliant sunrise that was beginning to light the sky.

NINETEEN

JESSA

Something was wrong. The closer I got to my house, the more I began to question myself. On the surface, it appeared to be a normal quiet morning, but there was an undercurrent of unsettling activity. I couldn't explain it, but it didn't feel right. As much as I wanted to get home, I moved at a snail's pace. I tiptoed through the yards, hiding in the dark shadows as I willed the sun to stop rising.

I stopped cold when I spotted her. Just beyond the tall shrubs I was using for cover, a girl quickly walked past on the sidewalk. She was talking loudly, using the telephone function on her slatebook.

"But she left the station about twenty minutes ago."

She paused for a second before continuing. As she started to pace, she turned toward me and immediately recognition gripped me. The young girl from the train. I hadn't bothered to ask her name. We'd finished our conversation, but she hadn't gotten off at my stop. If she stayed on the train, what was she doing here?

"Yes, I did as you said. I identified her, kept going and then came back here on the next train. Believe me, I searched the station high and low. She should be home by now. You should have her."

Another pause.

"I have no doubt that I confirmed the right girl. It was Jessa."

I inhaled sharply and felt my fingers turn to ice. *No, they can't have….*

"Because I was ordered to track her, not stop her," she said, exasperated. "Anyway, she can't be far. Like I said, I saw her less than twenty minutes ago."

Another pause. I held my breath and willed myself not to blink.

"All right, well, I'll be there in a second. I'm just around the corner."

The girl shook her head and slid her slatebook into her pocket. Turning on her heels, she started in the direction of my house. I didn't dare move. I crouched in the bushes and began a silent count in my head.

Just make it to one hundred. Then run!

One. Two. Three.

What am I going to do? I can't go home now. Someone is waiting for me, and I know that can't be good news.

Twenty-one. Twenty-two. Twenty-three.

Who is that girl working for? Faulk? Why didn't she stop me on the train? I can't believe they had a girl from my high school following me.

Forty. Forty-One.

Should I be surprised, though? I always knew I couldn't trust those people. I need to make a plan.

Fifty-nine. Sixty.

I have to get out of here. Can I go back to the palace? Pretend that I never left in the first place? No. Surely, there are cameras at the train station that can identify me. And anyway, that girl saw me on the train herself.

Seventy-four. Seventy-five.

I just want to get to my family, to help them. Where are they now?

Eighty-nine. Ninety.

I'm in so much trouble.

One hundred.

I took a step toward my house.

I should've run in the opposite direction. But I couldn't help it. I had to know. If I could get a view of the back window, I could see who was inside. Maybe if I knew my family was safe, I could turn myself into Faulk and deal with whatever punishment came.

Ducking low, I dropped to my knees and began to slowly crawl through the bushes. I was only three backyards away from my house. If I was careful, I could get close enough to check things out without being spotted. This was my territory. I'd spent my childhood in these trees. I could go unseen.

Well, at least that was what I told myself.

Something jammed into my back, sharp and direct to the spine. I tried not to scream as I lashed out at whomever or whatever was behind me.

It was the girl from the train. She sneered down at me as she held my face to the dirt and elbowed me again. "There you are. We've been looking for you."

"What are you doing?" I spat, trying to reach out and knock her off me.

She dug her knee into my back and pinned me down.

"What do you think, Jessa? You shouldn't have run away from the palace like that. How stupid are you?"

Pain shot up my arm as she bent it behind my back.

"Who are you?"

"Royal officer in the making. Didn't see me practicing in that gym yesterday, did you? No, you were too busy drooling over that alchemist pretty-boy, Reed. Now, hold still so I don't have to hurt you. Though, at this point, I'm sure Faulk wouldn't mind."

The realization slammed through me that she had been there just yesterday when I sought out Reed. But there had been so many people that my eyes had skimmed over the majority of them. Well, royal officer in training or not, if this girl thought for a second I was going to let her push me around, she didn't know me at all.

I held still long enough for her to shift her weight and relax. I bucked backward, slamming the back of my head into her face. A crunching sound proceeded her shrill scream.

"Be quiet," I hissed, jumping up.

She gripped my leg as I tried to run. Her fingers dug deeply into my skin. "You asked for it," she said as she spat blood from her mouth. It poured from her nostrils. I was positive I'd broken her nose.

I kicked at her fiercely as she grabbed my other leg and toppled me back to the ground. I slammed into the thick trunk of a tree. My head stung and my ears hurt. Immediately, I knew I was no match for her. She was trained. I'd never been in a fight in my life. I was strong from years of ballet training, but I couldn't defend myself from her attack.

She pulled my hands behind my back, twice as hard as before. Pain seared my shoulders. I cried out, begging her to stop. She was going to break my arm!

"Don't move." She leveraged her body so she could use one hand to reach into her pocket. She pulled out her slatebook and began to dial. Calling Faulk, no doubt.

Don't give up! You're stronger than her. You're the one with the real power.

It hit me. Maybe I couldn't fight with my fists. But I was a color alchemist. I could fight with my energy. I could fight with magic.

I need help! I don't know what color you are. I don't know where you are. But if you're out there, I need you. Stop her. Please, get her off me.

I craned my neck and looked back at the girl, her grip still tight on me. She blinked rapidly and shook her head in confusion.

"Drop it," I said. "Right now."

The girl stared at me, still confused as the thin device fell from her hand. It landed with a small bounce against the dirt.

It's working!

"Crush it," I said, never breaking eye contact.

In a daze, she stood up and slammed the heel of her foot into the slatebook. It broke with an audible crack.

"Stay here and count backwards from a thousand. When you're found, you won't remember what happened."

She nodded before sitting down hard and counting.

"One thousand, nine hundred ninety-nine." Her voice was dazed and hollow.

"In your head, please. Be quiet."

I studied her as she did what I asked. *How did I do that?* I had been so calm and sure of myself, as if I knew exactly how to control her.

I got up and brushed the dirt and grit from my clothing, looking around for an exit strategy. The girl sat still as the blood continued to fall from her nose. It dripped, gray and thick, in streams of iron down her neck.

Oh. I'd performed alchemy on blood. Red blood. And the implications of that truth rocked me. Because I used the alchemy to control her. To take away her free will. Possibly even her memory.

It will be like this never happened. I remembered the words I'd said to Lacey that bloody day on the playground. That must have been why Lacey never remembered the accident. And later, with Reed. What had I told him to do when he was upset about his cut? *Calm down Reed, you're fine.* He'd listened. He'd relaxed about everything, not actually in line with the situation or his personality.

And this is exactly why they want you. You're a weapon. You're the tool they will use to control minds and wipe memories.

I couldn't let that happen.

I hurried to the house, but stopped myself when I saw two royal officers through the window. Their backs to me, I knew I couldn't go inside. *All this way and for what? Is my family still in there?* I snuck around the side of the house, peering through each of the nearest windows. Not one sign of them. Where were they?

I forced myself to give up and quickly made my way back toward the train station. The morning commuters were beginning to leave their houses. Thankfully, no one appeared to notice me lurking in the shadows. Not yet, anyway.

What was I going to do? Where was I going to go now?

Public transportation was out of the question. So was asking any of my old neighbors for help. Because, honestly, who would help a fugitive?

What am I going to do?

My only option now was to run and hide. The suburban neighborhoods sprawled for miles beyond our own, but they were all broken up by forested areas. I could use that to my advantage. If I could just find a safe place to think, then maybe I would be able to come up with a plan?

I hurried to the end of my block. The train station was just around the corner, but that wasn't my destination anymore. I peered from behind the hedge at the unruly bushes and trees on the other side of the street. From years of adventures as a child, I knew there were several acres of unoccupied land beyond. Hiding there wasn't a solution, but it was a start.

A couple of cars drove past, and I knew that in a few minutes more people would be walking to the train station. A dog started barking. The world was waking up, and if I didn't hurry, I would miss my opportunity to find a hiding spot for the day.

I took a deep breath, double-checked the area, and sprinted across the road. The screeching of tires peeled around the corner. I looked back, horrified, as a small black vehicle came barreling toward me. My nostrils filled with the putrid smell of burning rubber. I momentarily froze. That only lasted for an instant. In the next moment, I was diving into the thicket of trees.

The car screeched to a stop, and a door opened.

"Get in, Jessa," a deep voice called out.

I stopped in my tracks. I was just barely in the sanctuary of the tree line. I peered out in astonishment at the person on the other side of the rolled-down window. Prince Lucas.

"I don't have all day," he said, his voice almost playful despite the circumstances. "I'm not supposed to even be here. Hurry and get in. I'll explain on the way."

"The way?"

"I'm getting you out of here."

I had to trust him. It was either that or take my chances on my own. The distant wail of police sirens shook me into action. I opened the door and slid into the passenger seat next to Lucas.

He threw the vehicle into drive, and we shot forward with a burst of acceleration. I yelped and grappled for the seat belt. "What's going on, Lucas?"

He didn't answer as he shot the car around a corner and toward the nearest freeway entrance. Few people drove anymore. It was easier to take the trains. The trains were free, and gasoline was expensive. Cars were for the elite.

"Could you slow down? You're going to give us away."

He growled with frustration as he slowed to the speed limit. We were headed south, away from the palace, away from my home. I watched in the rearview mirror as the downtown high-rises faded into the haze.

"I don't understand why you're here."

"What's so shocking about it?" His hands tightened on the steering wheel as he shifted into the right lane.

"Because you're Prince Lucas! For one, where are your guards? Aren't you, like, never supposed to be alone outside the palace? And for two, I didn't even know you could drive. And to top it off, why aren't you taking me back to Faulk? Aren't you mad that I ran away? Why are you helping me?"

The questions tumbled out of my mouth all at once.

"I know I have a lot to explain. But we're almost at the meeting point, and there isn't time to cover everything. But Jessa, you're going to be okay," he said, steering us toward the nearest exit. The area we drove through looked just like any other suburb, except maybe a little more rural than my own. Taller trees. Smaller houses. More space. Fewer people. The sleek black car probably stood out like a diamond in a bed of rocks.

"Where are we going?" I asked.

"Trust me," was the only answer I got. Great. He was always saying that.

After several minutes, we pulled into an empty field. There was no sign of civilization out here. Lucas turned off the car and peered around, looking for something. What could possibly be out here?

"Let's get out." He pulled the keys from the ignition. I sat there, gripping the edge of my seat, utterly dumbfounded. He wanted me to get out? *Here*? In the middle of nowhere? What was going on?

When I didn't join him so eagerly, he came to the passenger door and opened it. He kneeled, put his hand on the top of the door, and watched me. He didn't say anything. This close, I couldn't help but notice his beauty. The day-old stubble on his face. The way the muscles in his arms flexed. The intensity of his steel-gray eyes. He put one hand on my knee, and my body burned hot at his touch. "There's a lot you don't know about me, Jessa. And for that, I am truly sorry. But right now, you need to trust me."

"You always say that."

"This time, let me prove it to you. Someone is coming to pick you up, Jessa. Someone you know. They'll take you far away from here. Far away from New Colony where you'll be safe."

My heart raced. "Are you coming with me?"

He shook his head.

I looked past him and noticed the shifting of the tall grass beyond us. There was a strange rhythmic sound, like whirring air currents. As the noise increased, the wind picked up, and I realized all at once why we were here.

A black helicopter appeared above the trees and started to make its descent into the center of the open field.

"Your ride is here!" Lucas called out over the sound of the helicopter.

My gut tightened when I realized I would be leaving Lucas behind. I had no idea where I'd be taken, but I knew I had to leave. I unbuckled my seat belt and got out of the car. The wind carried my hair in a flurry around my face. I fought to push it back. Lucas joined in. Together, we pushed the tangle of dark strands away from my eyes. Once it was freed from the mess, our eyes locked. We held my hands against my face, each keeping our gazes on the other. Before another breath could pass between us, his lips were on mine.

The kiss was a flash of passion and movement. His strong arms wrapped around me tightly as we forgot ourselves in the embrace. His body pressed hard against me. I melted into him. My long hair whipped around us, stinging our skin with every blow. The deafening roar of the wind flying past and the sunrise heating my neck were nothing compared to the explosion of emotions racking my body. As our mouths explored each other, I could no longer tell where I ended and he began. I dug my fingernails into him, pulling him in even closer. A minute later, he stepped back, breathing hard. He closed his eyes for only a moment before opening them.

We stared at each other, grinning stupidly in disbelief. Then we turned and ran, hand in hand, toward the helicopter. Despite my fear of the unknown and the fact that I was about to fly away into an uncertain future, nothing could take away the joy of the perfect moment I'd just shared with Lucas.

We made it to the helicopter too quickly. The noise and wind were wild now. Lucas squeezed my hand as if confirming his feelings for me. Our hands released as he opened the door for me. He wasn't coming with me. I already knew that. And yet, Lucas was still a gentleman. I didn't want to leave him. Not now. Not after that kiss.

Stepping up into the small backseat of the helicopter, reality slapped me with what I saw. Or rather, *who* I saw. *She* was sitting in the pilot's seat, large earmuffs perched snugly over her smooth blond hair. Her blue eyes shone brightly as our gazes met. It was Sasha. The girl who was currently dating Lucas. And it was painfully clear from her stiff expression that she had just witnessed the most passionate kiss of my whole existence, at her expense.

TWENTY

LUCAS

"**Y**ou're coming with us," Sasha called to me over the roar of the engine. I shook my head. That wasn't okay. I needed to get back to the palace before anyone could accuse me of being part of this.

"We're not going to blow your cover, Lucas. Someone will hide the car, and you'll get to be the hero in the end. It's all worked out."

The hero? What was she talking about? There wasn't time to argue with her. Not with Jessa waiting. So, I decided to trust her. Sasha had never given me a reason not to. Not yet.

Jessa looked between us, her face flushed. She still didn't know the truth about Sasha and me. The fact that Sasha wasn't actually my girlfriend was finally something we could talk about openly. Guilt dug into me. Jessa probably thought I was a total jerk for knowingly kissing her in front of Sasha. But I didn't regret it. I could never regret a kiss like that.

"Stop wasting time. We need to get her out of here!" Sasha snapped.

She was right. And if they weren't going to leave without me, I wasn't about to put them at risk and keep them on the ground. Not for another second.

I jumped into the backseat next to Jessa and squeezed her hand. She pulled away and widened her eyes at Sasha. Trying to do the right thing and clue me in, I assumed. I couldn't wait to finally explain everything to her.

We quickly strapped ourselves in and put on the bulky headphones as Sasha began to lift the chopper from the grassy field.

"Where did you learn how to fly this thing?"

The headphones connected us so we could speak to each other above the roar of the helicopter.

"Oh, Lucas, I've got skills even you can't touch," Sasha said.

I laughed and took Jessa's hand again. She looked at me warily and shook her head. Her blue eyes matched the morning sky behind her. They were filled with confusion and longing. And hope.

"What's going on here?" Jessa asked.

"You go first, Lucas," Sasha said.

I thought about where to start, but I wasn't sure there was a good place. "First of all, we're not working with Faulk. And we're getting you away from her and my father."

"Where are we going?" Jessa asked.

"Someplace safe," Sasha responded before adding, "Oh, and Lucas and I aren't really dating. You can spare me the public displays of affection, though. I want to be able to fly this thing without barfing."

"You're not together?" Jessa shook her head.

We were flying fast and low over the landscape. It blurred by in a stream of color as we left the city behind us. Jessa glanced out her window and nearly flinched. She stiffened in her seat, settling in. I was sure she'd never flown before. Regular citizens certainly didn't travel by helicopter. Even the wealthiest ones didn't have that luxury. Helicopters were a commodity controlled by my family.

"It's okay." I put my arm around her. "We're safe up here. Sasha knows what she's doing." *How does Sasha know what she's doing?*

Jessa seemed to relax as the chopper shot through the morning air. Luckily, it was perfect flying weather.

"I think you two have some explaining to do," Jessa said.

I paused, and when Sasha didn't jump in, I decided to start.

"A few years ago, I started to suspect that maybe the GC wasn't as innocent as it seemed." I considered the best way to explain this. "I would notice strange things that concerned me. People would go missing. Royal officers would be sent with the guardians on missions, and everyone would come back full of secrets. I had no proof of anything. And I don't even think most alchemists noticed the things I did. Most of them were kept out of the loop, and they still are. But something wasn't right."

"So what does that have to do with Sasha?" Jessa frowned.

"Well, a few months before you got here, my father pulled me in on something that confirmed my fears. The GC is running secret tests on innocent people. Dangerous tests."

"What kind of tests?" Jessa asked.

"I don't know exactly what they're for, except to test the boundaries of alchemy. But you know how when the color is all used up, only gray is left behind?"

She nodded.

"Well, it has to do with that. They're testing to see if people can live off of gray food, gray land, gray…everything."

"And they can't?"

"No," Sasha interjected sharply. "They cannot."

"Then someone sent me pictures. They were horrible. Children starving. People getting sick or dying. As you can imagine, I was upset when I learned the truth. My father was behind the whole thing and expected me to understand.

He's been traveling to the test sites with Faulk every few months to check on the progress. I went with him on one of the trips. This has been going on for years. I didn't know what to do when I saw that people were dying. Richard's my father, you know? How was I supposed to stop him without tearing my family apart?"

"And that's when Lucas met us," Sasha's voice piped in. "The Resistance. We're part of a national network that was created in response to New Colony's inhuman tactics. I have been working with Lucas on behalf of those who also want to stop the king and people like Faulk. We're not violent. We don't kill people. But we have to do something before things get any worse."

"So why did you pretend you were dating? Why keep this a secret from me for a month?"

"I wanted to tell you. But I was following orders. The Resistance didn't know if they could trust you."

"Don't be so hard on him," Sasha added. "He tried to convince us to tell you everything. A number of times, actually. And if it makes you feel any better, everything between us was just a cover. Lucas doesn't have feelings for me. None whatsoever. He made that clear."

Was that true? When I first met Sasha, I had definitely been interested. But as soon as I'd met Jessa, that all changed. Again, I was amazed by how much this girl affected me. She'd changed me, simply by being herself. Simply by standing up for who she was and what she wanted.

"All right." Jessa's half-smile calmed me a bit. But she still didn't move back into the crook of my arm. I needed to feel her near me. We'd probably only been given a few extra hours together. I didn't want to miss a second with her.

"I believe you, Lucas. Now, where are we going? Do you know where my family is?"

"Don't worry. We've got them in hiding."

Jessa let out an audible sigh of relief. I hated the reminder of my own failure to take care of Jessa's family. I could only be grateful for Sasha's good news, for the safety of the Loxley family.

I peered out at the landscape again and realized where we headed, the shadow lands. This wasn't safe. This was the last place we should take Jessa. Ever. She needed to get away from the GC. Not head into their territory!

"Sasha, what is going on?" I asked, keeping my voice calm. I didn't want to alarm Jessa. "We need to get somewhere safe. This is not what I had in mind."

"This isn't just about Jessa's safety. It's also about making sure she understands what's at stake. She needs to be firmly on our side."

I willed myself not to punch the seat in front of me. "Are you crazy? Of course she's on our side!" *So much for calm.* "This is the last place she should go. Or any of us, for that matter! It will be crawling with GC royal officers."

"What's going on? Where are we going?" Jessa asked.

"Turn around," I said to Sasha. "Fly us somewhere else."

"No."

If I had to rip off my seat belt, shove her out of the pilot's seat, and fly this helicopter myself, I would.

"Jessa, look outside. Look carefully." Sasha pointed to the vast expanse of earth below. The changes in our field of vision were gradual at first. But then they came all at once. "This is what is left after these tests have finished." Sasha's voice was low, laced with the sour tinge of regret. We stared out from behind the shiny glass, our faces reflecting back expressions of disbelief.

The rolling hills, farmhouses, and the forest beyond were a sickening shade of gray. It was almost as if the land had been painted with a fine layer of ash. Only this wasn't ash. It wasn't anything.

"Where is all the color?" Jessa whispered.

She leaned in closer. The sweet scent of summer rain mixed with lavender brushed past me as her hair fell in a dark wave around her face. I breathed her in, wanting nothing more than to hold her hand, or better yet, to kiss her. I remembered how she'd pulled away from me earlier, and I decided that now wasn't the time to be distracted.

"It's all gone," Sasha said.

We stared at the vast landscape below us. The remnants of life and energy were only a memory now. We didn't have to guess how this happened. We were all too smart for that. We knew it was the result of color alchemy. *Serious* alchemy.

"You want to know what happened to the people?" Sasha asked what I was thinking. "They're dead. The life was sucked right out of them, as well."

"Why would an alchemist do this?" Jessa asked.

Sasha caught my eyes in the rearview mirror. As our gazes locked, I remembered her confession. She'd been taken as a child to work out here. She'd been a part of all of this. But color alchemy was usually strongest in younger guardians, and when her power had started to fade, she'd probably been moved on to other assignments.

Children. They made children participate in this.

"I'd known about the experiments. But I didn't know it was this big. This is so much land. How has this been hidden?" I asked.

Did my father's reach really extend this far? What he'd shown me on my one trip had only been a fraction of this. Could he really hide something so obvious, so massive, and so egregious as miles and miles of land, all in ruins? Why hadn't anyone said anything? Why hadn't the people rebelled?

Sasha was stiff, watching us carefully.

"The GC. Faulk. Your father, Richard. That's how. Any civilians who figured it out were either killed, imprisoned, or worse—they became part of the trial."

"What are these trials even for?" Jessa asked.

"Like Lucas said, it's all about testing the boundaries of color alchemy. To keep New Colony on top. To stop West America from starting a war. To gain more power. You were smart to keep your red ability a secret. Despite what you were told, there are others who've done it before. But poorly. That's why Richard is looking for someone who can sustain the red ability, hone it in a targeted way. So far, all it's done is cause widespread pain. And now? Well, they want to be very strategic with how they use it." She looked wistfully out at the landscape.

I noticed Sasha didn't include herself in the group of "others" who had been called upon to use red color alchemy. But, in her past, she'd been part of these ghastly tests.

"Thank you for trusting me on that one," I added, looking at Jessa. "I wanted to tell you about the red, but I didn't know how."

"What happens to the people?" she asked. "The ones whose blood gets manipulated by the alchemy?"

"At best, they become extremely forgetful. Most end up with some kind of brain damage. And the worst cases die from brain aneurysms. But there's definitely more to it, and I think you already know what that is," Sasha said. "We need to stop more innocent people from getting hurt."

Jessa just stared straight ahead.

"Tell us, Jessa. What happened? What is it that's made Richard pursue you so aggressively?"

A small part of me hoped it was all a mistake. That maybe there was still some good left in my father. Maybe *why* he was doing this was something else entirely than what Sasha believed.

"I know why." Jessa looked at me as if it was painful to confirm the truth. "I never told you what happened before you picked me up," she said. "Someone found me. A younger girl from my old high school. She was looking for me. She was working for Faulk. She's a royal officer in training, she said. She attacked me, and when I tried to defend myself, I broke her nose."

I smiled inwardly at the thought of Jessa knocking some royal officer girl's lights out.

"I used red alchemy on her blood. I turned a lot of it gray. I was just trying to get away. And it worked."

Sasha interjected, "The red helped you, didn't it?"

"Yes…because I controlled her mind. I told her to stop screaming, and she did. I told her to sit down and count backwards from a thousand, and she did. She did *exactly* what I said."

The weight of the news was more damaging than I could have guessed. I mean, I already knew about red blood. Sasha had told me everything weeks earlier. But still, the conformation shook me.

"I'm sorry, Lucas." Jessa reached out to me, but I couldn't even move to hold her hand. "But I'm pretty sure your father wants to brainwash people. To control them…by using me."

So it's true. My father's a bad person. What happens to me now?

I really didn't know.

"This is the news we've been expecting," Sasha said. "Thank you, Jessa."

"Thank you for what?" she replied, her voice rising. "I probably left that girl brain-damaged. And I did it to my own sister. I did it to Lacey back in January. She fell and got really hurt. I messed with her blood, and while I was doing it, I told her it would be like the whole accident had never happened. And guess what? She forgot everything! I could have killed her. I could have given her an aneurysm! And then she lived for six months with a small amount of that horrible gray dead blood flowing through her veins. What kind of damage have I unknowingly caused her? My whole reason for being in the GC, the one thing that is most unique about me, is the ability to hurt other people. To control them." She laughed in frustration. "The irony is, I hate being controlled. I hate that people like Faulk and Richard only want to use me. But I've been training only so I can help them control others! What do I do now?"

"You hide," I said.

"I'm not sure it's that simple," Sasha said.

"Sure it is," I scoffed.

"We've got company." Sasha's hands gripped tightly on the controls.

She dropped the helicopter low over the terrain as the jet appeared from above. It was coming in at an alarming rate, moving in fast. My heart slammed into my chest when I glimpsed our royal family emblem on its side. The three red stars were a stark contrast to the shiny white jet.

"It's my father," I said, knowing what those stars meant.

Order. Progress. Justice.

"Then you better hold on tight," Sasha said as she veered the chopper in a 180-degree turn.

Jessa slammed into me, her slender frame flush against my own, and I grabbed her hand. I squeezed it tight and caught her eyes. I was pleading with my every emotion that she could see how sorry I was. I shouldn't have trusted the Resistance to take her somewhere safe. I'd been so careless with Jessa, over and over. And now, this was it. These were the only moments we had left together. We'd definitely be caught. I didn't know what would happen to me. But if they discovered I was a traitor, it would be drastic. And Sasha would be executed. Would they do that to Jessa? No, she was too valuable to them. Her fate would be worse.

"What's going to happen to us? Are they going to shoot us down?" Jessa asked, panicked.

"Not if they suspect you're in here," Sasha replied.

We zipped through the air, and Sasha moved us as close to the gray earth as she possibly could. The line of decaying trees up ahead was becoming dangerously close.

"What's your plan here?" I asked.

"We're going to land in there and take cover. We have to hide."

"We can't go in there. It's all dead. We'll starve to death. Or get lost. We won't make it out."

"Do you have a better idea?" Sasha called over her shoulder as we approached the ashen forest. If we didn't crash in the landing, we'd be lost in this wasteland. Or get caught by the royal officers. I didn't know which fate was worse.

I knew what I had to do. Without a doubt in my mind, I knew I had to let it all go. All the secrets, the half-truths, and the lies.

It was time for me to save our lives.

TWENTY-ONE

JESSA

I'd sometimes wondered how I was going to die. Death by helicopter crash had never crossed my imagination. But there was no way out. We were going down. Even I knew that at the speed we were moving and the thickness of the trees up ahead, there was nothing Sasha could do to save us.

Was my life supposed to be flashing before my eyes? That wasn't happening. It was more of a sudden realization, in slow motion, that this was the end. An unwinding of stillness as everything around me took perfect form. The rough feel of Lucas's hand clutching mine. The comforting smell of the warm leather seat beneath me. The thumping movement of the chopper blades, spinning too fast to follow. The desolate gray land created such a stark contrast against the bright morning sun, the wide blue sky, and the large puffs of feathery white clouds that sat low.

"Go up!" Lucas yelled. "Right now, go up, Sasha."

Sasha didn't acknowledge him. She was still focused on attempting a successful crash landing in the forest cover. I didn't think it was possible.

Lucas ripped off his seat belt. He dove over the seat in front of us. He practically sat on Sasha as he shoved her away. They grappled for the joystick, and he pushed it down. The chopper rose.

"What are you doing?" Sasha hissed, grabbing the controls.

"Sit down," he yelled, shoving her back.

She didn't listen.

I watched in shock over their struggle.

Out of the corner of my eye, I saw a flash. The three red stars visibly announced our imminent capture.

"Someone will see you!" I yelled at Lucas, realizing he was now in clear view, sitting up front like that.

"No, they won't. We're almost there."

He pulled back with the entire weight of his body and we jolted upwards, much faster than before. In another breath, we were catapulted through a mass of white clouds. Dense and thick around the chopper, they provided momentary cover.

"Hover here," he said to Sasha, as he let her back into the pilot's seat.

"No!" Sasha scoffed.

"Just do it. And stay buckled!"

He put his hands up against the door. It slid open. I screamed, reaching for him. He didn't respond, just kept his eyes held shut and stretched his hand out into the white atmosphere. Utter concentration lined his strong features. His dark hair fell in waves, covering his face. As his whole body stilled, it was as if everything stopped, suspended in space.

Sasha gasped, realizing something I was seemingly missing.

"What's happening?" I asked.

Lucas shuddered, then looked up at her.

"Go," he said, slamming closed the door. "I got a lot, but I won't be able to hold this for long."

She nodded and threw us forward. We flew quickly out of the clouds, into the open blue again. I looked around for the plane and all at once, there was nothing. We were invisible!

"They can't *see* us?" I screamed. *Is this real?* "What's happening?"

It was like flying, but not. We were sitting. There was no wind. But the earth was barreling below and the inertia made me want to scream again. I heard the clasp of Lucas unbuckling his harness and felt him fall into my lap. "It's okay. We're completely safe. But this is quite exhausting. I need you to keep me awake," he said.

Keep him awake? Why? What was wrong with him?

"Just do it," Sasha called back. I couldn't see her, or anything besides the world flying by! But somehow she managed to maneuver the helicopter. "I'm serious, Jessa," Sasha yelled. "He can't fall asleep. He needs to hold this. He's our only chance right now. Do something!"

What in the world were they talking about?

I felt his warm hand on the back of my neck. His thumb rested in the small indent just below my hairline. An unexpected shiver ran up and down my spine. I lost my breath.

Forgetting all politeness, I leaned down and felt for his lips. The kiss was a slow burning answer to a question. With every movement, our bodies came closer to each other. Eventually, he sat up and pulled me onto his lap, our mouths never parting. I kept my eyes closed, and for that moment, I allowed myself to forget about everything. Not even the fear of death could pull me away from that perfect kiss.

I'd been pretending for weeks that I hadn't been affected by Lucas's presence. I tried to tell myself that I didn't long for him to be part of my life. But my true feelings were clearer to me now, more than ever. It was undeniable, especially in the heady caress of his touch, in the exhilarating sense of falling that was coursing through my body.

We continued kissing like that for a while before I slowly pulled away. His steady gray eyes were churning with passion—both intense and vulnerable.

"Are you sufficiently awake enough to hold this?" Sasha's voice chimed.

I looked around and saw that the terrain was no longer the lifeless gray we'd seen just before. It was pocketed with mountains, and we were flying high. There wasn't any gray in sight at all. There were just mountains and grasslands. And there wasn't another jet, another soul, in sight. Thank goodness...

It wasn't quite as terrifying as before, flying invisible.

"What happened?" It was magic, of course. But who, *and how?*

"Lucas can answer that," Sasha said.

"You're a color alchemist?" I whispered.

I didn't have to ask to know it was the truth, but I did anyway. The words were low on my breath, as anger threatened to break through. I wanted more than anything to see the look on his face. And the fact that I couldn't made me even angrier!

"So all this time you've been lying to everyone? To me?"

"I had to."

No, he didn't. "Who else knows about this?"

"Well, now, just you two. It's my best-kept secret," he said. "And now I assume the Resistance will know."

Sasha sighed. "I will have to report this, Lucas—I don't have a choice."

I didn't care about any of that right now. All I wanted was the truth, as painful as it might be. I shifted my weight away from Lucas, sitting back in my own seat and carefully adjusting the seat belt as I considered how to approach this. On the outside, I might have looked calm, but inside, I was seething.

"How did you keep your abilities a secret?"

"I know how to hide, and sometimes I can shut it off."

"One of the first things I *ever* asked you was how to turn this magic off. You said it was impossible. You lied." All that had happened to me, everything I'd been through could have been different if I'd known how to turn the alchemy off. "Why didn't you teach me?"

"Because no one else knows. Teaching you would have risked exposing myself. If I could go back and undo that choice, I would."

I shook with the hurt that he had chosen not to help me. He couldn't see my pain but I was sure he could hear it in my voice.

"It's too late to change it now. They already know what I can do. They already know that I can access red. They're just waiting."

"I'm so sorry, Jessa." Lucas put his hand on my knee. I quickly pulled it from his grasp.

All I'd wanted since I'd first met Lucas was to forget about the GC and go home. To live a normal life. To be a ballet dancer. And to actually be a part of my own family. Apparently, he was the only person who could have helped me create that. He could have taught me hide it, but instead, he'd chosen his own agenda.

166

"You're just like your father." I spoke each word sharply.

Silence. Thick suffocating silence.

"Where are we going?" he finally asked Sasha.

"How long can you hold this invisibility?"

"An hour," he said. "But this is a lot for me. Maybe not even that."

Sasha whistled. "You are one powerful alchemist—I'll give you that."

A memory from my studies surfaced as I realized what Lucas had done to get us out of there. He'd done the seemingly impossible.

"You can access white?" I asked him. "I thought that color didn't count. That's what I read..."

He didn't say anything for a while.

"White is a shielding color. A protector."

The alchemy of white was like red, one of the untouched colors. There was so much about it that was still unknown. As far as I knew, Lucas was the only one who could access it. If he'd known it could be used to cloak our helicopter that meant he must have practiced with white before. Sasha was right. He was incredibly powerful.

He was also a liar.

We sat in silence for at least another half-hour as Sasha brought us closer to our destination. With every passing minute, I wondered if Lucas was growing more and more exhausted. I could hear his labored breathing. Who could hold alchemy for so long? I'd never be able to do something like this with any color, let alone anything so insane as invisibility.

"You can relax now. Go ahead and drop it," Sasha said.

Lucas let out a groan. Slowly everything appeared again, as if coming out of a fog and into sharp focus. He laid his head against the window. I looked around for any indication of what had happened to us, but I couldn't see anything but the inside of the helicopter just as it was before.

Why would a prince hide something like this?

Within seconds, Lucas was lost to a heavy sleep. Guilt seeped into my every cell. He had saved us. And I'd insulted him. I'd called him *his father*.

"You're not the only one who'd like to shut it off," Sasha said.

I studied her for a moment. This girl was incredibly well trained, talented, and, of course, beautiful. I'd never considered the possibility that Sasha could be unhappy with her situation. What had she been through? There must have been something that caused her to start working with the Resistance, whomever they were.

"I'm sorry," I said. I'd become so self-centered lately that I'd forgotten to be a friend to Sasha. She'd always been kind to me, despite everything with Lucas. I knew now they were just friends, working on an assignment together. Yet there was a part of me that wondered, despite it all, if Sasha cared for Lucas. How could any girl get that close to him and not have feelings?

"It's not your fault," she said. "He didn't tell me, either. It would have been too late for me, anyway. I'm in too deep—no turning back now."

"But maybe I could have gotten out of all this?"

"Maybe. Probably not."

"He did." I looked at Lucas, who was still asleep.

"Yes, he *did*. But he's in this now."

After a moment, she adjusted some controls and pushed up on the joystick. We began to descend into a mountain range below us.

"Where are we?" I asked.

This area looked unfamiliar. We were moving so fast, I hadn't realized our speed as I'd kept my eyes closed for most of the invisible time. It freaked me out too much! I was sure this was a military-grade helicopter. This Resistance group, whoever they were, had strong connections.

"Canada," she said, "or at least what's left of it. There isn't much of a functioning government here anymore. We've got a hidden camp set up. Personally, I'm tired of being undercover. It'll be nice to have a break."

I considered this place. Is my new home near? Would I like it?

"You've always been undercover?"

I realized the amount of stress Sasha must go through daily. Just sneaking away from the palace had taken all my courage. I couldn't imagine what kinds of risks she must have taken to do the right thing.

"I got away from the GC when I was a kid. And then I found my way here. The Resistance trained me for years and recently helped me come back."

"Come back?" I shook my head. "How is that possible?"

Her face paled and her eyes glazed over, as if she were lost in her own thoughts. Tangled in the web of her life.

"It's complicated. Let's just say someone at the GC made an alias for me. There are enough kids who get shipped out young. It wasn't unbelievable when I showed up at the palace for more training."

I wanted to keep questioning her, but I decided to let it go for now. The thick green blanket of pine trees was getting much closer. I searched for signs of civilization. Strangely, I couldn't find anything. No houses or buildings, and definitely no people. The forest was wild and rugged. Thick underbrush coated the ground. The area certainly didn't resemble a rebellion stronghold. Not how I imagined one, anyway. We hovered above a clearing as she slowly dropped us into place. But there was nothing here.

"Sasha, what's going on?" I asked.

She turned off the engine, and the thrum of the machine began to relax. The blades, which had once moved at lightning speed, slowed to a dull whir.

Sasha turned in her seat, studying Lucas. He was still passed out. "He's going to want you to stay here."

"Well, that's the plan, isn't it?" I asked. I just hoped "here" was somewhere decent, not a tree fort. Because really, where were the people?

She frowned. "I'm sorry, but no."

"What do you mean?"

"We need your help, Jessa. You're the only one who can stop the royal family from hurting more people."

"No, I can't. I don't even know how that's possible."

"What do you think they want you for?"

"To control people. So I can't let them have me."

"Don't you get it? They're going to find a way to do it, anyway. They'll find another red alchemist eventually. Or find someone else who can separate primary colors like you did at the ballet. Do you realize that since that day whole teams are now dedicated to replicating that magic? One way or another, someone will get to the red."

"But there isn't another person. That's why they want me."

She laughed. "There was someone before you and there will be more after you. You are not the only one who will ever have red."

I paused. "The gray land. What happened there?"

"We call them the shadow lands. They're the result of intense alchemy. Someone using color for evil purposes. It was punishment to the people who lived out there. And it won't stop. The royals do it to their enemies. They'll do it to their own citizens if they must. There's plenty of ways color alchemy can hurt people. Worst part? It's all in the name of a stronger Protectorate."

"So how am I expected to stop it? Why me?"

"Because, Jessa, you have control over the blood. You've shown ability with red that few people ever have. You have a chance of giving them what they want. You have to go back. You have to learn everything you can, and then use it against them. Fight!"

"How?"

"Isn't it obvious? You need to use your abilities to control them. Control Richard. Control Faulk. Get into their minds. Figure out their secrets. Slowly change their thoughts. *Help us stop them.*"

I sat with that idea for a moment. Could I do it? Everything inside was screaming that I couldn't. It was too much responsibility for one girl. I barely knew what I was doing. How could I take on something so important? And yet...

"What's going to happen to Lucas?" I asked, looking at his sleeping body. The dark curls had fallen into his eyes. He breathed a long sigh and shifted his weight.

"I said he was going to be the hero, didn't I? That's because he's going to be the one to take you back in. He'll turn you into his father himself. That will help Lucas get back into good graces with Richard. We'll stop by and see your family first though. You can make sure they're safe. But then we need you to go back."

I was so relieved to know my family was near. And her reasoning, it made sense. If I pretended that he'd found me and forced me to go back against my will, then we could make up a believable story. "Can I have some time to think about it?"

"We don't have much time. If you stay here, you risk not being able to go back at all. We have to make this believable in order for Lucas to stay out of trouble. We need to get you on your way back before he wakes up, because he's not going to like the idea."

"Why?"

"He loves you, Jessa," she said. "He doesn't want you involved in something so dangerous."

She was probably right that he wouldn't be too happy about taking me back to the palace. He wanted me to keep my powers away from Richard.

But love? Does he really love me?

"So we're just dropping you off?" I asked. "That's why we came here?"

"It's not the only reason. Would you like to say hello to your family?"

I nearly jumped out of my seat. "Wait, they're *here*?"

"Yes, Jessa, they are. I want to work with Lacey. Just to see if she has abilities, too. To help her train so that she won't have problems in the future. So she can protect herself. We need you to convince your parents to let us find out if she has the same powers as you. As it stands, they're refusing."

I nodded. I understood now that this world we were living in wasn't the one my parents knew. To them, life was simple. Follow the rules and everything would be okay. But I knew it didn't always work out like that. It would be torture to see my family only to turn around and leave. But what was the alternative? Someone had to stop the king. Once I was successful, I would return to them. Only then could we be a family again.

"I'll do it. I'll help you."

TWENTY-TWO

LUCAS

I woke to the distant sound of muffled voices. My eyelids felt like they were about ten pounds each as I struggled to open them. Light poured in. I blinked it away. When I shifted my weight, my neck screamed in protest. A hard knot had formed against my spine. I tried to clear my head and think, but it was bogged down with exhaustion. Why was I so tired?

I was still in the backseat of the helicopter. I breathed in the current stillness. The silence was a welcomed friend.

"You're up early," a playful voice said. Sasha was sitting on the seat next to me, no longer up front. She ran her fingers through her long sunny hair and smiled.

I coughed, rubbing my throat. "How long was I out?"

"A few hours."

I looked around for Jessa. Where were we? Just beyond the clearing of pine trees, I saw a small group of people. They were standing close, hugging and talking. I couldn't make out what they were saying from in here, but I recognized Jessa instantly.

"That's her family," Sasha said.

So they were here. The Resistance had really gotten them out.

From here, all I could read was their body language. It was obvious that they were excited to see each other. Their movements carried a love that I almost didn't recognize. There weren't families like these in the palace.

Sasha looked away, her features turning dark.

"What's wrong?"

Seeing Jessa this happy only made me happy, too. But it seemed to elicit a different reaction from Sasha. There was something strange about her posture. It wasn't like her to be upset over someone else's good news.

"They're happy to see her," Sasha said. "Good for her."

"But?" I urged her to continue. What was she keeping from me?

"But they'd sooner abandon her if they could." She shook her head. "Isn't it obvious? They are afraid of alchemy. Too bad all of their kids were probably born with the ability."

"I don't think you know them well enough to say that." But, I could understand it a little if it was true. I had caught on early that my parents didn't care for the alchemists. When my abilities developed at the ripe old age of nine, I knew they wouldn't accept me. I figured out early on how to keep them hidden, and I moved on with my life.

There was something about Sasha's last statement that stayed with me and played with a memory at the back of my mind. Suddenly, I remembered the lost alchemist from my research. The girl who'd disappeared at the age of eight. What was her name? Francesca Loxley. I still wondered if there was a connection between her and this family. I hadn't found anything more. I almost asked Sasha if she knew anything, because I was beginning to suspect that maybe she did.

"Do you think Lacey is an alchemist, too?"

"Yes. The Resistance is pretty sure of it. Jessa should be talking to her parents about it now. We want to help Lacey. Train her."

I wondered how they would react to the news. I hoped that instead of trying to fight it, they could see that helping Lacey was the better choice.

"No one's going to let her join the GC though, right? No undercover spy-girl business for little Lacey?"

"A GC life is not the plan. She's too impressionable."

I reached for the door. "I think it's time I met some of your leaders."

Sasha shook her head. "We're locked in."

"What?" I pulled on the door handle. It wouldn't budge.

"Let me out, Sasha. Don't be ridiculous."

"They still don't know if they can trust you, Lucas. I'm just following orders. We have something planned for when you return home."

I laughed. Complete outrage was the first emotion to bubble up inside me.

"Are you kidding me? Would I be here if you couldn't trust me?"

"Well, there's nothing here," Sasha said. "The Resistance camp is miles away. And it's well hidden. We'll be hiking in. You're going home."

Looking around, I realized that although I could point out the thick forest, I still had no idea where we really were. And I'd been asleep for most of the ride here. We could have gone north. Or we could have gone west, but that was even more dangerous. Maybe a combination of the two. I had no way of knowing. I had lost my bearings. "Then have them come to us. And anyway, I need to know what your plan is. How are you planning to get me back fast enough without blowing my cover? This whole day has been ridiculous. I'm just supposed to go home and pretend I haven't been missing? I don't think so."

"Don't worry, Lucas. We know how valuable you are. It's handled."

Oh, great. Like that was supposed to make me feel better. I was losing confidence in this Resistance group by the minute. Who exactly had I partnered up with? I'd been so eager to feel like I was doing something right, to feel like I could help my country, that I hadn't really stopped to consider maybe I'd made a mistake. But now probably wasn't the best time to voice that out loud.

"And I'm just supposed to take your word for it?"

"What other choice do you have?"

Well, she had me there. She knew it. And she knew I knew it. For now. But there were choices. There were always choices.

"No offense, Sasha, but I'm struggling with this. I give you information, and I'm just expected to be patient and wait it out. But you said it yourself, didn't you? I'm a valuable asset. In fact, I think I'm probably your *most* valuable asset. I'm the prince, for crying out loud. What more do you want from me?"

"You *are* a valuable asset. But you see that over there?" She pointed to Jessa. She was on her knees, hugging Lacey and saying something to her parents. I caught the words "for the best" and saw them nodding.

"That's what we call our most valuable asset now. I didn't realize how easily Jessa would come around to our way of thinking. But all it took was one open conversation for her to understand how much we need her now."

"What are you talking about?"

"What you did back there with the white was remarkable, Lucas. Thank you for that. Who would have guessed white could do something so useful? I'm impressed! But I thought that amount of alchemy would have knocked you out for another few hours, at least. I hadn't expected you to wake up so early." Was she turning on me? Why was she talking like this?

"And your point is?"

"You have to take Jessa back to the palace."

"Absolutely not."

"We need her."

"We're not having this conversation. We didn't just risk our lives only to take her back there. It's not safe. They're going to hurt her. What they're doing is unthinkable. It's so much worse than what I could have ever imagined. To have the ability to control people's minds? To make them do whatever they want? That kind of power will probably kill Jessa by the time she's finished."

"This isn't about one person. If I could do it myself, I would. But I can't be there anymore. I've already received word that my cover was compromised. I'm needed here now anyway. You're the only one with a fighting chance of getting Jessa back in that palace. They know you took off, but they *don't* know you're with us."

"And what do I do when I go back?"

"You're going to show them that you're on their side. You'll say that she never left the capital city. You found her and brought her home. The end."

"And what about the jet. They saw us, remember?"

"These windows are tinted, Lucas. There is no way they could have known for sure who was in here. Or what we were doing. Sure, they're looking for Jessa, but they wouldn't expect to find *you* in a helicopter. Plus, we already moved your car. It's safe. They're looking for you back home."

Could it be so easy? But I still didn't want to take Jessa back. Saying goodbye to her would tear me apart. I'd known that going into today. As soon as we'd found out Jessa had gone missing, our plans had drastically changed. Our plan had quickly transformed from getting Jessa to her parents to finding a safe place for her to hide…and now Sasha was telling me that wasn't the case anymore.

Maybe it never was the plan. Maybe Sasha just told you what you needed to hear to get you to bring Jessa here in the first place.

The thought had me questioning my alliance with the Resistance more than ever. Once I got home, I was cutting them out. I was done. There had to be another way than dealing with these people. I would go home and Jessa would stay here. Here…where it was safe. Where she could live a comfortable life with her family. Where she could still be trained to control her abilities, without fear of being used by people like General Faulk and my father.

"Has she made up her mind?" I asked, looking back out the window.

As if sensing me, Jessa peered back at the helicopter. Even though the windows were tinted, I knew she could see me. She stared at us for a minute, smiled faintly, and turned back to give her family another round of hugs.

"Yes, she's sure. You won't be able to change her mind."

"And who's flying us back, then? Now that you're staying here, we're going to need a pilot."

"My friends are going to fly you back to a safe place, and then you'll be picking up your car and taking Jessa back. You can trust them to get you there safely."

I was pretty sure I couldn't trust anyone in the Resistance. I would play along long enough to get home. This little false mission of theirs was the last straw. "And then what?"

"No one will know you flew off. You'll create a cover story. Take her back to the palace."

"You've said that already. I mean, what happens to Jessa?"

She stared at me for a moment. "When you get back, make sure that Jessa gets initiated into the GC. We need her working on the inside. She's more valuable to us there than she is anywhere else."

That wasn't okay with me! The last thing I wanted was to put Jessa in harm's way. But it seemed that my opinion didn't matter. I felt so out of control. Not only were they leading me around without telling me their true plans, but now they knew about my alchemy. And that was something that could easily be used against me. *Why did I put myself in this situation?*

"So if you're staying, who will be my Resistance contact?" I asked.

"Jessa will be your contact. I'm pretty sure my superiors don't think you'll turn her in for treason. They know all about your romance."

So that was it, then? They would use my feelings for Jessa against me. Because they knew, just as much as I did, that I would help her no matter what.

"Are you trying to make me regret ever having met you?" I snapped.

"Oh, don't pretend like you ever really cared for me. You should be happy that now you and Jessa have another reason to spend time together."

Could I have misunderstood Sasha's feelings? Or maybe I was just a game she had played and failed. She'd been a good sport about our faked romance. But then last night we'd gotten closer than ever. I wasn't proud of it. At least I stopped it before it went too far.

"Is this about last night? You're mad because I didn't hook up with you?"

"Ha! Don't flatter yourself."

My reply was interrupted by pounding on the metal door behind me.

"That's your new pilot," Sasha said, reaching for the door. "Oh, and I lied. We were never completely locked in here. My door was unlocked. You're kind of naïve, Lucas."

Whoa! Why does she suddenly hate me?

She wrenched open her *apparently* unlocked door and jumped out into the clearing below. She hugged a very large, very tall, burly middle-aged man. He was wearing oil-stained brown jeans and a plaid button-up with rolled-up sleeves. His tanned skin, work gloves, and disheveled hair gave me the impression that he was probably a handyman of sorts.

"It's so good to see you," he said, "My, you're all grown up now, aren't you?"

"It's good to see you too, Hank." Sasha's earlier sour mood had gone.

The man gave her another smile, shaking his head before peering into the helicopter. He looked me up and down.

"Well, son," he said, "looks like I'm the sorry sap who agreed to see you home. You're not going to turn on me, are you? Some of the others think I'm a fool, flying a *royal*. You're not going to make a fool out of me, are you?"

"No. I'm pretty sure I'm the fool."

"Well, okay then." He turned to Sasha, "Let's get the girl loaded up. They told you Tristan is coming along too? He insisted on keeping an eye on things."

"Sounds like him," she laughed.

"We're already behind schedule," someone said, coming up to the helicopter. He was young too, probably in his twenties. He hugged Sasha and she smiled up at him, adoring. "Of course you insisted on going," Sasha said to him. "I'll see you when you get back, all right? We have a lot of catching up to do."

The guy hugged her again before sliding into the seat next to Hank. I noticed he made sure I saw the gun in his hand. Whatever. "I'm here to make sure you don't give Hank any trouble, so don't even think about it."

I only glared at the kid, then looked out of the window.

Sasha walked through the tall grass and tapped Jessa on the shoulder. Jessa pulled away from yet another hug with her father, and the two girls nodded. They exchanged a few inaudible words before they came walking back to the helicopter together. Jessa climbed in next to me, careful not to meet my gaze. Her cheeks were ashen, her eyes hollow.

"Don't do this, Jessa. Don't go back with me." I had to try and talk her out of this.

"I've made up my mind. There's no changing it."

"Are you sure?" I asked, unable to help myself.

She looked at me. Or rather, she looked through me. Through me to her small group of family members, circled in the distance. The longing on her face was replaced with an expression of fixed resolve when she focused her attention back on me. Did she blame me for my father's actions? Would she ever forgive me for choosing not to teach her what I knew about hiding color alchemy?

"Do you hate me? Are you doing this to punish me or something?"

She didn't answer. She just turned to Hank, who was busy switching on the controls up front. "I'm ready to leave."

He turned a knob. The heavy thrum of the engine came to life, an unseen answer to her request.

"What happened back there?" I asked. "Is your family okay?" I didn't know if she was talking to me, but I had to try.

"Well, let's just say they don't understand me anymore. But they love me. And I guess that's all that matters."

"So why not stay?"

"Because I love them, too."

■

"Are you sure about this?" I asked Jessa one last time.

We stood at the edge of the dim parking lot, hidden by the shadows of the setting sun. How was it possible for so much to happen—in the way of action and emotion, as well as revelation—in one day?

My car waited for me, silent and ready. I didn't know what would happen when I left this morning, but I never expected to be doing this. This was the last thing I wanted for Jessa.

"Don't ask me that again." Jessa folded her arms, bent her head down low, and ran for the vehicle.

I followed, quickly catching up to her as we sprinted across the empty parking lot. My car was the only one here, half hidden by an overgrown weeping willow whose roots had probably began tearing through the tarmac years ago.

Hank and the wannabe badass Tristan had dropped us off about a mile away and gave us directions before heading back north. This time, we'd flown so high that I couldn't really be sure where Sasha had taken us in the first place. There hadn't been any recognizable landmarks that I could identify. All I knew for sure was that north, in the mountains somewhere, a Resistance camp waited.

Once we loaded ourselves into the car, we went over our story a few times as we drove back to the palace. Within the hour, we pulled up to the gates. I hesitated, squeezing the steering wheel tight. My hands wanted to turn us around and get Jessa out of there.

Jessa studied me. "It's too late for that, Lucas."

She was right. Any more hesitation would raise too much suspicion in Faulk and Richard. I pushed on the gas and headed up the long, smooth drive. As soon as we pulled up to the front of the palace, we were surrounded by dozens of royal officers and guardians, their guns pointed.

"Stay calm," I whispered, before opening the door and casually stepping out of the car. "You can put your guns down," I called out, shaking my head. "Where's my father? This is no way to treat your prince."

A few hesitated and lowered their weapons, but most stayed put.

The massive door to the front entrance opened, and my father, mother, and General Faulk stepped out. "You heard the boy." My father's voice boomed. "Lower your weapons immediately!"

The men all stepped back as the three approached the car.

Faulk's eyes were bloodshot and angrier than I'd ever seen them. "Where have you been all day?"

Her tone, although tough, actually ignited a chain reaction of calm through every cell in my body. Suddenly, I knew that although I may be under great suspicion, no one had actually seen me doing anything illegal.

"Tracking this one down," I said, pointing to the car. "For you, Father," I added, with a smirk. "Maybe we can finally agree now that I'm not as useless as you may think?"

They stared at me for a second and then looked to the car. My mother leaned closer to the window, eyes squinting, before stumbling back. "It's her!"

Mom landed on the ground, and I ran to her as the rest of them—my father, Faulk, the guardians, and royal officers—swarmed the car.

Mom brushed herself off and looked up. Her eyes tried to focus on me, but it was difficult. She was grasping for something in her mind, but it was slipping away. A misty confusion filled her face, and she blinked rapidly. Had someone used more mind control on her today? Something was wrong. That *had* to be it!

"Are you all right, Mother?" I asked, lifting her up.

"I don't think so."

Her knees buckled, and she dropped into my arms.

TWENTY-THREE

JESSA

"I 've already told you," I said, leaning back against the cool metal chair. "I don't know where Sasha went."

Faulk stared at me, silent. She was waiting for me to say something, anything, that she could use against me. And though she didn't say it, she was waiting for me to incriminate Lucas, as well.

As soon as we'd pulled up the palace drive, Lucas had gotten out of the car and left me in the passenger's seat. It hadn't taken them long to figure out I was in there. They swarmed the vehicle, pulled me out, and threw me to the ground. They handcuffed me tightly and hauled me off. Of course, after everything I'd been through, it wasn't like any of their actions came as a surprise. These people didn't care about me. They didn't care about my freedom. As far as they were concerned, I didn't have any.

"Repeat your story," Faulk said for what felt like the hundredth time.

I looked around the concrete gray room. I knew there was no added color to be found in here, except for that of the people who came in and out. But I couldn't seem to stop myself from looking for something safe enough for alchemy, because I was beginning to think I'd made a huge mistake. "I already told you. Do you really need to hear it again?"

Faulk cocked her head. "Yes, I really do."

"I ran away. I jumped out of my window in the middle of the night. I broke my legs, and yes, I even screamed. But your royal officers never came looking for me, did they? You really need to increase security around here. So anyway, I healed myself with the grass. Green is one of the only alchemies I can do. That's the reason why I jumped from that high in the first place."

"What happened next?"

"I ran to the wall. It's big. I didn't know what I was thinking. I pretty much gave up. I got really upset and hit it. And I guess I used alchemy on something

178

there too, because one of the large stones crumbled. So I pulled it from the wall and crawled through the hole. You've confirmed all this by now, haven't you? You obviously found the open window. Was the grass turned gray just below? And I'm sure you already sealed up the hole in the wall."

She stared at me for a long moment. "Keep going."

"I rode the high speed train to my old neighborhood. You already know that. Some girl from my old high school was there and tried to make small talk. I thought that was strange, but when I got off the train and she stayed on, I let it go. But you and I both know what happened next. She attacked me in one of my neighbor's yards. That girl can pack a punch, I'll give her that. I thought she was going to break my arm."

"So what did you do in retaliation?"

"It was self-defense. And I had no idea what I was doing, actually. She was going to turn me in, and I freaked out. I think I broke her nose. Then I ran."

"And where did you go?" Faulk was ready for me to slip up. But I wouldn't.

"I hid. I spent most of the morning in one of the nearby forests. But I knew that I couldn't hide there for long. So I snuck into a neighbor's tool shed and waited it out."

"And what were you going to do? Who were you going to meet?"

"No one. I never got that far. I had no plan. I just wanted to see my family, I swear. But I knew I couldn't go to the house, not after what happened with that girl. I finally decided I needed to come back to the palace, but I also knew I'd be in trouble. You know, that girl told me she's a royal officer in training."

"She was. But it's funny Jessa. She doesn't remember the fight," Faulk said. Not for the first time, I wondered what had happened to her.

"You got me. I used alchemy on her. It made her forget. After that, I got scared, and I ran. I hid and tried to think of a plan. But honestly, I didn't have one. So when I got hungry, I just started walking back to the palace. I kept myself hidden, because I didn't want to hurt anyone else. Just in case a civilian saw me and got involved. I know it's lame, but it's the truth."

"But Lucas found you? How did that happen?"

"Blind luck, I guess. He told me that his father was angry with him for losing me. And so he spent the day driving around the city, looking for me. Just when he was going to give up and go home, he saw me darting across a street. He pulled up and told me to get in. By then I'd all but given up anyway, so I did. And here I am."

"And here you are." Faulk said. "You never saw Sasha?"

I shook my head. "No, what does she have to do with any of this?"

Of course, there was no answer.

Faulk got up and left the room without a word, the heavy door banging shut behind her.

The room was a box. No window. One door. There was a mirrored glass wall that I was sure was actually a two-way mirror. For all I knew, there were royal officers just on the other side, studying me. Looking for mistakes. But they wouldn't find any. I wouldn't mess this up.

After a few more minutes, Faulk came back into the room.

She wasn't alone. King Richard sat down across from me.

"Your Highness." I attempted what probably looked like a pathetic bow, considering I was handcuffed to the chair.

"Hello, Jessa."

"We're curious about a few things." Richard narrowed his eyes on me. "Why is it that one of our best guardians would also go missing on the same day as you, and yet you two never crossed paths?"

"How should I know? Maybe Sasha took the distraction as an opportunity to run. It might come as a surprise to you, but you don't always treat your guardians right."

We both watched as I tried to raise my hands from where they were cuffed to the chair. They barely moved. *Case in point, dear King Richard.*

"But, Jessa, you're not a guardian, are you?"

It was not a question.

"But I want to be," I said, quickly catching his attention.

This was the part that had to be convincing. Otherwise, I would be stuck in a room like this forever. And everything I risked to come back here would be for nothing.

"You think I'd let you join my Color Guard. I don't need you to be a part of anything so important to get what I want from you."

My heart dropped into my stomach, fear threatening to take over.

"General Faulk told me that if I could figure out red alchemy, I would be able to have weekly phone calls with my family. And I promise I tried, but I couldn't do it. I got desperate to see my family and I made a mistake."

"Oh, yes, you certainly did," Richard said. "There are rules for alchemists, Jessa. Rules that are there for a reason."

Rules meant to control us! I nodded. "And you're right. Because I ended up using alchemy while I was out there, Your Highness. And you probably already know by now that I changed that girl's blood, turned it gray. Don't you see? Just when I had given up, something got triggered within me, and I did it. I did what you wanted."

"So?" We both knew he had all the power right now.

"Well, when Lucas found me, he explained that you probably had my family on lockdown because I ran away. Personally, I didn't get close enough to my house to see much of anything. But I did see that they weren't there."

I began to cry, allowing the tears to fall as heavy as I could manage. "Lucas said that breaking the rules would only get me into more trouble. But if I was really good, if I worked hard for you and did what you needed me to do, then you'd let me see them again. Please, that's all I want. Don't punish them for my mistakes. Let them be free and let me join the GC so I can prove myself to you."

By the time I finished my speech, hatred boiled inside. But I worked harder than ever to maintain the outer appearance. I was the prodigal child, coming home for forgiveness. Maybe his pride would be enough to keep me safe.

I knew he didn't really have my family. The Resistance had gotten them out already. But he would never have to know that I knew the truth.

"I don't buy it," Faulk said, stepping forward. "From day one, she put on a show and lied to everyone. Who's to say she's not doing that now?"

Richard stood and looked down at me for several moments before turning his back. Just before the door closed, he turned to Faulk. "Immediately begin training her for the GC initiation," he said. "I want her."

■

I wasn't returned to my bedroom. Nor did I end up in a prison cell. Instead, I was taken straight to GC headquarters and was left to wait there alone in one of the training rooms. I was still dressed head to toe in the stale gray jumpsuit. The space was similar to the others, with glass walls and modern furnishings.

Nobody said anything about who would be joining me, or if there was something I was supposed to be doing here. So I just waited and watched as people walked down the hallway, glaring at me.

Great, these are going to be my peers. They hate me more than ever.

Reed materialized on the other side of the glass, talking to someone. About me, I was sure. I recognized Brooke, the girl from the ball and the gymnasium, the one who obviously had it in for me.

I couldn't hear what they were saying, but it didn't look like it could be anything good. I shrugged. The girl stormed away in a huff, but Reed gave me a tight half-smile before walking away.

I couldn't help but remember how he'd tried to use blue alchemy on me. How he tried to mold my feelings to reveal my secrets. Should I confront him? If I acted like nothing happened, would it be easier to become a part of this operation?

Jasmine walked into view and waved at me from behind the glass. The two guards at the door nodded at her and left us as she walked into the room. She wore her usual wardrobe. "Why don't you dress like the rest of them?"

She paused, looking down at her blue cotton dress. "I made a deal with the king. I'm his best healer. I do not ask to be reassigned. I do whatever he asks of me. But I get to be myself. And part of that means I dress how I want to dress. I have free range of the grounds here, too. Makes life a little easier."

"You do *whatever* he wants?"

"Yes. Is that a problem?"

"Nope," I said, faking a smile.

I could only imagine what talents Jasmine had that the king found so valuable. But I knew I would also do whatever he wanted with my own talents, at least for a time. I smiled at Jasmine, sorry I'd said anything at all. If I was going to pull this off and take Richard down from the inside, I couldn't raise any suspicion. At one time, I thought she understood me, but after what she'd just confessed, I wasn't so sure.

She studied the room, as if she was looking for something. But there wasn't anyone else in here. In fact, it was quite bland. She opened her palm, where a small blue flower lay crushed in her hand.

"How's Hank doing?" she asked.

My heart stopped. Hank was the kind older man who'd flown us back in the helicopter. How did Jasmine know about Hank?

"No one can hear us," she said, gently rubbing her thumb against the flower, the blue color staining her skin. "Don't worry. It's safe."

"You're part of the Resistance? Are you here to help me?"

"Yes. I was Sasha's handler," she said. "And now I'm yours. We have important work ahead of us."

A group of laughing teenagers burst into the hallway beyond the heavy glass, and I nearly jumped out of my skin. We watched as they continued down the hall, and it became quiet again. Even though Jasmine was using some kind of blue alchemy to mask the sound, it still felt risky to be having this conversation.

"Jasmine, I'm terrified. What am I supposed to do now?"

"Fit in," she said, not bothering to keep her voice down, evidently confident in her alchemy. "Train with the guardians. Be a team player. Then join them. Get initiated. Do whatever you need to do to gain the king's trust."

"Anything else?" I laughed. She made it sound so easy, but I knew it couldn't be that simple. And what did initiation even mean?

"Yes. Get over your squabble with Lucas."

"Why should I? He lied to me."

"Because we need you to be successful where Sasha failed."

"What do you mean?" I asked, beginning to question again what Sasha had really been here to do. Who was she, really?

"We need him to be absolutely committed to us," she said. "And we're convinced the best way to do that is to get him one hundred percent committed to you."

"How am I supposed to pull that off?"

"Easy. Make him fall in love with you."

I thought about that for a moment. Could I do that to Lucas?

"You must keep it all very hush-hush. After Richard found Lucas and Sasha in bed together, he was incredibly angry. That won't help us. So instead of being public, you need to keep your relationship a secret. I'm sure that a forbidden love angle will make it even better for him anyway."

My brain could only focus on the one thing she'd said: *After Richard found Lucas and Sasha in bed together.* My chest burned. Lucas had said that his relationship with Sasha had only been for show. Apparently, he'd lied about that too, and now I was expected to pretend it didn't matter? How could I?

I bit my lip and nodded, allowing my thoughts to return to my family. They were most important. I would do anything for them, even if it meant being close to someone as deceiving as Lucas. And the truth was, I still cared for him. Deep down, I still wanted to be with him. This wouldn't be too hard.

"I'll do it," I said, interrupting Jasmine. "I don't need convincing. I'm in."

She reached out her arms and pulled me into a hug. It caught me so off guard that I just stood there, frozen. She smelled like sandalwood and lemon. I allowed myself to melt into her embrace for a moment before she let go.

"You can trust me," she said, her eyes focused intently on mine. "We're doing the right thing here. We'll stop Faulk and Richard. We'll help Lucas make the changes needed. We'll stop the killings. We'll use alchemy for good."

I believed her. I wasn't alone anymore.

"There won't be royal officers or guards around you anymore. You're officially in training, which means you'll have freedom to move around the palace. Just don't try to sneak away anymore. Stick to the GC wing. We'll start tomorrow. But today, you need to go to Lucas. He needs you."

"What do you mean by that?"

"Just go."

I stood there, confused.

"I mean it, Jessa. You need to go now, and hurry. He's in the royal wing. I suggest you run."

I lost all my previous apprehension. She wasn't going to lead me astray. The Resistance needed me to hurry, and so, I ran.

■

Flying out of the room and down the hallway, I made my way through the palace. And Jasmine was right—no one stopped me. I got several strange looks, but there wasn't a single cry of alarm. I guess that meant I was finally on the inside.

Within minutes, I was approaching the large wrought-iron door that marked the private residence of the royal family. It was surrounded by palace guards. It was late, and I was sure I needed an invitation.

I hesitated, but the door opened and Lucas walked out. He beamed at me. Here was the boy I wanted, the boy I maybe even loved. And yet, he had betrayed me. He'd kept his secrets for too long.

"You came just in time. She's doing much better. Come see!"

What was he talking about? Before I could ask, he grabbed my hand and pulled me back through the door with him.

The room was large and beautiful, as one would expect. And in the middle of it all, Queen Natasha stood with her arms open wide. "I remember you! You're Jessa!" She rushed to me, her white silk robe fanning out behind her. Pulling me into a hug, she then spun me around and giggled. "You're so pretty!"

I just smiled, unsure of how to behave. Here was the queen of New Colony, a woman I'd barely seen in passing but who had always been untouchable. And she was spinning me around and acting like a whimsical schoolgirl. What was going on?

"It's an honor to meet you." I curtsied.

Lucas smiled and put his arm around his mother. "Why don't you sit down and rest? You've been ill."

"All right, dear," she said, flashing him a smile. "If you say so."

And then she ran and actually jumped onto the couch, landing in a pile of pillows. She leaned back and grinned up at Lucas, laughing hard. Her auburn hair fanned out around her, framing her pale face.

"She's been ill?" I asked, not quite believing it.

"You didn't see?" He knelt on the floor, holding her hand and staring at her with admiration. "She passed out earlier. When I got out of the car, she fainted right into my arms. The result of another headache, I'm sure. But then Jasmine came. She helped. You feel better now, Mother?"

"Yes, I feel better than I have in years."

I watched Lucas and his mother. Their bond was tangible. Despite her strange behavior, I was happy for Lucas. He deserved this small happiness.

Natasha sat up then and rubbed her forehead. Her face tightened.

"Are you okay? Is your headache coming back?" Lucas asked.

"Who is that?" the queen said, pointing at me.

Lucas's gaze traveled between us.

"That's Jessa. Remember, you just talked to her a moment ago? She's my friend."

"No, I didn't." Natasha stood up, wobbly on her feet. She put her hands on her knees and began breathing deeply. "Son, I need to lie down. Please ask your friend to leave and walk me back to my bedroom."

Lucas's mouth parted, as if he didn't know how to respond.

"It's okay," I started backing up toward the door. I didn't want to be here, anyway. Why had Jasmine sent me here? To see *this*?

Lucas nodded back at me and then focused on his mother, helping her across the room. Just as I was about to turn around and exit, the queen let out a pained scream.

She grabbed her head, her hair flying in wild fire streaks around her as she tumbled to the hardwood floor. Lucas was at her side in an instant, and I rushed to help.

"It's all gone!" she screeched. "It's all gone!"

"What's all gone?" Lucas asked.

She started convulsing, arching her back and banging her head against the wood floor. Lucas struggled to hold her down, to try to do something, anything to help her. And then the beloved Natasha, Lucas's mother, the queen of the New Colony, went completely limp. The color immediately drained from her face.

Lucas carefully slapped her cheeks. "Mother!" he cried, shaking her gently. But she didn't move. He looked around, panicked.

We spotted the potted plant at the same time, and I jumped up and practically dove for it, stumbling over my feet. I grabbed it and pulled the heavy pot to the two of them as quickly as I could. As soon as it was within reaching distance, Lucas put one hand on it and the other on his mother. I followed suit and did the same.

I concentrated as hard as I could, focusing all the energy within me on healing her. I knew Lucas was doing the same. We sat like that for several long moments, willing something to happen as we pulled the color from the plant in waves. The green was swirling around her, almost frantic. But it wasn't doing anything. She wasn't changing. It just moved for what felt like forever. Eventually, the color began to calm, and then all it once, it flew back into the many leaves of the plant.

I sat there, stunned, looking at the lifeless woman before me.

"No!" Lucas gasped, pulling her head into his lap. "No, no, no..."

I didn't know what to do. I just sat there like a statue and watched, horrified, as Lucas rocked back and forth with his mother's body in his arms. He sobbed, and I felt tears on my face, too.

Something stopped within him as he carefully placed his mother back down on the floor.

"I don't understand! What happened to her?" He was beginning to hyperventilate.

I didn't understand, either. But when I looked down at her body, I grew cold, because suddenly, I knew. Dark gray streams of liquid were dripping heavily from her ears, pools of death that could only lead to one logical explanation. Queen Natasha had just been murdered by a color alchemist. I was sure that someone had messed with her blood. But who? I *knew* I hadn't done anything to hurt her. Sasha said there were others like me, ones who could get to the red. And yet, would Lucas believe that? Would Richard? Faulk?

Who did this?

I crawled backward, my knees sliding across the hard floor.

"No. No, I would never," I choked.

Lucas stared up at me as he lifted his mother's body into his arms. I just sat there. I couldn't bring myself to move.

A moment later, the doors swung open, and Faulk appeared in the living room. She was saying something, but I couldn't hear it. I couldn't understand anything, as if I were witnessing the whole scene from behind a murky sheet of glass.

Lucas stood up. I expected him to explain, but he moved right past me and just stood there, dazed, his mother's body in his arms. And that's when several palace guards stormed the room.

"Queen Natasha has been murdered," someone said. Faulk? I thought it was her voice.

The moment slowed further. My ears buzzed. I sat there motionless as the men swarmed the room, pushing me out of the way. Would they blame me? I found my back against the cool wall, as I stared at the world around me. I studied the plush white rug, the dark wood floors, the disturbed potted plant with its spilled soil...and Lucas. His black shoes, motionless, as he held his mother. The pool of her gun-metal blood widened between us.

TWENTY-FOUR

LUCAS

I failed. I went off on some hero's mission, leaving my mother stuck here. Alone. Vulnerable. Hadn't she tried to ask for help just this morning? She'd acted so strange, worse than ever. *I knew* something was wrong but I'd gone anyway. Too caught up with the Resistance. And even that turned out to be a bunch of lies. In the end, the Resistance had used me. They got Jessa. I got nothing. And now, my mother was dead.

This is my fault. I clutched her body, unable to let her go.

"The queen has been murdered," Faulk repeated.

Her words shook me. Looking around, I took in the wide pool of gray blood circling where I stood. The liquid gunmetal streamed out of my mother's ears, her mouth, her eye sockets. Alchemy.

"Someone's messed with her blood," I said to myself. But I looked up and saw Faulk nodding.

"How did I let this go unnoticed?" Faulk questioned. "It was my job to protect your family, Lucas. I'm sorry."

I never thought I would see the day that Faulk would apologize to me. I took no glory in it.

One of the royal officers reached out and took the body.

"It looks like the color has been drained from her blood." Thomas stepped into the room. "Red alchemy."

My eyes flashed to Jessa's. She shook her head more. She didn't speak, equally in shock at what we'd witnessed.

"Jessa Loxley, you're under arrest." Faulk shook her head.

Immediately, palace guards and royal officers swarmed her. They pulled her into standing and shoved her wrists into handcuffs.

"No, it's not her," I said. "She just met Natasha today. I think my mother has been having problems for a long time."

The guards continued, ignoring me.

"I didn't do it, I swear," Jessa cried.

"The headaches! Faulk, her headaches have been a problem for years. It couldn't have been Jessa."

Faulk peered at me briefly before motioning for Jessa to be taken away.

"Aren't you listening to me?"

Thomas stepped closer and wrapped his arm around my shoulder. It did little to comfort me. "She's the most likely suspect, Lucas. And she was on the scene when we arrived. What are we supposed to think?"

"I at least have to question her," Faulk said. With a pitying glance, she left.

I looked around, unable to process everything. There was blood everywhere. Some of it red, but mostly gray. I grimaced. I was covered.

And my mom is dead.

Someone had laid her on the floor with a sheet pulled over her body. More people were coming into the room now. Where was my father? Did he know yet?

"Why don't you go get cleaned up?" Thomas said. He motioned me away from the horrific scene. He walked me to my bedroom and ushered me inside.

"Take some time, all right, son? Take a shower. Find your bearings. I'll come and check on you soon."

He was right. With shaky hands, I closed my door behind him and stumbled to my bathroom.

I don't remember getting undressed. I don't remember stepping into the shower. But I must have, because some time later, I found myself sitting on the shower floor. The water beat down on my stoic body. When it turned lukewarm, I considered getting up. But I didn't move until cold water pelted me.

I got dressed. What was I supposed to do now? There was a light knock on my door, and Thomas let himself in.

"How're you holding up?"

"I don't know." It was true. I didn't.

"Your father's not doing so great either."

I wasn't ready to face him. As much as I hated Richard for the awful things he did, he was still my dad. I didn't want to see him grieving. For as many issues we had, he always seemed to have a strong bond with Mom. Losing her wouldn't be easy.

"What about Jessa?"

"There will be an investigation," Thomas said. "It could have been her."

"No, it wasn't. It was someone else. I know it."

"What do you mean?"

"This isn't new alchemy. Jessa's only been here for weeks. Whoever killed my mother has been tampering with her blood for years. So much of it was gray. That couldn't have happened quickly. Plus, why else would she have all those headaches?"

"The headaches were chronic. Unrelated."

"I don't think so. They were a side effect of red. Someone was getting inside her mind. To control her and then take her memories."

Thomas peered at me. "Why would someone do that? Why take that kind of risk?"

"I'm not sure. Information about my father, maybe? Secrets about the alchemists. It could be anything. We're royal. We know more than we let on. Controlling one of us? That's valuable."

I was pacing the room at this point. Thomas crossed to me.

"Sit down, son," he said, motioning to the bed. "You're getting worked up. We'll get to the bottom of it. Don't worry."

I did as he asked and sat on the edge of the bed. But I didn't want to calm down. I wanted to figure out this. Who murdered my mother? They wouldn't get away with it.

The old man sat down next to me, putting his arm around me again. We were never too close, but he was a family friend. He'd been with us my whole life. His comfort was the only thing I had. "Tell me again. What do you think Natasha knew?"

I shook my head. "Could be anything. Like I said, she was royal."

Suddenly, a sting ripped my bicep. I jumped. A small pinprick of blood bubbled up on my skin. *What the?* I glanced around, confused. That's when I saw it. The thin needle in Thomas's fingers. I jumped back, slamming into my headboard.

"Stay away from me!"

"Don't fight me on this, Lucas." Thomas lurched toward me. For an old man, he was strong. His body loomed over me. He reached his hand toward the trail of blood running down my arm.

"What are you doing?"

"You know too much," he said. "It's okay. I'll be more careful with you than I was with Natasha. I never meant for her to die. It's too bad. She was rather useful to me over the years."

"You! Why?"

"Don't you get it? She found out who I am." An alchemist. It made sense now. A royal officer for all these years, hiding magic. He couldn't do both. That wasn't allowed.

"Get away from me." I gritted my teeth, catching his hands as they reached for me. We were in a tug-of-war. He pushed toward my blood.

"You royals think you have all the power," he sneered. "But do you have any idea how powerful I am? I'm a royal officer *and* an alchemist. I'm not a slave to Richard. I've controlled Natasha for years."

"You're crazy! You had nothing to gain from that. And you killed her!"

We fought harder. Locked in a tight grip. But I could feel myself gaining headway. I was almost free.

"Don't be so dense. You know what they say? The woman controls the man. Natasha was always his weak spot. She could get him to do just about anything, especially in the early days. Let him believe he's in charge. I never cared. I was in control."

"You're sick." With one final push, I slid from the bed, ready to run. But he was too quick. He grabbed my arm and pulled me back. His fingers were slick against my blood. The connection was instant.

"You lose," he said. "Now it's time to forget this conversation."

I could feel the alchemy starting. It was as if bits and pieces of this whole exchange were fading away with each passing moment. I reached out, looking for something, anything to help me. My free hand gripped my pillowcase.

"You don't know who I really am. You're convinced Jessa killed your mother. In fact, you're going to lead the charge against her. Make sure she's executed. We don't need another red alchemist around here."

I nodded my head.

He let go and stood up. Bits of gray blood were smeared across my arm.

"Clean yourself up. I was never here." He didn't even look back as he left the room.

I sat motionless.

All along the answer was right in front of me. Of course I wasn't the only alchemist hiding in plain sight. All these years Thomas was my favorite royal officer. I'd thought he was kind, but he was more evil than anyone. His need for power had caused my mother's death.

I slowly let the pillowcase loose in my hand. As it unfolded I stared at the gray handprint left behind. White. It was my biggest secret.

White was a shield. It was also the alchemy that came easiest to me. I'd used it growing up to keep myself from suspicion. I could hide my alchemy because of white. It was my buffer, my protection. Earlier I'd revealed myself when I'd hidden our helicopter from radar. And again, just now, white saved me.

What Thomas didn't know was that I too was an alchemist. He thought he was controlling my mind, erasing my memories, but I was fighting back. Pulling white into my body through that pillow, I'd blocked him. I shuddered to imagine what would have happened if I'd failed.

I jumped up and bolted out of my room.

◼

I went to the basement prison, looking for the action. Following the commotion, I found my father and Faulk surrounded by royal officers. Thomas stood front and center. The group was huddled outside a cell that I assumed was Jessa's.

"Son," Richard looked at me, his eyes bloodshot. "What are you doing down here? Go back upstairs."

"I know who killed Mom."

Thomas smiled faintly. "Jessa? Yes, we know."

I paused, staring into his dark eyes. How had I missed it before? His kindness wasn't kindness at all. It was manipulation. Arrogance.

"No. It wasn't Jessa. Thomas murdered her. He confessed."

Thomas took a step back, his eyes darting around. "That's ridiculous."

I looked from my father to Faulk. They were skeptical. "He's an alchemist. He just tried to manipulate my blood. He wanted to control me. But whatever he did, he messed up." I held up my arm. The evidence was all right there. I never had cleaned off the mess of gray.

Thomas sprang into action. He pulled open Jessa's door and ran into her cell. She was still handcuffed, still dressed in the gray prison outfit. He yanked her into his arms. Her body jarred violently in reaction. "I'll kill her. I know you need her. She'll be dead if you don't let me go."

"Thomas," Richard replied, "don't you dare."

"I mean it. I'll break her neck."

"Drop her," Faulk yelled.

"Then let me go. Let me out of this Godforsaken place."

There was no chance at that. He'd murdered the queen. What did he think he could gain from this? I watched Jessa carefully. If anything happened to her, I wouldn't survive it. I'd already lost my mother. I couldn't lose her too.

Jessa whipped her head back. A loud crack sounded. Blood gushed down Thomas's face. He swore, throwing her to the ground. His face dripped blood. He jumped back on her just as we swarmed the room.

"Stay," Jessa yelled as her hand connected with his bloody face. Her red alchemy went into full force in an instant.

Thomas froze.

My father and Faulk stared at the pair. It was all out in the open now. Here was the proof of Jessa's magic. Red alchemy. Blood alchemy.

■

It wasn't long before Thomas was arrested and thrown into a gray prison cell. I didn't know what would happen to him, but I hoped it ended in execution. He murdered my mother. He deserved nothing less. I was relieved to have caught her killer. But even still, her death rocked me.

I hid out for a couple days, grieving in my bedroom. I couldn't eat, sleep, or talk to anyone. I didn't know where to go from here. It was just me and my father now. A man I'd spent the last couple months of my life spying on. A man I no longer respected or trusted.

Pulling myself from my hole, I made it out to the gardens. Fall was approaching and the change of seasons left me depressed. I would give anything to go back and save my mother. But it was too late. I never saw what was right in front of me. And she was dead.

I found my favorite clearing and sat on a stone bench. I concentrated on my breath. In and out. I tried to picture my future. I saw nothing.

"Hey stranger," Jessa said. She walked into the clearing tentatively, wringing her hands. She was dressed in black alchemist gear, her brown curls loose down her back. "I saw you walking out here. I thought I would come and say hello."

I didn't know what to say.

"I'm sorry about your mother." She sat down next to me. "I just wanted you to know that I've been thinking about you. Lucas, you're not alone." Slowly she wrapped her arms around my torso in a side-hug. I breathed in her familiar scent, welcoming her touch.

"I can't believe after all that, we still ended up back here," I said.

"I know."

"I'm not going to work with the Resistance anymore," I whispered.

"I know."

"But you are?"

She nodded and looked up at me, her blue eyes glassy with tears. I hated that answer but knew there wasn't anything I could do. She'd made her choice. I'd made mine too. I leaned down and gave her a small kiss. She was the only good thing left in my life. I needed her.

We held each other as the day faded to night. There were no words between us, and a million reasons why we couldn't be together. But still, we were fighting for the chance.

EPILOGUE

SASHA

I honestly couldn't remember the last time I'd slept so deeply, without the constant worry that my whole life could come crashing down at any moment. It had been years since I'd been back here. Years since I'd felt this kind of safety.

Upon waking, I went outside. There was something about the mountains that brought me back to my center. I stared up at them and smiled, breathing in the fresh morning stillness and allowing the stress of everything I'd just endured to melt off me in waves.

"Those aren't mountains, you know," Hank's gravelly voice said from behind. "They're hills. If you want to see real mountains, you've got to go out west. The Rockies will blow your socks off."

I laughed. "I wish I could, Hank, but there's nothing that far west for me anymore. No reason to go when New Colony's capital city is near here. I'm a freedom fighter now, remember?"

I winked and put the words "freedom fighter" in air quotations, even though we both knew I wasn't joking. None of us were joking about this.

"For the view." He sat next to me on the fallen tree stump. "You should go for the view. It would be worth it, just for that."

"So I take it they got back safely?" I asked, changing the subject.

I was referring to Lucas and Jessa getting back to the capital city under Hank's supervision. He nodded, and as the moment stretched, a knowing silence filled the air. We watched the peaceful quiet morning that could only be found in places like these. Places away from New Colony, the guardians, and everything else a part of that life.

"Are you going to make me ask?" he said.

I folded my arms. I already knew what was coming. We could pretend that I'd been returned to base camp because of a blown cover. It wasn't entirely true though. Faulk didn't know for *sure* that I had taken that helicopter. I was here for something more. No one had to spell it out for me.

"They abandoned me. And now you expect me to forgive them just like that? Just pretend like nothing happened?"

He shook his head. "You don't have to forgive them, but we need you to push your feelings aside and work with the girl. For the good of everyone."

And what about what I need? I wanted to scream. They hadn't even recognized me yesterday. Never even blinked twice.

I only nodded.

"Thank you, Frankie." He stood up. "I knew we could count on you."

"Don't call me that. I haven't gone by that name in years."

He stared at me for a moment. "So you're not going to tell them?"

"I'm not telling them anything. Why should I? They don't care about Francesca anymore. And neither do I."

I stood and brushed the sticky pine needles and grit from my jeans. I turned to Hank, one of the few people who knew me from before, who was with me from the beginning. "Please, just let me be Sasha."

His expression was pained, but he only nodded. I knew he wanted to say something more. But what else was there?

I guess, of all people, maybe Hank understood me. He was the one who had gotten me out of the GC when I was still only a small child. He'd brought me back to the people here and taught me everything I knew. Hank became a father to me when I had no one else. When my real father had forgotten about me. When my real parents had let me be taken from them without so much as putting up a fight.

They never even tried to save you. They just moved on with their lives. Raising Jessa, forgetting you, and having another baby. You were replaced. These were the words I'd repeated to myself for years.

"When do I start training her?"

Lacey. The little sister I never met until yesterday. And even just during the short hike back here from the landing spot, Lacey had reminded me so much of Jessa. I had left Jessa as a toddler and didn't get to see her grow up. But still, little things about Lacey bore striking similarities to Jessa. It had nearly killed me to keep my anger at my so-called parents in as I'd led them back to camp, but I'd somehow managed to put on a show for them. I had managed to keep my cool.

And the whole time, they had no idea who I really was.

"As soon as you're ready to start training her, we'll get started."

But that was the tricky thing about this whole situation, wasn't it? We both knew there was no such thing as being fully ready. Not really. Not for us. There was just sucking it up and doing what needed to be done.

I peered back through the trees, into the brilliant wilderness of the forest, and drew in a slow breath.

"I'm ready now."

FRACTURE

THE COLOR ALCHEMIST BOOK TWO

ONE

JESSA

I bit my lip and rested my forehead on the large oak door. My first test in color alchemy waited on the other side. Nervous energy poured down my body in electric currents, setting me on edge. This was the beginning of my new life. I tapped my foot, ignoring the conversation that buzzed around me. I was surrounded by people who were taking bets—not on *if* I would fail, but *how fast* it would happen.

The other alchemists wanted me gone because I wasn't like them. They'd grown up together, and I was the new girl, reminding them of everything they'd missed out on. Not to mention, a typical alchemist spent years honing their magic before initiation. So it came as no surprise that my quick rise into magic wasn't well received. Of course, the king loved it. Everyone else? Not so much. Perhaps it was only natural for them to dislike the person who changed the way things were done—who cut in line. Because if I was initiated so quickly, then what else would change?

Ugh, this is so not how I thought my life would turn out.

As a prima ballerina, I'd been on the perfect track to living my dream. Sure, at times it isolated me from my peers. My single-minded passion wasn't relatable to the average teenager. Dance was my world, and I loved it. But everything had been taken away from me the day my alchemy was discovered. The last few months had been torture. But, as devastating as it was, I'd finally accepted that my life was bigger than the stage: I had a king to take down.

I ignored the cold glares and hostile mutterings of the many guardians lining the corridor outside the testing room while we waited. Guardians. That's what we called alchemists after they initiated into the Guardians of Color—GC for short. It was the elite organization, ruled by New Colony's royal family. The GC kept our kingdom powerful and prosperous.

Or so they liked to think. I knew better.

"She's going to crash and burn," someone snickered from behind. A chorus of laugher broke out.

Back straight, head up; I couldn't let them get to me. Still, an unwanted twinge of longing burned inside. Okay, if I was honest with myself, I shouldn't care about their approval, but part of me did anyway. I hated that. I had a mission to complete. Getting initiated was the first step. Once that was done, King Richard would put me to work on GC assignments and heaven knows what else. The plan was to become stronger. I would get close enough to him to use my red alchemy against him, ultimately ending his corruption.

I shuddered as I let out an overdue breath. Defeating the king and his many loyal, some even magical, subjects was a big mission for anyone to accomplish, let alone for a new alchemist. If caught, I'd undoubtedly be killed for treason. The worried thoughts crossed my mind on more than one occasion. *Is it really worth the risk? Maybe I should have stayed with my parents and the Resistance…*

I cut off the thoughts right there. No regrets.

I focused again on the door in front of me. On the other side, my first test would either end in success or disaster. I sucked in a breath, hoping for the former. I straightened my spine and turned around to face the crowd. A sea of faces glared back at me. Faulk and a couple of her officers approached, arms crossed, brows furrowed in skeptical lines. They took their jobs *very* seriously. It was almost comical, except they had the power to ruin me and we all knew it.

Stand tall, Jessa. Don't let them win.

"How's it going, Faulk? What's new in Officer Land?" I smiled inwardly at my sarcasm, knowing it would drive her nuts.

"Don't be cute," she replied curtly. Her eyes strained as she sized me up. I assumed the death of the queen and subsequent revelation that her own right-hand man, Thomas, had been the one to do it, were weighing on her career. I refused to feel sorry for her. At every turn, Faulk had made it clear that she wanted me locked up. Ever since the day she first met me, she'd hated my very existence. I was a dark stain on her otherwise shining record, the alchemist girl she'd missed.

The one who got away—kind of.

"We'll be watching you from the observation room," she continued, jabbing her finger at me as she spoke. "Don't try anything stupid. You're to get in and out as quickly as possible, obviously using alchemy to do it."

"I'll be fine," I said, keeping my voice level.

Of course they chose to keep the details of the tests a secret. If I knew what I was walking into, I wouldn't feel so unsettled.

"Good luck," Faulk said bitterly. Then she and her underlings marched away and through a door farther down the hallway, slamming it behind them. The observation room, no doubt.

"Are you scared?" a voice snickered.

"You should be," another called from the group.

These lame alchemists apparently had nothing better to do.

"She's not ready," another added with a chuckle.

I didn't bother to reply because I sort of agreed with them. Since when had I ever been ready for this? *Ready* was of little consequence. The king wouldn't wait for *ready*. Neither would I.

I pushed open the heavy metallic door, anxious to discover what color I'd be working with first. I had to show strong proficiency in at least three colors to make it to initiation. I knew red and white weren't on that list, as those magics weren't accessible to the typical alchemist. In fact, I was one of the only known alchemists able to access red. And white? That was uncharted territory as well, though Lucas had his own closely hidden ability with it. That left me with purple, blue, green, yellow, and orange. There would be tests for all of those. Three was doable. However, uncertainty burned in my body.

I stepped inside.

The room was dark. As I moved in farther, a rush of humid air kicked my senses into awareness. A large space, bigger than my old dance studio. A gymnasium, I guessed. Harsh chemicals assaulted my lungs. Chlorine?

I took another tentative step forward. Blazing lights shot through my vision, and I stumbled back. *Of course...*

I exhaled slowly. It was only a swimming pool, nothing to worry about. And *yellow*.

Yellow flowers, plants, and stones lined the edge of the pool. My gaze rapidly raced across the room, assessing the situation. They wanted me to perform yellow alchemy, but what was the test? What did yellow have *anything* to do with swimming?

A digital clock illuminated red numbers on a black square screen across from the pool. A countdown: 20:00.

19:59...

Twenty minutes! Only twenty minutes to accomplish what exactly?

The door slammed. A loud click echoed through the room. Panic threatened to tear me apart. I was locked in here. *Why?*

Breathing deeply, I peered over the edge of the pool. Hundreds of keys twinkled in a layer of scattered gold across the cobalt blue tiles, at least fifteen feet under water, like spilled treasure. The purpose of the test tumbled into place in my mind. It was so obvious.

I wasn't a good swimmer, but I needed to get to those keys. Fast.

I wracked my brain, drawing upon all my studies. What did I know about yellow? It was connected to energy and willpower, and, most importantly, it was an amplifier. Yellow alchemy had given me the strength to break through the wall surrounding the palace. Of course, I'd *wanted* to break through that wall. That was critical. Still, it was solid stone, and I'd been able to crumble it with superhuman strength. It was just one of the many miraculous things alchemy could do. At the time, I was convinced Lacey's survival depended on me getting to the other side of that wall.

Could I draw upon the same inner willpower again?

This time, it was *my* survival at stake. I had to pass this test. Although I was a dancer and quite athletic, I wasn't fond of water. I was a terrible swimmer.

Finding the right key to open the door would take time, and the eighteen minutes I had left wouldn't cut it under normal circumstances.

I inhaled a deep breath. *You can do this. No more analyzing.*

I ripped a flower from its stem and crushed it between two fingers. It only took a moment for the yellow to lift from the broken petals and rise into the air. Another moment and the color drifted into my body. I closed my eyes, breathing in the magic, willing the yellow to enter my lungs, my bloodstream, anything to make me a faster, stronger, and better swimmer. A burst of adrenaline pulsed through my veins. The magic ignited.

I dove into the water.

Swimming down, I ignored the immediate sweep of ice that attacked my body. The water was frigid! The biting sensation cut across my skin like a million needles, stinging. I fought the distraction, the instinct to flee, and swam deeper. I refused to be bothered by the black uniform that weighed me down. Determination raced through every cell of my body. I would *not* fail.

If I ever wanted to see my family again, to help Lacey, to save New Colony from the manipulation of the GC and the king, then I had to keep swimming. And I wasn't alone. Knowing an entire resistance of people was out there somewhere bolstered my spirits. I didn't know them all yet, but I felt their solidarity with every stroke.

Settling on the bottom of the pool, the water pushed me down, even colder than before. It oppressed all my senses, caging me in. A thread of panic stitched its way into my burning chest, binding me. I forced myself to focus on the yellow magic supporting me and allowed it to strengthen my resolve. I grabbed as many keys as I could, pulling them into a makeshift pocket by tugging my shirt up around my torso. The keys were slippery and harder to pick up than I'd anticipated. I was running out of breath. I needed to move. The urge to breathe overpowered me. My eyeballs twitched, and the weight of the water caused panic to rip through my body. I positioned my feet on the bottom, pushed off, and rocketed to the surface. I flew out of the water, yelping in surprise, and landed with a thud on the concrete.

Wet keys clattered in a golden arc around me.

I patted my body frantically, expecting pain. There was none. Nothing was broken either. I couldn't say the same for the concrete floor. A crack had formed where my body had taken the biggest hit.

Whoa... turns out I can control yellow alchemy. I paused for a momentary happy dance. *Go me!* Faulk was probably gritting her teeth in irritation by now. I grinned at the crushed floor, not hiding my gleeful smirk. I was going to own this test, and she was going to watch me.

I moved to pick keys up off the floor, my pace infinitely faster with the magic pulsing through me. With every handful, I sprinted to the door and tried to maneuver the lock into position with the different keys. None worked. Once I'd exhausted them all, I took another deep breath and dove back into the frosty water.

It wasn't just *possible* that I wouldn't make it out in twenty minutes; it was *probable.* Everywhere I looked, more keys reflected back at me. I swam anyway. As I got closer, it was as if they were mocking me and multiplying. Just how many were down here? Worry snaked through my thoughts, twisting me up and threatening to slow me down. Despite everything, the yellow energy kept me focused, moving quickly. I drew on it, the magic igniting confidence in me. And with each key I scooped up, I felt closer to my goal.

A few more flowers and three more trips into the pool, and I was starting to feel the magic wane. I was tired. The keys were beginning to slip through my fingers. I let out a frustrated yelp as yet another key proved incompatible with the lock. I shook away the urge to give up and pushed yet another into the keyhole. It clicked into the lock and turned with ease. My jaw dropped. This was it! I peered back—still ten minutes on the clock. I couldn't believe my luck. The tension in my body was immediately washed away.

"Take that," I muttered, "stupid lock."

I pushed open the door and stepped into the crowd. Their conversations silenced as shock filled their stupid faces. No doubt they didn't understand how a novice like me could complete such a difficult task.

"What? She didn't fail?" a female voice blurted, disbelieving, as the group stared.

"Nope," I boldly responded. "I didn't even lose my breath."

Then I glanced around at the thirty or so people, mostly teenagers, and winked. Okay, a little immature of me to rub it in their faces. But what did they expect? Just because I wasn't as trained as they were, I wasn't as powerful? Alchemy was still scary to me, but like it or not, it came naturally. I'd tried to fight my magic for so long, but I couldn't anymore. I was hell-bent on learning to control it so I wouldn't end up hurting someone again. I needed to be here for my own good. I needed to learn. And I wanted the chance.

A flip of silky yellow hair caught my attention. The flawless complexion behind them was familiar. Brooke. She'd made it clear she didn't like me, so I wasn't surprised to see she'd come to watch me fail. Too bad she hadn't gotten her wish. She leaned into Reed, whispering. She flipped her shiny hair back *again* and sneered at me. "You think you're something special, don't you?"

I was dang tired of her nasty comments. I'd mostly kept my mouth shut, trying to take the higher road, but I couldn't stand it any longer. "I don't know what your problem is with me, Brooke, but get over yourself and accept that I'm good enough for the GC." I glanced at Reed, my former friend. "That goes for both of you."

She laughed. "Being a guardian is about more than alchemy. It's about loyalty. We all know about your pathetic attempt to run away."

I glanced at the other alchemists, noting the interest rippling through the crowd. This was a dangerous topic. I needed to end it here and now. Of course, I didn't. "What's your point?"

"Loyal alchemists don't run away from the palace. They're honored to be here! You broke the rules. And we want to know why."

I held back a response. I couldn't give anything away. My secrets were more important than my ego, and even though I badly wanted to set Brooke straight, I didn't know how many of these alchemists were here to spy on me. I had to assume their loyalty was to Richard and Faulk.

It was possible some of them could be Resistance members, but I couldn't trust anyone until I knew for sure. Shaking my head, I pushed past her and through the hostile crowd. I held off the impulse to shiver, eager to get to my room. The adrenaline from the yellow was fading fast, and I needed to get out of my wet clothes and into a hot shower as quickly as possible.

"Jessa, fortunately for you, you've proven proficient in yellow."

I turned to the agitated voice, my internal guard on red alert. Faulk stood at the edge of the crowd, surrounded by her officers.

"If I didn't know you better, I'd think you were giving me a compliment."

She was the head of the royal officers, and their number one job was to keep the alchemists in line. In her mind, I wasn't an asset. I was a liability. I didn't have as much control over my alchemy as she would have preferred—not to mention, I wasn't easily controlled. And that's what really bothered her.

Complimenting me? Never.

She frowned, studying me. "Brooke is right about the importance of loyalty in a guardian. I guess we'll see how loyal you are during your next test."

I could recognize a threat when I heard one. My brain scanned through everything I knew about alchemy and loyalty, but I found no definite link.

"Report to my office tomorrow morning for your second test."

Tomorrow? A ripple of exhaustion pulsed through my muscles at the thought. I couldn't imagine being ready for another test so quickly. "I'll be there." I nodded with a slow grin. I needed her to believe I was on her side. I had to gain her trust, as impossible as that seemed to me now. Passing these tests would be the first step.

She turned to go. "Oh, and Jessa, make sure to eat a good breakfast first. You'll need the energy." She smiled coolly and left me to my doubts.

●

I sat, soaking in the shower, allowing the hot steam from the water to thaw my frozen body, the adrenaline melting away. In the heat of the moment, I hadn't allowed myself to fully consider the ramifications of my first test. The water had been frigid, nearly icy. And those cursed keys had been *everywhere*. If I hadn't gotten control over the yellow alchemy so quickly, I would have failed. True, I only had to prove myself in three colors, and I had five chances. But I couldn't afford any mistakes. And that cold water? It was dangerous! If the first test was that hard, *that dangerous*, how bad would the second one be?

The water began to lose its warmth; I peeled my exhausted butt off the floor and practically crawled out of the shower. I forced myself to dry off and dress in the black guardian uniform. Although I wasn't technically one of them yet, I'd been allowed to wear the clothing for training. It was customary, and I'd found I actually *liked* it. The black material was surprisingly comfortable and easy to move in. And since it was black, it didn't interfere with my magic. Alchemy required that I physically touch color, and more than once, I'd inadvertently used the color of my clothing. It was rare to be able to manipulate synthetics, but I could do it. The whole reason I'd blown my cover so easily to the royals in the first place had been because I'd turned my lavender ballet costume into a ball of volatile energy. I sucked in a breath. I couldn't allow myself to think about ballet anymore. It used to be my life, but I needed to forget about it.

Peering around, I took in my newly acquired surroundings. I still had my own space, thankfully, but I wasn't near the royal wing any longer. The luxurious room Lucas had set me up in upon my arrival to the palace was long gone. Now, I was housed in enemy territory: a small dorm located in the GC wing. The room was stark white and boxlike, with a bathroom and closet attached. Not that I was complaining. It was nice, but living in a box, surrounded by a bunch of less-than-trustworthy alchemists, bothered me to no end.

That didn't change the fact that I was lucky to be here instead of in the prison below the palace. At least this way, I would be right where I needed to be.

I needed to become a guardian.

I didn't fit in with them, true. But I was trying, wasn't I? My mind flashed to the scene earlier with Brooke. *Okay, I will try harder.* But more importantly, the king wanted me initiated. Faulk had insisted I pass the required alchemy tests first, but when push came to shove, I was sure Richard would have his way. He was our *king* after all. He wanted me for nefarious reasons. It wouldn't be long before he'd be calling on me to use my red alchemy.

I shuddered at the thought. It was like a stain I couldn't wipe from my mind.

I quickly applied my usual amount of light makeup and pulled a hairbrush through my unruly locks. My hair was always a mess, especially wet, and despite the thick curls, I had what my mom called a "tender head". I seriously hated to brush it after showering, and *especially* after swimming. All those chemicals wreaked havoc with it. I tried to focus on the task, but the pain of the movements did little to distract me from my anxiety.

Red alchemy was mostly unknown. I was only one of two alchemists in King Richard's possession who had access to the magic. The other was the imprisoned officer, Thomas. Red was the color of tribe, family, and passion. I didn't know everything it was capable of, but one thing I knew for sure, it could be used to control someone's mind—pulling the red from their blood to complete the horrifying task—and I'd done it three times now. First with Lacey by accident, second with an unknowing Reed, and the last time was to an officer in training who'd attacked me. *That* time had been on purpose. Once I connected with her blood, it was easy. I told her to sit down and begin counting so I could get away. She'd done exactly what I'd said, trance-like.

Thinking about that moment brought out a dark side in me, a shadow self. Because, although I hated what I'd done, a small part was excited by the power. And thirsty for more. It left me breathless.

I shook the feeling away, reminding myself of the truth. Manipulating the color from blood had deadly consequences.

Thomas had used red alchemy to the point of utter destruction. Alchemists weren't allowed to be officers, but he'd kept his magic hidden, using red to manipulate Queen Natasha. To get her to influence the king. Thomas went too far one too many times with red alchemy and killed Natasha. I'd seen it myself. The way she'd buckled under her own weight, the gray blood dripping from her eyes and ears. Being pulled away from the scene, watching the horrified look on Lucas's face, it had rocked me to my core. Luckily, Lucas had quickly discovered the truth. Thomas was now locked up, awaiting execution.

Again and again, the "what if" scenarios haunted me. What if Lucas hadn't figured it out? What if he still thought I'd killed his mother? My eyes burned.

And now here I was, training with the guardians to use my alchemy in service of the crown. The very crown that was killing its own people. That was the other startling reason I'd decided to join the GC—to help the Resistance take him down. King Richard was using the alchemists to interrogate people, control them, and in many instances, drain the color right out from their land and kill them. The memory of the shadow lands sent a chill through my body. It was wrong to utterly destroy like that. I didn't care what Richard's reasons were.

He had to be stopped, and I had to do it.

A soft knock on the door startled me from my thoughts. I quickly attempted to brush through my wet hair one last time. The brush literally got stuck. I cringed and pulled it out. Giving up, I moved to answer the door. Lucas stood in the entrance with his hands buried deeply in his pockets. He rocked back on his heels and stared at me, his signature smirk tugging at his lips.

"I heard you made quite the splash," he said.

"Oh, shut up." I laughed and opened the door wider. I adored that about him—his corny jokes *and* signature smirk. But I'd never tell. His ego would probably suffocate us all.

He peered around the hallway, making sure he wasn't being watched by any guards, and stepped into the room. He usually had a few with him, but it was his palace, so he had a way of extending his freedom to be alone when he needed it. Lately, he'd been using that freedom a lot.

Closing the door soundlessly, he pulled me into his arms.

"You smell amazing." He sighed. I snuggled into his broad chest. His own heady smell was equally intoxicating.

Since his mother's death, he'd been coming to see me daily. We never talked about the Resistance, or her untimely murder. Instead, we spent most of our time kissing, pushing our nagging thoughts to the furthest corners of our minds as we got lost in each other. I had to admit, I felt guilty knowing that my feelings for him were so convoluted. It shouldn't be so easy for me to want him.

I couldn't seem to help myself. I wanted Lucas. The knowledge terrified me. But also thrilled me.

We had a deeper connection than anything I'd experienced. He attracted me into his world like a magnet. It certainly didn't bother me that he was the most gorgeous man I'd ever seen. But he was also much kinder than he appeared on the gossip feeds. I didn't know how to explain it, but he was just so different from what I'd expected. And Jasmine, my handler with the Resistance, wanted us together. So that made it even easier to justify my growing feelings.

It also made them more complicated…

I couldn't forget *who* he was, no matter how hard I tried. He was a member of the Heart family. A prince. And his father was my sworn enemy. Could I still trust him? That was the question that kept twisting inside. It was no secret between us that Lucas wanted me to distance myself from the Resistance. He believed we could stop his father without them. He'd hated how the Resistance had used him. They brought him in without fully trusting him or giving him the information he needed, and in the end, it had backfired on them. They lost his loyalty. I was supposed to get it back.

I gripped his cotton shirt in my fingers, biting my lip. True, I felt a little guilty about that one.

And then there was the hard fact that his father had forbidden him from dating alchemists. After his relationship with Sasha, albeit fake, Richard had put his foot down. Richard believed that alchemists had no business wearing a crown. They were meant to serve the crown only, and the officers who swarmed the palace made sure that happened. Little did Richard know, his own son was an alchemist. Few people knew Lucas's secret.

"What are you thinking?" he asked.

I didn't know what to say.

He held me like I was a life raft and he was stranded at sea. And I longed for it, despite my better judgment. Lucas wasn't supposed to touch me, nor be alone in my bedroom with me. Holding me. Kissing me.

It was all so confusing!

Yet here we were again, wrapped up in each other. He pushed me against the door and bit down on my bottom lip. A rush of adrenaline pulsed through my veins. His hands moved to hold my hips, his fingers brushing against the exposed skin under my shirt, his body flush against mine.

I sighed and inched back, staring into his hooded eyes.

Sometimes I needed to put some distance between us, unable to handle the heat. I needed to clear my head—to stay in control. "How are you?" I asked, stepping back fully this time. I felt the distance like a knife.

A pang of sadness flashed through his eyes, and he ran his hands through his dark hair. God, I loved his hair. Even that movement attracted me to him, his hands so different from my own, so entirely…masculine.

Yup, I had it bad.

"I'm doing better. *You* make everything better."

And I thought he did too.

I smiled, shyly. "You know I'm here for you if you ever need to talk."

He nodded and paced to the window, visibly shutting down. I followed, a step behind. I wanted to comfort him, to ease his pain and the worry I had for him. He was using our relationship as his escape, and as much as I enjoyed our time together—maybe too much—I didn't want him to feel alone in this. I wanted to help.

"I don't know a whole lot about grieving," I continued carefully, "but I don't think you're wrong for not wanting to talk about it. I just want you to know, you can, if you want. Talk to me, that is. About…everything, or anything. Or nothing…" I gritted my teeth, annoyed with my rambling. *Right about now would be a good time to shut your mouth, Jessa.*

"I just want to get the execution over with. Thomas needs to pay for what he did." He turned and locked eyes with me. I let the words sink in.

That wouldn't bring Natasha back. I sucked in a breath. We both knew the execution wouldn't change what happened. And I highly doubted it would even make him feel better. Still, I was sure if it had been my mother, I'd want retribution too. I needed to support him, even if the idea of an execution made me want to hide under my blankets.

"He will," I said. "He'll die, because *he* was the one who did this. He's the one who did that to her blood. He pushed her too far, nobody else."

Lucas shook his head and moved further away. "I shouldn't have been so naïve. It was right in front of my face, in my own home." He slammed his palm against the window frame. "And I didn't catch it."

"Don't do this to yourself."

"I can't talk about this with you," he replied.

"Okay. That's okay. But let me just say one thing and then I'll shut up, okay?" He didn't move. "This. Is. Not. Your. Fault. And if you decide you need someone to talk to, all I am saying is I'm here."

Did he blame *me* for what happened? I'd wanted to ask, but was too afraid of what it would do to our relationship. Had I been too much of a distraction for him? If he hadn't been so wrapped up in my drama, in saving me from Faulk that day, maybe he really would have been able to save his mother. I sucked in a breath and pushed those thoughts deep into my soul.

He finally looked at me, his expression melting. "I know what you're thinking. It's written all over your face." He strode across the small room in his usual swagger, placing his hands on my shoulders. The warmth of them automatically sent a wave of comfort through my body. I leaned in. "But if anyone's to blame, it's me, not you. If I had been honest with you from the start, you wouldn't have left like that. You were only trying to help your family."

The guilt attacked me then. I felt my chin quiver as I fought the urge to turn away. Honesty?

How honest was it for me to be with him when it was the Resistance who'd ordered it? When Jasmine had told me to be with him, I'd been upset with him at the time. I wasn't mad anymore. So much had happened between then and now, and anger had left my heart. Still, how would he react if he knew our relationship was somehow part of the Resistance's plans? No doubt he'd end it.

Only a few weeks ago, I was convinced he'd been too close with Sasha for my comfort. I swallowed, grimacing at my behavior. I'd always thought boys were confusing but maybe it was us girls who were the source of the trouble. It wasn't long ago that I wanted nothing to do with him. Now, every time he sought me out, I easily allowed him to sweep me into his world, his arms, his scent, his mouth…

I met his pewter eyes and caught the flash that turned them dark. Unable to resist any longer, I pressed my lips to his.

●

The next morning came too quickly. I squared my shoulders and strode into the officers' headquarters, central in the GC wing. I ignored the furtive glances of the underlings and stalked up to Faulk's lair. Technically it was her office, but since I considered her the predator and me the prey, *lair* had a nice ring to it. There was little I could do to prepare today. Could they really judge loyalty using an alchemy test? No matter what faced me, I wouldn't let them break me.

Upon entering the office, I bristled at the occupants waiting for me. Faulk stood along the back wall with two hulking officers. Reed lounged next to Lucas. And none other than King Richard sat on Faulk's desk, his eyes trained on me.

"We usually leave blue for the end of the trials, but Faulk thinks we ought to get it taken care of quickly with your…situation," Richard said. He looked the part of a handsome businessman, in charge and decisive. And most importantly, at the moment, he had the power.

His eyes narrowed further as I held his gaze. *Show no fear. Show no fear. Show no fear…* He had to believe I was under his control, but that didn't mean I had to cower. He wielded his power darkly and would stop at nothing to gain more. But he couldn't hold it forever. Eventually his people would see him for what he was, and he would lose everything.

I peeked at Lucas, who stood in the corner of the room. Somehow he fit in well with the surroundings, all glass and steel and modern. His expression was one of cool interest. It was an act, since the true nature of our relationship was a secret. Or maybe I was reading the situation all wrong. Maybe he knew any chance of my passing today was hopeless.

"Blue is an unlikely color for most alchemists to control. We don't expect you to be able to do much with it." Richard smiled. He spoke smoothly, unruffled by the situation.

"So why am I here?" I cocked my head.

"When we already know an alchemist can't manipulate blue, we don't just drop it altogether. How fair would that be? No, we test it in a *different* way."

"I don't understand."

Reed stepped forward, smirking, and I suddenly understood. I understood all too well. He raised an eyebrow, and I groaned.

Blue was the color of communication. It was used to spy on conversations, to make arguments extremely persuasive, and it was incredibly useful for one other thing. My mind flashed to the memory of Reed in my bedroom, drilling me for information, and how easily I'd almost given it to him. The magic had gotten a hold of me, and I'd *wanted* to tell him everything. I'd been persuaded to open my big mouth and spill all my secrets. Luckily I'd been strong enough to hold off, and he'd gotten spooked and left without getting what he'd wanted.

But this time he wasn't going anywhere.

This time the interrogation wasn't a secret to anyone, least of all me. Could I convince them I was loyal? Icy fear prickled up my spine. This blue alchemy test was more than just a test of skill; it was a test to see if I deserved to keep my life.

"Have a seat, Jessa," Richard said. "Let's get started."

TWO

SASHA

We had the same eyes, the three of us. Eyes an indecisive blue that shifted shades depending on arbitrary things like the light or clothing or if our hair was down. Bright, cheery sky blue one minute, dark, angry ocean the next. Every time I worked with Lacey, I stared at her eyes, those six-year-old versions of my own. So innocent. I'd search them out, and before long, I'd be analyzing our similarities and differences. Her hair was lighter than my golden blonde locks, also tamed like mine. Jessa's hair had taken a different turn, raven dark and unruly. And yet we all had identical blue eyes and the same pale complexion. Traits that came from our father. Well, *their* father. I refused to consider him family.

"Are you ready to try again?" I asked Lacey. *I'm here to do a job. I'm her teacher and that's it. No more gawking.*

"You promise it's not going to hurt them?" She peered at the smattering of wildflowers growing at our feet.

"No, come here." I sat in front of the flowers and patted the space next to me. She joined, tentative at first, legs crossed, eyes still etched with worry. "I'll show you how to do it."

I grabbed hold of a tall, green blade of grass. It was wild, scratchy, and dry between my fingertips. Without much effort, I maneuvered the color out. Green alchemy was as natural as breathing, but I was careful not to take too much and risk killing the grass completely. Once the perfect amount of emerald energy danced in the air, I turned my attention to the overgrowth. Winter was coming, and naturally the flowers were dying off. For the purposes of this exercise, I set my intention and used the green to heal a few of the neighboring flowers. They perked up, visibly rising, restored to perfect health.

Lacey smiled with the kind of fascination that only young children could pull off. "See? That wasn't so bad," I said. "Are you ready to try?" I'd taken hardly any green from the plant, leaving only a small patch of gray. Not enough to kill it, but I also knew it would never be the same.

They never were.

"Why does it look like that?" Lacey asked. She was nearly seven and observant enough to notice the trace of gray.

"There's a price to pay for everything, kid." I smirked at my dry humor. She didn't get it. *All right then, let's try again.* "In order to give to something, like making these flowers feel healthy again, we have to take from something else. This grass gave a little bit of its life so that the flowers can keep living. Do you understand?"

"Does it have to be that way?" She bit her lip, her small face pinched. Her worry over one blade of grass was so ridiculously cute; I had to hold back a laugh. I didn't want to hurt her tender feelings, as innocent as they were.

"For what we do, yes. Alchemy is magic. And magic is never free. Taking color is the payment. But we can always try our best to make sure we don't kill anything completely. And the grass doesn't feel like we feel. It doesn't hurt. Sound okay?"

"Okay." She wrinkled her nose, not convinced. "But what if it does hurt?"

Okay, she was adorable, but we had to move on.

"It won't hurt you and the grass doesn't have feelings. Now, you try. In your mind, and with *your* feelings, I want you to ask the grass to give you a little bit of its color. Do you think you can do that?"

She nodded and reached her hand out to gently caress the wild stalks. I could hardly believe someone so young could hold so much power. It wasn't fair that alchemy came on so strong in kids. It was too much responsibility. But I was just as young when I'd been discovered and taken to the guardians for training. I understood the daunting emotions she faced.

"Look, you're doing it." I pointed to the emerald strands of magic that twisted above Lacey's hand. "Now move it to some of the dying flowers," I told her before she could get frightened and lose focus. All it would take was her intention if the ability was there. Luckily, green was one of the easiest colors to manipulate. And with a use like healing, that had come in handy on more than one occasion. Just as mine had done, her flowers perked up the instant they received the green alchemy. As she giggled something in my heart cracked open.

"How's it going over here?"

I prickled at the voice of the woman who approached. It appeared she still didn't know who I was. I planned to keep it that way. Placing a false smile on my face, I looked up and greeted Lara Loxley like I cared what she had to say.

"We're making progress. Lacey just healed these flowers."

"Mom, it was magic! They're pretty, don't you think?"

"Beautiful," Lara replied. I noticed the family resemblance, despite my annoyance. Jessa's dark curly hair and height obviously came from Lara, but her sense of style was entirely different. Lara was all-colorful, each article of clothing a bright hue not matching the next. I found it odd. She didn't match the picture I'd had in my head of a cold, calculating person.

"It turns out Lacey is a natural alchemist. Like Jessa. You have talented daughters, Mrs. Loxley," I said. "Magic must run in the family." She averted her gaze; I probably shouldn't have added that last bit. Sometimes my mouth ran away with me, no matter how much I tried to keep out of trouble. Something else Jessa and I had in common. The last thing I needed was for Lara to figure out who I was. I couldn't pretend some happy family reunion with that woman or her husband, even if they were, technically, my parents.

"Well, I think that's enough for today."

Wait, what? "But we're just getting started."

"I don't want Lacey to get too tired."

I stood and brushed the dirt from my pants. "I assure you that took very little effort on her part. Like I said, she's a natural. We have a lot of work to do and not much time."

"What do you mean, not much time?"

Oh, oops. Maybe I shouldn't have said that either...

It was likely that Lacey would be needed. The Resistance had big plans to take down the monarchy, and alchemy was an integral part of that. But Lacey's parents had only agreed to her training so that she didn't accidently hurt herself. They didn't actually want—and I'll admit, neither did I—Lacey anywhere near the Resistance or New Colony.

I backpedaled. "I just meant to say there's not much time before we move on to the next color. I want to make sure she's fully comfortable with green first."

"Please, Momma." Lacey grasped her hands together in a praying motion. "It's so much fun! I want to try some more."

"Really, I'll take care of her. The first sign of fatigue and I'll make her stop."

And it was true, I would. No one gave me that luxury when I was a kid, and while the Resistance would possibly need Lacey's help later, at least for now I certainly wasn't going to treat her like a workhorse.

"Okay, fine." Lara smiled fondly at Lacey before turning on me. "But I mean it. You stop the second she gets tired. You have to remember, she's only a child. She's my *baby*. And I want her safe at all times."

I nodded vigorously. Anything to get this woman to leave. I watched her retreat to the cropping of trees, no doubt to supervise from a close distance. Her momma-bear instinct drove an angry blade right down my center, fileting me wide open. The hot anger of rejection charred so painfully, I lost my breath. More than *anything*, I wanted to run over there and give that woman a piece of my mind. How could she now have such care for Lacey, her *baby*, when she'd had so little regard for me?

I had been her child too.

And while she didn't know who I was now, she'd certainly done nothing to protect me back then. Lara and Christopher didn't even try to hide me, like so many other New Colony parents often did. No. The second these so-called parents discovered my alchemy, they'd sent me straight to the wolves. I'd spent years burying that memory into the deepest recesses of my soul. But it flashed through my mind anyway, like nails on a chalkboard.

"Give me a hug, okay," Mommy says. I wrap my arms around her. She smells like sugar and roses. She pulls me in so tight that I squeal. She doesn't normally hug this way, but I like it. I laugh. She doesn't.

"What's wrong?" I ask. She's kneeling in front of me. Her eyes are all watery and blinking. She just shakes her head. Daddy comes into the room.

"Jessa's finally asleep," he says. She goes to bed before me because she's only three so she's still really little. But I'm a grown girl. I get to stay up later with Mommy and Daddy.

"Are you sure they know? They're coming?"

"I'm positive. Kareth Jackson saw her do it, Lara. You know how that woman is. She would never keep something like that secret."

Mrs. Jackson's our next-door neighbor. She isn't very nice to us. But she has kids our age that we sometimes get to play with. Mom says it's better that we play alone. She says my magic is a dangerous secret. But it doesn't feel dangerous. It's fun. Jessa loves it, too!

But since it's our family secret, I'm not supposed to do magic in front of anyone else. It's okay. I am really smart.

"What do we do?" Mommy stands now, whispering to Daddy. They think I can't hear. But that's silly thinking. Kids always hear.

"I don't know," Daddy replies. "Where would we even go?"

"Maybe we could get out."

"I have no idea how we would do that, Lara. We could all be killed."

"So what do we do?"

"Maybe they'll give her a good life. Better than we can."

"No."

"They'll train her. She'll learn how to control it."

"No."

"We'll see her again. Maybe we can work something out with them."

There's a long pause then. My heart begins to summersault through my body, like when we play tag and Daddy is just about to get me. Something is bad, and Mommy is crying. But they're both nodding. And hugging. So it can't be all-bad. Mommy and Daddy always know how to fix the bad things.

"We love you very much," Daddy says, pulling me into their hug. It's my favorite kind of hug, a Frankie-sandwich. But something about it isn't right.

"I love you too."

There's a knock on the door.

●

I trusted them. Loved them. They were my protectors. So surely they would have at least put up a fight, right?

Wrong.

●

I tucked my head under the hood of my sweatshirt as I began my evening run around the perimeter of the camp. Newly fallen leaves crunched under my shoes as I focused on the trail.

Our Resistance camp was located in a remote Canadian mountain range. It worked well enough, small and isolated, even though the winters were brutal. We said "camp", but it was basically a small village of log cabins. Mostly abandoned, our people had moved in one by one. Some were fleeing prosecution from New Colony, too fearful to go anywhere else, and others were looking for a place to hide out before moving on.

Canada didn't have much government left to care about us, even if they did know we were here. Plus, there were little villages like this all over the country. It was a nation of refugees and misfits, people happy to be left alone and willing to take care of themselves. West America was a big unknown, so no one wanted to try his or her luck there, and anything south was so poverty stricken and overrun with drugs, it was downright dangerous.

I headed around the edge of camp, behind the mess hall where they were still cleaning up from dinner. We all took turns, spreading the work out evenly. I didn't stop to chat. Not that anyone expected me to. Since returning from New Colony, I'd been less than talkative. Then again, I'd never been the friendliest of the bunch.

Nobody cared.

Our community was filled with rejects. We were a mix of alchemists and their families who'd run away in order to stay together, political dissenters who'd joined the Resistance, and social outcasts looking for a better life. Because of the shadow lands, it was nearly impossible to survive a trek out of New Colony by foot. Everyone had been smuggled here either through one of the Resistance's helicopters, or, more likely, by boat on the Atlantic Ocean. Plenty of the people who lived here met the Resistance with weariness, because as much as we stood for what they believed, they feared King Richard more. But, over the years, we'd figured out how to live amicably. We worked together in a commune of sorts, growing our food, raising livestock, and sharing it all with each other. Of course, it helped that the few alchemists we did have used magic to grow healthy crops, heal the sick and injured, and just generally make life easier for everyone. Alchemy could do a lot of good things for the world, given the opportunity.

I increased my speed for the next stretch, zooming past a group practicing combat. That was something that could be seen during all daylight hours lately. We were training for something big, even if we didn't know the logistics yet.

I wasn't in the mood to join them. I would later, but running was my salvation and I needed it after my day training Lacey. Part of me wanted to forgive Lara and Christopher. It wasn't their fault. And had I been born somewhere else, I probably would have been murdered. Most countries imprisoned or executed alchemists out of ignorance and fear of the unknown.

Then the image of gray things infiltrated my mind. No. What I'd endured, being forced to harm innocent people as a child, was worse than death. The smell of decay haunted me. The cries of agonizing death terrorized my dreams. My actions as a child were something I'd live with forever, because of *them*.

My parents.

The officers.

And the royal family.

The kings of New Colony were all the same. Power hungry. Fear mongering. Strategic. Each one worse than the last. Richard used magic to keep the kingdom protected by the uncrossable shadow lands—lands that grew larger every time we flew over them. He used alchemy to keep the people in line, just comfortable enough not to question the cage. And they used alchemy to keep their own royal family living in luxury.

Worst of all, they used magic to kill.

Needless to say, after my own painful experiences with the GC, I was more than grateful to be out of there. And also more than ready to take down the royals the second I got the chance. I'd thought Lucas was different, and part of me still held out hope that he was. But reports had come back that although he was helping Jessa, he was refusing to work with the Resistance. He foolishly blamed us for the queen's death, as if we knew who was doing that to her. He admonished us for putting Jessa back in the palace, but that was the most logical course of action to gain an upper hand against Richard. And he hated that he hadn't ever been let into the inner-circle—even though we'd planned for that to happen soon. He'd ruined it, and I hoped he wouldn't get killed for it. Every day Richard continued on his path, the likelihood of a peaceful rebellion grew smaller. We would succeed, no matter what, and if that meant removing Lucas from the equation, my superiors wouldn't blink an eye. Especially now that he'd left the alliance.

Stupid boy. Why does he always have to be so difficult?

I stopped to catch my breath, bent over.

I was just outside Hank's cabin. He usually spent his evenings alone, but I heard the sound of muffled voices coming from within. Someone jogged up the front steps and entered without even knocking. Tristan. What was he doing here? I knew it had to be Resistance business, and I wanted in on that.

I took a deep breath, squared my shoulders, and pushed open the door to Hank's cabin. Sure, I might have been dripping with sweat and red-faced from the run, but I didn't care.

"Frankie, girl, always a pleasure to see your smiling face," Hank said, clearly joking at the stoic expression I so carefully wore. "I was just going to send Tristan here to fetch you."

Anyone else, and I would have called bull. But Hank didn't lie.

"Thanks for thinking of me, old man," I said. "And don't call me *Frankie*; we already talked about this. It's Sasha."

"That's right, sorry, Sasha. Old habits die hard for this *old man*." He winked. Trying to be funny, no doubt.

I scoffed and shuffled into the cozy cabin. Three other occupants filled the space. I'd spent numerous hours here and considered Hank to be the closest thing I had to a father figure. I lived in a cabin with the other single girls, though I didn't connect with anyone very well. I struggled with relationships. Can we say, abandonment issues? But Hank had never treated me like the orphan I felt I was. I loved him for it, and I owed him everything. He'd saved me from the GC and taken me under his wing. And while I'd begged him for years to let me get more involved with the Resistance, he'd only agreed when they'd needed someone young on the inside. I'd started off at a few of the distant outposts, finally working my way to the palace to monitor Lucas.

Technically, my mission there was to get the prince to fall in love with me, to get him to turn from his father and join us beyond any doubt. And technically, I'd failed. Jessa had come along, and my long lost sister had easily stolen his heart. She didn't have to try. Just the way they looked at each other wasn't something I'd ever experienced, so I didn't blame her. Since I'd recruited her to our side, I still considered the mission a win. If anyone could turn him for good, it was Jessa.

And Jessa was one of us now.

"She's the alchemist?" One of Hank's guests stepped forward. I didn't recognize him. In fact, I only recognized one of the other three. This man had a different air about him, unfamiliar and almost hostile. He was clean-shaven and dressed well—he wasn't a regular in our camp. He was an outsider.

"What business is it of yours?" I quipped back.

Hank rested a hand on my shoulder. I instantly felt protected, and the hostility inside began to defuse. I looked up at the grizzly-bear of a man: mid-fifties, hair beginning to gray, and a scruffy beard to match. I smiled.

"We didn't expect to be working directly with your alchemists," the man pressured in a clipped tone.

"I assure you," Hank said calmly, "Sasha is an asset. She's here to help us, and we can't do this without alchemists on our side."

"And why not?"

Who is this guy? I wasn't used to people being so volatile against alchemy. In New Colony, while it was a crime to hide it, it certainly wasn't anything to be ashamed of. I was proud of who I was because I'd fought hard to become her.

"Ever heard of the phrase *fight fire with fire*?" I barked at the man. He raised an eyebrow, less than impressed. I didn't care. Whoever he was, he needed to back off. I'd proven myself time and time again, and I refused to let anyone doubt me. I studied him further and guessed he had some kind of military background. His cold eyes sparked with calculated intelligence as we faced each other.

"Sasha's right," Hank interceded. "The king has an arsenal of alchemists at his disposal. We need to take whatever magic we can get. And I promise, I've known Sasha nearly all her life. She can be trusted."

The man glared for a minute longer, then smoothly returned to his seat at the table. I followed and dropped into a vacant chair. I wouldn't shrink because of this man's opinion. He knew nothing of what I'd sacrificed for this cause.

"Sasha, this is Jacob Cole." Hank waved a hand at the jerk. "And you already know Tristan." Hank nodded to the guy sitting next to me. Oh yes, I knew Tristan all right. Before I'd left the camp, he'd been the closest thing I had to a best friend. He'd helped get me out of New Colony in the first place. And we'd spent countless hours together over the years since. He was one of those people who always had the best jokes and could diffuse any situation with his smile. Since returning, I'd worried things would be awkward between us. I hadn't had a lot of time to catch up.

"Hey, girl." Tristan grinned. "I heard you made out with the prince."

I nearly died.

Blood rushed to my face, and I rolled my eyes. "Shut up! You're just jealous. When was the last time you got any action around here?"

Tristan only laughed and nodded. "Too true. I need a girlfriend. I also heard the prince dumped your butt. So what do you say, want to go out with me?" He waggled his eyebrows and blew me a kiss. There were no feelings between us. He was more like an older brother, since he was twenty-five and I was nineteen.

We were just friends. Not that the thought hadn't crossed my mind on occasion—because it had, especially since I'd gotten back. He had smooth Asian skin and dark eyes that always seemed to ground me. He was tall, insanely ripped, and above all else, he had a wonderful personality. It was who he *was* that I loved most.

"You wish," I laughed.

"So this teen girl, this girl making jokes about fraternizing with our sworn enemy, this is the *alchemist* you're letting in on our plans?" A fifth member of our little party stepped out from the shadowed corner. Where had he come from? I couldn't believe I hadn't zeroed in on him immediately. He said "alchemist" like it was the dirtiest of dirty words in the English language.

Oh, this should be fun.

Like Cole, he also had that outsider look: clean-cut with buzzed hair. He moved like a predator as he stalked closer. His boots clomped on the wooden floor, and then he was standing to attention. Definitely military. My eyes traveled up his tall frame, noticing the way his khakis clung to corded muscles. I swallowed, unsure of what to make of him. And then I found his eyes. They bored into mine, and my brow creased, taking in their piercing green. I gripped my hands together under the table, and swallowed again. This man was dangerous. I shook myself to alertness and gritted my teeth

"For your information, Soldier-boy, I'm nineteen. And I only fraternized with Lucas because the Resistance ordered me to. I was doing my job."

"An alchemist and a whore."

I exploded from my seat. Tristan beat me to it, launching himself at the guy with a primitive growl. Unfortunately, Cole was too fast and held him back. Hank couldn't get to me in time. Not that he wanted to stop me. Knowing Hank, he was next in line.

I rushed forward and slapped Soldier-boy across the face. My hand burned with satisfaction. "Don't ever call me that again or I'll do worse."

Before I registered what was happening, he grabbed hold of me, twisted my

216

body, and swung me around. He had my arms locked against my sides, my back to his hard chest. One arm held me so I couldn't move, the other wrapped around my neck in a loose chokehold. Anger rippled through me.

"Like what?" he whispered into my ear.

Anger swept through my body. *Arrogant idiot! I'm an alchemist!*

He may have had me in a chokehold, but my beloved stone necklace still hung intact, filled with a myriad of colors for me to pick my poison. All it took was one second to connect with the yellow, and I had the strength I needed. I slammed him to the ground with a crack. His stunned expression only made me smile. From my peripheral vision, I saw Tristan smirk, before he doubled over with laughter.

"Like using alchemy to teach you never to touch a woman without her permission!"

"Lady has a point," Tristan added between fits of laughter.

"You slapped me first," Soldier-boy growled.

"You called me a *whore!*"

He relented, hands up. "Okay, I'll admit I shouldn't have said that." His face reddened at that. I wasn't sure if he was still angry, or embarrassed, or both.

"You're right. You shouldn't have." A voice grumbled. I swung my head around to see Cole's deadly gaze on his man. Huh? "That's no way for my top pupil to behave toward a woman, even if she is an alchemist," he finished.

And there it is, ladies and gentlemen...

"Why do you have such a problem with alchemy?" I turned on Cole, staring him down. Who did these people think they were?

"All right, everyone settle down. That's enough fighting for now," Hank interjected. The power of his voice immediately defused the situation, as if he had blue alchemy at work. But nope, that was just Hank. We all returned to our seats, though a fair amount of hostility still hung in the room.

Hank introduced us. "Sasha and Tristan are Resistance members. Tristan may be a joker, but he's smart as a whip. Sasha is our best alchemist and loyal to a fault."

The two men stiffened. I couldn't help it; I smiled with pride and narrowed my eyes at the younger one, meeting his glare head on. "Cole and Mastin are very special guests and new members of our Resistance. They are *valued* members and we're *lucky* to have them." Hank directed those words—"valued" and "lucky"—at me.

Whatever.

I still didn't get why I had to play nice with people who so clearly hated me. I bit my lip and stiffened.

"They're the beginning of our alliance with West America."

My eyes shot to Hank. He was serious.

"Why would we want that?" The question slipped from my mouth. West America wasn't part of our cause. They hated New Colony, sure. But we didn't work with them because they also hated alchemists. They imprisoned them and sometimes even killed them. "And you expect me to trust these two?" I continued. "Alchemy is illegal in West America. I can't work with them!"

"You can and you will," Hank said, his tone final.

"Don't worry, they may be jerks, but they can be trusted," Tristan added. "They want to take down New Colony as much as we do."

"And then what? Execute me?" I asked Cole, figuring he was the authority over that Mastin guy.

"We already signed an agreement. Everything is in place. Alchemy is still illegal in West America as of today. But we won't hurt *any* cooperative citizens of New Colony if we succeed with what we set out to do."

"And what's that exactly?" I asked.

"It's quite obvious, don't you think?" Mastin said, studying his fingernails in boredom. "We're going to take back what's rightfully ours. We're going to take back New Colony and unite America again."

My mouth usually ran away with me, but, this time, I was lost for words. This was *never* what the Resistance had been about. This was *not* okay! We knew practically nothing about West America. They were a democracy still, that was true, but they hated alchemists. How could we possibly trust them with this?

"Let me just ask you one question," I said, gathering my thoughts. I glanced between the two men before settling on Mastin. He drew me to him, like a moth to the flame. A moth he probably wanted to smash under his shoe. "What is your honest opinion of alchemy?"

He didn't hesitate. "It's an abomination."

I stood, body shaking, stomach clenched in a sickening knot. I caught Hank's pained expression. He'd been an officer when he'd left New Colony and taken me and Tristan with him. He wasn't an alchemist. Tristan wasn't. Most of the Resistance weren't. The vast population wasn't.

But I was.

I was, and he'd made an alliance with people who hated my very existence. Who hated my family—Lacey and Jessa. Even if they didn't know I was their older sister, I still felt a primal need to protect them. I barely had them in my life again, and somehow, despite all logic, I wanted it to stay that way. And Hank, he was supposed to be my family too. He was the only adult who'd ever really cared about me more than my magic. And now he'd done this.

"I can't believe you'd risk my life and the lives of all the alchemists we've been trying to save. What about Jasmine? What about Jessa? Lacey? And all the others?"

"Sit down and let me explain," Hank said, his voice filled with some kind of fatherly concern, like he knew what was better for me than I did.

He doesn't get it and he never will.

I shook my head. "Mastin said enough. Alchemy is an abomination, right? Well, until these two can prove to me without a doubt that West America won't *ever* hurt innocent alchemists, I'm out." I strode from the room, out the door, and didn't look back.

THREE

LUCAS

I was useless. I just stood there, watching, knowing there was nothing I could do. And Jessa knew it too. Her curly hair was wilder than normal, her eyes wide with anxiety, as she chewed on her lip—her nervous tic. I believed she would pass this test, but there was a possibility she wouldn't. And that scared the hell out of me. If she failed today, it wasn't just her secrets that would unravel, but mine as well.

I was an alchemist. That was my secret—and my burden.

I fidgeted uncomfortably against the wall as I studied the back of my father's head, boring holes into it. What was he going to do to Jessa?

My father, Richard, had a love-hate relationship with alchemy. He wasn't an alchemist, probably much to his frustration. No one in our line before me had the magic. Still, he used alchemy to keep the royal family powerful and New Colony isolated and controlled. He surrounded himself with an army of skilled alchemists, indoctrinated from a young age, and then used intimidating officers to keep everybody in line. But that couldn't last forever: sooner or later, the alchemists would rise up. He knew it. I knew it. Faulk knew it.

And everyone in the Resistance was committed to it.

Pained, I watched him gaze at Jessa like she was the key to winning whatever sick and twisted game he was playing. She shifted in her seat, waiting for whatever was coming. Whatever it was, knowing him, it wasn't good. I'd learned all about his experiments, and he'd even tried to get my involvement with a few when I first found out. He would use his lowest level citizens, or those who were acting out for whatever reason, and would test magic on them. Sometimes torturing them. Many times killing them.

And I couldn't forget. I'd seen the shadow lands with my own eyes, the miles of dead, rotted, colorless earth where alchemists had stripped all color. The people didn't know about it. In fact, most of them loved him and treated our royal family like we were handed down from God himself. Of course it helped that Richard's Guardians of Color used blue to spy and persuade, yellow for physical strength and agility, and green to heal those deemed worthy. Purple shades were useful to my father, though also extremely hard to manipulate. They could be used for telepathy and even for predicting the future.

And now that he had Jessa, he finally had red.

When an alchemist could pull red from someone's blood, they could control that person's mind. Make them do anything. We knew this because he'd had an alchemist in the past, Jessa's older sister, who'd been able to do it. But then she'd disappeared. She'd returned years later as Sasha, much older and unrecognizable, and somehow infiltrated the GC on behalf of the Resistance. Faulk had figured that one out too late in the game, and I was still annoyed with myself for not seeing the connection sooner.

The officers had figured it out once she'd disappeared. Sasha had shown up at an outpost with a false identity, then slowly worked her way to the palace. The Resistance had to have someone on the inside because they'd also added her cover story into the files.

Richard was livid about it, and I hoped he didn't take it out on Jessa.

Jessa.

The girl who not only could access red, but who could separate colors into their primary counterparts, another remarkable talent. One she hadn't been able to replicate; but eventually, she would. There was no telling what that magic could do. If Richard could unlock her power, and worse yet, duplicate it in other alchemists, he'd be unstoppable. And if that happened, I had no doubt this girl, the one person who was capable of breathing life into my broken heart, would be lost in the crossfire.

She sat across from my father, her chin lifted and eyes narrowed in an expression that could either be interpreted as defiant or focused.

I knew better than to assume the latter.

"Let me guess? We're testing blue today?" she asked.

"That's right, but I'll be the one testing blue on you." Reed smirked. That smirk just gave me one more reason to hate him. Reed had befriended Jessa when she was the most vulnerable she'd ever been in her life, only to use and manipulate her for Faulk. He was a lackey. Another brown-nosing, ladder-climbing GC prick. But he'd failed.

And for all our sakes, he'd better fail again. Or I swear, I will beat him to a pulp. The angry threats tumbled through my mind, but I still managed to keep my expression apathetic. I'd had a lot of practice in that department over the years.

"And how is that a fair test?" Jessa asked. "Aren't I supposed to get a chance to actually *use* blue?"

"We thought you'd ask that," Faulk said, sighing heavily. "And don't worry, you will. But first, we have some questions." With a sharp tap of her pointed boot on the concrete floor, she glided forward, her hair slicked and scraped back more harshly than I'd ever seen. A repulsive creature, who basked in the enjoyment of making Jessa squirm at every opportunity. She gripped her hands behind her back and set her lips in a thin line. I attempted to relax my shoulders, aware of how tense this woman made me. When Jessa was in her sights, there was no knowing how far this monster would go—it was no wonder she and Richard worked so well together.

"I guess I don't have a choice in the matter," Jessa said, her eyes darting between Faulk and Richard. She rolled her eyes and settled farther into her chair. Reed ran his hands through his blond hair. I noticed a slight grimace as he positioned himself behind her and placed his hands on her shoulders. A pulse of anger rolled through me. He had to touch her for this, but, logical or not, it still bugged the hell out of me.

The blue angular stone was about the size of my thumb and hung from a thick, black cord around Reed's neck. It gleamed in the morning light that poured through the office windows. It only took a moment of Reed's concentration for the color to begin rising from the rock. The blue tendrils swirled in rotations of menacing magic, before they shot around the room. A slice of the magic went into Jessa, with the intention of making her susceptible to persuasion. And more of the magic went directly into Richard, doing the exact opposite, making him the one with the persuasion. Even one thread of this magic had a powerful effect, but this was double time. My entire body went cold. Reed finally removed his hands from Jessa and stepped back. I ignored his wink in her direction.

"Great work, Reed." Faulk smiled at her little alchemist protégé. And even I had to admit it *was* great work. Which made me sick. I held my jaw still, resisting the urge to groan. Jessa was in a lot of trouble.

"Are you ready to begin?" Richard asked, holding her gaze. He sat on the edge of his seat. Jessa nodded eagerly and smiled. In the short time between being affected by Reed's blue alchemy to now, she'd visibly changed. Her eyes were no longer guarded, her expression open and vulnerable.

I bit back my anger. I'd wished I'd been informed in advance of this test today so I could've warned her. But it wasn't until breakfast that *Father Dearest* had decided to let me in on what was going to happen.

This test had clearly been twisted to suit Faulk's need to sniff out any disloyalty in Jessa. It was true that we could test blue alchemy by not only asking someone to perform it, which they usually failed, but by also seeing how resistant they were to someone else using the magic on them. Also, that usually resulted in failure. Blue was one of the hardest and rarest colors to control in alchemy. There was a reason the initiates *only* had to pass three of the five main colors to be accepted into the Guardians of Color. People simply didn't have the ability to master all the colors.

"Is your allegiance to the crown?" Richard asked.

"No," Jessa replied.

No? No? She answered honestly. Can't she fight it at all? A bead of sweat ran down the back of my neck. If she didn't hide some of her deeper secrets, we were both at risk for punishment.

"Why do you say that?" Richard countered.

"I lied."

"Lied about what?" he spat.

On the outside, Faulk was an attractive woman. But that only made her more frightening. Her single-minded obsession was showing now as sneers at Jessa's answer. But I knew my father well enough. This new development would cause problems for him. He was desperate to control Jessa. But I wondered, what would happen if Jessa failed? Would he demand her initiation anyway? Would he just store her away for special occasions?

"I lied about being an alchemist. To Faulk, when she first came to see me. I'm loyal to my family more than I'm loyal to the crown. You won't let me see them." The words Jessa spoke came out in an air of honesty and calm, like she was having a normal conversation with a trusted friend.

And it was true. She wasn't lying. What else would she be honest about?

"Okay, but are you loyal to the crown *now*?" Richard asked.

"Not completely. Why would I trust the ones who have my family locked away? I'm loyal to you only as long as you can reunite us. They are my true objective."

Now I knew she was lying. Pride rippled through me, and I stood a little straighter. She and I were both fully aware of where her family really was. Richard and Faulk were only pretending to have them under lock and key. Her family was with the Resistance, safe and hidden. And as it stood, there was nothing that anyone could do about that.

Richard shifted the conversation. "And you'll do anything to make that happen? You'll do anything I ask of you?"

Jessa paused, and I ground my feet into the floor. *Please, answer correctly.*

"I don't know," she said. "I don't want to hurt anyone."

Good girl! I exhaled a slow, shuddering breath. She needed to *sound* honest, not like she was saying exactly what Richard wanted to hear. That was the only way they'd believe Reed's magic was doing its job.

"Are you hiding any more secrets from me?" Richard asked. It was a tough question. Of course, she was hiding mountains of information from him. And he suspected it. If she said no, she'd likely pass the test. Pass, because everyone would know she'd been lying and they wouldn't trust her. If she said yes, she would have to divulge some information. And it was likely she would fail this color. I wanted her to fail. For her own safety. She had to fail.

"Yes," she said simply, calmly. "I do have one more secret."

"And what's that, little alchemist?" Richard asked. The room froze with anticipation. All eyes were intense on Jessa. She swallowed before speaking easily, with an open smile.

"I know you didn't like it when your son was dating that other alchemist girl. The one who disappeared?"

"And what's your point," Faulk spat, unrestrained. She stalked behind Richard, pacing, her eyes narrowed into slits. If the woman wasn't careful, she was going to give herself a headache.

Jessa didn't bother to acknowledge Faulk; her eyes stayed locked on my father. "I know you look down on the idea of an alchemist and a royal dating. You don't want an alchemist anywhere near that crown. Lucas told me as much. But you see, I think you don't have as much control over your son as you think you do."

"And why is that?" Richard folded his arms before turning back to look at me. Actually, there was an audible shuffle as everyone in the room turned to me.

"Your son wants me."

My mouth fell into a hard line. This was so not good for us, for whatever our relationship was growing into. I wanted to keep it secret until I could find a way to get Richard to agree to it.

"Is that true?" Richard faced me now, anger dripped from the question. And a fair mix of fatherly disappointment, which didn't actually mean anything to me. I didn't care what he thought anymore.

I let out a breath. If I lied, suspicion would be sent right back on Jessa. The questions would continue until she eventually gave too much away. But if I told the truth about my relationship with her, Richard would lecture me mercilessly, and I might lose my only lifeline. Still, I had no choice.

"Her observation of me might have some truth to it," I conceded.

Reed laughed, Faulk clicked her tongue, and Richard glowered. We both knew what memory was on replay in his mind. After Richard found Sasha in my room, he'd forbidden me to fraternize with alchemists. Richard had been livid, but things had gotten so out of hand that day—and then Mom had died. We hadn't had the conversation again.

"Everybody, get out," Richard said, ice piercing every word.

"But what about the rest of the test?" Faulk asked.

"She failed," Richard spat. "Now get *out!*"

They scurried from the room like frightened mice, not a backbone in sight. Jessa followed with a dazed expression. I had to admit, I was proud of her. Everything she did made me like her even more. She'd managed to act as if she was completely under Reed's magical spell, when really, she wasn't. Her power was growing stronger every day. And turning the attention to our relationship? While it caused a problem for me, it took my father's attention off the deeper secrets we shared. It was actually kind of brilliant.

Richard stood slowly from the chair, scratching it on the polished concrete floor. He stalked toward me until he stood only inches away. We were so similar in our physicality, it was almost uncanny. But we couldn't be more different. I stared back at the man who was my physical mirror. He was the "thirty years older" version. White peppered his dark hair. Storms brewed in his gray eyes. Deep lines pulled at his masculine face.

"Are you purposely trying to disappoint me?"

"No, sir."

"Was I not clear before? With that other…*thing*?"

"Yes, sir."

"Why are you interested in Jessa? She is a pawn. *My pawn!*" he challenged. "Alchemists are not to be trusted. *Ever.* They are too powerful to be anything other than our slaves. We have a duty to protect our *royal* bloodline. Do I make myself clear?"

I nodded, meeting the darkness in his eyes with my own. He knew nothing, absolutely nothing.

Your own son is an alchemist!

"You know we tracked that fake back to her, right?"

I paused. "What do you mean?"

"I mean that Sasha and Jessa have more in common than just alchemy."

So they'd combed through everything and figured out who Sasha really was–Francesca Loxley. The long lost alchemist, turned rebel spy.

"Stay away from Jessa," he continued. "You're no longer needed to oversee her training. She's fine to train like all the others. *Keep your distance.*"

A hard knot of tension gathered in my chest. Forbidding me to see Jessa would only stoke the fire I had burning for her. He may be my father, and he may think of Jessa as his slave, but I was no slave. I would do whatever I wanted. No matter what, I would find a way. Until then, I'd just have to be extra careful. In the midst of my depression over Mom, Jessa was the only thing that mattered. He wouldn't take that away from me.

"I understand, sir."

●

I paced the length of my bedroom, rubbing my hands across my face. I stopped, tilted my head and gazed up at the ceiling. I needed to see her.

I wanted to talk to her, make sure she still wanted me as much as I wanted her. Two days had passed since her blue test, and I was a man obsessed. But in that time, I'd forced myself to stay away. My security team normally kept their distance when we were home. With palace guards and officers swarming the place, there wasn't a huge need for someone to tail me at all times. But ever since Richard had forbade me from dating Jessa, I'd noticed more eyes pointing my way than normal. More guards watching me, more officers around than ever. It was obvious that my father had sent out some kind of order to keep me under observation. At the rate we were going, there was no chance I could just pop into her bedroom again.

Forget it. I stalked from our apartment and out into the corridor. I was heading into the GC wing, even if it meant I only got to catch a glimpse of her. That is, if I was lucky. It came as no surprise that eyes followed me as I walked. If they didn't catch me actually with her, then they had nothing to say to Richard.

There has to be something I can do…

There were fewer watchful eyes in certain areas of the palace. The royal wing—but obviously that was out. The gardens—but it was almost fall and there weren't many leaves left to keep us hidden. Not to mention, it was getting colder. And the servant areas had too many people.

No one seemed too bothered lately when I ate in the GC dining hall. But I went there again and again, just to catch a glimpse of Jessa. I couldn't help myself; I was seriously losing my mind over the girl. She was the best distraction

I had to keep myself from thinking about…darker things.

I entered the dining hall, my steady gaze searching for her. Jessa wasn't anywhere to be found. The room was filled with alchemists and officers, paired off in their respective parties. I frowned and bee-lined to the one person who might have an idea: Jasmine. I sat across from the older woman dining alone and threw my hands up in the air.

"I need to see her."

"Hello, Your Highness," she said warmly. "How can I help you?"

"I'm sure you probably know this by now, but my father has pulled me off Jessa's training." She was one of the only alchemists who didn't bug me. She dressed her own way, moved to her own beat, and the officers let her because she was so good at her job. Plus, she was trustworthy. She'd never drawn an ounce of suspicion her way.

Jasmine nodded and pulled her gray braid back over her shoulder, stroking the ends before meeting my gaze. Her eyes were bright as she nodded, a knowing smile playing at her lips. "And this isn't okay with you, because?"

I coughed. "Because…" I didn't know what to say. I didn't have a good enough reason. I just wanted to be with Jessa. The pull to protect her was as strong as the need to breathe.

"Because you're in love with her?" She spoke like we were talking about the weather.

A zap of energy ran through my body at her question. I thought maybe I was in love, but I wasn't ready to admit it out loud. It seemed so childish. I'd only known Jessa for a few months. There was still so much left between us to figure out, if we ever got the chance.

"I just…need to see her," I finally said.

She held my gaze, studying me.

"And since I've been tasked with her training now, you think I can help you with that?" she asked.

I nodded. Because I wanted to see her, yes. But I also wanted to talk to her about the Resistance some more. I hated that she was still working with them, whoever they were. I couldn't trust an organization shrouded in so much secrecy. That was exactly what had led me to distrust my own father in the first place. I needed her to understand, to get away from them so she could stay safe.

You couldn't save your mother. What makes you think you can save Jessa?

"Fine, you poor boy. I'll help you," she said, lowering her voice. A knowing smile lit her face. "I always was a romantic at heart."

"What do you need me to do?" I blurted the question.

"You two can meet in my classroom when it's empty. As you know, it has its own private greenhouse. You should find some privacy there. Not to mention, there are multiple entrances." She winked, and an iota of hope rose in my body. But the thought badgered me. Was she really willing to help us?

"I like you, Lucas." She smiled. "And I like Jessa. You two are good for each other."

"Thank you," I replied.

"Just promise me if you get caught, you won't drag me into it?"

"Of course not. And it's not like you're always in your classroom anyway, right?"

"That's true. I always lock my desk. But sometimes, I forget to lock the doors." She winked again and eased herself from her chair. Her floral skirt sashayed around her as she shuffled away.

I followed her with my gaze and froze. Jessa had just walked in. She had that serious expression on her face that she got sometimes. I loved that look, but I loved her smile even better. I would do anything to see it again. I stood. Just as Jasmine was leaving, the two stopped to talk. They both caught my gaze for a moment. Jasmine leaned in to add something more, and Jessa's cheeks flared. Then they left together.

This was my chance.

I strolled casually from the dining room, careful to make sure nobody followed. After that, it didn't take me more than a couple of minutes to find my way into the greenhouse. Jasmine wasn't at her desk on my way in, but Jessa stood just under the cropping of tropical trees. She was leaning toward a flower, smelling it. Her hair curled down her back, her body relaxed. When she turned to me, her complexion glowed radiantly in the evening light. Then she smiled.

"Do you think they believed it?" Jessa asked.

"What?" I couldn't concentrate. The heat and her flushed cheeks were distracting me in a very good way. We walked farther into the greenhouse.

The room was massive, humid, and filled with colorful plants curated from all over the planet. I watched as her fingers trailed across them. Lucky plants. It was vital that alchemists had access to many colors so they could do their magic. They didn't have to have natural elements like these, but it made things much easier. Life held the most magic of all.

"With the blue test? Do you think they fell for it?"

I smiled, shaking my head in amazement. "You were incredible."

"I hate failing. The competitive dancer in me won't accept anything less than perfection." She laughed, and the sound drew me to her.

I grabbed her free hand, linking her fingers between my own, and pulled her even farther into the foliage. Once I was sure we were out of sight, I backed her up against a tree and stared down at her parted lips. Her eyes flitted from my mouth to my eyes and back down again. I took pity on us both and decided not to prolong the inevitable. I kissed her. Molding my lips to hers, all my stress fell away.

There was something different about this girl. Somehow I'd let her in, allowing her to peer into the hidden places of me. And miraculously, she didn't cower at what she saw. I came with heavy baggage, and she helped carry my load. No one had ever cared enough to do that for me before. Not beyond the surface of what I could do for them. She never asked me to do anything.

I wrapped her in close, while also restraining myself as much as possible. It wasn't easy. But she was young and innocent. I didn't want to add any more reasons for her to leave me. After losing my mother, I couldn't handle losing

Jessa too. The break would fracture in too many places.

"So what do we do now?" she asked, pausing our kiss. I pressed my forehead to hers and breathed in her lilac and honey scent.

"Honestly," I said, "I'm not even sure myself."

"We have to keep this a secret, don't we?"

"Yes." I *hated* that word: secret. I groaned and stepped back, taking in every bit of her reaction. Was she upset?

"Okay." She smiled softly. "We can meet here until we figure something else out."

Relief washed through me. The greenhouse was one of many on the property. It wasn't the most romantic or secluded spot in the palace, but it was cooling down now as the weather changed, and it was private enough with all the plants to hide us from view. And, most importantly, it was ours.

"But Lucas? Will you please talk to me?"

"About what?"

"About your mother. About Thomas. About *everything*. I'm really worried about you. I just…what is this between us? Am I just a way for you to numb yourself?"

I felt myself hesitate. When her face crumbled, I mentally kicked myself.

"It's not like that." I leaned in to hug her before facing her. "I don't know how to put it into words, Jessa. Are you a distraction?" I smirked, thinking about how good it felt to kiss her like I just had. "Absolutely. But a really, *really* good one. And not for the reasons you think."

"Is that so?" She let out a teasing laugh. "Not for any of *those* reasons?"

I played along. "Okay, maybe a little bit. But Jessa, I like you a lot. Ever since you walked into my life, you turned my world upside down. I used to be so lost. Hell, I'm still lost, especially now, but you, you make me feel like I can be found again."

I knew it was cheesy. Every word would have had me rolling my eyes just months earlier, but it was the truth now. She was my truth.

I stood back and studied her face. Her wide ocean eyes that pulled me in every time I looked at them. Her curly, dark hair that, in the last few minutes of kissing and the greenhouse's humidity, had managed to grow larger than it already was. But I loved it, and I loved that about her. Her cheeks lifted in her earth-shattering smile and there was just so much *goodness* in her.

"Say it out loud," she dared me.

I smiled. "My whole life I've been surrounded by darkness. My mother was sick for years. My father, well, you already know what kind of man he is. The officers can't be trusted. And the alchemists come in as innocent children and leave as brainwashed guardians. What few friends I have are more like acquaintances to me." My voice grew thick. "I'm an only child, and I've always just been so…alone."

She frowned.

"No," I said, putting my finger to her lower lip. "I don't want you to feel sorry for me. I didn't know any different. And I know I have it better in here than a lot of people have it out there. I'm not trying to throw a pity party. I'm just saying, I didn't know what I was missing. I didn't know there could be someone like you."

She blushed and swooped in for a quick kiss. I forced myself not to linger. "I'm serious, Jessa. You love your family with a bigger heart than I've ever seen. You'll do anything for them. My family never worked that way. And somehow, in the middle of all this chaos, you decided to give me a chance. I'm so full of faults. I've made mistakes. And lost so much. And yes, I may be a prince, but I feel I have so little to offer you."

"I know you're doing your best. It's okay–"

"No, it's not okay," I spoke louder. "You don't deserve to be hidden away. But it's the best I can do right now. And I just…I don't want to lose you." I lost it then, my voice cracking on the last few words. I'd already lost too much. Truth was, if I lost Jessa too, I would fall apart for sure. But I also knew in my gut that I didn't deserve her.

"You won't lose me." She smiled and brushed her hand along my cheek.

I leaned into it, before moving into a hug. She burrowed her head into my neck, and shivers ran down my spine. It just seemed so illogical that I was here. That I was in this position, holding this girl, falling in love with this unattainable future.

"Lucas," she said, "I have to go now."

"Go where?"

She hesitated. "Resistance stuff."

I practically growled. That reminded me… "Are you sure you can trust them, Jessa? Maybe we don't need them. Maybe we can change things ourselves, without all the secrets and politics."

"You know I'm committed to this." She stepped back. Pain traced her features, and I decided to drop it for the moment. I nodded once and grabbed her hand, tracing the outline of her palm.

"Just promise me you'll be careful."

"I'll be careful, Lucas, I promise. It's okay, really, I'll be fine."

She kissed me quickly before disappearing. I was tempted to follow her, but decided against it. She would know. *They* would know.

I leaned against the tree, the same she'd used as her anchor moments ago. My thoughts turned angry.

She was too trusting. The Resistance could easily turn out to be just as dark and twisted as my father. What if they used her, hurt her, broke her spirit? She'd promised to be careful with them, but would they be careful with her? Not a chance. She was in danger. She'd willingly put herself right in the middle of a deadly situation, and there was nothing I could do to get her out.

That didn't mean I wasn't going to try.

The darkness rose inside me, blurring my vision. I gritted my teeth. She saw it in me, that demon. I knew she did. I needed to use it for something useful before it ate me alive. *Take down the Resistance. Stop your father. Save Jessa.*

I burst from my rigid stance and strode from the room, the demon hot on my heels.

FOUR

JESSA

Someone had been in my room.

When Jasmine told me where I could meet Lucas, she'd also told me to check under my mattress in an hour. So the whole time I'd been with Lucas, the back of my mind tinkered with the idea of what would be waiting for me. And who in the Resistance had access to my room?

I had few belongings: a high-tech slatebook with restricted access; a wardrobe of beautiful clothes Lucas had gifted me, of which I wore hardly any. Not when I needed to dress in the guardian outfits in order to fit in. I still had my lavender ballet costume from the night I'd been discovered, tucked away. And that was about it.

But still, my door was usually locked. So someone had used magic to open it. I wondered what color would do that. Or maybe someone had a key. That didn't narrow it down. I assumed many of the officers, guards, and even housekeeping staff had access to my room if they wanted it. It sent shivers all over my body just thinking about it.

But there was no doubt *someone* had come in, because sure enough, as I lifted the mattress, a typed note was waiting for me.

Officer Wallace plans to work late tonight. There will be no one else in the office after 10 P.M. Get him alone and find out the status on New Colony and West American relations. Specifically, anything regarding the shadow lands. Don't let him remember your conversation. Someone will be in touch tomorrow. Destroy this message.

I reread the note twice, clutching it between shaking hands. *Are you kidding me?* My heart exploded at the thought of this mission. Even thinking I had a *mission* was beyond bizarre. Who had I become? My whole life had turned completely upside down in a matter of months. At any moment, I could be discovered, tried for treason, and executed. Was I really going to use alchemy on an unsuspecting officer?

Yes.

I wasn't here to back down. Whatever the Resistance asked, I would do it. I had to. Too many people were counting on me. It was time to be brave.

The first thing I needed to do was pocket a knife. That was easy enough, considering the dining hall had all manner of utensils available. A steak knife would be messy and wasn't my first choice. I'd have to get my hands on something smaller and cleaner, and soon. Especially if I was going to start using red alchemy on a regular basis. I took a deep breath and rubbed at my temples, squeezing my eyes shut. My magic could be the difference between the Resistance succeeding or failing, I reminded myself. My magic could be the difference between never seeing my family again!

I began pacing the room, building the resolve deep in my belly.

I wouldn't use red alchemy on any one person more than a couple of times. A little gray blood was harmless. Lacey, Reed, and that officer girl in training had all forgotten what had happened to them because I'd made it so. But they'd all been fine. They hadn't turned out like Queen Natasha, who'd been abused for years with the magic.

I sat on my bed, anxiously waiting for the time to pass. When ten o'clock finally rolled around, I shuddered. I reread the note for what felt like the millionth time before flushing it down the toilet. Then I headed out to find a knife before I could talk myself out of it.

The note was right. This late into the night, there weren't any officers in the area. Not when I'd gone to pocket a knife. And not when I went to open the door to their office. It was locked. The guard at the end of the hall gave me a suspicious once over, shaking his head.

"It's locked," he said.

Duh… Well, now what am I supposed to do?

As luck would have it, a man rounded the corner. An officer. As he marched closer, I noticed he was probably in his early thirties. He eyed me warily. He was broad-shouldered and strong, with wiry, blond hair pulled back into a small ponytail. His dark eyes flashed as he realized I wasn't moving out of his way.

"Jessa," he said, stopping just feet away. "What are you doing here?"

So he knew my name. That wasn't a good sign.

"I came to report something. A crime."

His jaw ticked. "I was just grabbing my slatebook. I left it inside. Why don't I go in and call Faulk." It wasn't a question. "Stay here," he added, before swiping some kind of identification into the lock and walking through the double doors.

I peered back at the guard, who seemed to be distracted by a group of alchemists laughing as they staggered down the adjoining hallway. The sound of the polished floors tapped under their shoes. Now was my chance. I slipped through the door behind the officer, hoping to grab him before he got to his slatebook.

"What's your name?" I asked, gaining his attention.

He didn't slow. "Officer Wallace. You're not supposed to be in here."

My pulse quickened. "I know," I said. "I just needed to talk to someone right away." My hands shook as I gripped the head of the knife. I'd slid it into my pocket, but since it was a little big, I had to keep one hand on it at all times. Not suspicious whatsoever... *right*. I inhaled a steadying breath and relaxed my face; I could do this.

"I'll call Faulk for you."

"Actually, Faulk and I don't always see eye to eye, in case you hadn't noticed."

He turned then, a sly grin on his face. "I think everyone's noticed." He seemed stressed, but that grin transformed his features from ordinary to kind. For a moment, I didn't want to hurt him. I didn't want to do this, not to this man who seemed like he could probably be a friend.

I gripped the hilt of the knife a little tighter. What was I thinking? No way he was kind, not if he worked for Faulk.

"Yeah, well, would it be okay if I talked to you? Told you about the...crime that I saw. And then you can decide if we have to call Faulk."

"I really should just call her. And you really shouldn't be in here."

I followed him to his desk, a typical office cubicle at the back of the large room. All the monitors were off, the desks clean and locked up for the day. A quick glance up the open staircase to Faulk's large windowed office showed that it was also dark. We were alone.

"Please, I don't want to get yelled at again. Maybe what I saw wasn't a big deal. Last thing I need to do is drag Faulk away from whatever she's doing in her off time. You know what I mean? The woman doesn't like me as it is. I don't want to get in trouble." I poured as much trepidation and fear into my voice as possible. He frowned and studied me. With a slight nod, he pulled over a rolling chair from the cubical opposite.

"Sit," he said, gesturing to it. Then he settled into his own chair.

I sat, a few feet away, but still not quite close enough. I felt for the knife again, adjusting my position nervously to keep it from view. I peered around the space, double-checking we were alone. I also quickly assessed his person. He wasn't carrying a weapon.

"It happened yesterday," I said, catching his eye. "I saw some alchemists do something that I'm pretty sure is illegal."

"And what was that?" He held my gaze.

I tried to ignore the beads of sweat collected on my forehead. My story was a complete fabrication. Apparently, I hadn't thought this through. I dug my heels into the floor and rolled the chair closer to Officer Wallace, so our knees were almost touching. I leaned in as if to whisper my secret.

"You can tell me," he said, expression earnest.

"I wanted to say—" I shifted closer. "That I'm sorry about this."

I ripped the knife from my pocket and slammed it into his hand. Blood immediately squirted from the point of contact. The knife skittered to the ground. I winced at the sight, but determination ignited inside.

Wallace sprang into action, jumping away and up against his desk. His eyes darted to either side of me; he was about to make a run for it. I wasn't a complete idiot. But he wasn't an idiot either. He knew what I was capable of. I couldn't let him get away. My life depended on it. Just as he dodged to my left, I reached out and fumbled for his bloody arm.

"Stop," I said when I made contact. I felt the alchemy move between us. I didn't yell. I didn't have to. He did exactly as I asked. "Don't say anything. Don't move."

His features went blank as the red magic swirled violently in the air. His blood was already beginning to drip gray. I had to act fast.

"Log onto your computer, and print everything recent regarding West America." I figured that would be good enough. As he automatically did what I asked, I drilled him with questions.

"What can you tell me about the shadow lands and West America?"

"We're expanding," he said, his voice monotone. "The shadow lands are one of our best lines of defense. They keep us protected."

"What do you mean by expanding?"

"Right now they're mostly north and south. We're moving west." West? That didn't make sense. Canada didn't have much infrastructure anymore, nor people, and Mexico was in complete anarchy, controlled by the constantly warring gangs too busy to worry about us. But West America and New Colony had a nefarious history, and everyone knew it was best not to poke the beast.

"Going west, why? Just to keep us isolated?" I asked.

"To prepare."

Prickles of white-hot panic spread across my body. I had to lean up against the cubical wall to catch my breath. I feared where this conversation was going. "To prepare for what?" I asked, drawing out each word.

"War."

The mechanical sound of the printer stopped. Silence descended on the room. Thick drips of crimson fell from Wallace's wounded hand and splattered on the concrete floor. We'd need to do something about that.

I grabbed the thick stack of papers out of the printer. I flattened them between the waistband of my pants and abdomen, then pulled my shirt over to cover them. It was the best I could do. If I hunched just a little, no one would be able to see I was hiding anything. I hoped.

I reached out and grasped his bleeding hand. It was warm and slick, and rather large against my own. *All this power I have in my small hand.* I gulped.

"Let's go to the bathroom," I said.

Still in his trancelike state, he led me around the darkened offices until we found the bathroom. I kept my hand on his, even though it made me squirm. I had to make sure my alchemy was still working. But I also wanted to end this quickly. As much as I disagreed with what this man did for a career, I didn't want to permanently damage him.

We entered, and I instructed him to clean himself at the sink. I let out a sigh of relief when his separation from me didn't change the magic. I started searching the attached supply closet, rifling through the contents. There was a small kit in my dormitory bathroom, so I hoped there'd be one here too. I located a kit on the top shelf and pulled it down. I placed it on the counter next to where Wallace still washed his hand. The water ran over it, mixing in swirls of blood in the sink. I stepped closer. It looked pretty clean. Why was he still washing it then?

Oh, that's right. Realization hit me.

"You can stop that now," I said, guessing he needed a little more direction from me. "You're going to dry and bandage yourself, clean everything up, and forget this happened. If anyone asks you about me coming here to talk, you're going to say I got spooked and never said anything. And if someone asks about your bandaged hand, you're going to tell them you accidently sliced it on a letter opener." Ugh, I hoped that story would be believable enough. It was the best I could think of with so little direction from the Resistance.

He just stared at me.

"Do you understand?"

He nodded, and I bit my lip. His head was drooping at an odd angle, his eyes glassy and dazed. I hoped no one found him like this or it would be obvious what had happened.

"Clean this up, then splash your face with some water, and go back to whatever you came here for tonight."

He began, and I didn't allow myself to hesitate. I rinsed the knife and replaced it in my pocket. Then I hurried from the bathroom and out into the offices. Luckily, the area was still deserted. I exited, light on my toes. I sucked in my stomach, the paperwork burning against my skin. I kept my head down as I passed the guard still in his same position. I felt his eyes trained on me, but I didn't allow myself to meet them. I stalked around the corner and made it back to my room in record time.

I slid the papers under the mattress into the same place the note had been left for me. I knew that would be one of the first places Faulk and her people would look if they decided to search my room, but where else was I supposed to hide it? I certainly didn't know any magic for hiding classified documents! Whoever was handling these items for the Resistance had better work fast.

I forced myself not to panic as I stripped off my clothes. Then I jumped in the shower to wash off any remaining blood. I'd already rinsed quickly back in the officer's bathroom, but still, it was better to be safe than sorry. Plus, the thought of having someone else's blood on me made my stomach turn. The feel of the warm water soothed my shaking body as the adrenaline melted away.

After finishing up, I wrapped myself in a plush towel and twisted a second around my dripping mop of hair. I padded out into my bedroom to grab some pajamas. I stopped. A vulnerable sense of knowing pricked at my senses. Someone had just been in my room. Was anything out of place? The bed was still immaculately made, the items on the desk untouched, the door locked. I lifted the mattress.

The papers were gone.

I wasn't surprised, but a gasp escaped anyway. Part of me was relieved it was over and the incriminating classified documents were no longer in my possession. But another part was freaked out that someone had been in my room *while I was in the shower*. I mean, seriously, I was naked in my bathroom and they'd broken into my locked room. Logically, I knew it had to be done. But that didn't erase the worst part: I had no idea who had accessed my room. I felt violated by that truth, the lack of privacy in this place yet again setting me on edge.

●

"I think it's time you joined the other alchemists for classes," Jasmine said. Over the last week, since my confession to the king, she'd completely taken over my training. Jasmine had become my constant companion in magic. The more I got to know her, the more I liked her.

I groaned. "Why would I want to do that?"

"It's not about what you *want* to do, it's about what you *should* do."

"And you think being around people who hate me is going to help me?"

"I think it's time you at least tried to make some friends."

Oh no, I'd been afraid that this was coming.

As much as I hated to admit it, she was right. Since coming to the palace, I'd purposely separated myself from the other alchemists. And they'd done the same thing. At first it was because I didn't want to be one of them. And then it was because I wasn't sure whom I could trust. Jasmine was older, the strongest healer in the palace, and a teacher. I'd always felt comfortable with her. But I hadn't trained with any other teachers, and it didn't help that the one guardian I had befriended had turned out to be a terrible friend after all. I was still so mad at Reed for trying to persuade me to give up my secrets, but I had to let it go if I wanted to get anywhere with these people.

Still, even if I decided to play nice, it didn't mean they would.

"Okay fine," I conceded. I would *try*. But that didn't mean I'd have to like it.

"Let's start now, shall we?" Jasmine motioned for me to follow her from her office. I glanced back longingly at the space, with its clean modern finishes and attached greenhouse. Leaving the cocoon of this safe haven in the GC wing was not my idea of a good time. But, it was now or never. My heart kicked up a notch, unwelcome anxiety bursting to life.

As we walked down the hallway, Jasmine spoke, "We don't know when your last three tests are going to be. You could be done in a week, or you could be done in several months. You're being tested off schedule, so it's really just up to Faulk. As you know, everyone is tested in the five main colors. You have to pass three."

"And I'm currently one and one," I said, grumbling at my failure with blue. Even though that failure probably saved my life, it still bothered me that I'd had to do it. Stupid tests.

"Yes. And we have to assume Richard will want to do something with red as well," Jasmine continued, "but that will likely come after your initiation. Of course, we won't know until it happens."

I swallowed hard, rubbing a hand through my tangle of hair. I was naïve if I thought that wouldn't come soon. But it still scared me to think about it. Every time I used red, it got easier. Or maybe I was just getting better.

"So what does this have to do with training with the other alchemists?"

"Everything. You need to make allies here. You need to better learn the other colors. I can help you, of course, but there are other teachers. It would only be expected that you would start working with those teachers as well."

She didn't say more, but I could read between the lines: Jasmine wanted several things from me. She wanted me to pass my initiation so I could get closer to the king. If the Resistance was going to use me against him, I needed to be a full-blown Guardian of Color. I also realized, if I made friends here, I might be able to build some alliances and bring more people into the Resistance. It would be dangerous, but in the end, if we succeeded, if we brought down the monarchy and allowed people to be free again, it would be worth it. I thought about my family in hiding, about all the families torn apart by this kingdom and its many laws, and strengthened my resolve.

"Okay, where do I start?"

●

I should've known better. Cowering awkwardly at the entrance of the large training gym, I nibbled my bottom lip. At the far end were weight machines and treadmills, but most of the area was open for sparring. And all around me, people were doing just that. The smell of sweat and grunts of combat saturated the gym. It was like there was an extra layer of testosterone in here. *Wonderful.*

"But you don't fight," I muttered to Jasmine.

"Why would you think a silly thing like that?" The old woman winked at me and then strode in like she owned the place. *Well, okay then...*

The gym was filled with both officers and alchemists. Apparently this was one space in which the two groups mixed well. Obviously, the alchemists would have the advantage in a fight, but the officers were strong, lethal even, and there were five of them for every one of us. Plus, many carried weapons.

I followed Jasmine to a beast of a man calling off positions to a couple of younger boys who were, for all intents and purposes, beating the ever-living hell out of each other. One landed a punch with a sickening crack. Blood flew across the mat. They both had light amber necklaces tied around their necks. Yellow. It made sense. The one who'd been hit barely noticed the impact. He jumped up and pummeled the other.

I turned away, shielding myself from the sight.

"All right, that's enough," the man called out after a couple more minutes of brutality. The boys instantly stopped fighting. One helped the other off the mat, where only seconds before he'd been punching him repeatedly in the face. They both acted as if nothing had happened as they limped to a door at the back of the gym. I briefly wondered where they were going.

"Are they all right?" I asked, unable to stop myself from asking the question.

235

Fighting wasn't something that was tolerated by New Colony citizens. Violence of any nature was quickly quelled. Even the typical stuff that happened at school could end up in revoked privileges. Fighting was just not part of everyday life in New Colony. To see it so openly accepted, celebrated even, made me want to hide in a corner.

"Don't worry," the man laughed. "They like it. And there's a greenhouse out back. In a few minutes they'll be good as new." So they could quickly go heal their own wounds, I realized. I remembered the palace medical wing I had stayed in briefly, but I guessed that wasn't really for alchemists. It must be for everyone *else* who lived here. Alchemists could just heal themselves.

"Jessa, this is Guardian Branson," Jasmine said. The man was my dad's age, tall, but all hard lines and bulging muscle. Dressed in the typical black, he looked deadly. He probably could kill me with a single punch.

"Um, hi." I tried to steady my voice as I shook his hand. It was like shaking hands with a rock, his grip was so strong. "So I can assume you're good with yellow, then?" I asked. My voice shook.

He shot me a startled look and then cracked a warm smile. "You could say that."

I tried to hide my disappointment. I needed to work on orange, purple, and green, but I didn't say anything. Last thing I needed to do was make the guy angry.

"You're going to spend some time with Branson today, Jessa. Do whatever he says. Don't worry, he'll keep you safe," Jasmine said with so much confidence that I wondered if Branson was part of the Resistance too.

We'd be so lucky to have a guy like him.

"And tomorrow, I'll come find you again?" I asked, turning my attention on Jasmine. I bugged my eyes out at her, hoping she caught my meaning. I so did not want to spend days in this gym.

"Yes, we're going to start rotating you among all the best teachers here. Have you attend some of their classes, do private mentoring, and practice. You're behind on your training, and like I said, you could be tested at any moment."

I let out a squeak of anticipation.

She was right. As I watched her glide away, part of me was terrified to even think about what was next for me. But another part of me was excited for the opportunity. It was really happening. I was an alchemist.

"So, Jessa," Branson said, his voice gravelly. "I heard you passed your yellow examination with virtually no training."

I turned on him, smiling tentatively. "Yes, that's right."

"You got lucky," he said gruffly. *Oh shucks, thanks for the compliment.* "But luck won't always win. There's talent, and then there's hard work. Are you willing to work hard?"

"Of course." I meant it. This entire gym and everything that went on here terrified me, but I wasn't naïve enough to think I wouldn't need to know how to hold my own. These people could fight, officers and alchemists alike, and there would most likely come a time I would have to fight some of them. Maybe even for my life.

"All right then, I'm going to be teaching you some basic movements. But before we do that, let's see what level you're at." He handed me an amber necklace.

"I'm a beginner," I sputtered before I could stop myself. But he didn't acknowledge my embarrassing response. I followed him into the center of the gym, anticipation making me want to run in the opposite direction. That's when I noticed Reed had been hovering in the background. Just my luck, the second Branson motioned for him, he came running like a little puppy dog about to get his favorite bone. Remembering what Jasmine had said about making friends, I held back my glare and met him with a huge fake smile.

"All right, you two, fight. Reed, go easy on her. I have a feeling she's never done this before."

"Hold up. What?" I turned on Branson. Was he serious? He wanted me to *fight* Reed? Right here? Now? But, before I could get an answer, the little weasel swiped my legs out from under me. I fell on my butt and scrambled backward. I may have been a novice, but I was smart enough to know that I needed to get back on my feet.

"Oh, so you want to play dirty?" I asked, venom in every word. Forget this, Reed wasn't getting my fake smile for another second.

He only laughed that infectious laugh that had made me want to be his friend in the first place. His eyes squinted mischievously. "Oh, I would love to play dirty with you, Jessa."

I groaned and rolled my eyes. *Such* a boy answer.

He moved in for an attack, but I dodged him. "When are you going to stop being mad at me?"

"When you stop spying on me."

"You know I regret that."

I swung a punch, but he blocked it.

"Oh, do I?" I swung again, but faked, and head-butted him in the chest.

He stepped back, not affected. *Dang it!*

"I was just following orders, but I didn't *want* to do it. You know me better than that." He shrugged.

I did know him better than that. He'd been my friend, and I thought I could trust him. Even though he liked me, he liked his boy-wonder status with Faulk more. And at the times when I was most vulnerable, he'd used his blue alchemy to get what he wanted.

But I apparently needed to make friends, to fit in, and not to call suspicion to myself. Reed was the most popular alchemist in our age group. He was athletic, funny, out-going, friendly, talented, and attractive. Anyone who was in with him probably had a better shot of winning over the rest of the group.

I swung at him again—missing, *again.*

"Geez, you're terrible at this." He smiled, brushing off the shoulder of his black uniform. "Use your alchemy, Jessa. Seriously, you're not even trying."

"I am trying!" I yelled. Okay, maybe I hadn't thought of using my magic. Not that he needed to know. I wiped away a bead of sweat running down my temple and connected with the necklace.

"Well, try harder." He lunged, bringing me straight down on my back. His solid body loomed over me, pinning me to the mat. He had the upper hand, the chance to break my face if he wanted to. But, his position didn't scare me. Reed wasn't on my side, but he still had that persuasive thing about him— probably to do with his gift for blue. There was just something about the guy that made people like him.

"Okay, fine, I'll forgive you," I said, "if you get off."

"Make me." He smirked.

I grumbled, pulling on the magic from the yellow. I allowed the feel of the rock against my throat to weigh on my skin, focusing. A moment later, the yellow alchemy connected and a surge of adrenaline shot through me. I catapulted him off me in a single shove, then jumped to my feet, cat-like.

"Good girl. Now, you're trying."

"Oh, shut up." I fought the smile lingering on my lips and stepped toward him, ready to go in for another punch.

"That's enough, you two," Branson hollered. "This is a fight, not a date."

Reed laughed. I shuffled back, taking in the crowd of people who'd assembled around us. I'd been so involved in the task I'd hardly registered them. A pit of nerves landed in my stomach, and I bit my lip, sure my cheeks were flaming. It wasn't like that with Reed, but to the rest of the world, it sure looked like it was.

I caught a glimpse of stormy gray eyes at the back of the crowd. Lucas's expression held nothing. No evidence of jealousy. No amusement. Not even a peek of longing that I'd come to recognize whenever he looked at me. He was just…blank. We locked gazes for a heavy moment, before he took a step back and disappeared into the crowd.

FIVE

SASHA

The leaves crunched under my shoes as I headed down the path. The forest was alive today. I inhaled the fresh pine and welcomed the warmth of the evening sun as it caressed my face. I was alone at the moment, and I relished in that fact. Mastin and Jacob Cole were pretty much everywhere I went, and it would be a lie to pretend it wasn't bothering me. We didn't need them or anyone from West America to help us. We'd spent years getting to this point. Jessa was in the palace now, a red alchemist.

The Resistance had people who were either alchemists themselves or supported them. West America? They were anything but our allies. I didn't understand how we were suddenly buddies with them. But nobody seemed to care what I thought about it. If they did they sure had a funny way of showing it. Hank hadn't talked to me since the meeting in his cabin two days ago. Not that I was talking to him either. The sting of betrayal was too fresh.

My nightmares had started again. Dreams where the pain came in flashes, leaving me gasping for air as I woke. I'd been out running more than ever, dreading the snow that would arrive soon.

I continued down the path, smiling when a squirrel nearly ran into my foot. The little guy was probably used to us humans by now. I caught sight of Lacey then and sucked in a shallow breath. I'd been spending a lot of my time with her. It hurt, and was probably the source of my nightmares returning. Because as much as *she* didn't bother me, her parents certainly did. And it always seemed that one of them was hovering whenever Lacey and I worked. Granted, she *was* only six. But it wasn't like I was going to do anything to harm her.

"Hey, girl, are you ready to get to work today?" I approached her. She was sitting on a log bench—our usual meeting place. Her legs were crossed under her small frame. The crisp breeze caught a lock of her wavy hair, stretching it in ribbons across her face. It was probably one of the last hot days we'd have for a while, and she was enjoying it like any kid should be.

She smiled up at me, and I was struck again by her looks. She was a cross between Jessa and myself. Why people didn't question me about it had to be because few knew about my family history.

But our parents know. Don't they see the resemblance?

Of course Christopher, our father, chose that moment to grace us with his presence. Not surprising since Lacey was never alone. I really didn't want to deal with him.

Abandonment issues, anyone?

"Good evening, Sasha." He half smiled, but there was guardedness behind his hazel eyes. "How are you?"

"I'm doing all right." I wasn't. I was too distracted to care about things like happiness. It was depressing to see where I'd ended up emotionally after all this time. I needed to get it together and suppress the itch to run.

We both stood awkwardly for a minute, neither making a move. What was I supposed to do? I could barely even look at the man. He brought up too many feelings of inadequacy. And much to my own frustration, longing was mixed with that pain. A ridiculous need to impress him, or something equally pathetic.

"So, how's our girl coming along? Everything...safe?"

I cleared my throat. "Absolutely. Safety is my number one priority."

Okay, that wasn't entirely true. I had pushed her hard a few times in the last couple of days. But it was only because I knew she was powerful. She had to be! Three alchemists in one generation, in one family like that? Unheard of. And with the West American guys hanging around, she'd need to know how to control her magic. I didn't trust them to care about her safety.

"Well, we'd better get to work." I smiled at Lacey.

Christopher fidgeted, shifting his weight. He was lanky, a typical middle-aged man. His sandy hair was threaded with gray, showing the signs of age. "So, Sasha, where are you from?" he asked.

Are you kidding me? My throat pinched as I fumbled for the right words. *Yes, Daddy, it's me, Francesca!* I banished the thoughts. I was Sasha now.

"New Colony. I was a GC kid who was lucky enough to get out and end up here. I've mostly been up here for years," I said. "That's all I know." I ended it with finality in my tone.

The pine needles crunched under my boots as I took a step back and turned away. If he figured out who I was, then what? We'd all live happily ever after? Yeah, right. No way was I going to forgive them.

This camp, this little misfit village we had here, it was my home. The thick forest was my backyard. The morning fog, the ambient noise of small animals, the clear air, it all comforted me in a way the Capitol never could. These people who lived here were the ones I trusted. The only ones who cared about me. Hank and Tristan had gotten me out of the dark New Colony world, and I'd clung onto my new one ever since.

Christopher nodded, like he had an idea of what I'd been through.

I focused on the little girl who was beginning to follow me around with stars in her eyes. Hero worship, some might say. I guess that's what I got for training her. "So, what do you say, Lacey, ready to get to work?" I asked.

Christopher followed as I led her through the clearing of pines toward the nearest glittering lake. It was one of many that dotted the area. Small and docile, the lake was one of my favorite places to think. The rocky banks had been my friend and confidante too many times. I didn't mind bringing Lacey to my special place, but I hated that I couldn't tell her dad to bug off.

"So what color is your favorite so far?"

I matched her smile while she talked with animated hand movements.

"Well, I didn't know how to do purple. But I want to try again. Yellow was the most fun. But I really liked green too. That one is the best."

In time I would be testing all the colors on her, including red. And now that I knew about its capabilities, white as well. Red wasn't something I cared to relearn, but since I'd seen white in action, I couldn't stop trying to get it to work. So far I'd had zero luck. I hoped I could figure it out soon because *that* would be something valuable to have. White was a shield. It could be used for invisibility of all things. No wonder Lucas had been able to keep his a secret for so long. I wondered how many other alchemists knew about white, if any. I was dying to get it to work.

Red had been a brief ability for me, but it was gone now. My theory was that the horror of what I'd been forced to do with it had been too much for me, and I'd suppressed it. Good riddance.

"Would you like to try some other colors?"

A toothy smile spread across her face as she nodded excitedly, her blond curls dancing.

"All right, how about *orange*?" I laughed when she started jumping up and down.

"What does orange do?"

"Orange is passion."

She stared at me, a line deepening between her eyes, and I laughed harder.

"What's passion?"

"Well, think of it like this. Orange makes people happy." *Among other things.* "It lightens the mood, if needed. It basically takes a feeling someone is having and makes it ten times bigger."

Her eyes wavered, distracted by a couple of ducks floating idly on the water. Maybe I wasn't the *best* with little kids. I didn't know how to entertain her by *talking* about magic, but *showing* her would draw her back in.

I stepped closer to the lake, peering through the water until I found what I was looking for. My fingers slipped into the icy water, and I palmed a smooth orange stone. The lakes up this way were notorious for their colorful river rocks, and they came in handy more often than not. We didn't have access to the same crystals and exotic plants at the palace. I had my necklace, but I had to be careful not to use it up too fast. I mostly kept it on for safe keeping, just in case. I could find all the colors I needed in their natural elements. *So, take that, New Colony!*

"Are you going to show me?"

"You got it."

"And then can I try?"

"Absolutely."

Her gapped-toothed smile returned, and I mirrored it again. I had to be careful. She wasn't ever going to be my sister, not truly. The more I enjoyed spending time with her, the more it would hurt when she was gone. A rush of longing filled me at the thought.

"Tell me a funny story," I said, ignoring the feelings that threatened to overpower me. "What's something that made you laugh so hard that you couldn't stop laughing?"

I carried the rock as we made our way up to a tree to sit under. We both sat cross-legged, and Lacey wove a lock of her hair around her finger as she thought.

"Oh, I know!" Light sparked in her eyes, and she giggled. "This one time, Jessa told me the funniest joke, and I laughed so hard I peed my pants."

"You peed your pants?" I teased.

"I couldn't get my belt off in time. It was so funny!"

"Okay, silly girl." I shook my head, trying not to laugh too. I really didn't understand kid humor. That sounded like a mortifying experience to me, definitely not funny.

I waited for her to relax and the giggles to slow. Then, I pulled at my magic, allowing it to connect with the orange stone on my own palm. Thin wisps of color twisted into the air. With barely a thought, they found their closest entry point into Lacey—the tiny tip of her elbow.

"Was it like this belt." I pointed to my own.

That was all it took, and she shrieked into hysterics. This time, her enjoyment was tenfold. I watched, beyond amused, as the magic worked on her. I'd only used the tiniest amount, but it had been more than enough to keep her going for another five minutes. Finally she calmed, clutching her tiny torso, the pink shirt she wore rumbled around her belly. We'd probably have to get her into black soon. She was progressing so quickly. But the idea of taking away any ounce of her childhood, including pink clothes, could wait.

"Okay, now it's your turn," I said.

"Good." She smiled. "It's about time you're happy."

"Hey, I'm happy."

She shook her head, snatching the rock. "No, you're not."

"Okay, fine."

"Tell me a funny story."

Funny was a tall order. I didn't find a lot of things particularly *funny*. I didn't use it often, but when I did, I usually used orange to lighten up. Just to soften my mood and make my *shining personality* less grizzly. Not that anyone really knew just how depressed and angry I could get at times. I was a good liar. *Was* being the operative word lately. Lacey could see right through the illusion. Kids had a way of doing that.

"Well, let me think," I said, eyeing the rock in her hand. Small pulses of color were already beginning to filter out of the somewhat-muted orange. Was it really this hard to think of something funny? That was just sad. Footsteps edged around the lake, and my guard immediately shot up. I spotted the blue sweater vest and rolled my eyes. Christopher was walking around the lake, a little distance from us, making a ruckus as he did so, knocking rocks and weeds. He really didn't have the personality for roughing it in the wilderness. But at least he was far enough away that he couldn't hear whatever I had to say.

"When I met Hank, I was just a little girl," I said. "He helped me and Tristan get out of New Colony."

"Like how you helped my family?"

"Yes, like that."

"Except you forgot Jessa."

I sighed. "No, Jessa came here, remember? But she chose to go back to help us from over there."

She frowned. "This isn't a funny story."

"I know, hold your horses, I'm getting to that," I said. "So when I first met Hank, he had this silly mustache. It looked so bad. It wasn't the scruffy man beard he has now. It was a corny mustache."

She grinned. "Like right here?" She pointed to her upper lip and made a face. I crossed my eyes at her and nodded, sending her into more giggles.

"Yes, and one time Tristan… Have you met him? Well, he's kind of a jokester. He's always playing pranks and making people laugh." I smiled. "Well, one time, when we first got out here, Tristan shaved off half of Hank's mustache while he was sleeping."

She erupted into laughter, and I joined in. Tristan had been a teenager then, always creating havoc wherever he went. But I'd been gone for a while, and I wondered if he still had those prankster tendencies—I had better watch my back.

"Then Hank got up the next morning and came to breakfast without even looking in the mirror." We had a lot of communal meal times back then. We still had some, but as our encampment grew into a village, those community meals had dwindled down. "You should have seen his face when he found out." I grinned. "He was so mad! And that only made it funnier. He had to shave it off. Which was actually a blessing in disguise."

I eyed the magic, still ready, and nodded for her to send it to me. The second it attached I burst into tears. *Oh my stars, I still can't believe Tristan did that!* The memory of that morning mixed with the orange magic had my sides aching. I was doubled over in a fit, unaware of anything else going on around me.

I looked up to see Christopher had circled back, but he wasn't alone. Mastin walked with him, dressed in his typical combat gear. The man was kind of ridiculous. He stared hard when he saw us. Ugh, I didn't want him to see me like this. The image of Hank's half-'stache popped into my mind again, and I snorted and wiped the tears. *Awesome timing.*

"Is everything all right over here?" Christopher asked, a line drawn between his eyes. Always so serious.

"Yeah, Daddy," Lacey said. "Sasha is super funny. You should hear this story." I shook my head. No way.

"Okay," he smiled at her, trepidation still in his eyes.

"It's the magic," I said through laughs, which were, thankfully, beginning to die down. "Your daughter has quite a strong affinity for orange."

"I don't get it." Mastin uttered the first words I'd heard from him in days. Since observing him, I'd found he had a way of lurking. It was annoying.

"No one expects *you* to understand alchemy, Mastin." I sighed, exasperated, my normal self returning.

"I know more than you think," he said, deadpan. Why was he always doing that bored voice? It grated my nerves.

"Well then," Christopher interjected, "I think that's enough for today. Lacey's mom has a meal waiting for her."

I held back an eye-roll and nodded as they wandered off together. The two were like peas in a pod. I noticed how close they were and tried not to let it bother me.

"What's your problem?" I turned on Mastin as soon as we were alone.

"I don't have a problem." He glared at me. His blond hair glittered in the light. His face was *too* pretty. All high cheekbones and green eyes and full lips and... *Intense brooding nonsense!* I felt my pulse rise every time he was near, and it irked me to no end. He was equal parts off-limits and sexy. *Did I just say sexy?* I stomped my foot in frustration.

"Look, the orange alchemy is an amplifier of emotion. The emotion someone *is* feeling, not necessarily what they *want* to feel. We were talking about funny stories so we could see if Lacey could make them even funnier."

"You're training that little girl."

"Obviously."

"But she's only a child."

"Yup, all the best alchemists start young."

He shook his head, darkness flitting over his eyes and matching them to the color of the pines. "You think children can handle the...responsibility?" He said responsibility as if it were a synonym for sin or something.

Was this guy for real? He needed to back off.

"Actually, yes, I do. I was younger than her when I started."

"Oh, and you turned out great," he countered.

Prickly anger clawed at my hands, forming them into fists. "Haven't we already established that you can't talk to me like that?"

He didn't answer.

Someone that attractive and that mean was a lethal combination. I needed to distance myself from this man; nothing about him could be good. He shrugged and reached down to pick up the orange river-rock Lacey had left at our feet. As he flipped it over, we both noticed the alchemy that floated up. Lacey hadn't used everything she pulled. A trace of magic still remained, like an echo.

"Don't touch that," I said, grabbing it from his hands. A bolt of energy shot through both our veins. "Too late," I grumbled.

His eyes flashed again, alarmed. "What's it going to do to me?"

"Geez, no need to be afraid. A little orange never hurt anybody."

He furrowed his brow. Well, that was interesting. He was feeling afraid of me and only the orange alchemy had made it apparent. *Score one for Lacey!* Even with that panicked expression, I couldn't help but step closer to him. *Something about him, I don't know.* It was magnetic.

Oh wait, I *did* know. I'd been stupidly admiring his sexiness when I'd grabbed the rock from him. *Ugh, why?* Residual orange had made me lose all logical thought. Now all I saw was this gorgeous unreachable man, and that made me want to understand him even more. *What the...?* I breathed in, trying to calm the passion rolling through me, but all I smelled was his spicy scent.

I moved closer, closing the gap between us. His lips hardened. They were so...full. So soft. I wondered what they would feel like to kiss. A pulse of desire shot through me, and I dropped the stone.

"This isn't real," I whispered, stepping forward as he backed away. He pressed himself against the tree, and I continued until we were toe to toe. My emotions clouded my better judgment. It wouldn't be long before I turned the kiss in my head into reality, something that the back of my mind screamed at me to avoid. And I didn't care. That was only a small part of me screaming to *back off*. But, it was so insignificant compared to the burn of desire consuming me.

My eyes caught his, and I was done. I *had* to kiss him.

Just as our lips were millimeters apart, he shoved me away. Hard. I landed in a puddle of emotions on the dirt. Rocks pierced my palms. The pain was enough to pull me back to reality.

"Ouch! Geez, Mastin, what was that for?"

He shook his head, covering his mouth and stumbling backward. "Were you going to kiss me?"

Well, this is embarrassing. "No," I lied. "Are you afraid of me?"

"No." He glared.

Ha! He totally is. "I don't believe you."

"*I* don't believe *you*," he grumbled. "I know that look you gave me. I've seen it plenty of times before. You were going to kiss me."

"No I wasn't," I insisted. "You're so full of yourself!" Who was I kidding? I was such a liar these days. "And you *are* afraid of me," I said, changing the subject back on him. "I'm the big bad alchemist, out to get you, aren't I?" I laughed then, because it was kind of true.

"Orange is an amplifier of emotion?" he asked, eyeing the rock.

"It's not a bomb," I said. The thought brought me right back to the hysterics again. He was being such a baby!

"You people are so messed up," he said. "You're a crazy person."

"It takes one to know one."

"Whatever. I'm out of here," he said, stalking off into the trees.

I stifled my laughs and took a cleansing breath. *What just happened?*

●

A flash of annoyance rippled through me as I made my way down the path to Hank's cabin. It was dark, and I didn't use a flashlight. I knew this forest by heart. The chill had a bite, and I moved quickly, trying to keep distracting thoughts from entering my mind. Truth was, I didn't want to see Mastin again. Over the last couple of days, I had done everything in my power to avoid him. No doubt, he'd be at the meeting to go over whatever plan they were working on. When Hank had asked me to join them at dinner, I'd reluctantly agreed. I didn't want to associate with West America, but I also wasn't going to stop them from doing something stupid by staying away.

The lights shining out of the cabin normally were a comfort to me. Not tonight. I ambled up the steps and knocked on the door. No matter what anyone said, I refused to lose my cool. I was walking into a situation with people who hated me because of who I was. Because of something I couldn't change. That kind of ignorance wasn't my problem.

I inched taller as Tristan swung open the door. He pulled me into a hug before ushering me inside.

Mastin was draped across the couch this time, as if he didn't have a care in the world. At least that was a step up from hiding in the shadows. He wore some West America get-up, a kind of armed forces uniform. Most girls would probably take a double look at that. I refused.

"She's back," Cole nodded, standing to greet me.

"She's back." I smirked and joined him at the table. "But she still believes what she said before. She doesn't trust you."

"Let's not worry about any of that right now," Hank said as he maneuvered around the kitchen. He poured tea from the kettle, passing cups to everyone. The energy wasn't quite so tumultuous tonight, and I could tell Hank was making an effort to keep it that way.

I caught Tristan's eye as he settled in across from me. He winked. I relaxed a little. I was glad he was with us again tonight. He always had a way of lightening the mood, no matter how dark. It was one of my favorite things about him.

Everyone settled in, and I noticed Cole motioning for Mastin to come and take a seat. When he slid into the chair next to me, he asked, "Are you going to attack me again?" His tone was dry and unaffected.

"I was only defending myself."

"Oh, is that what you're calling it now?"

"And what would you call it?"

"Attacking an innocent bystander with alchemy," he clipped.

I laughed. I couldn't help it. Why was this guy so bent out of shape about color alchemy? And of course, West America had outlawed it completely. What did he even know about the magic? More than likely, he was scared of what he didn't understand.

"All right, that's enough," Hank sighed. I glowered at Mastin, but held back my retort.

"Yes, *Sasha*. Settle down," Tristan smirked. His eyes flashed when he said my fake name. I was sure he was dying to call me *Frankie*. But I was holding onto this new identity, and I was grateful people were going along with it. I was pretty sure Hank had told everyone to keep their mouths shut on the name situation, on account of my parents' arrival.

I let out a long breath, deciding to get to the point. "Why am I even here? We all know these guys hate alchemy, so what do you want from me?"

"It's complicated," Hank muttered.

Cole straightened his uniform as I rolled my eyes. Military didn't intimidate me. "Is she always such a contrarian?" he asked.

"No!" I answered, at the same time as Tristan said, "Yes."

"Traitor," I growled.

"It turns out that as much as we don't agree with you and your lifestyle, West America needs your help," Cole admonished. He straightened his back and stiffened in the chair. I knew it was hard for him to admit it.

Let him squirm.

"So, that's why you're here… You need *our* help?" I averted my attention and focused on Mastin. Raising my eyebrows, I asked, "You need *our* help?" A smile followed, willing him to challenge me.

"So it would seem." Mastin met my gaze, his emerald eyes sharp.

The look triggered a flash of memory. The tension between us at the lake. The way the orange magic had amplified our feelings. Him, utter fear. And me, complete desire. I shook my head slightly, fighting the burn of embarrassment I was sure was exploding across my cheeks, and took a deep, steadying breath.

"What do you want from us?"

Cole cleared his throat. Mastin opened a folder that was sitting on the table. He retrieved a stack of papers, which he practically threw in my face. I glanced at the men briefly before making a show of stacking the papers neatly to read them. Not my most mature moment. Tristan laughed.

I should've been surprised by the words. I wasn't. Very little surprised me these days. It was on New Colony letter head: communications between Faulk, Richard, and a few other officers. There were even photographs.

"Shadow lands," I whispered. I stared at the landscape in the photos. They were prairie lands with sweeping fields and endless horizons. A rock formed in my stomach at the thought that soon this beautiful land would be dead.

"Richard has guardians all over New Colony, as you know," Hank said. "We have information that he's going to use those guardians, along with his military, to expand into West America. Very soon. And that includes destroying parts of our land."

I blinked, trying to wrap my mind around the situation.

"So? It's not like you'd let him get away with that," I said. "Don't you guys have armies? Weapons? Couldn't you just stop him?"

"It's not that simple," Mastin interjected. "Whenever we've tried to engage in any kind of combat with New Colony, your people's guardians are too strong. They're trained like soldiers, are they not? But what's worse, they have magic and can trick us or hurt us in innumerable ways."

"So you're too scared to even try?" I shoved the papers sidelong at Mastin. "Do you have any idea how bad the shadow lands are?"

"I never said we were scared," he paused. "We won't let him do this." His fist slammed down on the table, sending a vibration through the wooden surface.

"We didn't see this coming," Cole said. "These are areas of our country that are mostly empty. Some farmland—actually some very important farmland, but not near an urban city. As much as I hate to admit it, we're unprepared to fight alchemists. We need more resources, more soldiers, more everything."

"And that's why they're here," Tristan joined the conversation, his tone serious. The playful energy that usually accompanied him was nowhere to be seen. Tristan used to be an officer in training. Hank had gotten us both out together. He was fifteen and I'd been nine. I trusted him just as much as I trusted Hank. "You know I hate the royals as much as you do. If I'm willing to talk this over with these guys," he motioned to Mastin and Cole, "then maybe you should too."

As much as I hated to admit it, my friend had a point.

"All right, so you need alchemists. Don't you have your own?" Mastin ran his fingers through his stubbly hair, exasperated. I turned on Cole. His face had paled considerably. "Or did you murder them? Isn't that what you do over there?"

Cole sighed. "As you know, we run a democracy. And alchemy is illegal. But we're not animals. We don't kill them! We put them somewhere they can't hurt themselves or others."

I shook my head. *Not good enough.* I knew what that meant. Richard did the same thing with many of his less qualified alchemists. Did he kill them? No. But he took away their quality of life. Some were probably even institutionalized, too drugged up to perform magic. Medicate the alchemy right out of them.

"Let me get this straight. You've ruined your own alchemists, so now you've come here to see if you can wrangle up a few of King Richard's runaways?"

Tristan smiled. "She's perceptive, this one."

"Look, we need your help, okay?" Mastin said. "If you don't help us, a lot of people are going to die. Do you want that on your hands, Sasha?"

"He's right. The bug we put on Richard's slatebook stopped working about a month ago," Hank spoke up. He fidgeted in his seat, rolling his shoulders under his flannel button-up shirt. "We've since learned that he upgraded his software and got a new device. Our people on the inside knew something big was going to happen with West America, they just weren't sure what. Just a couple of days ago Jessa was able to infiltrate the officers' computers and get the rest of the information we needed."

"And what's that?"

"Richard has plans for war." The air grew thick as we took that in. "He wants to take back West America. In the process, he will kill anyone who resists."

"How is that even possible? West America is bigger."

"Maybe, but are they stronger? He's now in possession of two red alchemists, as you know. We're not exactly sure what research he's doing on them, but he believes he can use their power for mind control. If he succeeds, what's going to happen? You know. You've seen it for yourself."

He didn't have to elaborate. We both knew he was talking about when I was younger. I had access to the red as well and I'd been trained to ruthlessly use it. Luckily, the stars had smiled down on me, because I grew out of the ability. That rarely happened, but it did for me.

Either that, or I'd forced it out.

But it seemed Jessa had grown into it. And Thomas, the queen's killer, could also use the magic. If there was a way Richard could use that magic on a mass scale, or replicate it in other alchemists, then it was true. Richard would be unstoppable.

Maybe Lucas had been right. Maybe we should have kept Jessa away from his father. But it was far too late for that.

"All right, so what are you going to have me do?" I conceded.

"We've been informed that you already have about twenty alchemists living here and many more throughout New Colony. That doesn't include the citizens who have joined the Resistance," Cole said. "You have the people in the right places. And we have extra resources. We can combine and beat him."

"And what of alchemy? Let's say you win, do you take back New Colony? Do we become our own nation? And in this new world, is alchemy suddenly going to be legal?" I shifted, running my fingers through my hair, laying it over one shoulder.

"Our president has already signed an executive order to give any new alchemists immunity in our country. After all this is over, we'll take another vote. Things are changing. We're a very political country and people are beginning to be more open to the idea. If this actually works, and if the polls are correct, I believe soon we will make alchemy legal for everyone."

"Oh, so is this why Richard is suddenly so interested in you?" I asked, putting two and two together. I sucked in a breath, uncomfortable at the thought of Richard controlling more alchemists. If he had reason to suspect West America was going to create their own strong army of alchemists, of course he would want to retaliate. He always wanted to be the one with the most power. That would be a direct threat against New Colony and his tyrannical position.

Mastin added, "With the way things are going, you'd be welcomed right in." The way he said it made it clear that he did not agree with popular opinion. Loser. He still feared and hated alchemists. He probably always would. "But of course, if your king has his way, you certainly won't have a place. Being an outlaw and all."

"Oh, I assure you, Mastin, I take pride in my outlaw status."

He raised his eyebrows then looked away.

"Fine," I said, relenting. "What do you need me to do?"

"Remember those West American alchemists we were talking about?"

"Yes?" I asked wearily.

"The strongest ones are on their way as we speak."

I took that information in, frowning. This was all getting to be too much.

"You're the most well-trained and powerful alchemist we have at camp," Hank said. He still held his tea, which had to be cold by now.

"Let me guess, you want me to take a bunch of untrained, deadly, and probably angry alchemists and turn them into a magical army?"

Tristan laughed once again. I loved that sound; his laugh was like liquid happiness. But this time, it did nothing to lighten my mood.

I turned on Mastin, meeting his prickly gaze.

"That's exactly what we need you to do."

SIX

LUCAS

For the first time in two weeks I looked at myself in the mirror and stared at the person I'd become. I hated what I saw. The man staring back was partly responsible for his own mother's death. I knew it. Part of me wanted to forgive myself like she would want. But the bigger part refused to let go of the truth. I let it bore into me, disfiguring from the inside out.

I splashed running water over my face, watching the streams of liquid fall in rivulets. I wiped my face clean and groaned. I didn't want to go through this today. My royal uniform was especially restricting. The starched collar stifled my airflow, a snake wrapped around my neck, squeezing the life out of me. I finished buttoning up the gold brocade buttons of the black suit jacket and pulled at the sleeves. It trapped my body heat in with its thick and scratchy fabric. I lamented the traditional garment with the royal family insignia stitched on the lapel.

I hated funerals. Who didn't? Coming together to say goodbye to a person who was already dead as if it could provide any semblance of closure was a joke. What did the dead care of funerals? They weren't there. It was for the living, and it was unbearable, every time.

I took one last look in the mirror. I couldn't avoid it. I was who I was. The prince of New Colony about to attend his mother's funeral.

Mom is dead.

One of our most trusted officers had killed her. Thomas had used her, continually, to influence royal policy. He wasn't supposed to be an alchemist, none of the officers were. No one knew. That's what they said. And he'd been strong enough to pull the red from her blood and control her mind. He'd done it on and off for *years*, slowly killing her. She tried to get help. She even came to me. She didn't know what was happening to her since Thomas always wiped her memory with each event. But she knew something was wrong. I was too stupid and distracted to be of any use to her. I was a terrible son.

Time's up.

I stalked out of the bathroom and went to meet my father. He stood in the living room, in the exact spot she'd died. I wanted to look away but forced myself to stare. Bile rose in my throat. He was dressed to royal perfection, even had the crown perched on his head. He rarely wore it, only when he wanted to remind everyone of his power. His people surrounded him on all sides—officers, advisors, guards, and even a couple of alchemists. The actual members of his court would meet us there. They didn't live in the palace; they just attended the parties. And the funerals.

"Are you ready?" Faulk said, turning on me. Her voice sent a shot of hatred needling up my spine. How could she have missed it? How did she not see Thomas for what he was? She was supposed to keep us safe. It was her *job,* and her own number two had murdered my mother. She, too, was responsible.

●

The dome of the Capitol Rotunda stood like a beacon in the early September sky. Inside, Mom had been laid out for viewing for the last two weeks. It was tradition for the citizens to have an opportunity to come and pay their respects before the funeral. Our procession approached the building. Masses of flowers were piled outside the building—gifts from people who loved their queen. They were laid atop each other in systematic reverence. Most were already rotting.

Crowds lined the streets as our car pulled to the curb. Escaping the claustrophobic space, we were greeted with camera flashes. I blinked rapidly as the media captured our solemn expressions. Security was everywhere, but at an event like this, people had enough respect to stand back. They even kept their voices down. That made it real, and I momentarily longed for their usual noise.

Once inside, I sat next to my father on the front row—the row reserved for immediate family. Not that there was anyone left. It was just us. The room was filled with a limited number of dignitaries, just the typical influential crowd I'd grown up with. These were the court of New Colony, the barons and dukes and all those stupid titles that meant little to me. I thought of the crowd outside. No one forced any of them to come. It wasn't a social engagement, standing outside. They were here because they wanted to be. Something about that gave me comfort. Mother was loved by her people.

The black casket, surrounded by huge bouquets of white roses, was open.

As much as I tried to look away, the scene drew me to her. My eyes couldn't look away from her plastic-like body. She was ungodly pale, her lips and cheeks painted a sickly red. She was dressed in an ornate purple gown, dripping in diamonds. Such extravagance wasn't her normal style; she had more class than that. Except for her long, red hair, she didn't even look like the same person.

That's because she isn't!

As the funeral began, I couldn't look away from her body. Nor could I retain much of what was said. All the speeches and accolades and crying, it was completely washed out. It was like I sat behind a pane of soundproof glass.

No tears. No thoughts. Nothing.

A familiar face in my periphery pulled me back. Reed stood off to one side. What was he doing? A knowing look passed between him and my father. Then my father stood and headed for the podium. As he walked by Reed, he slowed and brushed shoulders with the boy. They paused for a moment muttering between themselves, and the little brown-noser nodded imperceptibly. Reed shifted in his suit, then touched my father's elbow. It happened so quickly, I was sure no one would have noticed anything unusual about the exchange. But if Reed was here, it could only mean one thing.

Blue alchemy.

Reed had quickly become the best in the kingdom at that brand of magic. And the power for persuasion was useful to someone like Richard. Leave it to him to find an opportunity to sway public opinion. Even at his wife's funeral.

Richard strode to the podium. All eyes and cameras pointed toward him. He wore the perfect expression of a grieving husband and an angry monarch. He almost *glowed* with it. I knew it then. He'd used some of Reed's magic to make whatever he was about to say as believable as possible. Even though Reed couldn't infuse his magic to the entire kingdom, he could certainly make anything the king had to say utterly believable.

"I am a man standing in front of you today with a broken heart. For thirty-two years I have loved and cared for Natasha, your queen. She was my soulmate and the love of my life. Today we remember the kind, strong woman she was. Not only in motherhood, not only as a wife, but as a monarch to this great country." He paused, as if to wait for applause. Being a funeral, the room stayed silent, but the emotion was thick. Her loss was felt by everyone.

"Many of you are wondering what happened to end her life so early. As you already know, her cause of death has been kept private as we investigated her early demise." He looked through the crowd, surveying their reactions. Everyone sat, most with backs stick-straight, leaning slightly forward. The crowd was enraptured by his velvet voice.

I found myself among them.

"The truth is, your queen, my wife, and the mother of my son, was murdered."

A hush, followed by a flurry of whispers.

Was he going to tell them what happened to her?

Finally. A wave of tension left my body as I exhaled a quiet breath, knowing that Thomas would get his punishment.

"After conducting a thorough investigation," Richard continued, "we have discovered that West America was behind the murder. Our only recourse is to declare war on our neighbor. We will not sit idly. We will avenge the death of our queen. It's time to take back what is ours!" The final words were said with such finality, that not one person in the crowd disagreed. Applause broke out. A completely inappropriate action for a funeral, but the magic was too strong to resist. Even I couldn't hold back a few claps. And I knew the disgusting truth.

He was using her *death* for his own political goals. I couldn't believe it. But then again, I could. I hated him more than ever for this. Anger pulsed through my core, and I squeezed my hands into fists.

He returned to his seat moments later, and the funeral continued, the last condolences said. A depressing song about loss and letting go was sung by the royal choir. Through it all, my mind raced, focused on the uncertain future. *War?* Richard had used this to rally the citizens for war? We hadn't had a war, not ever. Not since America broke apart and we became New Colony.

When it was time, I joined the other pallbearers. But even that experience was weightless. The coffin—a feather—and me, unable to process the moment. How could this be happening? My mother was nothing more than a decaying body. And my father cared more about his political gains than seeking justice for her killer.

Thomas needed to be held accountable.

I went along with the rest of the day in complete misery. It could've been minutes, or it could've been hours, but I endured it all. Forcing myself to feel every painful emotion, because I deserved nothing less.

At some point I found myself standing in the crowded cemetery. Headstones seemed to litter every square foot of earth. Most were worn and unidentifiable. Her body was sealed in the casket. The waxy shell, locked away.

Slowly, the men lowered her into the hole, the earth becoming her home.

It was a beautiful, sunny day, one of those rare fall days that still felt like summer. How was that okay? It should have been raining. Should've stormed! The clouds dark, the air bristly, wind and hail assaulting us. I joined the others in tossing a little pile of dirt on top of the casket, but I couldn't look. I didn't want that image burned into my memory. I couldn't handle any more.

After a few minutes, it was time to go. Relief washed over me, the strongest emotion I'd felt all day. I hated myself immediately.

We'd left the largest crowds back at the rotunda. Still, many people had come to gawk outside the cemetery gates. At least they had dressed in black. A couple of officers and several guards kept them at bay as we approached our waiting car. I was so ready to be done.

Pop! Pop, pop, pop!

Instinct flared. I flattened to the ground. Screams erupted. Bodies fell. More *pops* echoed around me. Little plumes of concrete and dust, grass and dirt rained upward. Acidic panic filled me. Then shock. Then *realization*.

"Get down!"

More shots fired.

"Your Highness," someone said, practically jumping on top of me. "We need to move." The guard snatched my arm and yanked me toward the car. The door was open, my father already inside, his eyes wild. I was shoved in, toppling over the seat. The door slammed. More bullets rained, a couple pinged off the car. One right against my window. The glass barely cracked. They clanged, louder than expected. We were safe. This vehicle was bulletproof.

Outside, the officers and guards took over. They fired back at whoever had attacked us. I stared, horrified, as bodies continued to fall, as people, some with children in their arms, ran screaming. Innocent bystanders had taken the bullets for us. But everyone knew who the true target was, who it had to be.

Someone had just tried to assassinate us.

"Has that ever happened before?" I choked. I already knew the answer.

My father looked at me then, his eyes wide. It felt like this was the first time he had really *seen me* in years. "Thank God you're okay."

I nodded, and he continued, "No, this hasn't happened before. Not in the capital."

"I know." My voice sounded far away.

A hush had descended outside, the occasional cry or shout cutting through.

"Our citizens shouldn't have guns," he said aloud, mostly to himself. Guns were illegal. They'd been illegal for decades and were extremely hard to get. Any citizen caught with one was severely punished. We tracked everything, and only officers and guards had guns. Even then, not all of them had the privilege. I didn't have a gun, though I had been trained to use one.

"That's a good point," I said, but had a sinking feeling I already knew. The Resistance. When I'd left them, did that mean they'd suddenly changed their plans? When I was helping them, they'd agreed to no assassinations. But I was right. It turned out I couldn't trust them. Who else could have done this? Maybe it was their plan all along, and they were just looking for a good opportunity? Get us out in the open, away from the palace. Catch us off guard.

"No matter who this was, we have to blame it on West America." Richard closed his eyes and brought his hands through his hair, lines crossing his face. In that moment, he looked his age. Older than he'd ever looked before. "We'll have to work it into the war effort."

"I'm not even going to justify that with a response," I said, shaking my head. West America had *nothing* to do with Mom's death. Who was to say they had anything to do with this? Blame wasn't about justice, or even truth, but about political gain. And that was wrong.

A flash of darkness crossed his features, and he turned away. We would have this conversation later. He knew it. I knew it. But still, I found myself relieved he was alive. Guilt swept over me; he probably didn't deserve to be. It was confusing. I didn't agree with him. I didn't even like him. He was a terrible king. He hurt people. He was using Mom's death for his own ends.

But…I didn't want to be an orphan.

We sat in thick silence until Faulk finally banged on the car door. Blood was splattered across her white uniform, her face grim. Richard opened the door. "I have good news, and I have bad news," Faulk said, between panting breaths. "The good news is we got him. The bad news is he's dead."

"Who is he?" Richard said.

At the same time I responded, "I would think the bad news is all these other people are dead."

We slid out of the car to survey the carnage. It was worse than I imagined. Bodies littered the ground, carnage so gruesome I nearly vomited at the sight of it. Several more people were injured, either crying out or in shock. A few people were close to bleeding out, and they were swarmed with those trying to help. I had to look away. Luckily, the few alchemists we had on hand were already jumping into action. There was more than enough green in the graveyard to take care of those on the brink of death. The magic flowed through their hands into the injured. They would be okay. As for those who'd lost their lives, there was nothing anyone could do. Not even magic could save them now.

"And who authorized this?" Richard said, pointing to the healers.

"I did," Faulk snapped. For once, I agreed with her. She shouldn't have to defend this. *Alchemists should be doing this kind of thing every day.* If I were king, they would be much more public with magic. "It will be a blip," Faulk continued. "We'll get the media to sit down with some of our most persuasive alchemists. They won't report anything out of our control. But we have to save as many as we can."

And this was how it worked.

People like Reed would use their blue alchemy to sway a story in the direction the royals wanted. In this case, Richard would pin the deaths on whomever he wanted, whoever was most convenient. There would be no talk about the specifics. There would be no explanation for those who were healed. New Colony would be informed, of course, of something. But that something was not going to be the truth. They'd likely name the assailant as some West American assassin.

"Who is he?" Richard asked. We walked over to a man sprawled out on the sidewalk. He was dead, of course. Blood oozed from a hole in the center of his forehead, an assault rifle resting just beyond his gloved hands. He was dressed in black, probably mid-twenties, brown eyes glassed over. Nothing indicated his identity.

"We don't know yet." Faulk shook her head, kicking the heel of the dead man. She narrowed her eyes into slits. If looks could kill, he would be dead twice. No, he would be dead ten times over.

"I just buried my wife," Richard growled, "and we're about to start a war. The last thing we need are renegades running around. Find out!"

The metallic smell of blood and the faint assault of charred flesh was too much. I held back a gag. I needed to get away. I rushed back to the car like the coward I was. In silence, I waited until it was time to leave.

My mind worked through all the scenarios. Who would do this? Would the Resistance really kill innocent people? It was hard to believe. Rage burned a hole through me. I needed to say something about them, to tell Faulk and Richard what I knew.

But how could I do that? The truth would reveal way too much about myself. And it would put Jessa in danger. My mother was dead. Today should've been a day to honor her. I rocked forward and bit into my fist, my teeth ripping at the calloused flesh. A guttural scream erupted from somewhere deep inside, an ancient, foreign sound.

It was the inhuman battle cry of suffering. And I deserved to listen.

I stormed into the prison, ignoring the startled looks the guards shot my way. Locked in the bowels of the palace, it wasn't a typical area I frequented. But I had murder on my mind, and I needed answers.

I strode right to the door of Thomas's cell. "Open it," I demanded of the guard posted nearby. The hulking man shook his head for a brief moment before he caught my expression. "Now," I growled.

He immediately did as I asked, his hand swiftly opening the lock. I hadn't even bothered to change my clothing when we had returned home. I was still dressed from the funeral. I threw off the jacket, with its colorful ornaments, and strode inside. Only now in black and white, I had nothing to worry about.

Thomas lounged on his cot, meeting me with a lazy grin. "To what do I owe the pleasure?"

"Why did you do it?" I demanded.

"Do what?" he deadpanned.

"Don't play stupid with me." The old man was dressed in gray prison scrubs. His facial hair was beginning to grow into a white beard. His dark eyes assessed me, obviously catching the anger that radiated off me.

"You look upset. What happened?" he sing-songed and stood.

"I asked you a question. I expect you to answer it."

He laughed softly, the throaty sound filling the small space. "Faulk hasn't been able to get anything out of me. Even with her blue magic cronies. What makes you think you will?"

I stalked forward, pushing him hard against the wall. It was easy: his aging body was feeble without access to magic. His eyes darted from side to side. Did he think someone would save him from me? Not a chance. They finally settled on my own dark gaze.

"I still haven't been able to work out how you managed to evade my magic, Lucas. Your mother was always so...weak."

I shoved him harder. "Why did you do it?"

"I already told you I had my reasons."

"Did you work alone?"

"Ah," he scrunched his nose and winked. "Now that's a good question. One I won't be answering today."

"You're pathetic." I pushed him again, then stepped back. "You deserve to die for what you did to her."

"Oh my, so upset." He shrugged. "It was an accident."

"You knew she was sick because of it. You knew what you were doing to her, and you never stopped. You just kept going!"

"And what's your point? What's done is done."

"You're a disgrace of a human being."

"And you're hiding something." He smiled and returned to his cot, relaxing as if he didn't have a care in the world. "Why are you really here?"

Why was I here? Knowing that Thomas was still alive had been bothering me, that was true. But after witnessing what I had today, and seeing my father's reaction to it all, I had to come down here. To yell at the man? Make him feel bad for what he did? To find answers? It was pointless. He honestly didn't care. He was supposed to be a friend of the family, but his only regret was getting caught.

"You're going to die for what you did," I said, moving to leave.

"Maybe," he drawled, putting his hands behind his head. He crossed his legs and grinned at me. "Maybe not."

"What's that supposed to mean?"

"A red alchemist is hard to come by, you know. Richard may hate what I did to Natasha, but like I said, it was an accident. And well, now that he knows about my magic, do you really think he's going let it go to waste?"

A million nasty replies filtered through my head. The anger had each one ready to explode out of my mouth. But this man didn't deserve another word from me. I growled in frustration and left the room, slamming the door as I went. I didn't care what kind of magic he had. I didn't care if he was the most powerful alchemist the world had ever seen. He was going to pay for what he did to my mother. No matter what I had to do to make it happen, that man would not see the light of day ever again.

●

Hours later we met in our usual place, the heat of the sun pressing down, the thick plants hiding us. I was starting to love this greenhouse and the privacy it offered. With most of the alchemists wrapped up in the news, I was confident no one would find us here.

"Are you okay?" Jessa encircled me into a frantic hug, running her hands up and down my arms. She stepped back, her eyes searching mine. She wanted something from me. Validation that I was okay, perhaps. But there was nothing left to give. I looked away.

"Someone tried to kill me today."

"I heard. Everybody heard," she whispered.

"They failed."

"I can see that." She pulled me into another hug, her face finding the crook of my neck. A familiar anticipation ran through my body.

"Thirteen people—innocent people, *my* people—are dead."

Her body stilled. "I'm so sorry. Is there anything I can do to help?"

I paused, raking my hands through my hair. "How committed are you to the Resistance?" She moved away from me then. I studied her face as it paled.

"You already know."

"What if they were the ones who did this?"

"They weren't."

"How do you know?"

"I just know, okay?" She adjusted her body uncomfortably, her weight resting against the nearest tree. The lush plants surrounded us, tall and overbearing.

They hid us from the world, but in that moment, they suffocated us too. She shook her head. "I just *know.*"

"You just know?" I laughed, disbelieving. "How is that even possible?"

"It's none of your business."

"None of my business?" Was she kidding? She stood rooted to the ground with her arms crossed like a petulant child, unwilling to listen to reason. "How is a resistance group that's bent on ending the monarchy—*my* monarchy, I might add—not my business?"

"You were part of them!" she snapped.

"Not anymore. You didn't answer my question."

"I thought you wanted democracy too. I thought you weren't okay with what Richard's been doing."

"I'm not okay with what he's been doing. But I'm also not okay with murdering innocent people to remove him."

"And as long as there is a monarchy in this country, innocent people will be murdered." She was right about the past, and maybe about the future. Even if I somehow turned out to be an amazing king, there were no guarantees that future kings wouldn't be just like my father. Monarchy didn't work when it meant a small number of people got to control all the magic.

"I know that," I said. "But you didn't see what I saw today, Jessa. And to assassinate entire bloodlines; you think that's okay?"

"No. Of course I don't want *you* to die."

"Jessa, think about this for a second. Somebody, probably your precious Resistance, ordered a hit on my father and me. On the day we buried my mother! What about that is even remotely okay with you?"

She looked away, exasperated. What didn't she get about this? "I already said I'm not okay with that. But what I'm also saying is that you don't *know* it was them. And they already told me it wasn't them! And anyway, New Colony has loads of enemies. It could've easily been someone else."

I scoffed. Maybe. Maybe it was West America, or Mexico or Canada or any other number of enemies farther away. But we stayed out of their business, and they stayed out of ours. At least, we used to. With Richard's manipulation today, it seemed that wouldn't be the case much longer. But that still didn't answer the burning question. "Then how would they have come in without the help of alchemists? The only alchemist group I know of that opposes the crown is *your* Resistance. They are the most logical explanation, but you refuse to see it. You're part of a group who probably just tried to kill me, and you're standing there acting like it's nothing!"

"It's not like that, Lucas."

"Then what's it like? Please, enlighten me."

"You know I can't tell you anything. I'm not allowed to."

"See? This is exactly what I've been trying to say to you for weeks. First, they manage to pull on my heartstrings and recruit me. They get me to do a few things for them, all the while refusing to tell me anything. So I get out, but you turned into one of them, and now you say the same things Sasha always did. *Nothing*! And I'm supposed to just sit here and let them kill me? Let you be a part of all that? I won't do it!" The words flew out in a torrent of anger as I paced around the place. I couldn't believe I had gotten myself mixed up in all that crap. There had to be another way to stop my father. A *better* way.

"So what are you going to do? I'm the only Resistance member here, you know. Are you going to turn me in? Torture me for information?" she asked, her mouth set in a firm line, and the distance between us widened.

"Why do you have to be so difficult?" I paused. "Of course I'm not going to turn you in." She was the only good thing left in my life, but there would come a day when we'd have to choose the same path, or the space between us would suffocate our feelings right out of us.

I didn't want to think about the alternative.

She tentatively stepped toward me, the patterns of shadows and light flitting over her pained expression. Her eyes filled with tears. "I'm so sorry. I don't know what more I can say or do to make you feel better. I'm doing this for my family. For people like me, who need a way out. Richard controls me, Lucas. Or he will if I don't succeed. It's not about you. It's never been about you."

She was inches away. Her hair fell in curls, framing her face, ocean eyes filling. I wanted to reach out and wipe away the tear that rolled down her cheek, but I hesitated. "Then why do you keep meeting me? Jessa, why are you here?"

Trepidation crossed her features as she bit her lip. My gaze traveled between her mouth and eyes. A battle raged behind them, a dark ocean of fear. "Because I think… I'm pretty sure…that I'm in love with you."

Wait, she *loved* me? A wave of emotion pummeled me as I searched her face for hesitation. "You love me?"

My forehead fell to hers. She nodded. I shuddered, breathing her in. We were so screwed up. How was this going to work? We couldn't stop fighting, for one. We were opposite sides of the same fight. But I couldn't help it. I wanted her too. Desperately. She was the only thing that kept me going, the only reason I hadn't lost my mind completely.

"I love you, too."

I meant it. Every word, and I would mean it again and again. I'd never said that phrase to anyone who wasn't my mother. But the words just slipped out. So natural and heavy and *real*. Jessa, she was right there in front of me—all thin bones, warm skin, pumping blood and breath, and eyes, and hair, and lips…

I kissed her.

This girl, she might very well be the death of me.

SEVEN

JESSA

"I think your boyfriend is jealous," Reed said as he pinned me to the floor. I shoved him off and shamelessly glanced around the training gym for Lucas. He wasn't there.

"I don't have a boyfriend," I said. Okay, not officially. Lucas and I weren't supposed to be together. I still wasn't sure how we were going to find a way around that. Sneaking about could only last for so long.

Reed busted up laughing. He held his gut as he jumped to his feet. "You two are so full of it," he said. "If you don't have a boyfriend, then who are you looking for?"

"Oh, shut up and mind your own business." I laughed back.

"How's it going over here?" Branson came over, eyeing the two of us. I grabbed my water bottle. "I see a lot of flirting and not a lot of sparring."

I gagged, nearly drowning myself, and coughed. Reed just smiled. Reed was a flirt by nature, and it was hard not to get pulled in by his teasing. But there was nothing between us. There might have been an ounce when we first started hanging out, but once Lucas kissed me, I was a goner. Maybe it was foolish. Maybe I was naïve. But I loved that man, and there was nothing and nobody that would change how I felt. I kept going over and over the image of it in my mind. Me confessing my true feelings. His response.

He loves me too.

"Your boy is going easy on me again," I said to Branson. As a fighter, Reed was one of the best. Actually, all these people were so far ahead of me, it wasn't even funny. Not that I was laughing.

"You heard the woman. Do your job!" Branson huffed before stalking away to go chastise a group of unsuspecting students.

Reed came at me then. He was so much larger and stronger, so technically trained, and lethal, that I *shouldn't* stand a chance. But we'd been practicing for hours every morning, and I was finally starting to have a glimmer of confidence. One of these days I'd get him! Of course, it helped that I had magic to call on.

Reed toppled me in a matter of seconds. Again! I felt for the energetic connection with the yellow stone tied to my neck. I willed another burst of alchemy to flow into my veins. Seconds later, I pressed my knees into his chest. He rocketed off. I jumped up, landing gracefully on my feet, and threw myself into a combat sequence. I'd been practicing it so much I could probably do it in my sleep.

Block, uppercut, drop, kick.

I swept my foot out, catching him behind the ankle. As he fell back, I didn't allow a moment's hesitation. I pounced, pushing him to the mat. For good measure, I elbowed him square in the nose. The last part was something I added. But hey, he deserved it. A twinge of guilt grasped me as blood poured from his nose. *Oops.*

"What was that for? You play dirty, Jessa," he groaned, still smiling somehow. I ignored the double meaning—he was always doing that. I jumped off of him and back into a crouch.

"Nice one!" One of Reed's friends chuckled from across the gym. It didn't take long for all the other guardians to see what was going on in our corner. Since the shooting during Queen Natasha's funeral, the gym had become busier than ever. War was coming, and everyone wanted to be prepared. All I could focus on was how inadequate I was to fight. A flush of embarrassment ran through my body as I squared my shoulders and stood tall. In a real fight, I would break someone's nose if needed. Reed stood, shook his head, and then laughed as he ambled off to the greenhouse out back. A few nice green leaves, and he would be right as rain.

"How did you pin him?" Branson asked, returning.

"Using the sequence you taught me. Though, I might've gotten a little carried away at the end and elbowed him in the nose." I bit my lip and rocked back on my heels, trying to gauge his reaction.

The man's normally thin lips twitched up on one side. "Good girl."

Well, okay then...

I was getting stronger every day. As much as I hated to acknowledge it, I knew there might come a time I would have to fight for my life.

●

That afternoon, I followed Jasmine toward a new classroom. It was all work these days, training morning until night. She was happy with my fighting progress, and I would continue to work out in the gym every morning. But I needed to grow my abilities in *all* the colors—especially since there was no telling when Faulk and her lackeys would be calling on me to complete another test. I couldn't afford to fail again. Purple, orange, and green remained. I wasn't nervous about green—luckily it was one of the easiest colors to manipulate.

All I knew about orange was that it was used to enhance emotion. That's why the alchemists used it to replace alcohol—they could get a similar experience without the hangover. Made sense, and I didn't allow myself to get too worked up about the orange test.

I was too worried about purple.

Purple was something I could pull out, but what it *did* was still so elusive. I needed a lot of practice with that one. Jasmine assured me that if I could handle yellow then orange would be a cakewalk. So it was purple that needed my attention. I trusted her to be right about that.

●

It was one of the hardest colors. Very few alchemists used it. No one expected me to pass, because people rarely did. That was why I only had to pass three of the five tests. But I wanted to kick butt in every color! The few times I'd gotten purple out, the tricky color had split into primary colors—blue and red. That was another ability of mine that was apparently unique to me. I could separate the colors, but I couldn't do anything with them. And it made me way more exhausted than regular alchemy.

I rubbed my temples as I followed Jasmine. She knocked on a nondescript door.

A woman, not much older than me, flitted out of the room, her blond hair so light it was almost white. It was her defining feature, like it had a life of its own. It bounced around her shoulders in waves as if it was a translucent ocean. She was waifish, tall, with a way about her that didn't feel entirely grounded. Like she was half in this world and half somewhere else. Somewhere veiled in mystery. She had a carefree go-with-the-flow energy. Flightiness. Like trying to hold sand between your fingers.

"Jessa, I'd like you to meet Lily Mason. If anyone can help you with purple alchemy, it's her."

I stood awkwardly as Lily Mason glided over to me, her eyes calculating. They were such a disarming shade of light blue that I couldn't look away. I'd never seen this woman before in my life. She was a teacher here? Was she old enough for that?

"You're trying to guess my age, aren't you?" she asked in an apathetic tone, like she had zero attachment to my answer.

I nodded. It was true. So far all of the teachers I'd met were at least middle-aged. Sure, Lucas and Reed had assisted in my early training, and talent came in all ages. But the actual teachers who taught the alchemists weren't young. They were the most experienced, with years of training in the field before coming back to pass on their knowledge to the younger generation.

"I'm twenty-three."

"And she's been teaching for six years," Jasmine said. "Unheard of and impressive, I know. She knows. But there aren't that many people who are good with purple alchemy. And Lily isn't just good, she's renowned."

"It's my gift. And this way the king has better access to that gift." Again, she said things with no conviction. No emotion. It was as if she didn't care either way. They just *were*.

"Access to do what, exactly?" I asked.

Her eyes, which had been drifting, snapped back to meet mine. A chill ran up my spine. "What do you know about purple alchemy?"

"Umm... I can pull it out of things, but I can't use it. I've been told it can help people find their life purpose. Connected to intuition, something like that. I don't really understand what any of that means..."

She smiled then. It lit up her entire face. "Come." She opened the door wide and strolled into her classroom, which wasn't like the others. It was smaller. And there wasn't a glass wall on the side of the hallway. There also weren't any desks or even any tables. There were a lot of comfortable-looking couches and pillows large enough to sit on strewn across the floor, with a worn oriental rug underneath. It was dimly lit, with purple practically everywhere. There were amethyst rocks placed around the space, some taller than me. And smaller ones were neatly tucked everywhere. A few plants with purple flowers grew precariously in ornate pots.

She sat on one of the pillows, crossing her legs. Feeling awkward standing above her, I sat on a pillow as well.

"You know it would be better if you left," she said to Jasmine without breaking our eye contact. It seemed that she didn't care either way what happened. The woman was unattached.

"I know. Jessa, there is nothing to worry about. You can trust Ms. Mason. The kind of magic she's going to show you works best one-on-one."

And with that grain of knowledge, we were alone.

"So, purple, huh? What is it that you do? Does it do multiple things like blue or just one like yellow and orange?" I couldn't help the questions from forming. When I was uncomfortable, I tended to do that.

Lily cocked her head at me, unfazed. "The purple wheel of energy is strong in you. The chakra is open. It's the third eye. Intuition. You know so little, and yet you are so powerful. It's a dangerous combination."

"So I've been told."

She continued, "Do you want to know your future? I already know the answer. It's yes. They always want to know. But they shouldn't always know. And it isn't guaranteed. Prophecy is better. It has surer lines. It's rare. I can't choose it. It just comes when it comes. Fortunes, I can do those anytime, for anyone. But those lines move easily. They blur. Best not to plan your life around something so fluid." She said everything with a breathy voice, like she was talking to herself.

"You're a fortuneteller?" I asked. I'd heard about those people in old stories, but didn't know they still existed. A wave of excitement rolled over me.

"I'm an alchemist who can see fortunes...and misfortunes." She reached to one of the amethysts on the floor and held it in her palm. As expected the color leached out, dancing ribbons of purple magic. Then it split between us. I saw some of it flow into her and felt the color seep into me, calming my

264

nerves instantly. The prickly sensation of trust swept through me. The magic was connecting us.

I met her eyes again, but this time she was wholly in the other world. A glazed, unseeing expression descended upon her.

Please let this be good news.

"You have dark magic," she hissed. "It will be used against you." She paused, nodding, as if listening to someone who wasn't there. "You're on a dangerous path, Jessa. There is heartache. Betrayal. So much suffering."

Lovely.

"So how do I change it?" I hated the fear in my voice. Did I really believe this? But it was magic, I saw the purple, felt it…

"Do not trust him."

"Who? Who's him? Reed? Lucas? The King?"

The door burst open. Light flashed across Lily's face. Her eyes filled with recognition and she was lost from her trancelike state almost instantly.

"Who shouldn't I trust?" I pressed.

"You know the rules." Faulk snapped as she interrupted, moving headlong into the small space. As always, she was surrounded by her hordes of officers. They filled all available space quickly, bringing a claustrophobic cloud in with them. I wasn't happy about the interruption, obviously. Lily, however, didn't seem to care one way or the other. Her impassive expression never seemed to fade, no matter the circumstances.

"You *teach* purple alchemy. You do not *use it on anyone* unless specifically asked to by the king or myself."

"Yes, I am aware. I sat down to teach Jessa about this magic. I picked up a stone, and it just happened. I'm sorry," she added, her expression serene. Uncaring.

She's lying. She'd wanted to give me my future, had asked me. If she'd broken rules to do it, what did that make her? Part of the Resistance?

"And what did your future hold?" Faulk turned on me.

There was no use in lying.

"She said I had dark magic. And it would be used against me. But you interrupted before she had a chance to explain." I tried to keep the venom from my voice. But it was no use. I hated her. The feeling was mutual.

Faulk glanced between us, suspecting. What was she going to do about it?

"One short lesson and you already got your fortune told. I think that's enough for the two of you," Faulk said. "Jessa, come with me, please. Ms. Mason, you can stay, I think you've done enough."

"Where are we going?" I stood. I knew better than to ask Faulk anything, but I always seemed to do it anyway. I caught Lily's ethereal eyes again, but they were impassive. Nothing could be discerned from them. *Creepy.*

Faulk didn't bother to answer as she stomped from the room. As I followed her out and down the modern GC corridor, I thought about what Lily had said. I'd memorized every word. *Heartache. Betrayal. Don't trust him.*

The king kept Lily in the palace under the pretense of training alchemists in purple. But really, purple was so elusive that few alchemists ever figured it out. So that meant she was really here to be his personal psychic. She'd said that the future wasn't set in stone. Things can change. But still, she had to be useful to someone as bloodthirsty as Richard.

That didn't bode well for the Resistance.

"If we can't have you around Lily without her spontaneously reading your future, and who knows what else, then it seems to me that we might as well get your failure behind us."

She walked so quickly I had to run to catch up with her. "Umm, excuse me? What are you talking about?"

"Your purple test. Let's do it this afternoon, shall we?"

"Um, no, we shall *not*," I shot back. She couldn't be serious! "That's not fair," I continued. "I haven't had a chance to study purple *at all*. You're setting me up to fail."

"It's the king who wants you to take your tests before you're ready. He's already growing impatient. If anyone is setting you up to fail, it's him. If you've got a problem with it, you can take it up with him. My suggestion, however, is to keep your pretty little mouth closed and do as you're told."

This was ridiculous. Where was Jasmine? She'd stick up for me, wouldn't she? But then again, Jasmine was only tasked with training me. Anything more might look suspicious. I stomped my foot, annoyed as ever! I knew Lucas would help if he could, but he was supposed to stay away from me. His father wouldn't take kindly to anything Lucas had to say about me. Faulk could practically get away with anything where I was concerned.

There was no point. She always had the upper hand.

"Okay, so what exactly is this test? Am I supposed to read someone's fortune or something?"

Maybe I should just get this failure over with. There was only a small chance I'd miraculously know how to manipulate purple. I still would have green, which I knew was a sure thing. That left orange, and it was another easily accessed color. I would figure it out. I had to. There was no other choice but to pass at least three of these tests and be initiated into the Guardians of Color. Then I would get to work directly with the king and find a way to stop him.

"There's more to purple alchemy than looking for futures," she responded.

"What do you mean?"

Faulk stopped abruptly and gave me a hard stare. I was asking for her help, knowing full well how unlikely it was I'd actually get it.

"If you're lucky you'll be able to see the future. But there are more practical uses for the magic of intuition. You *may* be able to hear people's thoughts, telepathy even."

Umm...wow!

I stepped back and nodded. "Thank you." Now I was really curious. Mind reading? Telepathy? I hoped I would be able to do those things one day. Purple sounded amazing, but at the moment I was overwhelmed by it all.

She laughed. "Silly girl, don't count on it. Even *you* aren't that good."

Challenge accepted.

She turned on her heels, and I followed her out the ornate front doors of the palace. The cool air swept over me as I took in the sprawling, manicured yard. Where were we going? She stomped to the single black car waiting in the drive and motioned for me to get in. I didn't want to. I didn't trust her. But what choice did I have?

"The royal family *won't* be joining you on this one. With the recent attack, it's not safe for them to leave the palace grounds. So sorry your *friend* Lucas won't be there to cover for you." I had to force myself from rolling my eyes.

"Umm…okay." I smiled politely, sliding into the cool leather seat.

She threw a black blindfold at me. "Put this on."

●

There was a price to pay for everything, including magic. One of the most common prices of alchemy was energy. It made the user tired, especially if they'd been using a lot of magic. The day had been filled with alchemy already, and it was weighing on me. I might have fallen asleep in that car, had I not been so worried. With my next test looming, and the fact that I had no idea where we were going or what to expect, I wasn't sleepy. How long had we been driving? An hour? Two? Long enough that fat beads of sweat rolled down my cheeks.

"Hey, anybody up there? I know there has to be a driver in here. How much longer do we have?" No answer. I'd quickly figured out I was alone in the backseat. I didn't have anyone else to ask.

The smooth ride of the car changed as we drove onto some kind of gravel. That had to be a good sign, but the bumping vehicle only ignited my nerves. A few minutes later, the vehicle stopped.

I did a mental happy-dance, trying to hype myself up. I was probably going to fail, but I would try my best. I'd already decided that. The look on Faulk's face if I passed would be worth it. The car door swung open, and I took that as my cue to pull the blindfold from my face and get out.

I blinked as I adjusted to the filtered light.

There was no one there. *Actually,* there was no one *visibly* there. But I knew I was being watched as I stepped from the car and into a shady forest. The leaves were a hodgepodge of color. Some still held onto their green, but many were alight with the fire of fall. Brilliant orange, red, yellow, and pink surrounded me on all sides, interspersed with pine trees that gave off a comforting scent. I did allow myself to relax. I spotted a piece of white paper tacked to one of the trees. It contrasted so sharply from the rest of the scene that it stood out like water in the desert. I strode over, pulled it down, and read.

She's lost. You have one hour to find her. Take the amethyst at your feet and venture into the unknown forest. If you fail, she will stay lost.

The moment I finished reading the cryptic instructions, the car's engine turned on, and the vehicle backed out of the alcove and sped away. I peered around, and a chill prickled up my spine. *Maybe I really am alone.* I reached down to palm the crystal. The second it touched my fingers I heard it. A girl screamed.

I dropped the stone.

Frantically, I looked side to side. Nothing. My heart kicked up a notch as I picked up the stone again. Another scream pierced my ears. That's when I realized what was happening to me. *The purple alchemy is working.* That girl wasn't anywhere near, but I'd either heard her telepathically or glimpsed the future. I studied the stone in my hand, willing it to work again.

Nothing happened. *Seriously? Don't do this to me now!*

I stared hard at multiple hiking trails that led into the forest, wondering which to take. I squeeze the stone again. It was about the size of my fist, deep purple at the base and light purple at the tips, a jagged stone I could only describe as beautiful. Amethyst. The same stone Lily Mason used. I took a deep breath and pulled a wisp of color from it. It danced in the air for moment. I willed the color to enter my body. But it only poured back into the stone. Frustrated with little time, I picked the least worn of the three hiking paths and followed it.

I passed the stone back and forth between my hands and charged my way along the trail. Rocks jutted from the dirt floor. Weeds and tree branches brushed me on all sides. It was slow moving. I wondered if I should've chosen an easier one. This one seemed fruitless. I began to doubt I would find the person, the girl who needed my help, without the purple alchemy. I couldn't get it to work again. But what else was I supposed to do besides keep going? It wasn't like I was going to sit this one out. I had to try.

After a few minutes, I stopped to catch my breath and stared at the crystal again. I cleared my mind and relaxed as best I could. I tried not to imagine wild animals stalking me or what could be making all the cracking noises that came with the territory of a forest terrain. I allowed the sound of trickling water nearby to calm me. I focused on that and slowed my breathing. After a few moments of peace, I imagined the purple color of the stone seeping into my hands without opening my eyes.

An image flashed through my mind.

She was young, definitely close to Lacey's age. Her blond hair hung across her knees as she sat on the ground. Her face was buried against those knees, and she rocked with sobs. She sat against a tree trunk. There was nothing distinctive about her surroundings, other than that she was in this same forest. The image began to blur before fading to black.

I opened my eyes, trying to hold the image.

Who was she? A tiny voice of doubt rang through my mind. *Lacey?* But it couldn't be. Lacey was safe. She was with Mom and Dad, up north. New Colony had no clue as to her whereabouts. King Richard was only pretending to have them in his custody. He didn't know what I knew.

So who was this girl? Someone who looked like Lacey. A trick? My chest burned at the idea.

I pictured her sad little body, crying. It didn't matter who she was. I still had to find and help her. What had that note said?

If you fail, she will stay lost.

Would they really hurt an innocent girl, a girl who couldn't be more than six or seven years old, because of me? I wasn't sure, but either way, it lit a fire under me, and I started to run down the trail, hacking at the foliage in my way as I went. *Where is she?* I squeezed the amethyst so tightly the edges dug painfully into my palms. *Come on, please. Show me something!*

I was in the middle of nowhere, and so was this girl. She could be anywhere. I had to get this magic to work!

Please help me, a young choking cry sounded in my head.

"Where are you?" I whispered. Maybe she could hear me too?

Please help me.

Are you hurt? I asked, this time in my mind.

Please...

I listened to her thoughts, but she couldn't hear mine. I concentrated harder, pulling the images she saw into my mind. Trees. Just stupid trees everywhere.

I had an idea. *Water. Listen for water on her end.*

I stopped running and closed my eyes, hoping if I could see from her point of view, I could hear too. I could faintly make out the image of her huddled under a tree. But there was water. I could just hear it over the sound of her crying. It was close to her.

Okay. Sweetie, I'm going to find you. I said the words in my mind, hoping she could hear me. *My name is Jessa. I'm a teenage girl dressed in all black, and I have brown hair in a ponytail. If you see me, call my name. I'm here to help you.*

I need help. I'm lost. The voice an echo in my mind.

I'm coming, I responded. Maybe she'd heard everything I said and had responded? Part of me clung to that, convincing myself it wasn't coincidence, while the other part believed it was wishful thinking.

I took off, heading toward the sound of water. I wasn't sure how much of the hour I had left. I didn't know how far the girl was. But I had a fighting chance at saving her and passing the test. I'd give it everything.

Less than a minute later, I stood at the edge of the water. It looked almost the same here as it did in my vision. That was a good sign. How many streams could be up here that looked like that? I hoped for both our sakes there was only one. I took off at a run along the riverbank, half stumbling as I ran. I didn't trust Officer Faulk. Knowing her, that little girl really could be in danger.

Frigid water splashed, stinging my face, as I continued to trudge along the bank. Tree branches attacked my body as I pushed them out of my way. I squeezed the purple stone harder, thanking the stars I had figured out how to use it. No, I wasn't an oracle or anything special. I couldn't do what Lily Mason did. I wasn't seeing the future. I probably wasn't having some telekinetic conversation with the girl. But I was able to reach out and read her thoughts, *see* what she saw.

Checking back in with magic, it was easier this time to find her. She still sat where I'd asked her. But it could be anywhere. Her head popped up, and

I finally got a good look at her face. I already guessed she wasn't Lacey. But it was obvious they'd chosen somebody who came pretty close in appearance. She had blue eyes and blond hair and was about six years old. They must have picked her specifically to mess with me.

I'm coming to find you, I said, reaching out to her mind. No response.

I continued up the stream, heart pounding, breaths labored, determination pounding with each step. By this point, I could see her in my mind's eye and see my own reality at the same time. Like double vision, one clear and real image, the other hazy and in my imagination. *Incredible…*

How much time did I have left? I kept going, faster than ever. But I still had no real idea where she was, and the water had drenched me, sending my body into a shivering mess. I had an idea. Blue alchemy.

Frantically, I searched around for anything blue. My best bet was a river rock, so I started there. I all but jumped into the center of the stream and began lifting rocks, foraging for anything with even a blue tint. Holding onto the amethyst in one hand and searching for a new rock in the other was no easy task.

Finally, a flash of blue caught my eye. It shimmered under the moving water. I pried it out of the riverbed and palmed it. I willed the alchemy to work. I'd only done it one other time when Reed had shown me all those months ago in my old bedroom. But it had been easy then, so I could only hope for the best.

The hazy side-image of the girl began to fade as blue alchemy took over. She was still there, but this new magic was frenetic and excited. Standing still in the stream, I allowed it to take over me. The sound of the water magnified, but I pushed past that. Beyond was the scurrying of woodland animals: squirrels, birds, and even a few deer. It was as if my mind were a camera, flying over the forest, listening to everything with blue, viewing it with purple, and sending a signal back to where I stood.

It was easily the most amazing thing I'd ever done with alchemy. But I hardly had time to congratulate myself or get caught up in the wonder of it all because I found her.

And I was right. She was upstream. That was the good news. The bad news, she was much farther than I'd anticipated. At least another mile. I didn't have a clock, but I knew my timed test was nearing the hour mark. I dropped the large blue-tinted river rock, not wanting anything to slow me down. I ran.

Catching a glimpse of golden leaves, I grabbed a few in my fist, and willed myself to be faster. The yellow took effect immediately. I'd been practicing with it so much lately that I wasn't surprised. Pride warmed me at the accomplishment. I charged through the rocks, water, and aggressive tree branches at breakneck speed. Within a few minutes, I destroyed that mile. The little girl sat just on the horizon. I sprinted the final distance to her and wrapped her in what was probably a cold, wet, uncomfortable hug. I couldn't help myself.

"I'm here!" I exclaimed, joy bursting at all my seams.

She giggled, straightening her small frame into my embrace. "Good job, Jessa. The other initiates always fail this one."

"What?" I squinted. "You're in on this too?"

"Yes." She giggled again, as if it were the funniest thing in the world. It reminded me of when Lacey tried to pull her kid-pranks on us, always so simple to us but hilarious to her.

"It's okay." She stopped laughing and smiled at me. An adorable gap spaced out her front teeth, and dimples appeared on her freckled cheeks. "You did a good job. King Richard is going to be very happy about this."

Okay, this was just weird. I sat back and looked away, all adrenaline leaving my system.

She stood and waved at someone behind me. That's when Faulk appeared. Of course. It was all a test. *I knew that.* Still, the little girl being in on it too, that was beyond annoying. Maybe it was for the best. Even if my ego was a little bruised, it would have been much worse had the kidnapping been real.

"Lost forever, huh?" I said, glaring at Faulk, mentioning the words on the note.

"Halle is one of our youngest alchemists. She's been helping us out with this test for a few years now. Something about a little girl in trouble, lost and alone in the wilderness, puts a bit of skin in the game, don't you think?" Faulk smiled, her always-orderly appearance out of place in the wilderness. She walked to Halle and the two actually high-fived!

I didn't get why anyone liked Faulk, but it seemed many alchemists did.

"I guess," I muttered. Truth was, she was right. Halle had helped me gather the urgency needed to pass this test. I glanced at the girl, too young for this messed-up game. "Thanks for your help, kiddo."

"Too bad you failed," Faulk interjected.

"What?" I gasped. "I didn't fail!"

"Yes, you did. You are two minutes over the hour. Plus, this was a purple test, and you used several other colors."

"You've got to be kidding me!"

"Rules are rules."

"I was never informed of those rules. And two minutes? That shouldn't count. Why do you hate me so much? Why don't you want me initiated?"

She stared at me coolly, giving away nothing of her intentions. "It's time to go back to the palace."

"You *wanted* me to fail," I pressed. "Why? Isn't it your job to help me succeed so I can help the kingdom? Isn't that what King Richard, *your boss*, wants? Why are you trying to stop me? It doesn't make any sense, Faulk!"

My words fell on deaf ears as I followed her and Halle to a nearby path. I charged after them, anger fueling my entire body.

She turned on me then, meeting me nose-to-nose. "You cannot be trusted. Everything about you is defiant. You've lied on more than one occasion and I don't want you in my Color Guard. You are a stain on my reputation."

"You won't even give me a chance."

"Why should I? I am on to you, Jessa Loxley. I know you're hiding something. You'd be so lucky as to fail these tests and end up institutionalized, because if you join my ranks, I will find you out. And I will destroy you."

My mouth dropped open as she turned on her heels.

Did she know I was part of the Resistance?

Glaring daggers into her back, I vowed to do everything to best that woman. I'd passed one test and failed two. I had to make orange and green successes. I had to win. There was absolutely no way I would allow them to institutionalize me. I was a powerful alchemist, and I would use that magic to do what needed to be done. In the end, I would get what I wanted and she would just have to deal with it.

As we traveled back to the palace, a shadow of doubt followed close behind.

EIGHT

LUCAS

I sat back in my chair, my hands squeezing the base, and willed myself to keep quiet. Why must my father surround himself with idiots? We were in the main boardroom in the GC wing where the royal officers worked. His top advisers sat around the table with the king at the head and me at his side. We were going over strategy. War strategy. Papers littered the oval, wooden table, maps lit the screens on the walls, and multiple rounds of coffee had long since been finished.

"Do we have any more information on the assailant?" Richard asked, referring to the gunman—the dead gunman.

"No, sir, he is not part of our system. Everything he wore was untraceable, and his assault rifle did not come from here."

"So you're telling me an outsider got past the shadow lands?"

"It appears so, Your Highness. It shouldn't have happened. He must have flown in undetected."

"Are you surprised?" I interjected. "Whoever believed the shadow lands to be a perfect line of defense? All it takes is an aircraft with radar-jamming capabilities to get over them."

"We have constant patrols," the older man replied, his face red. He was the officer in charge of our military. A military that hadn't seen much action in decades, and in my opinion, was mostly for show. Everyone knew the alchemists were the real threat. This guy was a clown if he thought the shadow lands were uncrossable. Maybe by foot, but not by air.

"Well, your patrols aren't good enough, are they?" I shook my head.

My father sat back, studying me, a small smile playing on his lips. No doubt he thought I was following in his footsteps. Subscribing to his twisted way of thinking. *It's not that simple.*

Of course I wanted to keep our people safe. And the terrorist attack had shaken me to my core. I wanted to find out who was responsible just as much as anyone else, but I wasn't willing to lie about it. And I certainly wasn't eager to head off to war with West America, something my father was obviously gunning for. He and I both knew he'd lied when he had said that West America was responsible for Mom's death. In fact, everyone in this room probably knew by now, for one simple and glaring fact. Their previous confidant, Thomas, was down in the dungeons, waiting to be executed.

"We will figure out who did this and make them pay, Lucas," Richard said. "Rebels, foreign enemies, a resistance group, or otherwise, we'll find them. Either way, West America or not, we will be going over there."

My breath caught at his use of the word "resistance". Did he know about the group of his own citizenry, alchemists included, working to take him down? Did he suspect Jessa?

"And what about Thomas?" I asked, changing the subject back to one Richard and I had been arguing over since the day of his incarceration.

"What about him?" My father met my gaze, his eyes matching my own challenge.

"When are you going to execute him?"

"Soon."

"That's what you keep saying. But *soon* isn't good enough. He murdered Mom. The queen! He tried to pull the same control crap on me. He doesn't deserve another day of life, and you know it." The words shot out of my mouth with such venom I hardly recognized myself. But I stood by it all. That man was a traitor, a murderer, and he needed to go away. Forever. The heat rolled through my body, and I longed to take off my suit jacket. But I'd dressed professionally for a reason, and I made myself settle down into my chair.

"Like I said, son, he will die soon. In the meantime, you can trust me when I say he is wishing for death."

Trust him? How many times had he asked me to blindly trust him, only to put his own needs before mine? I was getting tired of his antics.

I held his gaze. "Like I said, father, that isn't good enough. Mom deserves justice."

There was something more going on, and I knew it had to do with red alchemy. Why else would Richard keep the man who killed his wife alive? There was no other explanation. He wanted to keep Thomas around in case he needed him. That had to be it. Thomas spelled it out for me that day I'd confronted him. He had the magic my father has been so desperately trying to cultivate for years. And if Jessa didn't work out? Thomas would be waiting, a willing plan B. But Thomas was not to be trusted, nor could I ever forget what he'd done to our family. He didn't even feel an ounce of remorse.

"You need to do it now. For her..."

Richard caught his breath, his teeth grinding. I'd pushed too hard. I didn't care. He always seemed to play this game with me, as if he liked it when I challenged him. Almost like he saw it as a leadership quality. But there was a line at which he became territorial with me, a border at which I should agree

274

to his every opinion. Kneel down to your king and father. I knew the line well. It showed up every time my lack of respect for him became obvious.

"That's enough." He slammed his fist onto the table. The mugs clattered, and cold coffee sloshed out of one and onto the mahogany surface. It spread, brown eating the edges of one of the papers. For a man who seldom yelled, I'd caught him off guard. It was stupid. I knew better.

"I apologize, Father," I said. "You know how passionate I can be."

"Don't we all." He smiled sourly. Turning to the room, charm warmed his features. Everyone nodded in agreement.

Oh, yes. Everyone knows how the prince can get.

Faulk, who'd been uncharacteristically absent from the meeting, chose that moment to interrupt. She strode into the room with the same air she always had, completely loyal to my father and her job. She was the type of woman who demanded attention with her ambition. There were no soft bits to her, only hard edges. I suspected she purposely chose to be cold because it gave her power.

Sometimes, I thought my father was in love with her because of it.

"I have some bad news to report, Your Majesty." She said *bad* as if it were quite the opposite. "We just returned from Jessa's purple alchemy test." My body tensed.

"And?" he asked.

"She failed."

My stomach formed into a hard knot. It took every ounce of willpower to keep my face stoic. I wanted Jessa out of this world and safe somewhere else, but as long as she was here, she needed to pass the tests. If she didn't, nothing good would come of it. She'd most likely be institutionalized, or maybe even become a prisoner downstairs.

"What happened?" I asked casually.

Faulk never took her eyes off the king as she answered. "She came close. She did use purple alchemy, it seems. But she also used blue and yellow. And she took longer than an hour to find the girl."

"Did anyone tell her not to use the other colors?" I questioned.

She didn't answer.

"But she was able to manipulate purple?" Richard asked.

"Yes, the most common way. Not quite back and forward telepathy but she did get into the girl's head."

"Well then, I hardly count this is bad news."

"But she failed."

"That may be up for discussion."

"I agree," I said, interjecting on Jessa's behalf. "If an alchemist can manipulate purple, an alchemist can manipulate purple. That's all there is to it. What other question is there? And who cares if she used other colors? From your lack of response to my question, it sounds like you didn't tell her not to do it. That's hardly fair. Plus, guardians in the field do it all the time. Maybe that should be counted as a good thing. Counted toward a pass."

"But it's not the way things are done during the tests."

"Maybe the tests need to change then," I challenged.

Faulk finally turned her steely gaze on mine, her lips in a thin line. I cocked my head at her, not willing to back down on this. She had the common sense to keep her mouth closed.

"You know what, son? I think you're right," Richard said, meeting my gaze. "Maybe it is time to change how we run these tests." He said it with a knowing tone. A glimmer of an idea brewing, perhaps? My body went rigid. What was he planning?

"That's it for now," he continued. "We'll meet again tomorrow to discuss the first attack on West America. I don't want to wait much longer. Every day we wait, the element of surprise could be taken from us."

The men and women surrounding the table stood to leave, nodding their agreements as they went. I put my head down, thinking heavily, as I followed close behind. I felt a hand on my back, and I turned. Richard. We were alone.

"I think it's time you and I had a discussion," he said.

"What are you talking about?"

"You are mighty defensive of Jessa. Some might say overly defensive of her. Are you still interested in her romantically?"

"What do you think?" It was an impulsive way to respond. Sometimes, I just couldn't help myself. I was a grown man and tired of living under the thumb of my oppressive father. He expected too much from me and gave me too little. Shouldn't I be free to love whom I wanted? I hated how complicated it was to be a prince with a king like Richard judging my every choice.

"No matter," he said. "I have arranged a party for tonight. It's time you met some eligible women. Women who will put Jessa to shame." He winked at me.

"I'm not interested," I said, pushing past him on my way to the door.

"Get interested, or your little girlfriend will be removed from the palace." I stopped, slowly turning back to him. There were other places in the kingdom they could train alchemists. Other places she could go. Worse places. Was it worth it to challenge him?

Taking in his firm expression, I decided to back off. He reached a hand around me and against the door. He clearly wanted to talk candidly.

Give him this, I had to warn myself

"Fine." I smiled. Fake, of course. "Let's meet these lovely ladies and see what kind of woman you think is better than Jessa."

There wouldn't be anyone. He didn't seem to agree. Instead, he raised an eyebrow, clearly amused by the whole situation.

He pushed the door open and nodded for me to leave. "That's my boy."

I stormed into the hall, my heels clipping as I walked. The depression from the last several weeks descended on me then, thick and heavy. I hadn't saved my mom. I hadn't gotten through to Richard about Thomas. I hadn't convinced Jessa to leave the Resistance. And now I had to deal with my father's disapproval at Jessa being a part of my life. I couldn't win.

I ground my teeth, lost in tumultuous thoughts that only spiraled into darkness. I couldn't lose everything, but I was so close to that edge.

●

I didn't have a chance to connect with Jessa. I'd spent hours going over things in my head. I still didn't have any solutions. I needed to talk to Jessa, so I'd gone to our usual spot in the greenhouse, but she wasn't there. I'd even gotten desperate enough to knock on her dorm door. No one had answered. I resigned to the fact that she wanted to be alone, recovering from the purple test failure. I hated the image that conjured in my mind. I should be able to comfort the woman I loved. Everything was falling apart, and the fact that I was hopeless to stop it was destroying me.

Straightening my tux, I gritted my teeth and entered the ornate ballroom. Immediately, I looked for her. But there were no alchemists in attendance. Relief washed over me. Good. She didn't deserve to witness the ridiculous spectacle that was about to take place. I took it all in: the people, the white linens, and tables overflowing with flowers and food. This was the last place I wanted to be.

The room was filled with New Colony's nobility. Only the most powerful and respected families had been invited to this event. It made for a smaller party, smaller than what we were used to. But in light of recent events, it probably made us all safer. Many women sauntered around the room with glasses of wine and champagne. The service staff carried trays of hors d'oeuvres and drinks. Everyone was dressed to impress. The younger women wore more revealing dresses than their mothers—all legs and cleavage and open backs, showing skin to get my attention. They had high hopes of catching a crown with this prince. To them, it was status that mattered most. I was good-looking and women liked that. Still, that was only a bonus. The crown was what everyone wanted most.

My father sat on his throne overseeing the party. I hated that thing. He loved it. It was made of cherry wood and red padded seats, raised on a platform at the far end of the room. Laughter and music filled the space, and a line of people were at his feet, waiting their turn to greet him. He caught my eye, and the laser focus of his gaze issued a challenge: behave and do what he wanted, or else.

Better get this over with...

"I don't believe we've met," I said to the closest woman who looked like she was here to *get to know me*. She was dressed in a skin-tight, black halter-top dress with an open back that left little to the imagination. Sleek red hair was tamed to perfection and an ungodly amount of black makeup was applied expertly around her green eyes. She was gorgeous. So what?

"Your Royal Majesty," the woman replied with a coy smile. "I am Celia Addington, only child of the Duke and Duchess Addington. I'm embarrassed to say we've met before."

"I'm sure I would've remembered you," I replied politely. That wasn't always true. I was used to women throwing themselves at me. It had been a normal occurrence ever since I hit puberty.

"Oh, we've met." She winked.

"Right," I responded dryly.

I stopped returning the attention pretty soon after I realized what these women and their parents were really after. An unplanned pregnancy was probably top of most of their lists, but it was bottom of mine. Some of them would do anything to trap the prince. The nobility of the kingdom lived in better conditions than anyone else. They really didn't have room for complaint. But ambition ran in their blood—they were the descendants of the families who had helped put the Hearts on the throne, after all. For their service, they'd become the Dukes and Duchesses, Counts and Countesses, and all other forms of New Colony nobility. It was all part of the fun of living with a monarchy.

The woman was still hovering, expectant.

"I apologize. Please, dance with me and let me make it up to you." I caught the approving eye of my father as I pulled her into a waltz. Ballroom dance had been just another class with another tutor, but I was an expert. I held her close, her name already forgotten, and tried to ignore the envious looks. This wasn't a typical party like the alchemists had—theirs were a little more relaxed and fun. No, this was a parade for the court, to remind everyone how special we all were. It was also a total farce.

After the dance with the redhead, I found a brunette. Same dance. Same show. This one was named Harlow something-or-other. Then it was onto a couple of blondes and back to another brunette. Each dance started with a little bit of flirtation and ended with a swift kiss on the hand and a quick cold shoulder. Onto the next and the next I went. Only because my father was watching the entire thing. This was what he wanted. For me to meet the kingdom's most eligible bachelorettes. By giving them each a few minutes of my time, I could meet them all, prove I wasn't interested in any of them, and get on with my life.

Prince or not, I wasn't going to allow my father to arrange my marriage. I would do what he wanted, flirt with the right girls, maybe lead a few on until I figured out how to get Jessa in my life permanently. Until that day, I would stay "single" as long as possible. In my mind, all I ever saw, all I wanted to see, was Jessa. *She is the one.*

My father stood and the music slowed and then stopped. Everyone bowed as his bellowing voice filled the room. *Here we go again...*

"My friends, I am delighted that you could be with us tonight. I hope you are enjoying yourselves," Richard said. The crowd quieted at his voice, enraptured as he began his speech. "As you know, our great kingdom has been attacked. Twice. As we speak, our military and our Guardians of Color are gathering their forces and preparing to attack West America. We will take back what is ours!" The crowd cheered. "Keep your eyes open. Report anything suspicious to the proper authorities immediately. Traitors will be punished to the fullest extent of the law, and if found guilty, they will be executed." I clenched my fists, knowing full well that Thomas was below us as we danced. He was the biggest traitor of all, killing the queen, and he was not dead.

It made no sense. A flash of memory played in my mind. The way he'd tried to blame Jessa for his crimes. My mother's dead body. She'd been struggling with excruciatingly painful migraines for years leading up to her death! Heat poured over me just thinking about it. *He will pay. Be patient, Lucas. You'll find a way to end him.*

My father's playful tone pulled me back to the present moment. "I hope you and your beautiful daughters take this time to relax before the battle ahead. Please, loosen up my son a bit, will you?" Everyone laughed, and the girls of the court giggled and shot me their most flirtatious smiles. "I don't know about you, but I think it's about time we had some merriment in this kingdom. My late wife, God rest her soul, wanted nothing in the world more than she wanted grandchildren." I shifted, uncomfortable with where this was headed. "I'm an old man. I don't plan on ever marrying again. However, it is my hope that we shall celebrate a royal wedding very soon."

I didn't often blush, but heat blossomed on my cheeks. *What in the world does he think he's doing?*

"My son, so he has told me, is ready for a serious relationship," Richard continued, a mischievous ring to his tone. He was using my feelings for Jessa against me, acting like it was all a big joke. "It is my deepest wish that he finds a bride in this very room." A gasp of excitement rippled through the party as more applause broke out.

I glared at him for a brief moment before pasting a fake smile on my face and nodding. I was ready for a relationship all right—with a certain dark-haired, blue-eyed alchemist. Not a woman in this room. This was low. "Thank you, Father." I laughed, going along with the game. For Jessa's sake, and her sake only, I needed to keep my mouth shut. Because he knew how I felt about her. Because he'd threatened to send her away from me. Instead, I said, "I am sure I will choose the most worthy girl in this *palace.*" My words carefully constructed to dig back at him.

He paused for only a moment. "As you were."

With the flick of his wrist, the party resumed, the atmosphere now entirely different. There was nothing fun about the hungry scent of ambition suffocating the Godforsaken ballroom.

I danced with more women than I could count. Probably between twenty-five and thirty, all within a few years of my age. Most too young to be considering marriage. Even I was too young for that. It didn't matter. They didn't care about me. Not one person in that room bothered to ask me how I felt about it.

It was all for show. I wouldn't be making any of these girls a queen. My father may be good at manipulating people. He may even be good at manipulating me. But he could not force me to marry.

Hours later, the last of the guests finally shuffled out the doors. I retreated from the ballroom. *Forget this. I just want to find my girl.*

Not that I needed reminding of how I loved her and she was the only one for me. But something about dancing with others left a hole in my chest that only she could fill. The first place I checked was her dorm room, but once again she wasn't there. She must be feeling dejected after the purple test, but she couldn't hide away forever. I didn't think I could give her any more space. I needed to see her. To hold her and kiss her and forget about this night.

But when she wasn't in our regular greenhouse spot either, or anywhere else in the public guardian areas, I had no choice. Time to give up. Frustrated, I headed back toward the royal wing of the palace. It had been a long day and an even longer night, and the exhaustion was beginning to wear on me. All I wanted was my bed and my dark cool bedroom.

The usual guards were standing outside the doors to our suite. But the added sight of a girl dressed head to toe in a black guardian outfit made my heart hammer. *Okay, I'm awake!*

"Jessa." My body swallowed hers in a tight hug. She fit so perfectly in my arms, like she belonged there. She *did* belong there. "I've been looking for you all day. I'm so glad you're here. You have no idea the hell I just endured."

"Sorry. It wasn't my best day ever, but I'm over it now and I wanted to see you. I know it's stupid for me to come and find you here."

"It's fine. Do you know where I've been tonight?"

"No."

I hated telling her; it would hurt her. But she hated secrets more. "My father threw a party for me. Well, not *for* me, but because of me."

"What for?"

"He had all of the most important families parade their daughters."

"For you?" She stepped back, her nose scrunching in annoyance. She bit her lip, and I was about ready to end the conversation there.

"Yes. Kind of. I never asked for it. It was for everyone but me. It was for him." I took her hand and led her around the hallway corner and into a nearby alcove. It was after midnight and we were shrouded in shadows. It was dangerous, and, of course, those guards outside our wing could find us easily. But I figured by now all of the families had left the palace. Richard was probably in bed.

I kissed her, long and hard. She returned the kiss, equally invested.

"What are you saying?" Jessa whispered in a low voice, pulling back.

I might as well come out with it. "He wants me to get engaged to one of them."

In the darkness, I could barely make out her face to gauge how upset she was. A small "Oh" passed her lips, and then she crumbled.

"It's not like that," I assured her, grabbing her hands. "You know how I feel about you. I won't go through with it."

"Are you ready to get married?" she whispered.

Was I? We were young, too young to be married. But it was different with royalty. There was a certain level of obligation to the country when it came to our marriages. I would be allowed to be a bachelor for a while. But before long I would have to have children. It was crazy to think about it, but it was the truth. It was how things were done. I wasn't ready for kids. And marriage also seemed wrong at only eighteen. But when I looked at the girl before me, I felt calm about everything. She made me feel like when the time came, if she were at my side, it would be a happy day. More than happy. She made me feel like maybe marriage wasn't such a bad thing.

A group of people approached, my father among them.

He walked down the hallway, talking to some advisor or other, laughing together. His laugh had an addictive quality. There was something about him that made people want to believe in him. A charisma that pulled others into his orbit. Made them want to follow him anywhere. Even into war. And if they didn't? Well, they had magic for that.

Jessa shoved me from our hidden shadow and out into the hallway before Richard could see me. He was engaged in conversation, and it took him a moment to notice me standing there. When he sauntered over, he was grinning like he'd done me some huge favor.

"Well done, son."

"Thanks," I replied coolly.

"You had those women practically eating out of your hand." He turned to his advisor, a mousy man I couldn't remember the name of at the moment. "He's always had a way with the ladies. Quite a scoundrel, this boy," he joked. "Time he settled down."

I grimaced, knowing this was the last conversation Jessa needed to be eavesdropping on. "I was only playing my part," I said between gritted teeth.

They both laughed. "You loved every minute."

"No. We need to talk about what happened tonight."

"You're quite right about that. Which one of those girls did you like best?" He smiled conspiringly. Who was this man? I was so unused to seeing him so…happy.

"Are you drunk?"

He bellowed, "Not at all. Okay, maybe a little. I'm just pleased with you, son. For once you didn't fight me on something. And with a looming engagement on everyone's mind, it will make the things we're about to do much easier."

"What things?"

"War. Among other things."

"What other things?" I pressed.

"I've decided to go ahead and expand the shadow lands. We'll see what the west thinks of us once we start draining their resources." He said it in the same tone he'd used when planning my future engagement. The thought of literally destroying land, *forever*, made him happy. What was wrong with this man?

I shook my head. "Are you sure you want to do that? It's such a waste. You know the shadow lands can't be reversed."

"It will be to our advantage."

"But if you really believe we're going to take over West America, then it makes for pretty inconvenient land for the future of New Colony."

"Sacrifices must be made. Don't question me, son," he continued. "Anyway, you never answered my question. Which girl do you prefer?"

"You talk of them like they are cattle. Of course I won't take any of them. You already know who I prefer."

We stood toe to toe. All joy drained from his face, turning it from red to white, then red again. He didn't scare me.

"What don't you understand, Lucas? You need to cut it off with that…*thing*. Alchemists are unnatural. Do not get attached."

"Too late," I challenged.

He shook his head. "I've been doing this job for a very long time. Trust me when I say I know what is best in the future queen. Leave the alchemist alone and date somebody appropriate. If you don't, I will do as I've said. I will remove her from your presence, from this palace. Don't tempt me any further."

With that final threat, he swept from the hallway, pulled the large set of doors open, and retreated into our home. His advisor scurried behind him and shut the doors before I could utter another word.

Worry washed over me as I moved back toward our hiding place.

Jessa stepped out from the shadows. Tears ran down her cheeks, and I nearly punched the wall.

"I have to go." She pushed me aside.

"I don't agree with him. You know that. I'll do anything for you."

"I can't talk about this right now," she choked.

"Please, Jessa. I'm with *you*. Don't you trust me?"

She didn't answer. She just rushed away, never once looking over her shoulder. Never once stopping to think that maybe this was hurting me just as much as it was hurting her.

My world grew a shade darker.

NINE

SASHA

The new recruits were out of prison or wherever West America had put them, but they were not free. I eyed Mastin warily. Trying to ignore someone like that wasn't easy. He was so intense. Always watching as I trained the new alchemists, those green eyes never missing a thing. His posture appeared relaxed, but he wasn't really. He was always ready to pounce. And the worst part? He had a gun.

Guns weren't easy to come by out here, and they made most people a little more than uncomfortable.

"I don't get this," one of the recruits said loudly with a haughty pout. She was that preteen age that made her attitude *extra special.*

We were working on yellow and green the most. I didn't have time to teach them everything, so I'd prioritized the easiest colors—which also happened to be useful in battle. Even then, things weren't going that well. I wasn't a miracle worker. I couldn't teach inexperienced alchemists everything overnight. Most of them spent more time looking over their shoulders than paying attention to me.

"This is hard," the preteen girl continued. "Why does it even matter, anyway?"

I figured if these people were going to fight, they'd need to know how to have extra strength and speed and how to heal wounds. Everything else would have to wait. It was such a disadvantage, but what was I supposed to say to her? The whole thing seemed ridiculous to me too.

"Remind me of your name?" I asked as I walked through the clearing of trees to stand at her side. She was one of the alchemists having the most trouble. It didn't surprise me. I stared up at the sky for a moment, the problem grating on me. With the exception of Jessa, the older you were when you got started as an alchemist, the harder it was going to be. Most of the people here were adults, and truth be told, they weren't great. But there were teens and even younger ones as well, yet they weren't doing so hot either.

"Sam," she sighed. "I've never done this before. Never really had the chance to try."

"When did they catch you?" We both glanced over at Mastin.

"When I was seven. I'm thirteen now."

It struck a chord with me and I stiffened, meeting her gaze. I remembered those years of my life and how hard they were. I could only imagine what she'd been through in a country where her very existence was illegal. The girl was timid, with black hair hanging in her eyes and a lanky frame. I turned her away from Mastin, putting both our backs to him, and whispered, "What did they do to you?"

"They locked me up and threw away the key. What else? I was shocked when they brought me here. I'm not complaining, but when they took us from the prison, they didn't tell us where we were going. Part of me hoped I'd get to see my family again. I mean, we're not like your country. We don't have cruel and unusual punishment, so it's not like I *never* got to see my family. We get visits every couple of months if we have good behavior. But when they came to get me, I hoped that maybe I was going home. Not out in the middle of nowhere to train in alchemy." Her entire body deflated. "I'm so stupid."

"Hey, I don't ever want to hear you call yourself names again," I said, wagging a finger at the kid. "Do you understand?" She nodded. "You're not stupid. And being an alchemist is a gift. *They* are the ones who made your existence illegal. That's not your fault."

I suspected part of the problem this girl was having with controlling her magic was that she had a deep-rooted fear of being punished. Her country had isolated her for who she was. They did nothing to help her. So it was no wonder she was repressing her magic now. If my theory was right, it explained the issues I was having training these people.

"All right, everybody," I yelled, stepping away from Sam. "Who is struggling with these colors? Raise your hands, please."

A sea of hands shot up. The mutterings stopped as they turned to face me.

"You do not have to hide who you are here," I boldly declared. I stood tall, my straight hair swept back in a ponytail. Dressed in black, I hoped I looked fierce. Hoped they would believe I was the kind of person who didn't mess around. "The time for fearing your magic is over. We are *not* in West America anymore. And if we are successful in beating New Colony, you will not have to return to your prison cells."

An audible gasp sounded as, one by one, they took in the news. It had been my one requirement for training these people. The last couple of weeks hadn't been easy. When I'd first agreed to do this, Cole said that any New Colony alchemists would be welcomed into West America. It had taken some pressure, but I'd finally convinced the West American commander to extend that promise to his own people as well. He'd gotten the order signed from their president.

West America had better keep their promise or there would be hell to pay.

It terrified me to think we could be going from one tyranny right into another. But I was learning to trust. And I was at the point where I didn't see any other options.

"Isn't that right, Mastin?"

We all turned to face the military man. He bristled. He hadn't wanted the deal to be made and had zero qualms about fighting for his beliefs. Alchemy was dangerous and needed to be kept away from regular society. That's how he felt, and he wasn't about to change his mind any time soon. Prick.

But their president was desperate and she was willing to see reason when he wouldn't. From what I gathered talking to Cole, the rest of their country was trending toward her beliefs as well. Everything there worked in a voting system. People voted for representatives who believed in what they did, and those representatives made the law. Apparently, the last election had caused some major upheaval, as many of those elected were outspoken in their sympathy toward color alchemists.

Mastin's firm line of a mouth twitched as I taunted him. "That's right," he said, eyes boring into mine. "It's been confirmed by the president herself just last night." He glared at me, because we both knew how much he hated that I'd won.

"And I will get the proof you need next time I see the commander," I said, taking in the many excited faces.

"The deal is, if you help us we'll pardon you," Mastin said.

"So here's the thing," I added. "You can help them and earn that freedom. You all can do this. I feel like most of you are holding back your powers because of your fear of the consequences, and the problem with keeping it in is the longer it stays inside, one of two things is going to happen. Your magic is either going to become weak and useless, or it's going to grow inside of you until it becomes dangerous."

I turned on Mastin. "I bet you didn't know that by keeping these people from their gifts out of your own ignorance, you've only made them more dangerous?"

He didn't respond. He didn't even move, his eyes narrowing to slits as he glared at me. But from the flash I saw there, I thought maybe he *did* know.

"Fine. Let's get back to work."

I had everyone using the yellow leaves to build up their strength. We'd gone farther into the forest than usual. There was plenty of space to do what needed to be done. The trees surrounded us on all sides, the sky bright blue and cloudless, the air crisp as an apple. I took in a deep breath before continuing.

"Take the yellow into your palms and imagine the color seeping into your body. Feel the adrenaline in your veins. Let it take over." I watched proudly when quite a few of them pulled the yellow and did as I'd asked. "We're going to try some things you've never done before. There's nothing to be afraid of. You're so much stronger than you imagine. Once you have the magic inside, I want you to pick a tree and climb it as fast as possible."

There was a moment of hesitation, and then one by one, they climbed. And they were fast. Smooth. Feline in their ascent, jumping from branch to branch, swinging upward, not a clumsy movement among them.

Not too bad, if I do say so myself.

I strolled over to Mastin and nudged him playfully with my elbow. "Well it's not nothing? Are you jealous?" I don't know why I taunted him like that. Something about this guy made me want to play the devil's advocate. I shouldn't even care. His jaw clicked, but as was his way, he stayed quiet and pensive. I turned back toward the alchemists.

"If you can still feel the magic inside of you, even just a drop, then jump to the ground," I called out.

"Don't do anything to hurt my people," Mastin growled under his breath.

"Oh, so now you're protective of them?" I folded my arms.

"You'll be fine! I promise!" I yelled toward the trees, ignoring him. After a couple of bodies flew down and landed in a safe crouch on the forest floor, the rest followed. His eyes widened, but he kept his mouth shut. If he was impressed, he certainly didn't show it.

"I know what I'm doing here," I said to Mastin. "My question is, what are you doing here?"

"My job."

I snorted and left him standing on the sidelines as I joined the new recruits. I clapped, beaming from ear to ear. We'd been at this for a while with little to no success. But I'd been right to press the issue on their freedom. Once they knew there weren't going to be dire repercussions for using their magic, *bam!* Magic in every last one of them.

"Okay, friends, I'm proud of you," I said, corralling them around me. "But that was just the beginning—child's play. Who's ready to get to work?"

●

I rolled the last bit of my dinner roll between my fingers and thumb, then plopped it in my mouth.

"Good job today," Mastin said, keeping pace with me as I skittered down the hill. "Looks like you finally got through to them."

"Yeah, no thanks to you." My stomach full, I was heading back to the cabin I shared with the other female misfits. The sun was already setting, casting a golden shadow through the woods. It was my favorite time of day.

"What's that supposed to mean?"

"Were you dropped on your head as a child?" I stopped to glower at him, and he almost careened into me. Was he serious? He really didn't know what the problem was? "They're scared of you, Mastin. Terrified! You come to all of our practices and stare everyone down. You've always got a gun on you. You're not one of them. You've made it clear you hate alchemy. I mean, hello? You're policing them! It would make anybody nervous."

"I'm just doing my job." He frowned, folding his arms. His biceps pulsed.

"Well, I'm trying to do mine. It would be a lot easier if you stopped coming around."

"Not gonna happen."

"So you're policing me too?"

He held my gaze, his green eyes catching the sunset, turning them the shade of a newly turned leaf in spring. A flame ignited in my chest, and I stomped away. *Forget him.* I was exhausted. I needed a good book and my bed. Fiction was hard to come by in New Colony. Most of the books the citizens had access to were state-issued propaganda. Here? It was a different story. A gloriously different story, no pun intended. I'd devoured everything in our makeshift library more than once over the years. Now with a paperback of *The Giver* snug in my back pocket, I delighted in the fact I had the freedom again to read whatever I wanted. I took off down the hill.

"Hey, wait up," Mastin said, catching up.

"You're still here?" His normally stoic expression flinched, and I smiled to myself conspiratorially. It was fun toying with his emotions.

"I wanted to talk to you about something."

"Talk away," I said.

"It's probably best if we discussed this—*issue*—in private."

"I'm not inviting you into my room if that's what you're trying to get at." I eyed him suspiciously. He turned on me, his face incredulous. I shrugged.

"I don't like you like that," he said.

I shrugged again. "I'm used to men hitting on me," I replied. It came in handy when I needed to use my looks to my advantage. I'd certainly used it with Lucas—while I could, anyway. But there were many times that it drove me crazy. Tristan was my only male friend even remotely close to my age. He'd never once come onto me. Probably because he understood the same thing I did. There wasn't time for romantic entanglements.

"You think you're pretty special, don't you?" Mastin met my gaze.

I rolled my eyes. "Takes one to know one," I said and laughed, lightening the mood. "Fine," I added. "Let me grab a jacket and we can go to the lake." It was private enough that we could talk. There weren't many alchemists here with access to blue to the point of being able to eavesdrop. We'd be fine.

I ran into the cabin I shared with the other women, women who ignored my existence, and headed into my small private bedroom. I grabbed a black hooded sweatshirt from my drawer and sped right back out.

Mastin waited for me, always looking so out of place in his military getup. We walked for a bit until we found a patch of soft grass to sit on by the lake. The sunset was magnificent over the water, turning the sky a brilliant fuchsia and reflecting against the barrage of autumn-kissed trees. "I've been here for years, and I still can't get enough of that view," I said, sighing.

"It's amazing. But nothing compared to the sunset over the Pacific Ocean."

"Always trying to one-up me," I teased. He laughed. He had a good laugh. Hearty. It made his hard edges softer and he seemed less…untouchable.

He should do that more often.

"So the Pacific Ocean, huh? What's it like back home?"

"West America, as you call it, is beautiful. And big. We still call ourselves America, by the way. New Colony gave us that name. Anyway, it's not bad at all. Democracy slows things down sometimes, sure, I can admit that. But overall the people are happy, and we take care of our own." He leaned back on his elbows, lost in thought. "We're free. We can pursue whatever careers we want. We can vote. We can do a lot of things others can't."

I pondered that for a minute, picking at the grass. "I'm in hiding, obviously, but I'm more free here than I ever was before. New Colony is *not* free. The government controls everything. Where a family lives, what jobs they're allowed to have, schools, food, pretty much everything. Some people have a great life because of it. Most people have it okay. And then there are those few who are treated like garbage. Or, you know, those of us lucky enough to be forced into the guardian program."

"What happened to you?"

I paused. I wasn't ready to share my story with this guy. He was still a stranger, an unknown. "What did you want to talk to me about?" I asked, changing the subject.

He let out a slow breath. "We received word that King Richard is planning an attack on America soon. We're not exactly sure what or when. We do know, however, that he plans to extend more shadow lands into our territories. We need to act fast if we want to stop him."

It took me a moment to answer, the images of my childhood burned on my mind. "That's some bad news, Mastin. So what are your plans?"

"Take our alchemists and some soldiers into New Colony and fight him."

I sat back, gazing at him. He was serious. How could he be serious? "Are you kidding? That's suicide. They're not even close to being ready."

"That's why I wanted to talk to you. How long?"

I shook my head. "Too long!"

"You don't get it, Sasha. Cole is going to make the order with or without your support."

"Wow, he must really care about them," I said, each word dripping in sarcasm. I shook my head. "Fighting the GC would be impossible. They've trained for years, not only in alchemy, but in combat too. They're deadly. Your people are toddlers compared to that."

"But our soldiers are the best. And I'll be there too."

"It's still a terrible idea."

"Will you come with us?"

"On a suicide mission? No thanks. I think I'll keep my life, if you don't mind." I couldn't believe this. No way could a bunch of uneducated newbie alchemists take on an army of guardians.

"We really need your help. We're going in with or without you. But I'm smart enough to know we don't stand a chance if you don't come. I've been watching the way they look up to you. They seek you out outside of training. They ask you questions. They trust you, Sasha. And I've seen what you can do."

I laughed because what he'd seen had barely even scratched the surfaced of what magic I was capable of. "Mastin, you don't understand, so please listen to me. I pale in comparison to some of those guardians in New Colony. They would kill me. They'll kill you! You have no idea what you're asking of me."

"Then at least help me delay the attack." His expression shifted, and he talked softly. "Help me convince Cole to wait a little while longer. At least so they can get some more training from you."

I jolted. Mastin always came off as so cocky. To humble himself in this way was disarming. I could tell he wasn't scared to fight. Or he at least had that soldier thing about him that kept it inside. But he was worried for his people and I found that admirable. Maybe he wasn't such a bad guy after all.

"I'll do what I can," I sighed.

He gulped, and I could tell he wanted to say more. "Out with it," I said.

"You have no idea how much I hate to ask." He sat up, running both hands across his buzzed hair. "But is there a way to use their magic to get Cole on our side of things? We're supposed to go meet him in a few minutes."

I sucked in a breath, considering. "There's two ways I can think of to make this happen. The first is red alchemy, which if used on someone's blood, can result in mind control." I met his eyes as they stared at me intently. "But I can't do red," I was quick to add. "If you aren't going to convince your boss to be reasonable, we'll have to do it the good old-fashioned way. I'll try the blue, which can be used for persuasion. No guarantees though, it's not my specialty."

He nodded. "Thanks."

"Have you ever been to the shadow lands?"

"I've seen the pictures."

"The pictures are nothing." I tried unsuccessfully to push the images from my mind. "They're dead. As in, no coming back. If Richard's going to do that to your country, you have to do everything you can to stop him. It can't lie in the hands of a few alchemists. You need to bring more than a few soldiers. You need an army."

"We're working on it."

"Good." I nodded.

"Have you been to the shadow lands?"

"You have no idea." I laughed, but it wasn't funny. "I helped create them." He let out a shuddering breath and bored holes into me with his crazy-intense gaze.

I looked away, unable to take the heat.

"It's not like I had a choice. But I was a kid, you know? It's messed up." I couldn't hold it in any more. Something about this moment had changed, and suddenly I needed to get it out. "They took me from my family when I was tiny. They trained me. And once they realized how good I was, they took me into the field. I was six years old when I went out there. I was there for four years until Hank saved me."

"I'm sorry."

"I don't want your pity," I said. "I just want you to know who you're dealing with. They care about their own agenda more than human life. Taking children from their parents is one thing. It's heartbreaking, but it pales in comparison to what else they do. The shadow lands had people on them. Poor people. Unwanted people. Uneducated outcasts… We didn't remove those people. They were part of a test."

"They died?"

"We killed them. I killed them."

"Thank God you got out."

"I don't know if God had anything to do with it," I scoffed. I was jaded, I knew it. "Hank and Tristan, I owe them my life. Did you know Hank used to be an officer? And Tristan was an officer in training. They defected and took me with them. I'd do anything for those men. They're my family."

Why was I telling him all of this? I needed to get a grip.

"It wasn't your fault." He said the same thing so many others before him had said. I studied his face, so earnest. He believed every word. If only I could believe them too.

"I know," I said. *Doesn't change what I did.* I'd learned a long time ago it was easier to agree on this point than to argue. We sat in silence as the sky turned dark.

Mastin stood. "We'd better get back."

He reached down and pulled me up. His hands were calloused, like he'd grown up working outside. We stood inches apart—the body heat between us suddenly electric. We were still holding hands when he squeezed mine before letting it go. He cleared his throat and took a step back. Looking for a way to break the tension, I grabbed the copy of *The Giver* from the ground. It must have fallen out of my back pocket. "Can't forget this," I mumbled before taking off down the path. He didn't say anything as he followed extra closely.

I had more important things to worry about than the weird moments between us. *Stay focused on the Resistance.*

Blue alchemy. Mastin understood and agreed, which I had to admit was kind of amazing. Blue was harder to find at this time of year, but, lucky for me, I had my stone necklace I could use. I quickly retrieved it from my room before heading out to meet the others. I slid it under my shirt.

"Lead the way," I said. Mastin led us to wherever we were meeting Cole and the others. If I had to guess, I'd say Hank's cabin again. Lo and behold, after a few minutes, we sauntered up his steps. I double-checked that the necklace was hidden as we entered the living room.

"Thank you for joining us," Hank said. He didn't have that usual twinkle in his eye or smile on his lips. His wrinkles were deeper than I'd remembered, and a few extra gray hairs had cropped up on his head. This must be serious. I steeled myself and took the seat next to Cole. I needed him close so I could work this magic inconspicuously.

"Well, there's no point in beating around the bush," Cole said. "Mastin told you what King Richard plans to do in America?" I nodded. "Then you understand why we have to act quickly. We need to get in there and take him down, take them all down, while we have the chance." He was so sure of himself. He was so clueless to the real risk. It was almost comical.

Except nothing about this was funny.

"Why haven't you tried something earlier? None of this would even matter if you could just deal with the problem with brute force," Tristan said, getting up from the couch and joining us at the table.

"We did. But we failed."

I wondered what that meant, but decided not to ask and draw unwanted attention to myself. I felt the stone against my neck and glanced around the room. It was just Mastin, Hank, Tristan, Cole, and myself. No doubt Hank and Tristan would recognize blue alchemy when they saw it. Mastin wasn't putting up any fights this time. I had to do it.

"And how would you suggest this is going to work?" I asked Cole.

"Some of our best soldiers and our alchemists, along with your people, go in and take over the palace. Take the royals and top people into custody. If they put up a fight, kill them. We can't allow war just because your king has decided he wants more land."

"He's not my king," I snapped. "And how exactly are you going to take down the hundreds of alchemists and officers who also reside in the palace?"

"We have weapons. We're smart. We'll hit them before they hit us, when they least expect it. We need that element of surprise."

I agreed that an element of surprise would be helpful, but enough time to prepare the people they were sending in was more important. And their alchemists were not ready yet, not even close.

"Give me more time," I said, making a last ditch effort to sway him without magic.

"There's no more time. As soon as I give the word, our soldiers will head this way. If all goes according to plan, we'll leave tomorrow night."

He stood. As far as he saw it, he was the one in charge here. But he didn't know whom he was dealing with. *We* were helping him, not the other way around. And we were the ones with alchemy. Whatever weapons he had at his disposal were nothing compared to magic.

I also stood. I reached out my hand and connected it with his arm. The blue alchemy was resting in my palm, barely the size of a button. Any visible trace was gone the second I connected the magic with him.

"We need more time."

He blinked several times and took a deep breath. "Okay," he conceded, "You can have more time. But we have to complete this mission soon." He appeared to be utterly dazed but sure about his choices. Then, not saying another word, he left the cabin and strode out into the night. Mastin nodded at us, his eyes stressed, before he followed Cole.

The door closed and the room fell into silence.

"I'm just going to pretend I didn't see that," Hank said.

"What choice did I have? The guy is crazy. Now we have time to try to figure out how to stop this whole thing from happening."

"You shouldn't have done that," Tristan said. I turned on him, scrutinizing his words. He brushed a lock of dark hair out of his face, his expression angry.

"Are you for real right now?"

"It's time we stopped playing it safe. This is the chance we've been waiting for. If we don't take Richard down now, when will we?"

"I don't know. How about when it makes sense and doesn't put innocent lives in danger?" I couldn't believe this. Mastin, the anti-alchemist, hard-core military American soldier, saw enough reason to let me do what I just did. But my own best friend, the man who'd been through some of the same horrible things I had, the man who saw what they made me do as a kid, was siding with Cole?

"I'm going to take a little walk and let you two work this out," Hank mumbled before slipping through the door. *Coward!*

"You know as well as I do what the guardians are capable of," I sputtered, looking Tristan up and down. "You know what the king is like. How ruthless the officers are. This plan to somehow catch them off guard is stupid! Stupid, naïve, wishful thinking that will get us all killed."

Tristan pinched his lips together and glared at me. His high cheekbones and thick brows created an expression of indignation that I'd never seen him point at me before. A lump formed in my throat, and I swallowed it down.

"Cole is on our side," he challenged. "You've always had a hard time with authority."

"Welcome to the club. It's not like you're any different."

He stalked closer, towering over me. He wasn't the teenager my kid-self was used to. I had to remind myself he was twenty-five now. And he was all dark. Dark eyes, skin, and hair. Add that with his Asian ancestry and a tall broad build, and he was the type of guy that made reasonable girls turn into bumbling messes. But I wasn't about to agree with nonsense.

He took a shaky breath, his voice low. "What I mean is, I feel like we can trust him."

"You're not an alchemist. That's easy for you to say."

"What other choice do we have? Honestly, sometimes—"

"What's that supposed to mean?" I cut him off. "There's always another choice. We were doing just fine on our own until those two showed up."

"Are you serious right now?" His eyes flashed. "Have we not been part of the same Resistance? Take a look around you, Sasha. Do you want to live here the rest of your life? Hiding? Is this enough for you?"

I didn't answer. The silence stretched between us.

"Because it's not for me," he finally said.

"It sure beats being a pawn. So what if we don't live in luxury? I don't care. We're free here, Tristan!"

"This isn't freedom," he grumbled. He ran his hand over the stubble on his jaw, shaking his head. I was just some idiotic, nineteen-year-old girl he'd babied all these years. He didn't see me as his equal. "What did you say?" he asked.

Oops. I must have said some of that out loud! "I'm not a child. I'm not stupid. I'm a grown woman with opinions of my own. Maybe it hasn't occurred to you, but it could be possible that I have a better grasp on the situation than you do."

"And using blue alchemy on a West American general is mature?"

Heat flooded my cheeks.

"I'll have you know," I said, "it was Mastin's idea."

"Great! So you trust Mastin more than you trust me now?" A flash of pain ignited in his ebony eyes.

"It's not that I trust Mastin more than you," I snapped. "It's just that he happens to listen to good ideas."

He stalked toward me and his body filled every inch of my personal space. "It's not a good idea to sit on this opportunity. We need to move out as soon as possible. But I guess you and your new boyfriend decided to use magic to get your way."

"He's not my boyfriend. Don't be ridiculous."

"And you don't think your good looks have anything to do with him being so nice to you?"

"No. It's the fact that I'm an amazing alchemist who could teach the boy a thing or two about how to kick New Colony trash."

He laughed. "Whatever, Frankie, keep telling yourself that." He slipped in my old name, my real name, and I flinched. It brought back so much history, that name. History he was an intricate part of.

He paused in front of me, only inches away, and stared down at my face. The tension grew thick. "Just for the record, I like you for *you*, not for what you can do for me. Not for your looks. Not for anything other than for who you are on the inside." He stepped back. Just as he reached the door, he turned back. "And believe me, I know you're not a little girl anymore." His eyes bored into mine, searching for something. He must not have found what he was looking for, because a moment later, he stormed through the door, slamming it behind him.

I unclenched angry fists and fought the tears. I never cried, but I also never fought with Tristan. Sure, I hadn't seen him in ages, but we'd always been best friends before I left to assume my new identity. I thought we could go back to that. Now what were we?

Hank chose that moment to return. He stopped the second he entered, scratching his head and staring at me. I didn't want him to see the tears pooling in my eyes. I held up a hand to him. "Not now." I stormed past him and through the door, ready to get back to my room and end this night. "Be gentle with him," I heard Hank say, but I didn't look back.

It was too dark to go for a run, but my body itched for it anyway. It was my salvation, the thing that took the heavy thoughts away and gave me some space. What was going on? It almost felt like Tristan had confessed feelings for me. And there was definitely something going on with Mastin, too. I had to stop whatever was forming before something happened that I'd regret. I didn't have time or energy for this kind of distraction.

Forget it! I took off running, not caring what consequences would meet me if I fell.

TEN

JESSA

The heart-pounding exertion of combat training still wasn't enough to take my mind off Lucas. As I walked back toward my room to shower and change, I wiped the perspiration from my neck with a towel, lost in thought. Every heartbeat hurt, my chest filled with a silent dull ache. Was this heartbreak? It was a *physical* pain, and I couldn't take it anymore.

Lucas came around the corner, an expression of relief on his face when he saw me. I froze momentarily, then turned and high-tailed it toward my room.

I didn't even know if Lucas and I had broken up. A huge part of that was my fault. I was avoiding him for fear of what our next conversation would hold. For the last couple of days, anytime I saw him, I turned the other way. I didn't see the point anymore. The thoughts kept nagging at me. Why go through all the trouble to be together if, in the end, Lucas marries another girl?

The only solution put me right back to why I was in this palace in the first place. If I could help the Resistance take down the current system, then maybe Lucas and I could have a chance. Maybe.

He caught up to me just as I was about to slip into my room and lock the door.

"Jessa, we need to talk." He sighed. I turned to face him. His expression was guarded and a knowing sadness reflected in his charcoal eyes.

"Look, I really didn't want to do this," I said, beating him to the punch. "Your father will never let us be together. And the more we try to defy him, the harder it's going to be for us."

He looked away, shutting his eyes for a moment. This was dangerous, for both of us. He shouldn't be seen with me.

"Jessa, please just let me explain."

"There's nothing to explain. I get it, okay? We can't be together." I lowered my voice. "Your father is in control, and there's nothing we can do about it at the moment. He's made it crystal clear that you can't date me."

"I don't care what he says."

I peered around, exasperated. Of course there were people everywhere, stopping by their rooms between classes. They watched us curiously. What did he think he was accomplishing here? He was going to get me into trouble. "You should care," I whispered. "If you want to keep me safe, if you want me to be initiated so I can do what I came here to do, then you should care what he says."

"I'll talk to him. I'll figure something out. I won't date those women. They mean nothing to me, Jessa. You're the one I want."

I reached my hand behind me, gripping the door handle to my room with a tight fist. "While that may be well and true, it doesn't change the fact that the king forbade you to date me. You shouldn't be here right now."

"So that's it? You just give up that easily?" He leaned back on his heels, his face reddening. The skin around his eyes tightened as he stared me down, but I had to stick to my gut on this one. It was too risky for us to sneak about at the moment.

"I'm not giving up. You know how I feel about you," I said. "But what you don't seem to realize is that your father is the king, which means he's in control of my future. You heard him just as well as I did. If you don't stay away from me, then he's going to remove me from the palace. I can't let that happen. You of all people should understand why."

I didn't have to say anything more; we both knew we were talking about my mission with the Resistance. My parents were somewhere north, in hiding, and more than anything I wanted to be with them. They were counting on me.

We can't be selfish anymore.

I needed to think about the bigger mission, even if he couldn't. There was more than just my love life on the line. Lives were at stake. We were on the brink of war. If Lucas couldn't see the truth, then I would have to do it for him. Even though it ripped my heart in two. Even though it was the last thing I wanted.

"Jessa, just please meet me in our spot. We'll figure this out, I promise." He reached out to move a loose strand of hair behind my ear, and I hesitated for an excruciating moment. With a fixed resolve, I opened the door behind me and stepped back.

"I'm not giving up on us forever. Maybe one day the timing will be right for you and me. But I have to do what's best. I have to give up on us *for now*. I'm so sorry, Lucas." It took everything to meet his steel eyes and hold my gaze firm, keeping my love for him bottled inside. His face hardened, and his lips thinned, but he turned and walked away.

I slipped into my room and immediately collapsed on the floor. I allowed myself five minutes to cry. Five minutes, and then I had to be done. Then I'd find Jasmine and tell her why the Resistance couldn't put me and Lucas together anymore. I needed to move on.

●

"Another party?" I asked, gaping at the glossy invitation in Jasmine's hand. After the big to-do they just had for Lucas, I was surprised the royals were throwing another party so soon. This time it was for the alchemists. It had only been two days since the break up, and I wasn't ready to pretend to have fun. I was too busy feeling sorry for myself, I hated to admit.

"There are a lot of parties here, in case you didn't notice," Jasmine smiled. I had come to train with her in green alchemy, and we were just finishing up. "The alchemists have a gathering of this nature every few weeks." We collected the remaining pots and carried them back to the greenhouse as I listened. "It's part of the perks of living in the palace. Train hard. Play hard." Then she whispered conspiratorially, "Live in luxury and don't notice all the things we have to go without."

Like our families.

"I guess, but I don't want to go." I frowned.

"Unfortunately, this one is mandatory," Jasmine said. She'd understood my reasoning for ending things with Lucas. Once I'd explained Lucas was to be engaged soon and Richard had threatened to send me away if we spent more time together, she'd reluctantly agreed it was best to hold off on the romance. She talked about it like it wasn't real, like it was just part of the mission. But it was real for me, and I ached every day without him.

"Why is it mandatory?"

"I guess we'll have to go to find out." She smiled her usual warm smile, but I caught a glimpse of worry. "Go and get ready. I'll see you soon."

I mumbled my frustrations all the way back to my room.

After a long shower, I let my hair dry in its natural curls loose down my back. I took extra care with my makeup and even used the dark eyeliner and mascara I normally skipped. My reasoning was probably flawed and idiotic, but I figured if I had a bunch of black around my eyes it would incentivize me not to cry and ruin it. I fished around in the grooming kit that came standard in women's dorm rooms until I found crimson lipstick. I matched it to a form-fitting dress of the same color and donned black heels.

I was dressed to kill.

I'd dressed the exact opposite of how I felt on purpose. If Lucas was there tonight I didn't want him to know I was moping about, feeling sorry for myself. I couldn't risk him trying to fix things for us. As much as I wanted to be with him, I knew I had to be the smarter one in the relationship and focus on more important things.

I was late to the party. Fashionably late, I told myself. The alchemists knew how to have a good time. This affair was less polished than the first one I'd been to months ago. There wasn't food, for one thing. The lights were darker, the music louder, and the dancing a lot…closer.

Well, okay then…

Totally out of place and awkward, I made my way to the edge of the room to hide out. Why was this mandatory? Seemed like an excuse for people to indulge in too much orange infused drink and rub up against each other.

Totally *not* my style. Especially not with people who hated me.

"You need to try harder to make friends," Reed said, sliding in next to me. "It will make it easier for you to be initiated if the guardians can see that you're one of us." I was trying, as per Jasmine's request. But so far, I'd not managed to make a single one.

"Easy for you to say," I groaned. "You don't even have to make an effort. People naturally want to be your friend. Everyone likes you."

"You don't like me."

I shifted to face him, noticing his tailored black suit and carefully styled hair. Maybe he did make an effort. "It's not that I don't like you, Reed. It's that I know what you did to me with the blue alchemy before. You tried to interrogate me so you could report back to your boss."

"I thought you wouldn't catch me and I could pretend it never happened," he said, eyes down casting shadows across his face. "I was selfish, and I'm really sorry about that. But I never didn't like you, just for the record. I would've gone after you whether or not Faulk had told me to befriend you."

"Sure," I mumbled.

"I swear. You don't know what it's like for us here. We have to do what we're told, even if that means hurting each other from time to time."

"That's not cool."

"No kidding." He nodded. We sat in silence for a moment, watching the crowd.

"Okay, fine, I forgive you," I said. "Tell me about something else, please? Like why is this stupid party mandatory?"

I caught his facial expression in the dim light as he chewed on his bottom lip. It was as if he was debating letting me in on a secret. "We're about to go to war. You already know that. Everyone does. My guess is this party will be the last in a while. No doubt King Richard will be out here soon to give us all a pep talk, maybe more. Faulk will be finding me in the crowd and asking me to help him with his persuasion. She always does. Like I said, I don't have a choice in these matters. I figured that out a long time ago."

"But if you did have a choice?" I asked.

"What do you mean by that?"

I shook my head and turned away. I'd said too much. Even if I could forgive Reed for his past, it didn't mean I could trust him with my secrets.

"Well, will you dance with me, or what?" He grinned.

At this point I realized I couldn't say no to that face. Or maybe I just needed to have some fun and forget about the heaviness of the last few days. "All right, show me what you got."

We moved to the dance floor, maneuvering through the crowd that pulsed to the thumping beat. I grabbed a flute of sparkling drink with an orange petal on top. I already knew what to do. I focused on building a happy feeling inside and touched the tip of my finger to the delicate flower. The orange alchemy danced into the drink, and I swallowed it in one gulp. The happy feeling swelled inside me, overpowering the pain. I welcomed it as Reed tugged me toward a group of his friends. Maybe I could have fun. It was better than crying.

I didn't allow myself to get too close to anyone. But I did dance my heart out. It wasn't the same as ballet. Nothing could beat ballet. But it felt incredible just the same. I lost myself in the thick crowd, the dark room, my eyes closed so I was cocooned from those around me. For all I knew they were glaring daggers at the weird new alchemist girl crashing their party. I didn't care. For once, I felt like myself, and I relished in that as long as I could.

"I think your boyfriend's here," a male voice shouted directly into my ear. I turned to see a dark boy with long black hair. I stepped away from him, not sure who he was. The kid just smirked and pointed behind me.

Lucas. He was brooding in the corner, looking gorgeous in dark jeans and a navy button-up shirt with the sleeves rolled up.

"He's not my boyfriend," I turned back to the guy; he was standing a little too close for comfort.

"Yeah right," he scoffed, and I shook my head before losing myself in the crowd.

What was Lucas doing here? Did he come here to check on me? Questions circled my brain. I tried to get back into the dancing, but I'd lost all the energy for it. I was officially done partying. I headed for the exit hoping my appearance at the party was enough for whatever higher powers had deemed it mandatory. Lucas caught up to me, pressing a hand to the door before I could leave.

"Please don't say anything," I said.

"Whether or not you care about me, there's something I have to tell you, Jessa. Because I care about you, and you need to hear it from me first."

I stopped. "Fine," I snarled. "Get it out so I can leave." I was being mean. But it was like some rude version of myself had taken over and was fighting back at Lucas for something that wasn't even his fault. What was wrong with me? Heartache did crazy things to people.

"I don't even know how to say this," Lucas said. He gulped as his face turned ashen in the dim light. "Things escalated very quickly this afternoon with my father. I did something I regret."

"What are you talking about? Look, Lucas, you need to stay away from me. We can't have this conversation over and over again."

He glanced around, clearly perturbed by our lack of privacy and my response to his confusing words. Just as he was about to say something, the music stopped and a voice boomed from the other side of the room.

"Good evening, my color guardians," King Richard bellowed over the crowd. Lucas stiffened next to me.

"I have to go over there," he growled. "Jessa, why do you have to be so hard on me? I just wanted you to hear it from me first."

I didn't know what to say, but it didn't matter. He left. I watched, exhausted, as he rushed through the crowd to meet his father. His behavior reminded me of the man I'd first expected him to be, brooding and unreachable. I shook my head, frustrated at the constant battles in our relationship. No matter how much we fought for each other, there would always be some bigger reason why it wasn't going to work. I was tired of fighting.

"Oh, there he is, the engaged man himself!" Richard called.

My heart dropped as I nearly doubled over. *Did he just say engaged?*

"Aren't they a beautiful couple?" Richard continued as Lucas climbed the stage. Then he joined his son's hand with a gorgeous woman's hand and held them up to the crowd. My thoughts ran a million miles, in a million different directions. But they landed on one thing.

Was Lucas tired of fighting for us?

When Lucas glanced at the woman, he smiled his perfect smile, and I almost threw up. This was exactly why we'd broken up. Because sooner or later, I'd get hurt and he would marry some trophy socialite of Richard's choosing. I'd hoped ending things would have diminished that hurt.

Nope.

The crowed cheered, clearly excited by this news, many of them still drunk on orange alchemy. From the blooming smile on Lucas's face, it seemed he was just as excited. Was he? I doubted it. Could it be possible that in giving up on us, he'd so easily moved his affections to a more worthy girl? I didn't want to believe it. Couldn't believe it. I knew him. Still, the nagging questions burned in the back of my mind bringing every insecurity I'd ever had to the surface.

Are we really done?

Maybe he doesn't love me anymore.

Maybe I'm too much work for him.

Maybe—

I pulled myself out of that downward spiral and focused my attention back on the stage. She was gorgeous, as to be expected. Porcelain skin and auburn hair slicked down her back. Big green eyes. Regal. She *looked* like a queen. Actually, she vaguely resembled the late queen, Natasha. I shouldn't have been surprised this was whom they picked. No doubt she came from a good family, was agreeable, well educated, and wealthy. *Not an alchemist.* All the things Richard deemed appropriate for his son.

Why had Lucas agreed to this? Surely he must be playing some other game here. I hoped...

"Thank you, Father," Lucas stepped forward to the microphone. That's when I noticed the camera crew at the front of the crowd. The media was rarely invited to the palace. And to have the alchemists and the media in one place was *extremely* rare. Practically unheard of. What was going on? "I look forward to our engagement and my future marriage to my lovely fiancée, Celia." He put his arm around her and kissed her sideways on the forehead, smiling his rakish smile. For all intents and purposes, he appeared to be a man in love. No doubt women all over the country would be mourning the loss of such a highly prized bachelor once the news broke out. I still couldn't believe it. Just two days ago we were still a couple, and tonight he was engaged.

No, there had to be a reasonable explanation. I needed to be patient until he came to me with the truth.

You should have let him talk, I chastised myself for blowing him off minutes ago. No way he'd actually go through with this marriage.

My heart ached. It was time for me to go. I pushed through the door when the king's steady voiced pulled me back into the moment. *Stupid curiosity!*

"The time has come for us to prepare for retaliation on West America. Not just for the death of our beloved queen, but for the deadly attacks during her funeral. Innocent lives were lost, and they will *not* have died in vain. I hope the news of an upcoming wedding will give us all something to look forward to as we begin the harrowing task of avenging those deaths."

War. He'd talked about it a couple of times before but never directly to the alchemists. There was no doubt about it now. We were his best weapons and this was our final warning. Get ready. The intensity in the room thickened as, one by one, the guardians stood a little taller. Sobering up, no doubt.

"It is with that happy thought," he continued, "that I must turn this conversation into something more somber." I bit back the annoyance at his use of the word "happy." Clearly, he was delusional if his idea of happy could resemble anything even close to what a war was going to look like.

"Bring him up," he said.

There was a scuffle on the side of the stage as someone was dragged onto it. At once, I recognized the man. He was dressed in gray prison scrubs and was handcuffed, his mouth gagged. Surrounded by way too many guards, there was no way for him to get away. Even if he could manage to touch the right color and use his magic, there were too many alchemists in attendance who could take him down. Still, he fought every step.

Officer Thomas.

Lucas and his fiancée had moved to the side of the stage. A thick hatred filled Lucas's eyes, almost consuming him. I'd never seen him look at anyone the way he looked at Thomas. I edged closer, around the crowd gathered at the front. First they made the party mandatory. Then Lucas announced his engagement. Finally, Richard brought Thomas out in public, in front of the media. Dread tingled up my spine. Something big was about to happen.

Richard and Lucas shared a knowing look, one I could easily read. I knew what Thomas did. But would it be revealed to the rest of the country when Richard had already announced something different at the queen's funeral?

"This man used to be an officer of the court," King Richard continued. "He was one of my father's most trusted advisors, and I admit that even I included him in my inner circle. But he is a traitor. We've discovered that he is the mole in our organization. For West America. It was only during an attempted murder on the prince that my brave son apprehended him and discovered the truth."

The crowd stirred, clearly vexed by the news. Journalists began calling out questions, but none were answered. A handful of officers knew the true story. But it seemed the truth didn't matter anymore. Not even to Lucas.

He was on the other side of Thomas from where I now stood, on the edge of the stage. He glared so intently at Thomas, it was unlikely anyone would break his gaze. But then, he met my eyes. I glowered back, not at Thomas, but at *him.* He startled.

I didn't care what his father had over him—this was too much, all of these lies. His expression softened, pained, fighting back at my own. Almost like he was willing me to understand. I shook my head and looked away. That's when I realized his depression over Natasha's death had clouded his judgment beyond anything I'd imagined. The Lucas I fell for wouldn't have let any of this happen.

"It's been ages since we had a public execution," Richard continued and the crowed hushed. "An attempt on a royal life is punishable by death. And the same goes for treason. This man has been found guilty of both. His only use to our country now is to be made an example of."

Thomas was squirming now, his old, bony body jerking. His white hair was matted to his head in perspiration. He screamed unintelligibly through his gagged mouth. The crowd mostly began to push back and out, but a few scurried closer to the stage. The cameras stayed where they were. That's when I noticed something horrible. A man dressed all in black with a mask over his face ascended to the stage. He carried a long blade. It glinted under the lights, sharp edges flashing death.

"Let this be a message to you all," Richard said, but he wasn't looking into the cameras anymore. He was staring out into the crowd, meeting the eyes of the alchemists. "This is no longer a time of peace. We are at war."

The men wrestled Thomas into a kneeling position. Someone yelled something into his ear, and he went still. I caught the words, "Or it will take more than one swing."

I clutched my stomach. I couldn't imagine the terror he must be feeling.

"There will be no mercy for traitors. If you betray this kingdom," Richard bellowed, his eyes bulging under his heavy crown, "if you betray *me*, you will die."

There was no time to turn away. Upon the king's final words, the executioner swung the axe wide. It was over in a moment, just one lethal movement. Blood splattered in a sickening arc. The body crumbled, the head rolled, then stopped a few feet away. Everything froze.

Bile rose to the back of my throat. I doubled over, sure I was going to either vomit or pass out. The message was clear. Somehow, some*way*, King Richard knew about the Resistance. He had to. And this was our warning. I'd assumed Thomas hadn't died yet because he was a red alchemist. But it seemed Richard valued loyalty more. And this? This was what his son wanted. What Lucas had been negotiating for…for weeks. When we broke up, had the pain been so intense that he thought *this* was the only way to feel better again?

Lucas still stood on the edge of the stage, comforting his bride-to-be, his lips set in a grim line, blood speckling his body. He didn't reach up to wipe it off his face. He remained motionless, glaring at what was left of Thomas.

Was it worth it?

His gaze landed on me then, as if he could hear my question. With an indecipherable shake of his head, he returned his attention to the woman at his side. He didn't look my way again.

ELEVEN

LUCAS

I applied pressure to my temples in a half-hearted attempt to alleviate the headache brewing. Celia and I sat awkwardly on the couch, our conversation stilted at best. She rubbed at the heavy emerald jewels draped from her neck as I fidgeted in my stiff suit. I cleared my throat.

"Did you want to say something?" she asked, perking up.

I shook my head, and she deflated.

Three parties in one week was not my idea of a good time. But here I found myself again, playing the role of dutiful prince. This time we were about to attend an intimate gathering to celebrate our engagement. I'd only met Celia earlier that week, even though she seemed to believe we had history together. Most likely we'd crossed paths a time or two, and while she'd held onto the memories, nothing remarkable had stuck around for me.

Couldn't everyone see that I wasn't interested, let alone *in love*, with this woman? Couldn't *she* see it? Sure, I was putting on a show for my father's sake, but even I wasn't that good of an actor.

"Come on," Celia said, snaking her arm around me. "You need to meet my parents."

"Goody." I smiled through gritted teeth.

We stood, and she led me to the door. Someone knocked politely on the other side. I pulled it open to two middle-aged people with hungry stars in their eyes. They looked just like Celia, both with red hair, pale faces, and green eyes. She was sent in right away to greet me while they were given a quick security briefing. Now that they were the parents of the future queen, they would be in the public spotlight. I'm sure they didn't mind. My father had already seen to it that Celia and her family were vetted, top to bottom. He'd chosen my fiancée, and I'd stupidly agreed in exchange for the execution of Thomas.

I am such an idiot.

I thought back to the events, still shocked that I'd been so impulsive. True, the fact that Thomas had been allowed to live had been keeping me up at night. But when Jessa broke up with me, something inside snapped. His execution become my sole focus, anything to avoid facing how bad Jessa had hurt me. A desperate part of me thought if I could just get justice for my mother, I'd feel better again. But I didn't feel better. Anger simmered just below the surface, threatening to eat me alive. I was out of control and would do almost anything to get it back.

"Ah, they're here." My father strode into the room. "I'll admit, I'm grateful you trusted me enough to give your daughter to my son. She's a wonderful girl. No doubt they will be very happy together."

They all blushed at the same time. *Who are we kidding?* We all knew every single one of those girls at that party had been dying to get my ring on her finger and a crown on her head. When Richard had proposed the idea of an engagement to me, he said he had a few girls in mind. I stupidly told him it didn't matter who he chose. In my mind, there was no way I was actually getting married to a stranger. Agreeing to an engagement wasn't agreeing to a marriage.

"I can hardly believe it myself." Celia winked. "I must have made a lasting impression." Little did she know that wasn't the case. "Lucas, I'd like you to formally meet my parents, Mark and Sabine."

I shook their hands. "Pleasure to meet you," I said.

"You'll be good to her?" her father asked. I could barely meet the man's eyes as I lied through my teeth.

"Yes, sir."

He continued, "Right, well, this all seems rather fast to me but as long as my princess is happy, then that's okay by me."

Princess... Yeah, I heard that. No doubt her father was just as thrilled as her mother despite his attempt to fulfill the role of the overprotective daddy.

"Let's eat, shall we?" I asked, focusing on the hearty smells wafting in.

We headed to my family's private dining room; extra guards lined the walls, their expressions stoic and searching. They were on edge lately. I couldn't say I blamed them. First their queen died, then a public attack, and then an execution. Not to mention my sham of an engagement.

I assumed dinner was delicious by the constant compliments of our guests. Mentions of "so tender" and "exquisite" filtered around me. But I could hardly do more than move my food from one spot on my plate to another. I wasn't the type to lose my appetite. With my morning workouts, and my age, I was always sneaking off to the kitchens for more food. But today my stomach was in knots. *How am I going to get out of this?*

Once again, Richard was getting everything he wanted and I was stuck doing his bidding. If it came down to it, I'd refuse to marry her. I wondered what he would do to me then...

"Well that was the most incredible apple fritter I have ever had." Celia smiled, her overly made-up face beaming. "Thank you so much for dinner, Your Royal Highness."

"You're welcome," my father replied, wiping his face with his napkin in satisfaction. "Why don't us old folks retire to the sitting room and let the couple have some time alone." He winked at Sabine and Mark. "No doubt you remember what it was like to be newly engaged."

"Oh, do I ever." Mark laughed.

My body went rigid. They got up to leave, and I stayed like an anchor in my chair.

"Lucas." My father looked back at me. "Don't keep your fiancée locked away in this stuffy dining room. Let the servants clean up. Show her your bedroom where you can have more privacy to talk and to…get to know each other better."

I expected her mother at least to protest but she only nodded in agreement. Wonderful. *How am I ever going to get Jessa back now?*

I bit my lip and stood. "Shall we?" As we walked to my room, I didn't even bother to look if Celia was following. Of course she was.

"Not many get to come back here," I mumbled.

"Oh, that's surprising." She followed me into my room and closed the door behind her. She was dressed in a short black dress and high heels. Her red hair was intricately braided down her back. She looked at me with expectant green eyes.

"Surprising?" I asked. "What do you mean by that?"

She smiled coyly. "You read the news. So do I." She was the picture of innocence. Delicate, yet brimming with confidence.

But I saw through the façade. She was dangerous.

I frowned and gripped my hands into fists behind my back. "The gossip columns love to paint me as a playboy. My father allows that to an extent because he thinks it makes me more desirable."

"So it's not true?" She smiled coyly.

I shrugged. "I won't lie and pretend there isn't a shred of truth to the stories. But overall? No, it's not true."

"Interesting."

"Besides, a lot has changed for me recently."

She nodded. "Your room is lovely," she said, walking around and running her finger over every surface. "Of course, I wouldn't expect anything less. You are the prince after all."

"And you're my fiancée," I said it as a challenge.

She squared her shoulders and smiled. "Yes. I am."

"Most women would be offended by the way that happened. I never even asked you." It was true. Once I agreed, Richard jumped into action and asked, or rather *told*, her parents to come to the palace immediately for the press conference. We'd only met again backstage. Some advisor hastily pushed a giant ring onto her finger and that had been that. My mother's ring.

I glanced at the rock, still planted on her finger, and a pang of regret shot through me.

"I don't mind unconventional," she mused. "We'll have plenty of time to get to know each other after we're married. Anyway, sometimes fast is more practical. And more exciting." She laced her tone with a level of innuendo as she approached me. Probably thought she was going to seduce me or something.

"I'm not going to sleep with you," I said.

She only smiled and raised a perfect eyebrow. "Of course not."

I shifted away from her, standing against the wall to put distance between us. She didn't seem to find it alarming in the slightest. The scenarios ran through my head. Should I try to push her away? Get her to break up with me? Was that even possible? Should I play along? Should I pretend?

But I can't cheat on Jessa. Even though we were no longer together, I wasn't stupid. Anything with Celia still felt like cheating, and I didn't want to hurt Jessa anymore.

"What's your endgame?" I asked, deciding to go straight for the kill. I needed the truth. I needed to know what Celia wanted most so I could use it as leverage. As bait.

She didn't falter. "I've been groomed my whole life to have an advantageous marriage. And, Lucas, *you* are the top prize. Not only are you the prince, you also happen to be rather attractive and intelligent. I couldn't do better. My endgame is simple. You."

"Well, at least you're honest."

"And you couldn't do much better either."

I eyed her confidence, skeptical. "You're rather sure of yourself."

"My father has a lot of influence in this kingdom," she replied simply. "And I will be a good wife."

"What if I don't want that?"

She sighed dramatically and placed a hand on her hip. "I'm not stupid, and I'm not romantic. I will let you do what you want if it comes to that." She paused, her expression grim. "Do you understand what I'm saying?"

I wasn't sure what to say. It wasn't like I needed her to spell it out for me.

"Don't be so obtuse. You can tell me you're not a playboy all you want, but like I said, we've met before. *I* remember how you behaved as a boy. And honestly, Lucas? I'm okay with you as long as you stay discreet, stay safe, and most importantly," she paused, careful to get her point across, "nobody gets near my crown."

I pushed off the wall and stalked toward her. "Your crown?" I laughed. "Has anyone ever told you not to count your chickens before they hatch?"

She only batted her eyes. "I know what I want. Our marriage will benefit both our families. Don't fight the inevitable, Lucas. You won't win."

"Is that a threat?"

She inched closer and pressed a soft kiss to my lips. I didn't kiss her back.

"Absolutely."

●

"We had the response we were looking for," one of the advisers said. "The people are rallying around the idea of war. Men are volunteering to join the army in droves, and of course, the alchemists are prepared for anything."

It was the next morning, and I sat with my father around the same conference table I'd been at far too frequently lately. I squinted and pinched my nose, resigned to the fact that this war was really going to happen.

"I want to move up our timetable. With the national broadcast yesterday, it's probable something was leaked and West America will be expecting us."

"Then why did you do it in the first place?" I asked. "Of course Thomas needed to die. But why broadcast it for everyone to see? Why do it in front of the alchemists and the kingdom like that?"

He turned on me, his eyes sharp. "Because we suspect there are spies and we won't have it." I held my breath, anxiety rooting me to my chair.

The men in the room nodded. "Not to mention, there is unrest," he continued. "The attack was performed by one of our own citizens. And Thomas lived in this very palace. I had to send a message."

"I think your message was received," I said, deadpan. My thoughts immediately went to Jessa. She needed to disassociate with the Resistance. I could only pray they didn't have her name written on some list somewhere. If Richard suspected an alchemist of foul play, it would only be a matter of time before he smoked them out.

"What's the prognosis if we launch our first attack tonight?" My father leaned in toward his highest-ranking general. The broad-chested man perked up at the attention, his military ornamentation gleaming. We hadn't been engaged in war in decades. Did this guy even know what he was doing?

"We're ready. We will need some of your best alchemists. Your fighters. And a few healers. But we have thousands of trained men ready to go and more who are preparing."

"We're going to send a message to West America. Going to suck them dry so they have no choice but to surrender."

"And why are we going to war again?" I interjected.

My father paused, his face sharpening. "Son, we've already gone over this. They killed your mother." *Lies.* "In all likelihood, they had something to do with the attack during her funeral." *Maybe.* "It's clear they want to start a war with us, so it's a war they will get. Besides, it wouldn't hurt to have more land. More resources. And to bless more people with our monarchy."

I gritted my teeth and nodded. There must be people in the room who didn't know the truth about my mother's death. War must be his priority because of his insatiable need for more land and resources. Lust for power. I tried not to think of the bloodshed that would happen because of my own father, but the reality of what was sure to happen haunted me.

He'd used his alchemists not only to destroy areas of our border, creating the shadow lands, but to essentially torture people. He'd used magic on them in so many unimaginable ways, most often ending in death. Maybe all those tests with magic had been his way of developing weapons. Maybe he'd been preparing for this war much longer than I realized.

"It's settled then. Round up your soldiers, and Faulk will deploy our officers. Together, we'll make a move on West America far worse than they can even imagine." A spark of excitement lit his eyes as the room burst into a flurry of action. The time for talking about war was over. It was time for action.

Richard had found a scapegoat in my mother's death and subsequent attack. He now had a reason to enact something he had long awaited. How many lives would pay the price? I left the room. I couldn't stand it anymore. This was not the way to lead the kingdom. This was wrong. But I wasn't king. And I was party to everything that was about to happen.

And there is nothing I can do about it.

●

I woke with a start. Sweat poured down my back as I caught my breath. I'd been so tired lately, but even sleep haunted me, turning dreams into nightmares. Images of my mother flashed through my mind, the blood pooling around her body, the smell of death, her eyes unblinking, the feeling of helplessness.

I jumped from the bed, changed into workout clothes, and headed to the gym. There was a perfectly adequate gym on this side of the palace, but I found my way into the alchemist wing instead. I needed to make sure Jessa was okay. I wouldn't talk to her. I didn't deserve that. But I could at least see how she was holding up. I knew she spent most of her mornings sparring.

A few people sent odd looks my direction as I walked into the gym, but most seemed unbothered. I worked my way over to the area with weight equipment and began to lift dumbbells. My eyes scanned the room for Jessa, finding her sparring with another girl I didn't recognized. She laughed at something the girl said, her face lighting up.

I finished my set and moved over to the leg-press machine. I added more weight than normal and got to work. I focused on my shoelaces as I thought about Jessa. She needed to get out of the Resistance. At least while Richard was on his witch-hunt. The fact that I still didn't know who her handler was ate away at me. Who else knew about Jessa's involvement?

I got up from the machine and walked over to the water station. I swallowed a cup in one gulp and threw it into the trash. I didn't have to sit back and let the Resistance have Jessa. *I'm an alchemist*, I reminded myself. I glanced around the room, watching the mix of color guardians and officers for a moment. What would they do if they knew about me? It was my biggest secret. I'd revealed it once only because I'd had to. That day in the helicopter, I had saved my life, Jessa's life, and Sasha's. Sasha said she was going to tell the Resistance about my secret, but I suspected she never had. So far, no one had confronted me. I wished I could talk to Sasha and find out for sure. But she was hiding in the mountains north somewhere, and I had no idea how to talk to her.

My eyes traveled to Jessa again, and I saw her training with a man this time— some guy I didn't know. He came at her, pummeling her to the ground. Every instinct in me fired. I began to move toward them, but I stopped myself. She had jumped up and taken control of the fight.

She doesn't need you.

I ran a few miles on a treadmill, watching her. She never looked my way. She either hadn't noticed me, or she was deliberately ignoring me. I pressed the incline and speed buttons to max level for as long as I could possibly go. Exertion was the only thing that could distract me from the frustration that had been stealing every thought. When she caught my gaze and looked away just as quickly, I'd had enough.

I jumped off the machine and stormed out of the gym. I didn't have to deal with this silent treatment. If she wasn't going to see reason and distance herself from the Resistance, then I would find a way to do it for her.

I'd been working on my white alchemy for years. And I was good. I didn't have proper training in all the colors, but I knew I could be initiated if I had the chance. But white? That was my specialty. As a royal, I would never be part of the guardians. It would upset the balance. None of that stopped me from using magic when I had to. *Maybe I had to.*

I quickly showered and dressed myself in black, moving into action.

It was the same for all alchemists. Natural elements like plants and stones were easier to manipulate than synthetic elements. The best alchemists could still use the color from things like cloth, which was why everyone wore black. It was best to avoid any mistakes. And I wouldn't make a mistake again.

I would do anything to protect her.

Our royal quarters were private, and I was alone as I walked into the dining room. I pulled the white rose from the large bouquet on the table, breaking its head from the stem. Nobody would miss it. It had been a while since I'd done this, and the thrill of excitement pulsed through my veins as I squeezed the soft petals. I calmed at the velvet feel between my fingers.

I watched as my body faded away, growing foggy at first, and then…nothing. I was invisible. I needed to be quick before I got too drowsy, as I knew from experience just how tiring this type of magic was on me. I took off running, careful to land softly with each step. I followed the corridors back toward the GC headquarters.

I'd noticed an extra level of anxiety at the gym earlier. I'd been too lost in my own cloud of depression to realize why. They must all be in a complete frenzy over the recent war announcement. Many of them would be leaving tonight. Faulk had been tasked to organize it and had immediately begun preparations. I had a strong suspicion Jessa would be connecting with her Resistance contact over the news. At this point, I hoped her initiation would be delayed. The thought of her being sent off to war wasn't something I could handle. But she wasn't ready, and Richard wouldn't risk losing her. She should be finished at the gym by now. I decided to follow her. If I was lucky, I could figure out whom it was I needed to blackmail.

Invisibility was an extremely useful skill. I balked when I rounded a corner, stepping into full view of a group of officers, but no one looked in my direction. I checked the gym just in case. She was still there. A few people came close to bumping into me as I went in, but I was able to dodge them. A small trickle of fatigue picked at my eyes, and I took a steady breath. I found a corner and watched impatiently.

Jessa, come on. Connect with your handler.

She was sparring with Reed. Again. She was always forgiving that guy. He grabbed her around her waist, and I was reminded why I didn't like him. He wasn't trustworthy, for one thing. But it was his obvious romantic interest in her that made me dislike him the most. He flirted ruthlessly, always worming his way into her life. He wasn't shy about what he was doing. I'd seen him around with plenty of different female alchemists. The kid knew how to get a girl. I never worried about it too much before, but now that we weren't together anymore, seeing Jessa with him killed me. The urge to go over there and rip the guy off of her consumed me. He had her pinned to the ground as she wriggled to get out of his grip. When they laughed, I almost lost it.

I stared at the wall as they did a few more rounds. Biding my time, I pushed off the exhaustion beginning to overtake me. I couldn't see the rose in my hand, since it was also invisible, but I wondered how much longer I had. A while, but not forever. I considered turning back.

If you don't keep her safe, no one else will. You owe her.

She knocked Reed to the ground and smirked in his face, letting out a whoop of victory. She helped him up, and he brought his arm around her as they walked toward the greenhouse out back, no doubt to heal their wounds. I followed, knowing this meant she was done fighting for the day.

I didn't anticipate that there would be so many people back there. I had to stop multiple times to let people pass, just in case. When I finally made it inside, I warmed at the sight. She had friends. The other alchemists weren't nearly so hostile toward her as they usually were. A few of them laughed with her over her knocking Reed out. I smiled. They would grow to love her if they just got to know her.

When she left, I followed close behind. It was most likely that she was going to her own room for a shower. I may be invisible, but I wasn't a creep. I would have to wait outside for her and hoped she'd be quick.

But as she approached the corridor that led to her room, she passed it, and continued down the hallway. She stopped abruptly, every muscle tense and still. Then she whipped around. I didn't move an inch, holding my breath. She eyed the hallway but nobody was in this area right now except me. Of course she couldn't see me. But could she feel me watching her?

She hesitated for a few long moments and then opened the door to Jasmine's classroom and office. I wasn't sure what that meant. Jasmine had been training her, and I'd helped put the two of them together. Jasmine was older and kind, matronly even. Jessa had been so vulnerable in the beginning. She needed somebody comforting on her side, which was why I'd originally asked for Jasmine's help. I sighed, knowing it was probably a typical meeting with her mentor. I was running out of time!

Still, I pressed my ear to the door and looked in through the glass windows.

But then something curious happened. The windows had a special feature to create privacy when needed. And that's just what they did. Jasmine walked over, and they nonchalantly switched from clear to opaque.

Why do they need privacy?

Mumbled conversation filtered from the other side of the door, but it was hard to make out the words.

"The war?" Jessa said. A scraping noise followed—most likely a drawer being opened. "Hold on…" Then there was nothing.

Absolute silence.

My heart rate skyrocketed. Jasmine. I'd trusted her. And clearly she was using blue alchemy to protect against eavesdroppers. There was no other explanation for complete silence on their end. She had to be Resistance, otherwise they never would have done that. It was dangerous to keep secrets here. That kind of behavior was forbidden.

How had I missed it?

I fought the urge to push open the door and confront her right there and then. I'd spent so much time with Jasmine while helping the Resistance. And all I'd wanted was some validation from them. If she was the Resistance's contact in the palace, why couldn't she have trusted me enough to reveal her secret to me? Knowing how close I'd been to her, and how easily I'd been deceived despite that, had me reeling.

I pressed myself against the wall, holding my breath, waiting for Jessa to leave. I had zero hesitation about what needed to be done.

Sure enough, a few minutes later, Jessa exited the room. Her face was reddened as she wiped a bead of sweat from her brow. She didn't hesitate as she ambled off toward her room. Once I was sure she was gone, and no one else was in the hallway, I took a deep breath and willed myself to become visible again. It worked, my body filling out into full color. The rose was only about half gray, divided down the middle by life and death. I pushed open the door.

"I know who you are," I said, slamming the door behind me. Jasmine sat at her desk, the blue stone still in her hands. "Don't try to deny it. I know you're with the Resistance. You're Jessa's contact."

She stood, her eyes widening. "It's not what you think."

"Save it," I said. "Let me make this brief. You're going to exclude Jessa from everything Resistance from here on out. She is no longer a part of your organization. Your only concern for her is her alchemy. And to keep her safe."

"You don't know what you're doing. We want the same things, Lucas."

"You don't know the first thing about what I want!" I yelled.

She shook her head. "Where are these threats coming from? Lucas, this isn't you." I momentarily froze, confused by her tone. She meant what she said.

I shook my head, resolved in my decision. "Oh, it's not a threat. It's an order. And if you don't do as I say, then I promise you will be the next one on that executioner's stand."

I meant it. I moved in close, leaning my palms against her desk. "Do not underestimate me."

"And what if I told your father all of your secrets?" she responded, leaning back in her chair. I wasn't sure she was alluding to my short time with the Resistance or if she knew about my alchemy. I wasn't going to stick around and find out.

"You have no proof of *anything*. It would be your word against mine," I said. "And who do you think my father is going to believe? Some healer with a distaste for the rules?" I peered at her clothing. She was the only guardian who didn't dress in black. She got away with it because she'd been one of my mother's only alchemist friends. I still didn't know why she went against the grain; self-expression had always been my guess. "Or is he going to believe his own son?"

Something threatening traced her eyes, as well as something else. Tiredness. Both were emotions I hadn't seen on the woman before. Either way, I seemed to have the upper hand. She nodded, lips pinched.

"Oh, and one more thing. Don't you dare tell *her* anything about this conversation." I headed for the door. We both knew whom I was talking about.

"You don't understand what you're doing, Lucas. You'll only put her in more danger by doing this," she called after me.

I didn't dignify that garbage with a response as I shoved the rose that had been hanging limp in my hand into my pocket. I slammed the door behind me.

TWELVE

JESSA

About a quarter of the guardians were gone. When they left the night before, everything went from chaotic to downright silent. Nobody wanted to talk about it. And nobody wanted to admit it, but worry followed us around like a dark shadow. Breakfast was a solemn affair as we all waited to hear news, knowing it was likely we wouldn't hear anything for a while.

I wasn't the only one pecking at my food as I sat at one of the tables surrounded by my new friends. It was weird, how far I'd come. Not to say I was friends with Brooke or her crowd. But ever since the last party, it was as if the other alchemists decided to stop hating me.

Over the last couple of days, the others my age had started talking to me. Inviting me to eat with them, spar with them, sitting by me in the few group lessons I attended. It was as if everyone was worried about bigger things, and I was suddenly invited to the party. It was part of what Jasmine wanted, so I wasn't complaining. As much as I hated to admit it, it felt good. I guessed deep down maybe there was a part of everyone who wanted to be accepted. Some of us just knew how to hide it better than others.

●

"I wonder when we are going to be called up," one of the girls said. She'd gone out of her way to be nice to me, which I appreciated. "Usually those of us under eighteen are stuck in training, with the occasional mission," she finished. I'd recently learned her name was Callie. I didn't question why she'd befriended me, because I quickly noticed she was one of those people who made friends with everyone. There were four of us: a boy, me, Callie, and a blond girl who sat across from me.

"Not this time," the girl across the table sighed, her brown eyes heavy. "Reed and Brooke have both gone, as well as about twenty others under eighteen. There were even a couple of fifteen-year-olds and one fourteen-year-old." She snagged a hair tie off her wrist and began pulling her hair on top of her head.

"Fourteen?" I frowned. "That's so young."

"It just depends on how good they are," Callie responded, spooning her grapefruit. "Reed's been going out on stuff for a long time. There are others who go even younger than that."

"But that's different, isn't it? This is an actual war. It's not like they're in New Colony territory. They went over to West America."

"That's true." The other girl nodded eagerly. "I can't wait until I get called up. I've been training like a mad woman. I need a real fight."

I sighed and looked back at my buttered toast, picked up a piece, and plopped it into my mouth. It tasted like cardboard, but I made myself swallow. I took a big drink of water, trying to dissect the conversation in my mind. It seemed they were all *eager* to get in on the action. Nervous, of course, but more excited than anything. Did they know what they were really asking for? Fighting or not, this preparation wasn't for an initiation test or a sparring round. This was war, and that meant to the death.

And I can't change their minds, so don't mess this up.

"What about you?" Callie asked. "Do you want to fight?"

"She's not ready." A guy piped in. He had shaggy blond hair around his ears and glasses. He shrugged from across the table. "No offense."

"None taken," I responded, though I was a bit put off. "Honestly, you're right. I'm not ready for battle like that. Plus, I haven't been initiated yet. I still have to pass two more tests."

"Which ones?" Callie asked. "If you don't mind me asking?" She blushed, but I got the feeling she liked to know the latest gossip.

"It's okay. I passed the yellow. But I failed the blue and the purple," I said, a little embarrassed. "Even though I can do a little bit with both. It wasn't enough, apparently."

Callie's friend, who I hadn't really met, smirked. "It's harder than it looks, isn't it?"

I bit my lip. *You're here to make friends, Jessa.*

"It's okay," the boy said. "*Nobody* passes all five tests. And you only have to get three. Green and orange are pretty easy. You'll do it."

"Are they the same tests for everyone?"

"Sometimes," Callie said. "Not always. But we can't give you any hints. It's against the rules," she was quick to add.

I nodded, already knowing this to be true. The element of surprise was part of what made the tests difficult. "I'll be fine with green," I said. "I just haven't used orange all that much."

"Everybody can do orange. It's going to be fine. You'll see."

I smiled at my new friend. She had caramel eyes, wiry blond hair, and thick glasses, but she pulled it off in an adorable smart-girl way. "Thanks."

"I wonder when her next test will be," Callie's friend said to the other two at the table, basically ignoring me. *Umm, hello? I'm sitting right here.*

"What's your name?" I asked the brazen girl in my friendliest tone.

"Tessa," she said, turning on me.

"Hi, Tessa, I'm Jessa." I laughed. Our names rhymed and something about that was funny. I guess she didn't think so. I decided to be nice. "I'm wondering when my next test will be just as much as you are. Truth is, with this war stuff happening, I have no idea anymore."

"Well, King Richard definitely wants you for something."

I bristled. "What do you mean by that?"

She shrugged. "Just that you're here because you have something he wants. So my guess is your initiation is going to happen sooner rather than later."

The shaggy-haired boy nodded. "Yeah, Tessa is right. I'm Nate, by the way." He reached out a hand across the table, and I shook it. "I wouldn't say the same thing for most alchemists. Anyone else would probably have their tests postponed."

Callie chimed in with a smile. "But you, my dear, are extra special."

"Lucky me."

"You should consider yourself lucky." Tessa got up with a huff and strode away from our table. What was with that girl? I had been nothing but nice.

"Ignore her," Nate said. "She'll get over it."

I realized something then. No matter how I acted or what I did, there would always be someone who didn't like me. Maybe that was a fact of life. Stand for something, and people hate you. Stand for nothing, and hate yourself. Plus people would still hate you. I decided to take Nate's advice and ignore Tessa's behavior. It wasn't my problem.

"I'm sorry, you guys," I blurted. "This is hard for me. I didn't grow up here, and I still have a family. I miss them so much. Don't get me wrong, the magic is amazing, and I can see how it can help a lot of people. And I like doing it. But war? I didn't sign up for that."

"No one signs up for it." Callie sighed.

"You'll get used to it here," Nate added.

I smiled. "Thanks. I'm sorry, I haven't introduced myself." I reached out a hand. "I'm Jessa."

"I know." He laughed, shaking the hair out of his eyes, but it just fell right back into place. He met my handshake with a firm one of his own. "Everyone knows who *you* are."

"You really have a family?" Callie whispered. She pushed her plate away and leaned in. Part of me wanted to hold back, but making friends wasn't about keeping secrets.

"Yes. It's me, my mom, dad, and my little sister, Lacey. She's only six. I *really* miss them."

"You're so lucky. I don't remember my family. I'd give anything to even have one memory."

"You can't think about it, Callie," Nate said.

"It's not as easy as that." Callie stared down at her plate.

314

"Nate might be onto something," I said. "Don't get me wrong. I'm doing everything I can to have some kind of connection with my family again. Let's just say the king has…leverage. And I would never choose not to remember them. But I can see how you guys have the advantage."

Maybe I said too much.

"You're right," Nate agreed. "The king doesn't have as much leverage over us." He blushed, cleared his throat, and got up from the table. "Forget I said that. I have to go."

Callie stared after him. "That was weird."

I shrugged. But actually, I didn't find it that weird for Nate to question the king. Maybe he would join the Resistance? What was weird was all these talented people going along with everything Richard wanted. Couldn't they see there had to be a better way? To see Nate behave that way signified that, perhaps, there were more people like me out there. More alchemists who weren't happy with the current state of things. And if that were true, maybe the Resistance really did stand a chance.

What was going on with Lucas? Was the boy I'd fallen in love with under the summer stars turning into his father's son? I didn't want to think like that, but I couldn't help the questions from turning over and over in my mind.

When I'd met him, he'd taken me completely by surprise. I'd thought I knew who he was. That he was just what the media presented him as: a handsome, spoiled, playboy and duty-driven prince—nobody I wanted to know. But then he'd showed me someone *completely different.*

And now we weren't even talking.

I pushed the remaining food around on my plate, lost in thought. He was clearly moving forward with his life. Forward in a completely different direction than what I wanted. It hurt to think about my future without him; the wound constantly reopened. When push came to shove, would Lucas stand with his father? Would I have to fight against the man I loved in order to save not only my family and countless others, but myself? Those were the questions that haunted me.

"Earth to Jessa?" Callie's voice rang out. "Are you in there?"

I shook myself out of it and smiled. "Sorry." We stood together and threw the rest of our meager breakfasts away.

The day continued—training, meals, whispered conversations, and anxious glances between the guardians. We all assumed the attack had happened and watched the newsfeeds on our slatebooks eagerly. But there was never any news.

●

I woke to sharp pounding on my door and catapulted myself from my bed. The gym training must be going better than expected because I landed expertly on my feet. I fell into a defensive crouch. My heart thundered as I glanced bleary-eyed around the room. Darkness filtered through the drawn shades on the dormitory window. Another series of booming knocks sounded. There was a cry and a shuffling noise. What was going on?

I didn't hesitate. I leapt for the door and pulled it open. The hallway was dim. Nobody. I peered from side to side, my ears trained in the direction I'd heard something. The shuffling sounded again, around the corner. "Help," someone mumbled, before the cry broke off.

I darted toward it, down the hall and around the corner, ready to jump in and aid whoever was in trouble. My instincts kicked into high gear. The hair on my arms stood on end. I was only wearing shorts and a tank top but hardly noticed the cold air as I swooped into action.

Again, nobody was there. *What in the world is going on?*

Then a blood-curdling scream erupted though the space. It sounded farther down. I squinted into the darkness. A figure was crouched down, much farther up the corridor. A few of the other dormitory doors flung open, but I took no notice as I sprinted down the hallway. Just as I reached the figure, it stood to full height. A man, much taller and much older, loomed over me. There wasn't a trace of emotion on his face.

"What's wrong?" I asked, confused.

"Sorry," he muttered.

A ripple of pain blasted through my side, followed by a clipped boom. He stepped back, lowering a gun into his holster, and disappeared into the darkness.

I gasped, the icy pain turning to tormented burning. I fell to my knees. Blood blossomed around the wound, forming a circle of crimson. *He shot me!* My mind grew dizzy. A few people surrounded me in a wide arc. What were they doing? Why were they just standing there?

"Help me!" I screamed, but the sound came out all wrong.

Someone moved forward. "Don't," one of them said. "She hasn't been initiated yet, remember?"

"Oh, sorry," another replied. Was that Nate?

I tried to respond. Only a low moan came from my mouth. What were they talking about? All at once, they retreated to their rooms. When the last door closed, panic ran through me. How could they be so cruel? I tried to piece it together—why someone would shoot me, why others would walk away—but I couldn't make sense of it over the pain. My mind wasn't clear.

I held my side, shocked at the blood. There was so much! If I didn't do something, I was going to bleed out. I struggled to look around the hallway, trying to figure out where I was. That's when I realized what the tall, darkened shadows in the room next to me was—one of the greenhouses. I gritted my teeth, pushing with both my hands against the wound and willed myself to a standing position. I shuffled to the room, gasping as I opened the door. I fell, grunting, crawling into the room. I reached out a bloody hand for the closest green I could find.

It didn't take long to get ahold of a plant, but the time it took me to reach my magic felt like an eternity. Finally, the green alchemy flowed through my body, penetrating the source. The healing was familiar. It was icy, tingly, as it wove through the wound. I kept one hand on the pain and another grasping desperately at the poor plant crushed between my fingers. Something solid oozed out of the wound and into my palm. The bullet. Relief swept through me as I stared, shocked. But the pain still held on as my eyes fluttered. A wave of tiredness overtook me, exhausted from both the magic and the wound. I managed to lie down just as the darkness took me.

●

"That was a harder test than most get," someone said, perturbed. "You didn't need to go to such lengths as to *shoot her*."

"We had you on standby," someone else responded coolly. "She was never in any real danger. And look? She passed. She's *fine*."

Where am I? What is happening? My thoughts were hazy. A wave of adrenaline pulled me to the surface. My eyelids fluttered, and a needle of light found its way into my vision. I opened my eyes, blinking repeatedly up at the women standing over me.

"Good, you're awake," Jasmine said, frowning down at me. I wanted to cry out and hug her. She brushed a bead of sweat from her forehead. She looked tired. Worried. I blinked a few more times, trying to gauge the situation and failing. Faulk was with her. A glint of disappointment flashed across her face before she stepped back. Why were they standing over me, and why was I lying on the floor?

"What happened?" I asked, sitting up, but the memory came flooding back just as I asked the question. "I was shot!" I hissed.

"Clearly. She's observant," Faulk remarked.

"You passed the test," Jasmine said. "I'm sorry, I wasn't allowed to warn you. I didn't know they would go to such lengths."

"You had me shot?" I gasped, glaring at Faulk.

She only shrugged and scribbled something down in a notebook. She and her people were clearly done with me as they began to exit the greenhouse. Well, at least I'd passed the test.

Jasmine knelt down next to me and brushed the loose hair from my face. I breathed a sigh of relief, allowing myself to be comforted. She'd become not only my mentor, not only my contact to the Resistance, but probably my best friend in the palace. It sounded weird to be best friends with an old lady, but it was the truth.

"The king wanted to see what you were made of," Faulk said, standing in the doorway. "We usually shoot a few other people for you to heal. But sometimes, the lucky ones get to be shot and heal themselves. You should be grateful; this will only raise your esteem in the palace. I, of course, didn't think you'd be able to do it. You're a more powerful healer than I gave you credit for." She stared at me for a moment, almost torn by her statement, her jaw tense. She slammed the door behind her.

Well, okay then...

"She's right," Jasmine said. "What you did was remarkable. I was in here the whole time. I would have stepped in if you needed me, but you passed that test with flying colors, Jessa. You should be very proud of yourself."

"Thanks. But geez, a little warning would have been really nice," I said, reaching for Jasmine as she helped me rise to my feet. I was a little unsteady, so I leaned against the woman for support. "That was terrible."

"I know. I'm sorry." Jasmine sighed as we moved toward a couple of chairs. "Believe me, it wasn't my idea." We sat. She faced me so her back was to the glass wall along the hallway. She opened her palm to reveal a blue stone. It was risky, doing that here. She must have good reason. A wisp of magic danced in the air before it split, going into me and then into her. In the darkened room, no one from the outside would have seen it. And with the magic now flowing, we'd be silent to the outside world. If someone looked in the window, it would appear we were just sitting here, resting for a moment.

"Don't say anything," she said. "You're facing the hall, and I don't know if someone is watching." I narrowed my eyes at her and nodded imperceptibly. I understood what was at stake. Normally, she used the switch to turn the glass wall opaque, but that was too dangerous with officers lurking outside.

"Your initiation is being moved up quickly. The king plans to pass you in the orange tomorrow no matter how the test goes, so there's nothing to worry about with that." She got up, tending to the plant I had used in my recovery, her back still to the hallway. "But it means he needs you to be a guardian sooner than we expected. He must want to use your red alchemy in the war, especially now that Thomas is dead. It's the best explanation."

I shuddered, but it made sense. I had to gain his trust. And then when the moment was right, I would turn on him. I would find a way to bring him under my control, under the control of the Resistance. That had been my mission all along. I was terrified of what it would mean for me, but I could do it. I fidgeted in my chair, pulling my shirt up to look at the mess of blood.

"There's more. Your initiation is set for just two days' time. You're not supposed to know this, but they're always similar. There will be another party, a nice dinner, and you will be asked to use your magic publically to do something for the king. There will be a large crowd of the alchemists and officers there to watch it all happen—bring you into the fold, so to speak."

This was news to me. But I could handle it.

"There's one last thing." She paused, coming back to sit down, grim-faced. "You're out of the Resistance."

"What?" I sputtered.

"Shhh," she said. "Don't talk, remember?" She leaned over, appearing to look at my wound.

I stared into her eyes, willing her to read my thoughts.

"Look, I can't explain what happened, but it's not good. For the time being, we need to lie low. No more missions until I'm sure it's safe. No more talking to me about *anything* other than normal guardian business."

I bit my lip, hating what she was telling me. The Resistance was the one lifeline I had left to my family. I was not okay with being cut off from them.

"I'm really sorry about this. But it can't be helped. I promise to bring you back in as soon as I can." *Fine.* "There's one last thing," she added. "I probably shouldn't be saying this, but you deserve to know. We have plans to use your initiation to stage an attack. You'll be fine. But you must stay out of trouble." My eyes were probably as large as saucers at this news. "There will be a lot of high-level people in one room at the same time. And with most of the best fighters gone, we can't miss this opportunity. But you, Jessa, must *not* reveal your alliance to the Resistance under any circumstances. I too will be sticking to the background, keeping my cover."

With that information-bomb, she slipped the blue rock into her pocket and gave me a quick hug. She left the room in a flash. "Get some rest," she said, disappearing around the door.

I soon followed, heading back to my room, the shock sinking into me with each step. So much had happened in the space of one night. I still couldn't believe it. First, I'd been shot, then I'd passed another test, only to find out that the Resistance was ditching me, even if it was temporary. It still hurt—the memory of the bullet wound *and* the news about the Resistance. And now my initiation into the Guardians of Color loomed. I was scared of everything that it entailed, but an attack? What would it mean? Who would they go after?

But this was what I'd wanted. I needed to chill and move forward. There was no turning back. No matter what, I had to make sure I passed tomorrow's orange alchemy test. I had to shine at that initiation ritual. Whatever it was, I would excel and earn my place.

I shuffled into my room and landed with a thud on my bed. I stared at my ceiling, going over every possible scenario the rest of the night. My mind couldn't stop spinning, but deep down it didn't matter. I couldn't control what Richard did to me, but I could control my own effort. And I would do everything in my power to impress him.

It wasn't until much later when my whole body had finally relaxed that I opened my hand. The bullet still rested in my bloody palm.

THIRTEEN

SASHA

"I heard it's your birthday," Mastin said. "Why didn't you tell me?"

"I hate birthdays," I moaned. It was a matter of fact. I didn't get what the big deal was. And I didn't want to celebrate. "So what? I'm another year older, who cares?" I shrugged.

He smirked and sat by me on the fallen log—currently my favorite thinking spot.

"How old are you?"

"Twenty."

"A new decade of life. What's not to celebrate about that?" He laughed. "I'm also twenty," he added.

I rolled that fact over in my mind for a minute. "You're young to be working so closely with a general, aren't you?" I tried not to sound impressed. His ego was big enough as it was—no need to inflate it more.

He shrugged and changed the subject. "So, do you come here often?"

I let out a laugh. Living in close quarters with other people meant I had very little privacy and space. I spent most of my time outside during the warmer months. Once winter came, I would get super cooped up. I watched a leaf as it fell in the wind, resting on the hard earth. A breeze blew my hair out of my face, and I pulled my collar up around my ears.

"How did you find me?" I asked.

I was a little off the beaten path, higher up on the mountain. Or "hill" as Hank called it. There was a clearing with a view of the whole camp, and now that there were more people here than ever, I'd needed to find a new alone spot.

"I found you by accident." He shrugged. "I was just looking for somewhere to get away." He held up a book. I smiled and held up the ratty paperback that I clutched in one hand.

So he wants to be alone and yet when he saw me, he chose to sit right next to me. I filed that information away as I peered over at him. He shifted closer and his warmth brushed my arm.

"You know, Hank has been to the Rocky Mountains. He acts like they're so much better than these. Is that true?"

Mastin laughed. "I wouldn't say better. It's beautiful here too. But yes, they're a lot bigger."

"I'd like to see that."

"You will."

I nodded, placating him. But I wasn't sure if it was true. I'd spent the better part of a decade hiding out in Canada. I was used to this place. To think I'd ever go to West America was almost unfathomable. What would it even be like? Would it be better than what I had here?

I looked over at Mastin, studying him. He was wrapped up in a coat and scarf, unperturbed by our proximity. "Why are you being so nice to me?" I blurted. Sometimes, I wondered if he forgot I was an alchemist.

"I don't hate you, if that's what you think."

But he hated alchemy.

Cole said laws on alchemy in his country would be changing soon. I knew better. It was probably a lie, a manipulation to get what they wanted from us. I didn't like feeling backed into a corner, and the truth was, maybe the Resistance actually did need their help.

"I don't know what I think anymore," I murmured as we fell into silence.

We sat for a while. I was more and more comfortable around Mastin every day. He wasn't my type, so rigid and by the book. But I couldn't pretend I wasn't attracted to him. I was. The accident with the orange alchemy had proven it. But at the end of the day, it was foolish to get close to a guy like Mastin. We may be from the same planet, but we were from totally different worlds.

And you don't have time for that right now. It was the truth I clung to.

"Do you still hate alchemy?" I asked, feeling brave.

He stood, pacing, but silent. I wasn't sure he was going to reply when he looked back at me. "I was raised to be a soldier my whole life. I was always the top of my class."

"And what does that have to do with alchemy?" I asked, pressing the question again.

"Our soldiers are trained to maintain order." He stopped, taking me in with his eyes. "Our job is to not only protect our country from outside invaders, but to protect our citizens from the alchemists that pop up. It was something I personally worked on."

"What do you mean?" I stood too. "Just tell me."

"If an alchemist was reported, I would go and apprehend them."

"So you're basically telling me that you were not only trained to hate alchemists, but you personally saw to it that they were put away? Awesome, Mastin. I think that answers it." I shook my head.

He squinted at me, jaw tense. "What I am saying, Sasha, is that I was trained that way. Magic doesn't fit in my world."

"So that makes it okay then?"

"I saw a lot of dangerous people."

"Most of them were children, though, weren't they? How can you hold them accountable for that?"

He didn't answer.

I studied his eyes, looking for something that would make it okay. But the green eyes staring back at me were unreadable. "Got it."

"No, you don't get it, Sasha. I was trained to hate alchemy. And I thought I would hate you. I knew I would…" He paused. "But I don't. I should, but I don't feel what I should feel for you." He shook his head. "I have to go."

He stalked off down the hill. I let him leave, somewhat relieved that he had. The last thing I needed was to get mixed up with a guy whose job was to put alchemists in prison. I needed to forget whatever weird feelings were building between us. Besides, if I wanted a relationship, there was someone else who would be a much better fit for me.

My thoughts traveled to Tristan.

He'd been my rock growing up, my best friend for ages. But in the last few years, Tristan had grown into a man. And I had grown up too. He was older than me by five and a half years. And for most of my life, he felt like the brother I never had. But lately, things between us had shifted. It had all started that night he'd confessed some sort of feelings for me. I hadn't been able to get him out of my mind since.

He is good for me. He brings out my best qualities. And I do feel something for him, too.

Mastin was like the forbidden fruit. And that was probably why I was suddenly crushing on him. I pushed all thoughts of romance out of my head, determined to be done with it once and for all. My focus needed to be on preparing these alchemists for the battle ahead.

I sighed and began to make my way back to camp.

Much to my annoyance, I found myself at Tristan's door. Our recent argument had been weighing on me. I needed to make things right with him. In hindsight, I could see why he was more comfortable going into New Colony as soon as possible. He'd been ready to fight years ago, and only now had the opportunity finally presented itself. Of course he wanted to take it. He was also ready to live a free life outside of this camp.

I knocked on his door, sucking in a breath.

The man had actually built himself his own small cabin with his bare hands. Being stuck up here for years on end caused the guy to be extra resourceful, and it was impressive. Even though the cabin only had a couple of rooms, he'd installed electricity and running water. It was just him; what more did he need?

He opened the door, running his hands through his wet hair. When it was dark and wet like that, it nearly reached his shoulders. I watched a drop of water fall onto his shirt. The blue cotton clung to his body. There were a few more wet spots, and I was pretty sure he'd rushed from the shower to answer the door.

"Hey," I said, smiling up at him. He towered over me, lean and athletic. "Can

I come in for a minute?"

"Always," he said, making room as he stepped inside.

I sat on the worn, puffy couch and patted the seat next to me. "We need to talk."

He sighed. "I'm sorry about our argument before."

"Me too."

"I just…really want to get this over with, you know?" The couch dipped as he sat next to me. He smelled of soap and citrus, and I closed my eyes momentarily as I took it in. "It's only a matter of time before we have to attack. I'm ready."

"I know." I nodded. "And maybe you're right about everything. It's just hard to think about sending those people in there. They aren't ready, Tristan. But the truth is, they may never be ready. I don't think even I'm ready to face that place again."

He laughed and leaned over, giving me a side hug. It felt good to be close to him, comforting. A moment passed and then he relaxed with his arm around me. "You need to give yourself more credit. You're good enough to beat them."

"Thanks," I mumbled. I was never any good with compliments.

"I mean it. You're extraordinary," he whispered, his voice scratchy. "I've never met anyone like you."

I swallowed hard. My heart pulsed, and I stood, breaking the connection. I was so confused by all these feelings. I almost couldn't believe myself. It wasn't long ago that I was attracted to Lucas. Sure, Jasmine had ordered me to get close to him, but he was easy to like. That didn't work out for obvious reasons, namely him falling for my sister. But it seemed that the second I got over Lucas, I'd found myself gravitating toward Mastin—the guy I most definitely needed to stay away from. And now Tristan was appealing to me in ways he never had before. He was my best friend. I wasn't supposed to feel this way because it would ruin that feeling of safety that we had together. How was it possible that someone who'd never been that person to me was suddenly…more?

Clearly, I didn't know what I wanted.

"I think we need to stay focused on the mission, you know? Overthrow the monarchy. Start a new life."

"Agreed."

Tristan's eyes flashed before he looked away, and he stood and headed to his kitchenette. He opened a cupboard, pulled out two glasses and filled them with water. Handing me one, he cleared his throat. We both gulped the water, as if trying to keep ourselves from saying anything stupid. From the strained look on his face, I would guess he was as uncomfortable as I was, but I wasn't sure. He was harder to read than most men.

"Are you okay?" he asked, his left eyebrow rising in a familiar gesture. Just one of the many things I loved about him.

"Yeah, why?"

"You look like you're trying to do a math problem."

I hated math. *Yup, I am obviously over-thinking everything.*

"Hey, I wanted to wish you Happy Birthday." He smiled.

Oh, here we go. My birthday. I didn't celebrate.

"Thanks."

"I got you something." He slipped into his room and came out with a box-shaped gift wrapped in brown paper. I was never good with stuff like this. Presents. Birthdays. Holidays. Being abandoned by a family did that to a person like me. But Tristan was the opposite. He'd always found a way to make everything special. And his homemade gifts were the best. They were the one thing about my birthdays I looked forward to.

I unwrapped the gift carefully to find a tin filled with brownies. The smell of chocolate made my mouth water instantly. "How did you pull this off?" I gasped. Cocoa was nearly impossible to get out here. We traded with the closest Canadian town, but they were just under a hundred miles west. Not a very convenient trip; plus, we didn't like people thinking about us too much.

"I traded with one of the new families. Helped them with their plumbing. They smuggled it in from New Colony, and then I convinced Mrs. Riley to bake them for you. I helped clean out her garden."

My eyes burned, and I pushed back the tears. He had done all that for me. He was always doing nice things for me. I didn't deserve him. I felt my eyes brim with tears.

"This is so nice." I smiled up at him as we stood close, the tin between us. "Thank you. Here, you have the first one."

We both plopped a square of the chocolate cake into our mouths. I moaned. I caught him staring down at my mouth, and I blushed again. I swallowed, licking the chocolate from my lips. He moved an inch closer.

"You've got something…" He reached up and brushed my lips with the pad of his thumb. Then his hand stopped, traveling to cup my cheek.

I decided to be brave and met his eyes. There was so much there. So much unsaid, burning in the darkness. Longing and torment…and love.

I wasn't sure if I was more afraid or less afraid by what I saw.

"I don't think I can do this right now," I whispered. He let out a breath and stepped back.

A heavy knock sounded at the door, and I jumped. He held my gaze for a heated moment and then left me to open the door.

Mastin stood in the doorway. They stared at each other for a beat and then turned to look at me. Agitation crossed Mastin's brow. Tristan had shut down again. Nobody moved.

"Hey, guys," Mastin finally said. He sounded a bit winded. He also appeared a bit flustered. "We're having an important meeting down by the fire pit at eight o'clock tonight. Everyone's invited. Spread the word. You both need to be there."

"Is this about what I think it's about?" Tristan asked.

Mastin nodded slowly. "It's time."

•

"We all have an important decision to make," Cole said. "Consider your options

324

carefully. The choice you make will determine your future."

About a hundred and fifty men and women stood around the large fire, crowding the area. It crackled as the night settled over us. Almost every adult and teenager who had defected from New Colony at some point were in attendance, a handful were alchemists like myself. Some were ex-officers like Tristan and Hank. But most were just regular, everyday people who'd caught word of us and fled here for one reason or another. The flickering of the fire danced off their faces, their eyes shining in the darkness.

"New Colony has attacked America. This is what we were worried about. King Richard has accused us of not only the death of Queen Natasha, but for aiding in a recent terror attack. His claims are completely false, but that doesn't seem to matter to him. We believe he's been preparing for this opportunity for a long time now."

"How many dead?" someone shouted from the crowd.

"We don't know an exact number yet. He struck a military base as well as the surrounding town. The reports coming back are…disturbing."

Which was to be expected with anything that man touched.

"His strongest alchemists and military leaders are out of the palace at the moment. We've decided to strike while the iron is hot. West America has helicopters on their way now to pick us up, armed with many of our own soldiers. Anyone who wants to fight is invited to fight with us. We'll be dropping in on the palace tomorrow after nightfall. But we're vulnerable to the alchemists, and we're asking for any alchemist who is willing to join us."

"But we're barely trained," someone protested.

"Don't take the children," another person yelled. I agreed, of course the kids had to stay behind. Lacey popped into my mind and my breath caught.

"I have an executive order straight from our president herself. To our alchemists sixteen and older, if you come with us, no matter what happens to you, your family back home will be excluded from the military draft, should we need to use it." The crowd was silent, apparantly considering. A draft meant they would force people to fight this war. No one wanted that. "And once this is all over, should West America be the victor, all your crimes will be pardoned." He then looked over the audience, catching my eye. "And to those of you who aren't citizens of West America, if you help us win this war, we will grant you citizenship and a good life. You will be free to enjoy our prosperous society."

A hush ran through the crowd, coupled with the buzz of excitement. The news infuriated me. *What?* These poor people. Alchemists punished for being themselves. *Crimes pardoned only if they agreed to fight. Ridiculous!*

The draft was new information. How many people were in their military? And how many more would be joining? Was it possible we could win this thing? I couldn't stop the images from popping up. The thought of having a better life ahead caused a ripple of excitement to burst.

"Sign me up!" someone called.

"We're in," a couple said, stepping forward. A man, holding a toddler in his arms, placed his son in his wife's arms and spoke in a calm voice, "So long as I can act on behalf of my family as well, then I'm ready to fight."

Cole nodded.

After a few minutes, about half the crowd had agreed to the mission. If we had a hundred volunteers from this camp, plus special-ops soldiers coming in, maybe we could do it. Maybe we could end this war right now. It was wishful thinking, but the hope bubbled inside just the same.

"For those of you who are in, meet us back here at first light tomorrow. We have a lot to go over in preparation. One last thing," Cole continued. "Thank you. Thank you for stepping up. We won't let you down."

It was a promise. But not one he could keep. We all knew the risk, but did the people around me really know how difficult this was going to be? Did these people have any idea what the alchemists at the palace were capable of? And forget about the officers. They might shoot first and ask questions later. Plus, there were the palace guards—not quite officers, but they still knew how to fight. And they were crawling all over the palace...

Not everyone is going to make it.

I peered around at the stoic faces glowing in the firelight and realized the truth. These people weren't stupid. They knew they might die. But they were willing to take the risk anyway for something they believed in. That was true bravery. I looked at Tristan standing to my left. He caught my eye and nodded.

"You're coming with us?" Mastin asked, joining Tristan and me as we observed the frenzy of conversation.

"I wouldn't miss it for the world," I said, my words dripping in sarcasm.

A head of blond curls squeezed through the crowd. Lacey. She shot through the people and dashed over to me. "You're going?" she asked. I nodded, and she hugged my legs. "You're going to kick their butts!" I reached down to rest my hand on her head. "Please be careful," she added, quietly. She sounded so grown up, so afraid. This stupid situation was stealing her childhood and there was nothing I could about it. She deserved so much better.

"Kind of a crappy way to end your birthday, huh?" Mastin said, frowning.

"The worst," I agreed. But hey, it wasn't like I expected much.

"It's your birthday?" a woman's shaky voice asked, moving in behind me. It was Lara. *Oh no...*

"Yup, our girl is twenty today," Mastin said, oblivious. But Tristan reached out to squeeze my hand. He knew my secret was dangerously close to being revealed.

"You're twenty. *Today*... Oh my God," Lara breathed. She was technically my mother, but I didn't consider her as anything other than a passing acquaintance these days. I wasn't ready for some happy reunion.

"Christopher," she called, her voice unnaturally high. "Come here."

Oh no. Double no!

"What is it, honey?" he asked, the shadows of the fire extenuating the lines on his face. His hair was graying and he looked...defeated. Tired. He was a completely different man from the one I remembered. But his smell...it was the same. It was leather and grass clippings and everything that broke my heart.

"*Sasha*," she said, drawing out my name, "is twenty years old. Today."

He blinked, his gaze moving from me to Lacey and back again. "I thought it might be. The resemblance… But I didn't want to get my hopes up," he whispered.

"All right, well, you two have a good night," I said, stepping back farther. I needed to get out of here immediately.

"Wait," Lara said. "Please. Don't go, Francesca."

I stilled, my whole body numb.

"Frankie, please," Christopher added. "We've been waiting for this moment for years."

"What are they talking about?" Mastin glanced to Tristan, who only shook his head imperceptibly. "Who's Francesca?"

"She is," Lara said, pointing to me, her hand shaking. "She's not Sasha. That's not her real name." Tears formed in her wide eyes. "She's Francesca, our daughter."

"Frankie," Christopher gasped, rushing and pulling me into a hug. Frozen, trepidation filled every cell in my body. *What do I say?* What was I supposed to feel? I wasn't happy. I wasn't sad. I wasn't angry. I was just…*nothing*.

"All these years, we prayed to find you again," Christopher whispered into my hair. His voice cracked. "We didn't think we would ever see you again."

"And all this time you've been here?" Lara asked.

At some point, she had also started hugging me. I was in the middle of two people grabbing onto me for dear life. Fight or flight response was firing through me. *I need out.*

"Why don't you let her go now?" Tristan said, resting a hand on each of their backs. His tone wasn't asking; he was telling them what to do. They caught the meaning and stepped away from me. Everything went hot and cold and hot again. I watched the ground, unable to look anyone in the eye.

"But…" Lara sputtered, turning to Tristan. "You don't understand. They took her away from us when she was only a child. We had no choice."

That's when I finally got my mouth to work again. "I remember it. I saw it all, okay? You didn't even fight. *That* was a choice." Indignation filled every word. Anger. Regret.

My head popped up, letting her see all the pain my eyes had held onto for years.

Tears began to cascade down my mother's face. "We made a mistake. We were in shock. Total shock until it was too late. And you were just…gone." Her voice broke and she sobbed.

I shook my head. Something wet caught my attention, and I wiped at the sensation moving down my cheeks. I was crying too.

"Please," Christopher begged. He was shaking. "Please forgive us. Please, let us be a family again. We've missed you more than you could ever imagine."

I glanced at Tristan, not knowing what to do. *He* was my family. My rock. He would know what to do, what to say. I willed him to do something. *Get me out of here!* He caught my sense of panic and grabbed my hand, squeezing it before nodding.

"I think this is a lot for all of you to process right now. Why don't you let Sasha go to her cabin and you can all talk about this later?"

"After the mission," I said. *I can deal with it then. Just, not now.*

"You can't possibly go on that now!" Lara continued. She had Jessa's hair, dark and wild, and it danced around her face in the firelight, causing something painful to rise in my chest. I didn't want her concern. I didn't know what to do with something like that.

"It's too dangerous," Christopher agreed.

"But we need her. She will save a lot of lives if she goes," Mastin said, the light of the fire igniting his features, making his cropped hair shine. Apparently, he'd caught up on the situation, but his mind was focused on the mission ahead, as it should be. *As mine should be.*

"I'm going," I said, finally feeling a moment of confidence and grabbing on for dear life. "I'll be fine. I'm really good at what I do."

"It's true," Tristan confirmed. "She's the best alchemist we have."

"Then I'll go too," Christopher said calmly. His back straightened.

What? No way!

I shook my head. "No, we promised Jessa we'd keep you three safe."

"Please don't go," Lara tried again.

Lacey had been standing on the edge of the conversation. She didn't seem to get everything that was being said, but she was smart enough to understand her father had just volunteered to go and fight. She crawled into his arms and hugged him tightly around the neck. Her little body trembled with fear and confusion, but she didn't say a word.

"I'm going," Christopher said again. "And I'm getting you and Jessa out of that horrible place." He turned to his wife. "And then we're all going to finally be together."

I cursed inwardly. There was already enough riding on this mission, and now I had to keep my estranged father safe as well. As much as I told myself I hated my parents, deep down, I *wanted* to forgive them. I wanted the hole in my heart to be filled. I wanted to be loved by a mom and a dad and siblings, just as any normal girl was. And if I was ever going to get the chance, I had to keep him alive. A man with no military training, no magic, and no advantage except an overpowering will to reunite his family. He was a liability, but from the conviction in his voice there would be no convincing him otherwise. I didn't want him to die.

Why can't I just say that? A small part of me longed to reach out and wrap my arms around him just like Lacey had. I squashed that part.

"It's a bad idea," I said, giving them both a pointed look. "You will probably die."

"I have to try," he shrugged. "Frankie, please understand, we *love* you."

I smiled half-heartedly, attempting to placate them, but I couldn't do it any longer. "It's Sasha," I said. They only blinked at me, confused. "Like I said, it's a bad idea. You can't come. We can talk about what's next when I get back." Then I pushed through the crowd and took off running. I ran like the devil was chasing me, and then I ran faster.

FOURTEEN

LUCAS

"She's what?" I exclaimed, clenching my fists at my sides.

"She's moving in," my father said.

I practically growled as I stared up at the ceiling. "You can't be serious."

He'd called me into his private home office, a place he didn't spend too much time in. Except lately. He worried about there being a spy somewhere in the network of the officers and had started to keep his plans even closer to his chest. Some I knew he even kept from me.

"I don't see what the problem is," he continued. "You barely know her, and she's going to be your wife soon. This is a great opportunity for you both."

I didn't know how to argue with that. He was right, but it still didn't want Celia anywhere near me.

"Besides, you two have wedding plans to make," he shrugged.

I stilled. "We have enough to worry about right now without adding a wedding."

"You're not trying to get out of this, are you?"

Obviously...

He stood, pressing his palms into his desk. "Lucas, we made a deal. Thomas was executed even though he was our only reliable source of red alchemy."

"At the moment," I spat. "Don't pretend like you won't pounce on Jessa the second she's initiated. I know why you're pushing her through."

"You're too protective of her."

"Someone needs to be!"

"It's not your place to be her protector!" He stalked toward me, his face losing its usual calm demeanor. "You are *not* her boyfriend. You are engaged to Celia. She is the daughter of an influential family, a duke and a duchess, charming, beautiful, and more importantly, she's a suitable bride." His voice quieted. "Jessa is and will always be an alchemist under our rule. She will get in line, just like everybody else. Just like *you*, Lucas."

I glared, matching his steely gaze with my own. We both knew I wouldn't back down so easily.

"You cannot be with an alchemist!" he pressed. "We have an established hierarchy here and order must be maintained. The royals. Then the officers. Then the guardians. That's it. We will not allow those lines to be blurred."

"Or what?"

My father sighed exasperated, like I was beyond reason. "Or we will lose our power," he said. "The alchemists already have more than they know. If they get too much power, it won't be difficult for them to overthrow us, eradicate us, Lucas. I know you don't understand it, but it's the way things have to be. Believe it or not, I do love you. And as much as I want you to be happy, I want you to have a promising future."

What kind of future was it to be married to someone against my will? He could tell me how much he loved me, but I didn't see him doing much to show it. "And an alchemist on the throne would ruin everything?"

"It could," he said. "Is that a risk you're willing to take? Because I'm not."

"Yes," I said. "For Jessa, it is. I love her, Dad. Don't you remember what it was like to marry Mom, the woman you loved? Please, don't make me do this." I'd never been so vulnerable with him before. It was probably a lost cause, but I couldn't help it. I had to try. I was a goner when it came to Jessa. I'd been lost to her for months. The thought that I would actually be married to another girl soon was something I couldn't swallow.

"The people need a distraction," he said. "A royal engagement and wedding will keep their eyes off the gritty details of war long enough for us to do what needs to be done."

I stared at the oak-paneled wall for a moment. And at the family portrait taken years ago centered there.

"So this is all about you then, isn't it?" I should have known. It always came back to what he wanted, even if he was twisting it to look like something else. "You're faking the motivation behind this war. We don't know that West America ever did anything to us. So why are you doing this?"

It was true. He could lie about it all he wanted, to the media, the country, the alchemists, himself…but he couldn't get past me.

"I don't expect you to understand," he said, moving for the door, but I stepped in front of it, holding it closed. This conversation wasn't over.

"Try me?" I said.

"We're confined. Our population is growing. Our people depend on us to provide for them. Millions of people depend on me. We need more land to grow our crops. We need more coal. It's about resources, Lucas. I don't expect you to understand."

"Okay, we need more resources. So you feel justified to just go and *take them*."

"We're the superior nation. Our kingdom is special. What we have here is special. Everyone is taken care of. Everyone has a place. New Colony has thrived because our people chose to go back to the monarchy instead of bickering over every law. And every day that American democracy exists is a day we have a threat to our way of life. They're *bigger* than us! They have more people. It's only a matter of time until they come for us. I would rather be the one to do it first."

"And what makes you think we'll even win?"

"We are stronger than we've ever been. And they're weak right now, having just gone through a politically divisive election. Their people are in turmoil, and ours are united." Crazed excitement filled every word. "We're ready for this. The Guardians of Color are incredible, don't you agree?"

I nodded reluctantly.

"And it's only a matter of time before they see the goldmine they're sitting on and begin to train their alchemists too. Their people have feared magic for generations, but a shift is happening. The new president is sympathetic to alchemists. It was a big part of her platform, the "untapped resource" as she called it. People want change there, and that might just be the change they get. We have to defeat them before they get smart enough to mimic what we've created here."

His reasoning made sense. But his lies? They were wrong and manipulative. His people trusted him, and he would keep that trust with lies and smokescreens. My engagement was just the latest proof of it.

"Father, there has to be a better way," I said.

"Lucas." His eyes held mine. "There is no better way. Get on board. Marry the girl. Please the people. Win the war. That's the plan, and you need to embrace it. It's your future."

"No," I said simply. I didn't accept it. I couldn't.

"I didn't want to have to do this…"

"Do what?"

"Get on board or Jessa will be joining the soldiers and alchemists in the field. We could use her out there anyway."

"She's not ready for something like that! You could get your only red alchemist killed."

"I know," he said. "I'm well aware of how new she is. But I'm also aware that her red alchemy could help us win this war!"

"So that's it, that's all that matters to you? She's a real person. She could die, and then what would you have left?"

"And that's the one thing keeping her here. She's here for her training, to grow strong, to become an asset to this kingdom. She's not here to be with you."

I'd heard enough. I slammed my way from the room, angrier with him than I'd been in ages. I knew what this meant. He was using my feelings for Jessa against me. And he would continue to use her as leverage over me, threatening her safety with my obedience. It only made me hate him more.

There had been moments since Mom's death that I felt myself growing closer to him. Wanting to trust him. Trying to make up excuses for his behavior. Looking for the logic in his seemingly insane choices. But that was over. If he was willing to trade my happiness to better deceive his own people, to win more power, then he didn't really care about me.

I had half a mind to hook up with the Resistance again, but it was foolish. I'd already gone down that path, and it didn't lead anywhere good. And now with this looming threat about Jessa over my head, I felt too nervous to seek her out. What if he saw an interaction with her as reason to send her away? No. I was alone, with a stranger for a fiancée as my only foreseeable company. I needed to find a way out of this. If he could find my weaknesses and use them against me, then I would just have to return the favor.

●

By that afternoon, Celia had moved into the palace.

And no one put up a fight.

I'd hoped her parents would decline the offer, wanting us to date more or something remotely close to normal, but I wasn't so lucky. This was probably their biggest dream come true, as if their only child couldn't amount to more in life than marrying into higher status. If her father really was as influential as she'd let on, then having his daughter at the palace would only increase his sphere.

The palace sprawled across acres of land, leaving plenty of room for residential living, despite all the government offices that operated here. The guests of the royal family were placed in our area of the estate, so Celia was now living just down a hallway from the entrance to my family apartment. If I wanted to avoid her, it would probably mean more white alchemy. And I didn't want to take the risk. The reason I'd kept my ability hidden as long as I did was because I only used it when absolutely necessary.

But if it got out? There was no telling how my father would react.

Suck it up. I knocked on the door to Celia's suite. *You did this to yourself.*

She smiled coyly as she opened it, stepping back to let me in. She was dressed in a simple, blue gown with a low neckline. "You're just in time, darling," she said. I noticed a crimson flush run up her cheeks, matching her hair. Her eyes widened when they met mine. Maybe this was just as awkward for her as it was for me? "Our wedding planner just arrived."

"Thank God." I smiled and winked. She smiled back earnestly. *She knows I'm being sarcastic right?*

"I hope you don't mind," she said, motioning her hands airily around the suite. "I brought some of my own furnishings."

And that she had.

These suites were all pretty similar in their overstated grandness. She'd replaced everything with frilly and feminine pieces, a lot of white, and way too much pink. Even the main couch was a pale shade of pink. It didn't fit her personality in the slightest. She pretended sweet innocence, but had a hidden side to her, like a viper. I had a feeling her mother had a hand in the decorating. "Of course, I was thrilled when my father suggested that I move in early. I know it's only temporary until we occupy our own suite as newlyweds, but this way we can get to know each other much faster."

So, her father had made the suggestion. *Figures.*

She stared at me expectantly.

"I like what you've done with the place," I said. Her lip quirked skeptically.

"Lucas." A woman I hadn't paid any attention to stood near the table. She matched the room. Unfortunately, that was the best way to describe her. I couldn't put my finger on her name, but I knew her. She'd been planning events at the palace for as long as I'd been alive. Her face was overdone, circles of pink painted on her cheeks. Her hair was styled in a huge yellow poof on the top of her head. And when she smiled, a small smear of lipstick stained her teeth. "I'm so pleased to be your wedding planner for this wonderful occasion," she gushed. "It's been a while since you've had any part in planning the parties here, but of course I expect you to have many things to say about this special day."

Sure.

We all sat, and she jumped into an array of options. My head spun as I half listened. I didn't care what flowers were chosen, or what food we served, or what music we played, because as far as I was concerned, none of this was going to happen. Celia, on the other hand, stepped right into the role of bride-to-be. She had a strong opinion on each and every detail.

I counted my breaths in and out while pathetically attempting to look interested.

"With a winter wedding, our flower options are going to be limited…"

"Wait, what?" I sat forward. "We're having a winter wedding?"

The wedding planner, whom I still hadn't paid enough attention to in order to remember her name, stopped mid-sentence. Celia smiled calmly, not the least bit fazed. "Of course, silly," she said. "The first of December."

"That's only a few months away."

"Yes." She reached out and wrapped her hand in mine. It felt wrong, calloused and cold. "It's very exciting. I can hardly believe it myself. A winter wedding will be so romantic. We'll have white roses everywhere, and I'll wear a fur cape over my dress for the outside photos."

"We can only hope for a storm the day before," the wedding planner added. "A white, untouched backdrop."

"Oh, that would be amazing!"

"There's so much to prepare with this short engagement." She returned to her normal tone. Back to business. "The ceremony will be televised, and the king has already told me to spare no expense. He wants to give the people something they can talk about for ages." She smiled, as if tickled by the thought. "He said that himself, you know." She winked at me.

Wow, lucky me.

How could I be so stupid? In my haste to see judgment served against my mother's murderer, I'd agreed to an engagement. *An engagement.* I'd never said I would be married. I figured I could draw the engagement out long enough to find a way out of actually marrying someone. But what I'd taken as one thing, my father had turned into something else: an arranged marriage.

Who was I kidding? An engagement *meant* a wedding, which *meant* a marriage. But I had to wonder. Why so quickly? And why *this girl?* It couldn't really be about saving face. There had to me more.

As the women continued on with the planning, my gut told me to bolt. But I stayed rooted; I was going to have to figure out Celia. There had to be some deeper reason why she was here. Of course becoming queen was good enough reason for many women in the kingdom, but there was something about her father. And the way she *talked* about her father.

He would be my exit out of this marriage.

If I could get enough dirt on him, could I use it as leverage to break off the engagement? I had to try. Part of me felt bad for Celia. She was just as much a pawn in this as I was. But she didn't see it that way. Our earlier conversation in my bedroom, the one where she'd all but told me it was okay to sleep around as long as I was discreet, said as much.

She was not in this for love, but she was not in this for money.

She was in this for power. For herself. For her family. And most definitely for her father. I needed to find out why.

After the wedding planner left, I stayed. Celia expected it; I could tell by the way she never let go of my hand, her fingers crushing mine. We sat on the couch and she immediately moved in closer.

"You know—" Her green eyes fired up. "You could have offered your opinion."

"About what?"

She scoffed, "With the wedding plans. It would help the situation for everyone if you at least tried to enjoy this."

I needed to tread lightly. She wasn't going to call off this engagement. That much was clear. And if I didn't play nice, she'd likely go tattling to her daddy, who would in turn go to my father. And I didn't want to deal with another of his threats. Jessa couldn't afford it.

"Sorry," I said. "I'm just…in shock, still, I think. It's not your fault."

Okay, it kind of *was* her fault.

"You can't be a bachelor forever," she said. "Eventually this was bound to happen. But marriage won't be that bad, I *promise.*" I wasn't sure I liked the way she said *promise.* Any promise she made came attached to strings I didn't want to pull.

"What aren't you telling me?" I asked, pushing for a weak spot.

She paused. "I'm going to be your wife. You need to trust me."

"How can I trust you? I don't even know you."

"Then get to know me." She stood and strode to the window. This was a game of cat and mouse. The problem she didn't seem to understand? I didn't want the mouse.

I changed tactics. "Let's have dinner with your family again." I swallowed, careful to keep my tone playful. "I didn't do a very good job last time, I'm afraid."

She turned, a smile back on her lips. "That's a great idea. I'll call and arrange it for tonight."

So soon...

But with a wedding date in less than two months, I didn't have a lot of options left. If I was going to get something on this family, I couldn't waste a day. The sooner, the better.

"I'm looking forward to it." I joined her at the window, kissed her gently on the cheek, and left her to daydream about a wedding that would never happen.

●

"We have news." My father strode into my room without even a knock. He rarely did that. My large bedroom—with a sitting area, bathroom, and adjoining office—had always been my own private space. But there was a light in his eyes tonight, an excitement, and he couldn't help himself from sharing it.

"Good news?" I said, standing from the couch where I'd been trying to distract myself with a book. I was meeting Celia for dinner in a few minutes, and the very thought of it made my stomach squirm.

"*Great* news," my father said.

He closed the door behind him and smiled widely. I stepped back. I couldn't remember the last time I'd seen a genuine smile on the man. Of course, Mom's death hadn't been easy for anyone, but even before that, he'd held a permanent scowl while around me. It was only in the presence of cameras that he seemed to transform into the charming king the people thought they knew.

"We've received more reports back from the attack. It appears that even though West America was expecting something, they weren't very well prepared. In just a few short days, we've taken over *thousands of miles* of their eastern territory."

My gut twisted in knots, but I nodded. I was stuck, unable to side with any end result the attack could have gone.

"Of course, there's work to be done. Their most populated areas is the west coast, but we've cut them off from a lot of important farmland."

His smile was magnetic. Gleeful. I was kind of disgusted to think he was excited about cutting people off from food.

"That's great, Dad. I'm glad things are going your way." I hated it. I hated lying. I wanted to go back to the days where I could tell this man off without such harsh consequences. But with the forced engagement and Jessa's safety on the line, I needed to play nice.

He was a fool too because his face lit up when I called him Dad. It was manipulative. I'd been using his first name for years.

"I'm glad to see you're starting to understand, son." He put his hand on my back, leading me to the door. "I want you to keep attending briefings with me. It seems it's doing you good."

I wanted to laugh. *No, it's called blackmail. That's why I'm playing nice.* I clenched my fists.

"I heard you're having dinner with your beautiful fiancée tonight and her parents," he said. "I would join you, but I'm going to be helping Faulk select which alchemists to send out next."

I stopped. "Not *her*."

"A deal's a deal. Keep up your end, and I'll always keep up mine."

Relief washed through me.

He walked me to Celia's suite, because I was apparently *picking them up* to come back to our dining room. They were waiting eagerly, dressed stylishly and regally. The women wore extravagant gowns and the men wore tailored suits, as was customary for a royal dinner. Not that I expected anything less. It's how we did things at the palace. It wasn't like when I was with Jessa, when I could wear jeans and a t-shirt. When I could just be myself.

The family exchanged pleasantries with my father before he took off toward the officers' wing, and I led them back to our home. I was distracted, barely paying attention to the conversation. I needed to focus. If I was going to get something on Mark, I had to get serious about what I was doing.

As we approached the royal suite, I almost missed a step. Jessa.

She stood at the door, biting her bottom lip. Our two guards glared at her. Her expectant gaze seemed to indicate she was hoping to talk to someone on the other side of that door. Me?

"Jessa." I narrowed my eyes, and Celia squeezed my hand. I'd forgotten we were even holding hands. It wasn't like I'd initiated it—or like I even would. "What are you doing here?"

"I was…" She faltered, taking us in. "I was hoping to talk to your father."

Of course. She knew to stay away from me.

"He's with Officer Faulk, dear," Celia's mother, Sabine, said.

Jessa nodded and skirted past us. I tried not to follow her with my eyes, but I failed miserably. In a second, she was gone.

As we gathered in the dining room, my mind wouldn't stop thinking about her. I wanted to talk to her so bad. I wanted to explain. I'd stayed away because she'd told me to. But maybe that was a mistake. And now she'd seen me holding Celia's hand, going to dinner with my fiancée's family.

"Was that girl an alchemist?" Celia asked coolly as I pulled out her chair. The table was dressed with silver domes at each setting, our first course waiting for us to dig in. She eyed it with an apparent lack of interest.

"Yes," I said, careful that my voice sounded indifferent.

"Dangerous little things, aren't they?" Mark said, adjusting his large frame in his chair. "But I suppose I should be thanking them."

"Why's that?"

"Without them we couldn't possibly face a foe like West America and expect to win. But with them? Well, it's good for business."

"Business?"

"Your father and I have an agreement," Mark continued and cleared his throat. "What's good for the war is also good for me."

Who was he? I wracked my brain, trying to remember what he did. At some point, someone must have said something. Celia caught my confusion because she added, "Daddy manages the food supply for New Colony. He's very good at getting the farmers to do what they're supposed to. And now, we'll have more for everyone."

Not more for everyone. More for New Colony.

It made sense. We didn't live in a traditional economy, far from it. Everyone was given a job according to their station, schooling, and skills. If someone wanted to move up, they had to apply to do so. The highest-ranking officials controlled everything, under the direction of the monarchy, of course. Mark must run the farming sector, controlling what seeds went where and who was paid what. It was an important job. One I'd paid little attention to.

Fortunately, dinner didn't last too long. When the plates had been cleared, I insisted Celia leave with her parents, pretending I had a headache. "They run in the family, you know," I said, rubbing my temples. They nodded, probably having heard about my mother's mysterious migraines before she died.

The staff cleared out as they said their goodbyes quickly. Celia even kissed me gently on the cheek. Then they left me sitting in my chair. The second they turned the corner, I grabbed a white rose and pinched the petals. The magic filled me in a rush of prickly heat. I watched as my body faded away. Yes, I was going against my normal way of conducting alchemy—which was not to do it at all. But was the risk worth it to follow Celia's father?

I intended to find out.

I held my breath and followed the Addington family out the door.

FIFTEEN

JESSA

I lay on my bed, counting all the reasons why I hated the tests. But I was starting to understand the purpose of them. All this magic was forcing me outside my comfort zone. And I was getting better with each one. Even though the tests themselves were pretty screwed up, so were the people who created such extremely dangerous scenarios.

First the water, then the interrogation, then trying to save the girl in the forest. They'd grown in intensity with each one, the worst of them being the experience with green alchemy. I still had the image in my head. The pain still fresh in my memory. And the blood, it had taken a scalding shower to get it off me. I'd had to throw my pajamas in the trash.

Would orange possibly be more terrible?

I trusted that Jasmine would tell the truth. I held onto that trust, because I was too terrified to imagine the worst. *No. Orange will be fine. It won't be so bad.*

I had gone about my day as normal on the outside, but inside, I was full of jitters. I kept expecting to be taken away for the test. Nothing happened. I couldn't handle the anticipation. The waiting.

Sitting up for a second, I plopped my pillows back into place and fell back with a huff. I couldn't believe how dumb I had been!

I'd gotten it into my stupid head to go and talk to the king directly. He wanted me initiated. I had reasoned that another test wasn't even necessary. I would pass since orange alchemy wasn't that hard for anyone. But pass or fail, I was confident I'd be joining the guardians. King Richard wanted my red alchemy. That was what everyone had been saying for weeks. So I figured I could just go right up to him and ask for my initiation.

Besides, I had an even bigger reason to get it over with: the Resistance.

Jasmine said I'd be tested in the morning, and the next day would be my initiation. Well, nothing had happened this morning. The Resistance was ready to attack. I didn't want there to be any delays. I was ready for this. Ready to help the cause.

I had sat outside the royal wing, waiting—hoping to catch the king and praying I didn't see Lucas. My heart was shredded because of that boy. But of course life being awesome, he walked right up to me with his fiancée's hand tucked perfectly in his own. I had scurried away as quickly as possible. So angry for putting myself in that situation.

I never should have dated him.

I groaned and rolled over. My pillow was all wet and pathetic. Of course after seeing Lucas and his new fiancée, I'd locked myself in my dorm room. I had thought for sure Lucas would have come to me with some explanation for his engagement, but he never did. And seeing the two of them like that? The tears I'd been holding inside for days came bursting out. More than anything I just wanted to go home. *You don't have a home.*

I curled up into a ball, so sick of feeling sorry for myself. This wasn't me. I needed to get past this.

A loud knock sounded on the door. I held my breath. I was so not ready to face anyone. Maybe if I was extra quiet, they'd go away.

"Open up," the unmistakable voice of Faulk said. "It's time for some orange alchemy."

"One second," I called.

I quickly ran to the bathroom to wash and dry my tear-stained cheeks. I ran my brush through my hair at record speed and called it good.

I opened the door.

Once again she was surrounded by officers. Was she ever alone? I was pretty tall, even taller than most of them. But from the way they assessed me skeptically, I felt small. I spotted the man on whom I'd secretly performed red alchemy at the back of the group and looked away. *No need to stare, Jessa.*

"How can I help you?" I tried to keep my tone level. Lately, I suspected Faulk was warming up to me as much as an ice queen could. She wasn't so suspicious around me. Nor was she so angry. She didn't snap at the things I said or watch me with cool contempt. I'd take any improvement I could get! Still, I didn't want to ruin it. If there was one thing she hated it was defiance, something I had in spades.

"It's time for your last test," she said. "This should be easy." Then she turned and marched down the hall. I followed behind, my thoughts flying in a million different directions.

"It will come as no surprise to you that this last test is in orange alchemy."

I rolled my eyes at her back. "Yup. Thanks for warning me this time." If she caught the indirect complaint about the green test, she made zero indication. *Deep breaths.*

"So when I'm initiated, then what? Will I be able to talk to my family?"

I really hated asking the question I already had the answer to. I knew for a fact the Resistance had my family and they weren't even in New Colony anymore. But Faulk and Richard didn't know where they were. They'd lied to me. They pretended to have them in custody. Leverage. I couldn't give away what I knew, so that meant acting like I believed their stupid story.

"Everything in due time," she said over her shoulder.

Liar!

"Well, I've worked really hard to prove my loyalty to you," I said. "But I can't help it. I'm worried about them. I just want to make sure they're being treated okay. They never did anything wrong."

She didn't say anything.

"I know you're not afraid to put people in prison," I pushed, "but you've got to have good reason to do it or it's just cruel."

I'd been detained in holding cells twice. Once when I was first discovered, and again when I'd been questioned about Sasha's disappearance after I'd run away. The places I'd been were completely gray, not a shred of color anywhere. Nothing an alchemist could get their hands on and manipulate to their advantage. I wondered where they put non-magical people.

She stopped abruptly, turning to meet my gaze. Hers was cold, calculated. She watched me carefully, scanning for something. A break. A lie, perhaps? Shivers ran up my body. I had to play into this game of theirs. If I didn't, I'd appear even more suspicious.

"They're fine," she finally said. "You have nothing to worry about. We'll talk about it more *after* your initiation."

I nodded and looked to the floor, no longer able to meet the eyes of someone who'd done nothing but lie to me. Her job wasn't to protect me. It was to protect everyone else from me, and use me to do it.

We began walking again. I kept my mouth shut.

One good thing had come out of our conversation. She'd basically confirmed it. I was going to be initiated! This final test was just for show, a customary event. The king wanted what he wanted, and even though I'd failed blue and purple, I could still do them. I was more than good enough. Besides, it was the red he cared about…

I tried to imagine what would happen tomorrow during my initiation. They would have their attack, and even though I couldn't participate, I could still pray they accomplished what they came for.

What if they hurt Lucas? That thought had been running circles in my head for the last twenty-four hours.

No. They won't.

Would they?

He used to be one of us, but lately, he'd gone so far in the other direction. He was spending more time with his father than ever and was engaged to the exact type of woman his father expected. He'd even been on the stage when they'd executed Thomas and when Richard had made his threats. *There will be no mercy for traitors.*

I shook the thought from my head. Lucas was all over the place lately, and it pained me to even think about what would happen to him.

"Tell me something, Jessa." Faulk turned. We now stood outside a closed door in the same wing of the palace I'd first stayed in. I had a feeling that I wouldn't like whatever was on the other side. "How much do you know about orange alchemy?"

"Umm." I faltered, eyeing the door. "It's an enhancer, used for emotions."

"And what else?"

I wasn't sure. My mind traveled back to when I'd spent weeks studying the color wheels and all the different attributes of each. "Creativity."

"Very good," she said.

"But I don't know how to use it for creativity," I mumbled.

"Orange can help you figure problems out. It can help you see solutions that you might not normally see," she said. "You just have to use it the same way you would for emotions, with the focus of trying to understand something."

That was interesting news to me. Useful.

"Why are you helping me?" I asked. I had every right to be skeptical of her sudden interest. What was in this for her?

"Because passing this test will not only guarantee your initiation, something I tried to fight but now see as inevitable—" She frowned. "But it will help your kingdom. More specifically, it will help me."

"I don't understand..."

"Of course not." She stepped closer. "Your test is simple enough. On the other side of that door are two people who may or may not be sympathetic to our enemies. They don't know what you can do. They don't know the nuances of alchemy."

"And what do you want me to do?" My voice cracked.

"Use orange alchemy to enhance their emotions. Help us figure them out, Jessa." She smiled ruefully, the skin around her mouth tight. "I already have a good idea they're against us. Your job is to prove it. It'll be easy."

I nodded as she placed a corded necklace with an amber pendant around my neck. Then she pushed open the door, and we entered a sitting room. It was much like the one I'd been brought into months ago when I'd first arrived here. Cozy and welcoming; everything about the space appeared safe. But I knew better.

A fire crackled in the wood-burning fireplace, and plush leather couches faced each other in the intimate space. A dark burgundy, plush rug covered some of the polished wooden floor. Orange pillows rested on the couches, and orange succulent plants were placed in a woodsy centerpiece on a large coffee table.

A young man and woman stood by the window, talking in low voices. They jolted when they saw us, but turned and smiled. Their nerves rolled off them in waves of fear as their eyes shifted between us. I didn't blame them. It seemed Faulk had brought them in for interrogation. But first, she wanted to see what I could do. Orange test, huh? I had a feeling this was a little different than a typical alchemist's test. I ignored my resentment and strolled into the room.

"Hello again," Faulk said. "How was your dinner?"

"It was great." The woman smiled weakly. "Thank you."

Faulk nodded. "Please, come and have a seat."

The couple moved to one couch, and Faulk and I took the other. The frantic energy was palpable; it wasn't just coming from them. *I can do this.*

Now would not be the time to use the orange alchemy. All I would get from anyone would be more of the same. And nervous didn't tell us anything.

"Jessa," Faulk said, smiling. Her face turned into the picture of joy, and she looked nothing like her normal self. I bit my lip and stared. "I'd like you to meet Jane and Parker Abbot. Remind me, you two are newlyweds, aren't you?" Faulk's charm was nothing but creepy!

"We've been married a year now," Jane said, reaching for her husband's hand. "But I guess you could say we're still new to this whole marriage thing."

He looked at her with fixed adoration, and she blushed. What they had was real. They loved each other and had gotten married for no other reason than that. It was how marriages were supposed to work!

"Wonderful," Faulk said. She turned to me. "These two were invited to the palace for a little tour. Isn't that wonderful?" I nodded, a little confused. People didn't just get invited for palace tours. "They were both there that day, you know? Terribly tragic."

"What day?" I asked. Jane's and Parker's faces flushed simultaneously as they looked at the floor.

"The day of the attack, of course," Faulk continued. "These two were rather heroic, I must say."

"Oh, I wouldn't say that," Jane said.

"We just did what anyone else would do," Parker added.

"Oh, nonsense." Faulk laughed amicably. "When everyone else was running away from the gunman, you two were running toward him. Tell me again, why on earth would you do that?"

There was a long pause. "Instinct, I guess," Parker said. He shifted, running a hand through his dark hair. "I had to take him down, and Jane came after me." He shrugged.

Jane nodded, her chin shaking. "I shouldn't have, but I couldn't help it. I love Parker. I wasn't going to let that terrorist kill my husband."

"Like I said, very brave."

So that's why Faulk had these two here. It was odd that two citizens would run after a gunman like that. But that hardly proved anything, right? At the very least, it was an act of bravery. Still, something about the discomfort between them told me there was more to the story. I briefly wondered if they were part of the Resistance and whether I should try to protect them. But if they were involved in that attack somehow, no way they were Resistance. A trickle of curiosity wormed its way in.

"You're very brave," I said. Putting my hand over the necklace so no one could see the magic, I allowed the orange to filter into me. Faulk was right. By using the magic during that moment, I had enhanced my feelings of suspicion. Suddenly, every rise of an eyebrow or held breath or shared look was part of a puzzle. I wasn't sure who these people were. My initial instinct was to like them, but that didn't mean I should. And it didn't mean they were innocent.

Maybe they really did have something to do with the shooting. Maybe they knew the shooter.

"Did you ever figure out who the shooter was?" I asked Faulk. Officially, King Richard had said it was a spy with West America. Maybe that was the truth, but what if it wasn't?

"Oh, that information is still classified," Faulk purred, then pointed to a tea trolley in the corner. "Jessa, will you do us the honors?"

I stood and wandered to it. I began pouring hot tea into cups. This was my moment; Faulk had set me up on purpose. I pulled a little of the orange magic into my hand while my back was turned and deposited it into the cups. It only enhanced the dark color of the tea and was pretty much unnoticeable. This would be easier than actually touching our guests, but it would work the same. At parties, orange magic enhanced true feelings. It would work here too.

"Well," I said, "you two are wonderful for doing what you did. You probably saved lives that day."

"They did," Faulk said. "They took the man down before we even got there. Of course, it would have been nice to keep him alive for questioning, but beggars can't be choosers, right?"

So that's what happened.

"You took him out?" I gasped, handing them the teacups at that exact moment. "How brave! You should be so proud."

They both looked down and then took sips from their cups.

"I'm not proud," Jane muttered.

"Why not?" I asked, placing my hand on her shoulder. A little more orange wouldn't hurt, would it?

"He didn't deserve to die," she said.

Guilt.

It was guilt they were both immersed in now. It was so heavy it clouded their better judgment. But I was sure it wouldn't last long.

"Why not?"

"He wasn't a—"

"She only means that it would have been better to question him," Parker jumped into the conversation, cutting his wife off. He was right back to nervous. I would have to focus on his wife.

"Of course." I smiled as I walked behind them, taking the long way back to the trolley to return the tray.

"He was a bad man, wasn't he?" I asked. On the way back to my seat, I lightly touched both of their shoulders, leaning between them for an answer. If that question elicited them to hide something, to disagree, we would know.

"He wasn't what you think," Parker said at the same time as Jane said, "He wasn't one of us, sure. But not bad. He was *good*."

I stepped back and caught the satisfaction on Faulk's face. "Is that enough?"

She nodded and licked her lips.

"What's going on?" Jane mumbled just as the door burst open and guards swarmed in. I moved to the side to make room for the guards, and Faulk joined me. She seemed pleased with me for once, and I didn't know how I felt about it.

"We already suspected they were working with the gunman somehow."

We watched the couple, still in a daze as they were put into handcuffs. It all happened so fast that they barely had time to protest.

"No worries." Faulk continued moving toward them. Her tone was back to the pleasant one from before. "Now that we're sure, we'll get all that we need from you during interrogation."

"But…" Jane sputtered. "What just happened?"

"Take them," Faulk ordered. It only took a minute, and we were left alone in the room. The teacups sat on the coffee table, still warm. I picked up my own and studied it. The liquid warmed my fingers. I squeezed my eyes tightly shut for a moment, hoping I had just done the right thing.

"That was impressive," Faulk said, moving to the door. "Can you imagine how easy it will be once we use red to do it?"

I gulped. *What have I done?*

I followed her out to find none other than King Richard waiting for us. He was talking lazily with Celia's parents in the hallway. My eyes darted between the three as they looked over at me. They seemed unfazed by what I'd just done. Maybe it wasn't a big deal to them, but my heart exploded in my chest just thinking about it.

"I knew you'd pass." Richard beamed at me. "But that was fast."

"Uh, thanks." My tentative happiness at completing the task evaporated.

"Good job, dear," Celia's mother said. Her eyes moved down me with contempt. It was clear she wanted nothing to do with an alchemist. Her husband did a better job of hiding his feelings, but even he held a grimace on his face. *Or maybe they don't like the way Lucas looks at me?*

Nonsense. He'd moved on. If he hadn't, he would have come to me by now. I hesitated, ready to leave.

"We'll make the announcement," Richard said. "Tomorrow night, there will be a banquet to celebrate your initiation."

"Wow," I said, my smile faltering. "Thanks."

"Your initiation will follow immediately after."

I nodded, the words no longer able to form on my tongue. I didn't know how I felt about all of this. The group left, and I rushed to my room.

As I walked, my heart thumped in my ears like the heavy beat of a drum. This was happening. I was being initiated tomorrow night. I was *in* with the king. I would be one of them. And at the same time, the banquet would allow for an attack. The odds of taking out Richard were pretty slim. The palace was crawling with people sworn to protect him. But an attack *would* weaken his forces, and it would send a message to all the alchemists: *there's another choice. Join us.*

No one had told me the specifics, and true to her word, Jasmine had closed up on all things Resistance.

Be careful. Stay out of the way. We need you to appear loyal.

That's what she'd asked. That's what I would do.

I rounded the corner to my dorm, eager to take a shower and get to bed. I needed to wash away all images of what had just happened. I was terrified I'd done the wrong thing, but that gunman had stolen innocent lives. How could anyone sympathize with that?

Sleep. That's what I needed. Not that I expected much of it. I was too nervous. This was happening. Really happening! One day closer to seeing my family again. One day closer to freedom.

I stopped abruptly.

"The guards told me where to find you." Celia was leaning nonchalantly against my doorframe. She still wore the extravagant dress from earlier, appearing as relaxed in it as I was in my pajamas. She yawned. "Let's get this over with, shall we?"

She was in GC territory. Was she not afraid of alchemy? No, if she was anything like her parents, she just hated us. Her hard gaze shifted over me, a question forming.

"Can we talk, woman to woman?" She reached out her manicured hand. I nearly stumbled as I stepped forward to shake it. I was a ballerina for crying out loud. When did I suddenly have two left feet?

She made me nervous. That was why. Everything about her reflected my own insecurities back to me. She had what I wanted. Pure and simple. Her grip was firm as she smiled.

"Sure, come in." I opened the door.

"It's...cute," she said, her gaze roving over the small, sparse room.

"It's fine," I said. "It's not like I chose it."

"That's funny." She smiled. "I thought being an alchemist was an honor. I'm certainly honored to have the opportunity to live at the palace."

"Such an honor," I quipped.

She raised an eyebrow, and I ran my fingers through my messy hair and bit my bottom lip. I needed to relax. This girl wasn't my enemy. Lucas had made his choices all on his own.

I sat on the bed and motioned for her to take a seat at the desk. "Why did you want to talk to me?"

"How long have you known Lucas?" she asked.

Of course she wanted to question me about him.

"Not long," I said. "I've only been here about four months."

"And in four months, you managed to get him to fall in love with you?" She didn't say it defensively, as a fiancée would. It came out more as a matter of fact. A question even, like, *how did I do it?*

My stomach twisted. "What? Why would you say that?"

Her lips twisted and she rolled her eyes.

"If he loved me, why would he be engaged to you? Lucas and I aren't even talking anymore."

"Then why were you waiting outside his door earlier?"

"I was trying to talk to Richard."

"You're on a first name basis with the king?"

"Kind of," I frowned. "I was going to ask him about a test I had to take tonight, okay? Why is that any of your business?"

She smiled, and it lit up her entire being. My heart ached as I realized that maybe she could find her way into Lucas's heart after all.

"You don't have to get upset. It was just a question," she said, kindness in her voice.

I shook my head. I wanted to ask her to leave, but I had to remember my place, and I didn't need to make any more enemies. She was the fiancée of the prince, and there was a real possibility she would become the next queen. I felt like puking and crying at the same time.

"Listen, your name is Jessa, right?" she asked. I nodded. "Listen, Jessa, I'm not here to tell you to back off my man, if that's what you're thinking."

My jaw dropped—like literally dropped—at the laugh that exploded out of her mouth.

"I know, not what you expected the second you saw me waiting outside your door, right?" she said. "But the truth is, I hardly know Lucas. And he hardly knows me. It's not fair of me to lay claim to his heart."

"Umm…okay." What was I supposed to say to that? It was so weird. Was this some kind of reverse psychology? Some kind of game?

"But I *am* laying claim to the crown."

"And there it is." I sighed.

Of course that's what this is about…

"And there it is." She nodded. This woman was bizarre. She had to be close in age to me, and she cared more about a crown than about marrying for love. A little jaded for someone so young.

"How old are you?" I asked.

"Eighteen."

"Don't you think eighteen is a little young to be married?" In New Colony, most people paired off in their mid-twenties, but younger marriages weren't unheard of. But still, I certainly didn't feel quite ready to get married. She was only two years older. And I could honestly admit I was *in love* with Lucas. How could she be ready for that level of commitment when she'd just admitted the opposite?

"He's a prince, Jessa. Come on, you're smarter than that. It's a monarchy, and he's an only child. The. Only. Heir." She smoothed her red hair, fingering a piece at the end, before turning her eyes back to me. "No doubt his parents tried for more. Just in case. But as it stands, Lucas needs to have children."

"And you're going to do that for him?" I was going to be sick. My body tense, I breathed in slowly as I waited for her answer.

She shrugged. "I am."

"So that doesn't explain why you're here."

"It's simple." She almost looked sorry for me. I didn't want her pity. "I'm not stupid enough to expect him to stay away from you. I saw the way you looked at each other, and I knew there had to be a reason why he's been so aloof with me. Men are never that way with me." No doubt; she was gorgeous and sophisticated. She was the type of girl to get her pick, no matter which men were on offer. "I'm just asking you to do me the courtesy of keeping things private. And safe, if you know what I mean."

Okay, now I really was going to puke!

I stood. "I don't know what you think is going on, but Lucas and I are over."

She studied me and finally shrugged. "Well, I thought I would ask. You know, woman to woman. Just in case it isn't *really* over."

"That boy has put me through so much, you have no idea. I refuse to be someone's second choice."

She stood, nodding. "All right. I guess I underestimated you."

"You did."

I'd had enough. I jumped off the bed and stalked to the door, wrenching it open. "Have a good night."

"Thank you," she said over her shoulder as she left. "I think I'll do that."

I had to keep myself from slamming the door.

I stomped to the shower. I ripped off my top, screwing it into a tight ball until my knuckles turned white. Peering down for a moment, I threw it at the wall and practically growled as I finished undressing. How could Lucas be engaged to that woman? She was truly sadistic if she thought I'd be her husband's mistress. That's what she'd alluded to. I would keep him happy, love him, and she'd run the household, give him children, and most important to her, she'd be queen.

It was wrong on every level!

It broke my heart to be away from him. I missed him so much. I missed our easy conversations and the way he challenged me. I missed the looks he gave that were only for me. I loved him. But I wasn't willing to share. I wouldn't stick around and be his side-woman. I had more self-respect than that. Besides, after the experience with Sasha last summer, my heart couldn't take it. Whatever had happened to cause his engagement was *their* business. Let him deal with it. I was staying out of it.

The water scalded my skin, pelting hot irons with each drop. I didn't turn the shower heat down. I wanted the distraction. *Don't think. Don't feel.* But for the second time that night, it happened anyway. I cried.

This time, my tears washed away instantly.

SIXTEEN

LUCAS

As I stood pressed against the wall, I realized that invisibility was a blessing and a curse. It was exhausting. Dangerous. Tailing people at a distance and silently slipping through open doors behind them was less than enjoyable. I didn't know what I expected to discover taking off after the Addington family. Would I have to follow the man *home*? And then what?

They first took Celia back to her new room, going in together before I had a chance to follow. I waited outside, trying to keep my eyes open as the minutes ticked by. It would've been a lot more useful to have an affinity for blue alchemy. But it wasn't my forte, and grumbling to myself wouldn't solve anything. I willed the conversation to filter through the door but couldn't make out a word.

Just when I'd about given up, thinking about where the closest and safest place to make myself visible would be, the thick door swung open. Inertia nearly landed me flat on the ground, but I was able to jump back and out of the way. I studied the family, but they didn't seem to notice anything. They headed toward the GC wing—a curious choice, considering normal people didn't venture over that way.

Celia broke off, heading toward the guardian dorms. Her parents didn't go with her. They kept going into the heart of alchemist territory. They didn't seem to be bothered about what they saw, not even cautious. Occasionally, a guardian would give them a funny look, but mostly they were ignored. I think everyone had the war on their minds: wondering what it all meant, if they were next, if their friends were okay. The whole palace was turned upside-down so apparently a couple of citizens taking a stroll down their hallway didn't seem out of the ordinary. The palace wasn't the same place it used to be. Not for any of us.

We continued down the hallway and when they met up with my father, I shouldn't have been surprised. I mean, really? But I was.

"How is she doing in there?" Mark said.

"She'll pass." My father nodded calmly.

The next moment, a door opened and a bunch of guards pulled a handcuffed couple from the premises. They looked a little confused, but definitely agitated. They were quickly whisked away. A second later, Faulk and Jessa exited the room. Jessa was pale as a ghost, but a wisp of accomplishment tilted her smile. At odds, to say the least. I wanted to help her. To touch her. Something.

I stood back, listening to their conversation, waiting for something out of the ordinary. My father placed a hand on Jessa's back. "We'll make the announcement," he said. "Tomorrow night there will be a banquet to celebrate your initiation. Your initiation will follow immediately after."

She smiled and responded appropriately, but I could sense something else behind those eyes. Worry? A few more words were exchanged, and Jessa headed back to her room.

I stuck around. Just as she was out of earshot, Richard rounded on Faulk. "I told you she was good."

She shook her head. "It was never a matter of Jessa's power, it was always a matter of her loyalty."

I sucked in a breath as my whole body went numb.

"You and I both know we can't *really* know who's loyal anymore, can we?" Richard's face flashed. My mind conjured an image of Thomas; my father was right. "It's not a matter of *if* we have more executions, but *when*. The least we can do is use up these alchemists' powers while we can."

Would he have done that with Thomas? Faulk shouldn't have missed the signs, and she had to know it. They could have used his red alchemy years ago.

Faulk pinched her lips and nodded. "We need to be extra cautious."

"Come." Richard patted Mark on the shoulder. "Let's get out of here, and we can talk more about our plans."

I followed the group, and the security detail that was my father's constant shadow. They went to the officers' headquarters, which were in another part of the GC wing, so it was easy to slip into the selected office with everyone else. When my father asked the security team to leave, I ducked into a corner. No one batted an eyelid in my direction. After a minute, it was only the four of them remaining.

Sabine stood aloof on one side, an older version of her daughter. The resemblance was uncanny if not a little bit disturbing.

"What have you found out?" Richard asked.

"We've been interrogating people all along the borders. Anyone who lives near there, asking them if they've seen people, helicopters, airplanes, anything," Mark said.

"And?" Faulk raised an eyebrow.

"So far we only have a few leads but they didn't pan out."

Richard narrowed his eyes. "That's not good enough."

"I know," Mark said. "We're not giving up."

"And what about that one helicopter? It was heading north the same day

Sasha went missing."

"We're still investigating. It must have been going to Canada."

"How did it disappear like that?"

"We still don't have the answer to that."

"Magic!" Richard began to pace.

"It's obvious they have alchemists," Faulk said. "The question is how did they use magic to get away from us like that? Invisibility is not something we've ever seen before, and we need to find out how it's done. What do their alchemists know that ours don't?"

That this was still under investigation was a problem. I realized I was utterly juvenile to believe the incident had been forgotten. Of course it hadn't been. It was still the forefront of my father's worries, and apparently Mark wasn't who he said he was. These people weren't in charge of managing farming and food resources. Or if they were, it was only part of the job. He was an investigator for my father. Someone undercover?

"Keep looking," my father said. "Keep interrogating."

Mark nodded.

"And what of your efforts here?" Sabine asked. She'd been standing off to the side, seemingly innocuous, when she turned to casually join the conversation.

"Like I said," Faulk interrupted, "we're being cautious."

"There must be a spy in the palace somewhere," Mark added.

"We know that," Faulk replied. "We're working on it."

"You think it's Jessa," Sabine purred, her green eyes focusing on Faulk.

"I think everything started the moment she showed up," Faulk replied defensively.

"Or it's merely coincidence," Richard said. "We've gone over this again and again. The girl is only sixteen. She was a dancer before coming here. What could she possibly know?"

"Her parents are missing."

The room fell silent.

"It is curious," Mark offered. "But it's not proof of anything. It could be that her parents were the spies and she knew nothing of it."

"Does she know about her older sister?" Sabine asked.

"We don't know," Faulk said.

"But the two were put together unwittingly," Richard accused.

"We've gone over this," Faulk said. "There *must* be a spy in the palace because otherwise Sasha never would have been able to infiltrate our system. Her cover was carefully planned out. I still want to know why she left."

They quieted for a long moment.

"You've combed through every person here, every alchemist? Every servant and guard and officer? You're sure of their history?" Mark asked.

"I'm positive," Faulk said. "No more false identities. We won't let that mistake happen again."

Richard shook his head. "She was Francesca, wasn't she? That girl who got stolen from us years ago?"

"We believe so," Faulk said.

"It was a blow to lose her. I can't believe she came back, and we missed her." He directed his words at Faulk, and she shrunk back. "It makes sense now that Jessa would be a red alchemist like her older sister. Talented family. Dangerous…"

"Then the damage is already done." Mark rubbed the back of his neck.

"Maybe," Sabine said, walking over to place a hand on her husband's shoulder. "Or maybe it was a blessing in disguise."

"Explain." Richard motioned to her, a flicker of hope crossing his features.

"Now that you know the parents have disappeared, and about Sasha, or should I say, Francesca, you know that someone is out there trying to get Jessa back. You can keep her close, protect what's yours." Sabine smiled. "Not to mention, now you know there's a mole in the palace in the first place."

"We need to start interrogating the alchemists." Richard nodded.

"I wouldn't alert them just yet." Mark relaxed. "If we can find the Resistance leader, we can cut them off at the knees."

They stood in companionable silence for a few minutes, possibly going through all the scenarios in their heads, weighing the options. They knew about the Resistance, that much was clear. From what I gathered, my father had called in extra help after Sasha had turned out to be a fake. Now they were searching for answers, trying to find her as well as Jessa's parents. And, of course, they were watching Jessa closely.

"How's Celia doing?" Richard asked, breaking the silence.

"She's unsure," Sabine said.

His eyes narrowed.

"Your son is obviously in love with Jessa. Even you know that much. But Celia isn't sure if it's just that or if something else is going on."

"Like what?"

An icy chill ran through my entire body.

"Richard," Mark interjected, "you already know Lucas went from dating Sasha to dating Jessa. It is suspicious."

"You don't think I know that?" Richard challenged. "What is Celia's take on it? Does she think Lucas is the spy?"

"She's not sure." Sabine shrugged. "But she's leaning toward no. However, it's likely your son knows something. Being involved with Sasha, did he really have no idea who she was?"

"The girl was gorgeous and mysterious," Richard said, defensively. "Not to mention being an alchemist and off limits. My son has always dated that type. He wants what he can't have."

Anger coursed through me. Celia was reporting back to her father about me! I knew I didn't like her, but this was taking things to a whole new level.

"How do you know Sasha wasn't just using him?" Sabine asked.

"She probably was," Faulk growled. "I just wonder how much that boy gave away to that traitorous filth."

"Celia will know more soon," Mark said. "She's talking with Jessa now, as a matter of fact."

Celia was with Jessa? I imagined my cold fiancée cornering the girl I loved. That was not okay. I wanted nothing more than to storm through that door and go and find them. Celia seemed to be some kind of spy with her parents—that much was more apparent than ever. She was a snake in the grass, and now she was toying with Jessa too. The whole thing had me dying to punch a hole through the wall right then and there!

"Celia had better make a decision soon," Richard said. "I need to know that my son is loyal. That's the only reason I agreed to this engagement!"

There it was. The real reason I was engaged. So my father could keep a closer eye on me. I swallowed angry words that needed to be released. He got the daughter-in-law he wanted, the one who kept me in line. The one who *worked for him*. And I got nothing.

"The engagement is beneficial to everyone," Mark said. "Your son will be lucky to have my daughter for a wife."

"Oh, don't get all fatherly on me now." Richard laughed, his voice filling the space. "We all know she gets a crown out of the deal."

"It's true." Sabine smiled. "She's very happy about that."

"Is there anything else?" Faulk asked. They shook their heads. "Then if you'll excuse me, I have some work to do." She headed up the stairs to her private office, her heels clacking loudly with each step.

"The minute you catch wind of anything, you tell me," Richard said, pointing at Mark.

"Yes, sir." He nodded.

They left in a rush of activity. I followed closely behind, my heart hammering. *I'm a suspect!* I should have never worked with the Resistance. Not because I didn't believe my father was a terrible king—he was—but because I didn't know enough about the Resistance to agree to do their dirty work. And now, not only was I in danger, but Jessa was too. I'd made a mess of everything, and she was bearing the weight of that.

I needed to find out what Celia was saying to her. I tried to clear my mind as I squeezed the rose in my hand tighter and rushed toward Jessa's room. Taking deep breaths as I went, I willed myself to be rational about my next action. If I was going to get out of this engagement, I had to prove my loyalty to my father. I needed to give him something he wanted more than marrying me off to that awful family. *What does Dad want more than anything?*

Control.

He wanted to dominate me by choosing whom I married. But it was more than that. He wanted to control more people and resources by going to war with West America, and getting in his way was the Resistance. He was searching for answers. If there was a way I could give enough answers to satisfy him, maybe I could protect Jessa at the same time.

I had an idea. But I needed to think it through. In the meantime, the need to comfort Jessa was overpowering. She needed to understand that this was all so much bigger than just our relationship. She shouldn't be afraid of someone like

Celia. I would find a way out of this, for both our sakes.

I ambled up to her room, waiting a few minutes until the hall was clear. I tapped at the door. A long minute passed before she opened it, in wet hair, no makeup, and pajamas. She peered around, seeming half annoyed and half relieved not to find anyone. Red rimmed around her eyes, and her cheeks looked shallow.

"Jessa," I whispered. "Please let me in."

She paused, her face lighting with recognition before darkening. I hoped she wouldn't be upset I'd come using white alchemy. I expected her to slam the door in my face, but she nodded and pulled it open just enough for me to squeeze through.

Once we were alone, I breathed out, dropping the rose from my grasp. After over an hour of being invisible, I was not only exhausted, but the rose was almost completely gray when it fell to the floor.

"You're sure no one else can do that?" she asked, picking it up. She studied the rose between her finger and thumb, twirling it, no concern for the thorns.

"Not that I know of."

"Hmmm..." She nodded. "You're engaged."

"I'm sorry."

"I met your fiancée tonight. She came here to talk."

"I heard." I shook my head, running my hands through my hair. "Whatever she said, please don't listen to her. It's not what you think."

"She basically asked me to be your mistress," Jessa whispered bitterly. She moved to sit on the edge of her bed and narrowed her eyes on me. "I told her no, by the way. Just in case you're wondering."

"I didn't know she was going to say that," I said. "I don't get her."

"She doesn't care about your heart, Lucas. Only your crown."

"Well, that I did know." I sighed. Then I laughed.

"It's not funny," she said, her eyes flashing.

"Believe me, I know."

I tentatively sat next to her on the bed. She scooted away. Only a couple of inches. A small amount, but it felt like so much more. She was communicating something with that motion: stay away forever.

"I spied on her family. They're working with my father. Celia is too," I said. "Believe me when I say that this mess is bigger than I imagined."

"Celia is spying on you?"

"And you," I said.

"Wow. She's bold." She ran her hands through her hair, and more drips of water soaked into her black, cotton top.

"Don't get me wrong, she wants that crown. But her father is trying to sniff out the Resistance. Plus, Richard and Faulk haven't given up on figuring out what Sasha was doing here, how she got in and out... all of it."

"I guess it makes sense." She nodded. "But why did you have to get engaged, Lucas? I've been trying to understand it. I'm sorry. I just...don't."

I hated this. She said the last few words with so much sadness. And it was my fault. "I was an idiot. My father was having second thoughts about executing Thomas. He wanted that red alchemy, and when you broke it off with me, I kind of lost my mind. You were right, Jessa. You're always right about me. I should've just talked to you about my grief, but I wasn't thinking straight. I thought the only thing to make me feel better would be Thomas's death."

"And do you feel better?"

"No."

"And you're engaged because of it?"

"My father made a deal with me. He'd execute Thomas if I agreed to an engagement. I *never* agreed to an actual marriage. I figured I'd call the engagement off or something, I don't know, I was stupid. But when I went to talk to him about it, he threatened to send you away."

"So I was right." She frowned. "I didn't want to be, you know."

"You were right. You broke it off between us because our relationship bothers my father. It's not what he wants, but Jessa, it is what *I* want." I reached out and grasped her hand. It hung limply in my own. More than anything, I wanted her to squeeze mine back, but she didn't. "You're all I ever wanted."

A tear ran down her cheek, and I shifted closer, catching it with the tip of my index finger. She turned her cheek. "I would do anything for you," I said. "Don't you see that? I love you."

"I know." She sighed, more tears absorbing into my palm. "But you're *engaged,* Lucas. I can't."

"I didn't choose Celia. She was chosen for me. I barely even know her. And what I do know about her tells me I can't trust her."

"So what are you going to do about it?"

"I can't marry her, Jessa. I won't do it. I'll refuse."

"So what's your plan then, huh?" She was jaded. It was my own fault.

I gathered every ounce of passion and looked her dead center in her eyes. "I'm going to find a way to convince my father to call off the wedding, to let us be together."

She laughed. "And how are you possibly going to do that? There's no way."

"There has to be a way. And I will find it. I promise."

She shook her head.

"Jessa, look at me." I carefully placed my hands on her cheeks again, moving her face to my own. We were only inches apart, and I stared into her ocean eyes with everything I had in me. I needed her to believe in me. In us. I needed her to fight for me as much as I was fighting for her. She was the only thing left. The darkness would consume me without her.

But I'd messed up. And I didn't deserve her forgiveness.

"Nobody else matters to me anymore but you," I said. "Please, I've already lost my mother. My father doesn't care about me, not really. You're all I have left that matters. Don't give up on me. I will find a way out of this. I'll do anything. Whatever it takes for us to be together, I promise I will find it."

I searched her eyes, waiting for the spark to come. The one I knew so well, the one I'd seen so many times before. It had to be in there.

354

"Please, Jessa," I said. "I love you."

It was the truth. It was everything. *I love her.*

"I love you too," she said, the words a sweet breath on her lips.

"I am not going to marry Celia," I said, my spine turning to steel. "I won't do it." It was true. I would do *anything* to be with this girl before me.

She nodded, hopeful.

"I'm going to marry *you*, Jessa."

A spark lit in her eyes, and she gasped. Surprise. Longing. Love.

I couldn't hold back. I kissed her gently, waiting for her response. Her lips felt like coming home. They were hope. They were passion. They were everything coming alive in one touch.

Our foreheads touched as I continued. "You will be my wife," I breathed. "When you're a little older, and when you're ready. I'll wait for you. I promise." She kissed me harder, her arms moving to wrap around my neck, and I came home.

I didn't know how long we went on that way, kissing to fill the void that only each other could fill. I'd always thought "butterflies" was a dumb expression. But that's what I felt with Jessa. Only more. It was so much more than butterflies.

"I know we're young. You especially," I said, pulling away, "but there's no one else for me."

"I know it too." Tears rolled down her face.

"Don't cry," I begged, kissing them away, the salt wetting my lips.

"I'm happy," she said, her smile making her cheeks move against my mouth. "I'm just scared, Lucas. I'm scared I'm going to lose you again. I don't know what it will do to me."

"I promise, we will be together." I laced her hands in my own and stood her up. Then I hugged her tightly to my body, ignoring the struggle to kiss her again. Right now, she just needed to be held.

I gripped her hands in mine. "Jessa, I don't know when, and I don't know how, but I *will* marry you. That is…" I coughed, nervous. When did I become this romantic guy? "That's if you'll have me." I kneeled before her. This was how a proposal should be done. I would do it again properly one day, with a ring and everything. But for now… "Jessa Loxley, will you marry me?"

Her eyes widened. A smile lit up her entire being. That alone told me everything I needed to know. But I waited for her to say yes.

She did.

I kissed her again, losing myself. I hated that my *real* engagement had to stay a secret for now. We'd have obstacles to overcome. But I would make it happen. Too many times, I'd rolled over, allowing my father and his people to tell me how to live my life. But not on this one. Not with Jessa.

We lay in her bed for most of the night, holding hands, kissing, but mostly talking about the future. We never brought up our problems or how we could potentially overcome them. Instead, we imagined what it would be like to be married. We saw a world without obstacles and talked about it like it was real. Where would we live? Would I become king or would we run away together? If

I was king, what would she do as queen? Would we have kids? Yes. And what would our kids look like? We laughed over some of the options and held our breath over others. But we held nothing back, and it was the best night I'd ever had. I kept her safe in my arms, as if that was somehow all it took. Just a boy holding a girl he loved, and deciding not to let go.

●

Time moved despite our best efforts. Reluctantly, I got up to leave, knowing I had already been gone far too long. She grabbed my hand, fear lining her eyes.

"What is it?"

"Lucas, tomorrow. Do you know I'm being initiated tomorrow night?"

I nodded. "I heard you passed your final test. Congratulations."

She stared up at me, the moonlight casting a blue glow across her face.

"You'll be okay," I said. "You're a champ. It's easy."

"It's not that," she whispered. Her face closed off for a second, as if considering something and deciding better of it. But then just as quickly, she opened herself up again. "Something is going to happen tomorrow night... with the Resistance."

I stilled, holding back the resentment that bubbled up at the mention of them. "What? What it is?"

She paused, eyes darting from side to side. "They're going to do something during my initiation. I don't know the details. Just promise me you'll be careful?"

I nodded, fear spearing through me. Of course they were going to do something during her initiation. It would put her in danger, but they didn't care about that. They never did!

"You too, Jessa," I said. "You can't fight."

She shook her head. "I won't."

I kissed her one last time. Then I snatched what was left of the gray and white rose from the floor, went invisible as quickly as possible, and returned to my room.

●

The next morning, I woke early with complete clarity. I knew what I had to do.

SEVENTEEN

JESSA

I floated on dreams all night and well into the morning. Dreams about Lucas and growing old together. Dreams about reuniting with my family. Dancing again, always, the dreams had dancing. Every time my consciousness pushed me toward waking, I was pulled back under. Back into the weightless surrender.

●

Lacey is learning to walk. Her chubby fingers grip onto my index fingers. They feel warm, sweaty. She toddles between my legs as we shuffle across the living room.

"Look, Dad, she's doing it." I laugh.

She peers up at me, startled by my laugh, I think. Her blond hair is curly around her face, like a halo. It reminds me of a wig because it's only a few inches long. Her blue eyes mirror my own.

"My girls." Dad smiles, and we walk toward him. One step. Two steps. Three. Four.

When we're only a couple away, I slip my fingers from her grip. She hardly notices, finishing the final few on her own before plunging into the safety of Dad's arms.

●

Mom stands over me as I sit on the bathroom counter.

"Let me see," she says, motioning to my feet.

I have big socks on, and after a moment, I peel them off one at a time. There are blisters on almost every toe, above my heel is rubbed raw, and the whole foot is beet red. "How long has it been like this?" she asks.

I shrug. I don't want her to get mad because I don't want her to make me stop.

"I'm going to talk to your teacher," she says. "See if we can get you a better fitting pair of pointe shoes next time." I exhale a sigh of relief. "You didn't think I was going to make you quit, did you?" she asks. "I would never do that to you, Jessa. I know how much you love this. I'm proud of you, honey."

I stick my feet in the sink, running cold water over the sores. I know the pain might not be temporary. Battered feet are part of ballet. Still, it's so worth it.

●

The dreams continued. Fragmented memories mixed with hope. Some made no sense and then perfect sense in the way dreams often did. What mattered was the right people were there. What mattered was how it felt. The sunlight started to pitter-patter across my face. I could feel the warmth pouring in, asking a question—but I wasn't ready to answer it.

I rolled over.

●

I run along behind her, my bare feet smoothing the dewy grass. The light filters between the trees, catching her blond hair. Her laugh has a way of calling to me. I want to play. She is taller than me, so I have to hurry to catch up. My legs are still chubby. Hers are sticks.

"Show me," I say, grabbing at a dandelion. She looks around, back at the house, at the fence.

"Come," she says, taking off again.

We go to our favorite spot: the trees where no one can see us. The place where it's safe to play.

"Show me," I ask again. Does she hear me? Does she know what I want? I push the flower at her, but she already has one in her hand. She smiles, and we sit, our knees touching.

"Don't tell anyone," she says. She squeezes the dandelion; the yellow comes off in her hand. It floats into the air, hovering just between us.

"Magic." I giggle.

"Shh…" she says, blowing it toward me.

When it hits, I erupt into a fit of laughter. I suddenly have the best idea. "Let's climb the tree. I go, up, up, up."

"No," she says. But I've already gone. It was easy. I'm high. So high. Too high. I'm scared to come down. I start to scream. "Frankie! Jessa!" Someone calls. Mom? I scream again. I want down.

"What is she doing all the way up there?" someone says. "How was that possible for her to move that fast?"

It's not Mom.

●

I sat up, my breath rushing out of me. The dreams were all so vivid, so real, but that last one was something else. And it wasn't the first time I'd had it, either. I climbed out of bed and I attempted to tame the mane that is my hair after sleeping on it wet. I couldn't rid my mind of the images. The dandelion. The girl.

Was it a recurring dream or a memory?

I tried to grab onto the last fragments of it, but with every minute, the dream slipped farther and farther from my mind. I held onto the memory of my mother calling my name. That was right, wasn't it? And whom else had she been calling for? I couldn't quite remember well enough. But it felt important.

I stretched my body for a moment, then flopped out of bed. Next, I opened my closet and dressed in the same thing I wore almost every day. At least it was comfortable. Checking the time, I groaned when I realized I'd slept through breakfast. I had combat training every morning and needed to get moving. Combat didn't scare me nearly as much as it used to, and today would be no different, even though most of the best fighters had been whisked away for the war. Plus, Branson was gone.

I went through the motions of training in a bit of a daze. Slumped against the wall, I sipped at my water bottle and took in the remaining alchemists who populated the gym. Part of me was training, going to class, going through the motions. The other part was wondering where Lucas was, wondering how we were possibly going to make it work. And I was absolutely giddy about last night, which was foolish. But I couldn't help it.

I sighed and wiped at the sweat on my neck with a towel.

I trusted him; he would figure it out. I couldn't wait until the day when we didn't have to hide our relationship anymore. And then another part of me was solely focused on the night to come. The initiation. I would swear my allegiance to the monarchy and perform a task in front of my peers. And then? The Resistance would do…something.

It was almost time, and whatever happened, I was ready. Throwing my towel and bottle to the side, I pushed off the wall and strode forward with confidence.

●

I brushed at invisible wrinkles in my satin gown. The dress was midnight black and hugged my torso in a sweetheart neckline, leaving my shoulders bare. It tapered out at the hips and ended just above the knees. Delivered in a velvet box, it had arrived courtesy of the king, along with strappy black heels and a gorgeous diamond necklace. I'd put the ensemble together and even spent an hour painstakingly straightening my hair. After applying smoky eye makeup and red lipstick, I'd been pleased when I'd left my room. And more than a little nervous.

I clutched the invitation in my hand, once more checking that I was at the correct entrance. I allowed myself a moment to breathe, then pushed open the doors and walked inside. Blinking, I stared wide-eyed at the scene before me. It was more than I expected. The place was packed, the ballroom filled with round tables and a sea of faces. White tablecloths adorned each one and a colorful floral centerpiece was placed identically in each center. All the guardians in residence were already seated, as were the officers.

In tandem, the whole room turned to face me.

I grimaced but quickly recovered with a smile. I quickly realized that since the invitation had been so specific about when and where I entered, I shouldn't be surprised to see everyone already seated, expecting me.

"And here is the guest of honor," King Richard's voice boomed through the speakers. Applause rang out, and I gave a little wave. Richard stood at a podium on top of a stage that appeared to be set up just in front of me. I quickly moved to join him and he continued. "Please, join the royal family for our meal, and then we'll get started. A little magical presentation during dessert, anyone?" The crowd tittered; I was going to puke.

Apparently the initiation meant I had to perform magic in front of everyone and swear my allegiance to the royal family. I could do it. *Breathe.* I scanned the crowd, frozen to the spot, when Lucas caught my eye. He nodded to me, smiling. I scurried off the stage to join his table below, sitting across from him and his fiancée. She smiled warmly at me, and my stomach seized. Richard joined us at that moment, taking the seat next to mine.

"You know, Jessa," he said, "you're a very special girl. It's usually the case that alchemists are initiated into the Guardians of Color once a year. We put on a big production that they all get to share. But you get the spotlight all to yourself tonight."

"Congratulations," Celia purred.

I quickly glanced her way, muttering my thanks, before turning back to my food. Her hand wrapped around Lucas's upper arm didn't go unnoticed.

"She *is* a special girl." Lucas smiled. My gaze shot to him, and I was unable to speak. His eyes glowed as he stared at me. He didn't try to hide it, even in front of Celia or Richard. My cheeks flamed, and I bit back my smile. He was gorgeous, of course—he always was—but dressed immaculately in a tux with his hair styled to messy-perfection and a cleanly shaved face was a *really* good look on him.

We ate a four-course dinner but I hardly swallowed a bite. I contributed almost nothing to the conversation. I was too nervous. Nervous to be at this table. To do the magic. To even *be here.* Whatever I was asked to do, I prayed I wouldn't make a fool out of myself. I couldn't even think about what would happen with the Resistance afterward; it sent my nerves into overdrive.

"Time to go," King Richard said into my ear before standing and heading to the podium.

I took a deep breath. Lucas nodded, and I allowed myself to be comforted— if only for a moment. Then I followed Richard onto the stage.

"My friends," the king said, "it is a special occasion that we get to initiate Jessa into our family. The Guardians of Color have long been a pillar of this kingdom, serving in a variety of important roles. It is because of you that we are so strong. Though you may stay out of the public eye, you are the cornerstone of our society. Thank you for all that you do."

The crowd applauded.

"And a big thanks as well to the officers." He motioned to their tables. Only a small fraction was in attendance, which sent a little wave of shock through me. I assumed the rest were helping with the war effort. But the palace was normally swarming with officers, and there were only a few tables of officers tonight. "Without your steadfast commitment to the law, none of this would be possible." More clapping. "Jessa came to us in less than desirable circumstances. As most of you know, she accidentally manipulated color during a ballet performance. Luckily for her, we were able to bring her in and train her like one of our own."

I climbed the five steps to the stage and stood next to the king. I smiled, hoping my discomfort was well hidden. It seemed the way he remembered how I was "brought in" and the way *I* remembered it were two different things. Typical.

"Now, I think it's time we dim the lights and get started, don't you?"

More clapping, even a few cheers from the alchemists. I blinked, somewhat amazed at the sound. Turned out, I'd come a long way with my peers over the last few months.

As the lights dimmed, a spotlight illuminated the stage. I was dizzy. Momentarily blinded. A longing burned in my chest. Memory. In my life before the palace, this feeling was accompanied by a ballet performance. The lights created a cocoon around the stage, shrouding the audience in darkness. It used to be a comfort for me, made it easier for me to relax. This time, the nerves didn't go away; they only increased. Everyone was watching, and I couldn't watch them back.

"Jessa passed green, orange, and yellow alchemy." Richard's voice vibrated around the room.

Someone must have removed him from the stage, because I was alone now. Frozen. Dazed under the lights. Alone on the stage. But not *alone*. Hundreds of eyes blinked back at me.

"She also showed signs of strong aptitude in purple. But what is most curious about her is a couple of unique abilities. Abilities we hope to study and replicate in more guardians. You see, when we first met her, she had inadvertently pulled the purple from her dress—a feat not uncommon, even though it wasn't the organic materials that come easiest with magic. No, it was the fact that the purple separated into primary colors: blue and red. Now *that* was rather impressive."

The crowd broke into whispers. They'd heard the rumors, of course, but this confirmed it.

"We haven't since replicated the act, but we will," Richard continued. The way he said it wasn't in disappointment; it was calm, assured. As if he was bragging about me: I was his possession, a new toy, and he'd almost figured me out.

An icy chill trickled down my spine, but I stood taller.

"However, we were able to conclude that she *can* manipulate red." More whispers followed his words. "Would you like to see it in action?"

They cheered, a thrum of nervous excitement rushed through the room.

Oh, no. I don't know if I can do this.

Part of me had wondered if Richard would continue to keep my red alchemy a secret.

Guess not.

Still, something nagged at me. He wanted to replicate it in others, sure, but that didn't mean he *could*. If it were true that he'd had access to this magic on and off over the years, he'd have already done that. Right? So why this big show? I fought the urge to run.

"Jessa, darling girl, are you ready?"

No! But I nodded. I had to do whatever he wanted. I ignored the ocean of panic that was rising, pushing it down.

"Now, I think her favorite *teacher* would be a wonderful help to us today. Who better to help demonstrate this than the woman who has taught you so much?" Richard purred. "Jasmine, please join us on stage. That is if you don't mind."

I gasped. I wanted to shake my head, to refuse, but my entire body was frozen to the spot. I had to play along.

Someone shuffled from the back of the room, and molten fear rolled through my body, creeping and hot. No! I couldn't do this to *her* of all people, it was too dangerous. What if I hurt her? What if she revealed her true identity?

"Ah, here she comes," Richard continued. His voice sounded as charismatic as ever, but I couldn't bear to look at his expression. "Please give her a round of applause."

The crowd clapped, but the applause was stilted. Slow. Nobody knew what this meant. Even *testing* red alchemy on someone felt wrong to me. Did they think so too? But this? Jasmine was one of the most respected alchemists in the community.

She ambled to the stage, a warm smile lighting her face. When she finally looked at me, a flash of something crossed her eyes. Something controlled. I didn't understand. What was I supposed to do?

"Please, Jasmine, have a seat."

A chair was brought onto the stage. I barely noticed as someone placed something in my palm. I looked down at it, my stomach turning. A small knife. The blade glistened in the spotlight.

"Red alchemy has long been sought after. We know that red is connected to belonging, family, and *loyalty*," Richard said. I finally glanced over at him, taking in his animated gestures as he spoke. "What's interesting is we haven't been able to do much with red materials, flowers, plants, rocks, and such. But blood, on the other hand, for some that is a different story."

I bit my lip, sucking in a breath.

"Jessa, please show us."

I stared at Jasmine, willing her to do something. *Tell me what to do!* She reached up and took the knife from me. I was barely holding it. Then she smiled at me, her eyes sad, and she cut herself across the arm. "It's okay," she

362

whispered. "Just do your best and everything will work out."

The knife clattered to the floor.

I fought back tears and reached for her arm. The blood wet my hand, slick and metallic. I cleared my mind, took a deep breath, feeling as the magic weaved its way into her blood. It pulsed out in tendrils of red magic and then shot up her arm. She jerked.

The crowd cheered, once again, as red alchemy swirled into the air. I expected Richard to interject and order me to tell her to do one thing or another, but he didn't. I wanted to get this over with as quickly as possible. I needed to show them what was possible with red alchemy. The more I pulled the red from her blood, the more side effects she would have.

I pushed the red magic farther into her, felt the power surging through me as well. "Dance!" I called.

Immediately, she stood and began to move to a beat only she could hear.

"Freeze!"

She did, one leg balanced in the air.

"Sit down."

She sat right there on the floor.

"What's your name?"

"Jasmine," she replied, calm.

"Where do you live?"

"The palace."

"Go and sit in your chair."

And now we're done, right? I looked out in the crowd, took a little bow, and made my way toward the edge of stage.

"Not so fast, Jessa," the king sing-songed. His voice echoed through the room. I stopped. "That was a charming little presentation of red alchemy. As you can see, manipulating the color out of a person's own blood and then using it on them allows for mind control." The crowd was utterly silent. The room even had a faint echo. "Now, I'm curious. Do you think we could control someone enough to tell us the *truth*?"

Terror gripped my entire body. No. I couldn't do this. I shook my head. "It's used for actions. Blue is used for communication," I protested.

The king laughed as he strolled over to me, carrying the microphone in his hand now. "Blue is very useful, that is true. Persuasion, listening, trying to figure out if someone is being honest. But red, now, I think red takes it to a new level, don't you?"

"I don't know," I breathed. What was I supposed to do? Run?

"I think you do know," he said. "But no matter, let's find out. Go to Jasmine, put your hand back on her wound, and repeat what I tell you. Got it?"

I stared at the room, blinking rapidly. Would someone save me? Where was the Resistance? Shouldn't they be here by now? Something was wrong.

I walked back to Jasmine and did as he said. Her blood was thick under my fingers, and I longed to make it go away. Just make it all stop!

"Ask her if she's loyal to the monarchy."

I gulped. She stared off into the crowd, dazed, her eyes empty orbs. She wasn't in control. This was wrong! I prayed she'd be able to fight this magic, but it was futile. The magic would work. It had every time before. I wouldn't be so lucky. Jasmine wouldn't be so lucky.

"Are you loyal to the monarchy?" I asked, my eyes filling.

She paused, her eyes moving from side to side. I hoped that meant she was gaining control again. But I felt the power coursing through me, felt my question fighting with her mind.

"No," she said, her voice steady and sure.

The crowd, so silent before, erupted in noxious whispers.

"Now that's a shame," Richard said, his voice flat. "I had hoped my suspicions were wrong."

Officers lined my peripheral vision. The heat of panic burned hotter.

"Ask her who she works for."

I paused.

"Ask her who she works for!" he bellowed, stalking toward us.

"Who do you work for?" I forced the question from my mouth, fighting tears.

"The Resistance."

I dropped my head in shame.

"Well, even I could have come up with a better name." Richard laughed, but he moved to put his face between Jasmine's and mine. A blood vessel pulsed in his forehead, and he gritted his teeth. "Now tell me, Jasmine, are you working alone?" He looked at me, eyes bulging.

Terror ignited through my entire body. What was I going to do? I stalled for a second.

The king yelled, "Ask!"

I started. "Are you working alone?"

"No."

I needed to stop this. I needed to help her!

He growled, dropping the microphone now. He moved in, his face only inches from Jasmine's languid expression. "Who are you working with? Tell me?"

I forced myself to speak. "Who are you working with?" I asked, the tears now free, running down my face. Any minute now, everything would be over. She would tell. And I would probably be dead because of it.

She fought, shaking her head, yelling nonsensically. She put her hands to her ears. Blood started to drip from her nose.

"We're hurting her," I gasped.

"Ask again!" Richard boomed, then straightened. I choked on a sob as he moved in behind me, squeezing down on my bare shoulders. Officers surrounded the stage, ready to intervene.

"Who are you working with?" Terror gripped me.

"I…I…" Jasmine sputtered. She ripped at her hair. "Get out of my head!"

"Ask again!"

"Who are you working with?" Tears ran down my face. I hated myself for it.

364

My grip loosened momentarily as I fought the urge to vomit.

Her mouth opened and closed in rapid succession. She dove. It all happened so fast. One second she was in the chair, the next she was on the floor. More blood. The knife gleamed between her fingers. There was no hesitation as she ripped it across her throat. *No!*

There was erratic screaming. It was me, sobbing, falling to my knees, reaching for her. I was wrenched away by meaty hands. I clawed at them. Thick arms wrapped around me, restraining. Jasmine was slack. Richard screeched words I couldn't understand. What was happening?

"Heal her," I yelled. Or maybe it was Richard. I looked around, frantic. I needed to help her. Several alchemists jumped to the stage. Someone dragged a green plant with them.

So much blood. Everywhere.

Alchemists surrounded her, pushing the green magic into her again and again. It wasn't working. It wasn't doing anything. I tugged at the arms around me, needing to try for myself. Nothing.

"We can't save her," someone said.

"She's gone."

Someone was sobbing.

It was me.

●

"Snap out of it!" Faulk shook me, minutes later. "It's over, done with. Jasmine is gone."

I didn't know what to say. I had nothing. It was empty inside. I looked around, finding myself in a ball on the floor off to the side of the stage. The ballroom was still filled with people. They buzzed, talking loudly over each other.

"You did a good job," Faulk said, her blond hair shining in the light of the stage. The room was still dark, the spotlight still lit. "I didn't think you had it in you. But Richard was right."

"What?"

"Come on, you have to finish your initiation."

I shook my head. I wanted to save Jasmine. I wanted to see Lucas. I wanted to get as far away from the palace as possible. I wanted to go home. Tears began to spring to my eyes again.

She slapped me. My head jolted to the side.

"Ouch!" The sharp pain cooled across my skin, focused me.

"Stop it." She stared at me, her eyes sharp. "Suck it up, Jessa. You will finish this initiation *right now.*"

I nodded this time. She was right. I was in this thing whether I liked it or not. And now Richard had the weapon he needed. Me. I stood, deep breaths filling my lungs, and wiped away the tears. And I did what she said. I sucked it up.

Faulk held my arm and led me back to the front of the stage. I tried not to look at the blood. The urge to gag was too strong.

"Sit down!" Richard called out to the crowd over the microphone gripped tightly in his white knuckled hand.

The room quieted immediately, everyone finding their seats. I could make out Lucas, just barely through the spotlight. His eyes were wide, staring at me.

"I hope I've made myself clear," the king continued. "*There will be no rebellion!* We are at war. We will win that war. This kingdom, my alchemists, my officers, you are all loyal to me! And if anyone shows even a moment of hesitation, I will use whatever means necessary to root you out and *end you.*"

The room was blanketed in complete silence.

"Now," Richard said. "Let's finish this initiation, shall we? Jessa, I know that was hard for you. Thank you for your loyalty."

I nodded, hands trembling. I closed them into fists.

"Repeat after me," Faulk said, taking the microphone into her slender hand. She wasn't dressed up as everyone else was; the officers had stayed in their white uniforms. Hers was stained in blood. "As a member of the Guardians of Color, I hereby swear my allegiance to New Colony and to my king. I will defend and protect the royal family with my life. I will be true to my word and swear myself to His Majesty."

I repeated every word.

"Long live the king!" she finished.

"Long live the king." I repeated that too.

The crowd cheered, less eager than earlier in the night. Fear had replaced me as the guest of honor.

"Now, somebody clean up this mess," Richard said, "and let's finish our dessert, shall we?"

EIGHTEEN

SASHA

I concentrated on the thumping rhythm of the rotor as we zipped through the night sky. True to their word, West America sent helicopters, guns, and soldiers. We had a troop of about twenty of their best men, and combined with our own, there were about a hundred willing and able to fight. Their helicopters were much larger than ours, each fitting twelve bodies plus the crew. We flew out after dinner, knowing it would take about four hours to get to the capital. My stomach in a knot, I hadn't touched much food all day. I absentmindedly picked at the hem of my long-sleeved black shirt and adjusted my combat boots under my weight.

I was strapped into a rudimentary chair, the two rows close and facing each other. Among us were Hank, Tristan, Mastin, Cole, and Christopher, much to my frustration. He had insisted on taking the trip and nothing would dissuade him. It was awkward, and every time I looked his way, I caught him staring at me. We'd all done our best to outfit ourselves in black, durable clothing and sturdy shoes, but the military men really looked the part. I sat quietly, going over every scenario in my head.

The palace was weak at the moment. Most of the best alchemists and officers were in West America trying to gain ground. King Richard had declared war, and in the process he had not only begun stripping areas of West America of color but had also taken over multiple cities. New Colony had a bigger army than West America expected. It seemed King Richard had been planning this for years.

"You don't have to do this," Christopher said, speaking loudly over the whoosh of the chopper. "You and I can stay in here until it's over." He pleaded with such sad eyes that it was hard to meet them. This man was my father, but he was a stranger.

I sighed and turned away. He already knew my answer was no. All day, he'd been hounding me to back down. But we were already on our way, no backing out now. I shot a glare his way, jutting my chin. "And what about Jessa? Are you going to forget about her now too?"

He frowned. "It wasn't like that. It was never like that."

"Fine. Explain it to me then. What was it like?"

"We would've kept you hidden." He rubbed his hand along his jaw. "We even did for a little while. If we'd known they'd take you away forever then we would've found a way to get out of there sooner."

"But you did know about my magic?" I asked.

The body of the chopper was lit with a red light. It shone on his face in the darkness, casting long shadows. I could just make out the whites of his eyes before he closed them briefly. "Yes," he said.

"Don't you get it, Christopher? I remember what happened!"

"We didn't know what to do." His voice shook. "When they came for you, it was because a neighbor had told on us. She saw something, I guess. They wanted to take you both. You and Jessa."

"So you let them take me to protect Jessa? Or to protect yourselves?"

He sat, quiet for a minute. "I am so sorry, Frankie. We made a mistake."

"Don't call me that. I don't use that name anymore."

He nodded. "I'm sorry, Sasha. You didn't deserve this. There wasn't a day that went by when we didn't think about you."

"I find that hard to believe," I muttered.

The other ten passengers had grown silent during our exchange. Some stared openly while others looked away, their faces taught. We were free entertainment. *Just line right up and see the cast-off daughter and estranged father put on a show.* But part of me wondered if he was telling me the truth. What if they really had tried to help me?

"I know we met before but just in case you forgot my name, I'm Hank." Hank reached out to shake Christopher's hand. "I'm sorry your family had to go through that. It's not right."

"Thank you," Christopher said, returning the handshake.

"I hope to get your other daughter out of there." Hank didn't say what I knew. Getting Jessa out wasn't the mission. Jessa was exactly where she needed to be, and no one was taking her out tonight. Not unless this mission went so well there was no New Colony at the end of it. Not likely. "I'll help you make sure Sasha stays safe in there," Hank continued.

They nodded at each other, like they understood what it was like to love me. To be my dad. I ground my teeth, refusing to be swayed by the warm, fuzzy feelings exploding in my heart.

This was too much for me.

"Let's go over the plan again," I said, changing the subject.

"All five choppers will land at the same time, and we storm the palace together," Tristan spoke up. He sat forward in his seat. "All of the major operatives will be busy for a few hours in the main ballroom, the royals too. So that's our target. Of course, we still expect guards and patrols. But we will move quickly."

The idea of landing five helicopters at once sent me into panic mode, but I didn't show it. This was how war worked. It wasn't supposed to be safe.

"Our targets are General Faulk and King Richard. We want them dead," Mastin said, his voice cutting through the darkness like a knife. "We'll give everyone else a chance to surrender."

"Jasmine is confident that most of the alchemists will be sympathetic to us," Hank nodded. "We can expect the same of the officers, but there shouldn't be as many of them there tonight."

"You're sure about that?" I asked.

"Faulk and Richard have been sending more and more people out every day," Cole's steady voice jumped in from the far side of the chopper, low and sure. It was the first I'd heard from him all night. "The king has left himself vulnerable for attack. It's the perfect opportunity."

It made sense. But still, not everyone signed up for this was equipped to do the job. Most of the alchemists were newbies, and even though we had trained soldiers too, I had yet to see them in action.

"Your boys any good?" I asked.

Mastin laughed. "We're men. And we're the best."

"I hope you're right about that."

●

We dropped quickly. The inertia did little to calm my nerves as I bent over to see out the back window. From my position, I couldn't see much. When I caught sight of the palace, lit up like a beacon, blood rushed through my eardrums. I felt my face get hot, and I inhaled a deep breath. We unstrapped our safety restraints and got ready, knees slightly bent, our bodies close together at the edges of our seats.

The alchemists had gemstone necklaces wrapped around their necks.

Everyone else had guns.

A lot of guns. And I worried many of those gun-touting men didn't actually know how to use them. Maybe West America had thought of that and some of those weapons held tranquilizers instead of bullets. But I knew that it was probably wishful thinking…

The second the helicopter landed on the grass, Cole slammed the doors open. We jumped out, crouching low. We all ran as silently as we could, arcing out in a fan across the palace lawn. More helicopters dropped in, and more people spilled from inside. We continued to fan out, low and quiet. It was so dark, and the heavy cloud cover blocked out any stars. The moon was only a faint glow.

I looked to my left and noticed Mastin taking off in a different direction. I could tell Tristan was staying close to me on purpose. So was Christopher. He wasn't trained for this. He should have stayed back, but heaven forbid that stubborn man listened to reason.

"Hide out here," I told him, pointing to a darkened cropping of trees. "I'll come back for you." And I would. Even though I didn't consider him my father, he was still Lacey and Jessa's father. I didn't want him to die.

"I'm not leaving you," he said, pushing forward to keep pace with the others. I sped up but he matched it. He must have been a runner. I wondered what it would be like to exercise solely for health. For me, it had always been a matter of training.

A matter of life and death.

The soldiers had walkie-talkies. One of the devices crackled, and a man muttered a reply. Then there was a yell and the snap of a gunshot. It sounded like a silencer.

"Let's go," Tristan said. He grabbed my hand, and we high-tailed it to one of the lower level windows.

Christopher followed on our heels. I jumped when my father picked up a rock and threw it through the glass. Then he reached in and unlatched the lock. "I'll go in first," he muttered.

Maybe I get my impulsiveness from him.

The plan was pretty simple. Everyone had already been briefed on where the main ballroom was located. We were to go in from all angles. There were several doors leading into the room so it would be easy. The alchemists were to fight the other alchemists and officers. The West American soldiers were the ones going in for Richard, Faulk, Lucas, and anyone who got in their way. If I was given the chance, I would do the same. I wanted to end the king. But it would have to wait. The plan was to kill Faulk and Richard. Lucas and the remaining officers and alchemists would be arrested. Anyone who put up a fight would also get arrested, and if we had to kill some of them to make that happen, we would.

As we scrambled through the window, a few others followed. The room was dark. Empty. I knew where we were, having spent so much time here. We were in a parlor right across from the ballroom. As soon as we left this room, it would be time. About ten other people crawled in through the window behind us. We all kept quiet, waiting for the signal.

It felt like an eternity. Every breath was like a full minute. I was hyperaware of each movement, each excruciating second that we sat there like sitting ducks. I wrung my hands out, fighting the urge to jump into action. I looked around the room instead, taking in the familiar palace decor. Being in this place brought up all kinds of mixed emotions. I had made friends here. Some would be on the receiving end of what was about to go down.

Then the walkie-talkie sounded. The voice coming through the other end was scratchy low, but I knew it was Mastin. "The fox is in the hole."

A soldier threw open the door, and we sprinted across the hallway. The door to the ballroom burst wide just as quickly. There was a second of hesitation. A moment of suspended belief that this was *really happening*. A couple of shots fired. A woman screamed.

And then it was chaos.

I raced into the room, my hand pushing my necklace under my shirt. It didn't matter if I held all the colors at once; I knew how to use each one as needed. Intention was enough. I willed the yellow into my system and felt the rush of adrenaline spread through my limbs.

"Get them!"

I startled at the king's voice as it bellowed through a loudspeaker, filling the room. Just the sound of it again ignited more adrenaline in my bloodstream. He was going to pay tonight for everything he'd done.

The alchemists hesitated, but the officers jumped into action immediately. A couple more shots fired off.

"Don't kill my guardians!" Richard bellowed.

The thudding sound of fists hitting bodies rang through the room. I made my way between the tables of alchemists; most were standing now but some still sat in shock. I ignored them and sprinted toward the action up front. I couldn't help but move in that direction. I spotted Lucas and a redhead sitting at a table next to Jessa.

My sister.

Dread overtook me as I took her in. Blood was smeared all over her arms and chest; her face white as a sheet. What happened?

"Jessa," Christopher shouted just over my shoulder. When he took her in like that, his expression completely crumbled.

"Don't go up there," I said, reaching out to calm him. "There are officers." It was true, they were swarming the royal family's table, desperate to protect them. Some of them formed human barriers. Others were locked in combat with our soldiers. But I noticed there weren't very many of them…

Somebody grabbed me, yanking me to my left and throwing off my center of gravity. I stumbled but quickly caught myself and turned. A middle-aged alchemist crushed a yellow flower between steady hands. A brief cloud of magic, and then they threw a punch. I ducked out of the way, barely grazing their knuckles, but even that would bruise. I caught a glimpse of the centerpieces on all the tables. Oh no! Why hadn't I realized this immediately?

They were filled with *all* the colors in floral arrangements and were easy access to anyone. We were on an even playing field. I fought back blow for blow. I didn't personally know most of the alchemists fighting around me, but I recognized most. It unnerved me, but I focused on the woman in front of me. I felt for the yellow alchemy inside and kicked her hard. She flew against the table, breaking it down the center. I leaped into position, ready to take her out, when another alchemist pounced. This one was a teenage girl and she was lethal in her movements. She ripped my ponytail back and kneed me in the kidney.

"What do you think you're doing, Sasha?" she growled in my ear. Hearing my fake name motivated me to fight back.

I head-butted her from behind. I felt the cartilage of her nose shift and break. She screamed. We turned toward each other and erupted in combat, our movements strong and catlike. The magic worked its way through our blood, enhancing every movement to dangerous levels. Tables broke. Chairs went flying. Table settings clattered to the floor, dishes splintering into glass shards.

I lunged for her, taking her down and bashing her head into the metal leg of the table. A sickening crunch sounded, and she passed out. I sighed and shot some healing green into her, enough to save her life, but not enough to wake her up anytime soon.

I glanced around the room and saw others engaged in combat. A lot of the newly trained alchemists that I had worked with were not as bad as I had first feared. The youngest had stayed home, obviously. But these people seemed to be holding their own against the guardians. Pride swelled as I watched them. And still, it helped that many of the color guardians stood back in shock. And even more pushed *away* to the edges of the room. A few darted out of the ballroom completely. But that didn't make up for the fact that there were guardians willing to fight any threat against their king. I needed to get back in there!

"Stop them!" I heard Richard boom again, his voice still attached to some microphone.

Why haven't they gotten to him yet?

More than anything I wanted to get up there and get in on the action. But I growled as I began to fight off yet another of these alchemists. If they knew why we were really here, what our mission really was, would they turn and join us?

I managed to get away from my attackers, immobilizing them both, as I headed farther into the ballroom. All that training was paying off, but this was taking too long. Then I glanced at my father. *Christopher.* He was stronger than he looked—a man on a mission. He had more motivation than most of these people had, and he was going for it, blow for blow.

This king had taken two of his daughters, and he was hell-bent on getting us back. But I watched in horror as he began hand-to-hand combat with a hulking officer. The man had a gun in a holster, and it would only be a matter of time before he used it. I veered in their direction, cursing Christopher. I needed to stay on task! I'd known he was going to be a distraction.

The officer had him in a tight headlock; the wrinkles around Christopher's eyes were deep as his eyeballs bulged. His face turned beet red as he struggled to breathe. I screamed and jumped on his attacker's back, beating my fists into his head. He didn't see it coming, and he didn't match my magical strength. Only a few hits were needed before the body beneath me went limp.

Christopher gripped his wrist. "I think it's broken."

"Come," I said. Quickly, I edged us to the corner of the room.

"Here." I reached out and gently held his wrist. During the fighting, my necklace had begun to press deeply into my skin under my shirt. The gems felt warm, and I knew they allowed me access to the magic instantly. I was lucky to be skilled enough not to mix the magics accidently. I'd coached the newer alchemists to keep their necklaces on the outside of their clothing for that reason.

I thought about the green gem and instantly sensed the magic coursing through my veins. It twirled out and into Christopher's wrist. He sucked back a shocked grimace as his wrist righted itself with a sickening crunch.

"That's amazing," he whispered.

"For someone who has three daughters for alchemists, you sure don't know a lot about alchemy."

He grimaced.

Welcome to the truth, old man.

"Please," I chastised. "Stay out of everyone's way. I've got to get back."

"But I want to help."

We turned to watch the action going on all around the room. We were gaining ground! Richard was not only surrounded by our people, but most of the officers had been taken out. Only a few alchemists still fought. The mood in room was shifting—on the verge of surrender.

"You did well. The best thing you can do now is to stay safe."

I didn't wait for a reply this time. I took off running. Cole held a gun against Richard's temple. It was all about to be over. I caught up to Tristan who stood on the edge of the action. Sweat dripped down his face as he huffed.

"I can't believe we did it," he said.

I laughed. "Now he tells the truth."

He shook his head, smiling. "Your friend is one hell of a fighter." He nodded to Mastin, who had one of the officers in a headlock. With expert skill he flattened the man twice his size.

I scanned the crowd until I found Faulk. She was handcuffed between three of our guys. I narrowed my eyes, studying her. She looked strange; a knowing smile pulled at her face. A wicked glint lit her features as she glanced around the room. I froze. I knew that look. What was going on?

Something was wrong.

"Put the gun down," Richard calmly said to the man who had him. Cole.

"You attacked my country, unprovoked. You've killed my citizens. You've destroyed vast amounts of our land. Tell me now why I shouldn't just kill you." Cole spat at Richard's feet, anger rolling off him.

Richard began to laugh. The laugh of a maniac, high and mechanical.

The room froze, all eyes trained on him. Had he lost his mind?

An echo popped through the room. A gunshot. A spurt of blood sprang out the front of Cole's head. He startled and collapsed in a heap. I stepped back just as screams echoed through the room.

Richard dove to the floor as more shots broke out. More people fell. Were they dead? I flattened myself against the ground. Then I frantically reached up and pulled Tristan with me.

"Get down!" someone shrieked. More screams. More shots.

Tristan and I crawled under a table. It was one of the only remaining tables that hadn't been completely destroyed from the fight. The tablecloth hung low, covering us.

"It's a trap," Tristan growled. He grabbed my hand and fixed his gaze on me, unease in his eyes. "We have to get you out of here."

Feet pounded across the floor. More bullets sounded.

"I said don't kill the alchemists!" Richard yelled again. No microphone this time, his voice howling from farther away.

I peeked under the tablecloth. Officers swarmed the room, securing the perimeter. Where had they all come from? There had only been a few tables of officers when we first came in the room. But now? Their numbers had practically quadrupled.

"Go!" Tristan said, forcing me in the direction of the closest unmanned exit. It was our only chance.

We crawled across the floor, dodging bodies at every turn. Most of them were alive, thank goodness. Many people were still lying flat on the ground for safety. Some had tranquilizer darts embedded in their skin and were unconscious. But I knew some were dead the second I laid eyes on them.

I recognized too many of their faces.

Tears stung my eyes. How could we have been so eager to rush into this place? Of course it had been a trap. We couldn't expect anything less from a man like Richard. We'd been led like lambs to the slaughter. I had willingly led people who weren't ready for this kind of combat into the situation. I should have trusted my instincts from the beginning. I should have never listened Mastin and Cole. Or anyone else.

We were all going to die. Innocent people were going to die.

"Go," Tristan hissed, pointing again to the unmanned door.

We jumped up, sprinting toward it. Just as we were about to push through, Mastin popped up at our side. He nodded, huffing quietly, his face grim. "Go!" he mouthed. We erupted into the hallway.

"Wait, where's Christopher?" I skidded to a halt.

The men exchanged a glance as they both shook their heads. "He's probably out already. We'll sort that out later," Mastin said. "We have to get out of here now."

Four or five of our people sprinted down the hallway from the same direction we'd just come in.

"The choppers are out here," one of them called, motioning to us. They didn't wait for us to follow.

"You go," I said, pushing the men in front of me. "I'll catch up."

"I'm not leaving you," Tristan said. Of course, it was only to be expected. He'd been my protector since we were kids. "Fine," I huffed. "But, Mastin, you need to help those people get out of here. We'll be out soon."

He hesitated.

"I'm serious, Mastin. If we're not there, you still have to go. Tristan and I know this city. We'll be fine. We'll get out. You have to get out of here. You have to get home and get reinforcements."

I could tell he didn't want to leave me, but he had to.

"I mean it," I said, nodding at him, then turning back to the ballroom. When I heard him take off, I exhaled, momentarily relieved.

Christopher! If he's not dead then I'm going to kill him.

Tristan and I edged our way along the shadows, peering into the doorway. There were too many officers. Several stood just beyond us now. It was hopeless.

We couldn't go in there.

The moment I was about to give up on Christopher, I saw him.

He was crawling on the floor, along the back of the room—in the *wrong* direction. He was moving toward the action, not away from it. He slowly crept nearer to Richard and Faulk, both of whom were now standing over Cole's body. Others were littered around them. The soldiers who'd been caught, I didn't think any of them had even been given a chance or a second thought. Bullets into the heads of each. Our alchemists had been spared.

I gripped my hands into fists. Magic…

"We need to go," Tristan whispered into my hair, his body against mine, tugging me away. "We can try to make the helicopter if we leave now." He needed to get out of here. We both did. We were traitors to our kingdom, and if we were caught, it would be an instant death sentence.

I nodded, and we began to back away. We'd already wasted too much time. There was nothing I could do for Christopher. He was in the thick of it and there was no way I could get him out without getting caught myself. That was a suicide mission. Impossible. They might save me, but Tristan would be killed on the spot. I just hoped they took mercy on Christopher, or that maybe, by some miracle, he got himself out of that room before someone realized who he was.

"This way," Tristan whispered, as he pulled us into a room and shut the door.

The window was open, but it wasn't near the ground. It was at least ten feet up. I didn't know this room. We hastily found a table to move and give us a leg up. The thumping of one of the helicopters starting back up sounded through the room. More gunfire.

"We need to move it," I hissed. Tristan was ahead of me, already on the table. I grabbed at my necklace, feeling for it under my shirt. "Yellow alchemy," I said. "I'll boost you up and then come over."

It only took a second for the magic to connect, igniting my veins and filling me once again with that burst of power and adrenaline. In a flash, I wrangled Tristan up and out of the window.

I crouched low and readied myself to jump.

"Are you lost?"

I shouldn't have looked. I should have just jumped through the window. Run. Moved. *Anything!*

But my curiosity got the better of me. I turned to the voice.

"We've been looking everywhere for you," Faulk said.

She pointed a gun. Everything burst into a flash of white.

And then there was only darkness.

NINETEEN

JESSA

As soon as the chaos started, Lucas grabbed me. He *never* let me go. When the first gunshot erupted, I thought we were going to die. It was a mess of bodies and bullets, and we huddled together in shock. There was no way we could overcome the attack sitting at this table. But they knew me, right? Even though I was sitting at the table with the royal family, had Jasmine told the Resistance about me? Did they know I was one of them? So much about the Resistance was secretive. People didn't tell me anything, so how could I expect her to tell them? That thought circled my mind over and over, bringing me to sheer panic.

I had allowed hope to come in once that man had Richard. But then that man was shot through the back of the head and the screaming started again. More blood. After Jasmine's death, I didn't think I could take it. The fear was exhausting, and it just kept coming. I focused on my breathing, letting the minutes tick by as Richard directed the room.

We lost...

"It's okay," Lucas said. He wrapped me in his arms, kissing the side of my face. "It's okay. It's okay."

I'd lost track of his fiancée. Not that he seemed to care, but I did. She had appeared to be just as terrified as me, if not more. And no one had been there to comfort her. "Where's Celia?"

"Some of the officers already took her away." He breathed into my hair. "She'll be fine. She's a big girl."

Guilt swept through me. If I'd been in her shoes, I certainly would have wanted Lucas to hold me instead of another girl. I must've said something out loud because Lucas squeezed me tighter.

"It's okay. I'm not with Celia anymore. I'm with you."

I didn't fully understand. Well, I kind of understood since we were secretly engaged. I couldn't believe that it had been less than twenty-four hours since Lucas had come to my room, begging for my forgiveness. Maybe that was what he was talking about.

"Things are starting to calm down now," Lucas said. "Why don't you close your eyes for a minute?"

I just wanted to get out of there, more than anything. I was sure he could see that. I looked at my hands. They couldn't stop shaking. "Can't we just go?"

"We shouldn't leave until the officers say it's okay."

"I really thought..." I mumbled, trying to sort through the events in my mind. It was all a mess. "I really thought the Resistance was going to win this time."

Lucas didn't say anything, his expression grew somber as he took in the scene around us. Too many people had died. Pools of blood circled the bodies. Alchemists, officers, and even some of the waitstaff had lost their lives. I glanced at the face of a waitress who had tended to me at dinner, and I grimaced. Tears filled my eyes as I took in the bodies of soldiers. Where were they from? And the Resistance? They had either fled, been shot, or been captured.

The wounded cried out around the room. Luckily, enough alchemists were helping out with that, green magic circling.

"I should go," I said, pointing to some of the wounded. "I can help them."

Lucas nodded his agreement. "But I'm not leaving you."

I stood on shaky legs and walked to some people who still needed to be healed. Even for those who seemed to be gone, we still stopped to see what we could do.

"Check for pulses," I told Lucas.

Then we began making the rounds—him checking for wounds, and me healing where I could. Even in my frazzled state, the magic came more naturally to me than ever. One after another I healed wounds, extracted bullets, pulled out tranquilizer darts, and even mended a few broken bones. It felt good to do something to help others. Right.

For once in my life I was actually making a difference.

The king yelled through it all, but at this point, I'd tuned him out. He'd gotten what he wanted. He'd won, and in the process probably squashed the Resistance. Jasmine was gone, as were most of those who came in to fight. It was a devastating blow, one I didn't imagine the Resistance could come back from.

I didn't know where I fit in anymore. The ache of loss threatened to tear me apart, but I just kept moving.

At least I had Lucas. I looked up at him, catching him checking more pulses. He handled everybody with care. That look of pain, it still held strong on his face. He was sweating, and blood was splattered across his suit. His hair was a mess, and he strained to lift somebody up into a chair. An officer. They cried out, and I rushed over to administer magic.

Technically, the officers were my enemy. I was Resistance. But I couldn't see somebody with that look on their face, the pain so terrible that they were on the verge of passing out, and *not* step in to help. That wasn't me. I'd learned that my magic could be a gift. Or it could be a curse.

I chose the gift.

The officer was coated in blood. His hazel eyes fluttered as I sent a pulse of magic into him. "Thank you," he croaked.

We finished up in our area. I scanned the room, sighing. It looked like everyone else had been tended to. So with the small bit of relief we allowed ourselves, we moved back toward the front of the room. The shock began to wear off as the reality finally set in. Deep into my bones.

We lost. The Resistance had *lost*.

"That was horrible," I whispered, sitting down at what was left of our table. Flowers were scattered about, dishes lying in shards, and everything was covered with splatters of blood.

Lucas reached out and squeezed my hand, before releasing it. "It's over now," he said.

Something tickled my ankle, then grabbed. I jumped! I almost let out a yelp, but I saw whose hand was attached to my leg. I sunk to my knees. Everything came into focus as I stared at the man before me.

"Dad?" I breathed out, shocked. Then I wrapped my arms around him and sobbed into his shoulder. I couldn't help it. "It's really you. What are you doing here?" The pain of missing him had dulled over the last few weeks, but now that he was here, it ignited, waking me up.

"I need you to help me get us out of here," he whispered.

Of course! He couldn't be here. I didn't mention that I would be staying.

We looked around, it seemed nobody had noticed us. Lucas sat still, staring down at us. His eyes were wide. A horrified expression had crossed his features, and he clutched his stomach.

"I'll help you." The words came out like a promise. But how was I going to help? The room was swarming with alchemists and officers. "Hide under that part of the table." There was a bit that was still standing, toppled to one side and covered by the tablecloth. It was plenty big enough. He nodded, and I stood.

I met Lucas's eyes. "You have to get him out of here."

He knew what I was talking about. His frown deepened, but he nodded imperceptibly. He needed to use white alchemy. If he went under the table where no one could see, he could make himself invisible and make my father invisible too. He could get him out. It was dangerous, but this was my dad.

We stared at each other, Lucas and I. He was thinking too much, I could tell. But so was I. My father was *not* trained. He should never have been here. The Resistance shouldn't have allowed it. How could they? They'd promised to keep my parents safe, and then they went and did this!

"Please," I whispered to Lucas. *You love me. I know you love me. Do this for me.*

Lucas glanced around the room. The king was still making the rounds on the other side. No one was looking at us.

"You can do it," I said, my voice low, and reached for one of the white lilies strewn across the floor. "You've done it before. You can do it with this, Lucas."

I handed him the flower. "You're more powerful than you give yourself credit for. No one will know. It will be fine."

He nodded again. "Okay."

He shifted, about to go under the white tablecloth with my father. No one would notice. I had to believe it. Someone patted me on the back.

"That was impressive," Richard said.

A rush of hatred covered me from head to toe. How had he gotten over here so fast?

Moments ago, he was on the other side of the room, and now he was standing inches away from my father. My father, the man he had pretended to have in custody. The man who was officially part of the Resistance. The man who had raised me. The man who had left the kingdom!

"Thank you?" I questioned. Everything that just happened was horrific.

"You're one of us now."

"Father, not right now," Lucas said, his body stiff.

Richard laughed. "So fickle. One minute you're begging me to call off your engagement with Celia to be with this alchemist, and the next you act like nothing is going on."

I glanced between the two men.

"I don't understand." I turned to Lucas. A small voice of doubt sounded in my mind. *Something is off.* "What's he talking about?"

Lucas only shook his head. "We'll talk about it later."

"Is your engagement to Celia called off?"

"It wasn't," Richard said. "But I keep my word. Lucas did what he was supposed to do, so I'll hold up my end and reconsider."

"Reconsider what?" My voice cracked.

"Reconsider you, my dear." He frowned. "Not the brightest, are you? I was always very clear with my son that he wasn't to get involved with an alchemist, let alone marry one. But I suppose, under the right circumstances, with the right woman, I could allow it."

I still didn't understand. What was happening?

"There's someone under this table," an officer said. In horror, I turned to find the hazel-eyed man I'd helped just minutes ago. Those eyes were fully awake now. He lifted up the tablecloth and pointed to my father.

"No!" I cried. "Don't hurt him."

"Who's this?" Richard ripped the tablecloth away. The remainder of the centerpiece and dishes flew in an arc. A clattering of broken pieces rang out, followed by a moment of silence.

"Please don't hurt him," I begged. "None of this is his fault."

Faulk appeared. I hadn't seen her in a while, and she strode up as if she had conquered the world, all confidence and pride. She sneered down at my father. He still hadn't said anything. His hands were up, but his eyes were trained on me. They never broke from me.

"That's Jessa's father," Faulk confirmed, flicking her wrist at him.

Richard laughed. "Are you brazen enough to think you could come back here?" But he got no reply from my father.

"Jessa." Dad's gaze held steady on mine. "No matter what happens to me, I love you. Do you understand? I love you. You are stronger than you know."

I had no words. I reached out to grab him, but someone restrained me.

"Get off me!" I screamed, clawing at the hands. The same officer whose life I'd saved with magic. I looked to Lucas. He would help me, wouldn't he?

"Traitor," Faulk spat at Dad. "We ought to execute him right now."

"Please, think it through, we can't just kill him," Lucas said, his voice somehow calm. "He's Jessa's father."

"Yes," Richard said. "You make a good point, son. As Jessa's father, he makes great leverage, doesn't he? Not to mention he could be full of valuable information about that disgusting Resistance."

I struggled against my captor. "Please."

"Don't you worry, my dear," Richard said. "We'll only put him back where he came from." He winked.

I couldn't say anything to that. It was a test. I wasn't supposed to know that my father had ever away from the kingdom. I was supposed to believe he'd been in holding this whole time. So I just nodded. I felt he wanted me to thank him or something. But I couldn't. I just couldn't! In prison, my father would not be treated well. And to use him as leverage against me? Now that Richard knew what I was capable of, he could use my father to get me to hurt more people.

I was so tired. I was so sad. And shocked. I needed to either puke all over Richard or claw his eyes out!

But mostly, it was anger running through me.

When was I ever going to get away from this awful king? When was I ever going to get to live a life on my own terms? And how in the world had the Resistance attack ended so badly?

It was almost as if Richard had known it was going to happen...

"Take them away," Richard said.

They yanked my father up. He didn't protest as they led him away. He was too smart for that. He couldn't win, everyone knew that. But in that moment, watching them take him away from me, I vowed to find a way to free him. To free all of us.

●

No one knew what to do with themselves the next day. Classes were canceled. The infirmary was filled with officers and waitstaff, sleeping off the last of their injuries. But with enough alchemists helping out already, they didn't need me.

I didn't know what to do.

Mostly, I stayed holed up in my room, trying to sort out the details of the previous day. I couldn't piece it together. It seemed that Richard knew Jasmine was a spy. How? Or he'd at least suspected as much and then used my ability to find out the truth. That seemed more likely. But I still wasn't sure. I felt her loss like I was missing a limb. I kept looking for her, expecting her to be there, and she wasn't.

She was gone.

And those friends I thought I had? Every alchemist I'd come in contact with since that night avoided me. They were afraid. I could see it in their eyes, the way they shifted gazes when I looked at them, and then shifted back to me when I looked away.

They were afraid of the red alchemy.

They were afraid to be the next Jasmine.

They were terrified I would somehow do something to make them suffer at the hands of the royal family. And I didn't blame them. I'd proved what was possible, so they should be afraid. I was dangerous. Lethal. As much as I hated it, it was true. Red alchemy destroyed lives.

I was alone in this burden. But at least I had Lucas. I got up and wandered around the palace, looking for him. He would know what to do. Except, I couldn't seem to find him. I didn't dare go to the royal wing, but I went to our greenhouse, to the gardens outside, and I looked for him in all the usual places. He was nowhere. I even went down to the kitchens and asked the staff if they'd seen him. Nothing.

I finally retreated back to my bedroom. That small dorm room was my safe haven. Even though it wasn't actually that safe, I could pretend. I would avoid the truth—that I was sleeping in the belly of the beast. In the most dangerous place of all. With the most dangerous people.

And I was one of them.

Another invitation greeted me when I walked in the door to my room. I shuffled around the small space, eyeing it suspiciously.

Really, again?

Someone had slid it under the door, like all the ones before it. I should be getting used to this by now. But I wasn't ready for another party, or dinner, or dance, or execution, or whatever the hell this was going to be. I just wanted a night off.

Please join the royal family in their private quarters for dinner. Formal dress. 7 P.M.

A wave of nervous tension rolled over my body. I wanted to see Lucas, but Richard was the last person I wanted to spend another dinner with. Last night's had seriously scarred me for life. And he was holding my father prisoner because of it. Jasmine and many others were dead because of it.

What would this one do?

But I did as I was told. I styled my curly hair on top of my head, pinning it into my best version of an up-do. Then I zipped myself into a gold velvety gown I had yet to wear. It clung in all the right places, and I groaned, tired of being on display. I fixed my makeup and slipped my feet into nude pumps.

●

"Doesn't she look regal?" Richard purred as I entered the elegant dining room.

Lucas and his father stood upon my entrance. They were as handsome as ever. It was just the three of us. *Okay, I guess this really is an intimate dinner.* And it made my stomach curl.

"Thank you," I said, my voice flat. I hated this man. I hated what he had done to me. And I hated most of all what he would do to my father. What he *was* doing! But he had all the power at the moment, so once again, I had to smile and pretend like I was the leader of his personal fan club.

"Please, join us." He motioned for me to sit next to his son. His son, whom he had forbidden from me. *Okay, this is weird.*

"I'm dreadfully sorry about last night," Richard continued. "Horrific business, isn't it? But sometimes what must be done must be done."

I nodded. My neck felt stiff, and I rubbed at it, pressing hard.

"Father," Lucas said, his face blushing. "Why don't we talk about something else?"

Lucas rarely blushed. I eyed him, once again getting the feeling that something wasn't right. Why was he blushing?

"Of course. Where are my manners?"

Good question, Your Royal Highness!

We talked about the weather. The upcoming holiday. The war, though that was mostly Richard's doing. We talked about anything we could besides what was really on everyone's minds: the night previous and all that it meant for us.

I pushed the food around my plate, hardly able to eat despite the warm texture of the potatoes and the juicy flavor of the seared steak. I'd grown used to the decadence of palace food. The novelty was growing old. I longed for a simple meal of pasta and vegetables, or even bread with cheese would suffice. The type of food I used to eat regularly with my family.

"I hear congratulations are in order." Richard turned his charm on and pointed it right at me. His eyes twinkled, but they'd never lost that calculating shine. I was beyond the point of ever caring what this man thought of me.

"Congratulations on what?" It was possible he was talking about joining the guardians, but I doubted it. He'd already congratulated me on that multiple times. This was something more.

"Your engagement." Richard smiled. He took a sip of his wine, studying me.

"What are you talking about?" I sputtered, sucking in a sharp breath.

He knew about me and Lucas? There was no one else. But everything between Lucas and I wasn't official. No, it was a secret. He had to figure out how to end it with Celia first. He had to convince his father...

"Yes, Lucas told me all about it. Your...love."

I turned on Lucas, incredulous. He paled and reached out to grab my hand. "It's okay," he whispered into my ear. "He's okay with it." I breathed in and out, but the oxygen just wasn't filling my lungs fast enough.

"I thought we mentioned this last night?" Richard asked. "Oh, but last night was all such a blur, wasn't it? Well, in any event, I've decided to be supportive of the union. I think you'll make a wonderful queen, certainly an asset to our kingdom."

What. Is. Happening? A ringing sensation began to sound in my ears.

"I'm sorry." I shook my head. "I don't understand. Lucas is engaged to Celia. Isn't he?" I stared down at our clasped hands. Mine didn't look right in his anymore.

"I'm afraid not," Richard sighed. "Of course, we had to keep that appearance up last night. I just had to make sure Lucas would hold up his end of the deal. That he was telling the truth. Of course, you understand."

Lucas squeezed my hand again. I ripped it away.

"No, I don't understand." The room began to spin.

"When Lucas came to me offering information about the Resistance's little assassination attempt in exchange for your hand, it was a deal too good to pass up."

The whole world crashed. My heart sputtered, then stopped. I gasped, and I also couldn't breathe. I stared at Lucas, taking in every inch of him. I needed an explanation. This couldn't be. He smiled, but it didn't reach his eyes. They were dark. Regretful. And also…hopeful. No!

I tore my gaze away and doubled over.

"Anything for love, isn't that right?" Richard laughed. "It turned out my son had heard a thing or two around the palace and had caught wind of the timing of that little attack last night. So, it was the perfect opportunity for me to end the Resistance, as they called themselves. Such poor souls. They never stood a chance. I really don't know what they were thinking, teaming up with West America like that. No matter. They're gone now."

I sat frozen. Numb.

"Well," Richard said, patting his mouth with his napkin. "I'll leave you two lovebirds alone." Then he met my gaze, winked, and stood. "If you need me, I'll be with the officers. We have quite a bit of planning to do. Not to mention, interrogations to continue."

He left.

We sat in silence.

"I'm sorry," Lucas finally said, his voice scratchy. "I never meant for it to get that far out of hand."

"How could you?" I whispered, anger clawing at my throat. "I trusted you." And that was what hurt the most.

Lucas turned on me then, gripping my hands again. "I love you. I was desperate. My wedding was only months away, and I had to be with you. I never expected that many people to show up. I had no idea your father would come."

"But you knew he was with them. You knew there might've been a chance!"

"No. He shouldn't have been there. He wasn't trained. It was stupid of me to do it, I know. I'm so sorry. I just thought that I would help my father get the upper hand in *one* attack. And I used that as a bargaining chip for you and me to be together."

"And then what?"

"Then we would figure it out. I would figure out how to fix everything, but we'd be together. And that's all that matters, right? That we're together now."

Nausea bubbled in my stomach. "No, that is not all that matters."

"Don't you love me? I did this for you, Jessa."

"Our love killed twenty people last night. Our love killed Jasmine! Our love is disgusting. I can't love you anymore. It's poison." I shot up so fast my chair crashed to the floor.

"Please Jessa." Lucas stood, his tone accusatory. "You're being unfair."

Betrayal ripped through me. Unfair? He had a lot of nerve talking to me about unfair. He had ruined everything!

"Don't you trust me? I'm telling you the truth," he continued. But I knew there was nothing he could say to fix this. "I'd have never done it if I'd known it would've ended like that. I didn't know they were going to send in all those people. I didn't know that was going to happen."

"But you did it. You still did it!" The words exploded from my mouth. "You betrayed my trust. Everything I told you, you took it to your dad."

"No! Not everything!"

"You said enough," I said. "Enough for Jasmine to be dead."

"I never mentioned her."

Lies...

"Enough for others to have died, in vain. Enough for my father to be in prison. Probably under interrogation right now. Probably being tortured!"

"We will help him," Lucas growled. "We can do anything together. Don't you believe in us?" A blood vessel pulsed in his forehead. He looked like Richard.

"You don't get it," I snapped. "You don't get anything I'm saying. If I can't trust you, then we can't be together."

His face darkened. "Nothing I ever do will be good enough for you."

"My father is probably going to die because of you. Others died because of you. I'll probably never see my mother or my sister again because of you, because you're so selfish, because you're so blinded by what you want. Because you're just like your father!"

He stilled. "Fine," he said. "Consider us over. You can go now."

"You don't need to tell me twice," I snarled, stomping out of the room and slamming the door behind me.

A fire ignited within me. The rage. The anger. How could he betray me like that? He was supposed to love me, and yet he could take something I'd told him in confidence and turn it over to his father. He knew how much the Resistance meant to me. He knew that was the only reason why I was still at the palace. I'd told him about the attack only out of concern for his safety. And he'd used it against me.

I would take this love and turn it into revenge.

I would burn it.

Bury it.

And no matter what, I would never trust him again.

"**Come with me,**" Faulk called, pounding on my door.

The night had been spent in a fire of rage, and I'd woken to an inferno. I'd gotten dressed and then stomped around my room in circles. I didn't leave it. What was the point? The palace was a mess, and I wasn't going to willingly participate in the clean up. I was done playing nice.

I climbed off the bed and stormed to swing the door open for Faulk.

"What?" I spat.

She raised an eyebrow. "Come." Then she took off down the hall.

I followed, hot on her heels. People stared at me as we passed them. I didn't care. Let them stare. I may have appeared broken to some, but I was stronger than ever inside. I'd spent the night thinking through everything, going over every angle in my head. I had painstakingly accounted for all the pain the people in this palace done to me.

Reliving it all, again and again.

Driving the heartache in.

Drowning in the anger.

And I was resolved. I was going to end the royal family, even if it ended me.

I followed her to a lift, and we descended. I'd been this way before. We were going to the dungeons. Well, I guessed it was technically called the prison. In my mind it was "the dungeons" since this was a deplorable palace. Even the very land it sat on was tainted by greed. Maybe they were going to lock me up? At this point, I wouldn't even care.

We walked down a hall and a rotting scent filled my nostrils. It was covered up by antiseptic, but not well enough. A female moan echoed from the far end of the hall.

"We have somebody we want you to meet."

"Okay." I nodded. *Let's get this over with...*

I noted that we were in the vicinity of the gray rooms. These were the sorry places the officers used to keep alchemists away from their own magic. I had been in these rooms. I felt a nudge of guilt for the alchemist I was about to find behind the door. Resistance, no doubt.

We walked inside.

The girl's blond hair hung heavily in her face. She was handcuffed to a chair, and, as expected, dressed in black. She peered up at me. Recognition lit her eyes.

It was Sasha.

"I already know her," I said to Faulk, sounding bored. "You said you wanted me to meet somebody. She is nobody new. So why am I really here?"

"Oh." Faulk laughed. It wasn't a pretty sound. "I guess I should've said meet *again*. In a new light. Under different circumstances."

"Fine," I said, striding into the room.

Sasha had bruises forming on her cheeks, some yellow and others a shiny, dark purple. There were a few cuts as well. The one that cut across her eyebrow looked deep enough to scar. Her eyes still revealed the friend I knew, though. Maybe I could help her.

Once inside, the door closed, and I turned back on Faulk. "What do you want?"

"Jessa." Faulk smiled. "I'd like for you to meet your *older sister*, Francesca. I think it's time the two of you were properly reacquainted."

The words rang in my ear, taking a moment to settle in. This made no sense. I shot my gaze to Sasha.

She just stared back at me, not a glimmer of surprise in her face.

Her blue eyes reflected my own.

I stumbled backward.

Francesca? A dream assaulted me. Not a dream, a flash of memory. A girl running through the grass. Blond hair streaming behind her. A dandelion in her small hand. Yellow magic twinkling in the air between us.

My sister.

BLACKOUT

THE COLOR ALCHEMIST BOOK THREE

ONE

SASHA

My head whipped back as the officer's knuckles cracked across my cheek. Pain exploded from the impact, jarring my consciousness. I sucked back a strangled cry, gritting my teeth and blinking rapidly. *I refuse to beg for relief.*

The coppery taste slid down the back of my tongue, thick as syrup.

"You're wasting your time," I growled, spitting the blood onto the concrete floor. It splattered like ink on paper. I shifted in the uncomfortable metal chair, careful not to tug at the handcuffs. They'd been biting into my wrists for far too long. Red rings of angry flesh wrapped around each, stinging like crazy. "I'm not telling you anything."

"Again," Faulk remarked coolly. I glared up through puffy eyes at where she stood in the corner of the small room. A punch landed in the next second, the same spot as before, doubling the pain. I held back a sob as something in my face gave way. The crack rang through my head and my vision blacked out for an excruciating minute.

"If you break my jaw, then I really can't talk," I gasped.

The officer struck again, unperturbed. I yelped, tears burning my eyes, and scowled at the man. He held no emotion. His expression was stoic, a machine ready to strike on command. No, it was Faulk who was causing this, even if her hands weren't exacting the blows. Blood was splattered across his white uniform. Hers was pristine, but she was anything but clean in this matter.

"Oh Sasha, don't be so naïve." She grinned, stepping closer. Then she cackled, a strange sound for such a hard woman. "I'm sorry, perhaps you'd prefer to be called Francesca? Oh wait, no…that's not right. I seem to recall you went by Frankie. You always were a bit of a tom-boy."

I turned away. Her boots clomped across the room until she was face to face with me, leaning down to glower. Wrinkles spread around her eyes. Her lips were thin and her complexion ashen, but something in her eyes gleamed. Didn't she ever get tired of this?

"Wake up, you fool!" she spat. "If we break your stupid jaw, we can have a guardian heal you. And then we can break you all over again. And again. And again. And again."

Of course, I knew that! Still, hearing it spoken aloud sent a shiver of fear down my spine.

Bam! Her fist slammed against my jaw, and my vision blurred. I gasped and fought the urge to cry. No, she would not get the better of me.

"You'd be better off to talk now." She leaned close and her icy cool breath swept across my burning face. "Before we try…other means. You know, eventually you will talk. And you know what our alchemists are capable of."

I glared up at her through wild strands of hair hanging limp in my face. She was right. Without any color to grasp onto in this prison cell, I couldn't pull on my magic. And enough blue sent my way would have me talking. I didn't even want to think about what they would do if and when they made Jessa use red alchemy on me.

It would all be over.

I shook my head. "There's nothing to tell," I rasped. "You caught us! You won. Now move on."

"Don't patronize me." Then she pranced toward the door. She lifted her hand to push her way through and turned her head nonchalantly to call back to her hulking underling. "Again."

There was no time to brace myself. His fist pummeled my face, my rib cage, my arms and chest, over and over. He was huge, muscles bulging, teeth bared, and he held nothing back. A guttural cry escaped my lips as the pain enveloped me, tormenting me in a never ending agony. The overwhelming stench of blood became too much, and soon, I choked on its heaviness.

What did I hate more? The pain? Or my own weakness? I didn't know anymore. I couldn't think anymore.

The darkness spilled over.

▼

A barking cough echoed through the room, waking me with a start.

I blinked rapidly, focusing on the source of the noise.

Christopher.

The lights were bright this time, assaulting my vision. My scream caught in my throat when I saw him, sounding helplessly in my head. He was Christopher, my father, but his face was barely recognizable under the immense swelling and cacophony of colorful bruises. He'd been beaten to a pulp. He sat hunched over on his own metal chair, also handcuffed.

"Are you okay?" I winced as the skin around my mouth stretched the wounds that had accumulated, one on top of the other.

He sat up, an agonizing groan escaping his swollen lips. He took in the full extent of my injuries, and sadness filled the space between his puffy eyes. Finally, he nodded. "I'm alive. We're alive. That's better than what I was expecting. Frankie, I'm so sorry..."

I froze, the use of my real name sinking in deep.

"They could still kill us, you know." I sighed, still stuck on the "we're alive" bit. I wasn't holding out hope that would still be the case once they got what they wanted from us.

"True." He swallowed hard. "But as long as they need information from us, then we're still breathing. We have to hold onto that."

I scoffed. "I guess so." While being beaten to within an inch of my life was technically still living, it wasn't what I'd had in mind when we'd first raided the palace. We should have known better. Of course, the whole thing had been a trap. Richard wasn't going to let us walk in and take the place.

"I'm sorry," he said again.

"For what?" But I already knew.

My teeth ached and it hurt to talk, but somehow, after everything I'd endured over the last couple of days, this conversation felt like salvation.

"For not listening to you. For coming in here unprepared. If it hadn't been for me, you'd have gotten out with your friends."

I wasn't about to argue with him. "Well, they caught a bunch of us, didn't they? It's not all your fault."

He shifted in his chair, the legs grinding on the concrete. He was dressed in the prison gray cottons, same as me, dried blood also splotched across the overly starched material. The collar of his shirt was torn, revealing the sweaty sheen of his chest. Swollen eyes squinted from his bruised face and bits of flaky blood crusted his wispy head of hair.

"But I heard the guards talking before they moved me in here with you," he said, the bruises stretching like taffy as he talked. "The other alchemists don't know the exact coordinates of the resistance camp. They killed Cole's guys and mostly everyone who got trapped in there. I was spared, you, some alchemists..."

"What's your point?" I really didn't want to relive our terrible failure. We almost had him. Cole had his gun pointed right at Richard but then...

The image of his body jerking and blood spraying outward from the impact of the bullet flashed through my mind. I closed my eyes and pushed it away, despite the rise of vomit that burned in my throat.

"My point is, I don't even have all the details they need to find the camp. I wasn't told all the specifics, I just know we were in Canada. You're the only one they have who knows exactly where the camp is. I think that's why they decided to stick me in here." He leaned forward, his arms also shackled to a chair, and glanced around the small gray room, eyes landing on the door. The room was empty except for the two of us and our godforsaken chairs.

"Figures," I muttered, glancing up. The lights burned bright as I stared at my distorted reflection in the metal ceiling. My attention turned to the gray walls, the floor of polished concrete, and the singular metal door. I fought hard against the rise of panic in my chest, but it was starting to get the better of me. I was trained to handle this kind of situation, and it still was wearing on my faith.

They knew who I was. They knew everything.

"What happened to you?" Christopher asked. I jumped, startled by his voice but more than that, I was nervous to answer him. *Doesn't he deserve to know? If you don't tell him, someone else will.*

I rolled my lip between my teeth for a moment and then spoke. "I'd originally been a color alchemist at the palace. After I got sent away from home." I couldn't meet his eyes when I said that part. The shame was still buried deep. "But I had been rescued from the Guardians by Hank and Tristan. It was while on assignment when I was only ten-years-old. That's how we'd ended up in the camp in the first place."

Silence stretched between us and I finally met his eyes. His were filled with regret. Even with the bruises and cuts, I could see that clear as day. "I came back into New Colony about six years later, undercover with a new name, Sasha. It worked, too. I eventually came to the palace and worked directly with Jasmine."

"Jasmine?"

"She died," I ground out the two words that hurt just as bad as the pain in my jaw. "Anyway, I had to blow that cover in order to help someone." That someone was Jessa, but I knew better than to say that here. She was still undercover. "Once I disappeared, I'm assuming the officers dug into my past and figured out who I really am. Faulk knows my real name, and that you're my father."

A lone tear fell down his face. "I'm so sorry," he said. "None of that should have been your weight to bear."

I shrugged and looked away.

The officers also knew I was a red alchemist. Well, I used to have that curse. I'd been able to successfully block it for years, but that wouldn't stop Richard from trying to rip it out of me again.

"I'm here because I'm their leverage," my father said, bringing me back to the moment. "Little do they know, I don't mean anything to you anymore."

"That's not true," I snapped.

He stilled, and I refused to say more. Yes, I was still mad about my past. But in light of everything that had happened, I was realizing that maybe I actually did want to be part of a family again.

Maybe.

I wasn't making any promises.

The door swung open, and Faulk strode in with an ugly conspiratorial smile ruining her face. "Of course you still mean something to her," she said to Christopher. "You are her father. No one could ever replace you."

"So then why take me away from my family? Why do that to little children?" I yelled, anger swelling as I tugged on the cuffs. The need to punch Faulk right in her beaky nose overwhelmed me. I imagined her crumpling to the cement floor, her head smacking it with a thud. I'd jump on top of her and match every single blow that she'd ordered on me and my father, until she begged for mercy.

The scene played out before me, but reality?

Reality sucked.

She glanced at me briefly, smiled, and then turned back to Christopher. "How are you feeling this morning?" She chirped. What was this? Good cop, bad cop?

I growled. "Morning? How long have I been passed out? Forget that, how long have I even been in this prison?"

She didn't bother to look at me as she ignored the questions. Living inside a gray box was not a fun thing for anyone, let alone an alchemist. But still, I hoped it had been days. My friends needed to get out of that camp. Innocent people would be caught and punished because of my stupid mistakes. Faulk was right: eventually she would get to the truth. But I would do everything in my power to make sure it was too late when she finally did.

"What do you want?" Christopher and I asked Faulk, at the same time.

She moved further into the cramped room, and a couple of her henchmen followed. They slammed the door shut and the space got tighter, the air thick and hot.

"Don't play dumb." She sighed. "You both know what I want. Sasha is going to tell us where the camp is."

"No, she isn't," Christopher said just as I snapped, "No I'm not."

I nodded my quick approval toward the man.

"We'll see about that," she purred, then flicked her bony wrist toward Christopher. Two hulking men strode toward him, arms raised, preparing to strike. He didn't cower.

"This is Jose," she pointed to one of the men. "And this is Carter." She pointed to the other. "They are two of my best officers, known for their fighting ability."

I glared at the men and quipped, "Pleased to meet you."

"It's not really a fair fight, though, is it?" She winked at Christopher and shrugged. "Oh, well."

"Wait!" I snapped.

She paused and turned, a smile playing at her lips. My eyes shot to Christopher, who was shaking his head. "Don't…"

"Just kidding." I smiled. "I'm only messing with you. Go ahead. Beat him. Beat me. Do your best, but it won't matter. I'm not telling you anything."

Crunch. A fist pounded across his face, and he cried out, ragged, as the men delivered punches that fell one upon the other. I flinched, but held my ground. It was what we both wanted. Besides, they could heal him if they needed to.

"Enough," Faulk said.

The room grew quiet, and she glared at me, her gaze cold and calculated.

"Bring her in."

The man she introduced as Jose threw open the door, and Jessa stood frozen on the other side. Her face was white as paper. Her eyes widened as she took in the extent of our horrible wounds. We were in huge trouble.

"What have you done to them?" she whispered and wiped at the tears that had immediately sprung to her eyes. They fell down her pale cheeks as she ran toward Dad. *Get it together, girl!* Jessa was apparently the emotional one in the family, but now was not the time

"They're traitors," Faulk replied. Jessa already knew that. Not only was she a part of our Resistance, but she was well aware that her parents and little sister had fled New Colony months ago. *My* parents and little sister, too.

And she knew who I was. Faulk had already brought her in the first day I'd been locked up in here to rub the news in everyone's faces.

"They have information we need," Faulk explained, "and, as you can see, we've exhausted our traditional means of extracting that information."

"And that's why I'm here?" She questioned, her voice squeaking. "But it could hurt them."

Red alchemy. How long could we drag this thing out? Would I be able to resist Jessa? I didn't have access to any color, and I wasn't able to do anything with white. I wasn't that talented.

Lucas, on the other hand…if only he were here. Leave it up to the prince to never be in the right place at the right time.

"Think of it this way," Faulk said. "If you don't do it, they'll only be hurt more. If you do what you're meant to do, what you were just initiated to do, then not only can we all move on with our lives, but we can heal their wounds."

"And then what?" I asked. "What happens to us then? You're not just going to let us go. Jessa, think about it." I turned on her. "Once they have what they need from us, we're as good as dead."

She glanced back and forth between us, her eyes somehow even wider than before. She was beautiful and sweet, to be sure, but at that moment, all I saw was weakness and I wanted to slap her for it.

"Don't do it!" I begged. "Refuse. She can't make you!"

"Shut up," Faulk roared. She motioned to her officers once again and this time, the pair separated, one coming at each of us.

The pain was nothing this time. Actually, it was awful, but it was nothing compared to the knowledge that I was right. I closed my eyes as Jose's fists pummeled me, forcing my mind into silence.

"We. Can. Take. It," Christopher gasped out between blows. "Sasha is right!"

"You have sworn an oath of loyalty to the royal family over all else!" Faulk yelled at Jessa. "Take this knife and take care of it, immediately!"

The pain kept coming, but Jessa did not. She'd backed up against the far wall, covering her face as she silently cried. Her tall, slender frame shuddered with her sobs as the emotions overtook her.

"Do it!" Faulk walked right up to her and dragged her back to us. Red splotches blossomed across Jessa's cheeks as she continued to cry. Faulk was right up in her face now, ready to explode.

"No," Jessa replied, finally ripping her arm free from Faulk's angry grasp. "I can't! Not until I have confirmation that you won't hurt them anymore, that you won't kill them."

Faulk laughed, shoulders bouncing, head down, and the sound anything but entertained. "I can't do that."

"Then I can't use red alchemy. I won't!"

"That's my girl," Christopher muttered. The officer that had been beating him responded with a punch to his face so hard that his body went limp. His head tipped, his arms dangled at his sides, the cuffs scraping against the metal chair.

I glared up at the two men, memorizing their faces. One day I would repay them for what they'd done, Faulk being first in line, of course.

Jessa was screaming and had crawled to Dad's feet. "Stop hurting them!"

"You know what we need. Get it, or we will beat them until they are dead!"

"No you won't," I challenged. "You need our information first!"

"I only need one of you," she replied, "and I'm guessing that one is you. Tell me why I shouldn't just end this man right now and get it over with?"

"Because"—Jessa jumped up and stood nose-to-nose with Faulk—"because he's my father. You're sick! You know that? You're truly sick to use him against us like this. I'll help you, okay, I said I'll help you, but I need a guarantee first."

"And how would you like me to do that?" Faulk spat.

They were toe-to-toe, wills battling. Faulk had the leverage, but Jessa was the one with the power. They needed her, and if she refused, what could they really do?

"Get Richard," I interjected. "Get him to agree to it."

Another fist slammed against the side of my face, followed by a ringing penetrating my head. I fought to regain control, to keep present in the moment.

To keep fighting.

Jessa stepped back from Faulk. "Sounds good to me. Let's get the king. You know he's my future father-in-law, right?"

Did I hear that right? I shook my head, trying to follow.

Faulk's cool exterior had cracked. She huffed before grabbing Jessa by the arm and dragging her from the room. I caught Jessa's determined expression and knew this wasn't over. The two officers followed like trained dogs. The door slammed, the lights cut out, and I was left to catch stilted breaths.

▼

The ambush came masquerading as mercy.

A light tugging on my hair caused the pain to heighten. I blinked, willing the exhaustion away. Something warm and wet slid across my face.

"Careful—" I sputtered, before she hushed me with the gentle press of her finger to my swollen lips.

"Hold still, we're going to get you cleaned up and healed in no time," Jessa said. Her voice was soft as comfort, like a mountain breeze. Just the thought made me long for home, for the pine scent and the stillness of the air.

Wait…

"What happened?" I forced myself back into the moment. I'd been dozing off when Jessa and another girl dressed as an alchemist shuffled into the cramped room. They had kneeled down before Christopher and me, warm rags in their hands. Rags now soaked through with blood.

"Shhh," Jessa said. "We're here to take care of you."

"Did I talk?" I asked. "Did something happen? Why are you here?"

It had to be. I must have been victimized by red alchemy and ordered to forget the whole thing ever happened. Why else would these two be in here helping us after the way Faulk had dragged Jessa out earlier?

Oh, no. All those people...

"Maybe we should heal them first and then we'll finish cleaning them off." The girl spoke with a gentle meekness that was unusual for a guardian. Her blonde, curly hair caught the light, creating a halo effect around her heart-shaped face. She wore thick-rimmed glasses that glinted as she turned a tentative smile my way. A familiar knowing flickered between us. She was one of the nicer teen alchemists I'd met during my recent time at the palace. Her name was lost to me now.

"Good idea." Jessa nodded, and the two girls hauled a potted plant over to us. It landed with a thud between Christopher and me. I longed to reach out to the green for relief. But, as I tried to lift my arm, the sharp pain in my shoulder felt like a million knives ripping it apart. Christopher was still unconscious, slumped in his chair, battered and beaten to someone now unrecognizable as my father.

"And after we get you out of here," Jessa said, putting one hand on the plant and reaching out to rest the other gently on my shoulder, "we'll get you changed and you can take a proper shower. I bet you're starving, huh? And when was the last time they took you to the bathroom?"

I shook my head. I had no idea but that didn't matter right now.

"Jessa," I begged as the magic worked its way into my body, filling me with healing energy. It was warm, wandering through my veins and calming all the hurt places. "Why are you allowed in here? What did I do? Did I talk?"

She paused then whispered low, "You didn't talk. No, it's not that. It's King Richard. He wants all the new alchemists down here in the prison to come up and meet him."

A glance passed between her and her friend, who was now busy taking care of our father's wounds and subsequent healing. I had to assume the girl didn't know the full extent of what was happening here, even though she could probably make an educated guess. I mean, she knew I had pretended to be someone I wasn't, everyone did by now. Jessa raised her eyebrows at me, her blue eyes bugging out. She didn't want us to say more in front of the girl. It would have to be enough for now. At least I hadn't talked.

I think. Maybe? Ugh, this is all getting to be too much.

Christopher stirred, and Jessa turned her attention on him. They hugged and talked quietly between each other while we waited.

A few minutes later, the four of us were escorted out of the prison and up into one of the finer areas of the palace. Armed guards swarmed us. In fact, they seemed to be everywhere, more than I'd ever seen here before. They normally blended in with the shadows, eyes always watching. But now they were patrolling, walking up and down the halls, guns at the ready.

Jessa, Dad, and I were brought into a generic but tastefully decorated suite, and dumped behind a locked door.

"Now what?" I asked, turning on Jessa.

"Now you two need to hurry and shower, eat, and get ready to meet with the king," she replied simply.

My chest hurt even considering the idea of facing Richard again, especially with Christopher here. But my stomach far outweighed that. The scent of cheese caught my nostrils and I dug into the tray of food while Dad took the shower first.

Chewing on a few raisins, I moved to stand by the window and stared out. It felt wonderful to see the sun, to have the pain gone and my belly full. But the undercurrent of fear threatened to take all that away any second.

The worry plagued me as I showered and dressed in the familiar black guardian outfit. Richard was up to something. Whatever it was, it couldn't be good.

The three of us left together, ready or not, to find out what that something was.

The second we stepped from the sanctuary of the room, we were met with opposition. "You can wait back here, please Sir," an officer said to Christopher. I recognized him as Jose, a man who's fists I knew sickeningly well. "You're not an alchemist." To know he'd beaten us only hours earlier, and was now tasked to guard my father, angered me completely. A shrill scream of anger threatened to escape me. More than anything, I wanted to beat this idiot down to a bloody mess.

"But if it concerns my daughters, it concerns me," Christopher challenged, his lips set in a grim line.

"No, sir, you are, under no circumstances, permitted to meet with the king today," the officer replied, stepping to stand in front of Christopher and block his path down the palace hallway. The two men glared at each other. Similar in stature, neither was about to back down. One had a gun, but the other had two magical, badass daughters. So really, if anyone asked me, there was no contest.

"It's okay, Dad," Jessa said, her voice calm and collected. "I'd rather you weren't there for this, whatever *this* is. I'll come find you afterward."

He gave her a stiff nod and sauntered back into the suite.

As Jessa and I walked down the hallway, escorted again by a pair of armed officers, I picked out other alchemists who were also being escorted by officers. They were the ones who had trained with me back at camp and joined in on the attack. Not all of them had been captured, but there were enough to leave me feeling ashamed. They avoided eye contact with me, their pace steady as they walked ahead. At least they looked clean and healthy. Hopefully, they'd been spared the pain I'd endured these past few days. These people were innocent and knew nothing that could help Faulk.

But that didn't mean she wouldn't punish them, or that Richard wouldn't ruin their lives. They'd stood against New Colony, and there would be a price to pay.

We were herded to the back of a ballroom. It was different from where we'd been arrested. It was much smaller, probably meant for more intimate gatherings. Just as decadent as the rest of the palace, with a gold chandelier that immediately caught the eye. It centered the room and dripped in gaudy crystals that reflected against the white marble floors. Gilded mirrors lined the walls, giving the room an endless look. I peered at the familiar faces, counting seven of us dressed in black, not including Jessa.

A pang of guilt gripped me as I locked gazes with the young Sam. Her black hair blended in with her clothing. She held her small frame in the same haughty stance, and her eyes pinned me down with a mixture of equal parts distrust and hope. Part of her still saw me as a leader. But most of her knew I wasn't even close to holding that title anymore.

The energy in the room stilled as two guards opened a large set of doors with a soft swish. Richard strode in, his steps purposeful, his dark eyes set on our group. Lucas followed a few steps behind, his head bowed, but his broad shoulders confident. He glanced up and looked directly at Jessa. Oh, yes, he was the same gorgeous guy I remembered, but he looked different somehow. Harder. Sadder.

Definitely sadder.

Wait, hadn't Jessa said something to Faulk about being engaged to Lucas right before I'd passed out? I made a mental note to ask Jessa about the status of their relationship as soon as I got the chance.

"It's been a long day and I'm tired of playing games, so I'm only going to say this once." Richard stood tall. "The sole reason you're still alive after attacking my family in my own home, is because you are alchemists. Perhaps, in West America, you were forced to endure savagery. Perhaps, they forced you to come after New Colony as if you were their child slaves."

There was a long pause as his words sunk into the group.

His lip curled into a smile and he continued. "In my kingdom we treat alchemists with nothing but respect."

Jessa had inched closer to me. She reached out and squeezed my hand. I waited. The urge to speak out and correct him burned inside, but Jessa tempered it with her steady grip. She was right. Play it cool. I didn't want to get kicked out before Richard got to the point of this showy speech.

"In New Colony, our citizens are well taken care of. We're prosperous, happy, and we're stable." Richard brushed off the collar of his velvet jacket, the gold buttons catching in the light as he began to step closer to us.

The room stirred, curiosity buzzing.

"I'm inviting you to choose one of two options," he continued. "You can join us, train with us, and pledge your loyalty to New Colony. If you choose that option, you'll renounce any and all affiliation with West America. And you will never want for anything again. You will live in our palace and enjoy your magical gifts the way God intended."

Oh, what does this man know about God? I dug my heels into the floor.

"What's the other option?" someone called from the back. The group stirred uncomfortably as the King frowned.

"The other option is you remain a prisoner of war."

Silence. I squeezed Jessa's hand so hard she had to pull it from my grip.

"Either way we're prisoners," I said, bursting forward, unable to listen to his lies any longer. I shook my head in fury. *He really thinks he can schmooze us over so easily?*

"Oh, Frankie." Richard replied, casually walking forward to meet me, "how I've missed you. Though I must admit I could do without the sass. It's too bad you never grew out of that. I was so angry at myself for not realizing who you were the first time you came back to us." His eyes traveled the length of my body, and my stomach churned. "But you really have changed, haven't you? All grown up and as feisty as ever. No worries, we'll wear that out of you eventually."

"Tell them what you did to me," I said, motioning to the group. "Tell them how you took me from my family as a child, how you forced me to work for you, to manipulate and *kill* for you."

"Oh, are you talking about that poor boy that you pushed off the roof?" He asked with a tilt of his head.

A wave of prickling guilt washed over me. "I didn't push him."

"Oh, right," he replied, "semantics."

The memory of the officer in training who'd jumped to his death the day I got away was something I'd never been able to get over. He'd tried to stop us and was willing to do anything to make that happen. My red alchemy had been too strong, and I'd accidently killed him.

"You were untrained and powerful," Richard sighed with sympathy. "Your training was for your own good. And those deaths, they were an accident, an unfortunate result of an unknown alchemy." He smiled again. "Let's put the past behind us, shall we?"

"Never," I replied.

"Very well. Anyone else want to join her in the prison again?"

I spun around. "You can't trust him. He'll ruin your life."

But the sea of faces were awash with pale fear, and even some indignant anger. Nobody moved. "Seriously," I cried, "he's evil. You can't agree to work for him. He'll use you to kill innocent people. He did it to me!"

"Get her out of here," Richard ordered, and within seconds I was yanked from the room. Jessa's sorry blue eyes were the last things I saw as the doors slammed behind me. Dressed in black, and with no color near, I was dragged back through the palace and into the stale prison below.

"Hello again," I said bitterly to the walls of the same forsaken, gray prison cell.

"I hope you rot in here," said one of the guards who'd so generously led me down here. I glanced back to glare as he spat on the floor and slammed the door. *Dramatic, much?*

I huffed and sank to the floor. In his eyes, Richard had offered me "redemption" and I had refused. There would be retaliation even greater than anything I'd experienced before. I prayed there had been enough time for the camp to have cleared out. Tristan and Mastin had gotten away that night of the attack. I was certain they'd gone back to help everyone flee.

It will be okay. They still have time, even now.

I relaxed against the wall and waited for the inevitable. Sure enough, not even an hour later, it came.

The door flew open with a gush of cool air, and Richard barged in. Lucas, Jessa, Faulk, Christopher, and a few officers followed. The room was filled beyond capacity, but at least this time I wasn't handcuffed to the stupid chair. It was across the room, and I wished it was closer, just so I could throw it at the king.

"What do you want?" I snapped, though I already knew. I stood, arms folded.

"Tell us what we need to know this minute," Richard barked. "And don't you dare lie. We have helicopters in the suspected area. We're armed and ready. We'll know soon if you're telling the truth."

"Oh, and what is it you want to know?" I asked sarcastically. My voice was cool but already I was scanning the people in the room, looking for a shred of usable color.

"Don't play cute." He stepped close and stared down at me with hate-filled eyes so dark they were almost black. "Tell us where you've been hiding. Where's Hank Reynolds? Where is your mother, and little sister, and whoever else is with them?"

"I'm not telling you anything!" I yelled right in his face. Changing my tone had startled him and I smirked.

"Tell us now or I will kill this father of yours without a second thought." He reached out and Officer Faulk handed him a black handgun. His fingers curled around it, and he pointed it right at my father.

"No!" Jessa and I screamed together.

"Don't tell him anything," Christopher said. He moved his hands slowly above his head and kept his eyes on me. Richard *would* kill him if he had to. Richard would do anything to get what he wanted. We both knew it.

"Father, there's got to be another way," Lucas said, voice cracking. He moved from where he'd been standing next to Jessa moments earlier.

"Nice of you to join us, Lucas," I growled. I owed him nothing.

"Lucas, if you're ever going to be able to live up to the responsibility of being a king you've got to learn how to make people obey your commands," his father said. "Frankie *will* tell us everything."

Christopher met my eyes again and nodded slowly. It wasn't confirmation for Richard. It was confirmation for me. I wasn't saying a word. Richard grabbed Christopher and shoved him to his knees between us. He went down without so much as a cry. Then, Richard held the barrel of the gun to the back of my father's head.

I needed to think, to find a way out of this. But panic began to overtake me as I realized there was nothing I could do.

"Tell me now or he's dead."

I caught the determined gleam in my father's eye, recognized the acceptance, and I knew, I just knew. He would sacrifice himself to save his wife and daughter back at camp. It wasn't even a question for a man like him. Hot tears slid down my cheeks.

"Please, no!" Jessa begged while Lucas held her back, one arm tight around her torso. She clawed at him and her breath became ragged as she lost control of her emotions.

Richard glanced at me one more time before his sure gaze landed on Jessa. "It seems I've been going about this from the wrong angle." He chuckled to himself. "Or I should say, wrong sister."

"What?" I shook my head, but he was fully turned on Jessa, completely ignoring me. He kicked Christopher to the ground in front of her.

"Okay, Jessa," he said, "I'll save your father *and* your ungrateful sister if you do one simple thing for me."

"Anything," she whispered between gasping sobs. Her bloodshot eyes shone back at him in eagerness.

"Use your red alchemy," he said. "Get your sister here to tell us what we need to know and they'll both get to stay alive. I won't touch them."

"Don't do it," I shouted, but it was too late. She nodded once, pulled out a dagger from a holster on her belt, and turned on me with bared teeth.

"What are you doing? Jessa, no!"

"I'm sorry," she said, "but I have to. I can't let them kill him."

"Don't do this. Think of the consequences." I slid back against the wall, squatting low and hands fisted, ready to fight her off. "They need more time. Jessa, your mom is there. Lacey is there!"

"It's been two days. Wherever they were before, they're gone by now. They have to be!"

"You don't know that!"

"Please try to understand." She narrowed her eyes, the knife glinting against the bright light. "This is the only way."

Everyone began to descend upon me, with Jessa a viper at the forefront. Quick as a flash, she slashed the dagger at me. I jumped out of the way, narrowly missing her. But when she tried again, it connected in sharp heat against my side.

"Get away from me!" I bellowed, but it was too late.

Her hands were pressing against my shirt and the wet blood already soaking through. The magic shot through me like a feathering of poisoned needles.

No!

"Tell us where they are," she said, her voice steady and calm.

My mind slowed, becoming heavy, and all emotion flat-lined.

The truth spilled from my mouth.

TWO

JESSA

Tears burned my eyes, trailing down my raw cheek. I held on tighter to my emotions and focused on my footsteps clipping the polished floor. Back in my room, I softly closed the door and fell to my knees, curling in on myself in a crying heap. Was Sasha right? Had I really just condemned innocent people to death, including my mom and sister?

No. I have to hold out hope that Mom and Lacey got out of there in plenty of time. I can't think about the alternative, not right now.

The clawing doubt threatened to choke me, but I breathed through it.

Tap. Tap. Someone knocked lightly on the door, and I grimaced.

"Who is it?" I called out. The last thing I wanted was to talk to anybody. I had to be strong— and I was anything but strong right now. My weakness needed to stay hidden in this place, but this was becoming more and more impossible. If King Richard discovered how much he'd affected me today with his threats, he would know exactly how to control me.

Too late, Jessa.

How long until he used Christopher against me again? The memory of violating Sasha like that, slashing her open and taking what I needed, was something I'd never be able to erase. It was as if a piece of my soul was lost.

Just like the night Jasmine died.

Oh Jasmine, I'm so sorry. I miss you so much.

The tapping at the door continued. "Who is it?" I called out again. Couldn't they have answered the first time? I wasn't in the mood for games.

"It's me." Lucas's velvet voice filtered through the door.

Speaking of games!

I lumbered to my feet and brushed myself off. Seriously? Lucas was the last person I wanted to talk to but still, I threw open the door anyway.

"What?" I clipped.

"Are you okay?" His hands were deep in his jean pockets and his shoulders slouched in a blue cotton shirt that complimented his eyes. But dang it, I was not okay!

I bit back my incredulity and forced myself not to laugh in his face. The whole reason any of this happened was because of him! Had he already forgotten? If he hadn't told his father about the Resistance's planned attack, it was likely Dad and Sasha wouldn't be in this mess.

Sister. It was still *so weird* to think that Sasha was Frankie.

"Am I okay? I don't know, Lucas, what do you think?" I glared at him, but still something inside me fought it. It just wanted to erase all the pain and jump into his arms again.

Traitorous feelings. There was no forgiveness here.

He scrunched up his nose, something I used to find adorable, but now only found incredibly annoying. He wanted to say more, but stayed silent.

"Really, what do you want, Lucas?"

"I want to talk."

"There's nothing to talk about." I glanced around the hallway where he stood. We knew alchemists and officers lurked at every corner. It wasn't completely safe to talk inside my small room, but I pulled him inside anyway. The touch of his hand in mine sent a rumble of emotion through me.

Get over it. He can't be trusted!

"You traded in *my* secret because of *your* bad decision. It's not my fault you chose to get engaged to Celia. I wanted to get married to you one day but not if the *only way* to get your father's blessing was to betray me. What were you thinking?"

He opened and closed his mouth, red creeping up his cheeks. He was a man who rarely blushed; this was affecting him. Then something hardened in his expression, and he shook his head. "I told you. I did it for us."

Was he serious?

"Well guess what?" I scoffed. "I don't want to be with somebody who would do that."

The anger that spread through his gray eyes reminded me of an icy frost, killing everything beneath. "Okay," was his only reply.

Okay? That's all he has to say for himself?

"I never would've agreed to it." I looked away, unable to stand the sight of him for a second longer. "I think you knew that, and that's why you went behind my back."

He didn't respond. He didn't move, drop his head in apology, or even try to look regretful. He didn't do *anything*.

I was right. And the truth of it burned deep inside my chest. He'd willingly broken my trust in such a terrible way. Jasmine and many others were dead because of it. The Resistance? Gone. And my family, the people I loved more than anything, were in more danger than ever.

And why? So Lucas and I could be engaged?

My stomach turned over.

"You should leave," I said, about to be sick.

"I just wanted to talk to you." His eyes were hard slits. How was it that his strongest emotion was anger when he was the one who'd hurt me?

"Okay, so we talked, now go away."

He stood there for a long minute. I studied him carefully, the planes of his jaw where stubble was growing through his smooth skin, the slight wrinkling of his brow. The pain in my heart nearly doubled. He finally relaxed, shaking his head, and stepped tentatively toward me. "Can I at least show you something?"

I didn't want to be around him any longer. It was too painful. What could he possibly show me that would matter at this point? But my curiosity was piqued, so against my better judgment, I nodded.

"One second," I said. I dashed to the bathroom to quickly wash my tear-stained face and brush my mess of hair. The curls were wilder than normal after my breakdown on the floor. For a moment, I stopped to study my blotchy cheeks and red-rimmed eyes, the blue irises bright with emotion. So much anger, sadness, and fear shone back at me. I shook my head and went out to meet Lucas, the boy who was responsible for most of that pain.

"This had better be good," I said, irritable as we rounded yet another corner. We'd long since left the GC wing and were in the belly of royal territory. The decadence of the marble floors and gold crown molding brought back memories of the night Lucas and I had become engaged, then the initiation the very next day when everything had fallen to ruin. I swallowed and shook away the memories.

We were nearly at the royals' private apartment, and the heightened security set me on edge. Guards swarmed the area. I was used to at least two practically anywhere I looked in this place, but the numbers were through the roof today. A particularly huge guard with bulging muscles sneered at me and I stumbled. I was seconds from turning tail and running. If Lucas was bringing me to see his father, I would officially lose it!

"In here," he said, opening thick double oak doors and ushering me into a shadowed room.

"I hope I don't regret this," I murmured, but followed him in anyway.

Someone was standing in the middle of the room, her posture oddly familiar. *What is-?*

"Madam Silver," I shrieked. I ran into the outstretched arms of a woman I thought I would never see again. She squeezed me tight, and I melted at the scent of my old ballet studio. The worn wood floors, the baby-soft fabric of the shoes, the balsamic fumes of the cleaner. They were all there, intermixed with her floral perfume. I cried out at the shock.

"What are you doing here?" I asked, stepping back and looking her up and down. Her dark hair hung in a bob cut around her chin, her eyes so dark they were almost black, her skin pale and ageless as ever. She carried a sophisticated attitude everywhere she went, but I knew her better than that. I'd been her student for years. Underneath the cultured exterior was a woman with a heart of gold and a deep love for her dancers. She was like a second mother to me.

"I've missed you, too." She shifted back to look at me and her ruby red lips moved into a smooth smile. "It hasn't been the same without you, Jessa. We've all missed you."

"It's been so hard to be away from dance," I whispered and hugged her again.

"You're telling me? You were my prized pupil. You shocked us all when you turned out to be an alchemist." Her voice rumbled against me, and a prickle of shame overcame me. I'd let her down. I'd let them all down.

"I shocked myself."

I frowned and took a few steps back, putting distance between us. Was she scared of me? Did she hate me for my magic? She must have sensed the worry in my expression because she shook her head and sighed.

"Too much talent for one person," she said with sadness. "It's not fair what happened to you."

She has no idea.

"You still haven't answered me. What are you doing here?" I turned to Lucas and raised my eyebrows. "What is she doing here?"

"I think you're ready to start dancing again," he said simply, the shadows in the room hiding his expression.

Joy burst through me like a sunrise. I was going to get to dance ballet again, and with my favorite teacher! A sense of peace warmed me just thinking about it. No matter what had happened in my life before coming to the palace, I had always had ballet. It was my salvation, the one thing I could do to calm the emotions inside. It was my outlet. My best friend. But I'd had to let it go in order to train as a color alchemist, and I had mourned that best friend every single day since.

"Are you going to work with me? Even though I'm a Color Guardian now?" I spun back to Madam Silver. I hated that I doubted her. But I did. She was normal, and I was the complete opposite. Normal people feared those like me. I'd learned that the second I'd accidently manipulated my stupid lavender ballet costume and the crowd of people had run away in horror.

Of course, the royals hadn't been horrified. They'd seen the opportunity and took it for their own.

"I would be honored to work with you, Jessa." She smiled, the kind that lit her eyes. I practically tackled her when I hugged her. Her petite frame shrunk under my height, but she only laughed.

"When can she start?" Lucas asked.

Madam Silver moved out of my embrace and peered around the space, her professional eye assessing the room. It was nearly perfect. The floors were hardwood, and all the furniture had been cleared. It wasn't quite as big as my old studio, but it would do just fine.

"I can get one of those bar things installed and some mirrors," Lucas continued, moving through the room and pointing to the walls as he talked. "I would like to get her in as many classes as you can fit in your schedule, and of course, we'll pay you double your regular one-on-one fee."

I began to wander around the room, imagining the studio it would become.

"You're very generous," Madam Silver replied. "I would be happy to meet her here three days a week for two hours each session. How about Monday, Wednesday and Friday afternoons from four to six, will that work?"

"Yes!" I whirled on them. "That's perfect!"

I couldn't believe it! I would not only get to dance again, but to study independently with the best dance teacher I'd ever known. I couldn't hold back my smile, it burned on my face like a brand. Sure, this wasn't the same thing as being in the Royal Ballet, nothing would ever replace that life-giving experience, but it was something. It was better than something! It was the best news I'd received in months.

Automatically, I began to move my body in long dancer's stretches that were ingrained into my body. Lucas and Silver began to discuss more details of the specific equipment and where to install it. Leaning over to stretch my leg, my mind wandered to the reality of my situation. I wouldn't forget my work here in this palace. I would still find a way to take Richard down, maybe rebuild the Resistance if I could.

I switched to the other leg. But this? This would make my stay in the palace at least bearable.

"I wish we could start today but I'm afraid I have other engagements. Can we start next week?" Madame Silver asked Lucas. "I trust you'll have this studio outfitted by then? She'll need to be fitted for proper shoes of course, and leotards. I'll send someone to meet her here Saturday at noon to take care of that. Does that work, Jessa?"

I nodded eagerly.

"And it's called a barre, with an 'e.'" She winked at him.

"B-A-R-R-E," I spelled it out for Lucas, and when I met his eyes, a confused feeling of gratitude washed over me. I wasn't going to forgive him. He'd ruined everything, and this wouldn't make up for it. I hated him. Or, something like that...

"Darling, I must go now," Madam Silver said. She gave me a quick hug before sweeping from the room, as gracefully as a professional ballet teacher would be expected to leave a room. I stared after her, the joy still dancing within me.

"Thank you." The words fell softly as I looked up to meet Lucas's gaze.

His expression was unreadable. He stood across the room, completely still, just watching me. The room was dark, the only light coming from the afternoon sun peeking through a partially shaded window. Long shadows were cast over his hooded eyes. Finally, he nodded slowly. "Can you do me a favor?"

"Depends." I bit my lip.

"Remember all of this." He motioned to the room that was to be my new studio. "Tomorrow night, I will escort you to meet with my father again. He will make his next move, and whatever it turns out to be, please just, remember I did this for you. No matter what, Jessa, I care about you. Everything I do, it's for you."

But that was the problem. He *still* believed that. What he'd done to betray my trust had been for him, not for me.

Tears filled my eyes. I wanted to nod, wanted to agree and just forgive him and be with the man I'd loved so deeply. Still loved. But the sting of betrayal was too hot. I didn't say a word. I couldn't. It was all too much. Instead, I turned around and left him there, closing the door behind me.

▼

I'd tried to check on my father and Sasha, or I guess her name was Frankie, but I wasn't allowed to see them. I had no idea if they were okay, or even alive. I'd spent the next day in a complete frenzy, trying to find out information but getting nowhere. I didn't even care about being discreet, either. I'd asked guards, officers, anyone who would talk to me, but nobody had information. Eventually, I'd had to give it up and get ready in the dress that had been delivered to my door. True to his word, Lucas had come to deliver me to his father.

I held his arm lightly, but kept my mouth shut and my eyes ahead. The day spent trying to help my family, who were still prisoners, had left me feeling helpless and angry. We walked into a ballroom that was lit with twinkling lights and black and white linens on tables scattered throughout the room. There were long-stemmed white roses in the center of each. In fact, it looked like everyone had been outfitted in elegant black and white, as well. We were instantly surrounded by tuxedos and exquisite dresses of all lengths and styles, but the colors were the same.

The crowd opened for us as we walked, everyone staring. I was sure we looked like a perfect pair. Lucas was styled to perfection, his suit crisp, his hair dark and gelled back, and his face clean-shaven. He smelled of ocean salt and citrus, a combination that made my mouth water. And I was wearing a full face of makeup. My hair was pulled back and adorned with crystal pins, and my sleeveless dress wrapped around me perfectly in crushed black velvet, fanning out around my hips and traveling all the way down to the ground. I hated everything about it; Richard had likely been the one to assign it to me. But I had to play along.

I planned to talk to Richard about my family tonight. Maybe I could work out some kind of deal to get them better accommodations.

"Ready for this?" Lucas whispered low in my ear.

I didn't reply. I wasn't sure what "this" was, and being here on his arm, against my wishes, made the wound between us fester even more.

He led me to a raised platform where his father sat relaxed on his throne. As we ascended the stairs, I noticed the media cameras set up again, a long row of black equipment with people buzzing around it. Last time the media was invited here was for the execution of Officer Thomas and subsequent proclamation of war. Not to mention Celia had been the one on Lucas's arm that night. My stomach flipped.

Celia. The woman was still in the palace. I'd seen her from afar a couple of times, and she'd barely even seemed bothered by her broken engagement. She was the same stoic, glossy, gorgeous redhead as always. But she was no longer

409

set to be the next Queen. How did she feel about that? And why was she still here? I glanced around the room, but didn't see her here.

"Hello, my dear Jessa." Richard smiled coolly as we approached. "I am very excited for you to see what I have in store for you, little girl." His use of "my dear" and "little girl" made me want to spit in his face. I curtsied and smiled carefully.

"Hello, Your Royal Highness," I replied.

"Please, call me Richard." He smiled. "I am to be your future father-in-law, after all. I would say you could call me "Dad", but even Lucas doesn't do that anymore."

Lucas was watching the exchange between us without revealing an ounce of emotion. His eyes kept flicking to me as I talked to his father, but that was the extent of it. He waited for me to nod my agreement to the King and then he cupped my elbow and led me to a chair, one that looked like a mini-throne with its red velvet seat and high back. He gently sat me down and sat beside me.

The mixed crowd of alchemists and officers turned to watch us now. Their faces were a mass of curious eyes and hesitant smiles.

Richard leaned toward his son. "It's showtime, boy," he said, his heady voice a mix of threat and anticipation. He stood. No blue alchemist to bolster him, I noted, as I looked around for one to pop into the picture. How long until Reed came back from the war? I bet Richard was missing his particular set of skills.

The King strode to a podium and pointed to the line of media with their row of black cameras. They adjusted with a few buttons and gave him a series of nods. He stood at the podium, rolling back his shoulders, his back to us. The spotlights were hot and bright. I resisted the urge to squint as the rest of the room was sent into shadows. Everyone quieted as Richard swept his arms wide and began to address his kingdom.

"My beloved New Colony, thank you for your attention tonight. It is with great pride that I can announce our war efforts against West America are succeeding. We've taken over vast amounts of land and continue to gain ground every day." He paused, the light reflecting off the gold ornate crown on his head. He rarely wore it, but when he did, it meant business. "Thank you to those who've volunteered to help, and of course, many thanks to those men and women in the field, risking their lives for our freedom. I trust that because of these heroes, I will soon have good news." His voice was smooth silk, practiced and confident. He didn't need Reed tonight. The crowd of alchemists and officers were nodding along with every word, as—I was sure—were the people at home, watching from their various slatebooks.

"That is all I can say for now without giving too much away to our enemy, but rest assured this continues to be our number one priority here in the palace. We will not let you down," he continued, straightening his shoulders, gold embroidered patches on each. He also had a red sash-looking thing across the outside of his suit jacket. There were tassels and shining buttons, a slightly more elaborate get-up from Lucas's. "West America has committed many crimes against us, from the tragic death of our beloved queen, to a public attempt on Lucas's life and my own. An act that, unfortunately, killed innocent people. West America will not get away with it. We will not rest until we've destroyed their evil ideology and taken back what is rightfully ours."

He paused, only for a moment, before the crowd exploded in applause.

"Thank you," he said, after they'd quieted. "I also have to thank the Guardians of Color and the Royal Officers." He motioned to the media, and on cue, they pivoted their cameras to face the crowd of guests, in all their finery. None of the small children were in attendance, of course; they rarely were. It was teens and adults, as usual.

"I know we have kept the vast majority of what we do here hidden from you," Richard said to the cameras as they swiveled back to him. "We made that choice to protect everyone involved. What we do with magic here at the palace has stayed classified from our enemies and we wanted to keep it that way. But I've come to realize that, while we should and will continue to keep some of what we do under wraps, it's not in your best interest to be blind to the advantages of color alchemy. This ability is the very bedrock of why we're so prosperous. It's high time you learned the basics of what it is and why it's so important to cultivate. For example, our alchemists who help to make crops grow are the reason our citizens have healthy food on their tables tonight."

The crowd cheered again. A distrustful feeling washed over me as he continued to speak of alchemy so openly to the press. People at home must be glued to their screens! Color alchemy had always been such a mystery. Seeing it was as rare as snow in July. Very few ever met an alchemist. Why was he talking about it now, when for decades, it had been mostly kept secret?

Bile rose in the back of my throat. Something was coming. Lucas reached out and grasped my hand, but it did little to calm my nerves.

Richard continued, "It's with this revelation that I've decided to hold a series of public exhibitions to showcase the power of color alchemy. It is my hope that you will understand not only why it's so important to willingly send alchemists to train with us, but for you to have faith that with these people heading our war efforts, we cannot fail. The exhibitions will be publically broadcast and a lottery system will select a small number of you to have the opportunity to watch live. There will be three of these events, one here in the capitol, one north, and one south. More information will be coming soon with exact times and locations, so please stay tuned for updates."

I glanced at Lucas. His eyebrows were pulled together in intense focus as he studied the back of his father's head. Did Lucas know about these exhibitions? Could it really be that the King just wanted to be open about alchemy all of the sudden, or was there something else going on?

"And finally," Richard said, his voice turning from smooth and serious, to amused. "I have one more item of happy news to share. I know, there's more!" He chuckled to himself, and even though I couldn't see him, I was sure he was smiling from ear to ear. The cameras shifted and slid back. Another tug of nerves gripped my stomach. They were filming Lucas and me. "As you can see, my son is joined by someone other than the pretty redhead Celia you've all come to love. I hate to say it, but truth is, I wanted that marriage more than the two of them. Poor Lucas, he's such a wonderful son, he'd do just about anything for me. But these last few weeks since the engagement, I've been feeling overwhelming guilt about it. You see, I knew it was another girl who had captured his heart. I fought it because I didn't know this girl well, and I already thought Celia was best for Lucas. But I've taken the time to get to know this beautiful girl you see seated here tonight and I've decided to let my son choose her as his bride. I'd like to introduce you to Jessa Loxely." He turned to us, no longer facing the cameras; his gaze was as sharp as ice.

Lucas grabbed my hand, and together, we stood.

I froze, a million questions running through my mind. I didn't want this. I should pull away. But I couldn't, not with the King's eyes pinned on me. He had my family downstairs in his prison. There was nothing I could do but play along. Besides, I *was* engaged. That was the whole point of why Lucas revealed my secrets, destroying the Resistance in one night, my dear sweet Jasmine gone with it.

I'm engaged but this makes it official. Time to buckle up and smile, Jessa!

"You two lovebirds can sit down now," Richard said with a wink. I fell back into the chair as my knees gave way. I smiled through it, somehow. Lucas placed a hand on my leg to temper the shaking, and when it didn't stop, he frowned slightly and removed it. I ignored the immediate sense of loss.

Richard had returned to the podium. "Part of why I'd like you to understand color alchemy better is because of Jessa. You see, there's something rather remarkable about the girl besides the fact that she stole Lucas's heart."

He paused, and I could feel the slight shift as the cameras zoomed in on my face. Was I breathing funny? Frowning or smiling? I couldn't even feel my cheeks anymore.

"She's a color alchemist," he declared. "One of the most powerful we've ever seen. It is my hope that you will accept her, knowing that not only does she make your prince happy, but she can potentially bring in a new line of remarkable power to our royal bloodline."

More cheers. More fluttering in my heart.

"The wedding will be a joyous affair in the midst of the tremors of war, but life must go on. Their wedding will be broadcast upon the completion of the three exhibitions. The wedding date is set for the first day of the new year."

I held my breath to keep the tears from falling. That wasn't even two months away! It was everything I had wanted, but had come in the worst package. I loved Lucas, I couldn't pretend otherwise. But I also saw too much of his father in him, too much greed and deception. I couldn't do it.

I have to find a way out.

Lucas squeezed my hand, and I smiled wide for the cameras and leaned over to offer him a quick kiss. On the outside, any tears in my eyes must have added to the presentation of the announcement. I probably looked so overcome with happiness that I was brought to tears. If only that were true.

"Thank you again, my dearest friends, for all you do," Richard continued. "I know there's a lot of change in the air right now, but rally with us and we will come out stronger than we've ever been before. Goodnight."

There was another blast of cheers followed by a pause and a release of air. The media began to take down their equipment, and Richard strode over to greet us.

"Congratulations again," he said to us and grabbed my hand, pulling me into a hug. The buttons on his suit coat dug into my chest and my whole body went rigid at his touch. He smelled so much like Lucas that I had to hold my breath. This man was a monster. And now he would be my father-in-law? The fact he could fool the kingdom so easily frightened me most. He could charm everyone at a moment's notice, all while killing anyone who got in his way. Was this an attempt to get closer to my red alchemy? Was it something else? I had a sinking feeling there was more to this charade than I knew. Even if I married Lucas, I would still be a prisoner.

Maybe even more of a prisoner than ever before.

"Enjoy the party." He released me and patted his son on the back. "Both of you. This is your engagement party, in case you didn't figure that out already." He laughed jovially, but it did nothing to quiet the fire in his eyes. They flickered between us for a moment. "You will behave," he threatened, then turned and briskly walked away, a flurry of people in his wake.

I followed. Now was not the time to be timid. "Wait, please, what about my sister and father?" I had to ask. I wanted to ask so much more. I wanted to know about the camp as well. Where were Mom and Lacey?

"What about them?" He continued to stride away, never bothering to look at me. We were nearing the back of the room, as if he was trying to get out of here before he was bombarded with guests wanting their moment with him.

"Are they okay?" I pressed. "If I'm to be royalty now, can't I help them?"

He stopped and whirled on me, expression hard, his eyes beat down on me with disdain. "There's nothing I can do for your sister, she's made her choice. She will remain in the prison for now."

I sucked in a shuddering breath. *For now?* Did that mean he would execute her? And if so, when?

"Your father, on the other hand," he continued, his voice dangerously low, "was smart enough to comply with our wishes. As long as he continues to stay out of our way, he can stay. He's already been set up with accommodations next to what will be your suite in our royal wing. Tomorrow you will be moving from your dorm and beginning preparations for your upcoming nuptials."

I nodded. What else could I do? Once again, I would be moved, like a piece on a chessboard. I was used to it now. "And what of my mother and little sister? Did you find them? Are they alive?"

I shouldn't have asked. I knew that, but I couldn't help it. And now I would pay. Rage was filling his entire body, his eyes widening and a purple vein bulging in his forehead. I stepped back, regretful. My knees began to buckle again.

Warm arms caught me and Lucas pulled me against him.

"Jessa," he said, loud enough for Richard to hear, "be careful how casually you address my father. He is your King. You must not make demands of him."

Richard's eyes danced between the two of us and he nodded, the anger fading slightly. "Quite right," he quipped, then pushed through the back door and disappeared.

I shifted away from Lucas and turned on him. "Since when do you talk to me like *that*?"

His eyes narrowed. "Your mother and sister weren't at the camp. Nobody was. They got out," Lucas said this wonderful news, emotionless, as if he was reading a math problem. "Now, let's do as we're told and go mingle with our guests."

He never answered my question about why he'd talked to me like that in front of Richard. Was he saving me from Richard's wrath, or was he really his father's son?

I followed him, no longer caring about having to feign happiness in front of all these people. I was elated! A swell of gratitude threatened to bring me to tears all over again. Sometimes it bothered me how quickly I was brought to tears, but that moment was not one of them. Mom and Lacey had gotten out! I had no idea where they were, of course, but they had to be okay. And maybe, just maybe, that meant there was still a chance.

Maybe there was still a Resistance.

THREE

LUCAS

I held Jessa close, breathing her in as we danced. It broke me.

We spent the evening dancing, making small talk with everyone who crowded us, held hands every moment. It didn't matter. She wasn't with me. Emotionally, she'd shut me out, not a single crack left in her exterior. She currently rested her head on my shoulder, the soapy lilac scent of her shampoo wafting through the air between us. I closed my eyes briefly and scoffed at my naiveté.

This meant nothing to her.

I'd hoped the ballet studio would soften her. I recognized the longing in her, knew how much she'd missed dance. When I'd seen her eyes light up at the presence of her old teacher, I'd thought, *this is it. She's going to let me in. She's finally going to understand our relationship is what I value most of all.*

Wishful thinking. She'd taken the gift and closed the door even tighter on me. I gritted my teeth, annoyed at my continued wishful thinking when it came to this girl. I'd always been such a cynic until she'd come along.

Lost in my thoughts, I hadn't realized I'd stopped leading her in our dance. We were now standing in the center of the dance-floor, curious eyes surrounding us.

"What's wrong?" Jessa asked, shifting back to look at me straight on.

My chest burned. I wanted to kiss her. So badly, I wanted to kiss her. But it wasn't what she wanted.

"Nothing," I muttered, then swept her back into my arms.

I never would have told my father what I knew about the Resistance, had I known it would backfire so badly on her family. Didn't she realize that? I couldn't have known that her father was going to show up. Or Sasha.

"How much longer do you think this thing is going to last?" she asked. "I'm getting pretty tired."

I sighed. *Tired of me, more likely.*

"I'll walk you out." I shifted to hold her hand and began to maneuver her through the room.

I noticed a couple new faces standing together in a corner and watching the two of us with distrust. Recognition passed between us as I locked gazes with one of them. They were some of the alchemists who'd originally attacked the palace with the Resistance. I was certain they saw me as the enemy. They had no idea that they could have succeeded if not for my intervention.

I only did it because Richard was already suspicious, already planning something. Telling them about the attack gave me the leverage to get to this moment with Jessa. It had worked. And then it had backfired.

I gently tugged Jessa through the crowd, stopping every few steps to thank yet another group of people. They swarmed on all sides to congratulate us, some taking photos with their slatebooks. It wasn't so much the Guardians or Royal Officers who cared, but my father's many friends.

"Thank you so much for saying that." Jessa smiled at a particularly pushy couple. "Richard picked it out," she said, gesturing down to her dress. It fit her in the right places and dropped to the floor.

"Actually, I picked that one out," I said. Since when did I care about getting credit?

Her expression faltered as she peered up at me, her smile slipping. She'd barely met my gaze all night, but now our eyes locked and heat flashed between us.

You may be fooling everyone else here, but you're not fooling me. I know you're too stubborn to forgive me. I know this isn't what you want. By the way her wide eyes turned into a hurt glare, it was almost as if she could hear the thought.

See? We're so connected you can read my expression and I can read yours. But you're still choosing to hate me.

She huffed and turned back to the couple. "I do like this dress," she said. "I just *love* how everything in my closet was picked out for me by someone else."

Touché.

Seeds of anger, long planted, were beginning to take hold, spreading, wrapping their roots around my nerves and pulling my heart in opposing directions. When had she *ever* chosen me first? I thought she loved me, but I'd never wanted love to feel this way. Love wasn't supposed to be one-sided. We were both supposed to want it, to fight for the other one's needs.

She isn't fighting for me. I buried that thought down deep because it hurt almost as much as her refusal to look me in the eye.

I shook my head and shifted so she was even closer. She'd come around. She had to. We were getting married; no way Richard was going back on that grand announcement. He'd never allow two canceled engagements. That would embarrass him, and embarrassment was not something he tolerated. This wedding was happening. It's what Jessa *had* wanted not too long ago, and maybe one day she'd want it again.

Once again, we moved through the crowd, almost to the door. Maybe I was ready to be done too. Sleep sounded amazing. At least then I could avoid the pain.

"Congratulations to the beautiful couple," Sabine said, sidling up next to me and smiling coolly. A prickle of heat ran down my spine. I did not want to have this conversation, but the inevitability of it was staring right at us.

Sabine's husband Mark, and thier daughter Celia, stood just behind her, eyeing Jessa with equal parts distrust and hatred. They wore smiles on their faces and expensive black dress clothes on their bodies. They nodded along with Sabine and portrayed a happy family in all its perfection. But there was something wrong with that picture.

"Umm–thanks," Jessa said softly.

They returned the smile tenfold, and Sabine stepped forward to shake her hand. I didn't like it. After following the group a few nights ago while cloaked behind my white invisibility magic, and seeing Sabine and Mark interact with Faulk and my father, I was beginning to think it wasn't Mark who led his household after all.

No, Sabine was the puppet-master behind her powerful husband.

"Thank you," I added as I cleared my throat, matching each of their heavy gazes one-by-one. They may be intimidating, but I wasn't intimidated. That was a distinction everyone in this little party needed to understand.

"That is very gracious of you to say," I continued, my voice hard. "Considering the circumstances." I refused to feel an ounce of guilt over getting out of that prison-sentence of an engagement with Celia. The whole thing had been for their benefit and not mine. No one had cared that Celia and I barely knew each other and certainly weren't in love. All they saw was the crown.

"You're very lucky," Celia said to Jessa, gesturing to me with the lift of her white-gloved hand. Her dress matched, accentuating her auburn hair. "I hope he doesn't drop you as quickly as he did me. He is such a fickle man, I've discovered."

"Celia," Sabine said low, her tone thorny. "Please, dear, none of that tonight." She wore a regal black number and was just as done-up as her daughter. She struck me as the kind of woman who agreed with the old adage that revenge was a dish best served cold.

"The girl does have a point," Mark said, glaring at me behind his thick lashes. I supposed that was what fathers were supposed to do when their daughters got dumped. "I believe Celia is owed an explanation."

Jessa tensed under my arm as silence spread through the room, both of us knowing the conversation had begun to travel. I inwardly groaned. Most of these guests would do anything to be privy to a royal scandal.

"It's fine," Celia chirped and looked away, her cheeks flaring red.

Jessa's body was still tense as stone when she spoke. "I completely agree with you, Sir." She nodded toward Mark. "Lucas does owe your daughter an explanation."

Heat prickled up the back of my neck, and I fought the urge to roll my eyes.

"Honey, why don't you dance with Celia and explain it to her?" Jessa purred, smiling at me. She was the picture of the blushing bride-to-be and I froze. Her eyes were flush with indignation. She wanted me to suffer in the hands of Celia and her family.

My jaw clicked as I held her stare, each of us urging the other to be the first to look away. The first to stand down. *Fine, if that's how she wants to play it.*

"Sure." I nodded, meeting her challenge, and turning a devilish grin on Celia. "I'd be happy to dance with Celia and have a little chat about what went wrong. I *do* need a chance to apologize."

"But what will you do?" I asked Jessa. I wanted to be the one to walk her back to her room.

She laughed. "Don't be silly, I have other friends." Then she slipped from my arm, spun on her heel, and joined a group of alchemists I'd seen her with a few times before, two teen girls and a boy. They walked off together and immediate worry replaced my frustration. I needed to get to know these alchemists and decide for myself how much they really cared about Jessa. If there was one thing I'd learned during my eighteen years in this palace, people usually weren't what they seemed.

I reached out my hand, and Celia placed her cold fingers in mine. We strolled to the dance floor. She gripped my knuckles so tightly that I assumed she was seething mad. She didn't want to dance with me just as much as I didn't want to dance with her. And her father, well, he would have punched me straight in the face if I wasn't the prince. But it was her mother I needed to watch out for. She was still scheming, still plotting, I was sure of it.

"You don't have to pretend to care about me," Celia said as I brought her into my arms.

"Good," I replied, flat, "because I don't."

She let out a huff and narrowed her eyes. "Wow, Lucas, tell me how you really feel."

I was fed up with the games and didn't need this.

"Fine." I shrugged. "I really feel like you're a social-climbing, gold-digging, crown-obsessed socialite who cares less about me than I care about you. Don't pretend like you're heartbroken; this is all about the status and we both know it. But I am sorry if your feelings are hurt, whatever *those* may be."

"I can't believe you," she growled, her voice hushed. "You think you're the only one who has powerful parents, huh? Did you ever stop to think that I was also pushed into our engagement?"

Pushed into an engagement with the prince? She'd run right into it. She wanted it, and now she wanted to play the victim.

To what end?

I paused and studied her face, searching for any sign of truth to her words. People danced around us, the orchestra playing a waltz anyone of high birth would know well. As we moved around the room, tears had formed in her eyes, and her cheeks were twice as red as they were only moments before. Her feelings could be boiled down to embarrassment, but that was nothing like heartbreak. I knew heartbreak inside and out these days.

But still, a pang of guilt lingered.

"Okay fine." I sighed. "Maybe I'm being too hard on you. But try to understand, I was already in love with Jessa when I met you. I didn't have a choice about you—that was all my father. What would you have done in my situation?"

Her brow rose. "Fair enough," she grumbled, "but you could have at least warned me, or broken it off with me yourself. For heaven's sakes, Lucas! Not only did you ignore me during that entire attack, but you got engaged to another woman without even breaking it off from me. I had to hear it from your father. How do you think that felt?"

"I'm sorry. But, it's done now."

"It sure is." She dropped her eyes and turned away, a curl whipping through the air between us.

By now, the crowd of dancing couples around us were doing little to hide their gawking expressions and wide eyes. A flurry of whispers circled the room as the gossip spread like wildfire. The phenomenon wasn't unusual for me, but it had to be far worse for Celia. Maybe I really had mistreated her.

But if she wanted me for me, she wouldn't have offered Jessa the opportunity to be my mistress. That was proof enough that she put the crown before the person actually wearing it.

I was done playing into the manipulations of her family. However it had happened, I was over it. I had my own life to sort out.

"You should go home now." I dropped my arms and stepped back. "There's no need for you to stick around the palace."

She shook her head, a sickly smile creeping across her crimson lips that bore a striking resemblance to her mother.

"Oh, you hadn't heard?" She cocked her head to the side. "I'm staying in the palace until further notice. The King wants me and my parents to help with the exhibitions, among other things."

"What other things?"

She leaned forward and whispered in my ear, the movement sudden. "You and your little girlfriend better watch your backs, Lucas, because we certainly are."

Was that a threat? I shook her off and glared down at her. "She's not my girlfriend, she's my fiancé, and soon, she'll be *your* queen."

Her face fell, the color washing away. I turned briskly and strode away.

They were "watching us", huh? I wasn't even surprised; already Sabine and Mark had jobs with my father that went far beyond what they told the rest of the kingdom.

Obviously, some kind of undercover operation. They could watch me all they liked but they had no idea who they were dealing with. It was *them* who should be watching their backs. They might be working for my father, but I was working for myself, and I wasn't going down without a fight.

▼

The echo of my shoes filled the musty stairwell as I descended to the prison. I stalked down the dimly lit hallway, noting the guard and an officer leaning against the wall. They jumped up when they saw me, bowing low.

"I want to talk to her alone," I said gruffly to the two bleary-eyed officers. They blinked rapidly, probably because they were bored out of their minds and fighting sleep, until I interrupted them. I'd chosen to come down here in the middle of the night on purpose. Anyone with a vested interest in Sasha was presumably asleep.

"Uh, I'm not sure you're authorized to go in there alone, Sir." One of the officers stared at me and scratched at his stubbly neck, his young eyes squinting. *Good, I'm glad they put one of the younger guys down here; they were always the easiest to manipulate.*

"It's Your Highness, not Sir," I snapped. "I'm the prince, what more authorization do you need? If you'd like me to drag my father down here in the middle of the night, I'll do it. He'll be raging mad, but I don't care, I need to talk to that traitor *now*."

"Of course. Please forgive me." The other officer nodded to his cohort who unlocked the door with a quick flick of his wrist. The keys moved in and out of his pocket in a flash, and I smiled.

"Thank you," I said. "I won't be long."

I slid into the darkened room. Sasha lay fast asleep on a cot. No blanket, just her legs tucked up against her body. Her face was bruised and swollen, as I was sure the rest of her was as well.

Why though?

We'd gotten to the Resistance camp and torn it to shreds looking for evidence. But maybe because it had been empty, Faulk thought it fair to continue punishing Sasha. Not getting what she'd wanted had warranted another beating, knowing Faulk. Shame burned in the back of my throat, and I loudly cleared it, the abrupt rumble filling the small gray cell.

Sasha stirred, rolling over. I pushed up the solo chair and sat down to face her.

"We need to talk," I said quietly. I pulled a blue stone from my pocket and slid it into her palm. She knew what to do. She'd used blue alchemy as a means to keep our conversations private before.

She blinked a few times and sat up. "Water," she croaked. She sounded so broken, her voice so scratchy that it was jarring. This wasn't the Sasha I knew. My spine stiffened. What had they done to her?

"I'll get you some water as soon as we're done," I said. "I promise."

Her eyes narrowed as she focused on me. It was mostly dark, but I could still make out the mistrust that shone in her searching eyes. After a moment, she nodded, the stone hidden in her hand working its magic.

"We have to be quick," I continued. "I wanted to run something by you."

"What do you want?" She leaned back against the wall and rubbed one of the bruises on her jaw, then winced.

"I want to help you," I whispered, my voice low.

She laughed, a desperate sound.

"I'm serious. I want to get you out of here."

"Why should I believe you?" She glared beneath the shadows. "Jessa told me

420

what you did. This is *your* fault. Years of hard work and planning were wasted because you had to tattle to your daddy." She punctuated her words with the quick flick of her wrist. "I'm not doing a thing for you."

Guilt ripped through me, but I forced myself to stay calm. Now wasn't the time to hash out the details of that night.

I shook my head. "Who else do you have? Getting a lot of offers for help in here, are you?"

She paused and looked me up and down. I could feel her distain for me, hear it in every word she uttered. "Why should I believe you? Why should I even trust you? You know, I could tell them *your* secret. Did you ever stop to think about that?"

I had. Which was a big part of why I was here in the first place.

"Look," I said, "if you stay here, Faulk will kill you. Maybe not today or tomorrow, but eventually, it will happen."

"Jessa will stop her. She'll figure something out." She leaned back against the wall, pulled her legs up against her chest, and closed her eyes. Even in the darkness, I could make out a rip in the knee. Her flesh shone in the dark, scraped and bloodied.

"Do you really believe that?" I scoffed, exasperated. "Christopher is staying upstairs. All the other alchemists, too. You're the only one Faulk has to beat on at the moment, in case you didn't know."

"You think I like this?" she hissed. "That psycho keeps having them heal me only to hurt me again. She's sick. I already told them everything thanks to that ridiculously emotional sister of mine."

I needed to change tactics.

"They got out." I leaned back in the chair and crossed my arms over my chest. "The people at your camp. They got out."

She chuckled, a coy smile filled her face, and for the first time I caught a glimpse of the Sasha I remembered. "Where'd they go? Are they okay?"

"West America," I said. "That's all we've been able to figure out so far. As you can imagine, Faulk and my father are pretty angry about the whole thing. I think they're taking it out on you." I smirked, despite my better judgment.

I expected her to punch me or something, but she didn't.

She grinned even wider. "Let them. I don't care anymore. I'm just glad those people got out. Now the alchemists here on the other hand, they're complete idiots for giving in to him so quickly."

"I have to agree." I nodded. "And the thing is, it won't be long until Richard comes for you, too. If Faulk doesn't kill you, what he'll do will be much worse."

"What's that supposed to mean?"

"What do you think it means? Think about it, Sasha." I paused. "Frankie? He remembers you as that powerful alchemist. He's going to get over his anger with you eventually. The way I see it, either Faulk kills you with one of these beat-downs, or Richard forces you to come out of this little hidey-hole and do his bidding."

"Red alchemy?" she groaned. "No, I don't do that anymore anyway."

"So you've told me. But don't you think he'll try?"

Her eyes shut tight in annoyance.

"Yeah, me too."

Her eyes popped open, and she cocked her head at me. "Fine. So what's your plan, Lucas?"

"Go along with whatever Richard asks of you."

She laughed. "No way!"

I shushed her. She really needed to keep her cool, and keep it down, just in case her blue magic was rusty.

"Yes," I whispered. "It's the only way we'll be able to get enough leniency to get you out of here. I think I have an idea. I'm not sure of all the details yet. But when I come for you, you have to trust me and do as I say."

She held my gaze, the silence stretching between us.

"Fine," she finally grumbled and shook her head. "I can't believe I'm agreeing to work with you, of all people."

"Yeah, yeah, I'm such a traitor," I sighed. "And yet, I'm your best chance of getting out of here."

"And what about Christopher and Jessa?"

"I'll try to get him out with you, but I'm not sure about Jessa. Not yet."

What I didn't add was that I was too selfish to let her go. I wasn't sure I could do that, even if part of me had accepted I might have to. I knew getting her out of here would probably be the only way she'd ever forgive me.

But then she'll be gone. What did you expect?

I pushed the thought away to deal with at a later time.

"I need to go now," I said. "If anyone asks about me being in here, tell them I threatened Christopher. That I said you needed to cooperate with my father in exchange for me looking out for your dad."

"Fine." She nodded. I reached out and she dropped the warm stone into my palm. "Good luck, Lucas," she said. "I think you're going to need a lot of it."

I rose and slipped the stone into my pocket. "Me too."

I didn't want to count on something so fleeting as luck, but it was all I had left. I turned back to her just before I reached the door. "One more thing," I said. I could barely make her out in the darkness now.

"What?"

"About my secret," I said. "If I'm going to be able to help you, I'm going to need to keep it *my* secret."

She chuckled sweetly, a stark sound against her ragged appearance. "No kidding."

I smirked and shook my head. "No kidding."

▼

"Are you going to tell her, or should I?" My father leaned back in his chair and smugly placed his boots on the desk between us.

I'd come to him here with my latest idea. His study was filled with books, paperwork stacked neatly on the desk, and a map plastered across the wall. Little pins spread across it. A photo of Mom sat in the corner of one of the shelves and my eyes kept flicking to it, despite my efforts to ignore it. Seriously, being in here with *him* wasn't something I was excited about, but I hoped my idea would help Jessa in the long run. I wasn't sure she'd see it that way, but lately nothing I did would turn her on to my way of thinking anyway.

"Actually, you better tell her." He threw back his head and laughed, gleaming white teeth reflecting the overhead light. "She's going to have to learn that's the way things are going to be in your relationship. You make the rules."

I held in an angry breath but didn't repeat the thoughts brewing inside my head. Richard didn't seem to even notice, or if he did, he didn't care. He just went about his business as usual, plopping his feet back down and returning to his paperwork. I was next in line for this job. Would the power consume me the way it did him? I shoved my hands into my pockets, shaking my head, just watching him.

After a minute, he stood from his oversized oak desk and restacked the already neat pile of papers. He gathered them into his hands, straightening them against the desk with a click.

"What are those?" My curiosity was piqued by the sheer amount of paperwork. I'd seen him labor over paperwork before, but never so much of it.

"The latest reports from the front lines," he replied.

"Anything important?" I asked.

He raised an eyebrow as if carefully considering the question. "Everything was going well, but we're at a bit of a standstill at the moment, neither side making a move. That won't last long."

Of course it wouldn't.

"They'll be expecting a retaliation," I stated, matter-of-factly. They'd attacked us in our palace. Even though they'd failed, it was only logical they would be bracing themselves for the backlash to come.

Even I was bracing for it.

He nodded. "And they're going to get it," he said. "But not in the way they expect."

I raised an eyebrow and waited for him to explain further, but he didn't.

"Go tell Jessa the plan," he said gruffly, changing the subject. "I want to get started on this immediately. Faulk will work out the details."

I stood from the leather chair and left in search of Jessa.

I hated this part. I didn't want to go along with any of this, let alone be the one to orchestrate it, but I had to think of the bigger picture. The endgame.

She was my endgame.

Brushing my balmy hands against the thick denim of my jeans, I willed myself to take on the persona of the old me. She'd liked the old me…

Since when did I care so much about what women thought of me? Since when did I bend over backwards for someone who didn't do the same for me?

Since Jessa, you idiot.

I scowled at my internal battle and knocked on her door with a heavy fist. I was tired of it. Nothing I did would be good enough, so I'd just have to do what I thought was best and hopefully, in the end, she'd finally understand.

"Lucas." Jessa swung open the door. The sound of my name on her lips buried me. Her cheeks flushed pink when her eyes met mine. Her lips quirked before she frowned. I wanted nothing more than to run my hand through her wayward curls.

"Why are you here?" she asked.

And that was the problem. As soon as I saw her, felt her presence, she changed me. The hard exterior I'd built during my walk over fell away in the space of a single glance of her cobalt eyes.

"Can I come in?" I asked.

She drew her eyebrows together but nodded and opened the door wider. A few days ago, she'd been moved back into the royal wing. Even though she was officially a Guardian of Color now, royalty took precedence.

Her suite was one of the nicest in the palace and was just next door to Celia. I hated that Celia was even still here, but my father wouldn't even talk about the matter with me. It pissed me off. After Celia's threat, she had no right to be here.

"Do you want to sit down?" Jessa asked, moving through the room in her usual dancer's way, her limbs long and elegant. She sat in a striped, pale yellow armchair. It matched the rest of the room—a room almost sickly sweet in its decoration. Her black Guardian's uniform stuck out with its practical uniformity.

I settled into the loveseat across from her. "You're not going to like this," I sighed.

She closed her eyes tightly. "Just tell me."

"You're going to start training the other alchemists in red."

Her eyes popped open. "What? How?"

"Well, you're going to try, anyway. You'll show them what you do and help them try to replicate it."

She shook her head slowly from side to side. "I don't think it will work."

"I hope it won't. In fact, I'm betting it won't."

We sat in silence, a silence so thick and awkward and long that a sudden urge to do something drastic overpowered me. *Do something. Kiss her. Yell at her. Something!*

I did nothing. I stared at the floor, like a coward, my hands fisted in my lap.

"Is that all?" she finally asked, her voice tepid. I looked up to find her also staring at the rug like it was the most interesting thing in the world. Like nothing we'd just talked about had an effect on her anymore.

No, that wasn't all! I wanted her to fight with me like I had expected. In the past, if I had come to her and told her she would be doing something she didn't want to do, something as dangerous as this, she would have challenged me. She would have gotten in my space, her eyes sparking, her temper flaring, and I would have met her there. She would have demanded something of me. But today she wanted nothing.

The loss sunk me. First, my mother. And now, Jessa.

"Yeah, that's all," I replied and excused myself from her room. She didn't bother to watch me leave.

Had she really given up? Was she so done with me in all aspects that she wouldn't even argue with me anymore?

The hurt suffocated me from the inside out. She might be ready to give up on me, but I wasn't ready to give up on her. Or on us. *And when will you be ready?* The question lived in the back of my mind. Despite how many times I buried it, it was still there. Still asking. Still waiting for me to face it.

FOUR

JESSA

I ce crystals crunched under our boots as we ventured outside. I tried to relax into the cold, but couldn't hold back the shivers.

"It can't be that bad, can it?" Callie asked with a friendly laugh as we walked further out onto the patio.

"Are we talking about the cold now or are we still discussing my sad lack of friends here?"

She quirked her lips. "It is that bad."

"Yes, trust me. You're the only alchemist left in this place that still willingly talks to me," I said. "After you saw what the red can do, even I'm surprised. I don't blame the others for avoiding me."

"Hey, it's not your fault." She smiled. A fog had coated her glasses, hiding her caramel-brown eyes. She took them off and rubbed them against her top. "It's not like you made the King do that." She glanced around and then whispered, "That was crazy. And all on him. It wasn't your fault what he *made* you do."

She was right, of course, but I couldn't allow myself to agree with her.

I bit my lip and looked down into the steaming mug of hot chocolate warming my fingers. I didn't even know what the drink was. I had certainly never tasted it. After Callie had seen me wandering around the GC wing with nothing to do, she'd invited me to try what she called "heaven in liquid form".

But first, she'd said, we would have to take it outside. Apparently, by her logic, I needed to be cold to get the full effect of the hot chocolate's goodness.

"Ready?" she asked, nodding toward our mugs.

My mouth watered as I sniffed the drink. I took a small sip. It stung at first, the liquid hotter against my tongue than I'd expected, but the taste that washed through my mouth was equal parts calming and amazing.

I closed my eyes and let it warm me from the inside out.

"Well," her voice teased. I popped open my eyes and grinned back at her.

"What do you think? Good, huh?"

"It's incredible," I said. I wished I'd had something like this growing up. All those snow days, hot chocolate would have been something to make the freezing, wet cold totally worth it. But chocolate wasn't easy to get for my family. Or really, any family that I knew. Our status allowed us enough money to buy the essentials. It was usually those of the Royal Court who had the best jobs and subsequently, the highest quality of life.

"One of the perks of living at the palace," Callie added, as if to make my point.

I nodded. I didn't know what to say to her that wouldn't make me sound ungrateful. The palace was nice. It was beautiful, decadent, filled with magic, and parties, and more food at each meal than I'd ever seen. But I would trade it, hot chocolate and all, for one more normal day with my family.

The winter air that had been nipping at me was starting to eat me alive. "Okay, I'm officially freezing, let's go back inside."

"Wait," Callie said, gripping onto my black coat. "I wanted to ask you a question."

I studied her expression, careful to keep my own relaxed. So, this wasn't about hot chocolate...

"What is it?" I asked.

"There's a lot of rumors going around about you," she said. I sucked in a breath. "Sorry, it's not like that," she rushed to add. "It's just, I wondered if you'd set the record straight for me. Since we're friends and all."

I hoped we were friends. In fact, if we were, she was my only one, at the moment. But that didn't mean I wanted to answer her questions.

Still, I slowly nodded.

"So, okay, you're engaged to Lucas. No surprises there, the guy has been following you around since the day you arrived. But your sister is apparently Sasha—"

"I didn't know about that until pretty much everyone else did," I interjected. I didn't want her to think I was hiding that because I wasn't.

"And then you've got this crazy powerful, albeit terrifying red alchemy thing going on," she continued, her eyes round orbs behind her thick glasses. I looked down on my friend with her wiry blonde hair framing her earnest face. I wanted to trust her, I did, but I was uneasy.

"Yeah, I didn't know about that part either, until pretty recently," I relented.

"Well." She faltered, orb-eyes shifting around us. "I guess I'm wondering if you're actually loyal to the crown. Like, do you even want to be a Guardian? I know you were initiated and all that, but something just doesn't feel right to me, like there's something you're hiding still."

"I don't know what to say to that," I croaked, hoping to sound calm, but I probably sounded guilty. "Of course I want to be a Guardian." My stomach flipped as I forced the lies from my mouth, and suddenly the hot chocolate sloshing around in there didn't seem so amazing.

"Because the thing is," Callie continued, "I wouldn't blame you, you know?

That attack on the palace, the one Sasha was caught up in?"

"What about it?" I asked. My eyes flickered away from hers and toward the palace just behind us. This was a dangerous conversation.

"I can't help but wonder if you knew it was going to happen. I mean, the way you reacted when Jasmine died."

The image of Jasmine's blood flashed through my mind, and I fought back the urge to scream.

"You were pretty intense. You really loved her, didn't you? But if she was a traitor, why did you have such a visceral reaction to her death? It's a little confusing." Callie and I were standing side to side now, looking out at the snow-covered lawn. I wanted to shake her! This was not safe. But what choice did I have but to answer?

"She was my teacher and my friend," I replied, my voice faltered. "She killed herself because of what I did." I stepped back. I shouldn't have to explain that to her.

"No." Callie shook her head, turning on me. "She killed herself because she got caught, because she was about to reveal who else was working with her."

Was this how all the alchemists interpreted that night? Just no big deal because Jasmine had turned out to have a traitorous secret?

"What's your point?" I asked.

My body was so still, the cold penetrated deep into my bones. I wanted to run away, anything but deal with these questions and the burning shame they brought to the surface.

"I think there's more to your story with Jasmine. And the thing is, I don't blame you."

My eyes shot to hers. "Be careful what you say here."

She nodded. "I just want you to know, that if you ever need help with anything, I want to help. If you know something more about what happened to Jasmine, or who she was working for, you can tell me. It's something I've been wondering about for a long time."

I held back the urge to nod, to pull her into a tight hug and tell her everything. Unloading these secrets would be such a relief. But I couldn't.

Reed had been a spy.

Even my old maid, Eliza, had been sent to spy on me.

Sasha was actually Frankie. Lucas was actually an alchemist.

No, I can't tell her. I barely know the girl.

I cleared my throat and rocked back on my heels. "I don't know what you're talking about," I said. "Let's go inside. It's too cold out here."

She sighed, her eyes sparked with disbelief, but she followed when I turned away. Her energy, a static curiosity, circled me as we walked back to the dining hall to return our empty mugs. She wasn't giving up on her theory, whatever her motives. And I was left to worry that either way, if she really did want to be part of the Resistance, or if she was another one of Faulk's spies, I was about to lose my only friend here.

▼

Their eyes followed me as I entered the classroom. The flurry of quiet whispers that followed was like an unexpected gust of wind. The other alchemists had seen me as a threat, at first. But their fear had settled over time and just when I'd started to fit in here, I'd shown them what I was truly capable of. It was no wonder they went right back to hating me.

I was so alone; even Callie couldn't fill the void. And Lucas, he left me loneliest of all. He was always around, escorting me to dinners with his father and their friends, helping with the wedding planning, checking in on the ballet classes. But yet he was farther away than ever. He wanted me to forgive him, to force his way into my life, but it wasn't that simple.

I sighed and found my seat in the classroom, keeping my head down. The industrial room had orderly desks pushed together in pods. I was sitting in an empty pod, well aware that everywhere else was filled with cliques of alchemists. Most of the classes had people my age, but today there was a mix of ages in the room. I ignored the awkward loneliness inside and stared at the row of crystals and potted plants on the far wall.

Someone audibly cleared their throat. I looked up to meet Faulk's impenetrable eyes.

"Did you not hear me the first time, Loxely?" she asked with a sneer that curled her thin upper lip.

I shook my head. "Sorry," I mumbled.

"Get up," she growled. "Have you not prepared anything for today?"

I blinked, confused. "Huh?"

"Figures," she huffed. "Lucas said he told you but who really knows with that boy. We never should have trusted him to get the job done when he treats you like you're made of tissue paper."

"What are you talking about?"

Her blonde hair was pulled back in her usual bun, enhancing the sharpness of her cheekbones. Her white uniform gleamed as she stalked to the front of the simple classroom. "I said get up," she barked over her shoulder.

It was Monday afternoon. We always worked on blue on Monday afternoons. Even if most of us couldn't do much of anything with it, we were still expected to try. I'd never had much luck with blue, but that didn't warrant her yelling at me. Blue was rare.

I stood to face her, and she spun on me with a look of complete annoyance, like I was the dumbest person she'd ever met.

Well, geez, nice to see you, too!

"You're starting your lesson on red alchemy today," Faulk said. "Or did you forget already?"

My stomach flopped. "That's today?" Lucas had warned me, but he said Faulk was supposed to let me know the details first.

"Yes, it's today. Did you not get the date?" She grinned slowly.

I scowled. What did I expect from Faulk? She was enjoying my discomfort.

Didn't matter. She obviously wasn't going to wait for me to tell her my *legitimate* excuse because she turned and continued her angry tirade. "If you're not prepared to teach red alchemy, then I'll have to help you along, won't I?"

I swallowed. Was she serious? Last thing we needed was that sadistic woman pushing us into attempting anything to do with red. I reminded myself to play nicely with Faulk. That would piss her off more than challenging her, which had to be the reason why she'd sprung this on me. But a little planning would have been nice.

"What did you have in mind?" I asked and shifted to face the alchemists sitting in the room. There were about forty, all ages, but two of the youngest children sat in the front row, gaping up at me. My hands began to sweat. I didn't want to let anyone down. But I also didn't want anyone to learn red alchemy. I wouldn't curse this magic on my worst enemy.

"Let's start with a question and answer period, shall we?"

I shrugged, and several keen hands shot into the air.

I pointed to the youngest of the lot.

"Hi, Jessa. I'm Charity." The child smiled. She reminded me of Lacey, and my heart dropped. "I was wondering if it's just blood that you can use, or have you tried other reds?" Her tiny voice was so sure, and her eyes lifted in complete fascination.

"No, I haven't been able to get anything besides blood to work," I replied. "I've tried, but it's just blood that has power so far."

She nodded enthusiastically, and I forced her into my peripheral vision to call on another raised hand. To think that a child wanted my power, my horribly damaging power, made me want to run far, far away from this classroom. I blinked and tried to focus on the next question.

"What do you feel when you do it?" a boy about my age asked. "When you make someone do something like that, make them do what you say, what does that feel like?"

I carefully considered the question. The kid's black, shaggy hair hung in his hooded eyes, but I could make out the sparkle of anticipation in them just the same. I recognized him, we'd been in several classes together, and he'd once teased me about dating Lucas before we'd been official.

"It feels amazing," I answered honestly, "but also, it feels terrible. Scary. Like I'm not actually in control of anything."

His smile quirked, the desire to learn red rose in him, like this power was our drug. And for him, red alchemy would be the ultimate fix to satiate his addiction. I shivered. Not because he scared me, but because sometimes, I scared myself.

"That's enough for now," Faulk said, stepping to the center of the room. "Let's try it, shall we? Everyone grab a partner, a dagger, and a plant." She motioned to the wall of tools. "I want you to take turns trying to pull the red from each other's blood, healing when necessary."

The room buzzed with activity as the students set out to work. I stood on the edge, arms crossed over my stomach, half worried someone would succeed.

430

After several rounds of the alchemists' failed attempts, however, I began to relax. No one was even close, and the blood was beginning to get messy. I hoped this would be over quickly. I watched the minutes on the clock as they ticked away. The frustration was growing within each person, only a small mirror to that of Faulk's. I forced myself to appear neutral.

When class was scheduled to end and nobody left, I began to get antsy. I found myself making eye contact with Faulk and frowning.

"That's enough!" Faulk finally snapped. "That's all for today, we'll try again next week." Then she strode over to me, her boots clipping on the polished concrete. "You better come prepared next time," she snapped. "Better have something to offer us." Then she stormed from the room, slamming the door behind her.

Maybe you should have told me about the proper time and place and I would have done that today, you stubborn cow!

My body eased, and I hurried toward the door. *So glad that's over.*

"She's right, you know," someone called out over the stir of conversation. I turned to face the boy who'd questioned me about what red felt like. Silence descended as every pair of eyes locked on me. He continued, his voice dark and filled with the same frustration that had built over the course of the lesson. "You need to try harder, Jessa. If you don't, we'll wonder why you're so selfish."

I froze, shame gluing me to the spot.

Then he added, "No one wants to bow down to a narcissistic queen."

The edges of my vision blurred red, and the anger filled me so completely, I felt as if I would explode. Why was I feeling sorry for myself, trying to fit in with these people?

He was being selfish, here.

"What's your name?" I asked.

"Dax." He stood.

"Well, Dax," I said coolly, walking closer, "next time I sit down to dinner with my future family, I'll be sure to mention your concerns to the King. I'm sure he'll be delighted to know all about the alchemist blaming the future queen for his own failure."

His face stilled, bright red, as he glowered. I regretted the come-back immediately. It wasn't me.

"You think you're better than us," he replied darkly, reaching out and putting his hand on my upper arm.

I shook him off of me immediately. "You have no idea what I think, so don't pretend to know the first thing about me."

So, why don't you enlighten me, Jessa. His voice echoed through my head. My eyes flashed to the purple stone strung to a black leather cord around his neck. I stepped back. Purple Alchemy…rare. I hadn't met many who could do it. But this was a challenge, a show of his own power.

He can only hear what I want him to hear. He shook his straight black hair out of his face and smirked. How far did his power go?

"No," I said forcefully, then turned and marched from the room.

You shouldn't have goaded him on like that!

I groaned and fell back against my mattress. All I wanted to do was crawl into a little ball and hide under the thick comforter for the rest of eternity. *Okay, but that lesson had actually gone great.* Nobody had shown an ounce of ability in red alchemy. Letting that guy get the best of me had been the one downfall.

I rolled over and stared at the yellow wallpaper. It was hideous, truly.

Okay, it wasn't hideous by everyone's standards. Just mine. Someone probably thought it was beautiful, but to me, it was not only my least favorite color, it reminded me of where I was. It was way too fancy. Of all the rooms I'd stayed in, the dorms had probably been the best. My room there had been nondescript, simple. This one was dripping in the trappings of royalty.

Not to mention how I was next door to Celia. I saw her more than I wanted lately. She'd always smile at me sweetly, but her eyes were daggers and she never said a word. I was bracing myself for some twisted form of retaliation.

So far? Nothing. And that didn't make a whole lot of sense. Maybe she was only here to spy? Maybe she was waiting for me to disappear so she could get Lucas back? There was nothing for her to wait on, not really. The Resistance, what was left of it, hadn't made contact with me since Jasmine died. I was merely surviving until the day I'd be married off.

There's got to be something I can do to get out of here.

I needed to think. I needed to stop feeling sorry for myself, stop complaining, and start making a plan. That's what Jasmine would have done. That's probably what Sasha *was* doing, even in her terrible circumstance.

My father was practically locked in his room, but at least we'd been permitted to visit each other. I'd gone to see him every evening after dinner, and tonight was no exception.

He let me in his room and wrapped his arms around me in a tight hug. "You're bored out of your mind in here, aren't you?" I said as we went to lounge on the couch.

He shrugged. "They gave me some books to occupy my time. If I mind my business, Faulk said I'd get more of a role in your life here."

"You trust her?"

He shook his head, his smile faltering. "Nope. She makes me nervous."

I needed a plan for both of us. I stood and paced the room. His was an exact copy to mine, just in navy instead of yellow.

"What's going through that head of yours, Jessa?"

I shrugged and plopped back down onto the sofa.

The plan had to be kept secret from him. I knew there were royal officers always outside the door. I glanced around the room, past the built-in bookshelf, the thick rug, and the huge picture window, my eyes landing on the potted plant in the corner.

"Practice," I breathed.

"What?"

"I need more practice."

Today, Faulk had made the alchemists practice something they didn't know how to do. Granted, it hadn't worked, but that was common in *all* my alchemy lessons. We practiced, day in and day out. We tried over and over again to master all kinds of magics that seemed impossible. But we did it anyway. We tried. And sometimes, we got better.

Sometimes, we discovered *new* abilities.

"That's what I've been missing," I said, looking back to Dad.

His eyes narrowed. "What are you talking about?"

I leaned over and closed the space between us, hugging him. His familiar woodsy scent washed over me. I pulled back and met his gaze.

"I gotta go," I said. I kissed him on the cheek. "I'll see you tomorrow."

Before he could argue, I sprinted from the room, out in the hall, and back to my own suite. This wasn't something I was ready to do in front of anybody, even my Dad.

Sure enough, the identical potted plant stood tall in the corner of my room, as well. "Hello there," I whispered, kneeling on the floor at its base.

There was something unique about me besides red. All the focus had been on red, but what about that other thing I had done all those months ago?

The memory rushed back. Dancing on that stage, when I'd had so little control over what was happening to me, I'd done more than just access purple alchemy. I'd separated the color into its primary colors—red and blue.

How had I done that? And more importantly, *what did it do?*

As far as I knew, nobody understood it. But what if that kind of magic was even more important than red alchemy? If I could figure it out without anyone else knowing, I might be able to use it to get us out of here. Lucas had done the same with white, another mysterious alchemy.

I picked a long, smooth leaf. It snapped from the stem. Then I split it between my fingernails, the green color oozed out and into the air in the space of a heartbeat. The swirling magic twisted into the air like thick smoke, eager for instruction. Normally, I would send it to heal someone, but instead I imagined the color separating.

Yellow and blue. Come on, yellow and blue.

Nothing happened.

I sighed as the color dissolved into a mist. Ruined. There was no salvaging a leaf that had the color stripped away.

I went to the closet and rifled through the garments, my eye out for something purple. Spotting something workable, I removed a dress from its hanger. It was made of silk, slipping through my fingers. I considered the material, knowing it would be harder to manipulate this way than if I had a plant to work with. But I'd done it before. I could do it again. I made a quick mental note to get a rainbow stone necklace as soon as possible. Now that I was officially a Guardian of Color, I was pretty sure I could get myself one without any problems.

Moving to my bed, I held the shiny fabric on my lap. I willed something to happen, but the magic wouldn't answer my call. I laid back with a huff. What was I missing?

I remembered that performance and the dance. I focused on each move, reciting it all in my mind's eye. Connecting with the passion, with life-purpose—that's what purple was all about. I allowed that passion to overwhelm me as I imagined the dance over and over. My muscles knew the movements by memory, and I ached to move. A tear leaked from the side of my eye.

Still, I missed it. The thrill of performance, the natural way I felt on the stage. It felt like home.

I blinked, forcing the tears away. *Get a grip, Jessa.*

Just above my body, the purple swirled in clouds of iridescent magic. I gasped and sat up, allowing it to envelop me.

The purple urged me forward, to reach out and connect. Could I connect with someone's mind again? Or maybe I could even do what Lily had; maybe I could use it to predict my future.

But instead, I imagined the colors separating into blue and red.

Unlike the green, the purple opened up in an instant. The color seemed to relax as it shifted into a bold cobalt blue and a fiery red. I reached out, willing the new colors to do *something*. I wasn't quite sure what, as I'd never gotten to color this way. This magic was different. It buzzed in a frenzy, as if it were restless.

When the red touched my fingers, it zinged away from me and vanished. I grabbed at the blue and the same thing happened.

Why can't I touch it?

A tide of exhaustion overwhelmed me, like a heavy flood pouring over my body. I blinked, fighting it, but there was no use. It pulled me under.

I almost had it! The excitement inside drowned, my body succumbing to the need for sleep.

Practice. I held the thought in my mind as my eyes closed.

I'll practice again tomorrow.

FIVE

SASHA

My soul longed for magic.

So, when I woke to a clicking at the door, I assumed it was my restless imagination and rolled back over to the comfort of sleep.

"Hey, wake up," a voice whispered against my ear.

I flipped over and shot my hand out into the darkness. Nobody was there.

Okay, now I'm really losing my mind.

I had been so bored in this drab prison, that it wasn't the first time my mind had played tricks on me. The ebb of sleep nudged at me again.

"It's me," the voice said. "It's Lucas."

I sat up, blinking against the darkness. My mind was foggy, but I was sure I'd heard something that time. I squinted. Still, nobody.

"White alchemy, remember."

I shook my head, annoyed for not catching on quicker. White alchemy. A magic no one else had, that I was aware of, except for Lucas. He had used it to make our entire helicopter invisible once. The magic had both shocked and relieved me. I'd always wondered if white had power, and the shielding magic made sense to my logical side.

"What is it?" I asked, clearing my throat from the sleep. I'd been out like a light, the kind of sleep so heavy it felt like swimming through quicksand to wake up.

"Here," he handed me the blue stone and I immediately used it to shield our conversation from the possibility of listening ears.

"Okay." I sat up and stretched my neck. "We're good."

"I'm going to stay invisible. I think it's going to be safer that way."

I stood and stretched my legs. "Out with it, Lucas," I sighed.

"It's time to get you out of here," he said. My senses kicked into overdrive, the buzz of adrenaline shooting through my veins.

"Let's do it."

"I've been invisible since I left my bedroom, so nobody should have been able to follow me down here. I'm going out on a huge limb to get you out of here, I think you understand that."

"I do. I promise, I'll keep your secret safe. Now, are you going to turn me invisible with you or what?"

"At the right time, yes," he said, his voice soft in the darkness. "Security isn't as tight tonight. My father has the first exhibition planned for the morning and most of the officers are currently en route. He and I are flying out first thing tomorrow."

"So what's the plan?" I asked.

"There's no time to explain. Just follow my lead."

Oh, that sounds awesome! "Okay, fine."

"And Sasha," he said, "I might need you to try red alchemy again."

I froze. I hadn't done it since breaking free of New Colony years ago. I wasn't even sure I could do it now, but even if I could, I didn't want to! "You've got to be kidding."

"Do you want to die in here or what?" he snapped. I couldn't see him, but I could imagine his face as his frustration grew. "We don't have to tell anyone about your red. But if you want out of here and if you want to go find your friends, you're going to have to get over it and do what needs to be done."

"Fine," I snapped back, partly knowing he was right, the bigger part of me hoping I could prove him wrong. I wouldn't use red unless I absolutely had to. If red even worked!

"Let's get you outside and then we'll use invisibility to travel together to wherever you want to go."

"We have a Resistance safe house not far from here," I said. "Get me there and I can do the rest."

"Let's go."

"What about Christopher and Jessa?" I asked. He was silent for a long moment and my stomach flipped. "We have to help them, too," I pleaded, worried about what the silence might mean.

"I know," he said, "and I wanted to, but unfortunately my father insisted they joined him at the exhibition. They left earlier tonight."

"What?" I sputtered. How did he think *now* was a good time for me to go then?

As if reading my mind, he answered, "I'll try to get them out later, I promise. But for right now, this is the best chance I have at helping you. Even Faulk is gone. Most of the officers and alchemists have left as well. It's now or never, Sasha."

I almost corrected him. *It's Frankie.* But I just nodded and walked to the door, steeling myself but ready to do this.

"There's only one guard outside right now, with security being what it is at the moment. I'm going to open the door," he said, "and I want you to take him out. It should be easy; considering he's asleep at the job. I had no problem lifting the keys off him five minutes ago."

I huffed. *Idiots.* If I were running this place, I'd have the alchemists guarding the cells, not morons. Faulk was going to be so angry. She just might lose her job over this. But still, only one guard? Something about that didn't seem right.

Lucas placed a hand on my back and I nearly jumped. "Here, I have more," he said, opening my hand and dropping a gemstone necklace in my palm. It had all the colors I would need. I quickly strung it around my neck. "I'm ready."

He swung the door wide with a bang, and the guard jumped up, blinking the sleep from his long face. I recognized him as the one who'd spit at me.

"How'd you do that?" he asked gruffly.

I didn't answer and I certainly didn't give him a chance to make the first move. I attacked. I'd been training in combat for practically as long as I could remember. It kicked in without a second thought. I charged him and brought him to the ground, then punched him right in the nose. The shifting crack of bone made me smirk but didn't slow me down. I continued the pay back for all those times he'd stood idly by while someone did the same thing to me.

He didn't even get a chance to retaliate as the yellow alchemy flowed through me. The magic was a sensation akin to coming home, so familiar and calming, the magic sweeping through me like warm water. I smiled, administered one perfect blow to the guard, and sprightly stepped over his slumped-over body.

"Remind me not to piss you off," Lucas's voice whispered, and I laughed. The guard would have a terrible headache and some intense bruising, but he'd live.

"Where to?" I asked.

The next several minutes we navigated our way through the dark palace, our footsteps soft. As we came near the entrance of the prison, I jumped into action and quickly took out the two guards. Up the stairs, we slowed at the first corner. There was always someone awake in a building like this, so we had to tread lightly, especially near the kitchens and laundry. The low rumble of nightshift worker's conversation, clang of dishes, and hum of machines did little to calm my pounding heart.

"This way," Lucas whispered and, "right" "now, left" were my only indication of where to go. At one point I had to jump back into a dark alcove as a few palace guests passed, and a minute later, a guard on patrol. But it wasn't long until Lucas and I were on the main level next to the gardens, a door unlocked and waiting.

No red alchemy needed, thank you very much.

We broke out into the cold night, the snow falling in heavy flakes. The cold immediately seized me but I didn't mind. I grinned and reached out to let a snowflake melt on my fingertip. The frigid air smelled like freedom.

"Over here." Lucas grabbed my arm and pulled me to the side of the palace where the gardens grew thick in the summer. Now it was all sharp angles, the trees devoid of life. He pried open a gardening bin where he'd stashed some boots and a huge black coat. The area was quiet and still, as was his voice. "Get these on and then I need to make you invisible, too."

He didn't have to ask twice.

"Do you have enough energy for that?" I asked. He'd struggled with the helicopter and no way was I making out with him to keep him awake. Any misguided feelings I'd had for the prince were long gone. *Where's Jessa when we need her?*

"I've been practicing and I can go up to three hours by myself. With you invisible, too? I think I can half it. I hope that's enough time to get you to the safe house and to get me back to my room before I have to be up for my flight."

It was jarring not to be able to see his expression, not to be able to see him at all. I could feel his presence, hear his steady breath, and even smell his clean scent. But not to be able to see him left me feeling a tad skittish.

"That's enough time." I nodded, trying to relax. I hoped I wasn't about to make a huge mistake. Trusting Lucas could be the last thing I do. Maybe I could take him out and go on my own, but that was also a huge risk. "It's actually pretty close."

"Of course it is," he mumbled, then reached out to take my hand. "I really hope my father doesn't figure that out one day."

"You're telling me," I replied, distracted. My body, with its gray prison clothes and now, black puffy coat, was turning into nothing but air. As I faded, the panic began to rise. I shook my head. *Unbelievable! I really need to practice white.*

"Is this why you insisted we wait to do this outside, just to be certain nobody saw me go invisible?"

"Yes," he said. "Now, let's go." His cold hand squeezed mine, and together we ran headfirst into the storm.

▼

Sharp guilt twisted in my chest as we trudged through the wet snow. Bringing Lucas to the safe house was never part of the deal I'd made with the Resistance. Especially after he'd abandoned the cause. And even more so after he'd turned on Jessa and ruined our plans. The streetlights cast disapproving shadows across the city streets, a stark contrast to the darkened alleyways. I'd considered ditching him in more than a few of those alleys. But the closer we got to the address, the more I realized I couldn't do that to Lucas. He'd helped me and was still helping me. The urban skyline gave way to the first of many neighborhoods, and it was too late to change my mind. We'd arrived.

I approached the yellow door, centered on the redbrick house, two square windows on either side. The layout reminded me of a smile. It was a small craftsman, in keeping with the neighborhood, old, but well kept. I longed for "what might have been" as I looked at it, but shook the thought away. The Resistance would rise up again.

Right now? It's time to focus so that it has a chance to happen.

The elderly woman who lived there was named Sally. Jasmine had recruited her and her late husband. I'd had her address imprinted on my brain for a few years, hoping I'd never have to use it. Knowing, realistically, I would.

A prickle of doubt peaked the closer we got to the quaint home. What if this

438

was a trap? What if I'd told Faulk about this place already, sometime during that interrogation with Jessa?

We continued up the short drive, the night silent as a dream. Our feet crunching against the snow, our breathing heavy, as the emotions continued to rage.

The porch light flicked on, illuminating the falling snow. We froze.

"Motion sensors," Lucas whispered.

I inwardly cursed and bit my lip. The wind had started to pick up, and my jacket was quickly losing its warmth. I shivered, no longer enchanted by the snowfall. I peered around. There still wasn't a soul out on the streets, just as there hadn't been the entire journey over. Our long tracks that were left in the snow had quickly been swept away by the storm.

"Come on." I tugged him up the steps. I knocked three slow knocks then two quick ones on the yellow door.

We hunched together, still invisible. I felt Lucas's energy begin to fade. No surprise as to why he'd slowed his pace significantly in the last few minutes, his footsteps lagging, his body leaning on mine. He needed to get back and get some rest. Morning would be here before we knew it and there couldn't be an ounce of suspicion against him.

The old woman opened the door, squinting into the night. Her bathrobe wrapped around her, pink and fuzzy, large circular glasses sat atop her nose giving her an owlish stare. Wrinkles lined every inch of her pale face in deep lines of age.

"Are you Sally?" I asked.

She startled, her mouth popping open. "Who's there?"

"Are you Sally?" I repeated, louder this time.

Her eyes grew wide, and she nodded, taking off her glasses and putting them back on again, blinking several times. "Yes, I'm Sally."

I took a deep breath. "I'm a friend of Jasmine's. I'm with the Resistance."

She began to turn her head from side to side, peering out into the darkness, obviously trying to locate the source of my voice.

"I'm going back now," Lucas whispered in my ear. Before I had a chance to react, he released my hand. Immediately, my body returned to visibility. Sally yelped.

"Are my eyes playing tricks on me?" she asked shakily. "I didn't see you there." I decided not to explain.

"Can I come in?" I asked, eager to get off the street as quickly as possible. I lifted my arm to shield the porch light from my face and tucked my head down.

"Of course, dear," she cooed. "You're a friend of Jasmine's? Poor thing, I heard what happened to her. Such a shame. Just tragic. Come in, come in."

I stepped into the warmth of her home and shut the door behind me. Her front room was small and cozy with matching red furniture and the remnants of a fire in the hearth. The whole place smelled faintly of sugar and butter, like she baked regularly. All of these clues, and the proximity to the palace, pegged her as a wealthy woman. She was old now, but either she, or her late husband, must have been assigned high-level jobs before hitting mandatory retirement age. She shuffled ahead, her slippers cupping her tiny feet, as she led me into her kitchen.

"What's your name?" she asked.

I didn't hesitate. What would be the point? "Sasha, or Frankie, I guess."

"You guess?" She chuckled. "Well, Sasha Frankie, let's go get you something to eat. I think you'll be pleased with the company. You're not my only visitor tonight."

The kitchen was filled with white cabinets, a white and black tiled floor with a square oak dining table right in the center. My heart slammed in my chest as my eyes settled on the man sitting there, his body taking up the space with his familiar height. He looked up with black sparkling eyes and stood with a smile spread across his face. The chair tipped backward as a moment later his towering frame enveloped me into a tight hug.

Suddenly, the world, tipped off its axis, righted itself.

"Tristan," I breathed, the oxygen about all squeezed out of me. "What are you doing here?" Tears prickled.

He stepped back and looked me over, up and down several times. He then peeled off my heavy, now dripping, coat and ran his steady hands along my rib cage. My body purred against his touch. "Are you okay?" he asked, his smile thinning into a grim line. "What did they do to you?"

"The wounds have all been healed," I replied, "if that's what you're asking."

"I'm so sorry." He choked on the words. "I never should have left you there."

"It's okay." I glanced away, not wanting to go into the details of how they'd tortured me. "I'm okay."

"Did they hurt you?"

I guffawed at the question. "What do you think?"

When our eyes met, his were brimming with hatred. "I'll kill them."

The silence spread between us. Sally cleared her throat. "I'll just go hang this up." She peeled the coat from his hands and waddled from the room.

We sat at the table, the wooden chair catching my weary body. Letting out a tired sigh, I frowned at Tristan. Excitement made way for confusion. "What are you doing here?" I asked the question again.

"I came back for you," he said, leaning close to slide a warm hand down my arm. "I just got here a few hours ago, actually. I was going to find a way to get you out of there."

I shook my head, staring at him in disbelief. "You wouldn't have been able to."

"I had to try." He shrugged. "You'd have done the same."

He was right. I would have. I leaned my head against his shoulder for a minute, breathing him in. His arm flexed as he nudged me closer.

"Thank God, you're okay." His breath burned against my temple. "How did you get out?"

I sighed, sitting back up. "Lucas helped me."

He squinted at me, shook his head, and ran his hand through his hair, as he thought it over. I caught the scent of a fresh shower and it took everything in me not to climb into his lap and melt into him right there. "I honestly didn't think he was still on our side."

"Guess so," I replied. "Though, I do wonder if he has help that he didn't tell me about. He got me out of there pretty seamlessly."

"What do you mean?"

"Maybe there's still Resistance at the palace. Maybe they followed him, helped him get me out somehow? I don't know, sounds stupid when I say it out loud."

"There is still Resistance at the palace," Tristan interjected.

"Who?" I wracked my brain. Jasmine had been my contact, but surely there were others.

"I only know one personally, a trainee when I was in Royal Officer school."

I shrugged. I'd never met anyone like that through Jasmine.

My limbs still shook from the mix of adrenaline and cold. That funny sensation of being light-headed was creeping in. I closed my eyes, pushing it away. "Lucas was the reason we failed before," I said. "He's the reason the King knew we were coming. Jessa told him about the plans and he told his father. She's furious with him, and I guess he thinks helping her family out will make things better between them."

"Fat chance." Tristan whistled.

I laughed, but didn't say more. I didn't want to get into it. Lucas was in deep and he had to find his own way out. But that was his problem. I had my own to contend with, starting with the obvious.

"So what's the plan?" I asked. "How do we get out of here? Actually, first, explain how you ended up here?"

"Don't get mad." Tristan raised his hands and leaned back in the chair. He'd been holding my freezing hands in his warm, rough palms, and the release of them left mine aching. "When we got back to the camp we evacuated immediately. Mastin led the group out and I chose to travel back here on foot."

I gaped at him, lips parting and shame flashing through me. "You traveled by foot in the winter? Through the shadow lands? How?"

A journey like that was absolutely crazy. What had he been thinking? He could have been killed. *Should* have been killed. The shadow lands were a barren wasteland, not to mention, everyone in New Colony was on the lookout because of the war.

He only shrugged. "I packed plenty of food and water and I know how to take care of myself. The shadow lands were a little tricky but I managed to make it out all right."

I ground down on my teeth, breathing in slowly. "You could have died." Saying it aloud only caused the fear inside to grow. He should have never taken that risk.

"And you could have died in that prison," he replied as he squeezed my hands. "I will never leave you behind again. I'm always going to look out for you." He added, "Don't you know that about me by now?"

My heart leapt in my chest. It was true. Starting when I was only a gangly preteen kid, he'd gotten out of New Colony with Hank, and at the last minute, he'd risked everything to bring me along. He didn't even know me then, and yet he'd recognized the torment I carried with me. He'd saved me.

I let the image of him trekking through the shadow lands to sink in. The cold bitter air, the barren landscape, the snowstorms. It had to have been a couple of weeks since that night we'd been separated. He must be far more exhausted than I was after completing something so reckless.

"Let's get some rest," I said, "then we'll figure out how to get out of here."

"I have to make contact with Mastin," he said. He was wearing a black hooded sweatshirt with a pocket on the front. He rummaged around it to pull out an industrial-looking slatebook. He held it up. Military grade. And not ours. "I have a secure line to communicate with him. He said he could help us out of New Colony once we're ready. We even have a location picked out."

Wow, my boys had planned all this just for me? I grinned, glad that I hadn't been forgotten.

"Where are we going?" I asked, thinking of camp. My heart still ached to know it was long gone now. I could never go back.

"West America," he said. "We have asylum. It's too dangerous for us here."

"He's right." Sally waddled back into the room. "You two are welcome to stay with me but there will be a kingdom-wide search for you soon enough." She pointed at me, her eyes alight with mischief. "You broke out of that palace, Missy, and that makes you a fugitive."

She didn't say more, just busied herself making a pot of tea, as if it was no big deal that she was entertaining what was left of the Resistance.

"I'll let Mastin know we want to be picked up as soon as possible," he said. "We're going to have to travel on foot tomorrow to get to the drop point. It's not safe in the capitol city, for obvious reasons."

As if any of this is safe.

We sat in silence for a few minutes, listening to the teakettle. First the buzz of water boiling, and then the high-pitched whistle as the steam built inside. I felt like that teakettle, like I too was about to burst open.

"You ought to head out tomorrow. The snow will keep most people inside and the exhibition is happening down south. That's a pretty good distraction if you ask me." Sally said with a cackle. She smiled conspiratorially and joined us at the table, placing piping-hot mugs in front of us with a soft thud. The sweet scent of lavender and chamomile filled the air. I took a deep breath and wrapped my shaking hands around the mug. I needed to relax, really think this through.

As much as it terrified me, Sally was right. Tomorrow was our best chance.

I nodded, meeting her honey eyes, and took a long sip. I allowed everything to sink in just as the hot tea warmed my thawing body. "Tomorrow it is. We'll leave at first light."

▼

I should have known it wouldn't be easy. Getting out of the palace was simpler than I would have imagined. Tristan already being at the safe house was the last thing I'd expected to find there. But life wasn't easy, and I knew better than to assume luck was on our side. I leaned back against the seat and gripped the seatbelt strap that cut across my chest.

Our truck ambled along the snow-packed road. My heart raced at every turn, sure that we were going to hit ice and lose control. Tristan kept his eyes glued in front of him and his hand squeezing my knee. Somehow the torturous snow had become our salvation.

"How are you doing back there?" Jerry asked.

"Just fine," I muttered.

Tristan was more amicable, as was his way. He leaned forward, his face right behind Jerry's left shoulder. "Hanging in there. How much longer?"

"Oh, I'd say another hour, at least." Jerry was a weathered man. He had cracked knuckles and calloused hands from years of manual labor. He was also an old friend to Sally, and an ally to the Resistance.

"Good man." Tristan patted the back of Jerry's seat before sinking down into the cracked bench seat where we'd hunkered down for the journey. It was slow going, the snow picking up every now and then, flying past our window. As soon as it would start, it would stop, but that did little to relieve my stress. The roads were beyond anything I'd driven on before.

Sally had been able to connect with Jerry as soon as we'd made our decision to meet Mastin at the drop point. The hardest part of our journey had been the walk. We'd had to amble through the city streets for two miles. Public transport would have been simple, but that wasn't an option, so it was on foot to meet Jerry and hope he turned out to be someone we could trust.

The three of us had been in the pickup for four hours, Jerry at the wheel. There wasn't a lot of chitchat. Not because we didn't have anything to say, I could have talked Tristan's ear off. It was Jerry. I didn't know him. He was a necessary evil, someone I didn't want to let in on any extra information. Not to mention, the terrible roads kept my anxiety at maximum level. Tristan seemed to handle it like a pro, but me? I was jumpy and stiff all at the same time. It made my stomach ball into a tight knot by the time Jerry pulled off the road.

"This is it," he said. "These are the coordinates you gave me."

"Thanks man," Tristan said.

"Good luck."

Tristan swung open the door with a loud squeak and we jumped out of the tall truck. Our boots sunk into the snowdrifts, the cold wrapped over us once again, and we trudged into an open field. There was nothing here but snow.

Jerry didn't wait. With a quick salute and nod, he backed his truck around and drove away. The fumes of exhaust were all that was left, and soon, even that was gone.

We huddled close and waited. *What if they don't make it? What if we freeze to death out here?* The thoughts circled my mind like vultures.

Something faint sounded in the distance. A thudding echo.

"There!" Tristan pointed to a black speck in the otherwise white sky.

The West American chopper came in fast and low, until it was right above us. A door slid open and a ladder rolled out in uneven movements, the end landing at our feet. The noise of the rudder screamed through the landscape as I took the ladder first, Tristan close behind. We toppled into the belly of the chopper and a bulky soldier slid the door closed behind us.

"Ready to go?" he yelled.

We nodded and fell back into the seats, strapping our harnesses as the helicopter swooped up and away.

It was all so easy. Again, I should have known better.

I sat next to Tristan, my head resting on his warm shoulder, watching the landscape fly by in a stream of endless white. There were two other men, West American soldiers, and a pilot up front. They'd introduced themselves, but I'd quickly forgotten their names, too overcome with exhaustion to retain much. My body was still cold, and now that the anxiety of the day was melting away, the heat of my nerves was easing as well.

Mastin isn't here. I studied the thought in my mind, turning it over. Why did it bother me so much? Why did I care that he hadn't come along?

My stomach gave a little tug. It was stupid. Not important. He had other things to do and these guys were certainly capable. They'd picked us up on time, hadn't they? Still, the thought bothered me. And it bothered me that it bothered me!

Something pinged off the side of the chopper with a clatter.

"What was that?" I asked, but before anyone could answer, it happened again, louder.

One of the two men next to us drooped forward, blood pouring from the side of his face. Or…what was left of his face. Adrenaline flared through me as I scrambled to undo my safety restraint.

Gunfire!

"Get down," Tristan yelled. Not that I had a choice, he was practically on top of me, pushing me to the bed of the chopper.

"We've got a tail," the remaining soldier called out to the pilot.

"Hold on," the pilot yelled back. The chopper took a deep swerve to the left and dipped, knocking us all off balance. The pilot moved us even lower to the ground in a quick move that sent my stomach flying.

The moment we steadied, Tristan rolled off of me and reached for the guns strapped above the seats. He tossed one to me, and we scrambled to the back, around the slumped body. The remaining soldier had already opened the back window. He hunched over a gun much than ours, firing a barrage of bullets at our enemy. Army trained, the soldier maneuvered the thing like it was an extension of his body. An ounce of comfort warmed me, but I pushed it away. Tristan and I readied ourselves on either side of him.

Just behind us, a New Colony fighter jet zoomed in and out of our wake.

We were in big trouble.

Still, I waited for the perfect opportunity.

When it came, I didn't hesitate. I pulled my trigger and let out a round of ammunition. It ducked, slowed a fraction, before gaining speed.

"Oh, hell no!" The soldier let loose a string of profanities as he let his firearm loose on the jet.

Ping. Another bullet flew through our machine. The man next to me collapsed, his gun still firing. Tristan jumped on top of him to get ahold of the weapon. I continued to shoot, but something seemed off about this whole thing.

"Shouldn't they just be trying to bomb us?" I asked. "Kill us all?"

"Not if their orders are to bring you back alive," Tristan growled.

Horror flashed through me.

"We have backup on the way," the pilot hollered back. "ETA one minute. Hang in there."

We glanced at each other, eyes wide, hair blowing wildly in the freezing wind. It was them or it was us, and I wasn't ready to die, nor was I ready to lose Tristan. He gripped the huge gun and pressed the trigger. His muscles fired along with the bullets as he followed the path of the jet. I pressed my body even further to the cold metallic surface and steadied my gun again; one eye closed as I took aim. As I shot, my mind returned to the man beside me. He was splattered with blood across his face from the other fallen men, and I thanked God he hadn't been the one in their place. I didn't even know if I believed in God, but if He was real, I thanked him for keeping us alive and prayed it stayed that way.

And then I chastised myself, guilt overwhelming me. Those two soldiers had come to help us, and they'd died for it. Someone would mourn their loss just as much as I would mourn Tristan if he had been in their place.

"They're here," he called out. I glanced up and watched three combat planes drop into the sky, seemingly out of nowhere, shooting at the enemy, taking the jet down in a matter of seconds. It fell in a roll of fury, a blossom of fiery orange in the otherwise white landscape.

I choked back a sob as relief washed over me, quickly ducking my face. As I sat up, Tristan pulled me in to a hug. My body gave way.

Our chopper took a sudden dive, and our bodies flew apart. Alarms blared. Lights flashed. My eyes shot to the pilot, slumped forward in his seat, his head covered in a dark blossom of blood. The inertia of falling overwhelmed me. We slid with the fall, moments from death. My scream pierced the world as I dove for the controls.

SIX

JESSA

The train rumbled beneath me as my head bobbled on Dad's shoulder. I stretched my neck and I sat up, limbs stiff, bleary eyes on the changing landscape outside the foggy window.

"You doing okay, kid?" Dad said, shifting in his seat as he rolled his neck from side to side. He smiled softly when he caught my eye.

I nodded, my stomach instantly raw with hunger. It growled and Dad stood, reaching out a steady hand to help me up from the seat I'd just spent the night in. I was a breakfast person, always had been, which he knew. I'd always envied my friends who could skip it, no problem. That would make starting the day easier than only being able to think about my stomach. Oh well.

"This way," Dad said, opening the door to our tiny cabin and stepping out into the narrow hallway. I brushed off my clothes, standing to shake out my legs. I ran my fingers through my mess of hair and grimaced. No use. I joined Dad and we ambled down toward the dining car. Now that the day had started, the bustle of others waking carried through the train, a soft undercurrent to the worries lumbering around in my head.

The exhibition was to be in the southern part of New Colony, an area I'd never traveled to before today. That was normal. Most citizens lived their whole lives in the same cities.

Many of the officers and alchemists still in the palace had been summoned to the event. I thought I'd be staying behind, but just as everyone was getting ready to load up and head out, Faulk came for us. She said Richard wanted to parade me around to the country. "The main reason he's even doing these exhibitions is to get the people to accept an alchemist as their future queen, so you better behave," she'd threatened. Her words had stirred me in a way I didn't like. I was on display now? At least I got to bring Dad along for the trip.

We'd loaded up and had a simple dinner on the train. Faulk had announced that Lucas and Richard were travelling separately by air, something about their protection. I no longer cared. Finally, after a late night of conversing with Dad, I'd fallen asleep, my head pressed awkwardly against the windowpane, another snowstorm raging on the other side of the glass.

After breakfast, we retreated back to our private cabin. The snow was long gone by now. We watched the world outside whirl past us in silence. A few hours later, the train slowed, signaling our arrival.

"I think we're just outside of Marthasville," Dad said, pointing to the skyline of an urban city in the distance. "It used to be called Atlanta."

I nodded. I already knew this from school. Marthasville was one of the original colony names. Everything got a new name when New Colony rose to power. Or, in most cases, an old name restored.

Peering out of the window, I looked for similarities to the Capitol city that I knew so well. The land here was different. The air was thicker and the buildings older. There was none of the shine that the Capitol boasted. But it was much greener.

"Ready?" Dad asked.

"No," I sighed, but I put my hand in his anyway. He squeezed it once and then we exited the train together.

"The air," I muttered.

Dad looked at me, eyebrows raised.

I smiled. "It's so much cleaner here."

"Over here," Faulk barked, pulling me from my thoughts. She motioned to us, and we went to her, because what else were we supposed to do?

We were formed into lines and then escorted into a hotel just across the plaza from the train station. I marveled at the size of the trees. They were double our own, with gnarled knobs and stringy moss that hung like curtains. It was slightly chilly and the breeze had a bite, but that was nothing compared to what we'd left behind at the palace.

Royal Officers surrounded us, their guns at the ready. They eyed the onlookers with suspicion. No surprise there, not after the terrorist attack at Queen Natasha's funeral. But the crowd didn't seem fazed. Some gaped curiously, some clapped, and many had expressions twisted in fear as they followed us with their suspicious eyes.

They're not afraid of the guns. They're afraid of the magic.

"Boo!" Dax, the kid from my disastrous class earlier, yelled at one of the gawkers. The crowd jumped back, and he laughed, a dangerous ring to the sound. A few of his friends snickered along with him, as if taking pleasure in making fun of regular folks. "Did you come out to see the show?" he called back to them as we continued our walk.

I rolled my eyes and Dad and I shared an annoyed look.

Faulk shot over to Dax, grabbing him by his upper arm. She began hissing quiet instructions in his ear and his body deflated, moving toward the center of the Guardians. He didn't so much as look at the crowd after that.

"Shouldn't have teased them," Dad whispered low. "Not when King Richard wants the people to accept alchemy."

I glanced back at Dax and saw his lips set in a grim line. He caught me looking and glowered.

"That's her!" someone called out cheerfully over the buzz of the crowd. It took a moment for me to realize I was the "her" they were so excited to see. The alchemists around me seemed to split, taking their distance from Dad and me. As they did, the Royal Officers moved in closer.

"Jessa!" Another voice yelled, this time frenzied.

I studied the crowd, noticing the camera crews. The media was well-controlled by Richard, so I had no doubt he wanted my face plastered across slatebooks all over the New Colony. I smiled and waved politely, inwardly groaning to myself.

Be good. Stay in line. Go along with what Richard wants. And then when he least expects it, make your move.

That was the plan. But as I was surrounded by my fellow Guardians, all of us dressed in our black gear, with hordes of armed Royal Officers gleaming in white uniforms, and a crowd of everyday citizens surrounding us, that plan felt beyond impossible. It was as if it was on one end of the world and I was on the other.

"In here." Faulk strode up next to me, a rare smile on her face, as she pointed to the front doors of the hotel. Her blonde hair gleamed in the sunlight, making her look younger. What kind of woman would she be if she weren't an officer? Would she be happier? But her smile was for the cameras, since she wasn't the type to smile, and the thought made me a little sad. "We've got you and your dad a suite. You'll be expected to smile and say only positive things while you're here. Always assume you're on camera."

I laughed, grinning beautifully. "Got it." I nodded.

"Let's go inside, then," Faulk replied.

"Hold on." I pushed past her toward the crowd. I used to be just like these people. Before coming to the palace, I was living comfortably enough, on the outside of magic and not asking questions, but curious. Always curious.

Did they feel the same way? I wanted to see who they were. See if I saw myself in them.

I approached a family. A mother, holding the outstretched hands of two identical twin boys not much older than Lacey. A man with a full beard stood behind her, one hand resting on one of his son's shoulders.

"Hi!" One of the boys grinned up at me. He had a hole where his front tooth should be, smooth brown skin, and black, curly hair. He was adorable.

"Hi there," I said, squatting to meet his gaze. I reached out to shake his tiny hand. "I'm Jessa, it's very nice to meet you. What's your name?"

"I'm Theo," he gushed. "You're so pretty."

I blushed. "Thank you."

"Are you really magic?" he asked, his eyes lighting up.

"Theo!" His mom chastised him. "Be polite."

I grinned at her, meeting distressed eyes. "He's all right. I don't mind the questions," I said, and she visibly relaxed. I studied the twin boys, both now smiling at me with wonder that danced in their eyes. It wasn't my engagement that had them interested in me, it was my alchemy, and something about that felt satisfying.

"Yes, I am magic," I said. "It's a very special thing. Will you be at the exhibition tomorrow, so I can show you?"

"We didn't get tickets," the dad said in a gravelly voice, "but we'll be watching from home, won't we boys?"

They nodded, their heads bobbing.

Faulk choose that moment to come up behind me and tug on my arm. "It's time for the lady to go," she said to the family. They nodded along with her, eyes wide as saucers. It probably wasn't everyday an officer of the court addressed them. The crowd had started to cram around the family, every person seemingly eager to hear our conversation. A cameraman stood off to my left, trained on the whole exchange. I gave it a little wave and the crowd cheered.

"Faulk," I said, "can we please get this nice family tickets for tomorrow's exhibition?"

I turned to meet her steely gaze, her fake smile still plastered on her face. It didn't stop me from adding, "please," in a feathery sweet voice. By now, I'd become used to being on Faulk's bad side. The crowd liked me, so did the camera. They oohed and awed over my question, my public support of a simple family.

"Unfortunately, we already vetted the exact number of live attendees," she said slowly.

"Oh, but there must be something I can do," I challenged with a coy smile, winking at the family. I added, "I am Prince Lucas's betrothed, after all. That has to count for something." The crowd laughed jovially. The camera slid closer.

There was a long, weighted pause as everyone waited for Faulk's reply. Finally, she nodded. "Fine. I'll see to it that they get four tickets." She smiled out toward the onlookers, "But no more." They laughed, and she leaned in toward me, "Now, it's time for us to go."

"Oh, thank you so much," the mother called as we walked away. Her boys waved their hands so wildly, I was sure they were going to smack someone in the face. I beamed and waved back, following the last of the group into the fancy hotel. Dad laughed under his breath.

"What?" I asked him quietly.

He shook his head, the smile soft on his lips. "I'm proud of you. You'll make a fine queen, if it comes to that."

If it comes to that. My heart burned in my chest, conflicted.

The moment we were away from the cameras, Faulk turned on me. "What was that?" she seethed, eyes bulging, that youthful smile now twisted into an angry grimace.

I shrugged. I'd just achieved something important. I'd not only undercut Faulk, but I'd furthered my approval rating with the people. Richard would love that. And if I wanted to get closer to him, I'd need to get Faulk out of the way.

"You do not get to make the rules," she spat. "You do not get to flex any kind of power. You are here to look pretty and smile and *that is it.*"

I blinked innocently. "Whatever you say, boss."

She huffed and stormed away, a brigade of wannabes hot on her heels. I caught Dad's knowing expression and winked.

"That's my girl," he whispered under his breath. I slung my arm through his and leaned in. Maybe we were going to be okay, after all.

▼

The room was dark and cool, the air-conditioning causing a chill to spread over my exposed arms and legs. I shifted in my too-short dress. The flashing of the photographers' lights momentarily brought the room into illumination, followed by blinding darkness.

I sat in the front row, lines of chairs behind me filled all the way back to the end of the huge room. It was even bigger than the largest ballroom back at the palace, and whenever I turned around to look, the overwhelming amount of people staring back shocked me.

Such a long trip over, and so far, we'd never even left the hotel. The exhibition was being hosted in the same location as our rooms. At least when I'd been ushered down here, Dad got to sit right behind me. His nearness was the only comfort I had at the moment. But since Richard and Lucas were on either side of me, and all around us were Royal Officers and Color Guardians, that comfort wasn't enough.

I shivered as I watched the guards and soldiers lining the walls.

"Don't worry," Lucas leaned in and whispered into my ear. His closeness brought a mix of warmth and worry careening through me. I still didn't know how to settle on one emotion when it came to him. "You're not going to have to do anything but watch."

I already knew that. Faulk had been very clear that the alchemists performing in the exhibition had trained for it and if I intervened in anything, she'd kill me.

"Okay," I replied anyway. He shifted closer and kissed me gently on the cheek. I stiffened.

"For the cameras, remember?" he whispered, a trace of hurt in his voice. I reached out and laced his fingers through my own. My ring pressed against my finger. It was weird wearing an engagement ring. Earlier, Richard had handed it to me like it was nothing. Maybe it was. But when I'd slid it onto my finger, it had felt like everything.

Lucas frowned and glanced down at our hands, his face paling. "Where did you get that?"

I laughed quietly, but laughed all the same. Where did he think I got it? "Your father gave it to me this morning. Who do you think?"

His eyes darkened and flickered over to his father. Richard was busy talking to Faulk on his other side. "He should have had the decency to let me give it to you myself," Lucas said bitterly.

"It's okay," I said, sighing and turning once more to look at the guests

450

assembling in their seats behind us. Big mistake. I caught the eye of Celia. She sat with her family, just a few rows back and glared at me haughtily before looking away. Her mother said something and then all three of them turned toward me. A guilty pit formed in my stomach. I shouldn't feel bad. She barely knew Lucas when they got engaged. Besides, I'd been coerced into our engagement.

"It was my mother's," Lucas said.

"What?" I turned back to him.

His expression became even darker. "The ring."

"Oh—yeah, well, it's beautiful," I stammered. I'd had no idea it was Queen Natasha's ring. Geez, Richard really was heartless.

Lucas released his hand from mine.

I studied the ring, admiring its beauty. It was silver, featuring a large circle diamond in the center with two rectangular green emeralds on either side. It sparkled like it had been dipped in glitter. It was perfect for someone like Queen Natasha. But on me, I wondered if it looked silly. Wasn't seventeen too young to be engaged? Apparently, nobody else thought so. I caught a cameraman nodding at me, and I smiled proudly and flashed the ring.

"Time to get started," Richard said and stood from his chair. Sitting so close to the King had me in fits of nerves, but as he left, I found those nerves multiplied. Within seconds, he climbed the stairs to the long rectangle stage in front of us. It had been assembled just for this event. A podium and attached microphone stood off to one side. With a few sweeping steps, he took his place behind it and smiled out toward the crowd. Dressed once again in his royal regalia, he was a sight to see. A sight I was entirely sick of. *Better get used to it.*

"Ladies and gentlemen," his voice boomed over the microphone. "My beloved citizens across our prosperous kingdom, welcome."

Applause rang out.

I clapped along but bit my lip in worry. When Richard held an audience, nothing good ever came from it. What would he do next?

"This exhibition will feature the incredible magic of color alchemy. Today, specifically, we'll be showing you the power of yellow and green. These are two colors that our alchemists often use together in combat."

With that, four of the alchemists surrounded the corners of the stage. All teenage boys. I recognized Dax immediately. His black, greasy hair that normally hung in his face was tied back. He grinned at his competitors, ready to pounce.

"Oh brother," I mumbled.

"What?" Lucas asked.

I shook my head. "It's nothing."

I snuck a look behind me to catch Dad's eye. He rolled them, the silent exchange between us calming me for a moment. I chuckled and turned around. Lucas wasn't looking at me anymore, his eyes were trained on the scene in front of him, his body tense.

The boys jumped at each other, engaging in combat without holding back.

The yellow alchemy flowed around them, tendrils of strength. The crowd ate it up. Every time one of the alchemists pulled color from their stones, the energy in the crowd heightened. The alchemists were enhancing the magic as they continued hand-to-hand combat. They sent the magic out into the air, displaying it, before calling on it.

This was a show, after all.

The excitement that coursed through the crowd was palpable, like a collective pulse that rose and rose with each blow. Soon, two of the guys were knocked out. Officers swept in to drag them off the stage, leaving Dax and one of his friends to finish the exhibition. Dax grinned, another blast of magic surging through him when he landed the final blow. His opponent's body smashed against the stage with a dull thud, splitting the wood. He stood, staggered against the unevenness, and then crumbled in on himself.

Blood ran down Dax's arm as he raised it into the air, victorious.

Richard had long since removed himself, beaming with heady satisfaction from the sidelines. The stage was destroyed. Dax jumped off the edge onto the floor, coming to stand in the center of the room. I could smell the salty sweat and hear his labored breath as he stood only feet from me.

His friends were now laid out on the carpet. They weren't dead, but the slick blood and swollen bruises that covered them was enough to make bile rise to the back of my throat.

"That's enough fighting," Richard's voice rang out. He stood at the side of the room, the microphone tight in his grip, as he strode to join Dax. I sunk further into my seat. "Now please, show them how green is done."

An officer hauled a potted plant over to us.

"Now, this is something to watch closely," Richard said and nodded to Dax.

Dax smirked at the closest camera as he grabbed a large palm frond. The crowd of people stood, everyone vying for a better look. But now that there wasn't much of a stage, they didn't have a good view anymore. Someone must have thought of that because even though I had a perfect view, nearly every other head in the audience turned toward a ten-foot screen that was off to one side of the room. It displayed the alchemists in a clear view, zooming in close on Dax's hand as he manipulated the green leaf. The green color wafted out in strings of iridescent magic, spinning in the air above his bloodied hands. With the quick flick of his wrist, he sent the magic to his friends. It soaked into their skin like water, gone.

Broken bones straightened into place. Oozing blood stopped. Pale faces returned to normal. One-by-one, they blinked and sat up.

"It's a miracle," someone called from the back. And that was it; the room was swamped in the chaos of applause. People talked over each other, the noise rising, as the realization of green alchemy stoked what was already an excited fire.

"There you have it," Richard said, his voice booming over the crowd. "That is yellow and green alchemy. That is the reason our soldiers will survive and thrive on the warfront. They have magic at their aid, to make them stronger and keep them healthy."

How much of that was actually true? There were a lot of alchemists out at war right now, but how many of them were helping everyday soldiers?

"For those of you looking for adventure, for a noble cause, this is it," Richard continued. The gold buttons on his jacket gleamed as he leaned toward the camera. His salty black hair, his steel gray eyes, his square jaw, trusting smile, tailored royal clothing, everything about him seemed perfect. "Join our war, avenge our queen, spread the truth, and do something you can be proud of."

Again, the crowd burst into applause.

"Thank you, and goodnight!" Richard boomed once more through the microphone. I startled, letting the gravity of it sink me deeper into my chair. I glanced at Lucas from the corner of my eye. He was expressionless. Unreadable.

Did he agree with his father? Did he want this, too?

It was over. Just in time, too, as I was beginning to shake, the frenzied kind I couldn't control. *Get back to the room, get away from all these people, and you'll be fine.*

They had no idea of the costs of magic, not when it was controlled by a man like Richard. I shook the thoughts away and focused on Faulk. She'd taken Richard's microphone. "Everyone, please rise and stay in your places so that the royal family can be escorted from the room first."

I stood, but Lucas's warm arm quickly threaded through mine.

That's me. I'm the royal family now.

Richard led us down the center aisle. We smiled and strode to the back of the room. Hundreds of eyes followed. A camera, too. My cheeks burned. My jaw ached. My dress felt even tighter than I remembered, and I ran my hand down the black sequins, finding the roughness somehow soothing.

"Can you use that green magic on more than just people?" a voice bellowed.

Richard stopped, his shoulders tensing under his jacket. A wave of panic rushed through me. We turned to the man who dared speak. He stood tall, a tense look about him. It was the same bearded man from yesterday, his wife and children sitting next to him. They were gaping as they stared up at him, as if speaking out wasn't something they expected of their father. From the way his eyes shifted, I thought maybe he was just as surprised as they were.

Oh please. Please be careful what you say to Richard.

"Do not address your King like that," Faulk said, striding to stand next to Richard. She glared at the man, one hand resting on the gun at her hip. "I'm so sorry, Your Majesty." She swung back to Richard. "I thought we properly vetted everyone and coached them on what was and wasn't allowed here tonight. Well, we did, but then Jessa invited this family and—"

"Hush." Richard put up a hand. She shrunk and stepped back, silenced, her glare shooting to me. How was I to know the man would do that?

"Yes," Richard said to him, "to answer your question, we can use it on any living thing, depending on the severity of the wound. We can't heal disease or bring back the dead."

"But crops? Can you heal crops?" He raised his chin.

The crowd had completely quieted.

"We can, and we have."

"My entire crop died earlier this year. Not just mine, but the whole area was hit with early frost. Thousands of acres were lost, and our pay was cut. Where were your alchemists then?"

The room stirred uncomfortably.

A couple of the cameramen who'd come up behind us, filming the whole exchange, turned away. Richard was completely still. "We didn't arrive in time, unfortunately. But rest assured, we would have helped if we could have."

The man blinked, as if suddenly coming to realization as to where he was and whom he was addressing. He'd been brave, but now he bowed quickly, muttered a thank you, and sat down. As we filed from the room, I was certain he wasn't the only farmer in there.

I couldn't smile about it. But I wanted to. I wanted to champion those families and challenge the King myself.

"Find out who that man is," Richard said to Faulk once we were alone, "and punish him accordingly."

"Father!" Lucas chastised, stepping forward. In the brightness of the lobby, he looked even more like his father. The two were dressed almost identically but that was only where it started. "Punishment is hardly necessary. First of all, you had to expect there to be questions after the exhibition. Secondly, he was right! We didn't come to their aid. Or did you forget about that already?"

Richard and his son stared each other down.

"It doesn't matter," Richard finally replied. "He can't talk to me that way. Nobody can."

Lucas shook his head.

"No, it's my fault this happened," I said. "I invited that family here. Faulk didn't vet him, didn't coach him. He just saw the green alchemy and like Lucas said, he had questions. Please don't punish him. That will only make it worse. You're doing this to get the people to like alchemy, right?"

There was a long pause as Richard turned silvered eyes on me. A chill ran down my spine, but I held his gaze. "I'll consider it," he finally replied.

I nodded. "Please, do, Your Royal Highness." I sunk low into a curtsy, something I rarely did for Richard. But I was playing a game, and part of that was appealing to his arrogance.

"We leave first thing in the morning," Richard said to his son. "I'm tired of this place already. The rest of them can follow on the train in our wake."

We began to move toward the bank of gleaming elevators.

"Sir." Faulk cleared her throat. "I have something I have to tell you. I'm afraid you're not going to like it."

Richard's already angry face turned beet-red. "Out with it, Faulk!"

The elevator dinged, and the door opened. We all stepped inside, the four of us and two other officers who I recognized as Richard's personal bodyguards. We were crammed inside. Richard's growing irritation made the space even smaller.

"I think I'd better wait until Jessa is back in her room." Faulk sneered at me. Something burned deep inside my chest.

"I think Jessa might have more logic in her pretty little head than you do in your entire department, lately," Richard snapped.

Faulk paled. "We lost Sasha," she said bluntly. "Or Frankie."

The doors closed, and we began to rise. Nobody said a word. Mirrors surrounded us on all sides, so nothing was hidden. Only Richard and myself had any measure of surprise on our faces, as if the rest of the party already knew this information. I studied Lucas, biting my lip.

"What are you talking about?" Richard finally asked. Lucas grabbed my hand and pulled me behind him.

"She escaped," Faulk said.

There was a long pause. "How?" Richard asked darkly, his hands forming into tight fists at his side.

"We still haven't figured it out, but we have to assume with magic."

"When?"

"The night I left to come here."

The door opened and chimed. We'd reached our floor. One of the guards placed his hand over the elevator door so it wouldn't close, but still, nobody made a move to leave.

Finally, Richard spun on me.

"Did you do this?" he growled.

My jaw dropped. I hadn't seen Sasha in days.

"How could she?" Lucas questioned. His sturdy frame blocked me from the rest of the group. "She was traveling to get here. So was her father."

Faulk and Richard both glared at me.

"We'll figure out what happened," Richard said, eyes bulging out of his head, "and when we do, I can promise you someone will pay for this." He turned on Faulk. "And you, I'm beginning to wonder just how incompetent you truly are."

Then he stormed out of the elevator and down the hall. Lucas walked me to my room, gripping my hand tightly in his. For once, I let myself lean into him. As we approached my door, Faulk blocked us.

"I'm watching you, Loxely. Don't think I'll ever let another one of your family members slip from my grasp again. Because I won't. You will live the rest of your days under my watch and you will learn to behave, or else those days will be numbered." Her eyes were ice blue daggers directed right at me. She meant every word. It wasn't a threat. It was a promise.

▼

My body relaxed as I danced, trying to let anxious thoughts go. My feet pressed against the hardwood floor; my toes crammed against the points of my shoes. I felt the emotions in the movements, felt it all with each step, with each jump, each turn. The fear of my situation came crashing down on me as heavy as iron. I fell to the floor and sobbed, giving in. Finally, giving in. Gasping, awful sounds that I could hardly recognize as my own echoed through the empty room. Still, I didn't care, I just let it all out, an unstoppable catharsis.

The door squeaked open. "Jessa, what's wrong?" Madame Silver rushed into the room, draping her petite frame over mine in a hug. "Darling, it's okay. It's going to be okay."

I stilled. "You're early," I stated, my voice croaking. "I'm sorry. I wasn't expecting you for our lesson for another twenty minutes."

"Oh darling, no. I'm right on time."

"Oh," I sighed, wiping the mess of tears from my face. They stung against my raw cheeks. She sat back, and I looked up to meet her kind eyes. "I was practicing. I must have lost track of time."

"You do that often," she teased with a wink, and I laughed softly. It was true. There had been a time in my life where ballet had carried me away on a daily basis.

"I think I've cried enough for one day. You must think I'm so weak."

"Actually no," she said, standing and reaching out to help me up. "You're one of the strongest people I know."

"It's just this place," I confessed. "It's not as glamorous as it looks."

She paused, studying me. We stood close together in the empty dance studio, with its wood floors, white walls, mirrors and ballet barre on the far end. The light filtered in through the windows just the same as it had in my old studio, soft and muted. It had immediately become my favorite room here, and the only place I could fully be myself. Madame Silver's lessons were my saving grace, but after the exhibition and Faulk's threats, I was beginning to think grace didn't exist.

And hope. Don't forget hope.

"Darling, I believe you," Madame Silver said, stepping closer. Her rose scent filled me, stirring old memories. "I know you didn't ask for this. I know what your dream was, and this wasn't it."

I looked around the room and fought the urge to burst into tears again. I wanted to spill it all, to open up and tell her *everything*. She was one of the people I trusted most in the world. But how many more people would get hurt because they cared about me? I was dangerous to love.

"Can I help you?" she asked. "I mean it, Jessa. What can I do?"

This wasn't safe.

"Maybe there's something," I whispered. I was still weak, weaker than ever. A strong person wouldn't bring her into this. I knew better, but still, the words grew from my tongue like thorned weeds. "I think you might be able to help me."

456

SEVEN

LUCAS

The landscape stretched out, as dead as the horizon. I turned around and surveyed the farm from a different angle.

"Still dead," the farmer said, and I nodded, though it gave me no satisfaction.

When everyone had loaded on the train, Richard taking to the air, I'd stayed back. It had been easy to talk him into the idea. He'd been distracted. I said that I wanted to get a better feel for the issues facing the rural farming communities, see if I could brainstorm ways to help them. He left me with an army of bodyguards and plans to send the family jet back for me in a couple days.

"When we can't produce crops," the man continued, his tone gruff, "we get our wages docked. Trouble is, this is all we've got. There's no other job for us. Farmer's kids are almost always assigned to take over the trade. My old man passed away years ago and I've had this land in my care ever since."

We ambled along the dirt path, right through the center of empty fields. The back of my neck itched as the sun pressed down through the cool breeze.

"What do you grow out here?" I watched the farmer as he talked, noticed the way he thought over his words, as if tasting them first.

Taysom Green was the same man that had challenged my father at the exhibition. I'd instantly liked him and wanted to learn more. I also suspected he might be Resistance, or would be if given the opportunity. It was the way he'd first approached Jessa, as Faulk had described it, and the sureness in his voice when he'd challenged my father. This was a man who wasn't afraid of standing up for the little guy.

I hoped so, anyway. If I was going to get his help…

"In this part of the kingdom, we can grow all sorts of food. My farm is mostly wheat, though we *usually* have a nice tomato crop as well," he said forlornly. There was no trace of a smile now. It had struck me as sincere when I'd come out here. It glowed against his dark skin, magnetic. "It's been a rough year. Everything keeps dying. You name the problem and we've probably had it. Too much rain. Not enough rain. Frost. Wind storms." He rubbed his hand through his curls and faced me. "I'm okay. It's my wife and kids I worry about. We keep getting our pay docked but we're not allowed to find other means for work. Now you tell me, how am I supposed to take care of them? Feed them? How are any of the farmers out here going to make it until next harvest?"

My face burned at his questions, ashamed. What use was a prince in this kingdom? I examined the churned-up fields. "You're right," I said. "We need to be doing more. We should have a few full-time alchemists living out here to help with the crops. I know it's something we used to do, though my father has kept all his alchemists busy with other things lately."

"I've never seen an alchemist on my farm, but I believe it," he said. "There's been a few times where someone's crops were close to dying and miraculously, those same dying crops returned to full health overnight."

I nodded. It was what magic was meant for, if you asked me.

"Now that how it's done is no longer some big secret," I said, "I can work on convincing my father to help you. He should agree since this food helps to feed the kingdom."

"You're a good man." Taysom smiled, "You'll make a good king someday. Much better than your father."

I glanced back to the bodyguards trailing us, hoping none of them had heard that. Any one of them could be a spy for Faulk or Richard. But they didn't seem to care either way. Maybe they agreed.

What would Mom think of all this? Of me? I wondered suddenly.

We'd come down near this part of the kingdom to go to the beach, but never to the farms. Mom had loved the beach when I was a kid. I could picture her there, sitting on the sand, the morning sun hitting her red hair in just the right way, lighting it up like fire. I shook my head, momentarily erasing the memory so I could focus.

I cleared my throat.

"I'm so sorry." Taysom stepped back, looking ashen. He gulped and raised his hands carefully. "I shouldn't have said that."

I must have looked pretty bent up over the thoughts of Mom and he'd interpreted that to be offense over Richard.

"Oh, it's okay." I hesitated, peering at the guards several yards away. "I often think the same thing."

He raised a curious eyebrow and I shrugged. "Come on, show me more."

The next few hours were spent walking the length of the farm, answering each other's questions. I liked the guy. There was something so organic about him, so honest.

"And what of this war?" Taysom asked. "Do you support it?"

I swallowed.

"We were attacked at my mother's funeral and innocent people died," I said simply, as if that answered it. He nodded, seeming to accept the simple answer.

Truth was, I didn't know. There wasn't definitive proof that West America had anything to do with that attack. And the war certainly was an opportunity for my father to be greedy with other people's lives. Growing up in the palace, I'd learned the politics of greed with the best of them.

I looked out again at the land before me, stretching in endless fields of emptiness. "If we leave the dead crops, it will rot," Taysom said, standing next to me. "It's painful to do it, but we have to get it out, roots and all."

Richard wanted to expand his territory. And he also created the shadow lands, used alchemy to destroy entire expanses of terrain in a vain attempt to garner more control. He was an oxymoron, a walking contradiction, and my biggest fear was that we were the same, and maybe my roots were rotting, too.

"Come eat dinner with us. My wife has been preparing a meal all day."

Ahead stood his family's white, two-story farmhouse. It had dormer windows, a wraparound porch, and a grassy lawn with a towering willow tree. It looked centuries old, but well cared for over the years. How many wars had this farm home endured? And how many more before it was lost to the violence of humankind?

"I couldn't possibly eat your food," I said, "not after everything you just told me. But thank you for the offer."

"Nonsense! Samantha will never let me live it down if I had *the* prince here and we didn't dine with him. Trust me, she'll be the talk of the town after tonight." He laughed heartily, his tall frame towering over my own 6 feet 2 inches. I followed him inside.

▼

After enjoying tender roasted chicken and butternut squash that could rival any meal at the palace, Taysom led me down to his cellar to show off where he brewed his own beer. Samantha climbed in the other direction; two floors up to put the twins to bed. The bodyguards were left to their own devices. Some waited at the top of the stairs. Some crowded the kitchen, finishing off the leftovers that Samantha had offered. And others cased the perimeters of the house, at the ready to defend me in the event of an attack. But none had come down to the cellar, and with that, I'd found my moment.

"If I asked for your secrecy, for your trust, and most importantly, your help, would you offer it to me?" I asked.

Taysom didn't even hesitate. "Yes."

▼

I stepped out of the black executive car, legs aching from walking for hours yesterday with Taysom. The sight of the familiar sleek jet calmed me. At least I'd get to rest today.

It sat centered on the tarmac, large, pearl white, and with the royal family insignia of three red stars, painted across the side. I climbed the stairs, wind whipping through my hair. I hurried to one of the white chairs, relaxing into the heated leather seat. I was only going north into more cold, but I'd get to see Jessa again soon—that made it worth it.

I hoped she would be happy to see me, too. The likelihood, or rather the lack thereof, left me feeling raw.

I glanced out the window. A man struggled with a bulky suitcase. He had a limp, and was dragging the case across the ground with a strangled expression. I glanced over to the bodyguards huddled together outside talking. They'd be inspecting everything before we took off if they hadn't already done it. That was their job. But to make this poor man, whoever he was, battle with loading the cases all on his own? Not okay.

I sighed and stood, making my way out of the plane.

"Here, let me help you with that," I called out, climbing down the stairs and approaching the man. I grabbed the handle of the case. The suitcase was made from black fabric, bulging at the seams. It probably belonged to one of the guards flying back with me.

"No, Your Highness," the man spluttered. "You couldn't possibly."

I lifted it to the cargo hold and winced. "I *could* possibly," I said. "Really, I'm happy to help out. You don't have to treat me like my father, you know? I don't like to be waited on hand and foot."

"Well, okay, thank you," the man replied with a weathered smile. He looked pretty old, but that could have been from his manual labor job outside. He wore a black coat and a reflective orange vest that flashed in the sunlight as he moved. "I pulled a muscle this morning, but a job's a job. Gotta work."

I opened my mouth to ask if he could get the day off, but then decided better of it. Most likely, that answer was no. People worked in New Colony. They had what they needed, but they worked hard. It was what we believed in: give a man work and give him a roof over his head.

"Hey." A guard trotted over. "Your Highness, what are you doing? You're supposed to be inside the plane. This isn't your job."

I eyed the guard and caught the patronizing look he sent to the injured man, like it was his fault I was out here. If anything, those guards should have seen a man in need and stepped in to help. Getting mad at me for doing the right thing and taking it out on this innocent guy was not okay. "I can do as I please," I said coolly to the guard. "It's no concern of yours if I decide to lift a suitcase."

"Yes, but," the guard went on, shaking his head, "you need to get back on the plane. It's cold out here and we can't have you catching your death."

I rolled my eyes. These guys? Seriously? They thought I was made from feathers or something. "I think I can handle it."

"Are there more bags?" I turned back to the lone worker. "Can I help you finish up?"

"Sure." The man shrugged and waddled away, still limping.

We walked to a car parked ten yards away from the plane, piled high with luggage.

"That was the first one in the pile," the man said. "I still got all of these to load up."

Well, at least I can call this my workout for the day.

"Your Highness, I really must insist that you board the plane and relax." The bodyguard had followed us to the car but did he offer to help load bags? Certainly not. I shook my head and hefted another bag into my arms.

Boom!

It pulsed through the air, pushing me to my back. Hard. I gasped for breath, pain and heat shuddering through me.

What the—?

Adrenaline raced through my veins. Sweat bubbled on my skin. A strange crunch echoed through the air. I stared, mouth agape, at what was left of the jet.

"Get away from there!"

The remaining bodyguards swarmed me, pulling me away from the scorching flames as they grew wild into the sky. Still, the heat pressed down. The inferno was maddening, overcoming the jet in seconds. I blinked rapidly, trying to take it all in. As the faces of my bodyguards leaned over me, realization sunk in deep. Where was the man that had been so insistent I stay on the plane?

"Where is he?" I demanded of the guards. They'd now surrounded me, aiming their guns outward.

"Where's who?" The guard closest barely looked at me as he surveyed the area.

I shook my head and focused past the ringing in my ears.

"The bodyguard who just tried to kill me!" I yelled.

They all exchanged worried glances as they looked around.

"He's gone."

▼

After returning home and debriefing with my father, Jessa was the only person I wanted to see. I knocked on her door.

"Are you okay?" Jessa asked as she swung the door open. Her eyes filled with tears, blue oceans of worry. "I heard about what happened. That's insane. I can't believe it."

I nodded, even though I wasn't sure if okay was the right way to describe how I felt. The attack on my life had come way too close to ending it. The danger of it still pulsed through my veins. My mind couldn't stop replaying the scene over and over again, nor could my body relax. I kept catching myself shaking, my pulse climbing.

I'm so lucky to be alive.

She laced her arms around me in a hug and I held her tight, lingering in her familiar scent. I finally relaxed. After a long moment, she led me into her room and closed the door. Staring up at me, she frowned. "I know things between us aren't what they used to be, but I would never wish you dead. I'm really sorry you had to go through that. I'm still shaken up about it, but I can't imagine what you're going through."

My heart ripped in two at her words, part of me relishing in her closeness and gratitude that I was still alive; but the other caught up on her words. *Things between us aren't what they used to be.* Would they ever be normal again? Did she even want them to be? The more time I spent with her, the more I realized it was hopeless.

"Can I help with anything?" she asked.

"You can." I nodded and moved toward her couch, sinking into it.

After the attack, our plane was nothing but a heap of ash and metal. I'd taken a train home, traveling all day. It was getting late and I needed sleep, but there was something I wanted to do first.

"Did they find out who did it?" she asked.

"Oh, I know who planted the bomb," I said. "It was one of the bodyguards. But I'm not sure who they were working for or where they are now."

Faulk and a few of her best people had gone in to clean up the pieces and run a full investigation. Richard had been livid when I'd returned home. I could only imagine how he must have reacted when he'd first received the news. I wondered how much longer Faulk had here. If it was me, she'd be fired.

"So the bodyguard got away?" Jessa sat down next to me. I nodded.

"The easiest explanation is that West America had planted him—," I shrugged. And that was the interpretation my father had taken. But I had questions. Up until the war, West America had left us alone. We'd been the one to initiate the war. Not them. Maybe it was the Resistance behind these attacks; maybe it was someone else entirely. What happens next time?

I peered over at Jessa. She sat inadvertently close now, her face twisted in fear, a faraway look in her eyes. I knew she hated this place, but I loved having her here. Once we were married, we'd have the option to move into my bedroom or takeover a different suite. We'd move, of course. I'd let her decorate it however she wanted, and we'd only have to see Richard when necessary.

You really think that's going to happen? Get real...

"What do you believe happened?" she asked.

"Something isn't adding up," I finally said. "I don't know if West America is truly behind these attacks."

"Maybe you could go question that couple?" She shrugged, pulling the elastic from her hair and letting the locks loose. Curls tumbled around her shoulders, and when she ran her fingers through them, I had to look away. My gaze inadvertently flickered to the bed beyond her and I closed my eyes, pushing my emotions down. "You know the ones Faulk brought in a few weeks ago? They might know something," she continued.

I racked my brain, annoyed with my lack of focus. "Remind me?"

"The ones that Faulk used for one of my alchemy tests, remember? Did you ever know about them? It was a man and woman that had something to do with the attack at your Mom's funeral. Well, at least, I think they were closely related to the gunman. And they definitely had something to hide because the orange alchemy amplified that tenfold. I'm pretty sure Faulk has them locked up somewhere."

How has nobody told me about this? This could be the key.

"Help me," I said, grimacing at what I was about to ask. "Use your red alchemy and come interrogate them with me."

She leaned back, her brow furrowed.

"No way." She stood and lifted up her hands in protest. "The second I start doing something like that, it's over. Richard is going to be using my red alchemy left and right."

"That logic makes no sense. You already did it on Sasha before she broke out. Plus, you know it's only a matter of time before he makes you use it again. At least this could help save my life. And who's to say you won't be interrogating them tomorrow anyway. At least this way we can learn what we need to know together."

She bit her lip. "It'll become an endless cycle. That's my *logic*. Once I start doing it, I won't be able to say no. I'll just keep doing it." She turned away and walked to the window, quiet for a moment. Then she looked at me, shame pulling at her lips. "Part of me likes doing it and I don't want to feed into that."

The guilt tore at me. I strode toward her, stopping inches away.

"Please, Jessa," I pleaded. "I really need your help. My life is at stake here. I know you're angry with me. I know you don't want to be with me anymore. But please, at least help me find out who's trying to kill me."

She looked into my eyes, her resolve softening. I reached out and grabbed her hand, placing it on my heart so she could feel what I felt. It raced underneath my skin. For fear of death. And for her closeness.

"Fine," she relented, sighing and biting her lip again. She did that all the time and I *always* noticed. My heart raced faster, and I dropped her hand. "But let's go now while Faulk is gone and before I chicken out."

"Deal," I said. "We'll go down to the prison and I'll get the guards to tell me where they are. Once we're in there, we'll make it quick, in and out. I just have to know if that gunman was really working for West America or if it was someone else."

She was pale now and looked like she was about ready to be sick, but she nodded, heading for the door. "Okay, Lucas," she said. "I really hope we don't regret this."

▼

We descended the stairs to the prison quickly. The palace was crawling with guards and officers tonight. Since Sasha's escape and my own near-assassination, they seemed to have multiplied again. With that in mind, I expected the prison guards to put up some kind of fight. I tucked Jessa's arm through mine when we entered the dim corridor.

"Where is the married couple located?" I asked the nearest guard. He stared at me, mouth hanging open.

"What? Do I have food in my teeth or something?" I joked.

"Oh, sorry." He bowed. I didn't recognize him and wondered if he was one of the new guys.

"Your father said to let you do whatever you want," he said, then shrugged and pointed toward a steel door.

Interesting. Whatever I want and report back to him, most likely.

"There's only one couple here. They're in there."

With the rustling of keys, he opened the door and stepped aside.

The couple sat close together on a cot that was pushed against the far wall of the cell. Beat down and tired, they didn't seem the least bit fazed by me, but a flash of interest lit in the woman's eyes when they ran across Jessa.

The man glared up with a sullen expression. "What do you want?"

"We don't have anything left to say," the woman added and leaned against her husband, exhaustion stretched across her face. Their hair was ratty, and their limbs looked skinny in their prison garb.

"Let's be quick about this." Jessa and I walked closer to the couple. I couldn't help noting the bruises along their arms. I inspected them for the best place to poke them with the needle that was hidden in my hand. We didn't need much. Jessa could use a drop of blood and it could be enough to use her alchemy.

I rolled the needle between my thumb and forefinger. It glistened in the dim light as I stepped forward and poked the man first, right in his upper-arm.

"What was that?" He balked and jumped up, crazed eyes leveled with mine.

Jessa pressed her palm to his bicep, covering the bubble of blood that had formed there. "Sit down and relax," she said. Immediately, his countenance changed and he sat on the floor.

I moved in for the woman. She slid back against the wall, thin hands in front of her a face. "Stay away. I'm so sick of you crazy people and your magic. Please," she begged. "Just leave us out of it."

But I was much bigger than her, and I swiped the needle at her arm before I could change my mind, the needle striking the skin. There was a small prick of blood and she grimaced.

Again, Jessa was quick. She reached out her arm, connected with the magic, and told the woman to sit down and relax next to her husband.

They looked up at us with pliable, vacant expressions, relaxed and open for anything. I fought the urge to feel guilty. *But they know something. They could have been involved in the attack during Mom's funeral, and maybe even the one yesterday. Don't feel bad, just do what you need to do and get out of here.*

"Stay relaxed. Don't get up. You two are going to answer our questions with complete honesty and zero reluctance." Jessa knelt in front of them.

"What do you know about the attack during the Queen's funeral?" I asked, squatting to study their expressions carefully. I watched for any break in the magic, but they were as lost to it as anyone had ever been.

"My brother was the gunman," the woman said softly and slowly, but with no hesitation. "We hadn't expected him to kill so many people. That wasn't what he was trying to do."

"Who was he trying to kill?"

"You and your father."

464

I figured. "So why kill all those other people?"

"We don't know," the man cut in. "Maybe he had a problem with his gun or maybe he lost his mind or something? We don't know."

I shared a glance with Jessa, and she nodded slightly, urging me to dig deeper. "Was he working alone?"

"No," the woman said. "He wanted us to help but we refused."

"Do you know who he was working with?" I pressed.

She shook her head adamantly. "We don't know. Some woman. He kept referring to his contact as a 'she' but we never learned more."

"Did they call themselves the Resistance?" Jessa swung her head to look at me when I asked the question, frustration in the tilt of her mouth. But I had to ask it. I had to know.

The woman shrugged. "I never heard him say anything like that."

"Was it someone from West America?" I continued, desperate for something more than this.

"We don't know," the man said. "We've told you everything."

"Who gave him the gun?" I remembered the sickening ping-ping-ping of the semiautomatic rifle's gunfire.

"We've never seen him with one before," he said. "We don't think he was very well-trained. I mean, why would he be? Maybe that's why he ended up killing so many people."

Such recklessness. Who would be stupid enough to do that?

And this only confirmed what we'd assumed anyway, that someone put him up to it. Supplied him with the weapons and told him where to go and when. A she? It could have been Jasmine or someone else in the Resistance. It could have been someone connected to West America. Their president *was* a she, after all. But she wasn't our enemy until recently, as far as I knew. Dad had started the war, not her. I doubted she was somehow secretly interacting with someone all the way out here. Then again, there was no way to know for sure.

"Do you know how she, whoever she was, got in contact with your brother?"

"We don't."

I growled and stalked to the back of the small cell. The lights were soft, casting long shadows over everything. "Do you have any other information about your brother, that attack, the woman, anything you can tell me?"

They sat in silence.

"I give up," I sighed, exasperated. "These people shouldn't be here."

"But they *were* hiding something," Jessa pressed, talking to me but pointing to the couple. "I'm certain they were."

I turned back on them and stalked in close. "That night you first met Jessa and you got so nervous that Faulk decided to throw you in here, what were you hiding?"

"We don't support the monarchy," the woman said simply. "We haven't for a long time. My brother knew that, which was why he tried to get us to help him execute the royal family. But we never signed up for something like that. We're not killers." A tear slid down her cheek. She still appeared completely relaxed, but I wondered if Jessa's magic was starting to wear off, or if she was so upset about her brother's ultimate demise that the tear had leaked through.

"They don't know anything," I sighed. "Let's go."

"After we leave, you won't remember ever seeing or talking to us today. Got it?" Jessa's voice cracked as she gave her last command.

They nodded, and we left them there. The guard quickly locked the door. I was tired, the weight of it all suffocating me. I usually took the stairs, but not tonight. I glanced back to four men who stood along the wall. They'd been my tail ever since I'd gotten home, my bodyguards. I'd ignored them because they had kept their distance. I wondered if they could be trusted. Who among them was a spy, or worse, an assassin sent to kill me?

I shot them a distrustful look and turned back to Jessa.

"Well that was a bust." I sighed. We made our way to the elevator, stairs be damned.

"They're not that different from me, you know?" She shook her head. "Do they really deserve to be locked up in here? They don't support the monarchy, sure, but they didn't do anything. They didn't take action against anyone."

She had a point.

"I am not in control around here," I replied. "And it isn't fair for you to always get mad at me for someone else's actions."

She sighed. "Fine." She ran a hand through her hair and looked up at the ceiling, I think just to avoid eye contact with me. We strode into the elevator, my bodyguards filling in any empty space. We rose to our stop, and we stepped out onto the marble-tiled floor, never uttering a word.

"I'm going back to my room. I need to get to bed. I'll see you tomorrow, Lucas," Jessa said. She stood looking at me for a moment, then turned and walked off without a backwards glance.

There was nothing else to say. She didn't get it. She was never going to get it because she wasn't me, and didn't know the constant pressure I was under. And maybe she didn't care.

I ground my teeth and strode toward the royal apartment, in search of Richard. As much as I hated it, I needed to tell him about the failed interrogation. He might be convinced of West America's hand in this, but I believed there was someone else trying to kill us. We needed to take it seriously before it was too late.

When I found him in his private office, he motioned me in with a cunning grin. "I was wondering when you'd come to me," he said.

I shut the door behind us.

It's not like I'm on the same side as him. It was easy to tell myself things like that, but part of me was beginning to wonder if it was just another lie.

EIGHT

SASHA

"It's a good thing we learned to pilot a helicopter, or we wouldn't be here," Tristan said, shaking his head once again in disbelief. We'd come so close to death, but those lessons years ago had paid off with our lives once again. I kept replaying what had happened over in my mind, how just a few more seconds falling or a few more inches in the wrong direction and we'd be dead and gone.

But I'd gotten ahold of the controls, and our backup had escorted us to our destination. Tristan and I had followed, shockwaves of adrenaline slow to wear off.

"We're so lucky," I mumbled and met Tristan's familiar gaze. *So lucky.*

"Well, you're here now," Mastin said as he stood across from us.

That we were. The airport below had looked enormous when we'd flown into a private runway. As we'd deplaned, soldiers surrounding us, Mastin had instantly locked gazes with me.

Something flicked through his mossy eyes as he studied Tristan and I. Jealousy, perhaps? Tristan was mine just as much as I was his. We'd simply been through too much together. We were used to jealousy. But something about the look in Mastin's eyes made me lose my train of thought.

"How did the debriefing go?" Mastin asked.

"The usual," Tristan said. "We were placed in holding for a couple of days to corroborate our stories and go over details."

Nobody had protested. Of course they'd want to make sure we could be trusted before letting us into their country. I understood that. With everything going on, with death and war, it only made sense. Tristan seemed annoyed that Mastin still hadn't showed up to help. In his opinion, Mastin should have gotten us through this process immediately. But Mastin was only one soldier. How much pull did he *really* have? This wasn't some outpost of Resistance hiding up in Canada. This was West America.

America. It's just called America here, I reminded myself for the millionth time.

In the end, our stories had checked out and we'd been transferred by plane to the capitol city of Los Angeles.

"This is crazy," I said, looking around at the terminal. It was gorgeous, all white surfaces and shining steel. "I can't believe I'm here."

Outside, palm trees swayed in the wind. Sunshine shone through the window, warming my shaking limbs. My eyes kept returning to the trees. I'd never seen palms in person before, but I'd learned about them. Even though I wasn't officially in school, Hank had made me study. Geography was important to him.

"Believe it." Mastin nudged me and pointed toward a group of people gathered outside. "Because it's about to get a lot more apparent that we're not in New Colony anymore."

I lifted my eyebrows, my curiosity piqued at his statement. We followed him out the sliding doors. A team of security surrounded us as we walked into the pleasant sun and made our way across the sidewalk. A soft breeze brushed against my face, and I smiled. I could get used to this weather.

The chanting tumbled through the air and I nearly stumbled.

"No magic allowed!" they screamed, holding up signs with things written across them like "GO HOME OR DIE" and "GOD HATES ALCHEMY" and "MURDERERS ARE NOT WELCOME." But that wasn't all; there were also those chanting, "Alchemy is Progress" together with signs reading "WELCOME HOME FRIEND" and "MAGIC IS AMAZING" and "WE LOVE YOU JUST AS GOD MADE YOU."

Tristan tugged me close, his arm around my hunched shoulders, as he and the security cleared a path through the crowd. Mastin ushered us into a waiting car and slid in after us, shutting the door with a thud. It left only muffled sounds of the frenzied crowd. They swarmed the car and the driver took off before I had a chance to put on my seatbelt. My hands shook so wildly I couldn't get the belt secured. Mastin reached over to help, his cool hand brushing against mine. I didn't move.

"What was that?" Tristan asked, twisting around to watch the crowd disappear. "Who are those people?"

"Alchemy is a very politically charged issue here," Mastin said.

"But why were they doing that?" I asked. It wasn't anything I'd ever seen before. There was no such thing as that kind of crowd in New Colony. Sure, there were crowds, but they showed support. That was it.

"They're just protestors," Mastin said.

"Protestors?" Tristan raised an eyebrow.

"It's a normal thing here. People assemble to yell about their rights or opinions. It doesn't really do much most of the time. People are pretty set in their ideas. Not everyone would agree, but protesting is a waste of time, if you ask me. People have to vote."

I'd never voted, and I wondered if it made anything better. *What happens when you vote, and you don't get what you want?*

I turned to look back out the window, looking for more protestors. Maybe that's what you did.

"Your president?" I flipped back around and watched Mastin carefully. "You told me she was in favor of alchemy. Is that true?"

"Yes," he said, "she is. As are about half of the country." His eyes fixed on me, so intense and sure. "And me too, after meeting you."

My face burned, and I looked forward, watching the road in front of us. I couldn't face either of the men.

"You better be," Tristan snapped. "This girl has been through hell and back."

They both shifted toward me, sandwiching me between them, and the backseat grew infinitely smaller.

"What happened to you at the palace?" Mastin asked.

I decided to be blunt. I'd told the story so many times over the last couple of days; it wasn't like there was anything left to hide. "They tortured me. Used my sister's red alchemy against me so I gave them info about our camp, but they were too late getting there. Lucas was the one who broke me out."

"Lucas?" Mastin replied, surprised. "As in, Prince Lucas?"

"The one and only," I muttered. "But *that* part isn't public knowledge, okay?"

He nodded. "What's his endgame?"

"How should I know? He's not like his father, never has been. He's not evil. But he is self-serving. He's the reason we were ambushed that night. He thought he was protecting Jessa by giving us away. But now he's back to helping the Resistance. I think he's trying to play both sides of the fence to keep her happy. I'm not really sure where he stands."

"That's not going to work." Tristan chuckled, but I could tell he didn't think it was funny. Nobody did.

"No kidding." I leaned back against the seat and watched as palm trees passed outside the window. Loads of green waxy-looking shrubs, and buildings of all shapes, colors, and sizes flashed by. It wasn't as urban as I'd been expecting. Everything was close together, but small. Actually, Los Angeles wasn't anything like what I'd seen of New Colony and was certainly a world away from Canada.

And the people. Some strode along the streets as if they didn't have somewhere to be. Didn't they work? And others, they were dressed in rags, sitting under trees or walking slowly down cracked sidewalks. New Colony had plenty of diversity, but for the most part, everyone was fed and clothed in similar fashion, they all worked, and always had things to do.

What was better? Guaranteed mediocrity but nobody was left behind? Or a free life, with the guarantee that some people wouldn't make it out of poverty? I didn't know. And now I was here, too, stuck between two lives. Two choices.

I peeked at the men on either side of me, my feelings conflicted.

They were so similar in certain ways, but so different in others. One had been my friend for years, and I loved him more than words. There had been times when I'd been sure we'd end up together. But now there was this other man. He'd come marching into my life against my will, but had taught me to see things differently, forced me to grow. To fight even harder than I already was.

Mastin caught me looking, his eyes narrowing, so I quickly changed the subject.

"So, where to next?"

I figured I'd be joining the others from camp. I hated to admit it, but I wanted to see my mom. And I wanted to see Hank and Lacey, too. I missed them all, a feeling I had kept hidden away while I was in the prison. But now that I was here, so close to them, the longing hit me with an unexpected force.

"That's the thing I wanted to talk to you about." Mastin shifted uncomfortably.

"Are they okay?" I sat up straighter, glaring at him.

He raised his hands. "They're fine. They're great." Then lowered his voice, "But nobody knows Lacey is an alchemist. We've chosen to keep that a secret for now. She's with your mother."

"Okay?" What was his point?

"It's *your* identity that we weren't able to keep secret."

Obviously, considering the protestors, that was true.

"What are you getting at?" Tristan pulled my hand into his lap, holding it tight.

There was a long pause as Mastin leaned back against his window and studied us. "Okay, so Cole might have taken some creative liberties back at camp."

"What are you talking about?" I glared at him, my heart about to beat out of my chest. I had a sinking feeling I knew where this was going. Cole, the general who'd died, had said if the alchemists would help him then we would get to come to West America and be free. I'd seen the paperwork signed by their president herself. If that wasn't the case, what was?

"You don't exactly get amnesty here, though you're not about to be thrown into prison," he said, his expression shifting to shame.

Good! He ought to be ashamed!

Tristan's tall body tensed next to me as he squeezed my hand, like he was about to fly out of his seat and over me to beat the crap out of Mastin.

"How bad is it?" I asked.

"When those men died getting you out, your identity was compromised. There are a lot of people here who hate alchemy. It broke as a huge story. You're not safe here. The others have been given temporary living arrangements but you need to be kept in a more secure location."

"So, put her with me. I'll protect her," Tristan said.

"You've noticed all the security everywhere, haven't you?" Mastin interjected.

"I sure have." I rolled my eyes and leaned back against my seat. The air conditioning was starting to add to the chill and I shivered. "So where am I staying? Out with it, Mastin, you're driving me crazy."

"My father is a general. We've been stationed at a base here and you're going to be our guest."

"No, she is not," Tristan spat. He leaned over me and glared at Mastin. "I got her out of there, she stays with me."

"It was the best I could do. Either that, or another prison. She'll be safe with me on base."

"How convenient for you," Tristan growled.

"As far as America is concerned, she's enemy number one. They hate New Colony and this war. They want someone to take it out on and Sasha is it."

"Can't Tristan come stay with us?" I felt his body slightly relax against my side.

"He'll go stay with the others." Mastin shrugged. "My father doesn't know him well enough to trust him."

I laughed. "And he trusts me?"

"No," Mastin said simply. "But he's curious, so that's enough."

"Did you forget the fact I was the one who went back for her while you saved yourself?" Tristan yelled.

"I have other duties," Mastin snapped back. "I'm a soldier!"

"Stop!" I shouted over their rising voices. They turned on me, hurt, each wanting me to take their side. "Seriously, you two are like kids fighting over their favorite ball on the playground."

I spun toward Tristan, touching his face gently with my fingers. "It makes sense. We'll figure out a way to spend time together, and to bring my sister to see me."

"You need to continue her training. Hiding her alchemy or not, she needs to learn before she accidentally hurts someone."

"I agree," I said. "And thank you for coming back for me. Nobody else would have done what you did for me."

He quieted and studied me with thunderous frustration in his eyes, but he nodded.

Then I turned on Mastin. "And you, give Tristan some credit, will you? He crossed the shadow lands to get to me. He's amazing and if you have as much pull as you seem to think you do, you'll find a way to get Tristan some sort of security clearance so he can help with this war." Then I added, "Hank too, for that matter."

Mastin's mouth had thinned into one long line. I took that as his way of appearing chastised and I held back a bitter laugh. Had he already forgotten what I was like? Of course I was going to stand up for my guy. He was my best friend, almost like a human security blanket. He centered me like nothing else. And Hank, he was like a father to me. The fact he'd gotten out of that palace alive in the first place was a miracle. I wasn't about to let him sit around and do nothing; the man was useful. Mastin was a fool to overlook these men.

"Fine," Mastin relented, relaxing back against his seat. "I'll talk to my father."

"Fine," I said, grinning. I turned to Tristan and winked.

"Fine," Tristan said, studying my face. I willed him to be happy, and he must have sensed that because he winked and smiled, returning to his happy-go-lucky self. I had to admit, it was an impressive ability. And one the always-grumpy Mastin should've adopted. A pang of longing ached in my chest. I rested my head against Tristan's shoulder and tried to relax as the car drove us onward toward our uncertain future. Would I fit in on an American military base?

I considered the magic that flowed through my veins and laughed.

▼

"This is your room." Mastin opened the door and revealed a simple bedroom. It was nicely decorated in sage greens and cotton fabrics. A queen-sized bed sat in the middle, with wooden nightstands on either side, and a wicker chair in the corner by a large window overlooking the yard. A closet was open, empty hangers on the rod. "Mom is kind of the ultimate hostess," he continued, "so she's going to go shopping for you once she gets your sizes."

"She doesn't have to do that."

"Believe me," he replied, "She'll love it. You'll be like the daughter she never had."

The house was the largest on the base, which made sense considering Mastin's dad was some kind of general. It was bigger than most of the homes I'd seen on our drive in, red-brick, with white columns and green shrubs lining the sidewalk. I had immediately teased Mastin about it, delighted when he turned bright red.

The second we'd walked in the door, I'd been met by Mastin's mother, Melissa, who was the older female version of her son, all pale skin, white-blonde hair, and sea foam eyes. She'd immediately fed me, talked my ear off, and treated me like we were old friends. She was quick to inform me that though Mastin was an only child, his father would be there that evening and we'd all have a proper family dinner.

I'd caught Mastin staring at me as she'd told me about their family, about *him*.

And now we stood together in this bedroom, a tangle of emotions between us. We used to hate each other, and that had been easy. Trying to be friends was hard. Weary, I rubbed the back of my neck and yawned.

"Would you mind if I took a little nap and met you for dinner later?"

He nodded. "Sure, and don't worry about the dress or anything, we're pretty casual around here."

I looked down at the simple jeans and black t-shirt I'd been supplied with and shrugged. "Your mom will be playing dress up with me soon enough."

"I'm sorry about that."

"Why? Are you jealous? Need a little shopping time with Mom?" I teased.

He shook his head, laughing. "You really are a brat, you know that?"

"I know." I smiled.

"Alright, get some rest," he said, knocking on the doorframe once and closing it as he left. I sat on the bed, taking everything in. I still couldn't believe I was staying with Mastin's family. It only made me want to see my own. I didn't know when my icy opinion of them had melted, but it had. After everything we'd been through the last few weeks, I was ready for a fresh start with them.

I noticed a slim slatebook charging on the nightstand and powered it on. It was a different style than the ones I'd grown up with, but I figured out the differences quickly and began to scroll through the newsfeeds. It was filled with stories, with countless sides of the issues. The main ones being about alchemy and about the war, all sorts of sources gave their varying opinions. There were comment sections where people waged verbal battles on each other. Some of the things they said to each other made my skin crawl.

Was this what it was like to be free?

In New Colony, the palace controlled what news was released. They controlled the story. And there wasn't a comment section. But here? There were no restrictions. Some of the headlines seemed completely bogus, and others drew me in like a moth to the flame, especially the ones about me. I read through story after story. I quickly found one thing they all agreed on. King Richard Heart was an evil dictator, controlling both his people and their magic, with greedy intentions to take over their America and control them, as well. They weren't generally a country who supported war, from what I read, but this was different. This was personal and they were going to win, no matter the costs.

Wow. I sighed and laid back. There was no chance of napping now. I'd read the afternoon away and I needed to get freshened up for dinner. I went to the bathroom, and before I knew it, someone came knocking.

"You ready?" Mastin asked, his steady voice muffled through the door.

"Yup," I replied as I swung open the door and stepped into the hallway. I was still in the same clothes as before, but the shower had helped. He raised his eyebrows and I was suddenly annoyed. Why did he affect me so much? He was just a stupid boy, and I'd reserved my heart for Tristan long ago!

I followed him down the stairs to the dining room, with its table set with blue and white patterned china and its scent of seasoned meat and fresh baked bread. Mastin's parents were already seated. This was so weird, like I was meeting my boyfriend's parents or something. But I was *not* with Mastin, nor did I want to be. *I don't think. Maybe. I don't know.*

"There she is." Melissa beamed from the table and stood. "Honey, this is Sasha." Then she said with a conspiratorial smile, "The alchemist girl."

Her *honey* glared at me, looking me up and down with a sneer on his lips. "Oh yes, Sasha? Or Frankie? Which is it?"

I gulped. As if I knew anymore.

"Dad, we've been through this," Mastin clipped. Apparently, they had. They seemed to know all of my business.

"Sasha works fine," I added with a weak smile. My eyes shot to Mastin, bulging. *Hello, introduce me?* He squinted before getting it.

"Sasha, I'd like you to meet General Nathan Scott."

"Pleased to meet you," I replied smoothly. It was at that moment that I realized I didn't even know Mastin's last name. We'd shared a few conversations, a few almost-kisses, and battled together, but we didn't really know each other.

Nathan harrumphed at me, folding his large arms, and turned to his son, "Mastin, would you bless the food, please?"

We sat, and I followed along as they clasped hands and Mastin asked God to bless their family and their meal. I watched the family, thoroughly confused as to why God would bless us. Mastin's Dad caught me staring and I blushed, quickly closing my eyes and bowing my head.

I've never heard a prayer before, so what?

It wasn't something people did in New Colony. It wasn't illegal, but it was customary to keep religion private within the family. And there certainly had been none of that at the palace or in the camp with Tristan and Hank. I nearly laughed at the image of Hank praying. He wouldn't know what to do.

But this family treated God as if He were in the room with us.

"Amen," I said when the rest of the family did.

"In this family, we pray over every meal, attend church each Sunday, and read the Bible," Melissa said gently. "You'll learn."

That's probably why you hate alchemists, I thought. Maybe that wasn't fair. Melissa didn't seem fazed by my magic. But as we ate, General Scott certainly glared at me like I was the devil come to dine with his precious family.

"So, how long have you been in this home?" I asked politely, pushing the food around my plate and trying not to look as uncomfortable as I felt.

"Oh, not too long," Melissa said. "We've moved every few years, depending on our assignment but I hope we'll stay here for a while now that the war's broken out."

"I don't expect Mastin and myself will be here long," Nathan said with a grunt. He cut into his steak with a knife, his movements brisk. "I'm needed elsewhere, for obvious reasons."

"Just waiting for the right timing," Melissa chirped.

Mastin smiled. "It's killing him," he said. "Me too. We're made to fight."

The general nodded.

I chewed my food slowly and tried to ignore Melissa's worried expression. Unfortunately, I related with the men in the room, eager to fight. "Me too," I said. "I want to help."

Nathan laughed. "I wouldn't count on it."

"Dad—" Mastin interjected.

"And why not?" I asked, urging myself not to glare back at the man. He looked nothing like his son, except for his tall muscular build and his buzzed cut. He was all dark hair and olive skin and black calculating eyes.

"You're here, in my home, because my son has vouched for you *and* because I am going to be watching you carefully to make sure you are who he says you are. But let's just make one thing clear," Nathan replied, jabbing his finger at me, knife still in hand. "I don't know you and I don't trust alchemists, so I don't trust you. Men died to get you here. If you turn out to be as useful and as trustworthy as Mastin says you are, you *might* one day get off this base and be allowed to help with the war. But until then, until I say so, you will behave yourself as any self-respecting guest would."

Wow. Someone is used to getting his way! No wonder Mastin had been such a jerk when he'd first met me. I pinched my leg under the table, pushing the anger down deep, and smiled sweetly, nodding. "Of course, sir. I wouldn't dream of crossing you."

He was lucky I knew how to control my alchemy. He was on the receiving end of a hailstorm of dangerous emotion.

"Dad, I know you don't trust her, but you also don't know her. Don't be so quick to judge," Mastin cut in.

I smiled, despite myself. I had befriended Mastin, hadn't I? Pretty sure to the point that the man wanted more than friendship. I could get his father to trust me and take me with him to the warfront. I just needed to play my cards right.

"Thank you so much for this delicious meal, Mrs. Scott," I said, sending a practiced smile to the woman. "Please, I would like to help out wherever I can while I'm here. Whatever you need, just let me know."

I turned to Nathan Scott: man of this house, a man who strategized for a living. He had no idea who'd he just invited into his home. "That goes for you as well, General Scott. I'm here to help."

"We'll see about that," he replied.

I smiled. "Yes, you will."

▼

My feet echoed a familiar rhythm on the pavement as I ran along the path. My stone necklace thumped against my chest, reassuring. The sunrise was just beginning to peek over the mountains, a small bit of warmth tickling my face. I brushed away the beads of sweat dotting my forehead and pushed on, running faster. An ache twisted deep into my side, but I ignored it for as long as I could. Eventually, I stopped to catch my breath. My throat burned, and my heartbeat raced. I wasn't in the same shape as before being in the palace prison, but I would get it back. I was determined to come out stronger than ever.

Nathan had assured me I would be safe on the military base, so when I'd woken extra early, my body clock messed up, I'd decided to do the one thing I always did when things got weird, when I needed to think: run. But that early trust had started to wear off as I stood catching my breath and took in my surroundings.

The base was huge, expanding much wider than the tidy neighborhood where the Scott family lived. Nondescript buildings littered the area, with sprawling green lawns and several apartment buildings. I'd stopped on a bluff. On one side the glorious blue of the Pacific Ocean stretched out far below, and the mountains loomed on the other. The base was nestled in between. There were far more people out at this hour than I'd expected. Men and women were doing their morning exercises, some alone, others in units. I watched them move, their routines practiced. It was every time I crossed paths with one that my senses fired. They stared like they *knew* I didn't belong, expressions a mix of curiosity and mistrust.

I shook it off, ready to head back to the house.

A group of four men jogged toward me. I glanced around. The path had cleared out except for these men with cruel eyes trained on me. Worry crept up my chest. I turned, ready to flee, and ran right into the chest of another runner. His chest was akin to a brick wall, and I fell back onto my butt. I cursed.

"Sorry," I mumbled.

"Watch where you're going," he yelled, his voice harsh and scolding. His cheeks flushed, as his muscles bulged out of his khaki shirt.

"Yeah, my fault. Sorry." I brushed myself off and stood, wincing at the pain in my hip. If I were alone I would just use some of the grass to heal myself. But five men, much larger than me, all glared in a way that told me I'd better keep my magic to myself. But so what? Should I hide who I am? They would never understand alchemy if it was always kept hidden away like something shameful.

"You don't belong here," the same man said, stepping close and towering over me. "We ought to just take you out right now and get it over with." The other four surrounded me and nodded, like it was the best idea they'd ever heard.

Not today, buddy!

I straightened and met his gaze head on. "That would be a very bad idea."

"Nobody will know it was us. Sun's barely out," he said.

"I knew those men who died for you, you know that?" the youngest of the men sneered, moving in closer as he looked me up and down. He pummeled his fist into his palm. "Wasn't worth it."

Guilt burned, a twisting knife. The death of those men had been added to the memories that haunted me. It wasn't my fault, I knew that. Nobody made West America come pick us up. If these guys had a problem, they should take it up with Mastin and his father; but no, they'd rather pick on the girl practically half their size. If only they knew…

"Have you ever seen an alchemist in action?" I lifted my chin in challenge. One thing I'd learned about bullies, they liked to prey on the weak.

He spat on the ground. "Of course not."

Interesting. So, he hadn't been to the front line yet. If he had, he'd have seen the Guardians, would have first hand knowledge of how powerful magic could be.

I lifted the necklace out from under my shirt. I knew a rainbow of stones were visible even in the dim light. "I could use yellow to beat the crap out of all five of you, by myself. Hmm, or maybe I should use purple and spy on your thoughts, tell all your friends here your deepest, darkest secret. Oh, the possibilities." I smirked.

He rested his hand on his holster. They all had guns here. It was the first thing I'd noticed about the soldiers on base. They could kill me with a single bullet to the head. But that would make noise, and bullets could be traced.

"Who's first?" I asked. I wasn't bluffing anymore. If I needed to take these guys out, I would.

"Watch your back, little girl," the guy said, pointing at me, before backing off. His buzzed hair glistened in the sun as he and his gang jogged away. I sucked in a breath before sprinting back to the house. My limbs shook, and my hip throbbed the whole way, but I pushed past the pain. Mastin stood on the front porch, hands on his hips, his glare visible from across the street.

"Why on earth would you go running alone?" He snapped, his eyes running up and down my body as I caught my breath. "And you're limping. What happened?"

"It was nothing. I fell." I wasn't about to tell him the truth and prove his point. Mastin wasn't someone who needed any more validation. I leaned down to stretch out my legs, making sure to point my butt away from him. Because, let's be honest, that's embarrassing.

"Just because my father says you're safe here doesn't mean you are," he said, running his hand along the back of his neck. "If you want to go running, you go with me. In fact, if you want to leave this house at all, you don't do it alone. Understood?"

My, my, aren't we bossy in the morning?

"I was fine," I said. "I can handle myself."

His expression darkened, and I relented. "Fine," I huffed, exasperated.

"Good," he replied, his body relaxing. If you could call it relaxing. Mastin probably didn't have the word "relaxation" in his vocabulary. "Because you and I are going on a little excursion tomorrow and I need to get you there in one piece."

"Where?" I asked.

"You'll find out tomorrow." He glowered and then walked back into the house.   Wait; did he seriously think I would be patient about this? I pushed through the door. "Where?" I pressed.

He turned on me then, eyes flickering across my face. I was lucky my cheeks were already red from running. The sudden urge to kiss him slammed through me, a reaction I hated and loved all at the same time. I bit my lip, weighing the possibility in my mind. How much would change between us? And what would it mean for my relationship with Tristan? I tried to think through it logically, but Mastin was too close for that. I leaned in a fraction of an inch, my lips parting.

"You need to learn some patience," he said, eyes flicking up and down my face. Then he turned and walked away. I stood awkwardly in the dark entryway, wondering if he was talking about our trip tomorrow or about our almost-kiss.

NINE

JESSA

The problem with red alchemy was the blood. There was no other red that came to me, no matter how many times I tried. Stones, synthetics, plants—none of it worked. Only blood. Purple, however, wasn't too difficult and didn't require such a high cost as blood. It got me into this mess, maybe it could get me out.

Madame Silver and I finished our dance lesson early today, just as we had planned for the foreseeable future. We were going to do a little more than dance with the rest of our time.

"Are you ready?"

She smiled wisely, coming to stand in front of me. She put her cold hands on my shoulders, still warm from dancing, and nodded. "Whatever you need."

"Let's start with this." I skipped to my jacket and found the stone that I'd put in the pocket earlier. I ran my thumb along the smooth purple and flashed it to her, so she could get a better look. "Alchemy is typically a magic where we have to touch the recipient of the magic to do anything to them, but with purple, that isn't always the case. And I'm wondering," I trailed off.

Madame Silver smiled tentatively and nodded for me to continue. She didn't fully know what she was getting into, and for that I loved her even more. Our eyes met, and her bravery steeled me. The tingle of magic found its way inside and filled me. I reached out to her first with my hand, and then with my mind.

Can you hear me? I asked.

Her hand jumped to cover her mouth, eyes wide as she nodded.

I continued, speaking to her in my mind. *Try talking back to me. It's like thinking a thought but directing that thought at me instead of just to yourself.* I wasn't sure if a non-magical person could reply but since the connection was strong, it might be possible.

This is so strange, she said. *Can you hear me, Jessa?*

I nodded, excitement bursting out. "Okay," I said, breaking the magic. It washed away like sand swirling under an ocean wave. "I want to try again but this time let's go to opposite sides of the room and turn the music on really loud."

She flipped a switch on the stereo-system. The classical melody I'd been practicing to just minutes before blared through the room like thunder. I yelled out, "Can you hear me?"

She scrunched up her face and cupped her ear. I gave her two thumbs up and reconnected with the purple stone warming the hollow of my neck. It was an odd alchemy, like lightning as it made contact. When I directed it at Madame Silver, the magic seemed to both zap through me and settle on her at the same time.

Can you hear me? I asked the question again, this time with the telepathy weaving its path between us. I couldn't see it, but I could feel it, could sense the way it wound around its two hosts.

She burst into spontaneous laughter, once again pressing her palms to her cheeks. When she replied, it came straight through to my mind. *This is amazing. I can hear you as clearly as if I were thinking the words myself. You can hear me too, even with all this music?*

Sure can.

She jumped and clapped, then steadied herself. I'd known the woman for years, but I didn't think I'd ever seen her so excited. She was one of those people who took a while to read because she was usually so demure and classic. But not today!

I smiled and shook my head, our grins mirroring each other as she danced over to the stereo and shut off the music.

"So what's next?" She placed one hand on her hip.

"Hmm, that's a good question," I said. "I don't want to try anything that might hurt you, so red alchemy is out. I'm terrible with blue, so we could try that, though I bet it will be pointless. Yellow isn't really something I need to work on. Orange…well, we won't even go there."

"What does orange do?" she asked, her eyebrows rising.

"Ha, well, it just enhances emotion," I said. "An angry person becomes more angry, happy becomes happier, that kind of thing."

"What about white? Black? Do those do anything?"

I bit my lip. "No." The lie came out before I had a chance to consider the different angles. She was helping me, trusting me, so shouldn't I trust her too? But the amount of people who knew about white alchemy I could count on one hand and I wasn't sure she needed to know about it anyway.

Madame Silver ran her hand along her chin, her signature inquisitive pose. She always did it when solving a problem in her brilliant mind. I fought the pang of guilt knowing I'd lied to her.

Well, half-lied, as I didn't know if black did anything.

I think we should keep working on purple together and I'll work on the other colors alone, I said through our telepathy. *I want to set a time where we can* connect again, but this time you'd be outside the palace and I would be here.

She nodded and smiled wickedly. *Do you think that would work?*

It's worth a shot, I continued our telepathic conversation. *I've done it long distance before, just not that far.* The memory of the purple test and the young girl I'd "saved" flashed through my mind.

Well then, let's do it tomorrow and we can report our findings on Friday if we don't know right away.

I pulled her into a hug, sinking into her small frame. *Thank you.*

As I left our lesson, a sense of hope stirred in my heart. It was the first time in weeks that emotion had found its way to that broken place. Could I trust it? Probably not, but just for today, I desperately wanted to try.

▼

I pulled the coat around my shoulders, shivering in the cold.

"What are we doing, Lucas?"

"There's something I want to show you," he said.

"Do I have a choice?" I asked, attempting to rub the exhaustion from my drooping eyes. It didn't work. My vision blurred when I opened them to find Lucas's hurt expression staring back at me. His breath fogged as he thought of what to say. Regret crawled up me, but I squashed it before it took root. *Can't let that in.*

We'd spent the morning finalizing things with the wedding planner, and I'd agreed with everything Lucas had said. I'd figured that was better than voicing my true opinions on this wedding, a wedding that was only a few short weeks away.

"Please," He tried again, concern etched in his brow. "I promise you'll like it."

"All right." I nodded. He wasn't going to back down. "Let's go."

"Oh, we're not going for a walk out here," he said with a boyish grin. "We're leaving the palace."

I squealed in delight, the idea of getting out of the palace instantly perking me up. He led me to the drive and soon we were climbing into one of the royal armored cars. A heavy security detail joined us both in the car and in three others. Ever since the attacks on him and his father, his security had tripled. With things so dangerous for him lately, Lucas must have gotten permission from the King for this outing. The idea set me both on edge and gave me chills.

We drove for over an hour until we had left the city and its suburbs. We took a winding road out into the surrounding forest. The snow had melted into murky piles of slush in the capitol and around the palace, losing its fresh scent and becoming ashy and putrid. But out here where it was still mostly untouched, the snow had hardened into shining sheets of white ice under the December sun.

I watched the scenery both in interest and as an excuse to ignore Lucas. I was still angry with him. Our relationship was so far beyond repair that I was doubly frustrated with his persistent efforts to mend things between us. The ballet studio, Madame Silver, my father's close proximity, they were all bridges he was trying to build to reach me. And while they were appreciated, they didn't matter. Not really. How could I *ever* forget what he'd done? I couldn't. I wouldn't be so naïve again. Taking him back would be the mistake of a lovesick girl, something I refused to ever be again.

After a long ride, we pulled up to a large maroon brick estate. I decided it was called an estate because the main house was enormous and had smaller outbuildings around its perimeter. It had "grounds" similar to the palace with a sprawling lawn, pastures filled with horses, and a neat garden, all frozen under the winter tundra.

"What is this place?" I asked, finally turning to Lucas in the seat next to me.

"It's one of our royal residences," he replied. "We have the main palace, a beach house in the southern province, and this place up here."

"It's beautiful," I said, stating the obvious. It really was gorgeous. But did he think he'd win me back by flaunting his wealth? By showing me what kind of life we'd be sharing together? My stomach dropped, and I sank back into the leather seat.

"It *is* beautiful," he said with a knowing smile. "That's why I convinced my parents that we didn't need to keep it to ourselves. We rarely came up here and it has a fulltime staff, seemed such a shame to let all that beauty go to waste."

So what is it used for now and what does it have to do with me?

We stepped out of the car, our boots crunching on the mix of gravel and ice. The cold wrapped around me like a wet blanket, and I shivered deep, pulling my coat around me. Lucas took that as an invitation to wrap his arm around me and while his warmth was nice, I took no comfort in it.

He didn't ring the doorbell, just pushed open the huge black door and called out, "Knock, knock, we're here!" We stepped inside.

"Prince Lucas!" a young boy squealed and came running, socks sliding on the hardwood floor as he dashed to Lucas. Although he only had socks on his feet, he was dressed in a blue school uniform. He smiled wide, revealing gapped teeth. Lucas reached down to rub his mess of blonde curls.

"Hey there, Joey." Lucas laughed, hugging the boy. "How's it going, man?"

"We've been decorating for Christmas. Do you celebrate that at the palace? I know most people don't anymore. You probably don't. But Ms. Franklin does, and she said we could decorate this year. We actually got to cut down a tree. Did you know they do that at Christmas? It was so fun! I helped, I did. It's huge. It's in the main room. And we made strings of popcorn to wrap around it and—" The boy prattled as he led us to the sitting room. The home was old, but it was gorgeous. It reminded me of how Queen Natasha had decorated her parts of the palace, only this was the real thing; the original style.

I could easily see why she found inspiration in it. It felt safe. Welcoming.

"Prince Lucas, how have you been, dear?" An older woman padded in, her eyes shining with affection for Lucas as she pulled him into a tight embrace. "We've missed you around here. I know you've been so busy with this ghastly war business and of course, your exciting engagement, but do come visit us

481

more often or I'll have to travel out there and drag you back myself. You know how the children adore your visits."

He laughed and apologized for his unusually long absence. And then he introduced me to the woman, the little boy, and a myriad of other people, a handful of adults and dozens of other children who crowded the sitting room. At first, I sat in stunned silence, realizing this was an orphanage. But it wasn't long before I loosened up and began chatting with some of the children.

"Would you like to help out here for a few hours?" Lucas leaned in and asked conspiratorially in my ear.

"I would love to," I replied.

We started by reading to the younger ones and then helping a few of the older ones with math homework. That didn't last long for me because I hated math.

"Are you hungry?" the older lady, who I'd learned was called Mistress Grace, asked. My stomach pinched at the mere mention of food.

The large dining hall had been set with plates for the forty-three children and eight adults who lived here full-time. We dined with the kids, laughing at all their childish jokes.

"Are you two getting married?" Joey's little voice rose in disgust. "Do you kiss and stuff?"

My cheeks burned.

"I'll let you handle this," I whispered to Lucas who'd turned on me with a wicked grin.

"Yes." He leaned toward Joey. "We are getting married."

"So do you love her?"

My chest throbbed when Lucas nodded and said, "Yes. I do."

The conversation changed as dessert was served, but I felt Lucas's eyes heavy on me for the rest of the meal.

Soon it was time for us to go. The sun had set hours ago and I couldn't fight the tiredness any longer. Maybe I could sleep on the drive back. I hugged the children tightly and had to pinky-swear promise most of them that I would return after the wedding. It was a promise that came with a stab of regret, because if I had it my way, I wouldn't be keeping it.

We walked quickly back to the car, huffing in freezing air, and climbed inside. The heater was a welcomed friend, and my body softened against my seat. Exhaustion overtook me, and my eyes fluttered closed.

Lucas sat beside me, and even with my eyes closed, I could feel him watching and waiting.

"Okay, you win," I said softly. "That was worth it. Thank you for taking me here. Those kids are wonderful."

We were alone in the car this time. One of the security team had climbed up front but the partition window was up so it was just the two of us. Was that Lucas's doing?

I peeked open my eyes to see his turned on me, two shining orbs in the darkness. A hint of light cut an outline against his cheekbone and forehead. He was so unbearably handsome that I had to hold my breath. "Those kids used to live somewhere that wasn't very nice," he said. "Let's just leave it at that."

"And you convinced your father to let them take over one of *his* residences?" I asked, though I already knew the answer. "Wow."

He nodded. "Mom loved the idea," he said in a choked voice. "Really, she was the one to convince Dad. This was about four years ago. We hadn't been up here in a while and after a trip to the old orphanage for a charity thing, I brought up that this place was probably collecting cobwebs."

"Good for you, Lucas. You did a good thing," I said earnestly. I shifted away to watch the world rush by outside the window. My breath created a circle of fog on the glass, and I resisted the urge to reach up and doodle in it. As a kid I wouldn't have thought twice.

"I didn't bring you here to boast about something good I did years ago. I brought you here so that you could see the kind of thing we can do once we're King and Queen. We can do so much good, Jessa. We can fix things."

And how long will it take? Richard wasn't going anywhere, certainly not anytime soon.

My hand rested against the seat, and Lucas placed his on top. His thumb ran the length of my hand, and my chest burned. His touch warmed my frozen fingers, which only served to anger me.

"I don't want to talk about this," I snapped, pulling it free.

"When will you talk about it? Because like it or not, the wedding is only three weeks away."

"Don't you think I know that? I don't need a reminder."

He stiffened as he replied in an icy tone, "I'm sorry. I'm sorry about how this all played out. I'm sorry about Jasmine—you have no idea how sorry. I can keep saying it and it will still be true. But we're here now, we're engaged, we love each other, so why can't we just find a way to be happy?"

I gaped at him. "You think it's that easy? You broke my trust, Lucas. And not in some small, insignificant way, either, in case you forgot. You got my mentor killed. Because of you, my father and sister were locked up. My dad still is. And my mom and sister are who knows where."

"But Sasha got out." He leaned close, his jaw popping.

Seriously? Had he not heard anything else I said? "No. Just no. I'm not talking about this again. I'll marry you because I must, because your father has commanded it and I have no choice. But that's it, Lucas. Don't fool yourself into thinking it's real."

"But it is real," he sighed. "I know you love me as much as I love you."

"My love was destroyed. You destroyed it!" I yelled. There was a long pause as the air between us crackled. "I will play house with you in public, but I won't pretend behind closed doors. I won't open my heart to you *ever* again. You would be better off to end our engagement and find someone who will give you what you want."

His expression hardened as he shook his head, and turned away. My heart ached, beating a steady rhythm of *liar, liar, liar,* as it pushed my angry blood through my veins. I did love him. The second I'd said I didn't, the lie nearly choked me. But I refused to take it back. It was time I grew up. I was finding a way back to the Resistance and a way out of this palace. It was either that, or I had to turn on the royals and use my magic against them. Jasmine would have loved that. That's what she'd wanted all along, wasn't it?

Either way, it would be what was best for me. Not for Lucas. Not for *us*.

I shifted away as well, pressing my body against the door and staring through blurry vision out into the deadened night. I imagined doodling in that fogged up window once again. As a child I loved to draw hearts. Much like the children at the orphanage, I'd only seen the good in people, the light in the world. The love. But tonight, that drawing would no longer be a whole heart, but one left in pieces. One broken and battered and looking for revenge.

I wasn't trying to be cruel. I wanted him just as much as he wanted me. It killed me to be so cold, colder even than the frozen tundra outside. But I had to do what needed to be done. I had to step up, even if it meant giving up my first love.

▼

At the agreed upon time, I retreated to my room and used purple alchemy to reach out to Madame Silver. Nothing happened.

Either she didn't hear me, or I couldn't hear her reply, but the attempt proved fruitless. Frustrated, I tried it again and again. Fifteen more minutes ticked by before I gave up, deciding to wait until our next appointment to see if she heard anything. And then, if she agreed, we'd keep trying.

In the meantime, I had another class to teach.

I quickly found myself standing in the corner, bored, counting down the minutes until we could be done with this. I observed the students, each having zero success with red alchemy. Faulk had started the class by trying other red sources, to no avail. Now the students were attempting again with blood. It was a waste; the sight of it made my stomach churn.

"You could at least pretend to try," Faulk said with a sneer, her boots clipped the floor as she walked over.

"What's the point?" I asked. "Seriously, it's not working. Nothing is working. Maybe we should just give it up and focus on a color that actually matters."

"Red matters. Or haven't you figured that out yet?"

I gulped. Oh, I had.

"Fine," I muttered, scooting from the wall. I strolled around the room, giving encouragement and tips to the students. They weren't very receptive. They ignored me or rolled their eyes, some even made sarcastic remarks.

"Hey, don't worry about it." Callie was working with her two best friends, Tessa and Sam—the trio was normally together. I could tell Callie wanted me to be part of their pack, but Sam seemed indifferent either way, and Tessa hated me. "It's not like anyone actually expects this to work," Callie continued. "It's just one of those things, I guess." She shrugged and returned to her red flower, which didn't have a speck of color missing.

The trio had pushed their desks together and were chatting before I'd interrupted. Sam watched me with equal parts expectancy and curiosity, waiting for me to add something to the conversation. And Tessa ignored me, healing a small cut on her hand, her face twisted in disgust.

"I'm sorry," I said. "I wish there was more I could do to help." Another lie. I wished red alchemy didn't exist; my opinion was probably obvious.

Tessa huffed. "Whatever. I'm going to the bathroom." She rolled her eyes and left. Sam watched her go and then turned back to me.

"Is there any other way?" he asked. "Maybe something we haven't tried yet."

"If there is," I said, "then I haven't thought of it, yet."

He nodded pensively and went back to twisting the petals of the poor flower. The room was full of plants. A bushel of colors sat atop each desk, the large red exotic flower blooming in the center of each.

Are you still with us? a male's voice echoed through my mind.

I blinked, peering around the room. The voice sounded familiar, but also muddled somehow. And it was most definitely coming through with telepathy. My eyes shot to Dax, the boy who'd already revealed his talent for this kind of alchemy. But he was joking around with his friends, not even paying attention to me. And his voice sounded nothing like the one I'd just heard. I turned around in a full circle, looking for something out of place, someone staring at me, perhaps.

After Jasmine, you can understand how I've decided to keep my identity from you a secret, the voice said.

I bit my lip, attempting not to look startled. If this person was using purple alchemy to talk to me, I should be able to respond.

Who is this? I asked, pushing the question through the bond.

Like I said, it's best for you not to know my identity. But I was a friend of Jasmine's before she died.

You're Resistance?

I am, the deep voice said. *And I wanted to know if you're still part of our mission.*

I paused, considering my options.

At this point, my only mission is to get out of this palace before I'm married off.

That's a shame. You're closer now then you ever were before.

Jasmine had urged me to turn my red alchemy against the King, to bring him into their control. But it was too dangerous. Wasn't it?

You want me to control the royals? I asked.

Who better than the red alchemist engaged to the prince?

My heart raced and my fingers tingled. He was right. Who better?

I'll think about it, I finally replied, *but I can't make any promises.*

I continued to search the room, trying to catch the eye of someone who could be communicating with me, but nobody seemed fazed, let alone like they were in the middle of using powerful telepathy magic.

Who are you if you can't follow through? Jasmine died to save you, died so you could do this.

It felt as if a bucket of ice was being poured down my back. I surged for the door, ready to face whoever this man was. I whipped my head back and forth, looking up and down the hallway, but there wasn't a soul.

How can I find you again? I asked desperately. *We should meet.*

The voice didn't respond.

TEN

SASHA

I met Mastin at the door, hand on my hip, my head cocked casually to the side, but a fire burned low in my belly, one I refused to extinguish. "Let me go with you."

It was the third morning in a row that I was being forced to stay back in the house while the men went off to trainings and meetings, and I was beyond sick of it.

"I've said it to you the last three days and I'll say it to you again," he replied with the same flash of annoyance I'd learned to ignore. "No." He wasn't dressed in his typical khaki. He looked sharp in a military suit, and it seemed to me he was meeting important people today.

"You won't even give me a chance," I huffed.

"Only because the entire reason you're here in my home instead of somewhere else is to protect you." He eyed me wearily. "Did you forget that people hate you in this country?"

I laughed. "Right? Like you think that ever stopped me before?"

He shook his head and squared his wide shoulders. The sunlight hit his eyes, turning them emerald. Honestly, he looked better than ever, and it was starting to get on my nerves. I wanted to train, to fight, and to help with the cause, not to crush on this idiot. *If Mastin doesn't see my value, well, that's his problem, not mine.*

"Fine, I gave you a chance, but you leave me no choice." I brushed past him. I strode into the kitchen where I knew his father would be finishing breakfast before leaving for the day. We ate dinners in the elegant dining room, but the rest of the food was shared in here.

"Hello dear," Melissa said with a warm smile. "Are you still hungry? Would you like some more?" She held up a heaping bowl of scrambled eggs in one hand and a plate of bacon in the other.

She placed them on the table and patted her husband on the back.

"No, thank you," I replied, pulling out the chair next to Nathan and sliding in.

His gaze flicked to me, guarded, and he gave me the rise of thick eyebrows. Although they didn't look alike, the action reminded me so much of his son that it almost slowed me down. Almost.

But then again, I've never had any trouble giving Mastin hell before, have I?

"I want to help," I said, leaning forward and meeting his glower with one of my own. "I'm used to being on the inside. I've worked with the Resistance, hand in hand, since I was ten years old. I went undercover for them when I was seventeen and spent two years at an outpost before making my way into the palace." My heart raced as I continued, "I know more about New Colony than most of your operatives, even your spies. There's no point in having me here, in your home, on this military base, no less, right where you could use me, only to lock me up in a *guest room*."

He stared at me, considering. I took a deep breath and continued, "I have friends and family back in New Colony, so I have more on the line than most. I'm an alchemist, yes, but you should use that to your advantage instead of ignoring the opportunity you have right in front of you."

He leaned back in his chair, folding his arms across his bulky chest. Mastin had come to stand behind him, glaring down at me. I shook my head, not quite finished.

"You think King Richard won't use alchemy to destroy you? Because he will, he is, and there's a lot you who need to learn about alchemy if you're going to fight it."

"Sasha," Mastin cut in, "that's enough."

"I'm not talking to you," I spat, turning back to General Nathan Scott.

"Did you know you gave King Richard *your* alchemists? Yup, that's right, he recruited all the people you'd sent to the slaughter in some foolhardy attempt to assassinate him. They are being wined and dined, trained, and turned into weapons."

"And what would you have me do about that?" Nathan finally said, his jaw tensing.

I laughed. "I think it's about time you invite me to come along to whatever it is you have planned and put me to good use. He recruited your alchemists? So, you recruit his."

"Father, I'm sorry," Mastin said. "She's not used to civilian life."

Nathan held up a hand to shush him and studied me for a long moment. His face had slowly darkened to a deep red as I'd gone off at him. He was either going to agree with me, or punish me.

"Anything else you'd like to add?" he asked darkly.

"You will have no idea what I'm capable of if you don't try me," I replied.

There was another long, stretched-out pause, and the color drained from his face. *Yup, I'm right, old man. Deal with it.*

"She does have a point," Melissa said, strolling over and placing her hands gently on her husband's shoulders. She began to rub his tense muscles. "If you want to win this war, you should know everything you can about your enemy and Sasha could be the answer you've been searching for."

"Mel," Nathan replied, shutting his eyes. "You really think this is a good idea?"

"No!" Mastin interjected. "It's not a good idea. It's too dangerous for her."

I shot him a glare, annoyed and also a little hurt. Hadn't I proven myself to him by now?

"I think it's a great idea," Melissa replied, then she patted him on the back, picked up his empty plate, and began cleaning up the kitchen as if everything we were dealing with wasn't as important as keeping her house clean. But I liked her for it; she had a happy nurturing quality that I certainly didn't have myself. I didn't envy it. I liked who I was.

Nathan stared at the table for a while before he finally nodded. A surge of triumph rushed through me. "Fine, Sasha, you win. We'll start today."

I wanted to turn to Mastin, stick out my tongue, and yell *I told you so*. But I was twenty, I reminded myself. Be cool. Instead I smiled at his father and leaned back in my chair. "Trust me, sir, you won't regret this."

He shook his head and stood from the table. "Trust is a mighty big word for such a little girl," he said. I froze, ignoring the impulse to jump up and smack him. Oh, I'd show him what this *little girl* was capable of, with or without his support.

▼

"Okay, you wanted your chance," Nathan said. "Let's see what you can do."

The morning sun beat through the clear blue sky. Several long rows of soldiers were lined up on one of the vast lawns. No kidding, probably three or four hundred soldiers stared at me like I was an alien, an evil demon, or something. Each stood at attention, camo-style green-brown pants and tops like a second skin over taut muscles. They eyed me warily, but stood at attention for their General.

I peeked at Mastin, wondering again why he'd kept his father's position a secret from me for so long. Was it a trust issue? A pride issue? Mastin stood with a stick-straight back, his mouth set in a firm line, arms behind his back and eyes ahead.

Nathan Scott turned on me. "Well, are you all talk or are you going to do something."

I shook away my nerves as his comment seeped into my bones, the realization settling deep. "What do you mean?" My heart sped up with the questions. "You want me to do alchemy here? Right now?"

"You tell me," Nathan grumbled. "You were adamant that your alchemy is so useful, so show me. Do something."

"Fine." I smiled despite myself. "Hand to hand combat with one of your men." That could be fun.

"We use guns and bombs," Mastin spoke up. He didn't bother to move to offer his opinion. Not that anyone asked him!

"Not always." I'd seen men practicing their fighting and it looked much the same as it was back home. "Besides, I can use green alchemy to heal any wounds that don't immediately kill me." I walked nonchalantly to stand in front of Mastin. I winked. His mouth quirked ever so slightly as he stood at attention like all the other soldiers. *Ha! Got you!*

I used to wonder how he stayed so aloof most of the time, even if he did have a temper, it was nothing compared to mine. But seeing him here in his element, and meeting his powerful father, I understood.

"My son has a good point. How would you use an alchemist to fight against bullets and bombs?" Nathan asked. I turned to meet his smirk, shaking my head. He had no idea.

A bead of sweat formed on my temple, but I didn't wipe it away. "The alchemists working with Richard have trained military with them, it's not as if they're defenseless in that area. Alchemists aren't the soldiers, they're the weapons."

His eyes were hard black slits as he leaned in. "Interesting choice of words."

I shrugged.

"I don't think a little *healing magic* is going to save them from real weapons," Nathan quipped loudly, his voice carrying over the lawn. He put the words healing magic into air quotes. The group of men close enough to hear our conversation laughed at his joke. I didn't find it funny.

"Maybe not," I shot back, hands fisted at my sides, holding my temper at bay. Scott was the General after all, and I was keenly aware that I was probably the only person on this base without a gun. "But I've seen alchemy do more than just heal wounds, even life-threatening wounds. I've seen it turn people mad with emotion. I've seen it convince whole crowds that obvious lies are the truth." My voice roared, echoing across the lawn for everyone to hear— the blue resting against my chest aiding me. "I've seen it used for telepathy, to read the future, to eavesdrop on conversations happening miles away. Some can use it to control people's minds, make them do things they never would otherwise. It gives people super human strength. I've even seen it turn an entire helicopter invisible, completely invisible, *even* on radar."

The snickering had long since dissipated now, and I stared out into the crowd of naysayers. "So yeah, any one of your men can shoot a gun, and believe me, New Colony has those too, but not just anyone can do what an alchemist can do, and as far as I can tell, I'm the only willing alchemist *you've* got."

It was my second tirade of the day and it left the people around me more speechless than the first. I steeled myself for the fallout, not at all regretful of what I'd said. It had all been the truth. And these people needed to hear the truth. Everyone did. I was so sick of the lies, and wasn't going to let my time here be used to create more.

I studied the faces of the men in front of me and was instantly hit with a wall of hatred and fear—hardened eyes, clenched jaws, and fisted hands. Here I was, what they saw as a *little girl*, someone who clearly didn't belong, and I was holding my own with their General. Not only that, I'd revealed to them things about color alchemy that they didn't know, things that should terrify them.

Mastin broke protocol and stepped up next to me, muttering under his breath. "Are you trying to get yourself killed? I swear to God, Sasha, you're going to give me an ulcer."

I elbowed him in the side. "Don't swear."

"Let's start with your super human strength," Nathan cut in, loud enough that it also echoed across the lawn. His body language wasn't defensive anymore. Dare I say, it was proud? "Show us."

I nodded. "I can't do all those things I mentioned, no alchemist can. But I can do that one."

"What else can you do?" He turned, his eyes narrowed slits, along with hundreds of others. I quivered under the pressure, swallowing hard.

"The healing, the super human strength, the enhancing emotions," I said, "pretty much all alchemists can do that. But I can also block people from hearing me if I need."

"But not the rest of the...powers...you mentioned?" He studied me.

"That's all."

Liar.

If I told them about red alchemy they'd probably kill me on the spot. Or maybe just lock me up for safekeeping. And besides, I hadn't done it in years. I wasn't even sure if I could still do it if I wanted to.

"The invisibility? The telepathy? Mind control?"

"Super rare." I gulped. "But King Richard has alchemists at the palace who *can* do all of those things."

He stilled, then nodded and flicked his wrist toward the space of lawn between the three of us and the rest of his men. "Like I said, show us this super human strength."

I took five long strides forward until I was between Mastin and his father, and the rest of the men. My rainbow rock necklace rested under my clothes, flush against my skin. They didn't need to see the color. It was safer for me if they didn't know quite exactly how I accessed my magic, better if most of these men thought I could do it at any time. Though I figured Nathan and Mastin knew well enough that wasn't the case, that I actually needed access to the organic colors.

I reached out to the yellow with my mind and it met me like an eager puppy, excited by the attention. The magic shot through me with a jolt, a tickling burning sensation rolling through my body. I used the momentum to start running. I ran between one of the rows of men. Startled, they had no issue getting out of my way. I was fast, zipping down the row, blood pumping. To everyone else, I was a blur of blonde hair, white skin, and black clothes.

Getting closer to my target, I jumped, easily clearing thirty feet, before landing with a thud in the sidewalk with such force that it cracked the pavement. A huge army tank was parked just in front of me. I hunkered down and placed my hands under one of the rubber tires. It was taller than me! Taking a deep breath, filling the magic through my entire being, I lifted the tire off the ground, the tank tilting as I stood tall. I strained against the insane weight, the ridges from the tire digging into my arms like rubber knives. After a few seconds I couldn't take it much longer, so I dropped the tank and stepped back, brushing myself off.

Swinging back toward the crowd, I issued a bow. Admittedly, it was not my brightest move. Tristan would have laughed.

"She's unnatural."

"A witch!"

"Get her out of here!"

Mastin and Nathan jogged toward me. I didn't miss the fire raging in Mastin's usually mossy eyes. I couldn't look away.

"That was amazing," another voice boomed over the crowd.

"I wouldn't mind some of that magic on the battlefield."

A few snickered.

"Show us more, little witch!"

"I really don't appreciate being called a witch, thank you very much!" I yelled back.

Mastin stopped in front of me, putting both hands on my arms. He pulled me away from the soldiers, moving his body to block me like a human shield. "Let's get you out of here," he growled low.

"No," Nathan said, his voice soft enough that only we could hear. "You don't want to appear to be too friendly with her, Mastin. Step away."

The crowd was stirring, growing louder.

Mastin froze for a second but did as his father asked.

"Squadron, attention!" Nathan called out sharply. The men immediately stood at attention, their bodies tall, feet at 45-degree angles, their fists balled at their sides, and their mouths? Oh, they shut those real fast. It made me wish I was a General. Nathan had earned the kind of power that came from respect, not magic, and it was a sight to behold.

"You will treat Sasha as if she were one of our own," he said, his voice clear. "This is a direct order not only from me but from our Madame President. Sasha is here to help us, and she will be shown utmost respect at all times. Not only that, but you will protect her as if she is our biggest asset in this war, because quite frankly, she might be."

There was a long pause and then he finished with a single nod. "Please continue on with the rest of your scheduled activities for the day. As you were!"

The men disbanded. I watched them go with the kind of curiosity that lifted my spirit ever so slightly. I could relate to these people and maybe I would be one of them soon. True, most of them ignored me, others nodded their approval, and even more eyed me with suspicion, fear, or hatred. But I didn't let it get to me. These people had just seen their first bit of color alchemy, and whether positive or negative, it had made a lasting impact on each and every one of them.

They wouldn't forget me, and maybe that's how change would start.

▼

Nathan brought me along to all his meetings that day. It was like getting a bucket of cold water dropped over the head.

A wake-up call.

That night as we sat around the dining table, I didn't have anything to add to the conversation. I stirred the food around my plate, lost in thought.

First, the war was not going so well for West America.

Richard's troops were gaining ground every day. And if the American citizens didn't go along with whatever he wanted, they faced some nasty consequences. Torture and death in most cases. Color alchemy destroying land in others, but it seemed that particular problem had started to let up the more ground New Colony gained.

In the last two weeks, West America had tried several times to bomb the New Colony troops, but nobody got through. People were starting to wonder if the bombers should just go and bomb the palace. Never mind the fact that there were plenty of innocent people living there, many of them children. The very idea of it made me ill, and I hated Richard. But it wasn't right to send others to an early grave because of him.

The President had felt that way too, apparently.

That had been why they'd started with the original plan they'd involved me in, the one that had failed miserably, delivering a boat-load of alchemists right into Richard's hands.

And now everything was a mess.

War was a mess.

I sighed and leaned back in my chair, watching the family on either side of me. They seemed to have it all, the perfect home, perfect careers, love and respect. Would all of that become a casualty of this war as well?

The very idea officially ruined my appetite. I dropped my fork down with a clatter.

"May I be excused, please?" I turned on General Scott.

He studied me for a moment and nodded.

I took the stairs two at a time, retreating to my bedroom. I didn't want to watch that family downstairs anymore. Not with what I knew was coming. It wouldn't be long before Mastin and his father were out on the frontline, leaving Melissa to worry.

I plopped down on my bed and rolled onto my stomach, groaning into the squishy pillow. Would they let me come with them? I had to go! I needed to save who I could. Get Christopher and Jessa out somehow. Help those innocent West American alchemists I'd let down. Plus the many others who were Resistance, or who simply didn't deserve to die.

And it wasn't going to happen sitting on this military base.

Someone knocked on the door.

"Come in," I muttered.

Mastin walked in, rubbing his hand along the back of his buzzed hair and watching me with trepidation.

"I'm fine," I said, sitting up. "Really, it's all good."

He nodded once.

"Are you up for a surprise?"

I rolled my eyes. "Is it a good surprise?"

"It is. We get to leave base. It's already been cleared for approval."

Adrenaline shot through my veins as I jumped up.

"Are we going to the war?"

He stared at me, his mouth turning down in a frown. "No," he replied. "We're going to the beach."

Oh. Well, fine then.

I followed him out to a black, shiny SUV that turned out to be his. As we drove out of the base and into the city, down winding roads that led to the ocean, I was plagued with guilt. I shouldn't be here, shouldn't be going to the beach. People needed me. I rested my forehead on the window, telling myself it was okay to enjoy this moment. Having a good life when others suffered, that didn't mean I should suffer too. Right?

I closed my eyes against the setting sun and drove the thoughts from my mind. *Just breathe.*

We turned into a parking lot. The view unfolded before us, a spectacular horizon. The sun was setting over the ocean, transforming the sky into a vibrant mix of oranges, pinks, and purples. The second he parked, I was out of the car. I sprinted, kicking off my shoes as I reached the sand.

"The water is super cold this time of year," Mastin called after me. "Don't go in there!"

But I didn't care what he said, and besides, I was hardly listening. I planned to dive into the water and lose my worries to the thrashing waves. The salty air whipped past me as my feet buried deep with each heavy stride. The crashing sound drew me to it like a relief I didn't know I needed, but now that it was here I *had* to be a part of it.

"Well it's nice to see you, too!" a voice called out and I jerked from my run and spun, sand flying, to see Tristan coming down the beach. He walked toward me, Mom and Lacey on either side of him. I cried out, abandoned the water, and darted toward the group. I tackled Tristan as I jumped on him, my body wrapping around his in a full-body hug.

"Whoa, hold on there!" He laughed. "It's only been a week."

"Shut it," I said, nuzzling into his warmth and squeezing tighter for a second longer. Then I released him and hugged Lacey, and a surprise to us both, I hugged my mother.

"I've missed all of you," I said, putting special emphasis on the all. "This has been a crazy couple of weeks and I'm just so glad to see you're safe and healthy."

"We agree," Mom replied, though I could see lines on her face that weren't there the night I'd left her behind. The very same night Christopher had insisted on coming on that foolhardy mission and gotten himself captured.

"He's all right," I said, answering the question I knew was on the tip of her tongue. "Last I saw of him they'd moved him up into the palace, in a room right next to Jessa. They're treating him good, as leverage on her, I think. But he's all right. And so is she." *For now.*

She breathed out a sigh of relief and nodded.

I kneeled down to Lacey and wrapped her in a second hug. "I missed you." Her little body melded against me and I breathed in her sweet scent. A pulse of love went through me, so strong, I nearly cried out.

"Mom says you're my sister, too," Lacey said when I'd finally released her from my grip. "I'm so happy to have another sister *and* I'm so happy that it's you!"

She grinned up at me, her blonde hair wild in the wind. The sun reflected off of her blue eyes, mirrors of Jessa's, and the longing for all my family burned deep.

"I'm glad I'm your sister, too," I replied, the words a catharsis on my lips. "You have no idea how much I've missed my family."

We all sat down on the sand and talked, watching the sun set, the colors fading from bright, to pastel, and then to nothing at all. When the darkness overtook us, the chill set in.

"I'm so cold." Lacey started to whine as kids do and it was clearly time to go.

"It's okay." We stood, and I hugged Mom and Lacey goodbye. As they walked up the beach, a heaviness weighed me down. Tristan leaned into me and I rested my head against him, drawing on his strength.

A few military men stood in the parking lot. They helped Mom and Lacey into the car, then nodded toward Tristan. My gaze drifted toward Mastin who waited patiently, leaning against the side of his car. He gave me a quick wave, but that was all. I bit my lip, pondering.

"I'll walk you back," Tristan said, tucking his arm around me. I realized that I'd begun to shiver, and only now could I feel it.

We ambled toward the parking lot, moving slowly. We weren't ready for our time together to end. I didn't think I was ever ready for my time with Tristan to end. He was home to me. He was comfort. Some people have comfort items or blankets or animals, I had him.

"Where's Hank?" I asked.

"He couldn't come. He's been in so many meetings," Tristan replied. "He's working with lots of high-ranking people these days. But I'm sure you'll see him soon. I know he misses you."

I nodded. "I miss him. And I've missed you," I added, rubbing my forehead against him. We stopped and pulled each other in for another hug. He rested his chin on the top of my head and relaxed into me. I lingered against the hard plains of his body. They did something to my insides, something that caused the opposite of relaxation. I buzzed.

"I missed you, too," he whispered. "How's it staying with Mastin's family? Do you feel safe there?"

"Safe enough," I said, careful to keep my mouth shut about how there were just as many people who hated alchemists inside the base as there were off of it. But I didn't want to worry him.

I looked up to meet his pained expression. "What is it? What's wrong?"

He shook his head once, the wind flipping his black hair to one side. It blended in with the sky above him.

"Just tell me."

"It's selfish," he muttered.

"I don't care." And I didn't. I would do anything for Tristan.

"Can I ask you to do something for me?" He stepped back, only slightly, so we were inches apart. My gaze flicked to his lips and then back to his eyes. They were dark pools. Unreadable. Dangerous.

"You can ask me to do anything and I'll do it."

He cleared his throat, like he was afraid to ask. And that was weird because Tristan wasn't afraid of anything. "Don't date Mastin," he said. "I know there's something between you, but I also know there's something between us."

I stilled, my chest icy hot.

His thumb trailed up the side of my arm until his palm cradled my face. "I want my chance. I know it's not the right time, and I might not get to see you for a while. It's not your fault that you're spending every day with him." He had started to ramble and a smile tugged at my lips. He let out a shuddering breath. "I don't want to lose you, Frankie. Please, wait for me."

I blinked rapidly, trying to process everything. Was Tristan confessing feelings for me? For *years*, I'd dreamed of this moment, fantasized about it, wanting nothing more than to hear those words come from that perfect mouth, directed at me. And now it was here—I didn't know what to do or say.

And I hated it. I hated that my heart was unsettled. But I couldn't turn him down. I just couldn't, because I did love Tristan. And I wanted him, too. I just wasn't one hundred percent sure in what way. To lose our friendship would destroy me.

When I looked him in the eye and nodded, he smiled. Then he tugged my hand into his. We wrapped our fingers together and everything felt good again.

ELEVEN

LUCAS

Acrashing thud slammed through my sleep, followed by a sickening roar. The very foundation of the palace rattled, shaking my bed and waking me with a start. I ran to my window, threw open the curtains, and peered out into the inky darkness. A billowing cloud of fire raged just off the horizon, glowing so wildly it was almost mesmerizing.

Two guards rushed in, shouting orders. They pulled me from the window and ushered me to the entrance to our family's safe room. It was hidden behind a nondescript paneled door off our main living area. I stumbled into the tight space, my shoulders brushing either side. It had been years since I'd been down here, and then, only for drills.

"Lock it from the inside," one of the guards said, throwing the door shut in my face.

Hands shaking, I gripped the metal bar that clicked into place, securing me inside. A few steps and I began to descend the narrow, winding staircase. With each step, the adrenaline only rose in me.

Below, I heard Richard muttering to someone. They were already heading down the stairs that led into the underground bunker. I hurried to follow close behind, trying to ignore the cold air. At the bottom was a concrete room, no more than fifteen feet by fifteen feet, fortified with food cans, water jugs, and three sets of bunk beds. Along one of the walls gleamed black guns, rested on several racks. The sight was unsettling and reassuring at the same time. I knew how to use one if it came down to it, but I'd rather not. At the far end of the crammed space was another door. It was solid metal, the huge lever locked in place. Behind it was an underground tunnel. It led out of the palace to a secret exit almost a mile away. I'd never used it before. Never had to. War was new for me.

And yet one thing I can count on is everything changes, and this has, too. I'm not safe as long as this war continues.

I shook out the nerves and then sat on one of the bunks. The adrenaline that was coursing through my body threatened to make me sick. I glanced at the only other door down here, knowing it led to a bathroom. Resting my head against my hands, I breathed slowly. Someone sat next to me and I glanced up at my father. I stiffened. Did he think I was weak?

"Where's Jessa?" I asked. "She should be down here."

Richard rubbed at his temples, ruffling his messy sleep-rumpled hair. It always caught me off guard to see him out of his normal formal dress, instead donning black silk pajamas. He was clearly out of his element.

"Well?" I prodded.

He shrugged. "I don't know. But I am guessing she's fine. They didn't make it to the palace."

I frowned, unsatisfied.

"Look, son," he continued. "When you're married, she'll be with you, so this won't happen."

I huffed. He tugged at his hair, trying to straighten it out. It was one more thing changing lately. He'd lost so much color in the last few months. It used to be lightly streaked with gray, but now it was succumbing to the color. The lines that marked his face were carved especially deep in the dim light. When he exhaled, I could feel the exhaustion. But all this was his own doing. He hadn't protected Mom. He'd started the war. Lied about so many things. No wonder he was exhausted.

"How did they get through our men?" Richard asked, looking up at the three men who'd somehow been prioritized over Jessa because they were with us in this stupid hidey-hole. And where, exactly, was she?

"Only one of their bombers made it past our fighters but we were able to stop him before he made his target," the man replied, an officer, one of Faulk's best.

"I'm guessing the palace was his target?" I interjected.

Everyone looked at me, like I'd said something obvious, before continuing on with their conversation. Okay fine, the palace had been their target—it didn't take a genius to realize that. They wanted to murder me in my sleep. Me, and so many others, so many innocents, would have died with me. Nerves rolled through my body again, uncoiling like a snake.

I locked eyes with one of the other men who'd been granted access down here. Mark, Celia's father, and the man who I'd suspected was up to something for a while. Clearly, he was working for my father in more than just some kind of agricultural capacity. He was a war advisor, or he wouldn't be in this room.

The man regarded me as if I were of little consequence, focusing on my father.

"We were coming to wake both of you and move you down here when the plane crashed," Mark said. My eyes adjusted as I took in the frustrated set of his shoulders and the hard line of his jaw. "But our bomber was able to drop them before they got to the palace," he continued.

"They got too close," I huffed, thinking about how large that ball of fire had been, and probably still was.

"We should have been woken at the instant our territory was breached!" Richard yelled, standing up and breaking out of his exhaustion in a moment of fury. The group of men staggered back and cowered, but the challenge in Mark's eyes stayed put. He wasn't openly defiant, but it was there, just the same. Was he Resistance? Was it something else? My curious mind buzzed.

"We had it all under control," Mark said slowly. "Your Royal Highness." He bowed to Richard. "We didn't want to wake you with these trivial details."

"I don't think a West American bomber crashing into our capitol city qualifies as having it under control," Richard snapped.

I have to agree with that!

I thought back to what I'd heard and seen, and it clicked. It wasn't a bomb exploding but a plane being taken down. Which neighborhood had been hit? How many were now dead, injured, or without a home because of this?

"We have patrols on it and Faulk is already on her way," Mark continued. "They'll clean up and get a body count within a few hours. The bomber crashed in a field, so we don't expect the casualty count to be too high. Still, some of the neighboring homes caught fire pretty quickly, unfortunately. We're waiting to get word about the damage done there."

"Faulk," Richard huffed. "She and I are going to have to have a little chat. I have a feeling she's not going to like it."

A long pause followed; Richard's anger settled in. I noticed Mark's small smile. Was he gunning for Faulk's job? I wouldn't be surprised if he had it by the end of the day.

Dad stood and marched from one side of the bunker to the other.

"All right, we'll have to use this for our own benefit," he said, continuing to pace. His eyes filled with his trademark spark of excitement and my heart sank. What was he up to now? "We will let the people know what kind of savages we're dealing with, targeting innocent homes like that. I'll make a statement about it to the press first thing in the morning," Richard said. "Is it safe for us to go upstairs?"

I clenched my hands into fists and fought the urge to roll my eyes at his immediate plan to spin yet another problem toward his own favor. But nobody seemed to notice me, nor care. Did it not matter that the plane had been taken down by us? That they hadn't been targeting random people but the leaders of this kingdom? Of course it didn't matter. This was politics.

Mark slid a slatebook from his suit jacket and called one of his men on the outside. After a moment, he nodded the go ahead to leave the bunker.

"And one more thing," Richard said as we made for the stairs. "We're not postponing or canceling the exhibition. We're leaving this afternoon."

"Wise choice," Mark replied.

"Wait, what?" I sputtered on the question as I followed the men up the staircase. "Am I going? Is Jessa? Why didn't anyone tell me about this? It's *today*?"

"Always so full of questions, Lucas, but it's not my fault you missed the meeting on this," Richard said, not turning back to look at me. "You need to pay attention, and show up. If you had, you'd know we decided to keep this one quiet. We'll *all* go, do the alchemy exhibition for a few hand-selected families, and then air the segment after we've returned home. It will be a quick trip. Less than twenty-four hours."

"Why so secretive?"

"I'm not risking any more chances for someone to catch wind of our absence from the palace," he replied. "The less people who know, the better. The palace is the safest place for us, and being away puts us at risk."

I wasn't sure that was true, considering the circumstances, but I bit back the remark. He never listened to me anyway, not when he'd already made up his mind.

"Well then," I said sarcastically. "Sign me up."

"Don't worry, Lucas. I already did."

▼

The hunting lodge loomed ahead as we shuffled from the cars. Immediately, we were assaulted by freezing wind, the kind that clawed angrily at any exposed skin. I tucked my scarf tighter around my face and neck, wrapped my arm around Jessa, and hurried us toward the building. It was a massive log cabin, with wide gleaming windows and several wraparound porches. I'd been here a number of times; this was one of Dad's favorite places to schmooze his court. Still, the initial sight always sent a shiver of anticipation up my spine. I loved this place.

Tall pine trees surrounded the lodge on all sides, except for the front where we'd driven in our procession of armored cars. Now the cars were quickly emptied, hordes of wide-eyed alchemists, officers, guards, media crew, and even military men ambling around the drive.

The northern province wasn't very populated, and besides the lodge and forest, there wasn't much to see up here. But still, the crew filmed it all because Richard said it was a great opportunity to show off different parts of the kingdom. All of this was meant to build popularity among the people. Popularity was the lifeblood of the royal family, and now, the alchemists needed it as well. I hoped it didn't backfire but I could easily count a million ways why and how it eventually would—starting with the fact that these alchemists being televised used to have families. What would happen when parents recognized their stolen children from long ago?

I shook my head. *Not my problem.*

I tugged Jessa in closer as we stumbled into the entrance of the lodge, a tail of security close behind us. The warmth of the space was welcoming, and I relaxed into it. Jessa stepped away, rubbing at her ears and jaw, her cheeks and nose bright red. Her smile faltered when she saw me watching her, but then she wrapped her hand in mine and smiled, dropping a small kiss on my cheek. I ignored the cameras in our faces, documenting the royal love story. I also ignored the cool doubt that was chillier than the air outside.

Seeing the way she fought against me with every passing day was killing me. Betrayal and anger clawed at my confidence like puncturing wounds.

Her hand was icy cold in mine. She peered up at me with a coy smile. "Show me around? You said you know this place pretty well, didn't you?" Her eyes flicked to the camera as it zoomed in closer.

I froze, anger burning me up. I wanted this to be *real*.

An overwhelming need overtook me to either warm her small hand against my lips or push it away. Instead, I left it tucked in mine and led her out of the crowded foyer.

▼

I gave her a quick tour, starting with the game room, then on to the various living rooms stacked with comfortable chairs, leather couches, and pillows. We passed the dining area briefly—we'd be eating in there soon enough. We finished in what would be her room for the night. A burly cameraman, who'd kept his equipment trained on us up until this point, stepped back and saluted me.

I smiled conspiratorially as I closed the door.

"I'll just go out here for a few minutes to give the illusion that we're as happy as ever and then I'll get out of your way," I said. I dropped her hand and pointed to the balcony off the back of the bedroom. Nobody would see me up there since it was at the top of the lodge and tucked back against the tall pines.

"Are you sure?" Jessa asked. "It's really cold outside and your coat is still downstairs."

"I'll be fine. We only have to put on this show at dinner tonight and at the exhibition tomorrow. The rest of your time here is all yours. Don't worry about me."

"Okay," she said softly, her lip pouting. Did she actually have the nerve to be hurt by this?

"You can't have it both ways," I snapped, stepping through the balcony door and closing it behind me before she could respond.

She'd made it aggressively clear that she had no interest in forgiving me, let alone actually trying to make our relationship work. And I was done. With the camera following us around, the fact that she was *acting* had become excruciatingly clear. I had to let her go. It killed me, but it hurt worse to force it with her. My feelings were real, which only made her fake ones stand out in contrast.

I need to get her out of New Colony. That's what you want for her now, I told myself, forcing myself to believe it.

I breathed in the cold air, no longer affected by it. My body had settled into the bitterness. The pine scent washed over me, giving me a moment of tainted joy. I leaned against the wooden railing. This place only proved to bring back memories of Mom. This was another one of our vacation spots when I was a kid. I always knew I'd have this lodge to visit. It would be mine, too. And someday, I planned to bring my own wife and kids here to enjoy the stillness of the forest.

The way things were going, my future looked a lot like my parents' past. I closed my eyes and tried to picture it being any other way.

Tired of self-loathing, I pushed off the railing and let myself back through the bedroom door. Jessa startled, sitting on the bed with a slatebook in her lap. I didn't even look at her. Didn't say a word. I continued out into the hallway and down two sets of stairs. I found my coat on the rack, and bursting through the main doors, I let myself outside. I didn't mind the wind smacking my cheeks or the bright sun glaring in my eyes. I just needed to get away. When my bodyguards followed, I turned on them.

"Give me five minutes," I barked, and they faltered.

I strode into the thick set of trees, my feet carrying me down a hidden path I knew like the lines on my own palm. Dad had always said it was a deer path since it wasn't made by humans. Instead, it was barely visible to the eye, just a line of dirt to follow between the trees. As a kid I'd spent many summer afternoons walking it until I'd get scared and turn back. Then I'd go again the next day, always pushing a little further each time I ventured out.

In the winter, however, it was much harder to follow. That didn't surprise me. Even though it was more overgrown than I'd remembered and there weren't any leaves to block the way, there was snow. Mostly it was pines, and hibernating bushes and trees lined the path. The snow was muddied from where the deer and other animals had come through, so I found it and followed as best as I could, driving deeper into the forest.

Think. It's time to think.

I need a better plan. So far, all I have are a couple of addresses. Those won't be enough, will they?

A twig snapped. Boots crunched against the icy snow. Stillness descended upon the forest like a blanket.

I crouched against a tree and waited. It was most likely a bodyguard. I'd snapped at them, but this was their job. They probably followed anyway. But what if it wasn't a guard? The image of fire flashed through my mind. The planes. First the family jet. Then the bomber plane. Not to mention the gunman at Mom's funeral, the way the bullets had pinged off the pavement.

Coming out here alone was reckless. What was I thinking?

"Lucas? Is that you?" a soft, feminine voice called out.

The crimson red of Celia's hair appeared between a couple of trees, and I exhaled my breath.

I relaxed, and I slid out from behind the tree.

"Yeah, it's me," I said, approaching Celia. "You shouldn't be out here. You could get lost. It's going to be dark soon."

"I could say the same thing to you," she said. "Anyway, I was just heading back. You want to walk with me?"

"No," I replied.

Her mouth clenched. Was she surprised? Offended? Not that I blamed the girl. I was surprised with myself, but I was tired of the games, and Celia was certainly one to play puppet-master whenever she could. I wasn't dealing with that today.

"Well, then," she huffed, "so much for chivalry."

I shrugged. "I'm not ready to go back," I said. "I just came out here. But I'll see you at dinner."

There was a heavy pause. A gush of wind weaved through the trees, rattling the pine, a few dropping needles around us to rest on the white snow.

"Was it worth it?" She stepped close and peered up at me with intense curiosity.

"Was what worth it?"

"Choosing love over the logic?" She smirked, tugging the hood on her white fur coat over her hair.

"I assume you're talking about my engagement to Jessa."

"Of course." She cocked her head and smiled demurely, her bright red lips a contrast to the snow.

I wasn't going to talk to her about this, not right now. "Go home, Celia," I said, brushing her off and turning to head further up the barely-there path.

"I see the way she looks at you," Celia said. "I don't know what you did, but you certainly have an angry fiancé on your hands. What *did* you do, Lucas?"

I walked away. She didn't follow me, and I didn't care.

That family was trouble.

They were nosy, attention seeking, and lately, they were everywhere. Was I going to confide in Celia about my betrayal of Jessa only to betray Jessa's secrets even more? *Not likely.*

A few minutes later the scraping sound of boots on snow returned.

"I told you to go back," I said, turning to look for Celia. There wasn't a reply, only a sharp stillness. I paused and listened, then froze when I heard the sound once again. This time it was slower, softer, like whoever it was, was trying to be quieter.

"Who's there?" I called out.

Silence.

The sensation of being watched spread through me.

If it was a guard or someone meant to protect me, they'd have replied. Celia would have replied, and anyway, now that I thought about it, the sound of her boots had been different. These were heavier somehow, but also, quicker.

They sounded again, closer this time.

I took off at a run, ducking through low-hanging branches and working my way up the path. My breath was hot in my ears as I worked out where to go next. I probably knew this forest better than anyone. Would that matter?

I stopped abruptly, stilling to listen. The distinct sound of boots on snow crunched through the air once again. I jumped behind the biggest and closest pine, hoping I was hidden. I ripped off my glove, grabbed some snow in my hand, and turned myself invisible.

Please don't let them have seen that!

Then, I waited.

I waited for whoever was looking for me to pass so I could know without a doubt who they were. Maybe if I caught a glimpse, I would discover who wanted me dead. Could they be one and the same? It seemed a likely scenario as I stood motionless and invisible in the cold winter landscape.

Realization sank deep. Whoever they were, they were in the inner circle. They had to be if they were here, at such a private event, an event that only those invited knew about in advance.

I waited eagerly, wondering if I'd see Faulk stumbling through the trees. Or maybe Mark or Sabine. Maybe an officer, one of the alchemists or teachers. Maybe someone I'd never expect.

But the sound of boots was gone.

The forest once again fell silent. They must have retreated. No longer able to bear the cold, I slowly maneuvered back to the lodge. I didn't take the same path, in case someone was waiting for me. I stayed invisible as long as I dared, despite leaving incriminating footprints in the snow.

Visible or not, every step I took these days was a step in a dangerous direction. The trouble was, I didn't know how to course-correct. People wanted me out of the picture, many of them, and all I could do was continue on a path that might one day lead to my death.

TWELVE

JESSA

Jessa, are you there? Can we trust you? The smooth voice filtered through my mind, familiar and deep. I fought to hold onto sleep, my body cocooned by the fluffy comforter and my emotions exhausted. The nap came without much thought, but I wasn't ready to wake up quite yet.

Jessa, are you in there? The voice jerked at me once again.

Jessa…

I sat up, realizing what was happening. My heart sped, and my hand swept to clutch the rainbow stone necklace that hung around my neck.

I'm here. I reached out with my mind. *What do you want?*

Are you still with the Resistance? they asked boldly.

I stilled, weighing the decision on whether or not to tell the truth. What if the person on the other end of this conversation was a spy for Faulk?

If you're really with the Resistance, I said, *tell me something to prove it.*

There was brief silence. *Your sister was never really with the prince; it was a deal they made together to get her closer to the King and Queen.*

Relief washed over me.

I could accept that. As far as everyone else knew, Sasha had played Lucas. They didn't know about his brief interlude with the Resistance.

I got up from the bed and paced the room, my feet padding softly against the hardwood floor. I peeked outside the main door and into the hallway, hoping maybe I'd see someone acting suspicious, but there were only guards. All the bedrooms were on the top two floors, so whoever was talking to me could easily be in their own room, hidden.

There had been about twenty alchemists and officers, plus a few higher-ranking families loaded into those cars this morning. And guards. Lots of guards. And I couldn't forget the camera crew.

Whoever it was, I was just going to have to trust them if I wanted answers.

If there's still a Resistance, then I'm still with them, I replied.

We thought so, but we had to make sure. Why did you tell the royals about the attack?

We? I bit my lip and sighed. *I told Lucas because I thought I could trust him. I wanted to save him from getting hurt, but he betrayed me.*

We've already received word about that. But it looks like Lucas may be on our side again. We're being cautious about it.

Why would they think he was on their side again?

Doesn't matter, I replied. *I'll never tell him my secrets again.*

There was another long pause. The wind howled against the windowpane, rattling the frame. I shivered and sat back on the bed, pulling the comforter over my jean-clad legs. Even with the white sweater I'd thrown on that morning for good measure, I was freezing, the cold wind relentless.

Are you going to use your blood alchemy against King Richard? the voice asked. *If you can get him close enough, get him alone, you could end this all right now. End him and end the problem.*

But wasn't the issue deeper than just one man? What about the officers? Faulk? What about the alchemists who willingly participated in hurting innocent people in the name of New Colony? If Lucas took over, he might turn out to be the same. After everything, I just didn't know anymore.

I'm not a murderer. Jasmine never mentioned murder and I won't agree to it.

You say that now, but you might change your mind.

I mean it.

Okay, so what's your plan then?

I laughed. *Plan? I just want to get out of here before I end up married to a Heart. I don't want to end up like Queen Natasha.* Guilt ripped me at the statement. Lucas might be misguided, but he wasn't Richard. And I wasn't Natasha.

Maybe things would be different?

But still, my chest burned at the idea of a loveless marriage. I thought about what my parents had, how they treated each other, and the trust between them. That was what I wanted. A love that came before politics and circumstance.

Who are you? If you want me to help you, I deserve to know who you are.

There was another break in time, and I waited as patiently as I could. It was as if the person talking with me wasn't alone, like they were conversing with someone else. He had said "we", hadn't he?

I know there's at least two of you, I said, trying to see if I was right. *I know one of you must be a purple alchemist. I'll figure it out eventually, so you might as well reveal yourselves.*

And have us end up dead like Jasmine? the voice shot back. *How do we know you won't go to your fiancé about us?*

Prickly tears burned at the back of my eyes. Not because I was upset with him but because he was right. People had died because I'd told Lucas too much.

I already explained how I feel about what happened with Lucas. I won't say a word to anyone about you. I swear it.

More silence. I waited once again, but my nerves were beginning to get the best of me.

Besides, you need me, I added, *or else you wouldn't have reached out.* I jumped up from the bed again and paced the length of the bedroom. The longing to get back in with the Resistance, to not be alone in this, pulsed through my veins.

Come out on the balcony, the voice said.

I grabbed the fuzzy throw-blanket from the end of bed and wrapped it around me. I opened the door and stepped out onto the small wooden balcony. There was an overhang from the roof so no snow had reached the porch, thankfully, but the planks froze my bare feet. I ignored the cold and surveyed the back of the lodge with its identical balconies, searching for another alchemist. A few guards were posted along the edge of the forest, but nobody else was on their back balcony as far as I could tell.

Where are you? I asked again, getting annoyed. *I'm not standing out here all day. I'll freeze.*

A door opened a few rooms over, and Lily Mason slipped out. Her white-blonde hair whipped in the wind. After a long pause, she turned to smile at me.

"Hi, Jessa. How are you?" she called out, her voice nearly lost on the wind.

"Hi," I yelled back, narrowing my eyes.

I know I'm talking to a man, I said back to the voice in my mind. *Does Lily have anything to do with you?*

The pause this time was short.

We had to be extra careful with you, so Lily shared her magic with me.

Then another person swung open Lily's door, joining her. An officer. Not just any officer, either, but one of the men who worked directly with Faulk. I didn't know his name, but I knew him to be an enforcer. Brute strength. And worst of all, one of the men who'd beaten up my sister and father right in front of me.

I stilled at the sight of him, bile rising in my throat. How was I supposed to trust a Royal Officer, let along *this* one?

He turned his cunning smile on me, his dark eyes flashing, and ran a hand through his curly black hair. *As you can see, I need to be extra careful about anyone knowing I'm Resistance.*

I pushed my suspicion down and focused on the matter at hand.

I don't get it. Can Lily give you her purple magic?

He reached out and placed his hand on her shoulder. She leaned into him, her cheeks pink. *Yes. Most alchemists could share their magic if they really worked at it. It takes practice but it's possible. She can transfer yellow to me, purple, green. I can administer the magic, though it fades quickly. I have to keep getting hits from her every minute or so.*

I stumbled back and leaned against the railing as this revelation sunk in.

Why doesn't the King do this? Wouldn't he want that kind of power?

And would he want me to give him my red magic? What would happen if I refused him?

The man met my eyes across the space. *He does.*

My breath caught.

He's very sparing about it because he doesn't want anyone else to know about this kind of power.

Why not?

For the same reason he polices the alchemists with us officers in the first place. So nobody will get strong enough to rise up against him.

A bitter gust of wind flung my hair into a million different directions, but I ignored it as I studied the man with Lily. They weren't quite touching but I could *tell* they wanted to. There was something there. A familiarity that went beyond friendship. The way they stood near each other, looked at each other, revealed it all. They were lovers.

So you're both Resistance, I asked for the confirmation again. The link between us was strong despite the howling wind. I could hear every word as if I were the one thinking them.

We are. And as far as I know I'm the only Royal Officer in the Resistance. I've been in and out of the palace on assignment, but I've been called in for the time being. I'll probably be back to the war front soon.

And you're with Lily? Are you a couple?

He stiffened and paused, then whispered something in her ear. She shifted to meet my gaze and nodded ever so slightly. For anyone watching us, perhaps the guards below, we'd look like people standing on balconies, having nothing to do with each other. And except for the initial hello between Lily and me, we hadn't spoken another word.

You can trust me, Lily's ethereal voice drifted into my mind. *Things aren't always as they seem, and your path has been laden with misfortune. It's not over yet, but stay strong and you'll find your way. You're the key to everything.*

What does that even mean? Why do you have to be so cryptic all the time?

She smiled one more time in my direction before going inside, the officer following. They shut the door with a slam, that I wasn't sure was from the wind or some sort of anger at me. And still, they'd never answered my question about being together.

What's your name? I called out, hoping to connect with the man again. He was so much easier to understand than Lily.

Jose, he replied, his voice calm through the link.

Okay, Jose, what's the plan here? I asked. *What am I supposed to do?*

We know you want to leave New Colony, to run away from this engagement, he said with certainty. *Don't. Stay. Stay and fight.*

Shaking my head, I glared into the white forest and then rushed back into my bedroom. That wasn't a plan. That wasn't anything! Don't run away? Stay and fight?

What did they expect? I needed to get Dad out. *I* needed to get out.

Jasmine was dead. Others would perish as well if I stayed here.

I thought I could help your Resistance. I was wrong.

Richard had used me to interrogate Sasha. He would do it again as soon as he needed to. The Resistance would have to complete their mission without me. I was a weapon in the hands of the wrong people, and the only way to stop more pain from happening was to remove myself from the equation as soon as possible.

Don't give up so soon, he replied. *Lily knows what she's talking about. You're the key to everything. You have to stay and marry Lucas.*

I'm sorry but I can't help you.

I broke the connection.

Lily and Jose would have to find someone else to lead their rebellion.

▼

"Miss Loxely." Faulk smiled coolly. "What are you doing all the way back here? You're supposed to be going to be on camera with your fiancé." She pointed to the front of the room with a long bony finger and I groaned.

I wasn't ready for this! The exhibition had come *way* too quickly. We'd only just spent the night here and first thing the next morning, we were expected to perform. The largest of the living areas, called the "great room" had been mostly cleared out of furniture, and I waited like a stubborn mule in the corner, desperate to sneak away and hide. Chairs lined the back wall for the spectators. Up front, a few strategically placed couches and chairs waited for those who would be on the cameras, and unfortunately, that was where I was heading.

"I'm going there now," I replied. "It's nice to see you back, Faulk. I hear you've had your hands full with my sister's escape and the assassination attempts on the royal family. Your job certainly is important." I did little to keep the sarcasm from my tone.

"It is important," she agreed, eyes narrowing.

"I know," I replied, just to throw her off. "I would hate for you to lose it."

I pushed myself off the wall and strode toward Lucas.

When the makeup artist and hair stylist had woken me before the sun, they'd said it was because I'd be on camera longer than ever before. The result was hair that was perfectly curled in long waves framing my face and falling past my shoulders. My makeup had taken an hour, expertly applied to look like I wasn't wearing any at all. As if anyone would believe my lips were always this full and pouty, my cheeks this naturally blushed, skin this smooth, and eyes this big? Yeah, right.

Lucas was already sitting on a loveseat off to one side of the set, and I joined him, trying not to blush at my perfect styling. "Hi Lucas," I said, sinking into the cushion and brushing my dress so it laid perfectly smooth.

I wore a cranberry sweater dress that fell just above my knees and sleek brown boots with white fur along the top. Natasha's ring caught the light and sparkled on my finger as I placed my hands on my shaking knees.

"Hi yourself," Lucas replied. He looked so good. I had to admit my heart was more than a little fluttery at the sight of him. He was styled in dark jeans and a white button-up shirt that fit him perfectly, showing off his muscular body underneath without trying too hard. His hair was done in that messy yet planned look that he pulled off so well. He noticed me checking him out and his charcoal eyes darkened. He didn't say anything, but he did reach out for my hand. I wrapped it in his and ignored the fluttering feelings inside.

"Don't worry," he commented after a few minutes of silence. "I made sure that we're not part of the exhibition. Dad wants us to tell our love story to the cameras when we start. Answer a few questions, that sort of thing. Just follow my lead and you'll be fine."

"Okay," I replied with a gulp, suddenly aware that the cameramen were turning on their equipment and pointing it right at us.

Callie sauntered into the room. I perked up, seeing my friend. She was equally made up with hair and makeup but dressed in the typical black guardian outfit. They'd tamed her normally wild hair into a smooth blonde sheet, and her cute glasses were missing.

"Contacts," she mouthed to me, rolling her eyes and giggling. She sat down gingerly on the other loveseat across from us, smiling brightly.

Lily Mason stepped into the room next, an energy of quiet power following in her wake. She didn't smile, but a knowing glint shined in her eyes as she joined Callie on the loveseat. She was in her early to mid-twenties, I couldn't remember which, but she was gorgeous. She too was dressed in her regular black guardian gear.

Finally, King Richard swept into the room, his energy bigger than anyone else's here. The buzzing conversation quieted instantly and the silence that hung in the air became thick and stifling. He sat in the big chair that was between the loveseats, the center of the action, brushed off his collar, and rolled his shoulders in his heavy navy sweater.

"Let's get started."

▼

"I can't believe I got so lucky," Lucas said, pulling me in close and leaning over to kiss my forehead. He lingered for a moment, and his scent filled me, making this pretense easier than it should have been. I grinned and snuggled closer.

"Yes," I said to the camera. "We're very lucky it all worked out."

I turned back to Richard who'd been conducting the interview. "Thank you again for accepting me into your family. I hope I can make your son happy."

"You already do," Richard replied, smiling at me for a long moment.

"Well, then," he continued, breaking the eye contact and returning his attention to the main camera. There were two more on either side, and spotlights behind those that reflected in our eyes. "As much as we all enjoy a good love story, I think it's time we get to what everyone is most excited about: color alchemy."

He shifted and focused on Callie and Lily who sat patiently on the other loveseat. The cameras followed.

"Our first exhibition featured some of our best male alchemists, of course the ones who aren't off winning the war." The spectators laughed accordingly. "In our second, I'd like to introduce you to some of our best female alchemists."

Callie blushed deeply at the compliment, her eyes lighting with the praise. As far as I knew, she'd always been treated like the others. And actually, she wasn't sent out to the war because she said she wasn't a good enough fighter. Maybe being chosen for the exhibition was a great honor to her. Or maybe there was something else going on.

I watched her carefully, looking for a break, but there was nothing. The way she smiled openly, the gleam in her eyes, her upright position on the couch, they all indicated that she was genuinely excited to be here. And that made me question again why she'd sought me out before to inquire about joining the Resistance. I wanted her to be my real friend. But was she just a stand in for Reed? Another lackey sent by Faulk to spy on me?

"This is Lily," Richard said, motioning to the women. "And this is Callie."

They nodded at the camera.

"Now Lily, let's start with you. Will you tell us what color you specialize in?"

"Purple. Or some may call it lavender. Violet. Lilac. Plum. Amethyst." Her voice tapered off as she thought. "Periwinkle," she added.

Richard laughed. "Well, I'm sure our viewers at home get the picture. Will you show us what you can do with it?"

"Of course," she said. "Whose future would you like me to read?"

"Why don't you read mine," he said.

She nodded, reaching for the purple stone that hung around her neck. A second later the color floated in the air, a cloud of sparkling hues, and then drifted into the top of the King's head and then her own.

"There will be more assassination attempts on you in the coming weeks," she said, her voice darker now. "But you will survive them all. You will be the victor."

Richard nodded, eyes heavy on her. "Thank you. Anything else you feel would be beneficial for us to know right now?"

I suspected that she was holding back. Or possibly, she was lying.

It was the look in her eyes. They didn't have that same faraway gaze she'd had when she'd done my reading. Not to mention, she was much more direct with her words and not as confusing. And this kind of magic had a way of twisting words, leaving too much to the imagination.

"You will make more progress in the war," she said. "But it won't end quite as soon as you have been planning."

"Thank you," Richard replied.

He raised his eyebrows at the camera. "Lily doesn't always get her predictions correct as the future is fluid and not set in stone, but she's been right about a lot of things." His voice became deep, certain. "It's been helpful for our planning. Now, I know it sounds like this war is going to get more dangerous than we expected, but in the end, we will prevail."

Everyone nodded encouragingly, even me. Not that I agreed or knew Lily to be telling the truth, but because of the watchful eyes of the cameras.

Are they going to show telepathy with purple? But my question was answered for me when Richard turned on Callie next.

"And Callie. Tell us, what is your magic?"

She faltered for a moment. "Um–orange, yellow, green, and a little bit of blue."

"We saw green and yellow at last exhibition," he said. "Why don't you show us some blue and orange?"

"Okay," she said. "Which one first?"

She blinked rapidly, like she was fighting back an avalanche of nerves. Her eyes flicked around and she briefly made eye contact with me. I nodded my approval. *You can do this, Callie.* I knew she couldn't hear me as I wasn't using magic, but I hoped our friendship connection would be enough. *Just relax.* She nodded back before beaming a bright smile on the King.

"Let's start with blue."

He addressed the camera again. "Blue is very useful. One of its uses is for listening in from far away. Right now we have someone outside, about forty feet away from the lodge. There's a camera with them as well. They're going to say something at a normal volume, and Callie here is going to relay the message back to us, here, in this room." He paused to let the explanation sink in as his eyes traveled from one audience member to the next. "Callie, has anyone coached you on who that person is or what they're going to say?"

"Oh no!" Her eyes were as wide as saucers. "I would never cheat." Even if she was going to cheat, nobody would suspect it with the innocent look on her face. Maybe that's why Richard had chosen her? She was just so sweet, opposite of the ruthless Dax of the first exhibition.

"Of course you wouldn't cheat." Richard laughed. "Let's get started, shall we?"

She nodded, and an officer quickly handed her a blue flower, stepping off-camera. She held it in her hands, and the magic twirled out of the petals in a tiny blue stream. It bounced around her and then formed a cone shape before entering her ears.

I bit my lip, wondering what this meant for our friendship. She'd never told me that she was a blue alchemist. Reed was, and look how that had turned out?

There was a moment of silence while she closed her eyes in concentration. "They're repeating two words: progress and order." Her eyes popped open. "Is that right?"

Richard smiled. "That is right. Good job, Callie. The camera outside will now confirm it for us."

The spectators applauded lightly, just the right amount for this intimate gathering. They sat in three neat rows of chairs along the back wall, a mix of alchemists, officers, and Richard's favored family. As I watched them, I knew that although Callie might not have been coached, they had been. I scratched my lip, trying hide the smirk.

"Progress and order," Richard said, "that's exactly why we're doing these exhibitions and showing the world what we're made of here in New Colony."

More applause.

"Now let's move on to orange," Richard said. "It's a much more common color for our alchemists to be able to perform."

"It enhances emotions," Callie said, shifting excitedly in her seat. Next to her, Lily almost looked bored. "But only if they're already feeling it. It's great at parties! We have a lot of those at the palace." She giggled, appearing again as the perfect picture of sweet youth and wide-eyed innocence.

I studied the way the crowd looked at her. They were enamored. No wonder Richard had chosen Callie for this job. It was a brilliant move by an expert strategist.

"Would you say you're treated well as an alchemist?" Richard asked. "Are you happy at the palace?"

"Oh, *very* well," she gushed, her cheeks turning rosy. "We all love it at the palace. We get our own bedrooms and plenty to eat. We get to learn about our magic, help other people, and have a great time together. We're a family. I wouldn't change it for the world."

And there it was. If anyone at home was wondering if their long-lost children were happy, they had their answer, straight out of Callie's pretty mouth.

Okay. Callie *had* been coached. She was a happy girl, sure, but I'd never seen her quite this excited about anything. And I *did* think she missed her real family, it was the same vibe I got from a lot of the alchemists.

I shifted uncomfortably in my seat, waiting for whatever was coming next. Lucas gently squeezed my hand. I met his eyes, and he stared back, his expression guarded. Something lifted for a moment, and I saw a vulnerable pain there I'd only seen when talking about his mother's death. I wanted to reach out and bottle it up, hide it away so he'd never have to feel it again. But then his eyes darkened, and he looked away.

"I'm pleased to hear you're happy here," Richard continued.

"Thank you, Your Royal Highness," Callie replied. "It's an honor to be part of it all."

He chuckled. "Well, all right, let's get on with the orange alchemy, shall we?"

She stood eagerly as an orange orchid was passed into her hands. She lifted it to her nose and smelled it, then leaned back with a wide grin and looked out to the small crowd of observers. "I need a couple volunteers, please," she said. She shifted toward me and Lucas. "Unless you two would like to volunteer?"

Lucas stiffened. My eyes probably looked like they were about ready to pop out of my head. If our feelings got enhanced, we might not be able to put on this charade any longer. After his behavior last night, I knew he was mad at me. And I was still angry with him. There would always be something between us, but it didn't feel like love anymore. It was tainted.

Richard laughed, swooping in to save us from the embarrassment. "Oh, I don't think we need to guess what those two are feeling, nor should we enhance it. There's been enough public displays of affection from those two lately."

The crowd snickered.

"Don't be shy." He flicked a wrist toward the audience. A few brave souls raised their hands to volunteer.

"How about you?" He pointed to a young woman who had most definitely *not* raised her hand: Celia. Her face flooded with color as she shook her head and sank deeper into her chair.

"Don't be scared, we don't bite," he teased. After another moment of hesitation, and a nudge from her mother, she stood and strode toward us.

"As you can see," Richard said, "this is Celia Addington, my son's first fiancé. I already admitted my mistake in pushing two young people together who, it turned out, didn't have romantic feelings for each other. Luckily for everyone involved, we're all still friends, aren't we, Celia?"

By now he was standing next to Celia, draping one arm laboriously over her petite shoulders. Her mouth twisted ever so slightly, skin turning paler than usual. Her ill expression cleared quickly, however, as she turned to the camera with a demure smile. "Of course," she purred. "My family is happy to serve in whatever capacity is best for New Colony."

"Considering who your parents are, The Duke and Duchess Addington, I'm not surprised by your loyalty. Though, I am grateful." He squeezed her shoulders once and stepped away, sweeping his arm wide. "Callie will give you a little boost with this orange and I'm going to ask you a few questions. Whatever emotions you're feeling will be clear to the audience. Should be easy enough."

I gripped Lucas's hand. This was bad. And cruel. I wasn't her biggest fan, but even I wouldn't subject her to this. How was she supposed to save face with orange magic working against her?

Callie made quick work of the orange alchemy as she teased it from the beautiful orchid. It flowed elegantly from the flower and into Celia, seeping into her skin before disappearing. Immediately, her body tensed, becoming much more guarded than she was before. Gone was her cool exterior and in its place was an insecure woman with shifting eyes. She wrung out her hands nervously as she waited for Richard's questions.

"How do you really feel about Lucas's and Jessa's engagement?"

I stilled, holding my breath.

Orange magic didn't make her say anything, but it did make her feel it, and enough would have her talking.

"I feel good about it," Celia hissed. Her expression darkened considerably, mouth turning down and eyes thinning into angry slits.

"Again, I'm sorry for my haste in setting up the match," Richard said, acting the part of the admonished and regretful man. "Did you get hurt by what happened?"

Still standing, her knees began to wobble as she looked at the floor.

"It's okay," he pushed.

Tears fell down her face as she turned to look at Lucas. I stood, wanting to end this, but Lucas tugged at my hand, holding me back. "Don't," he whispered in my ear. "Don't interfere with Richard. You'll only make it worse."

"More," Richard motioned to Callie.

Celia's parents were no longer sitting either. They glowered from the back row of spectators, eyes wide with undeniable fury. Mine would be too if it was my daughter made to cry on a national broadcast! But trained guards and Royal Officers surrounded them. I watched as Mark eyed the people around him, tense. He knew, as well as anybody, that he'd have to wait and see how this played out.

Callie hadn't moved. The magic swirled around her, ready, but she held it at bay, her mouth open in a small pout.

"More!" Richard barked, no longer caring to appear polite. Callie's hesitation vanished. The orange magic twirled through the air. It fell upon Celia quickly, like a drop of food coloring seeping into the exposed skin of her arm. She broke down into sobs.

"Tell us," Richard said, resting a hand on her back in feigned comfort. "Let it out. I promise, nobody will judge you."

"It's not what you think," Celia gasped between sobs. "It wasn't as if we loved each other. I'm just so…embarrassed."

Her cries continued.

"And whose fault is that?" Richard asked.

Celia looked at me again. "It's Jessa's fault. She took him. I offered to share but she wanted him all to herself," she sobbed. "And Lucas. He didn't even try to care about me. He never gave me a chance."

Lucas and I grasped onto each other, motionless and chastised.

Slowly, Celia's sobs relaxed and her demeanor became filled with something else: anger. She whipped her head around, hair flying in an arc, and glared at me.

"More." Richard motioned to Callie. When she didn't move, he said it again, louder, and she jumped into action. The magic once again went to Celia.

I stepped closer, wanting to stop this. It was wrong. Celia didn't deserve this. Whatever she was feeling, it wasn't right to enhance it this much and embarrass her further.

"Whose fault is it, did you say?" Richard asked again.

"Jessa's fault," Celia growled. She glared at me, hatred seething in her eyes. Her face contorted as she watched Lucas pull me closer against him.

"I'm so sorry," I replied, my voice cracking. Guilt ripped at me. "Nobody ever meant for you to get hurt. It wasn't your fault, just bad timing."

"More," Richard said.

The magic shot through the air. The moment it hit Celia, she pounced.

One second, she was across the room, and the next on top of me. My head bounced against the floor with a sickening crack and she clawed into me, screaming profanities. Lucas grabbed at her waist, pulling her off.

"Stop!" I gasped. She had a fist locked onto my hair and wasn't letting go. Pain ripped through my scalp. I yelped, my vision blurring. Instinct kicked in, and I fought back, grabbing at her wrists.

She was up now, in Lucas's arms, and guards were swarming, but she wouldn't let go of my hair. I was half up and half on the ground, trying to get free. The pain burned, shocking me, as she yanked and yanked.

"You're a monster. A home wrecker!"

Reaching up, my nails dug into her wrists. I recognized the wet slick of her blood. I called to my magic. It only took a second. The red danced between us and then it was exactly where I needed it.

"Stop," I yelled. "Get off me!"

She did. She stepped back, all the emotion clearing from her face. It was a complete 180, one second she'd wanted to hurt me, the next she barely even cared about me or about anyone else. She slumped against Lucas and stared at the floor.

"Go to your room and clean yourself up, forget this ever happened," I ordered. I turned from her and assessed the damage she'd inflicted on me. There were a few small cuts on my arms but overall, I looked okay. It was my scalp that hurt. I needed something green…

When I looked up to make sure Celia was long gone, my heart raced in my chest. The room was silent. Everyone watched me, their faces confused and shocked. A few shook their heads. A few smiled knowingly. And that stupid camera was right in my face!

I closed my eyes for a second, counting down from five. Then I spun on Richard. "What did you just do?" I was careful to keep my voice down.

"That got out of hand." He raised his hands in protest. "I'm so sorry. Are you okay, Jessa?"

"I'm fine." I gritted my teeth. Then I took a deep breath. "I just feel bad for Celia. She didn't deserve that."

"But she attacked you," Richard pressed.

"Only because of the orange alchemy." I sighed and found my place back on the couch. Lucas joined, looking for wounds while I canvased the room.

What just happened?

"Well, it's a good thing you're a red alchemist," Richard said. He turned to the camera. "As you just witnessed, red alchemy, when used on blood, can be very useful." He paused for dramatic effect and my blood burned hot. "It can be used to control the mind." More silence. "Jessa is very special. She is our only red alchemist and that makes her our most powerful alchemist. Can you think of anyone better suited for the throne? To not only protect Lucas, but to aid him in leading this kingdom one day? I certainly can't. We are all very blessed to have Jessa as our future princess and one day, our queen."

The group applauded, the cameras zoomed, the lights just above them burned my eyes but I stared into them anyway. I couldn't bring myself to smile. I finally looked past the lights to the audience. A mix of trepidation and fascination had filled the expressions of any spectators who didn't know about my magic before today. The alchemists and officers, however, glowered at me in the way they always did, like I was the odd one out.

"That's all for today," Richard said. "Be sure to tune into our next exhibition. It will be broadcasted live from the palace in one week's time. We have a *very* special surprise for you that I am positive you won't want to miss. Goodnight all."

I waited until the cameras powered down, then I whirled on Richard. "What was that?"

"Explain yourself, Father!" Lucas said at the same time.

Richard held up his hands in surrender, but his eyes were awash in power.

He walked over, squatted down, and smiled. His eyes flicked back and forth between us. His face shifted to the same threatening expression I knew well. "Jessa, my dear girl, you couldn't have handled that better if I had told you what to do. You see, there was a lot of sympathy for Celia still, which didn't look good for us, so I needed to squash that. And at the same time, I needed the people to see you use your red alchemy, but in self-defense. That would be considered proper, and well"—he paused—"justified."

He straightened up and patted Lucas on the head. "Good job picking this one, son. You were right. She's perfect."

Rage poured over me like boiling water. This man was crazy! And way too smart for his own good. He would never stop manipulating people, never stop hurting whomever he needed to get what he wanted. The worst part was, there was nothing I could do about him. My chest rose and fell with my angry breaths as the thoughts circled through me.

I caught Lily's "I told you so" expression. She was still sitting in her spot. Never once had she moved. She raised an eyebrow and cast me a knowing look. I nodded. I understood now.

Do you have something to say to me? Lily asked. The telepathic link between us pulled like a tight string.

I smiled, and for the first time that day, I actually meant it.

Tell your boyfriend I'm not going anywhere. I'll help you. I'm in.

THIRTEEN

SASHA

I knocked on Mastin's door for the tenth time that day. Okay, I pounded on it. But I was *not* very happy and wanted…no, I needed, an explanation.

"Not right now," he called out.

"No!" I knocked harder. "I need to talk to you right now, Mastin."

"Hold on."

"You've been avoiding me all day and I'm sick of it. Let me in!"

No response. I wiggled the handle but it was still locked.

"That's it," I muttered, employing a dash of yellow magic and breaking the lock with a quick snap of my wrist.

I flung open the door. "You better have a good explanation for what you did last night," I said, bounding into his room. He stood by his closet, a towel wrapped around his waist, and from the looks of it, nothing else. I swallowed, fighting the blush that blossomed on my cheeks.

He glared, but I barely noticed, too busy staring at his six-pack. Sometimes I annoyed myself. Why was I looking at his abs? It wasn't like they were all that special. They were amazing, but so were about a million other guys. Whatever. I huffed and crossed my arms over my chest, tapping my foot.

"Did you break my lock?" he asked, incredulous.

"Get dressed." I turned around so he could have a bit of privacy. And because I needed to get a grip. His room was perfectly tidy, as expected. I blew out a breath.

"You did, didn't you? You broke my lock with your magic. This is what I'm talking about, Sasha! You're going to do something at the wrong time in front of the wrong person and get yourself killed."

I glowered at the white wall, listening to him rifle through his clothes. "Serves you right for locking me out all day."

"It's Saturday," he said. "I'm off work. I don't have to talk to you if I don't want to."

Oh, excuse me!

I flipped around. "Am I work to you?"

He chuckled low but didn't reply. Apparently, he was far too busy buttoning his jeans and pulling a t-shirt over his stupid head to be a grown up and have a conversation.

I stomped over and shoved him against the wall. That got his attention. His eyes flared. "I don't want to fight you," he growled, staring down at me, "but I will if I have to."

"And how did that work out for you the last time?" I scoffed, referring to our first meeting where I'd beat him with my magic. We both knew he couldn't fight me. I'd always have the upper hand and I didn't care what kind of guns he had—I had yellow alchemy.

I took a half step back, the proximity beginning to cause me to lose my train of thought.

You're mad at him. That's why you're here, nothing else. Focus.

"Why did you sell me out last night?" I peered up into his green eyes, hoping to find a suitable answer in their depths. But they were masked and shrouded in secrecy, like they always were.

His jaw ticked as his eyes narrowed.

For the last week I'd been invited to shadow Nathan everywhere and give my input in meetings. *I loved it!* I was proving myself to be invaluable. And when it came to training, I was showing everyone on base that I could hold my own and then some. And the best part was that my magic was stronger than ever. Each time I used it, it grew. It felt so good to be myself in an environment where I could actually make a difference. It was only a matter of time before I'd be allowed to fight in the war.

But last night, during a fighting session, Mastin had downright refused to spar with me. When nobody else would either, I'd found out he'd threatened anyone who would. No one wanted to cross Mastin, not only because he was talented, but because he was the General's son. I'd been left without a partner.

"It's simple. You shouldn't be training with us." He shrugged.

"Says you."

"Not just me. Says most of those guys. Do you keep forgetting that alchemy isn't very well accepted here?"

"I'm trying to change that!"

"No, you're trying to convince my dad to let you play soldier so you can run off to the war. This is serious, Sasha. You're here to be safe, not to get yourself into more trouble."

I folded my arms, the black active clothes that Melissa had found for me stretching with the movement.

"Oh, so that's what this is about? You're afraid I'll get hurt? Guess what, Mastin? I never asked for your opinion. I can make my own decisions."

He fisted his hands and stepped close, leaning his face closer so it was only a couple inches from mine. "Just because you *can* fight doesn't mean you *should* fight."

"Why do you even care?"

"Because you're going to get yourself killed!" he yelled.

Silence stretched between us, the room growing hotter by the second.

He moved back to lean against the wall, his chest rising and falling in heavy breaths. Then he squeezed his eyes shut for a few moments. "I just don't want to see another one of my friends die, okay?"

I could understand that. I could even respect it. But it didn't change the reality of our situation. I shook my head.

"This is bigger than your fear. Your country needs me right now and, quite frankly, so does mine. You're just going to have to trust me. I know my limits."

"Don't you get it?" he said in a strained voice. "War isn't a training drill. It's not a situation where you can choose whether or not you'll be the one to get shot. Nobody wants to die, but thousands do. What happens if you're one of them?"

My anger began to dissipate. I turned around, really checking out his bedroom. I'd been so hyped up, I hadn't had a chance to take it in. But the room was similar to mine. Nondescript. Neatly decorated. No personal effects.

This wasn't his childhood home.

Or maybe he'd never stayed in one place very long. Something about it tugged at me, a lingering sadness. Even I could think back fondly on the Resistance camp and consider it as home. And that too was gone. But maybe it was okay. Maybe home wasn't a place. It could be a person. Tristan.

I still had Tristan.

"I'm sorry," I said, turning back to Mastin and talking as calmly as I could manage. This wasn't some passing fancy. I was serious about everything, just as much as any one of those soldiers out there, and he needed to understand. "Nothing you say or do is going to stop me. I'm going to continue to work with your dad and as soon as I get the chance, I will be first in line to get out there and fight. It's who I am. I'm a fighter."

The energy between us softened. He nodded once and then strode toward me, pulling me into a tight hug. The animosity dissolved like ice in sunshine. "I don't think you know how much you matter to me," he muttered, his voice a tender vibration against my body.

But I did know.

Heat radiated off his entire body, drawing me in. He smelled like the clean shower intermixed with his own spicy scent. The mood in the room shifted, like a cloud passing over the sun. I tensed. My stomach dropped. Heartbeats sounded in my ears, picking up speed. He leaned back to peer into my eyes, searching for something. He must have found what he was looking for because the next thing I knew, his warm lips covered mine.

I couldn't allow myself to react, to give in. I pushed him off and took several steps back, wiping my mouth and staring at the hardwood floor.

"What's the matter?" he winced.

"I can't." The image of Tristan on the beach was all I could see. And my promise to him. Because as much as I was attracted to Mastin, it was Tristan who felt like home. That had to mean something.

Promise me you'll wait for me.

"You want to, though, don't you?" Mastin stepped closer, his eyes studying me for cracks.

But I couldn't answer. I didn't want to hurt him. I didn't want to hurt Tristan. And most of all, I didn't want to lose myself in something that would only end in heartache. I'd had enough of that in my life.

I was here to fight. That was all. Maybe one day, when all this was over, I'd be able to find it in my heart to love.

"We need to stay focused on what matters most." I strode toward the door. Swinging it open, I walked through, leaving him behind.

He called after me, "That's what I was doing."

▼

"Do we send out a call for more alchemists?" The man's wrinkly red face lit up with the idea. "We could offer to pay if they come forward. Then we'll train them, of course." He motioned across the table toward me. "Sasha can do it."

Thanks for offering my services. I rolled my eyes.

"Like that would ever work," Mastin replied.

"It's worth trying," the man shot back. Lip curled, he glared darkly at Mastin like he was the ultimate traitor to America.

"Mastin is right," Nathan said from his spot at the head of the conference room table. "This country hasn't been very kind to alchemists."

That was the understatement of the year.

"It's going to take some time before anyone willingly gives themselves over to us, especially if they know it's to fight in the war."

We sat around a long table, windows on one side that overlooked the base, stark white walls on the others. We'd been brainstorming ideas to combat New Colony's alchemists for the better part of an hour. So far, nobody knew how to stop the havoc they were wreaking on the frontline. The only logical explanation was to fight fire with fire. But how, when I was the only willing alchemist they had at the moment?

"What about the kids?" the man asked. "King Richard uses kids, doesn't he?"

I turned on him, shocked at his horrible suggestion. Did he want to send children to war? He sat at the other end of the table, second in command to General Scott. He was a weathered man, with a red face and judgmental eyes. "King Richard trains the kids in his palace, and they stay there until they're initiated as a Guardian of Color, usually around age eighteen." I said. "Have you seen any children out on the frontline?"

There was a stilted pause as the man regarded me coolly. I'd forgotten his name, but now I wished I had it, just so I could put a name to this face I hated.

"No, you haven't," I answered for him. "I went through hell because of that King, but I can say even he wouldn't send children to the slaughter."

521

"It was just a suggestion." The man glared.

"And anyway, what do you mean, 'what about the kids?' What are you talking about?"

There was a heavy silence. "You don't have the high enough security clearance to be asking about it," Nathan finally said.

I looked him up and down, no longer believing what I was hearing.

"Screw security clearance. I think we're long past that." He'd been taking me to meetings with him all week. Now he wanted to shut me out?

I glanced around at the others in the room, but they also avoided my weighted stare. It also wasn't lost on me that I was the *only* woman in the room. Finally, it was Mastin who had the nerve to meet my gaze and when he did, he grimaced and shook his head.

"You have child alchemists locked up, don't you?" I snapped.

"It's not what it sounds like," Nathan Scott grumbled. He fiddled with some of the paperwork in front of him for a moment.

"It's not? It sounds like you had all the alchemists locked up and you sent the ones you deemed old enough to work with me, and the rest you left in some kind of prison. Young children, am I right? And probably some elderly alchemists, too. You only sent the most able-bodied up to Canada."

Silence.

"And you call King Richard the monster," I huffed, standing. The chair scraped across the concrete floor, echoing. "I'm not helping you until you give those people a real life. Locking them away just because they're different is wrong and you all know it."

I slammed my weight toward the door. I'd had enough of this too small room, filled with too big egos. They thought they could get together and somehow save the world with their idiotic backwards ideas? Not likely.

"Just hold on a second, Missy." The man who'd originally suggested that kids be used in war stood. His face had transformed from scarlet to plum as he met me at the door, slamming his palm against it before I could leave.

Oh, you do not want to try me, old man!

"It's only been very recently that some people in this country have become accepting of you alchemists," he said, spit building in the creases of his thin lips. "There's still plenty of us who find it unnatural and evil."

I scowled, my temper rising. "Oh, plenty of *you*, huh? Great to see you leading a military that's going to lose to a bunch of those evil alchemists. Now, get out of my way before I physically move you."

"Are you threatening me?" he snapped. "Are you hearing this?" He looked around the room. "She's threatening me. *Me*, a two star General!"

I laughed, beyond done. I didn't care how many stars were in this room. These people weren't going to get anywhere with such terrible attitudes toward alchemy. I pushed past the guy, shoved him hard, and reached for the door, but as I was about to go through it, it opened and a blast of air conditioning washed over me.

Hank strolled in, followed by Tristan. My mood lightened and I squealed. I didn't know which one to hug first. I froze, letting their presence settle over me, then I dove for Hank.

"You have no idea how much I've missed you, kid," he said, wrapping his arms around me. His scruffy facial hair rubbed against my cheek.

I breathed him in. "What are you two doing here?"

"About that..." He smiled, and stepped aside. "It seems you've been causing a bit of a stir on this base. Can't say I'm surprised."

Tristan chuckled.

"Well, we've also been in quite a few meetings lately," Hank's voice trailed off.

A barrage of security streamed in, and we shuffled to the side. Tristan sidled up to me, nudging me and smiling down. Our eyes connected, and any lingering effects of anger melted away. We turned back to the door and I watched, transfixed, as an elegant, older woman in a black pantsuit sauntered into the room. Everyone stood.

"Madame President," Nathan said, eyes wide. "It's an honor to have you here. I must say, we weren't expecting you. We can move to a bigger room if you'd prefer."

"Oh nonsense, this is fine." She shrugged and slid into the closest empty chair. "I know my trip to your base was unexpected. But my new friends Hank and Tristan here have been talking with me at length, and we decided it was high time we *all* got together and figured out how we're going to end this ridiculous war that New Colony has decided to launch on American soil."

Since cheering would probably be frowned upon, I shot the room a wicked smile as I followed Tristan and Hank to the last of the empty chairs.

I'd quickly learned to call this country America, not West America as I'd grown up doing in New Colony. As far as these people were concerned, New Colony had seceded from them, but they were still proud as ever of their heritage.

Studying the American president, I felt myself wanting to like her. She looked so put-together and smart in her black suit. A knowing twinkle filled her eye when she talked, her white hair cut into a professional long bob that bounced when she moved her head. Her presence commanded the room far better than anyone in here, and with attendees such as these, I was impressed.

When the room had finally settled, she asked her first question, her eyes sweeping from person to person. "So, any marvelous plans you'd like to pitch?"

The two-star general I'd been arguing with cleared his throat. "We were considering bringing the alchemists we do have onto the base so Sasha here can train them."

He motioned to me like we were old friends and I rolled my eyes. *Figures.*

"And what use would that be?" she replied. "We only have children and elderly left."

I straightened in my chair. "That's what I said. But I still think we should remove them from whatever prison they're in and give them a proper life."

She smiled and studied me. She wasn't annoyed by my input like so many of the men had been. It was quite the opposite. She looked at me like I had valuable opinions that deserved a chance. I perked up, confidence building.

"It's already done," she said. "We've moved them to a much better facility where they can live as normally as possible given their particular set of circumstances. Even their family can stay with them as often as they'd like."

"Oh, thank you so much!" I gushed. "If only I'd had that kind of treatment as a child, so much would have been better for me."

"Don't thank me," she replied. "Hank convinced me of it. It was his idea. He's even offered to train them."

I leaned into Hank and gave him my biggest megawatt smile. He wasn't an alchemist, true, but he knew more about the magic than anyone. And he was the most patient person I'd ever met. He would be perfect for the job.

"That's wonderful," I said.

"It is wonderful," she agreed.

Over the next hour they dived into the current status of everything war-related, factoring in the tumultuous political climate and what could be done about it.

In the end, it was decided that more troops would be leaving in two days' time to go shore up those already fighting against the New Colony soldiers and alchemists. The plan was to beat them with sheer numbers and weaponry.

I kept my mouth closed. Hank, Tristan, and Mastin would never support me going with those troops. But I was brimming with excitement. It didn't matter what anyone else's opinion was on the matter. I was done letting other people control my life.

One way or another, I would be joining those soldiers.

I'd be getting out to where the action was, making all those people who worked for King Richard see that they'd made a huge mistake. Going to the war would mean fighting my own kind. It caused my heart to pound so hard I could hear it in my ears. But I refused to be afraid.

I was ready. I'd been training for this my entire life.

I would fight those who'd stolen my childhood. I would reunite my family. And I would prove to all these closed-minded Americans that alchemy was a gift.

Mastin caught my eye over the table and his jaw tensed. Ever so slightly, he shook his head. It didn't matter. I didn't need his support.

I nodded once and then turned my attention back to the President. She was a woman who'd climbed her way to power, who wasn't afraid to do what needed to be done, even if the men around her hated her for it.

I smiled. She would understand.

FOURTEEN

JESSA

The music moved through me like my body was another instrument in a grand orchestra. I danced for everything I couldn't say, my arms and legs extensions of the feelings playing inside. The song ended, and I plopped down in the middle of the studio floor, flat on my back, looking up at the ceiling and catching my breath. While my chest rose and fell, the faint scent of floor polish wafted around me. The room was dim since the lights were off and the curtains drawn, only some of the afternoon sun peeked in around their edges. It relaxed me, dancing alone in the dark.

This studio was the perfect place to spend as much time as possible between alchemy classes and training in the gym, but it still wasn't enough to quiet the stress. It was building to something bigger, louder and louder.

My eyes fluttered closed, and I forced it down.

Madame Silver would arrive any minute. Surely, she'd seen the disastrous broadcast. Maybe she'd have some sage advice to offer about my situation. She always did have a level head about these kinds of things, even though ballet issues and life issues didn't always cross over.

Dad was livid when he found out what happened with Celia. He hadn't been invited to the exhibition, and now we knew why. He would have intervened in King Richard's publicity stunt! The broadcast aired around the same time we'd come home that night. I refused to watch, locking myself in my room. Dad had come knocking an hour later. When I'd opened the door, terrified at what he would think of me, he'd buried me into a comforting hug, letting me cry it out. Eventually, as my tears mellowed, his anger grew. He'd stormed from the room, demanding to speak with the King.

Needless to say, I didn't let that happen.

I'd been able to talk him down, and eventually he'd relented, not because Richard deserved the benefit of the doubt, but because his entire stay at the palace was precarious as it was. We *both* needed him to stay under the radar as much as possible, to get in line and behave like everyone else. The next day we'd had an interesting Sunday dinner with Richard and Lucas. It had been filled with awkward silences and three uncomfortable people trying desperately to avoid eye contact. Richard didn't seem to care.

I groaned. Why was this my life now?

And where was Madame Silver? She should be here by now. I sat up and rolled out my neck. A quick glance at the clock confirmed she was five minutes late, and that woman was never late. It was in her DNA to be early to everything.

The stray image of Celia attacking me flashed through my mind. I rubbed my scalp, wincing. It was all healed now, of course, but the memory lingered. Even though she'd been manipulated, the look on her face would haunt me to my grave. The girl *despised* me. Did I blame her? The way she saw it, I had taken the crown.

It had been two days since the incident. I couldn't shake the feeling that my confrontations with her weren't over. Lucas must have thought so too because he wanted her gone. He'd lobbied hard with his father for Celia's immediate removal from the palace. Richard didn't care. He had brushed his son's demands off with the flick of his wrist, citing the orange magic as the reason for leniency.

But wasn't Celia humiliated? She seemed like such a prideful person. If I were her, I would want to leave. Geez, I wasn't her and I wanted to leave.

But she didn't.

She was still a permanent guest and her parents, permanent fixtures. Lately, I'd seen them every day, always talking with Royal Officers or Faulk, even going into private meetings with the King.

The studio door opened, flashing a stream of light from the hallway. The overhead lights blazed and I covered my eyes. Madame Silver pranced in, a flurry of energy. "So sorry I'm late, Darling. We had an impromptu meeting at the company that I simply had to attend."

I smiled weakly up at her, unable to share her enthusiasm. That should have been *my* dance company. Recognition gleamed in her eyes and she rushed over to me.

"Jessa, what are you doing on the floor? Are you okay?" she gasped, kneeling down and gently placing a cold hand on my arm.

I raised my other hand to quiet her worry. "I'm fine," I said, trying and failing to make my voice sound happy. "It's nothing. I've just been dancing for hours and I was resting up before our lesson." Okay, it was more than that. It was *everything*.

"Don't you have an exquisitely decorated bedroom somewhere for your beauty rest?"

I laughed bitterly, patting the hardwood. "Aw, but this is so much better."

She laughed along. Then she stood gracefully and reached down to help me up. Her eyes searched mine.

"Do you think it's safe to talk," she whispered, looking behind us at the closed door. On the other side were guards, of course, but there could just as easily be a spying alchemist around here as well. I'd thought Reed was the only blue alchemist who could listen in like that, but Callie had obviously proved me wrong.

I held up a finger. I skipped over to the corner of the room and snagged my stone necklace from where I'd left it, on top of my hooded sweatshirt, next to my stainless steel water bottle. I strung it around my neck, noticing all the colors individually. It amazed me that each could be manipulated in such different and incredible ways. The sheer magnitude of it hung heavy around my neck like another responsibility.

"Are you okay, dear?" Madame Silver asked.

"How is it, that out of all the people in the world, I was born with this ability?" My voice cracked on the question. "Sorry, I sound so ungrateful," I rushed to add.

Her gaze held mine for a moment. "I don't know, Jessa. I don't know why things happen the way they do. Sometimes it doesn't make sense, there's no explanation. But hear me." She reached out her hands and placed them on my shoulders. "You're this talented for a reason. Don't doubt yourself. Embrace who you are now so you can grow into the person you're meant to be."

"But how do I know who I'm meant to be?"

"That's the great thing about it. You get to choose."

I smiled softly and ran my hand along the stone necklace. Some were smooth, others jagged. The stones had been drilled with holes to allow for the black leather cord to pass through. It was mine to wear proudly, nothing to cower from.

And I was lucky. Not everyone could use stones as I could. My magic was strong enough that I didn't need to use plants, though I could. This necklace added a convenience, a security, to my already dangerous life.

"What color is your favorite?" Madame Silver carefully ran her fingers along the necklace. "Some of these are faded," she added.

"I need to replace a few of the stones soon. They're almost used up." I paused to consider her question. "I want to help people," I said. "All the colors can be used to help, so it's hard to choose a favorite. But for now..."

It was time to talk.

She stepped back and I placed my forefinger on the purple, knowing I still had plenty of color left for what was needed. My energy pulled at it purposefully, and I felt it sink in like ink.

What's going on, I asked Madame Silver, reaching out with the thought. I felt the magic working between us, an invisible string of energy. I walked over to the ballet barre and started the beginning exercises. We always started class the same way. Nobody would ever have to know that we were doing more than just dance in here.

The ballet company is going on tour, she said. *We had expected it to be delayed or canceled because of the war, but we just got word that it's been approved.*

My heart sank, and I faltered in my current set of stretches. *That will be fun.* I paused. *So, does this mean you're leaving the capitol?*

She met my eye with a quick nod.

When? For how long?

She came to face me at the bar, going through the same stretches. She often did that, even though she wasn't a professional ballerina anymore, she still danced. I guess the same thing could be said about me.

Tomorrow night, she replied. *We'll be traveling, the whole company, to all the large cities in New Colony. We'll be gone for two months.*

I frowned for a brief moment, then pulled myself back together. This was her job, it was normal. *I shouldn't be surprised, as you do this every year. I just forgot about it with everything else going on. I'm really going to miss you.*

Her eyes caught mine. *I want you to come with us.*

What? Confusion settled deep. My heart raced even thinking about it, the pain a dull thud-thud-thud in my chest.

That's not possible, I said. *I'm getting married in a few weeks. And even if I wasn't, Richard would never let me leave the palace. He doesn't care about ballet. I'm a Guardian now.*

She kicked her leg up gracefully and bent at the waist. I followed, grateful for the momentary break in eye contact.

What I mean is, I've met with a few of the other staff and we want to sneak you out with us, she replied, her voice confident as it filtered through my mind. *Our first stop is all the way down south and then we're working our way back up. You know how many trucks of scenery we have for these kinds of things. And I get my very own trailer, as I'm the lead choreographer. We could smuggle you out, get you to the border, and then you could use your magic to take refuge in West America.*

It seemed too risky. But something stopped me from refusing. It was a plan and I needed one of those.

Would they accept you in West America?

I think they would, I replied, excitement beginning to stir.

And if that doesn't work for you, she continued, *then stay with us on the road, but keep hidden. In two months, once we make it up to the north for our final stop, you can venture up to Canada. It will be riskier to wait that long, but the Canadian government accepts New Colony refugees without question.*

How do you know that?

There was a long pause. *It's a more common subject in this kingdom than those in the palace would like to admit. But anyway, I have a sister who left many years ago for Canada. She sent word back that she'd made it safely. She wanted me to go too, but I couldn't leave the company behind.*

But there's a chance?

A very good chance.

A flicker of possibility danced between us as our eyes connected. She thought I was leaving with her, but it was another thought that burned in me.

I could save Dad.

Lily and Jose weren't going to lose me. I was sticking around to help the Resistance—at least for now. Someone had to stop Richard.

That someone was me.

But I needed to get Dad out of here. It was only a matter of time before he ended up hurt, or worse. Besides, he was the exact kind of leverage against me that wasn't safe for either of us.

Could you get my dad out, too? I wouldn't outright refuse my own escape at this point. She wouldn't understand my reason for staying. I broke our eye contact, guilt coursing through me. But I needed to get her on board with getting Dad away from all this.

I met her eyes again, and pleaded with my own.

Of course, she finally said. *It will be more dangerous but I'm sure we can handle it. Didn't you tell me that your mother and sister are in West America? Your whole family could be reunited again.*

Smiling at the thought, I forced the smile to stay in place. They would be reunited and that was wonderful, but I'd still be here.

Here, until I changed things.

And if I had to stay back for some reason, I asked cautiously, *like if I wasn't able to make it because something happened to stop me, and my dad could make it, would you still help him?*

I'm not sure, she faltered, her head shaking slightly.

His life is in grave danger here, with or without me, he needs to run.

Your life is in danger, too. That broadcast… We all saw it, it was how I was able to convince the others to go along with this plan. Jessa, it was terrible.

We turned around and began stretching the other leg. Now facing away from each other.

I know that, I practically shouted the response in my mind. *Of course I know that. But they're using Dad against me. If I can't get out and he can, it would benefit us both. It could save us both. I need to know if he can come with you, just in case I can't.*

Her soft hand rested on my shoulder, I flipped around.

She nodded.

I exhaled and closed my eyes. *Thank you.*

We're leaving tomorrow night. Do you think you can get out and meet us in time? We will have someone waiting for you at the stage door all day tomorrow. They'll know where to hide you.

I'll find a way, I replied.

Once more, she nodded.

"Are you all stretched out?" she said, her teacher-voice filling the studio space. If anyone was listening in, they'd hear the best ballet teacher in New Colony giving her lesson and that would be all. "Do you feel warm enough for our lesson? I have a tough one planned."

"Let's do it." I gave her a quick smile. "I'm tough." But I was no longer talking about ballet and from the insightful glint in her eyes, we both knew it.

▼

"We're getting you out of here." I tackle-hugged Dad, the sheer excitement of everything causing me to forget about using my telepathy. "For a walk, of course," I added. After letting me go, he stepped back, confusion wrapped in his usually steady eyes.

"Let's grab our coats. It's so stuffy in here tonight," I continued, playfully. After a few minutes, we found ourselves outside, the bitter cold wrapping around our bodies. But the fresh air really did feel amazing. Breathing in deep, I allowed it to steel me for what I needed to do next.

The purple stone, still around my neck, hung warm against my skin. I quickly connected with it and reached out to dad. Once it was established what I was doing, he'd stilled, but let me explain everything to him.

You have to come too, he insisted. *I'm not leaving without you.*

Absolutely not. I need to stay here since I'm the only one with enough power to stop King Richard.

It's not your job! You're only seventeen, Jessa. You don't have to do this.

I glanced behind us, noticing a couple of guards trailing behind us. I turned to dad and wrapped him in a tight hug. The cold was beginning to bite through my clothes, and his warmth poured into me.

You don't have to understand it. But I'm staying.

He shook his head against me. *No. I'm your father. Listen to me. You need to come with us. You have to get out of here. What if I leave tomorrow and never see you again. How am I supposed to live with that?*

"I'm getting cold," I said aloud. "Let's go inside."

Jessa, just listen to me. With a sharp breath, I severed the telepathic link and walked toward the palace doors.

"Jessa," he growled. "We're not done here."

"Yes, we are." I shot a knowing look toward the guards. His mouth fell into a grimace and his eyes narrowed, but he didn't say another word.

We parted without continuing the argument, both upset with the other. I hated going to bed mad at someone, especially him. It was one of those things, that no matter how it happened, it always felt terrible. But one of Mom's old sayings came back to me just as I'd drifted off to sleep. *Things that look scary in the dark always look much different in the morning.* She was right.

The next day at breakfast, he was waiting for me. He'd never said a word as we picked through our food. But as we got up to leave, he'd pulled me into a hug.

"Okay." Was all he had said, but it was enough. The tears burned, and I'd quickly wiped them away.

The hours had moved at lightning speed after that, no matter how much I tried to slow them. My magic seemed utterly useless without control over time. Unfortunately, I didn't get to make the rules.

Classes ended for the afternoon and I found myself pacing back and forward in front of Lucas's suite.

I had no idea how I was going to get Dad out of this palace by myself. The national ballet was located within walking distance of the palace, so that was lucky enough. But with security everywhere, we'd never be allowed off-property, let alone to go downtown in the middle of the day. And even if we could, people would recognize me.

I didn't exactly have a getaway plan.

I could possibly get him out to the street. But that wouldn't end well. He might be recognized. There would be witnesses, adding extra risk to Madame Silver and the others who'd agreed to help me.

▼

I huffed, strolled past the guards with their suspicious eyes, and knocked on the Royal's door.

Nobody answered.

"Can you let me in, or what?" I tossed toward the nearest of the guards. He raised a cool eyebrow. "I need to speak with my fiancé."

He cocked his head, but then with the quick rattling of keys, let me into the royal apartment.

"He's in his room," the man barked after me.

Head up, I strode down the hall, past the family room, past Richard's private office, toward Lucas's bedroom. I knocked softly. No answer.

Okay, don't worry. Maybe he didn't hear it the first time.

I knocked louder, expecting the door to swing wide, but nothing. Was he here? I pressed my ear to the door and heard the faint sound of ruffling bed sheets. My hands began to shake. What if Lucas didn't want to talk to me? What if he wouldn't help me?

I pounded on the door this time, the noise three heavy thuds.

"I don't want to talk about this again, Father. You already know how I feel about it," Lucas called out from the other side in his sharpest tone.

"Um–sorry," I said. "It's me. Jessa?"

Why did I just say my name like it was a question? I wanted to kick myself. Lucas didn't need to know how nervous I was coming to him.

The door flew open.

His pewter eyes, cast in shadows, ran the length of me. "Come in."

I did, closing the door carefully behind me. We stood in the center of his bedroom, a distance between us that felt like we may as well have been on opposite ends of the earth.

I chewed on my lip, gathering the courage to tell him my plan.

"If I asked for your help, would you help me?" I said, my insides twisting.

"Anything."

Expression guarded, shadows still cast over his eyes, he hid his depths from me. But he'd said yes, so it was now or never. My truth burned in my throat.

"Okay." I bit my lip, reaching to my necklace. I connected with the purple. Then crossed to Lucas and placed my hand on his chest.

Showtime.

It's about my Dad, I said, the telepathy snapping to life between us.

He leaned back and studied me with a shocked expression.

"Since when can you do that?" he asked incredulous, "That's rare magic, Jessa."

I hushed him.

Since, I don't know? A week ago? You can talk back to me through the link I've created, I said. *All I have to do is touch you with it once, and it's there to use again and again, depending on the distance between us. It's safer for us to talk this way.*

He eyes flashed when I mentioned the distance but I didn't let myself dwell on the double meaning there.

So you can hear me? he asked, and I nodded slowly, trying not to smile. It was pretty cool, and something I was proud of. *What do you need, then?*

I explained the situation as carefully as possible, making sure not to leave any important details out. I walked to the window, appearing as natural as I could. He followed, his face grew darker and darker.

What's the matter? Spinning on him, anger bubbled up inside me. I knew we were about to argue over this. *You won't do it? I thought you said you would do anything.*

I'll do it, he snapped back. *But why aren't you going along? Isn't that what you want, to leave this palace and never look back?*

Not anymore.

He scoffed. *I'm confused. You suddenly want to stay and marry me?*

No.

So what is it? You just want to stay?

I had my reasons. And he should know better than anyone why I wasn't eager to tell him my secret plans. *Will you help me or not?*

The silence sliced between us, like an impenetrable wall.

This is his chance, Lucas. Please.

He'd gone completely still, watching me like he didn't know me.

Fine, he said, his tone a sharp knife through our link. *But you should go, too. There's nothing here for you anymore.*

I relaxed, exhaling deep. And at the same time, pain buried in my chest, like he'd put the knife there himself.

We don't have time to argue about this, I said. *If he's going to make it in time, he needs to leave as soon as possible.*

I guess I better get my coat. It'll be a cold walk to the theatre.

"Thank you," I breathed aloud. The telepathy waned, and I pushed it back between us.

You want my white magic, obviously, Lucas said. *Guess I'm good for something. It's not like that.*

He held up a hand. *Tell him to meet me in the garden in twenty minutes and to bring whatever he needs. Twenty minutes should be enough for you to say goodbye, right?*

It wouldn't. But I nodded.

Or if you're as smart as you think you are, maybe it will be enough for you to change your mind.

I guess I'm not smart. I glared, annoyed at his jab at my intelligence.

Suit yourself. He brushed past me to open his door. *Better get moving.*

As I left, I reached out to Madame Silver with my mind, hoping maybe this time she would be able hear me. We'd talked through the link enough times that it had grown. It was almost as if I could feel her, this far-off person attached to a tether reaching back to me. I tugged on it.

Can you hear me?

Jessa? Jessa, is that you? Where are you? Her voice sounded grainy, but it was there just the same. A thrill poured down my body. I was getting stronger. Last time the telepathy hadn't reached that far, but this time, it did. Maybe I would be able to communicate with Dad after he left. Could I be so lucky? We'd established the mental connection, but it was newer.

I'm in the palace, I replied. *I just wanted to let you know that the plan is a go.*

That's wonderful! We'll be waiting for you.

Guilt gripped me as I ended the connection. I couldn't explain to her why I wouldn't be showing up with Dad. There wasn't time and honestly, I didn't have the courage. I hoped she could forgive me.

A heady mix of emotions swirled through me as I walked closer and closer to Dad's door. Gratitude that Lucas was willing to help. Excited that my father was getting out. Nervous at the possibility this plan wouldn't work. And most of all, broken. Broken that I was about to say goodbye to another family member, another piece of me.

But most of all, broken by Lucas's words, now etched into my heart.

There's nothing here for you anymore.

FIFTEEN

LUCAS

We trudged along the sidewalk, arm in arm, invisible and careful. Being that it was broad daylight and late afternoon, people were out and about. As soon as the workday ended, they'd pour out from their buildings in droves. I needed to be back to the palace by then to avoid getting stuck. Christopher and I had already dodged a few unsuspecting bystanders, and also had a near miss. Rush hour would be a nightmare. I sighed; maneuvering through the city streets under the guise of magic wasn't as easy as I'd thought. Especially not with my fiancé's father lumbering against my arm.

"Were you the one who got my daughter out of there?" Christopher asked under his breath.

"Unfortunately, Jessa refuses to leave."

"Oh, believe me, I know all about that nonsense," he said, his frustration matching my own. "No, I'm talking about Francesca. Or, I guess you know her as Sasha." He huffed. "I'll never get used to that new name. Hopefully, it's just a phase. I've missed my Frankie for way too long."

I understood the feeling and my heart went out to the guy. "Oh, yup, it was me who got her out. This invisibility magic is my secret, and now it's yours too." I cleared my throat and tugged him along.

"I'll keep your secret safe," he replied.

"I wanted to help all three of you, but you and Jessa were already en route to the exhibition the night I got Sasha out."

"And now, here we are," Christopher said.

I nodded, though I knew he couldn't see me.

We walked in silence, and I wondered if he knew this part of the city. Was he observing it like it would be the last time he'd ever see it? And if I were in his shoes, would I feel good about the idea? The palace was my home, but the urban city that surrounded it was my backyard. Before things had gotten so crazy, I'd spent a lot of time here. I didn't think I could leave it behind, if it were me.

The city buildings cast cool shadows across the sidewalk as we moved at a steady pace. The architecture was a mix of old and new, though mostly new. And most of the buildings reached up into the sky, pillars of innovation. I looked down at my feet, momentarily stunned that they weren't there. Invisible magic had a way of doing that, no matter how often I used it. Luckily, all the snow had melted, the puddles mostly dried up. That was good for our ability to stay hidden, but I could have done without the prickly wind. It cut against my face, traveling down into my coat despite the zipper being so far up the plastic was nearly in my mouth. I fought the urge to complain. The cold was the least of our worries.

"You're not a bad kid, you know that right?" Christopher's gravelly voice floated gently through the air. He nudged me with his shoulder when I didn't respond. "Jessa seems to think you take after your father, after everything that's happened between you two, but I have to disagree."

My heart twisted into an angry lump. "She told you about us?"

"That girl, she used to tell me everything. We always had a strong bond, you know? And then she kept her alchemy hidden. I wish she hadn't. We would have helped her. After losing Francesca, we would have done anything to keep Jessa. But anyway," he paused. "Yes, she told me about what happened between you two. I can't say I agree with you, but I understand it. What you did…you were blinded by love."

"She doesn't see it that way."

"I know. But I get why you did it. Sometimes we men do stupid things when we're trying to keep our loved ones safe."

"Well, I think it's all too late, anyway."

"Either way, I just wanted you to know that I don't see your father in you. You're his spitting image, yes, no denying that. But your personalities couldn't be more opposite. You're a good kid, Lucas."

"Thanks," I replied, so quietly I wasn't sure if he heard or if it was lost to the wind.

Was he right? Could I believe that about myself? I wanted to, I really did. I had never wanted to be my father. But lately it felt like everything I did ended up hurting someone, usually someone innocent. And that was exactly what Richard did. At least getting Christopher out of New Colony could be one positive strike on my record.

At least I had that.

"We're almost there," I said, changing the subject. "Any last words you want me to pass along to your daughter?"

"No, we already took care of that back at the palace. But Lucas, can I ask you to do something for me?"

I stiffened with uncertainty. "Sure," I replied.

"Take care of her."

Something caught in my throat. "I don't think she wants me to do that. Besides, she'll be back to you eventually," I said. "One day she'll realize the palace isn't what she wants, and nothing will stop her from finding you again. And I'll help her when that day comes."

He was quiet for a long moment.

"I wouldn't be so sure." He tugged on my arm. "This is hard for me to admit, but I don't see how this marriage can be avoided. She's not even eighteen but you're going to be her husband very soon. Just promise me you'll be a good one."

I swallowed hard. "I promise." For months now, thinking about Jessa had consumed me. And now the idea of our future marriage terrified me. Not because I didn't want her, but because she clearly didn't want me.

The theatre loomed in front of us. It stood tall with huge, shiny glass windows and white stone pillars lining the front. We swept around the expansive plaza, dodging puddles, to the alleyway in the back where we found the stage entrance. True to their word, a man stood at the door, tall and lanky in block stage clothes. His brown eyes shifted as if waiting for someone to jump out at him. I doubled-checked we were alone.

"I guess this is it," Christopher said, clearing his throat. "Thanks again."

"Good luck." I released his arm and took several steps back. He materialized instantly. The man at the door startled, rubbing his jaw, his eyes opening wide. "I'm not even going to ask," he muttered.

Christopher laughed then turned back to where I was standing. Even though his eyes couldn't see me, it felt as if he were staring into my soul. Like he knew everything dark there and didn't mind the view. "I meant what I said. You're not your father."

Before I could utter a response, he turned toward the man and they disappeared behind the rusty door.

The white magic flickered through me, burning at my fingertips. The beginnings of exhaustion crept toward the surface. All the practice lately at invisible alchemy had allowed me to go for longer sprints each time, but the magic still demanded a physical payment on my body. Knowing my time was short, I took one last look at the barren alleyway, and sprinted toward home.

Nothing could have prepared me for what I found.

As I neared the palace, lungs burning, I caught the faint scent of smoke. A prickle of panic gripped me, and I ran faster. One hand still in my pocket, the head of the white rose between my fingers, I squeezed at the magic. My thumb caught a thorn, sharp as a tack, but I didn't care. My shoes echoed against the pavement, a mistake for an invisible man, but I didn't care about that, either.

All that mattered was figuring out where the sound of sirens was coming from. They drowned out everything else around me, blaring through the city streets, a rolling thunder. I hurried around another corner, knowing it was a straight shot down the road to the palace. I screeched to a stop. Even from here, I could see the flames.

"No!" I cried, gasping for air.

The palace was burning.

▼

Jessa. She was my first thought. My father was my second.

My feet slammed hard against the pavement, toward the gate. I didn't have to wait for a car to come through this time, as it had been left open for the fire trucks and ambulances. They zoomed through the gate and up the drive in a stream of noise and flashing lights. I followed on foot, holding on to my invisibility for as long as I could manage. Knowing I'd lose my concentration at any moment, I jumped into a cropping of trees to turn myself back and discard the rose. I took off again.

My eyes stayed glued on the raging fire, smoke billowing into the gray winter sky, flames climbing along the rooftop. It was consuming the side of the palace I called home: the Royal Wing.

I'd been there an hour before, resting in my bedroom. It was where Richard usually took his afternoon siesta. Where Jessa might be at that very moment.

I exploded with speed, my morning running habit paying off tenfold as I raced toward the palace entrance.

"You can't go in there!" someone called after me, but I didn't know the voice. I never turned to see who it was, nor did I waver or stop my crusade. I climbed the marble stairs in seconds.

"Jessa!" I screamed, pushing through the doors. "Jessa!" I yelled again, coughing as a wall of smoke hit me. I pushed past it toward her room. Since it was across from our apartment, it had to be on fire.

She could've been in a lesson, in the GC wing, as she most often was.

Or the ballet studio, not quite where the flames raged.

But I wasn't willing to take the chance. Knowing her as I did, she'd have skipped all of that to have a good cry alone in her room after her father had left.

I pressed on. My eyes burned, my throat too, but it didn't matter.

I had to find her. I ran deeper into the palace, the darkness of smoke surrounding me as the heat became suffocating. The acrid stench of smoke, mixed with the sweat from my own face, filled my nostrils. I coughed over and over again, but I pushed on, arms covering my face. My skin screamed, like I'd been dropped into a furnace. My throat burned. My eyes prickled.

But I was almost there.

Lucas, her voice rang through my mind. *Where are you?*

I stopped, nearly crying out in elation. Her telepathy! I'd never been more grateful for magic as I was in that moment.

I'm coming for you, Jessa. Don't worry. I'll get you out.

No! Don't go into the fire.

It's okay! I fell to my knees and crawled. I should have done it sooner. The heat and smoke weren't nearly as thick down here.

No, Lucas. I got out. I'm fine. I'm with the Guardians. It was just the royal wing that got hit. Arson, they think. You can't go in there.

My vision started to blur.

You're safe? I begged.

Yes! Where are you?

I coughed again. *Where do you think? I had to make sure you were okay.*

I'm fine. Get out of there, Lucas!

Okay. I'm turning back.

I was outside our own apartment. The doors had fallen down and the fire crept up the walls. I coughed, falling to my stomach. I got a hold of myself, turning to leave but the sound of a heavy, hacking cough stopped me.

Dad?

Bear crawling, I bolted into our apartment, toward the coughing.

His body was flat on the floor, one arm over his face, soot covering every inch of his skin, his eyes tightly closed. But he continued to cough; he was alive.

"Dad! Are you okay?" I knelt beside him and shook his torso wildly. The fearful thought that I was about to become an orphan shot through me.

He coughed again and opened his eyes, blinking several times as they searched my face. "I came back for you," he gasped. "When you didn't show up at the evacuation, I came back for you."

"It's okay. I'm here," I said. "Get up. Let's go."

He nodded and rolled to his knees. Another string of hacking coughs followed. When we shuffled toward the entrance of the apartment, the roof caved in directly ahead. The sound was deafening, like fighter jets swooping overhead. Or maybe that was also happening at this moment.

Sparks flew, and we jumped back.

"It's blocked," I said, shaking my head in disbelief. I considered going to a window but we were two stories off the ground and I wasn't sure emergency ladders would be up fast enough. "Let's go into the bunker," I said. Our family's go-to evacuation plan.

"It's locked," he growled.

"No. It can't be locked. It only locks from the inside." My throat burned as I spoke, the smoke growing thicker by the second.

"Then someone locked it," he coughed.

I stared at him, stunned as the realization sunk in. Whoever orchestrated this attack knew about the bunker and blocked it.

"I already tried it after I came to find you," he said. "I exerted myself so much trying to pry open the damn thing that I must have passed out from the smoke."

The fire continued to rage, the heat getting closer and closer now. It was silent, but everything it burned screamed and popped in a sickening chorus.

We were surrounded and there was no way out.

"Let me try," I said. "Maybe you loosened it."

Or maybe it just needs the magic touch.

He ignored me and stumbled away to fiddle with the nearest window.

I approached the door in the paneling, careful to keep clear of the fire. It was mostly on the far wall, but it was moving in fast and would be consuming this wall soon enough. The wallpaper here had yellow in it. I sent out a silent thank you that it wasn't covered in soot, and that yellow was easy for me. I placed one had on the wallpaper next to the doorframe and one hand on the door itself. The heat nearly burned my hands, but I pressed into it.

I glanced back to Dad through the haze of smoke. He was cussing, pushing on the stuck window. I held my breath. It was do or die. I had used my magic in front of him and hope he wouldn't see.

The door burst open.

"Got it," I called back. He turned around, disbelieving before relief washing over him. Together, we dashed inside and down the stairs into the bunker.

"Lily had said an attempt would be made but I hadn't expected it to be this bad," he mumbled behind me as we descended the stairs. The smoke was gone but it still burned in my throat, still stung my eyes. We stumbled downward, arms outstretched, lungs hacking.

Lucas, are you okay? Where are you? I still can't find you. Jessa's panicked voice tumbled through my thoughts.

We're okay, I replied, once again grateful for our connection. I needed to keep practicing that kind of magic as soon as I had time. It was far too useful to continue to overlook. *I found my father. We're both okay. Tell someone to check the bunker. I don't want anyone to know about your telepathy so just tell them I told you about the bunker and you think that's where we are.*

What about my dad? Is he okay? Did he make it to the theatre?

He's fine. He made it.

I don't want him to get blamed for this, she said, her voice rising.

He won't, I replied, but I had no way of actually knowing that. *If anything, we can act like he used the fire as a chance to escape, after his body doesn't turn up. But that doesn't mean he started it. Richard is going to think it's West America.*

Who do you think started it? She put extra emphasis on the you. It was a good question, one I'd give anything to have a definitive answer on.

Could be the Resistance, I said. *Or maybe someone working for West America. Whoever it is, this isn't their first attempt on my life and it won't be their last.*

I don't think it was the Resistance, Lucas, she said. *I honestly don't.*

I wasn't so sure, but didn't want to argue.

Then maybe it really is West America. I don't know.

There was silence, followed by the severing of our connection like a snap in a taut wire.

We took the final two stairs and Richard pulled me into a hearty hug, something foreign to us. My body stiffened and relaxed at the same time. It was the strangest feeling, and one I didn't want to repeat anytime soon.

"Thank God you're okay," Richard said, stepping away. "I really thought I had lost you. And after losing your mother…"

We stared at each other. The soot had turned his face black, his eyes red, but he gazed at me with a renewed sense of purpose.

"What are we going to do?" I asked. "This keeps happening. They almost got us."

"We will retaliate," he said. "If West America wants to turn this into a blood bath then we can make that happen. Until then, the palace is going into lockdown. Nobody will be allowed in or out until we sort through everyone's stories and find out who started the fire."

It made sense, but I doubted he would find the culprit so easily. The front gate being left open was just one reason why. But for the time being, it seemed our royal wing would have to be shut down for extensive repairs. We'd be fine; the palace was massive. But who was to say it wouldn't happen again? Eventually, our luck would run out.

I sat on the edge of a bunk, dropping my head between my knees and breathing in and out as slowly as I could manage without coughing. My skull tingled, and the edges of my vision tunneled into a blur of color. Unable to resist it, I gave into the coughing again. It rushed from me, over and over, as I hacked the thick soot from my lungs. Through it all, the adrenaline still raced through my veins.

An arsonist in the palace...

The fire was expertly done, so quick and all-consuming; so strategically placed. It had to be someone who knew what they were doing. And someone who wanted the job done swiftly and effectively.

Whoever just tried to burn us alive in our own home had to be a trusted member of the staff, or maybe even an alchemist.

"There is an assassin under our roof," my father said, mirroring my own dark thoughts. "I promise you. I am going to find them, and I am going to end them."

SIXTEEN

SASHA

As I sat down for breakfast, I immediately sensed the crackle of tension in the kitchen. Mastin stared at his plate and wouldn't meet my gaze, wouldn't even look at me. Lately, the guy didn't have an issue following me around with those emerald weapons.

Sorry, they were gorgeous. Not my fault.

Nathan appeared the perfect picture of a pensive and angry military leader. His jaw was clenched, and his hands were fisted on either side of his plate. And Melissa buzzed around us all, a ball of nervous energy. She dished the food in little spurts of action followed by long pauses, lost in thought.

I didn't realize how much I'd come to enjoy these breakfasts together until this one, since not a single person was acting happy to be here. This family had showed me kindness when I'd been in need. That had helped me to appreciate the family I'd lost. I wondered what life would be like once we finally had the chance to be together again. Would we ever have a normal breakfast together, too?

Melissa sat in her chair and the silence continued.

Something was definitely off.

Perhaps a normal person would wait for one of them to acknowledge what was going on. Or maybe a normal person wouldn't want to intervene, at all. But I was not that person.

Quickly losing my patience, I set my fork down next to my scrambled eggs, and looked between the three of them, batting my eyelashes. "Is anyone going to tell me what's going on?" I put a strong note of sarcasm in my question.

"She hasn't seen the news?" Mastin asked forlornly, looking to his parents. I shook my head.

The news? Today was the day these men would leave for war. Had that been on the news when it wasn't supposed to be? Or maybe it was that they'd be leaving Melissa today and that's why they were acting so weird. But they hadn't seemed the least bit fazed about the war stuff yesterday or the day before. Well, okay, maybe they'd been a little apprehensive, but they'd hardly acted like *this*.

"King Richard sent out a broadcast directed at America this morning." Nathan sighed, throwing his half-eaten toast onto his plate. "Excuse me, West America, as he calls it." He scoffed. "Apparently there was an incident of arson at their palace yesterday. His son almost died and now he's blaming us. Sure, we've taken our shots, I won't lie about that, but this isn't the first time he's blamed us for something we didn't do."

I mulled the information over in my mind. It was war, right? These things couldn't be out of the ordinary. A sense of relief filled me, knowing Lucas wasn't dead. Even though we were on different sides, he'd proven himself to me.

"Okay, so what's the problem?"

"The problem is the man followed his little broadcast with a raid on Nashville, which just so happens to be near the edge of our border. In his broadcast he said he would be taking his revenge on our military stronghold. But did he? No, the bastard bombed a civilian hospital, ending hundreds of innocent lives."

My blood pulsed through my ears in a whooshing stream. I took a deep breath, trying to settle my nerves. But the anger was building and the fact that I didn't have anything to take it out on coursed through me.

"So what do we do about it?" I finally said, lamely, as if there was anything to be done. Those lives were already gone. Families already devastated. More unsuspecting families torn apart because of the vile King.

"We were leaving anyway but now we're being redirected to Nashville to help. New Colony has already begun to occupy parts of the suburbs and their troops are moving in fast. It won't be long until they completely take over Nashville. This is our first large urban city to deal in this situation and, quite frankly, they're not equipped to handle it. Civilian militias are forming as we speak, and that's hardly going to be the solution."

"It's not your fault, honey," Mel said softly, placing her hand over his fist that seemed to be glued to the table.

"It's my job to protect the citizens in this country," he said. "I'm one of the highest-ranking Army Generals. I am responsible. We should have sent more troops out the second they attacked the first time. All along the border, not just the points where they were already attacking."

I didn't know what to say. I agreed with him.

"We'll make them pay for this," Mastin snarled and stood. "I'll be upstairs," he called over his shoulder as he left us, probably to finish packing.

And as for me? So far, I wasn't slated to travel with them, but I was determined to remedy that little issue.

Melissa wandered off, likely to check on something in another room.

This is my chance. You can do this. You must.

It was the very first moment Mastin had left me alone with his father since the meeting with the President. I'd no doubt he wanted me to stay back on base, to play house with his mother and stay safe. And I also figured he must be temporarily distracted by the news from this morning. Too bad for him; I'd take his distraction and use it to my advantage.

I won't feel guilty for it, I told myself, though the feeling was buried deep.

"Take me with you." I turned on Nathan. "I *know* I can help. You need me."

"We need you here even more," he replied. "We might need you to train alchemists—not kids—but if we can find any willing adults, they'll need a teacher and you're all we've got."

"That's not true. Hank is already on it. He taught me so much about magic. Trust me, he's fully capable and he wants the job," I pleaded, meeting his determined eyes. I would do whatever was necessary to get him to agree. If he didn't come around through begging, he would through magic.

"I would be useless here," I added. "But out there, I could be the difference between winning and losing the war."

"I don't know." He chewed his lip as if mulling over the idea.

"Think about it this way. Those people in the hospital? I bet I could have saved many of them. Green alchemy works quickly to heal flesh wounds, even the worst kind, and I'm an expert with green. There may come a time where I save *your* life." I added for dramatic effect, "Or maybe your son's life."

His eyes zeroed in on me; I had him.

And if he didn't, there was a knife awfully close to my hand that I could use to draw blood. One minute and it would all be over, assuming I still had the ability. If not, I'd be dead. The idea lingered. I imagined jumping into action, slicing him open and using the magic before he could respond. I could have the General healed and cleaned up in moments, unable to remember a thing except for the solid realization that he needed to take me with him today.

I shook the thought away. I didn't want to do it.

It had been years since I'd sworn off the magic. It was a massive risk, and something I never wanted to return to again.

"Well?" I pressed, staring at him head on.

I wasn't here to sit on the sidelines and watch America lose their war, their country, and everyone I knew and loved in the process. There was no way! My pinky finger rested on the edge of the knife, my ring finger beginning to draw closer as well.

"Fine," he said, blowing out a slow breath. My hand snapped back.

"You won't regret this," I replied, filled with anticipation.

He smiled mischievously. "I'm starting to see why he likes you so much."

A new sense of excitement washed through me, this one even more frantic than the first. I bit my lip and looked away, blood rising to my cheeks.

He didn't utter another word about it. He just chuckled, stood, and left the kitchen. I stood and busied myself with the cleanup, emptying the plates and bowls of their half-eaten food into the trash, adding the dishes to the ones already in the sink, and then wetting a towel to wipe everything down.

Through it all, my thoughts hung on Nathan Scott's comment. I didn't need him to say anything to know that he was hinting at the attraction between me and his son. But I couldn't think about Mastin right now, anyway. It was time to make plans for Nashville and prepare myself for all possible scenarios of what I could do there once we arrived. That's what I need to focus on, but my curious mind had already wandered to the boy upstairs.

▼

We flew in a stream of massive choppers, bigger than the ones we'd been outfitted in for previous missions. These were sleeker, faster, and outfitted to transport an entire squadron of soldiers at once. When I'd first climbed inside the expansive belly of mine, I was struck by the irrational fear that it wouldn't actually fly. It was just so huge. But I kept all wonderment to myself, musing that I might be able to pilot this thing if given the chance.

Okay, maybe that was too cocky, even for me.

Strapped into a seat next to Mastin, I tried to ignore his cold demeanor and the way he avoided talking to me. He was angry that I'd gone behind his back to convince the General of my worth. Either that, or it was the unsaid confessions between us that bothered him. After all the times I'd nearly kissed him, he'd been the one to make the first move, and my response was to run away. We still hadn't talked about it. I watched him from the corner of my eye, studying the way his hair glistened under the lights, the way his jaw moved as he swallowed or talked. He was careful to keep his arm from brushing mine, to keep his body turned away. *Fine by me.*

And on my other side, was Tristan. His scent traveled to me every time I turned toward him, a familiar wash of woodsy forest and sweet citrus. Tristan, the best surprise guest a girl could ask for. The moment I'd seen him approaching the chopper, I'd exploded into a ball of both excitement and worry. I wanted him with me, always. And I didn't want to see him involved in this war, ever.

And isn't that how Mastin feels?

I bristled at the thought. Tristan wasn't an alchemist. He wasn't *needed* out there, though maybe it was me that needed him. In any event, Tristan had also seemed slightly peeved to see me standing at the base of the helicopter. But Tristan didn't let his opinions or moods ruin things. It was one of his best qualities, the easy way he could brush things off. Once we'd strapped into our seats, he'd reverted to his usual adorable self, covering his trepidation with the kind of jokes and teasing that left me in stitches nearly the entire journey. And not just me, the soldiers around us immediately took to him, laughing along.

He provided an element to the group that was greatly needed: comic relief.

The flight took hours and by the time we approached our destination, I was aching to stretch my sore legs on the solid ground. If I could just go for a run, everything would feel better.

"What's the running situation like on these bases?" I turned to Mastin, forcing him to engage with me.

"Running situation?"

"You know? As in, I want to go for a jog when we land. I wondered what the possibility for that is like close to a war zone?"

He frowned. "We're heading into a war zone and you're worried about exercise?"

Tristan laughed, leaning in to join the conversation. "I thought you'd been living with this girl for the past couple weeks? Don't you know, if she can't go running every day, she can't be held responsible for her actions?"

I laughed. "It's true, Mastin. I need my runner's high if I'm going to have to put up with you." I winked, and he rolled his eyes, cracking the smallest of smiles.

There we go!

"You should be fine in a couple of days, maybe even by tomorrow." He shrugged. "These war zone bases are huge. But they're still fortifying this one."

I smirked, leaning into him. "It's your funeral!" I teased.

The group fell into companionable silence as we continued our flight. I noticed a few of the soldiers eyed me with suspicion, and one's glare was downright hostile. I narrowed my eyes on one of the soldier's who'd threatened me my first day on base. He could hate me all he wanted, it wasn't going to stop me from being part of the mission.

I turned away. Most of my critics would come around eventually. I chuckled to myself. Not likely.

"What's the matter?" Tristan whispered in my ear. His nearness sent a shiver down my spine and for a moment, I lost my train of thought.

"I think a lot of these guys hate me," I whispered back.

He sighed. "Yeah, well, they should be focusing on themselves and not worrying about you. But I'm here now," he continued, his lips so close now they brushed against my ear. "I'm not letting you out of my sight."

A rush of relief washed through me, because I knew what he said was true.

Whether or not he'd started this mission because of me didn't matter. He would stick to it, stick with me, because that's what best friends did.

I turned slightly toward him. "I hope one day they see me as another member of the troop, you know?"

He leaned back and studied me, eyes sparked with admiration.

"It doesn't matter how they see you, but how you see you," he leaned back in to whisper.

I giggled at how corny this conversation had just turned.

"No fraternizing!" a voice called out, teasing. Tristan and I both turned back in our seats as embarrassment crawled up my spine. Mastin bristled in his seat, folding his arms, his biceps flexing.

Being a woman in the middle of all this testosterone was tough.

Not only was I one of only *three* women on board this chopper, I was the only color alchemist in this army. The likelihood that I'd ever fit in was about the same as King Richard turning himself in for crimes against humanity. Maybe Tristan was right about what mattered most. It was my opinion of myself that mattered.

Besides, I like standing out.

There were a few windows in the chopper, and I fiddled with my fingernail as I anxiously watched the scenery below. We would be making up our own base on the other side of Nashville, close enough to the action to jump in when needed, but far enough away for us to have time to fortify a stronghold. Just as we neared the area, the descent of the chopper sending a thrill through my belly, a bomb exploded below. The immediate boom echoed over the land, an audible crack followed by a thunder.

Everyone tensed, ready to move.

"Oh hell no!" a man shouted. Angry cussing erupted among the rest.

"Arm yourselves," General Scott shouted out, his voice loud over the sound of the rotors and angry troops. "We're taking out whoever did that. We'll make them wish they'd never set foot on our soil!"

The men shouted in agreement, pumping themselves up. They quickly unstrapped themselves and loaded their weapons. I watched Mastin do the same as a nervous sensation tugged deep in my chest.

Nathan turned toward the pilot up front, barking orders. "Drop us off as close to the explosion point as you can manage."

The pilot nodded and we began to descend much faster. The inertia of free-fall shot through my body like whiplash, and I grabbed hold of my own gun resting on my hip, grateful someone had finally armed me. Once I'd boarded the chopper, I'd gotten the weapon, and thanks to Hank's training, I knew how to use it. But it was the stone necklace, newly refreshed and fastened under my shirt that I was most grateful for. It was the weapon that would make the most difference down there, and I intended to use it.

We landed softly, the impact a contradiction to the way we jumped out of the chopper. Heads ducked low, we emptied from the machine in a wave of soldiers. We ran, our training taking over as we found cover in the surrounding trees that dotted the base, as well as the few metal-sided buildings that littered the area. A few of the guys took refuge behind a handful of bulletproof vehicles that were parked.

Mastin was at my side even though I never asked for it. Tristan was as well, but that was expected. The three of us stilled behind a tree, assessing the area. Mastin took point, motioning to the rest of his troop with a series of quick hand movements.

"Stay here." He pointed at me.

"Not happening," I replied.

"He's right," Tristan added.

"I'm not having this discussion with you two."

Mastin cussed, and we ran, moving closer to the building, which was alive with growing flames. Up ahead, a group of people battled. I recognized the black Guardian outfits. Only these were slightly different. They had full body armor attached to their clothes and the alchemists wore full coverage helmets. Bullets would be hard pressed to slow them unless they hit the perfect spot. Stone chokers, in a myriad of colors, wrapped around the Guardians' necks. The color shining in the sunlight most was a yellowish amber.

Super soldiers. Just as Richard had planned.

The way they moved stunned me. These fighters were a sight to behold. They shook the earth when they ran, tore it away in clumps when they jumped, and when they hit someone, the blow was fatal. A body was thrown twenty feet in the air before crashing against a tank, and I had no doubt that life had just ended.

I screeched and ran at them, my own magic blaring to life in my veins.

I pounced on the nearest one, recognizing him instantly through the visor of his helmet. Reed. Popular Reed, the boy who'd had a little fling with Jessa all those months ago. He was a fierce fighter; I'd sparred with him a few times back at the palace. He chuckled as he pushed me to the ground with ease.

"We were wondering when you'd show up." He laughed, leaning over me.

"Here I am!" I shot back, jumping up. "So come and get me!"

"Oh, I plan on it."

He charged, and I met him blow for blow. The second a pain shot through me, I eased it with my green magic. But it seemed he was doing the same; we were an even match and this time, neither one fell. Finally, I ripped off his helmet, tossing it aside. He watched it, momentarily distracted. I swiped at him, gouged my fingers into his skin of his cheeks, fully intending to use my red alchemy and gain the upper hand. But he jumped back and scowled.

"I won't let you do that to me," he shouted, his shadowed eyes two angry black pellets. "Yeah, I figured out your secret after you left, and Faulk told us who you really were, Francesca! I remember you now. I remember your magic. I won't let you be near my blood. I know your sister already messed with me once! She tried––"

I didn't care about his stupid monologue.

I dived at him, reaching out toward a line of blood that dropped down his pale face. A slam knocked me aside and I rolled to the ground, losing my breath. Reed took off running like the coward he was.

"Fall back!" The man who'd tackled me yelled toward the group of alchemists. "Go!"

I recognized that voice, too! Branson, the fighting instructor from the palace. A trickle of fear shot through me as our eyes met. I'd seen this man fight before. He was a machine, and if I didn't manage to use red, I didn't stand a chance. But I pushed that thought aside and attacked him anyway.

He let me. He fell to the ground as if he wasn't even trying. *It must be a trick.*

"Wait," he growled, his voice soft. "I'm Resistance."

I froze, leaning over him.

"What did you just say?"

"Resistance," he spat and then turned to look at his Guardians. Most of them had disappeared but a few were still engaged in combat. One was laying on the ground, their body oddly shaped and a ring of blood around a mess of long blonde hair. He pointed to Reed and widened his eyes at me.

I nodded. That's right, Reed could listen but not if I could counter it. Blocking blue magic was one very useful ability that I did have. Before I allowed myself to question it, I felt for the blue.

"If Reed is listening, he can't hear us now. What do you want?"

"I can't stay or I'm dead," he said in a low voice. "But I'm Resistance and I want to work to help you, help from the other side. I need to make a connection with your leader. Where is he?"

"You can make a connection with me," I whispered firmly at him.

Tristan jumped forward, his gun pointed at Branson, finger hovering over the trigger. I held up a hand and shook my head. He raised an eyebrow but lowered the gun.

"Fine," Branson snapped. "I don't have time for this crap, anyway." He pulled a piece of paper from his pocket and slipped it into my hand. "That's a secure address," he said. "Give it to your highest-ranking officer as soon as possible."

I glanced at the crumpled slip of paper, at a nonsensical email address written in hurried script.

"Fine," I said. "You'd better be the real deal, Branson, or next time I'll kill you."

"I am." He chuckled, as if this was a laughing matter. "I've been working with Jasmine and the others at the palace for years."

"Who are the others?"

"Hank knows." He nodded to Tristan, who towered over us. "He probably does too. You're Tristan?"

Tristan raised his head once in confirmation. Branson used his magic to push us both back. We fell to the ground and before we could react, he was running away at top speed. He slipped behind the nearest building and was gone.

"What was that about?" Tristan knelt beside me.

"He's Resistance," I hissed back. "That's Branson."

Tristan's face lit with recognition, a knowing smile on his lips. "I know the name! Yeah, he's telling the truth. He's been loyal to the Resistance for years."

I shoved the paper into my pocket with shaky hands, still sitting on my butt like a total idiot.

"Sasha," Nathan called out, "over here." His commanding voice and presence embodied every bit the General he was. Soldiers surrounded him, looking to him for direction. The sun glinted off his dark hair, slick with sweat and even some blood.

I sprinted, quickly noticing the body lying motionless in the dirt. Her frame was petite and strong like mine. How easily could it have been me in her place? Blood soaked her tangle of blonde hair and when I pulled it aside, I knew the pretty face below me. Brooke.

"Make sure she's dead. No one wants to touch her," Nathan said with a grimace.

I stilled, studying her. From the looks of it, she was just passed out, not dead. She'd always been such a brat, but she didn't deserve to die like this. She was a product of her environment. *But aren't we all? At what point are we held responsible for our actions?*

I sighed, fell to my knees, and double checked for a pulse. Below my fingers the thick vein in her wrist moved with the faintest of flutters.

"She's alive." I looking up at Nathan.

"Kill her," Mastin added, striding to us with murder in his eyes. Blood dripped down his temple and a dark bruise was already forming across cheek. "She nearly took me out along with the others." I looked over his shoulder at three bodies being zipped into black body bags.

"Can you save her?" Nathan asked.

I nodded. With green magic, it would be easy.

"Do it," he replied. "Don't bring her to full health. I don't want her waking up for a while. Just give her enough to not have any permanent damage."

He turned to Tristan. "Any idea how we can safely put this girl into prison and interrogate her?"

He reached down and carefully unlatched the necklace from around her neck, tossing it aside in the dirt. "Start with removing any color from her." He motioned to me. "But honestly, it's Sasha you should be asking. She just broke out of an alchemist prison, after all."

All the nearby soldiers stared at me. There were about thirty of them altogether, and they glowered at me like I was a bomb about to explode.

"It's true," I said, relenting. "If I can break out of King Richard's prison, then maybe I can help you keep Brooke in ours."

"We don't have a prison for alchemists," someone grumbled from the back of the crowd.

No kidding.

I stood and brushed off the dirt and grass, taking my sweet, sweet, time. The fear that I was making a huge mistake prickled at the back of my mind, but what choice did I have? It was time to show these people just how valuable I was.

"You don't have one *yet*," I said, "but with my help, you'll have the best one on this side of the border. And maybe if you listen to me and we do things the right way, we'll be able to add a few of her magical friends in there to keep her company."

They erupted in shouts of agreement, and I smirked. Mastin stalked away in a fury and Tristan put his hand on my back. I knelt down to take care of Brooke, and as I did, the thought pricked at me again, demanding attention.

Be careful. You might just find yourself locked in that prison as well.

SEVENTEEN

JESSA

Since the fire, the palace wall, gate, and grounds swarmed with security. But on the inside, only the most trusted of the guards, officers, and advisors were allowed to move freely about the palace. Even the newer alchemists weren't allowed to leave the GC wing. No exceptions. They had come from West America, so suspicion was cast upon them. In the meantime, Faulk was conducting interviews. She was shriller than ever, and I didn't envy anyone on the receiving end of that woman.

Somehow, the fire had traveled through the royal wing, but had stopped just before reaching my dance studio. I'd still been permitted to use it, thankfully. And I did, every moment I could. After the stress of everything, my legs were sorer than they'd been in ages, but I didn't care. Dance was my only solace left in this place.

I was back in my old dorm room. Work crews had set out to restore the burned areas of the royal wing, but it would be months before anyone would be living there.

Either way, I wouldn't be in this dorm for long. The morning sun filtered in through the small window, and I stared at the stark white walls. They wouldn't be my walls for long.

Some of the other guest rooms had been taken over for Lucas and Richard. By this time next week, I'd be living with Lucas as a married woman. I could hardly bring myself to think about it, but it was coming whether I was ready or not. The wedding planning was complete. The date was set. Richard refused to let the fire slow things down. He said postponing would show weakness. The marriage was a fast-rolling ball nobody could stop.

I'd accepted it, deciding to enjoy my last week to myself.

Today, however, not so much…

Exhibition number three, the final one, was taking place in the palace's largest ballroom tonight, in the very same place as the first attack. My stomach churned, thinking about what another exhibition would mean. And again, every time I remembered that terrible night Jasmine had died. As I laid in bed, blinking away the sleep, watching the room grow brighter with the rising sun, I knew I'd have face the scene of the crime again tonight.

I rolled over and groaned into my pillow. I still missed Jasmine. She'd been someone I could lean on, someone to tell me what to do. Now I was on my own. Sure, I had Madame Silver. Maybe not at the moment but she'd be back in a few months. And I had Lily and Jose, but they felt more like allies, not mentors. It was up to me to stop the King.

I had to do it. Get Richard *alone*. Use my red alchemy.

An impatient series of quick knocks sounded on my door. I rolled out of bed, stretching as I padded to answer it. The same two cosmetologists from the disastrous exhibition at the lodge stood outside, smiling at me from ear to ear.

"You, dear Jessa, are going to have an amazing day!" the woman said. Her name was Lainey; she did the makeup. Lars did hair. I only remembered because their names went together comically well. I sighed and held open the door.

"Come in."

They pushed past me, assessing the space.

"Oh, this bathroom is quite small," Lars said with a huff. "But I guess it will have to do. Such ghastly news about the fire. So glad your beautiful fiancé made it out okay."

Lainey opened a tiny black folding chair in the center of the bathroom and promptly proceeded to lay out a million makeup and hair products across the counter.

"What time is the exhibition?" I eyed the things they'd brought along today.

"Oh, it's not until five," she replied.

Tonight?

"Then why are you here so early?" I questioned. "I haven't even had breakfast yet. Come back this afternoon."

They shared a knowing look and my suspicion burned deep.

"Don't worry, someone will be delivering your meals today," Lainey said. "We have very specific instructions about how your hair and makeup are to be done and it's going to take quite some time and effort."

"For an exhibition? It hardly seems worth hours of effort."

"Oh, but remember Richard announced there would be a surprise?" Lars jumped on. "Trust me, honey, you're going to want to look perfect for this. Now, we'll step out so you can take a shower. No offense, but you stink."

"Wow, thanks," I grumbled, shooing them from the area that they'd already taken over with their stuff. I probably did stink. I'd danced until midnight and then stumbled back to the dorm to crash in bed.

"Don't forget to shave your legs." Lainey waved at me, winked, and shut the door with a kissy face.

Dread filled me, as I suspected this extra-special surprise would mean the end of my freedom. There was nothing to be done about it now. The shower welcomed me, and as the warm water fell, I allowed my tears to fall, too. Soon, I would have to step out of this shower, and when I did, my tears wouldn't be allowed any longer.

▼

The hairdo was the biggest clue.

The top had been braided back expertly into two loose fishtail braids that met at the back where I usually put my ponytail. Down the back, Lars had somehow managed to curl and braid everything together in such a way it reminded me of a Viking Queen. It was incredible, and he was right, it took hours. Finally, he twisted in glittery, white rhinestone pins down the length.

Lainey hadn't gone for the natural look, like at the last exhibition. She'd given me perfect cat eyes with just the right amount of smoky eye shadow on top. My lips were painted a matte rose color that matched the blush on my cheeks. She called it "ballet slipper pink" and I had to agree. She highlighted my nose and cheeks with pale white shimmer and finished off the look with huge fake eyelashes. I had worn false lashes plenty of times for dance performances in the past, but they always felt strange and heavy. Today was no different. I stared at my transformed appearance.

I still looked like me, so that was good news. But I also looked so much older. It was as if the two had taken an eraser to all my imperfections and to every bit of me that made me look seventeen. I looked at least twenty-five now, like a woman who knew exactly what she wanted in life and just how to get it.

I laughed at the thought.

"Is everything okay, honey?" Lainey asked.

I smiled and lied through my teeth. "It's perfect."

As they finished up, my mind wandered back to Dad. I hoped he was okay. I'd tried to reach out through our telepathy, but I wasn't able to connect that far. I would keep trying. Ever since it was discovered that Dad was missing, I'd expected some kind of retaliation. There hadn't been anything. Not yet. Faulk hadn't even interviewed me. She'd been so absent from my life lately, it was a little odd, but I wasn't complaining. Richard never said a word about Dad to me, either. Lucas had said nobody was blaming me for his disappearance. They suspected that he'd simply used the opportunity of the chaotic fire to run and was in hiding somewhere. That he'd left because he didn't want to be used as collateral against me. It didn't take a genius to assume that. It was true.

"Now for the jewelry!" Lars clapped and removed a diamond necklace from a black velvet jewelry box. He took off my alchemy necklace and replaced it with this imposter. It sparkled brilliantly and ended with a huge teardrop diamond at the hollow of my neck.

He winked. "It's real."

My breath caught as I stared at what could only be royal jewels. More dread spread through me, more worry about what was coming next.

Then he pulled something else out of his bag, a delicate diamond tiara, and fastened it to the top of my head. A pin poked my scalp and my eyes watered.

"Ouch!"

"Sorry, girl. Price of beauty, and all that."

"Okay, what's going on?" I asked. My fingers had gone numb, and my heart felt like it was about to jump out of my chest. Really, there was no question. I already knew.

"Haven't figured it out yet?" Lainey squealed. "We're not allowed to tell you about the surprise but that doesn't mean you can't guess."

"No," I whispered. "No way, he wouldn't."

Oh yes, he totally would.

"Come," Lars said, wagging his finger at me. "It's time to put on your dress."

I stood on shaky legs and followed them back into the bedroom. The dress hung over the closet door, posted there like a warrant. I recognized it immediately and winced. The tailor had measured me for it only a few weeks ago. Shining brilliant white underneath, with fragile lace covering every inch, it fell to the floor in a wide train, the lace just peeking out over the edge.

Even I had to admit it, my wedding dress was stunning.

"I'm not getting married next week. I'm getting married tonight," I said, accepting the truth. I took several deep breaths. They didn't help. The panic began to crawl up my neck, gripping. The heaviness of the diamond necklace, a noose. The ring on my finger, a promise. The tiara perched atop of my head, a cage.

"Yes, you are," Lainey said. "I just knew you'd love this surprise! Now, let's get you dressed. Your groom is waiting for you."

And so was my entire future.

▼

The second I stepped from my room I was faced with cameras. They were everywhere, and more than ever before, as if they'd multiplied.

"Jessa, how are you feeling?" A man shouted from behind one of them.

I smiled, knowing these cameras wouldn't be going anywhere for a while. What did I expect? This was a public event for the beginning of what would be a very public life.

"I'm so excited," I gushed, running my hands along my dress.

"Are you happy about the surprise?"

"I couldn't be more pleased." I stared into the camera, my reflection shining back to me in the lens. "I want to thank Richard for this day. I don't know how I'll ever repay him, but I promise to find a way."

A barrage of security swept me away.

I wasn't brought into the palace ballroom. That plan had all been a ruse. Instead, I was whisked into a town car and driven to the oldest church in the capitol city. Saint Patrick's Cathedral may have been the oldest building in the kingdom, considering so many of others were deemed too patriotic and torn down decades ago. Out with the old, in with the new. There weren't many practicing Catholics left in New Colony, and as far as I knew, this church was used strictly for weddings and funerals. But then again, I wasn't religious. How would I know? Religion was a freedom we had in New Colony, but it just wasn't something people were fanatical about. There were too many reasons for us to stay in line.

As we pulled to the curb, I watched the guards and Royal Officers as they swarmed the area. There weren't many citizens here to gawk, as I'd been expecting and like I'd seen in the old footage of other royal weddings. That was probably because the wedding happening *today* would be a surprise for them, too. Maybe this earlier wedding day was Richard's way of making sure it happened exactly as he wanted. A surprise for everyone else but him.

I climbed out the car, struggling with the tight dress and its long train. A cacophony of people instantly surrounded me, like moths to the flame. My heart hammered, and my breathing picked up, making my dress feel ten times tighter than it had back in my bedroom. Someone handed me a bouquet of white roses, bound in shiny white ribbon. I'd specifically chosen blush pink and pale green for my colors. But looking down at myself and my flowers, everything that touched my body *in any way* was completely white.

I swallowed a shuddering breath, frowning at the genius of it. Just another one of Richard's tactics to keep me from going off-script.

Keep her dressed in white.

Keep her magic inside.

I bit my lip and lifted the flowers to my nose briefly, relaxing in the rose scent. Catching me off guard, not alerting the public ahead of time, what else would King Richard have up his sleeve? He must have been convinced I was going to mess this up somehow, to go to all the trouble.

I wasn't convinced I still wouldn't.

Or maybe he was just trying to throw off anyone with plans to assassinate the royal family during such a public event. Maybe this was all for my protection.

The cathedral loomed ahead. As a kid, I'd loved to study its uniqueness in the city, always picking it out from the modern buildings when my family had come downtown. Now, it would forever be remembered as my wedding location.

It was large, but not as big as I'd pictured. Composed of gray and sandstone bricks, it had gothic-inspired arched doorways and windows. Perfectly manicured hedges lined either side. New state-of-the-art buildings surrounded the cathedral, making it stand out as a gem even more.

The air wrapped around me, still and cold. My usually pale arms turned pink. I shivered and peered up at the large circular stained-glass window embedded above the entrance, trying unsuccessfully to count the number of geometric shapes. Anything to focus on but the reality of the moment.

"Time to go," someone said in my ear.

The ornate crimson front door beckoned to me.

It's going to be okay. This is just a necessary evil to get closer to the King. And it's not like Lucas is going to make you behave as a real wife would. Right?

It was a question that flipped my insides upside-down.

The nerves raged unbearably as I stepped into the church, my sparkly heels clicking against the stone floor. A string quartet played the standard bridal chorus, the music filling the space. A room brimming with people stood and turned in my direction, their gazes heavy as they stared. Someone whispered "now" in my ear, and then Richard slid in to take my arm and walk me down the aisle.

My heart froze. It should have been Dad. None of this was right. If it was right, then Dad would be escorting me down the aisle at my wedding, not this awful imposter who made my skin crawl.

I smiled sweetly despite the angry pit in my stomach. Along the edges of my vision, Color Guardians lined the walls. They stood at attention, manipulating magic in their hands that swirled out and over the crowd. The stunning sparkling colors of sea foam, cobalt blue, lavender, magenta, honey orange, and canary yellow danced around the room. It was magnifying. Stunning.

And absolutely the perfect touch for a wedding between a prince and an alchemist. Just like at the other two exhibitions, the cameras zoomed about the space to catch it all.

Tilting my head, I saw him. Prince Lucas. Lucas to me, and yet to the rest of the world, he was a prince. Today he looked the part, dressed in fine maroon and cream regalia to match the title. Atop of his head, a gold crown, inlaid with pearls, rubies, and diamonds. It was a smaller one than the monstrosity I could see Richard wearing out of the corner of my eye.

We began to walk forward.

The closer I got, the more Lucas's eyes shone. They narrowed on me with a mix of shock and intensity in their gray depths. Love and pain and regret and hope and everything in between flashed across his face as I moved closer with each step. Lately, he'd been so good at covering his feelings, at shadowing his truth. But seeing him now, I *knew* he loved me. I *knew* he was sorry and heartbroken. That he'd nearly given up but so desperately *didn't want to give up.*

Maybe he didn't want to control me. Maybe he just wanted my forgiveness.

Could I forgive him?

I still didn't feel ready. As I walked toward him, my chest ached with the knowledge, and I hated myself for it. I wanted to. I wanted to be with him, to love him, to forget about our past and move forward. But the betrayal burned bright, brighter than ever with Richard on my arm instead of my own beloved father. Things could have been different for me and Lucas. They should have been different.

Richard deposited me in front of his son, then moved to the side.

"You are so beautiful," Lucas's voice cracked as he said the words. Then he took my hand and together we faced the priest.

I didn't pay attention to a word the solemn and elderly man said as he officiated, but when the time came, Lucas said, "I do." And I said it, too.

"You may now kiss the bride."

The priest's crackly voice rose over the congregation. Lucas and I leaned in at the same time. I expected to recoil at his kiss after all the anger I'd been holding inside. But instead, I fell into his lips as I always had. I breathed him in and a peaceful calm settled over me. I'd missed that. Missed *him*.

It was possible that we were going to be all right. Maybe he wasn't going to turn out like his father. Yes, our love had changed, and we'd probably not be the most romantic couple in the world, but I hoped we'd be able to find mutual respect. Maybe that would transform into something more, something beautiful.

I was relieved, having decided on a place to start.

Respect.

As we strode back down the aisle, hands clasped together and smiling faces beaming back at us, I soon realized the night was far from over. Richard announced that we'd be going back to the palace for a dinner, reception, and dancing.

This time, we rode together in the armored black car. Lucas held my hand softly in his as he explained that he'd had no idea about the surprise wedding, either. He insisted that he wasn't okay about being deceived but looking at him, he didn't seem all that perturbed.

"Are you happy to be married to me?" he suddenly asked with a hopeful expression. A stab of guilt jabbed at me.

I held my breath for a moment. If it was respect I wanted, I needed to start with the truth. "I'm not unhappy about it," I said, my lips twisting as I tried to think of how to explain what I was feeling.

His face dropped slightly, and that familiar shadow overtook him: that shadow not as anger, or as frustration, but as heartbreak.

"It's not like *that*," I said. "Will you hear me out?"

He peered up at me and nodded. The sunlight caught the planes of his face, accentuating his jaw, and I nearly pulled him in for a kiss. I was so attracted to this man, and yet, so conflicted; I hardly knew how to handle myself.

This man is your husband.

I took a deep breath and explained. "After how we got engaged, not the first time but the official time, I thought I would have to be dragged down that aisle kicking and screaming. I was so mad at you, Lucas. You know that. And I can't say I'm totally over it because I'm not. I don't know if I ever will be."

He waited for me to go on, squeezing my hand once. His warm palms sent relief through me.

"I have to admit." I bit my lip, a little embarrassed. "I'm glad you didn't marry Celia. And I think maybe with time, we might be able to build something again. I can't stop thinking about what you did for me that day of the fire." I was talking about my dad, but with no purple near, I couldn't make the telepathic connection. He nodded in understanding. "And about how you went into that fire looking for me," I continued. "I know you care about me. I do."

Silence stretched between us.

"I can work with that." He smiled faintly.

We turned to face forward, and I leaned into him. He stilled for a moment, then placed a gentle kiss on the top of my head.

We pulled into the palace drive and were met with even more cameras. They escorted us into our reception in the main ballroom. It was decked out with white crystals that hung in long strings from the ceilings. White tablecloths were laid over the round tables with rose-flowered centerpieces standing tall in their centers, in the exact shades of pink and green I'd picked with the wedding planner.

The night flew by in a frenzy of food and dancing and talking with nearly everyone I'd ever met in the palace and a few more of the King's closest confidants and families. Even Celia and her parents attended the reception, ignoring the hostile glares people shot their way. They congratulated us on the marriage and left early.

After a few hours of everything, I had to admit, I was starting to get into it. I found myself relaxing, and my cheeks were beginning to ache from all the smiling. Lucas held me in his arms while we danced, my head resting on his shoulder, his face tilted in, breath tickling my ear.

"Are you happy yet?"

I chuckled, teasing. "I guess you could say this feeling is happiness."

I leaned back a little to catch the expression on his face. "Are you happy?"

He nodded once, eyes flicking to my lips. "Yes."

"Oh, you two." Richard stepped in right next to us, snapping us from the moment. "Aren't you a picture?" Lucas still held me as we turned to the King. "You remind me of me and your Mother." His face darkened, pain flickering across it. The crown on his head was a little off-kilter, the red around his eyes a little too noticeable. "We used to be like this, you know? Young, in love, the world at our doorstep…"

Lucas sniffed and furrowed his brow. Richard seemed a tad too drunk, a rare sight, and more than a little unsettling.

"I miss her, too," Lucas said, voice careful.

Richard's face twisted, eyes landing on me. "But we have *you* now." The words came out sharp, sounding like a threat. "Better do as you're told, Princess. This isn't a game."

Then he stalked away, party guests stumbling out of his way. A prickly doubt coursed through me as Lucas and I continued to dance; the earlier happiness washed away.

A few minutes later, Richard issued more reminders of the truth.

He'd found the microphone, and his voice bellowed out over the crowd. "Friends and esteemed guests, thanks again for coming tonight. I want to congratulate the happy couple."

Lucas and I turned from our dance to Richard, the crowd parting in an arc as they clapped. We stood in the center of the dance floor, the King on the other end.

"This marks the beginning of not just a loving couple's life together, but the beginning of a new era for the Heart family. Jessa and Lucas have united the Royal Family with the alchemists, making our kingdom even more powerful."

I swallowed a lump in my throat. Lucas's arm, draped around my side, grew tighter as his father continued.

"We will win the war, take back what's rightfully ours, and unite West America and New Colony under one prosperous kingdom." His voice was strong, determined, and the guests ate it up. They cheered with shining eyes and nodding heads.

He motioned to us once again, a glass of champagne now in his other hand. He raised it high. "To the happy couple, may you live long and be prosperous." He winked. "And give this kingdom lots of magical little heirs."

"To the happy couple!" The crowd cheered, a few snickering at the joke.

But it wasn't a joke.

Lucas and I smiled wide at our guests, but inside, I burned with anger. Richard's speech had once again shattered the illusion, waking me to my true reality.

I wasn't here to play house with Lucas, or to make alchemist babies for the Heart family. I wasn't here to be friends with the royals and I refused to play right into Richard's hands as I'd always done.

No. I'm here to complete my mission for the Resistance, gain control over Richard, and end his corruption once and for all.

I owed it to Jasmine. To my family. To everyone who'd lost a life because of King Richard.

"All right you two lovebirds." Richard strolled to us, microphone now gone. He seemed a little steadier on his feet, as if the speech had sobered him. "It's time for you to retire for the night."

But I could still smell the acrid scent of alcohol on his breath.

"I want grandkids, it's true." He laughed, patting his son on the back. "But don't worry, I don't expect any for at least a few more years."

Embarrassment washed over me as Lucas tensed at my side. It wasn't the thought of being intimate with Lucas that bothered me, though I hardly felt ready. It was the fact that Richard was joking about our children as if it were a done deal. And he was right. If things continued the way they were, I eventually would have to produce an heir for this family.

Lucas grimaced and hushed his father. "That's enough, Dad."

"Let's go," I said, tugging him back. I couldn't stand the sight of Richard for another second.

As Lucas and I strode from the ballroom, hand in hand, the guests cheered in a wild frenzy of hoots and hollers. It seemed as if their party was just getting started, judging by the amount of energy they exuded. The second the ballroom doors clicked closed, another flurry of nerves erupted within me.

Lucas took my hand and led me down the palace hallway, a security detail close on our heels. We moved quickly through the palace, toward what I could only assume was his bedroom.

No, not just his bedroom anymore.

Our bedroom.

EIGHTEEN

LUCAS

I never thought I would become a romantic.

The entire notion of romance felt antiquated and too vulnerable for my taste. And yet here I was, asking my wife if I could carry her over the threshold of our shared suite. *Nobody warned me that love came with embarrassing moments like this one,* I grumbled inwardly.

She looked at me like I had completely lost my mind. Maybe I had.

But she also looked gorgeous.

I laughed. "So what? It's our only chance to do something this corny. We have to take it."

She lifted her arms and giggled. "Okay, fine, but if you drop me I'll kill you."

"There will be none of that tonight."

I picked her up, kicked the door open, and stepped over the threshold. Then I set her down gently and closed the door, locking it. "That wasn't so hard, was it?"

She shook her head but smiled the biggest smile I'd seen all day. That was good. That was more than good. Ever since our conversation in the car on the way back from the ceremony, a flame of hope had rekindled that I didn't know was still there. And I liked it.

"Since when are you such a romantic, Lucas?" she teased back.

I smirked. What could I say? I'd had relationships before. And I wasn't a total jerk, but I'd never fallen in love with any of those girls. "The lovey-dovey stuff is reserved for you, Jessa."

She rolled her eyes. But it was true. She brought something else out in me; I guess that something was romance.

I shook my head, a tad shocked with myself as well. Eight months ago, she'd taken my world and turned everything upside down. And now, she'd made me a married man. She tilted her head to meet my gaze. Some of her hair had fallen from her braid, brushing the side of her neck.

A nervous hush fell over us as she turned to take in the room.

The bed was in the middle, with a loveseat and small desk by the curtained window. Across from the bed a wood fire burned in the fireplace, casting the room in flickering orange light. On one side was the closet door, and on the other the bathroom. But I didn't think it was the layout that had her chewing her bottom lip and her cheeks flushing pink. No, I'd say it was the satin and the red rose petals strewn across the white bedspread.

I gulped, my body instantly tensing.

"Okay," I said, "I swear I didn't have anything to do with that." I motioned in a circular motion at the general area of the bed, but we both knew what I was talking about. "That must have been one of the servants or something." I coughed.

She turned a scathing look on me, and then busted up, doubling over at the waist. When she looked up at me again, a few loose tears streamed down her face. "Oh my gosh, you should see yourself right now, Lucas," she said between bouts of laughter. "I've never seen you blush like this before!"

I shrugged, but inside I fought a torrent of emotions. I didn't really think any of this was a laughing matter. It was a lot of things, but funny wasn't one of them.

She met my eyes again, and instantly shifted, her laughs catching in her throat as she gasped. I couldn't help it. Her dress fit her like a glove, perfectly cut to show off the curves of her body. Her elaborate hair and makeup were starting to come undone, which was only making *me* come undone.

"Oh," she breathed.

She opened and closed her mouth a few times, so I beat her to the punch.

"You're my wife," I said. "But that doesn't mean I expect anything from you, now or ever. I won't push you into something you don't want, no matter how *I* feel about it."

"And how do you feel about it?" she asked shyly, her eyes fluttering. I groaned inwardly. She really needed to stop that.

"Do you really have to ask that question?" I wanted her. We both knew it. But I also didn't want to be teased for it. I had some pride left in me somewhere.

She chewed on her lip again, and it took everything in me not to pull her into my arms and kiss her until her body agreed with mine. "I'm not ready," she finally said, sighing and walking to the bed. A tingle of disappointment tugged at me, but I ignored it. My feelings didn't matter here. What mattered was winning Jessa back. I wasn't going to blow it.

She sat on the edge of the bed, twiddling her fingers for a moment. Then her face tipped up to study me, a touch of embarrassment rimming her eyes. "But that doesn't mean I won't ever be ready," she added. "It's just that you were my first real boyfriend, you know? And everything happened so fast with us, and then the attack happened..." She paused and studied her nails, the blush in her cheeks growing. "Our engagement was so quick, and the surprise wedding threw me off, too."

"You don't have to apologize," I said. Even though she hadn't, I could hear it in her tone. "This isn't your fault. This wasn't even what you wanted."

Bitterness rose inside me, and I pushed it down to hang out with the disappointment. I'd do anything to avoid her getting upset with me again. We'd finally turned a corner today. I really *was* okay with waiting, given the circumstances, but I wasn't okay with ending the night in another argument.

I stepped forward and gently tilted her head up to me, cradling her warm cheek in my palm. "Let's just get our pajamas on and go to bed." I held her gaze until she nodded.

I strode to the chest of drawers, pulled it open, and tossed cotton pajama pants and a t-shirt at her and found some long athletic shorts for myself. "We'll cross that bridge when we get there. For now, we can do what you said. Let's start with rebuilding our friendship."

"I'd like that." She smiled as she shuffled into the bathroom to change.

I changed quickly and brushed all the rose petals into the small trashcan. I closed the thick curtains and climbed under the heavy comforter, taking the side I was pretty sure she didn't prefer, and tried to relax. The fire was dying down; it wouldn't be long before the room would be completely black. That would help.

A few minutes later Jessa peeked her head out of the bathroom. "You ready for this?"

I sat up. "Umm…"

She threw open the door, sprinted across the room and jumped onto the bed. She leaned over and kissed me on the cheek, then slipped under the covers. Her sweet rose water smell wafted through me so intensely that I had to ball up my hands. I wasn't going to touch her. As much as I wanted to, I needed to respect her feelings more.

"Goodnight, husband," she said, rolling away and burrowing into the blankets. I stared at the back of her head for a long moment and then closed my eyes. The familiar dragging sensation of sleep tugged at me, as I sank deeper into the mattress. Today *had* been an insane day. Sleep would make everything better.

"Goodnight, wife."

▼

I woke with a start, my heart pounding. I reached out.

Jessa was gone.

Blinking away the sleep, I turned on the lamp. Still gone. Panic prickled at the back of my neck as I stood up and checked the bathroom. I even opened the closet door, but she wasn't there.

Did she already leave me?

No, that was stupid. But the fear was real and the thought nagged, like a little prick in my brain. So small and insignificant, but enough of a sting to demand attention. I went out into the hallway, peering around but she wasn't there either. It was getting late in the night. A guard was posted just outside our door.

"Have you seen Jessa?"

"Said she needed to get a snack." He shrugged, leaning against the wall. One hand was tucked on his gun, the other rubbed the side of his face. He was obviously tired, and that didn't bode well with me. "One of the other guards escorted her and then on her way back Richard stopped to chat, and they left together."

I stilled. "Where'd they go?"

He shrugged again. Useless. I glared at the guard, making a mental note to get him moved to another service, and went out in search of them. Richard's room was just down the hall, so it was the first place I checked. But there wasn't anyone in there.

What's going on?

I grabbed an ugly purple pillow from his bed and tried to reach out to Jessa through our mental link, but it didn't work. I didn't have that ability. It seemed she'd have to initiate the telepathy. But she didn't have her necklace. She'd taken that stupid diamond necklace off in the bathroom earlier, her normal necklace probably back in her dorm.

I threw the pillow at the wall and stormed back into the hall.

I racked my brain for possibilities as I paced the hallway. A faint sound of muffled voices filtered from a nearby room. I pressed my ear to the door, and recognizing Richard's voice, threw it open.

I nearly exploded into a rage at what I found.

Jessa was on the floor, cowering. Her hair was a mess, arms up in defense, whole body shaking. He stood above her, his hands in angry red fists.

"What's going on here?" I yelled.

He spun on me with murderous eyes. "Why don't you ask your wife to tell you what she just tried to do?"

I dropped to my knees to gather her in my lap. Her body still shook wildly, defenseless, and I kissed her forehead. "It's okay, baby," I murmured. She turned into me with a pleading expression and my eyes latched onto the beginnings of a purple bruise blossoming across her jaw.

"Did you hit her?" I glared up at my father in horror. I'd never known him to hit a woman; if this was his doing, it would be his last.

"Tell him what you did, Jessa!" He growled again. "Tell him now!"

"I–I tried to use red alchemy on him," she cried, bursting into tears.

For a split second, I didn't believe it. And then the world lost its balance. "Oh no. Jessa, you didn't."

What was she thinking? Now he would *really* treat her like a prisoner. Or worse. Obviously, whatever she'd done had failed miserably.

"Oh yes," he said, pacing in front of us. He strode to the open door and slammed it closed. We were in another one of the palace bedrooms, this one apparently vacant. "This little witch saw blood on me and assumed it was mine. She said she needed to talk to me about something in private, got me alone in here, and then proceeded to put her hand on the blood, spewing some nonsense about turning myself into West America and ending the war!"

He cursed and glared down at us with a fury that I'd never seen before in him. If I wasn't holding her at the moment, I was sure he'd hit her again.

"You need to get a hold of yourself," I snapped. "This is my wife!"

The silence stretched between us, thick and heady.

"Lucas, you need to take your new *wife* back to your room before I kill her," he finally replied between heavy breaths. "I'll figure out what to do with her in the morning *after* I've had a chance to discuss the ramifications of this treasonous act with Faulk."

That would make things so much worse for Jessa.

But not waiting a second longer for him to change his mind, I pulled Jessa to standing, half carrying her

"Come on," I hissed at her. "We have to get back."

"Be careful with that one, Lucas. It seems she's a traitor not only to her country, but to her own father-in-law," He spat the words as we stumbled from the room together.

This was bad. This was so bad.

The second we were back in our suite, I wrapped my arms around her in a tight hug. She sobbed against my chest.

"I'm sorry. He seemed a bit drunk and when I saw the blood, I thought the two things combined would be the perfect opportunity to end all this right here and now."

I couldn't emotionally process this disaster. I shut that side of me down, and instead jumped into fixer-mode. If there was one thing that needed to be done, it was to get Jessa the hell out of the palace before morning.

"Use your purple," I whispered against her ear. "We need to talk."

She nodded and walked over to the chest of drawers, rummaging around in frustration until she found her stone necklace. So it hadn't been left in her dorm after all. Her clothes had been moved over since the wedding, luckily, it had been brought along.

Okay, what is it? she asked, and the link between us snapped to life.

I know where a Resistance safe house is, I said. *I also have a few addresses of people throughout New Colony who've agreed to help you. You need to go down to a farm in the south and from there you can make contact with West America. They won't be able to get you out up here; there's just too much going on with the war for you to be safe in the Capitol. But I think they could help you if you make it down there.*

She stumbled back and stared at me in complete bewilderment, her eyes wide. *Lucas, how long have you been planning this?*

Ever since Jasmine died. I ran my hand through my hair and sighed heavily. Then I strode to her and pulled her close to me again.

I'm not ready to lose you. But this was a reality I'd accepted long ago, though I hated it. The only way you'd ever forgive me was if I showed you that the choices I've made really are for you and not just me. She sunk into my chest, brought to tears again. The whole thing with Jasmine had been a stupid mistake, a plea of a man desperate to be with the one he loved.

Her mouth found mine, initiating a kiss, confirming what I knew.

To win her back, I had to let her go. And it ripped me apart. But I took her lips, her body, her soul and held it close, savoring every moment I had, even if they were our last.

Thank you, she said, releasing me. *I'm so sorry. I messed up. I was so close and I had to try. If only that had been Richard's blood I would have been able to do it! That was Jasmine's plan all along, you know? Get your dad alone and turn him around. I actually think she wanted me to reform him, but with the war I thought it would be best just to surrender.*

I wanted to know about the blood, too. Whose was it? None of it made sense. But Jessa's foolhardy idea that Richard turning himself in to West America would make everything better? It was too risky. I wish she would have discussed this with me first. How would surrendering to our enemies be safe for her or for me? We were royals too! I didn't press the issue. It was pointless.

She was going to end up in West America anyway, and soon.

We'll use my white and your purple to get you out, but we have to go now. The safe house isn't far, and the gate should be open, as people will be cleaning up from the reception. A few of the guests probably haven't even left yet, if I know how these events can go. I'm taking you out the same way I took your dad out.

She frowned, questioning. *How do you know where a Resistance safe house is?*

How do you think your sister broke out? I added with a shrug. *I helped her. Anyway, we need to move. I need to get back before I'm locked out and have to climb that damned wall.*

You helped my sister? Her face fell. *I underestimated you, Lucas. I'm sorry.*

I reached out and took her small hand in mine. *It's time to go.*

▼

There was nothing worse than a goodbye kiss.

I delivered her to the safe house and before I took her inside, she kissed me deeply. Her lips curved perfectly to mine, her body following. We stayed like that for far too long, lingering in each other. The regret between us was palpable. It buried me in what might have been. Finally, she pulled away. She reached down and opened my hand, placing something gently in my palm. I felt the cool metal, the cut of the stones, and squeezed.

My mother's ring.

I still love you, you know, she said, her voice breaking. *Thank you for this.*

I love you, too.

Maybe she didn't forgive me entirely but to hear those three words again was like being brought back to life. Brought back, only to have it taken away.

I let her go before I lost my nerve and stepped back. We were in the drive of the house, the night black and silent around us. Her form materialized, and when I saw the agonizing stretch of her face, I nearly ran back to her.

"Goodbye, Jessa," I said, my throat catching on the pain.

She sighed deeply and lifted a hand, then turned and hurried up to the porch, ringing the doorbell and knocking at the same time.

I waited as a house light turned on and a minute later, an old woman swung open the door. They exchanged a few words, and then Jessa was gone.

I walked home alone.

I didn't know if I believed in God, but I prayed to him that night. I looked up at the cold sky and I begged for Him to keep her safe and to bring her back to me one day.

After a while of this, I was back at the palace gate. It wasn't an issue. A van came through right as I approached; I had no problem getting back onto the palace grounds in my invisible state.

I strode up the front steps, my body feeling heavier as the weight of everything pressed down. A few party guests stumbled out, a couple clinging to each other. I moved to the side, watching in disgust as they ran to a nearby car, stopping every few strides to kiss. I hated them. They were happy, unencumbered, and able to do such trivial things when I had none of that.

Storming into the halls of the palace, I checked on our room first. The door was still locked. We'd come out together, locking it behind us and telling the guard we were getting a midnight snack. Before he could bring himself to follow, we'd darted into darkened alcove to turn ourselves invisible.

Now, I stared at the door handle like it was the source of my pain. I wasn't ready to go back in there and lay in a bed that would smell like my wife. The wife I'd only had for not even a night. Who I never really had at all.

I wandered, ending up in the GC wing. It, too, reminded me of Jessa. But didn't everything? The area was silent and mostly dark except for a few lights always on at night to light the halls. Everyone down here was probably fast asleep by now, not that I cared either way.

Something trailing along the concrete floor caught my eye. I squatted down, one hand still on my white rose, and reached the other to touch it. Blood.

Like an idiot, I followed the trail. The little red drips led me around a few corners and into one of the empty classrooms.

I didn't see him at first, not until my eyes adjusted to the darkness. He wasn't moving. He just sat like a statue in a chair.

Who was that? I moved in closer.

His hand snapped out and grabbed me.

Startled, I dropped the rose to the ground. It was the same one we'd taken from Jessa's bouquet earlier. The rest of the bouquet was probably still there, left in the bathroom.

My body materialized, and panic swept over me.

"You!" Mark growled up at me. "How did you do that?"

I snatched my arm away, annoyed but also a little unnerved. Quick as a flash, the man sucker-punched me square in the face. I fell to the ground with a thud.

"What was that for?" I gasped.

He jumped up and kicked me. His heavy boot connected with a rib. It snapped, pain shooting through me and I groaned, curling in on myself.

"You bastard! You broke my little girl's heart. Do you know that? Are you even sorry?" he yelled, landing a blow right in the kidney. I reached toward the nearest plant, desperate for relief, but it was too far.

"And earlier, your father had the gall to hit me when I challenged him. He's put my family through hell and he hit me! *Me!* A loyal servant to him for *years* and this is how he repays me? He humiliated us in front of the whole kingdom!"

I raised my hands in front of my face. "Please stop!"

"So I'll hit *you*!" His voice was wild. "And you're an alchemist? God, just like your whore of a wife! What a match made in heaven. I hope you two will be very happy together."

He chuckled, and I crawled to my knees, the physical pain vibrating through my entire body.

"Oh wait, no I don't," he spat.

Anger clawed at me. He was right to be angry; I would be too in his position. But he had *no right* to touch me!

Then his hulking boot connected with my face. A searing heat enveloped me followed by a confusing heaviness. My vision blurred. Something wet fell into my eyes, and I pushed it away. Blood. I gagged on the salty copper liquid. Once again, I staggered up, forcing myself to stand.

"I'll kill you," he growled. "I'll kill your whole family."

He struck again, kicking me in the same spot, but this time with double the force. I heard it before I felt it. A crack.

"Finally."

I blinked rapidly and fell. My head slapped the cement floor with a wet snap.

A gasp echoed. Was it his or mine? The question faded as my vision turned to black.

NINETEEN

SASHA - TWO WEEKS LATER

"How much longer are you going to hold on to that?" Tristan asked, startling me.

I quickly shoved the small slip of paper back in my pant pocket and turned on him. His eyes squinted at me, shiny black hair hanging in his face. A flicker of challenge passed through his eyes and his lip quirked.

"Shut it," I growled. We'd already had this conversation. I'd turn over the email address when I knew *for sure* that these people could be trusted, that they really weren't going to toss all alchemists in prison once this was all over.

We were walking back from the dining tent toward the barracks to settle in for the evening. The setting sun shone bright against the base, lighting the tents, buildings, and tanks up in a golden tint. Long shadows fell across the scene as a familiar figure jogged toward us.

"You need to come straight away," Mastin called out, motioning with his arm. "It's about your father."

Worry catapulted me forward, Tristan at my side, as we took off, following Mastin toward a nearby building. Men with enormous guns guarded the entrance. They saluted as Mastin approached and stepped aside.

"He's in here," he said, swinging open the door.

"What do you mean he's in here?" Last I had heard, Christopher was still back at the palace. A jolt of excitement shot through my chest.

Tristan put a hand on my back and ushered me forward.

Sure enough, inside the building, sitting on a chair with soldiers buzzing all around him, was my father. His head was drooped, and he looked beat down and bone tired. But when our eyes connected, the same joy I remembered from back when I was a kid spread across his face. It was as if the years of sorrow melted off of him.

"Frankie!" He jumped up and tackled me in a hug. I didn't bother to correct him. Sasha had been an alias for a few years now, but Francesca was *me*. Eventually, I'd probably have to adopt my old name again.

"Are you okay? What are you doing here?" I asked.

"I just got here a few hours ago," he said. "I came through the border on foot." *He what?* I stepped back and studied him. From the sheen of sweat and the layer of grim and dirt on his clothes, his story seemed plausible.

"How did you not end up getting yourself killed?" I gasped, shaking my head. My hair was braided down my head and the long end of it whipped my shoulders like a rope.

The room had turned on us now, everyone growing quiet. Tristan and Mastin stood the closest, but there were about ten others who were also waiting for an explanation. A few had a hand resting on their holsters, and I glared darkly at them.

"It's a long story for another time. Listen, I have to tell you something. It's time sensitive." Dad's voice turned frantic.

It clicked into place. Jessa had been missing from the palace, everyone knew about the nationwide manhunt Richard was conducting. I was terrified to think of what he'd do to her if he found her.

"You know where Jessa is?" The question came out as incredulous, but hopeful.

He nodded, his eyes round circles of concern. "As I was leaving, she connected with me through her telepathy."

"Her what?" Mastin stepped forward, eyebrows drawn in disbelief.

I nodded. "It's rare magic, but it can be done. She must have learned it recently."

Dad agreed. "She established a link between us before she left, but we have to be in close proximity for it to work. Not the same room close, but a few miles or so. I'd already started on my journey through the border when she connected."

"Is she okay?"

"She's okay, but she's in trouble. She told me where she's staying right now. She's at a farmhouse, not too far from here. We have to get her out of there, out of New Colony. From the way she sounded, I think Richard's officers are closing in."

"Let's go get her," Tristan said.

My eyes shot to Mastin, expecting some kind of argument. He stared at us hard for a couple of seconds before nodding. "Okay, Tristan and I will go."

I held back a laugh. Did he not know me by now?

"No! If I don't go, she won't trust you. She doesn't know either of you."

He motioned to Dad. "Can you tell her we're coming?"

"I'm too far, and besides, she has to start the connection. I can't do it." He rubbed his palm against the side of his head, ruffling his wispy hair.

"So it's settled," I shot back at Mastin. "I'm going. We're leaving the second that sun sets."

Mastin grumbled but didn't argue again. He and a couple other soldiers began to make preparations while dad rattled off the address of the farmhouse.

My mind drifted to Jessa, wondering if she was okay. Sources said that everyone in New Colony was looking for her. There were patrols, random searches, and even helicopters with blaring spotlights roaming the kingdom at night. Richard had even gone so far as to issue a kingdom-wide curfew.

All because Prince Lucas was in a coma. Maybe even dead.

We didn't know for sure what had happened to him. General Scott told us that the prince was rumored to be on the edge of death, in a sleep so deep, not even the alchemists could wake him. But Scott also speculated that was a lie, a temporary cover up for the murder of the only heir to New Colony. Two weeks ago Richard had made a statement that someone had tried to kill the prince, yet another assassination attempt. This time it had come the night of royal wedding, one of the most publicized events in New Colony's history, and yet, there were no pictures, no witnesses, no proof whatsoever.

Speculation ensued like wildfire.

Richard had also said the princess was missing. When he'd issued a massive reward for her capture, people questioned. Had she been kidnapped? Or had she been the one to hurt Lucas? With her disappearance that same night, nobody knew what to believe. I didn't know what to believe!

"Are you okay?" Tristan pulled me to the corner of the room, his hand cupping my elbow. I watched my dad carefully, apprehension building within, as he answered question after question. The soldiers around him didn't seem too keen on the situation. Would they trust him here? Would they help him?

I sucked in a breath and met Tristan's gaze. "Yeah. I'm fine. Is it time to go yet?"

I was suspicious of how they might treat Jessa once we brought her back, but we had to get her out while we had the chance. On base, she was a subject of extreme speculation. I'd felt questioning eyes on me everywhere I went these last two weeks, heard boisterous talk fall to snickering whispers when I walked past. I'd lived in close quarters with plenty of women before, but they had nothing on these gossips.

They called her the blood bride.

That was the one that got to me the most.

I had to admit the nickname was catchy, but it still made me cringe.

I leaned against the metal sheeted wall, leaning against Tristan, and watched as Dad took it all in. I wondered what he thought. Was this place better or worse than he'd imagined? Soon, I'd figure out how to get him back to California where Mom and Lacey were staying. That's where he belonged, somewhere safe.

The door swung wide and General Nathan Stott strode in, his hand outstretched toward Christopher. Nathan was dressed in his usual black and gold uniform, a rainbow of decoration adorning his chest. But even without it, he'd carry himself with the air of importance. The room stood at attention.

"It's a pleasure to meet you, Christopher Loxely," he said, his voice booming. "I hope you don't mind, but I'll get right to the chase. We have to take you in for more questioning before we do anything else; with you coming out of New

Colony, you're considered a liability."

"What?" I gaped at Nathan, rushing forward. "Are you kidding me? He's helping us!"

Nearly all the men in the room reached for their weapons. Nathan held up a hand and glanced quickly at Mastin, as if it was Mastin's job to calm the screaming female. "Not now, Sasha," he pressed. "We did the same due-diligence with you, didn't we?"

That may very well be true, but I still didn't like it.

"He can be trusted," I said between gritted teeth. "He's my father. He's been through enough suffering to get here and now he just wants to help us."

"We just have to make sure he's the real deal. How do we know he wasn't planted here?"

"Oh, you've got to be kidding me!"

I turned to Mastin, waiting for him to back me up, but he stood back, never meeting my eye. So he agreed with dear old dad, did he?

"It's okay," Christopher interjected, meeting me with a sad but knowing smile. "I get it. And I don't have anything to hide."

I shook my head, but he shrugged and willingly accompanied Nathan through a door that led further into the dank building. In a matter of moments they were swallowed up by a cacophony of more soldiers. The door slammed, leaving the three of us left to wait in silence.

"This is garbage." I whirled on Mastin. I strode right up to him and shoved him in the chest. Hard. "You're going to let your dad do that to him? He's been through hell and back getting here and this is how you greet him?"

He was busy looking over my shoulder, ignoring me. I shoved him harder and he finally met my eyes.

"Actually, it was my idea," he said.

Disbelief overpowered me and I stepped back.

"Why?"

"He may be your father, but he's also the father to a royal. A princess. You saw the wedding footage, right? Saw the way those two looked at each other? They were clearly in love. And we don't know what happened after that. This could be a trap."

"It's not!" I felt Tristan coming up behind me. He put his hand on my shoulder but I shrugged him off.

"Be logical. You're getting your emotions involved," Mastin continued.

I wanted to slap him for that comment.

"It makes sense." He frowned and looked into my eyes, pleading with me. "Do you *really* know them, though? I thought you barely made contact with your family again this summer."

He was right, and I hated it. Twisting things around to look a certain way didn't mean they were true. My family was innocent. They were on our side.

"What does this mean for the mission tonight? Are we still going to get Jessa out or what?"

He sucked in a breath. "I'll go, for you. But I'm not risking any of my men on this. It's just going to be the three of us, and a pilot, as planned."

"I can fly the chopper," I snapped. "Even better."

"You're not authorized."

I let out a sharp laugh and turned around to find Tristan's expression. Concern was written all over his face, causing a stab of guilt to go through me. I ignored it and raised an eyebrow in his direction. He sighed and ran his hand through his raven hair, shaking his head ever so slightly.

"Are you still in, or what?" I finally asked.

"Where you go, I go." He shrugged.

"Wow! Don't let me twist your arm," I snapped.

I stood rooted in place. A wash of anger rolled over me. Anger that they didn't fully trust my judgment on this. But also anger at the small seed of doubt that had been planted by Mastin's logic. He had a brilliant mind for war and strategy, inherited from his father. And what if he was right? What if it was a trap?

Over the last few weeks, I'd witnessed awful interrogation tactics as General Scott had dealt with Brooke, who so far, didn't know much. But his men had certainly exhausted all their efforts in figuring that out. Were they about to put my father through the same? Would trying to be the hero only to put Jessa through more pain? But no, anything was better than Jessa getting caught by King Richard. I didn't know what happened that night between her and Lucas, that was true, but whatever it was, it couldn't be good.

"So let's get out of here." I whipped back around and shoved Mastin with my shoulder as I made for the door. No matter the consequences, it was time to get my sister out of New Colony.

▼

We flew in the middle of the night, the black sky our best asset. And by the way Mastin acted, our only asset. As the helicopter landed silently in the open field, I stood and tensed one hand around the stone necklace, the other rested on my loaded weapon. The three of us peered out the window at the white farmhouse where Jessa was supposed to be hiding. It loomed up ahead, silent and still in the night. I glanced around the farm, looking for hidden dangers. The whole area gave me the creeps. I shuddered. This place was so desolate, so marked with shadow, and dark as midnight.

Mastin nodded, and we jumped out of the belly of the chopper, the three of us running low toward the house—Mastin on one side and Tristan on the other. What was it with me always being thrown in between these two men? Well, at least they were hot.

I smirked at the childish thought as we trudged on.

We stopped behind a tall oak tree, its shadows long and all-encompassing. Carefully, we cased the area one last time. There wasn't a soul in sight. Just the farmhouse up ahead, empty fields surrounding us, and the moonless sky. Stars watched over the scene. A small critter ran across the lawn.

"I should go," I whispered, already holding up my hand in protest. "Don't argue. She knows me. She might spook if someone else does it."

Before they could reply, I took off. My feet landed softly on the grass, and I imagined I was moving like a cat. Silent. Swift. Predatory.

Dad had claimed that the farmer knew she was here. But the farmer's wife? Not so much. So, we needed to be extra careful as not to draw unnecessary attention to ourselves. Nobody knew if she could ruin this for us or not. With the bounty on Jessa's head, I figured it was more than likely.

Approaching the cellar door, I crouched down and another tingle of nerves swept through me. I knelt at the base of a long sheet of metal, fastened down over a large box like a protrusion coming off the side of the house. I knocked softly three times and then unlatched it. It swung open with a loud creak that pierced the silence like a knife. I cringed.

"Jessa, are you in there?" I whispered down into the dark space. It vaguely reminded me of my time spent in Richard's prison. Pushing the thought away, the feeling still lingered.

There was a moment of silence followed by a soft, "I'm here."

"It's me. We gotta move."

"Frankie?"

"Or Sasha, whatever. No time to debate the pros and cons of that whole name situation right now." I rolled my eyes at my own obnoxious rambling.

She crawled out of the space, her eyes round orbs in the darkness. Her hair was knotted around her shoulders, her clothes threadbare and hanging off her thin frame. She wrapped her arms around her torso and shivered.

"Where's your coat?"

"Lost it."

"How?" I asked before quickly adding, "Never mind." I pulled her into a quick hug, murmuring softly into her hair. "It's okay. You're safe now."

"It's not me I've been worried about. But thanks."

Her body, taller than mine, still felt smaller against me somehow.

"Lucas will be fine," I replied, guessing that it was her comatose husband on her mind. "He's tough. Anyway, he wanted you out of New Colony, right? So let's go."

She nodded and I grabbed her hand, tugging her along. We ran to the oak tree and met up with the boys.

"Who are they?" Her wide eyes tracked up and down the two men. Men who she knew nothing of, but who had become my anchors.

"They're trustworthy," I said, tucking her arm into mine. "They're okay. I promise. But we have to go."

She nodded and the four of us turned to peer out from the shadows. Mastin took point, casing the area one last time and nodding his go-ahead. Just as the four of us were about to sprint back to the chopper, the door to the farmhouse flung opened. A man stumbled out into the darkness, his hands waving.

"Wait!" His deep voice rolled over the cold landscape and I jumped, ready to take action.

"Don't," Mastin said, placing his hand on my arm.

"It's okay," Jessa replied. "We can trust Taysom."

I don't know about that!

"Taysom! Over here!" she called out loudly and the rest of us cussed under our breaths. Was she for real right now? With all our training, we couldn't help her if she was going to pull stupid stunts like this!

"Shh–" I hissed out at my sister. But then, super intelligent girl that she was, she took off running *toward the man.* I began to take off after her, but Tristan yanked me back and slammed me against his hard chest.

"Just wait," he growled. "See what he does."

In the darkness, I could barely make out the farmer's expression. Jessa was the tallest in our family, but this man towered over her. He said something to her, his gravelly voice coming out with a twinge of regret, and she fell to the earth. A sob escaped her, echoing through the landscape.

"Get off me!" I shoved Tristan back and ran to my sister, my footsteps slamming against the ground. One hand on my gun, I ripped it from the holster and pointed it at the hulking man. His eyes flashed when he saw me, and he raised his hands slowly.

"Hey now," he said, nodding toward the gun. His eyes two bright white spots in the darkness. "No need for that. I just thought she should hear it from me first."

"Hear what?" I spat.

Mastin and Tristan ran up behind me, their guns also pointing at the man. I caught the rage in Mastin's eyes, the frustration in Tristan's, and looked away. They had no excuse. I'd come after her. They'd come after me. Same story.

"Lucas is dead!" Jessa cried out, her voice so hollow and pained, it sent an ache through my core. Lucas and I didn't always see eye to eye, but he had proved himself to be a good man. His death didn't please me, but I also didn't have time to dwell on it. None of us did. If Richard's people really were closing in, we should have already left the area by now.

"I'm so sorry." I dropped my gun to my side and squatted next to my sister's sobbing body. "But we have to get out of here. It's not safe. We can talk about it more on the way back to base."

She didn't respond. She continued to cry, as if she hadn't heard a word I said. Either that, or she just didn't care.

"Seriously, Jessa." I grabbed her arm and tried to pry her off the cold grass. "We really have to go. We can't get caught out here or we're all dead."

Tristan strode forward to help, his long arm reaching to tug her up.

"Don't touch me!" Jessa bellowed. She turned on us, her face streaked with tears, her eyes wild. She scrambled back on the grass, pushing away. "I have to go back! I have a connection to him. If I can reach out with the purple I can see if he's still alive."

"But he's dead, sweetie." The farmer looked down on her with pity. For such a large man, his tone was gentle. "There was just a national broadcast about it."

"I don't believe it. Did you see a body? How do you know?" she pressed.

The farmer's dark face was hard to decipher in the night, but even I saw the flash of doubt. "Well, no body. Not yet."

"See! He might not be dead!" Her body snapped to attention and she jumped up. "I'm going back."

"You can't!" I gasped, but she didn't care.

She spun around and took off running, kicking dirt into the air behind her. Her yellow magic must have been coursing through her veins because her speed was unnatural as she tore through the night. I swore under my breath.

"Don't you even think about it!" Mastin said, turning on me.

My eyes flicked once to him, and once to Tristan, before settling on the path ahead.

"I have to," I said simply.

The tug of yellow magic ignited in my veins, the necklace warm against my skin. I bolted forward, legs burning with insane speed as I sprinted out of the yard and into the field, pushing onward.

She wasn't going to endure this alone. I had a family again. For most of my life, I'd let the pain of abandonment push any thoughts of my family away. But really, they'd missed me just as much as I'd missed them. I knew that now. The same blood coursed through us, tying us together, and it always would.

Jessa's head bobbed up in the darkness, a beacon for me to follow. My lungs burned and my breath was labored, but my mind cleared as I gained ground. This was the right thing to do. Helping her, being there for her in her weakest moment, it was what family did for their own. I was ready to embrace what it meant to be a Loxely, what it meant to be a big sister.

Saving Jessa from her grief was the perfect opportunity to start.

COLLIDE

THE COLOR ALCHEMIST BOOK FOUR

ONE

SASHA

"You need to give this up before you get us all killed," Mastin huffed, his voice a low timbre that rolled over the dark landscape. *Traitor.*

I spun on my heels and shoved him. Hard. He didn't budge. The man barely even blinked. Me and my "nice side" shouldn't have been on such good terms at that moment. He was lucky I was currently choosing to refrain from using my magic on him. One touch of yellow was all I needed to knock him out—we both knew it. Our eyes met, his narrowed into slits, and I glared.

"Nobody said you had to tag along," I snapped, stepping back. Tristan moved in between us, head cocked and arms folded, his stance diplomatic, ready to mediate.

"Keep your voice down," Mastin hissed. "Or have you already forgotten where you've so wittingly led us?" He motioned to the barren field that spread wide around the three of us. We were in the middle of no man's land, shrouded in darkness.

I forced the annoyance down, trying to replace it with humility. This was New Colony, and I knew better than to test my luck here.

"You're right," I said, the two words nearly killing me. Still, my eyes rolled. They couldn't be controlled.

Fingers pressing the blue stone on my necklace, I drew on its power until I was sure we were silenced. We could hear each other, no problem, but my form of blue magic worked as a noise-cancelling force field, preventing our conversation from straying too far. And for someone like me in a place like New Colony? That could mean the difference between life and death.

A shiver ran up my spine, both from the winter night and the weight of our situation. As if sensing my discomfort, Tristan placed a steady hand on my shoulder. The pressure of his touch calmed and grounded me. I breathed in deep, forcing the nerves to retreat.

"Arguing isn't going to get us anywhere." Tristan's voice of reason made me want to scream. He must have sensed it because he gently shifted my body toward him. He held steady hands on my shoulders and leaned down to meet my gaze. "Your sister is gone and obviously doesn't want to be found. We're in enemy territory. If we stay here, we'll end up getting killed."

"Or worse," Mastin added.

A flash of my time in the palace prison jolted my memories. My muscles tensed. I could practically feel the pain of the beatings I'd endured. *Just breathe.* I forced my lungs to fill with air and then slowly relax, clearing the emotions. Tristan was right. Mastin was right. Of course, they were only speaking the truth. And yet, the idea of giving up on Jessa made tears prick at the back my eyes.

I turned away. "Let's go back and talk to that farmer. Maybe he has an idea of where she could have gone." When they didn't answer, I glowered back at them. "Well, are you in or not?"

Mastin shook his head as Tristan nodded.

"We don't have time," Mastin ground out, his bright eyes flashing.

"We could hurry," Tristan added.

A robotic ping sounded. I jerked back, heart accelerating. Mastin pinched his lips and pulled out his slatebook from his back pocket. It was a smaller device than most, but industrial and boxy. Military issue.

I eyed him wearily as he put it to his ear to take the call.

"We're almost done here." He paused for a long second, his pursed lips falling into a deep frown as he listened to the hurried voice on the other end, loud enough for me to make out the tone but not the actual words.

"What is it?" I asked.

In the shadows cast by the faint glow of the moon, it was tricky to make out his full expression, but he obviously wasn't happy. He lowered his head, essentially ignored me, and finished the call with a quick, "Yes."

"Well?" I questioned again.

"It's our pilot. He's not willing to wait much longer. If we're going to make it back to base, we have to leave now."

Another reason why they should've let me pilot the thing.

"Pull rank. Call him back and tell him to wait!"

"It's not that easy. I'm not going to ask him to risk his life any more for us. Let's go."

I growled but nodded. The three of us sprinted toward the chopper, kicking up clumps of hard earth in our wake. The dusty scent filled my nostrils and my eyes watered. The urge to cough gripped my throat. Inwardly, the battle between guilt and practicality raged. Jessa had been *right there*. How could I have let her get away? Just as I was about to get her out of this God-forsaken place and reunite her with our family, she had to run off like a total lovesick fool. Now what was I supposed to do, leave her here? Why would she choose this?

Love. That word again. There was no questioning that love was why she'd gone back. It had pushed her to find out for herself if Prince Lucas was actually dead.

Even if that meant risking her life, it was worth it to her to find out the truth.

The emptiness spread around us in a kaleidoscope of gray and black. I studied the horizon, searching for a flash of her. In every sway of shadow, I questioned. Was it Jessa? It hadn't been long since I'd lost her to the darkness, maybe twenty minutes, so there was no way she could have gone *too* far, even with the magic. But as I scanned the scene, I knew in my gut that she was long gone. She had vanished, and so had my hope of finding her tonight.

Our speed increased as we neared the location where the helicopter had dropped us off. It waited, part of the darkness, our saving grace, our way out. Guilt ripped through me. A hand found mine and he tugged just enough to get my attention. Tristan. I met his eyes, trying to read his torn expression. He nodded once. He understood. Despite the undesirable circumstances, my lips quirked up in a smile.

"Are you sure about this?" he questioned, his voice barely a whisper above the intake of our hurried breaths. Our legs continued to pump us forward as we moved behind Mastin. He was in soldier-mode and paid us little attention, so zeroed in on his target he didn't catch what I was planning. I didn't mind. Mastin was good for a lot of things, but not for this. He wouldn't understand.

"I have to try. Don't I?" I panted.

"It's what I did for you." His full lips spread into a smile so wide, I could see his teeth shining in the dark.

Once again, I nodded, my heart swelling as I remembered how he had crossed the Shadowlands to help me. I squeezed his hand and then dropped it. I switched directions, taking off for the white farmhouse on the edge of the horizon. My boots thudded against the ground, the cold air rushed against my cheeks.

A few seconds later Mastin broke his protocol and shouted, "You have got to be kidding me!" His voice carried over the landscape and I cringed, but also, I had to suppress a laugh.

I felt for the energy of yellow and allowed it to pulse through me, the magic connecting like an internal power source. In a burst of alchemy, my legs swept me forward, and I left the two men far behind.

Mastin could head back to basecamp. That was his right. Tristan, too, though I doubted he'd leave me here. But I just couldn't give up on Jessa so easily. I'd spent my whole life running from family and I wasn't going to do that again. If needed, I'd hide out in New Colony, give it a couple of days. Most likely, my sister didn't have a plan. She was powerful, but not cut out for this kind of thing. If that farmer had a clue as to where Jessa was hiding before stowing her away in his cellar, then I would retrace her steps until I found her.

As I shot up the porch steps, the hum of helicopter blades caught my attention. It flew overhead, disappearing into the inky blackness. I didn't let myself turn to see if Mastin and Tristan were still on land. But at the back of my mind I wondered. Were they hiding out somewhere, watching, ready to jump in at any minute if things went south?

Of course they were.

And I owed it to them to focus, to make sure this didn't turn into another disaster. The house was silent and dark. I calmed my breathing, swallowing any panting leftover from the run. I stepped forward, clenched my fist and raised it to the oak door. The moment I was about to knock, a massive figure appeared from around the side of a wraparound porch. I jumped, adrenaline slicing through my chest. A man held up his hands in surrender as he inched closer to me.

"Hold on there," he said in a deep baritone.

Recognition calmed me; it was the farmer. He towered over me in both height and width. He wasn't overweight, just carrying a ton of thick muscle on his already large frame. His unruly beard framed his dark face, eyes shining like two small lights in the shadows.

"This is your fault," I snapped, folding my arms. "She was about to come with us when you had to run out and tell her about Lucas. Why did you do that?"

He sighed and cleared his throat. "Yeah … not my brightest idea. I see that now," he said. "But I've met the prince. He's a good man. I thought … I don't know, what I thought. That I was honoring his memory by telling her. That's his wife, you know? He really cared about her, made me promise to help her if she ever showed up here."

I squinted, making out the most earnest of expressions on his face. A tiny part of me understood his reasoning, even if it was the definition of stupid. Lucas had shown him kindness, and from the looks of this guy's barren farm and weathered features, he'd needed it.

"Fine. It's done. But now I need help finding her. Do you know where she was before she came to you?"

An upstairs light flicked on, the interruption illuminating the yard. The man's eyes widened, and he shot toward the door, fumbling with the handle.

"Wait. Where are you going?"

"My wife doesn't know about all this."

"Just answer my question."

"I don't know anything. Okay? Please, you need to get out of here. Treason is not something I'm going to subject my wife and children to."

"You're a little late for that." I laughed, shocked that he would help Jessa if *this* was how he was responding to me.

As he pushed open the door, a woman in a blue bathrobe stood in the doorway, one hand rubbing the sleep from weary eyes. Part of me wanted to shake her! *Really, lady? You slept through everything else tonight.* Behind me, leaves rustled and boots crunched against the frozen grass.

"Taysom Green," the woman chastised. "What on earth is going on? Who are these people?"

I spun around to find a smiling Tristan walking up the steps, his hand raised in greeting.

"So sorry for the inconvenience, Miss," he said, his voice as rich and smooth as butter. "We're Guardians of Color on assignment to check on your farm. Is there anything that my associate can help you with? She's a master healer." He winked at me.

"Uhhh," I faltered, but I quickly recovered and turned back to the woman with an equally pleasant smile. If anyone could play this game of make believe, it was me. After all, I'd had years of experience.

"Yes, we're so sorry for waking you," I said pleasantly. "We check on things at night when the citizens are asleep. We're not supposed to draw too much attention to ourselves. It's part of our protocol. But it turns out that your husband is a light sleeper."

Her eyes flicked back and forth between the three of us, as if she knew we were lying through our teeth. I continued to smile, until finally, her tense face relaxed, eyebrows softening, lips parting, and intense eyes losing a bit of their focus. She gave us a quick nod.

"I'm afraid everything's dead this season. Ground's already been tilled. We're planting again in a few months. Will you be back to help us then?"

I nodded eagerly, the shame of my outright lie ripping through me. There was nothing I could do for these people's dying farmland. And besides, we had a war to win. Once that was sorted, then I could help as many farmers as possible.

"Well, it's late, best be off with you," Taysom said, sliding into his home, his frame blocking his wife from our view. He shut the door in my face with a thud.

I clenched my teeth and fists, burning to bust that door wide open. But instead I closed my eyes and sighed. Inviting hothead Sasha to the party wasn't a smart idea, given our situation.

"Now what?" Tristan asked, putting a warm hand on my back. It only accentuated the cold night.

I took a deep breath, watching it hang in the air, as I considered our options. "I'm not convinced that man doesn't know anything." I leaned into Tristan and laid my head on his shoulder, pulling him into a hug. "Thank you for staying with me," I whispered. At least I wasn't alone in all of this.

I felt him nod and breathe me in. I did the same. He reached out and coaxed my tight fist to relax, threading long fingers through mine.

"Come on," he said into my hair. "We don't know the area. Let's hide out in that cellar while we figure out what to do next."

"You think we can trust him?"

"I do. He's spooked, so we'll have to move on soon."

I still wanted to stomp on the porch, to bang on the door, to demand answers. But Tristan was right. I let the frustration go, forcing it away with each step as I followed the man who would follow me anywhere, who was undoubtedly my best friend. We rounded the house hand in hand. Exhaustion ebbed at the corners of my vision. My body heavy, I reflected on my appalling lack of sleep lately.

I blinked as my eyes adjusted. Someone was waiting for us.

Mastin.

He leaned against the house with his arms crossed over his chest, a tightly wound expression held on his face. I knew deep in my core that he was livid with me, but I also knew just how grateful I was to see him still standing here.

"I can't believe you stayed," I choked on the emotion, smiling and scrunching my nose.

He didn't look at me, didn't acknowledge me in any way. He only pushed off the side of the house, threw open the cellar door with an angry clang, and stormed into the blackness below. His boots sent a mist of stifling dust wafting back out after him, as if to taunt me for what I had done to land us here for the night. I didn't blame him for being angry; this had never been in the plan. But my entire life hadn't gone according to plan and you didn't see me slamming doors. Typical Mastin. I refused to feel guilty.

I turned to Tristan, ready to make my argument, but he only chuckled.

★

Tristan took first watch. When he woke me a few hours later, I expected to trade positions straight away, so he could get some much-needed rest.

"I want to show you something first," he said, his voice a low whisper that tickled my cheek.

The sleep had come quick and heavy, despite the cold, hard floor. Mastin was still out cold, his back pressed against the side of the small room. The walls were dusty stone, the floor damp earth. There were a few blankets and crates pushed alongside one wall.

"Okay, I hope it's something good," I whispered, standing in a crouch because of the low ceiling and following him back up the short set of stairs.

Outside the sun met us in a brilliant pink light that illuminated the landscape. There wasn't another structure for miles, just dark earth kissing a new sky. Warmth caressed my face, and I sighed with a soft smile. I relished the peace— soon this feeling would be gone.

"So beautiful," I said, leaning against the house.

"Yes." Tristan nodded, watching me. His gaze had turned intense, a side of him he rarely showed me. His eyes were two questioning depths, staring back at me. A twinge of anticipation ran down my spine. I couldn't stop thinking about what he'd said that night on the beach. *Wait for me.*

Didn't he know I'd always been waiting for him?

"I wanted to talk to you about something," he whispered, his voice catching ever so slightly, but enough for me to know he was nervous.

It made me nervous, too.

What is there to be nervous about? This is Tristan. He was my best friend and the person I trusted most in the world. I'd known the guy for years, had seen him grow from a boy to a man. And truth be told, I'd spent several of my teenage years pining over him, a secret that I was pretty sure he'd known about. But we were almost six years apart in age and I'd always been too young for him before. Of course he'd never acted on anything. Tristan always did the *right* thing.

But things were different now.

"You can tell me," I said, shifting to get a better look. His dark eyes burned behind a fallen lock of midnight hair. The corners of his liquid eyes crinkled as he studied me for a long moment and then he shifted closer. When those same eyes flicked to gaze at my lips, anticipation burned inside. Was he going to kiss me? Did I want him to kiss me?

The truth rooted me to the spot. *Yes, I wanted him to.*

"I shouldn't have asked you not to date Mastin," he said, suddenly creating distance between us. He stepped back. The passion in his expression vanished, replaced by the familiar understanding and friendly gaze he always wore around me.

"Wait…what?" I sputtered, confusion and shame coursing through me like boiling-hot water.

"I know there's something there between you two. It wasn't right of me to ask you not to pursue that." He cleared his throat. "You're my best friend, but I don't own you like that, you know? It wasn't right."

So what was he saying? That he didn't have interest in me? That he thought Mastin was a better fit?

Or maybe he knows about your stupid crush on him and he's rejecting you.

A razor-sharp pain tore at me. All the insecurities of being a young girl fantasying over an older but romantically uninterested guy, surfaced in an instant. The embarrassment that rocked me sent burning hot tears to the back of my eyes, which only made everything worse.

Please don't cry. Please don't cry. Please…

"Thanks for your permission," I snapped. "I'll take it under advisement."

I kept my head down, sure my cheeks were bright red. This was so embarrassing! I stumbled back to the cellar door and down the stairs, steadying my breath as much as possible.

"Wait," he called after me, his voice torn in frustration.

But he didn't follow.

I plopped down in the corner of the cold room, glaring at the boxes of root vegetables in across from me, the rudimentary brewery next to those, and Mastin's hunched over form in the other corner.

He wasn't asleep anymore. He watched me like I was up to something. Had he heard any part of my conversation with Tristan? The thought of it sent another wave of shame crashing over me.

"Everything okay?" he finally asked, his voice laced with a protectiveness that I hadn't heard from him before.

"He talks," I muttered, referring to the frustrating silent treatment he'd given me before we'd gone to sleep. I knew I was being a brat, but I couldn't seem to stop myself.

"When I need to talk, I talk," he replied, his voice softer this time.

I closed my eyes and rested my head back against the cool stone for a moment. "Yes, everything is fine. We're trapped in New Colony, but other than that, things are great." I made sure my tone dripped with sarcasm.

"You don't have to be such a brat."

I laughed because he had called me out on what I'd just been thinking moments earlier, though I wasn't amused. *I need to get a hold of myself. No more arguing with my guys.*

"I'm sorry," I finally relented, blowing out my breath and meeting his inspecting gaze. "I know this is my fault and complaining won't help the situation."

He studied me through the filtered light, flecks of dust floating between us. We hadn't turned on the lone light bulb, instead opting to keep the cellar door open. At least for now. Once the family woke up and found us, all bets were off.

"I'm going to get an extraction team out here as soon as possible," Mastin said. "Our base outside of Nashville isn't far at all, but I'm afraid it might be a few days with everything going on. I don't know yet, but I don't like sitting here. Richard's men are hunting Jessa and all we've managed to do is take her place."

"And women." I crossed my arms over my knees.

He raised a questioning eyebrow.

"You said Richard's men. But it's men and women. His number one officer, Faulk, is a woman."

He nodded. "Well, either way, I don't know if we can trust this guy," he said, pointing to the house above, "or his wife."

"Who else is there to trust in this kingdom?" I sighed.

But as I asked the question, an idea came to me. How hadn't I thought of it earlier? I'd been so distracted that I'd overlooked something important. I lifted my hip to the side and reached two fingers into my front pocket, digging for a moment. The thin slip of paper slid out like an answer to a prayer. I held it up to the light, a smile pulling at my lips. I pictured the day Branson had given it to me, remembered the shock of the moment when I'd learned he was Resistance. An email address had been written there, meant to give West America an inside source in New Colony's warfront. I was supposed to hand if off to General Scott, but had instead held onto it. I had worried that it was a trap. Or that if it wasn't, Nathan Scott wouldn't treat Branson right because of deep rooted prejudice. Tristan was the only other soul who knew about the email address. He hadn't liked that I'd kept the paper, but hadn't tattled on me to anyone, either.

"What's that?" Mastin's eyes narrowed, catching sight of my secret.

I stilled. Mastin and his "live by the rules set, adhere to your higher ranks" attitude was going to be pretty pissed when I revealed this secret. But hey, I wasn't known for following the rules myself. What did he really expect from me?

"Sasha, what is it?" A twinge of panic rose in his voice and I smirked.

I avoided his question by asking one of my own. "How much charge is left on that slatebook of yours?"

His lips thinned, but he pulled it from his pocket and tapped at the screen. "A few days."

"Good." I flashed the slip of paper once more. "Because this just might be our ticket out of here."

TWO

JESSA

I crouched behind a dumpster, waiting for the already thin crowd of theatre-goers to disappear into the night. They streamed from the building, chattering voices floating on the cool air. Nobody looked my way. The stench of food waste and musky city streets wafted around me, encouraging me to move on, to take the risk now if only to get away from the stench. I didn't. Pressing my hand harder against my nose, I waited for my chance. It needed to be perfect.

The second it had been dark enough, I'd slowly traversed through downtown Marthasville. Careful to keep my head down, I'd dodged pedestrians and hidden in the darkest shadows I could find. If anyone got a good look at my face, I'd be in big trouble. Since the engagement, I'd become one of the most recognizable people in the kingdom. At least I was dressed better and more put-together than yesterday, since I'd stolen clean clothes this morning on my trek into the city. I had to steal the clothes right off a clothesline from one of the farms outside the city. No coat, but there wasn't snow here in the winters like up north. The dark green shirt was a little big for my frame, but it was long-sleeved and helped keep the shivers away.

The downtown area was compact, so it wasn't too hard to find the theatre. The people here weren't quite as well-to-do as the ones in the capital, but they still dressed in fine clothing and chattered like they didn't have a care in the world. Nobody noticed me in my hiding spot. The marquee across the street shined bright, the sight sending both hope and dread careening through me. I read the blocky words again: New Colony Royal Ballet. Tears pricked at my eyes. If only I'd been here a week ago, even a few days, I could have seen Dad. Held him, hugged him. But by the time I'd made it to Taysom Green's place after weeks of hiding with sympathizers and travelling in the dead of night, it was too late. Reaching out in the farm's cellar to Dad via our telepathic connection,

I'd discovered he was just crossing the border. I squeezed my eyes shut and let one tear trickled down my cheek. I hoped Dad had made it into safe hands. I couldn't think about the alternative.

I slapped my cheeks, determined to be strong, to think back on my journey. Why couldn't I see just how brave I really was? None of it had been easy, but I had done it, I had made it through. And I would make it through tonight, too.

The possibility of failure needed to fall to the back of my mind for now. I needed to focus on the building in front of me, on the task at hand. This was my only chance at getting back to Lucas. I clenched stiff fingers against the inside of my sleeves and wrapped my arms around myself for warmth. Soon, I would be inside and wouldn't be cold. Soon, things would be better. I thanked my lucky stars that the ballet was still in town and I could find a way to get help.

It made sense the ballet was still here, even though I'd been plagued with worry they wouldn't. When the company traveled, they would stay a week or two in one place before moving on to the next. Most citizens couldn't afford a ticket, of course, but those with the best jobs and highest wages prided themselves on going. There was always an audience for ballet. Dressed in their finest suits and gowns, people would make a public spectacle out of the event. It seemed that was the case even in war time. Ballet was an old aristocratic tradition, even from way before New Colony, one of the few things that had stuck in the new kingdom.

The once-busy crowd had disappeared, voices fading as they went their different ways, some on foot, others in vehicles. The once-bustling area had emptied. The night had grown silent. This was my chance. I stilled, ready to make a run for it. I needed to make it across the street and around the back of the theatre. And I needed to be quick, in case someone was out here that still recognized me. That part of the plan was doable. But then I'd have to break into the back door of the theatre and find Madame Silver, *also* without anyone recognizing me. Considering I'd trained with these dancers, knew most of them by name, that part of my plan was *not* so doable.

Didn't matter, I had to try.

Head down, I darted across the pavement, eyes focused on the ground, lights and shadows dancing in the corner of my vision. I walked as fast as I could without running. Since I didn't want to draw attention to myself, I didn't connect with the stones around my neck or use yellow magic to quicken my strides. For all I knew, there was someone watching from a window, or lurking around a corner. My heartbeat pounded in my chest. Biting air whooshed against my cheeks, my clenched jaw aching, my ears burning. Seconds later, I made it to another darkened alleyway and pressed myself against the wall. Eyeing the street, I made sure I wasn't being followed. Nothing stirred. Nobody was there. It seemed that the street was still mercifully empty.

I crept around the side of the building, running my fingers along the smooth whitewashed stone as I searched, eager for a service or crew entrance that I could slip into undetected. It didn't take long to find a nondescript black, steel door with rust around the edges. Perfect! Using yellow, I pushed the magic from my stone into my body, channeling it instantly, and broke the lock with a snap. It creaked open with the faint grinding of metal against metal. I cringed, scrunching up my face. If only I had access to silencing magic. But I couldn't think about that, I needed to move. I stepped inside.

The familiar scent of being backstage surrounded me as I slipped into the darkest shadow. It was the mix of dust, heated plastic, floor polish, sweat, and paint that calmed me and also called to me. For the first time all day, I smiled. This was home. Longing enveloped me, but so did the comfort of what I loved. This was where I should have been all along. If only things hadn't fallen apart all those months ago.

"Good show tonight." The familiar stagehand's voice carried through the space. *Toby.*

I'd worked with him just over six months ago, but now those memories felt like they'd been years ago. Another Jessa. Another life.

"Another great performance," he called again, down a set of stairs. That meant the dressing rooms were down below—a common set up. I slipped further into the shadows, pressing myself against the wall and praying with every fiber of my being that Toby wasn't about to find me. He was the ballet's light guy, a ruddy character with a thick mustache and a round belly. I liked him; he always had a smile on this face. But that didn't mean I could trust him now. Heavy footsteps clopped across the stage and his familiar round outline protruded into my sightline, followed by the rest of him. He ran a finger and thumb down his peppery mustache as he hummed to himself.

Same old Toby.

Madame Silver had said others in the ballet company's management agreed to help me and Dad, but I didn't know if that included Toby. Nor did I know if things had changed since Lucas's reported death. No, it was Madame Silver who I needed to find first. I couldn't expose my presence to anyone but her. Everyone else was too much of a risk.

Toby strode across the stage again, a satisfied grin flashing from under his bushy mustache. The urge to run and enfold him in a hug overcame me. Instead, I held my breath and clenched my hands into fists. The velvety maroon curtain was down, its bottom barely brushing the floor, and most of the area back here was shadowed in inky darkness. I hoped it would stay that way. But Toby walked up to a light on the far side of stage right and started flipping a row of switches.

No! I stumbled along the wall, darting for the closest hiding place. The plywood scenery piece was my only shot. It hid me, but only barely. It wasn't very large, the shape of a shrub, and there was nowhere for me to go from here. I crouched and watched Toby carry a ladder to center stage and begin setting it up. Either he was adjusting some lights for tomorrow's performance, or he was collecting a few things before the company moved on to their next location. I wished it was the second option—that meant I could hitch a ride back north. Maybe.

I'd be one step closer to finding out if Lucas was really dead.

Grief threatened to overtake me. It would claw at my every thought if I let it, so I pushed it aside for the matter that was right in front of me, for what I could try to control. Where was Madame Silver? I had to find her. It was possible she'd already left, but knowing her, that wasn't likely. Always the professional, she liked to see to it that all the dancers were out of the building before leaving herself. Were things different on tour? Perhaps this wasn't like dancing back in the Capital. I didn't know, and I hated that. I rolled my eyes and bit my lip, coming to grips with my desperate reality. Just as I was debating the best way to go about finding her, realization hit me. How had I been so stupid as to overlook it before? The solution was obvious.

It lay in the purple and gray stone warming my neck.

Madame Silver, I called out through our telepathic connection. *Can you hear me?*

I slunk even further behind the scenery piece and waited, grateful I had this magic tying me to her. *It's me, Jessa. I'm here and I need your help.*

Still nothing.

My head dropped into my cold palms. Overwhelming fear poured down my entire body, sinking me deeper into the floor. What if I was stuck here in Marthasville? What if coming back for Lucas had been a terrible mistake? Maybe I should have gone with my sister. I could be reunited with my family right now. But then, wasn't Lucas my family, too?

Jessa? Is that you? Our connection flared to life, like a lighted match dropping into a stream of gasoline. I gasped and slapped a hand over my mouth as the relief roared through me.

Yes, I'm here in the theatre. I'm backstage. My words would be flowing through her mind just as hers were in mine.

What are you doing here? We've been worried sick about you. Your father is gone now; I hope he's safe. We thought you'd be with him after your disappearance. Her words rushed at me, the flood of worry overflowing in her tone. *At least you're alive*, she added.

I smiled wider, once again filled with awe at this magic. Lucas's white invisibility would've been really handy at a time like this, but purple's telepathy was just as good. I rubbed the necklace around my neck, grateful for all it provided. But also, a little worried about where I'd find more purple once this stone was used up. It was almost gone as it was. There wasn't time to be concerned, I'd deal with it as soon as I had the chance.

Where can I meet you? I begged. *I need your help.*

Use the stage right stairs and head down to the lower level. I'll be in the first room on your left. Be quick. I don't know how long this hall will be clear.

Toby is up here right now.

She paused, as if talking to someone else for a moment. Unease rolled in my belly, but I reasoned that Madame Silver had always done right by me. She had saved my father's life, after all. And I hated that she was all I had. I was asking for her help, help that put her and many others in danger.

Madame Silver?

I just sent someone up to fetch him. The moment they head down the stage right stairs, you need to bolt for the left stairs and beat them down here, then hide in the room on your first left. I'll meet you there.

My whole body tensed. If I ran into anybody here, red alchemy would be my only saving grace. I didn't want to risk that. I *couldn't* risk that. Not on these people. They'd once been my second family.

"Hey Bossman, we need another pair of hands downstairs for a bit. Can you take a break from this?" A young man ambled up the stairs, dressed head to toe in black. I flashbacked to the Guardian uniform and shuddered. But no, this was just typical stagehand dress, nothing about this was formal, nothing about it spoke to the authority that had ruled my life these last months.

The kid had shiny blond hair and a youthful sureness to his stride. He must have been assigned to an apprenticeship under Toby. I didn't recognize him; he must've been new. Possibly as new as this tour.

"All right, Kenny," Toby replied. "But help me out here first, will ya? I've almost got this unscrewed. I'll pass it down."

Toby carefully lifted a large stage light from where he balanced near the top of the ladder, moving it into Kenny's upstretched arms. My heart raced when Toby leaned a tad too far for my comfort, but Kenny secured the light in his hands and strode back. Toby righted himself with the ease of a master.

"There you go," Toby said cheerfully, stepping down the rungs of the ladder.

I moved into a runners pose, calling on the yellow to flow through me. The second these two were out of view, I'd make a run for it. With the magic, I had no doubt I'd beat them downstairs.

"Whoa," Toby's voice ground out just as Kenny snapped, "Careful!"

But it was too late.

Toby slipped. It was his job not to slip, not to have an accident. And yet…

He crashed to the ground, the ladder rocking and toppling in the other direction with an ear-splitting shatter.

"No!" Kenny yelled. Another, smaller crash echoed through the area. The light was in pieces on the floor, an arc of glass around it, and Kenny was already on his knees in front of Toby.

I stared, horrified. Toby's body was bent at an awkward angle. An unnatural spread of limbs. He screamed out in pain, the sound so wild and guttural, that I jumped up.

I ran, all thoughts fading away. I slid next to Kenny, falling to my knees and running my eyes up and down Toby. I reached out, green magic flowing from my fingers in strings of effervescent light. The one measly stone on my necklace might not be enough for an accident this bad. I suspected his back was broken.

"Hurry," I said to the kid. "Can you find me a plant?"

"Don't touch him," he challenged, eyes drawn in confusion. "I need to get a medic. His back could be broken."

"I said get me a plant! I don't think I have enough with just a stone."

I widened my eyes at him, and his eyebrows drew in. Confusion and then recognition and then something like horrified-awe spread over his face. He nodded and sprinted off.

Toby's eyes were squeezed shut in two deep lines sunken into his reddened face as he howled in pain. I pushed the magic into him, feeling it work through his broken pieces. It would find the source and begin healing immediately, but I needed to act fast to mend bones properly. At least he hadn't snapped his neck because then he'd be dead right now. There were some things even magic couldn't bring people back from.

"Jessa!" Madame Silver ran onto the stage, her dark hair streaming behind her, her eyes round and frantic. "What are you doing?"

Her face drained of color as she took in the gruesome scene. Then she too fell to her knees beside me, her black skirt tucking against her thighs. "Is it working?" she asked, voice turning eerily calm. "How much longer? We have to get you out of here before anyone else sees you."

"Too late. Kenny already did. He went to find me a plant. I need more green."

Toby was whimpering now; I felt terrible that I hadn't been able to completely numb his pain. I whipped my head from side to side, I searched, needing to get my hands on some more green. Where was that kid?

As if on cue, Kenny stumbled back onto the stage, footsteps hollow in the vastness of the theatre. "This was all I could find," he said, dropping a bouquet of fresh-cut yellow roses into my lap. I eyed the stems and leaves, and inhaled the scent of performances gone-by.

"Thank you." I pressed one hand into them, avoiding the thorns as much as possible, and held the other hand against Toby's arm. His flesh was warm and sweaty under my palm. At least he wasn't cold. "This should be enough."

I concentrated and sent the green magic flowing into Toby. After a long minute, his eyes fluttered open. His body relaxed. He shifted his head to one side, moved a hand to rub his head, and then slowly, he sat up. Bewilderment filled his entire expression as he blinked at me. I threw a worried glance at Madame Silver. "Jessa," he breathed. "I thought that was you. What are you doing here?"

Before I could answer, he added, "You saved my life."

"Your guy Kenny found the green," I supplied lamely, my cheeks heating. Kenny sat across from us now, equally shocked by everything he'd just witnessed. He stared at me like he either wanted to get my autograph, or run away. Either way, it was not a good sign. My heart sank.

"Please don't speak of this," I begged of the men, looking from Toby to Kenny. My voice trembled. "Please don't turn me in."

"We'd never." Toby smiled, eyebrows drawn in concern. He took my hand and patted it reassuringly, like a father would to his daughter. He helped me up and my heart rose with it, hope, foolish hope, filling me.

I stood wearily, shaking out my legs and getting ready to make a run for it, despite the pulse of a headache forming between my eyes. Maybe this had been a huge mistake. But as I turned around, fear slammed me, rooting me to the spot.

Streaming from the staircase was a crowd of familiar faces. The entire crew of dancers and staff must have had heard the commotion upstairs, and now, they were all gaping in my direction. Equal parts fascination and fear lined their features as they stared at me, the girl they all knew, the one who had been lost to magic. The one who was a wanted woman, a bounty on her head. My eyes burned. Dread washed through me. I stumbled backward.

Were they more shocked at seeing color alchemy in action? Or was it my presence that alarmed them? I was the runaway queen. And yet here I was, randomly showing up on their stage, once again disrupting their lives.

"Please," I croaked, my voice not sounding like my own. "Please don't turn me in." I stepped back, panic building.

But then, one by one, they did the strangest thing. The thing that I would have never expected: they lowered their heads and bowed.

"Your Royal Highness," someone called from the back, "you're alive!"

My heart exploded in a flurry of shock. Yes, I was very much alive. But with this many people privy to my whereabouts, there was a real possibility that I'd be dead by morning.

The train rumbled beneath me, a steady vibration that should have rocked me to sleep. But sleep wouldn't come. Not for me, not at a time like this. My guard was up, and I wasn't planning on taking it down. I couldn't.

I rested on the hard bed of the sleeper train, my back pressed against the cool wall, going over everything again and again. After explaining myself, the entire company had sworn to protect me. That was the part I hadn't seen coming. And still, I questioned if I was safe. I knew I wasn't, but I was also out of options.

When the crew had finished cleaning up and we'd loaded the train, I'd taken the offer to stow along. I desperately needed to get north, needed to find out the truth about Lucas. The train was the only way I knew how to make that happen. My connections with the Resistance were lost since being dropped off at Taysom's farm.

I could do this. I could make this work.

A light tapping pulled me from the bed. I stood and brushed past the paneled wall, opening the pocket door. Madame Silver waited on the other side, her downcast gaze sending a fresh panic through me.

"We need to talk," she said.

I ushered her inside and closed us into the tight space. "I'm not safe, am I?"

"I don't know." Her makeup now washed clean and hair brushed loosely around her shoulders, she looked older and younger at the same time. She sat down on the bed and patted the spot next to her for me to join. "Probably not for long. You can trust these people, but there's just so many of them, and that's what worries me."

"Me too," I agreed. "A few could have been locked down, but that was what, like forty people? Fifty? It's dangerous and not just for me. I keep thinking that every minute I stay with the company is another minute I put everyone at risk, including you. Especially you, given our history." My voice cracked on the last part as guilt swelled.

She sighed. "We've agreed to help you. That's already done. What you do next is up to you."

But what could I do?

"I've come to show you something," she said, slipping her slatebook from her silky pajama bottom pocket. "There was another broadcast earlier tonight. I think you need to see it."

I stilled, something deep within me knowing that the broadcast was about me. I took a deep breath and forced the tears burning in my eyes away. She fiddled with the device and then passed it to me gently. The screen lit up, basking the room in a blue glow, and King Richard filled the screen.

I recoiled, struck by his appearance. He was more worn down than ever, with dark circles under his eyes and a grim line to his lips. Even his hair looked to have grayed another shade since I last saw him a few weeks ago. None of that stopped me from hating him.

"Dear citizens, as you already know, my son has been murdered." His voice was as strong as ever as it boomed out of the slatebook speaker. "We believe a West American assassin is responsible. We've gone over everything from that night, and the startling truth is, one of the most trusted members of the palace was the assailant. We have him detained and a public execution is scheduled for tomorrow."

Richard hadn't named me as Lucas's killer? The stark realization allowed me to release the breath I'd been holding tight in my gut. The camera flashed from Richard to a man's photo. I squinted in disbelief.

"That's not Lucas's killer," I gasped. "That man has been in prison for weeks."

It was the same man I'd interrogated with Lucas, the one whose wife had been related to the gunman from Queen Natasha's funeral. I highly doubted he was a West American assassin, not when I'd used magic to question him. He was just someone caught in the crosshairs, someone who'd known too much.

"They're using him as a scapegoat." The truth hit me hard, like whiplash, throwing off everything else Richard had told the press. My eyes widened. Hope burst into flame within me. Did this mean Lucas wasn't dead? Or did it confirm the opposite? It was confusing, but I was leaning toward the former. Madame Silver sat still as a statue next to me and didn't offer a word.

"Because of the horrible murders that occurred during my wife's funeral," Richard continued. "I have decided Lucas will be buried in private. Thank you for understanding. I am burdened with more grief and anger than ever. I will stop at nothing to defeat our enemy and avenge not only my wife and my son, but also my daughter-in-law."

"What?" I sputtered. "Avenge *me*?"

"Just watch." Madame Silver squeezed my shoulder before resting her arm around me.

"We believe that our newest princess was kidnapped from her wedding bed. It happened the very night her husband was murdered, possibly before her eyes. Now that we've had more details come to light and a chance to interrogate

Lucas's killer, we know the assassin wasn't acting alone. Princess Jessa Heart has been kidnapped. It is very possible she is still in New Colony. Please, if you find her, or know of any information leading to her discovery, call this number immediately and report it to the proper authorities."

A number flashed across the screen as dread prickled up and down my entire body. This wasn't good news for me.

"It is my belief the princess is being held against her will and is in grave danger. Help me in returning her to her rightful place, if not for me, do it for the prince you loved dearly. My son never would have wanted his beloved wife to be in such danger. Please, bring our princess home. A reward will be offered to anyone who can help us in this most important endeavor."

My image filled the screen along with a startlingly high reward price that flashed across the top. In the photo, I was standing next to Lucas at our wedding reception, smiling from ear-to-ear, happiness radiating from my eyes.

Madame Silver gently pried the slatebook from my shaking hands, but my eyes followed the image of Lucas's handsome face until she shut it off.

"Have they watched it?" I didn't have to say whom I was talking about; I was surrounded by people who knew exactly where I was.

"They watched it in the dressing room, before they found you," she said. "That's the good news—they already had this information before they agreed to help. The bad news is I don't know how long it will take for someone to second guess themselves and call that number. Not to mention, that reward…"

I nodded. "Okay," I breathed. I needed to run. "At our next stop, I'll sneak away. I won't say a word to anyone about where I'm going." Not that I knew where that would be.

"I'm going to prepare a pack for you," she said, concern etched in her words. Her faint wrinkles deepened around her eyes as her shoulders sagged under the weight of her words. "Food and clothing, whatever I can find that might help. I'll do that now."

We stood, and she hugged me tightly, my tall frame towering above her. I could practically feel the guilt she had over this.

"It's not your fault," I whispered. "I'll be fine. I promise. I've made it this far, haven't I?"

"You need to get out of New Colony." She stepped back and looked me up and down, her mouth falling into a sad frown. "You can't stay here."

I nodded.

She had no idea just how right she was. This was the worst possible place for me to be, but still, I had to know the truth. I still didn't believe Lucas was dead, and that broadcast had only solidified the burning questions in my mind. Why would the King accuse a false killer? Why hide the body like that?

Something wasn't adding up.

"I know. You're right." I smiled weakly. "But I can't put you in any more danger. Thank you so much for all you've done for me. I'll never forget your generosity."

She nodded, hugged me once more, and then slipped out the door.

I fell back onto the bed, overcome with the weight of the situation. How had things gotten so off track? Lucas should have come with me when I ran. Or I never should have tried to manipulate Richard's blood in the first place. Oh, there were so many things I could have done that would have avoided all of this.

All the regrets, they pressed down, threatening to suffocate me.

No matter. Don't focus on the past. I repeated the words in my head, trying once again to find the sleep that eluded me.

Don't sleep. You saw that broadcast. You're a wanted woman. There's a huge bounty on your head. You can't afford to sleep with so many people near.

So, I sat back up and I waited. Waited for sunlight. Waited for my chance to flee. Waited for the moment that I'd be on my own again, running for my life.

THREE

SASHA

"Check it again." I nodded at Mastin. My eyes flashed toward his pocket where he kept his slatebook. He shook his head slightly but still did as I said. Despite the warm sun, I shivered. Why was I suddenly so nervous? I should've been used to this kind of thing, this life and death thing. But no matter how many times I was faced with it, the possibility of dying always sent a cold shiver down my spine, always caused a shaking nerve, always made my breath quicken.

His mouth fell into a frown as he swiped the screen. "No news."

"I don't like this," Tristan added.

The three of us were bored, struggling as we waited in yet another cropping of overgrown bushes and trees. The afternoon sun had cut into me, pushing a sort of heavy lethargy deep into my bones. The constant rise and fall of temperatures weighed on me, but I didn't want the others to catch on to my weariness. I needed to stay strong, not only for them, but for myself.

"You hungry?" Tristan changed the subject, shifting the backpack that rested between the three of us. He rummaged inside and pulled out a canteen and a couple of long leafy carrots. "Lucky for us that farmer was willing to give us some of their winter provisions, eh?"

Mastin scoffed, rubbing the heel of his boot into the dirt. "Only to get us off his property as quickly as possible."

"It's better than nothing." Tristan smiled and tore into his sad lunch.

I shrugged and grabbed the extra carrot from Tristan, biting into it with a crunch. I rolled the thick pieces around in my mouth, trying not to think about the odd taste. I'd always hated carrots.

"Truth be told, I don't really fault Taysom for wanting us to go," Tristan said.

He was right to think so. We were a liability, a threat to the man's family. The kind farmer may have made an agreement with Lucas, but that was about

Jessa's safety, not ours. He'd certainly never bargained for the three of us to come knocking on his door in the middle of a war.

"Neither do I, but that doesn't change the fact that we're stuck out here," Mastin said. I sighed and focused on my measly carrot.

We'd been traveling northeast for the better part of two days, keeping out of sight during the sunlit hours and moving through the long dark nights as quickly as possible. The area was a mix of farmland and forests, with a few rolling hills for good measure. But mostly, the land was desolate and under-populated. That played into our favor. Now we were only a couple miles from our destination, and the closer we got, the more tense I became, my thoughts turning toward all the worst-case scenarios I could conjure in my mind.

Just breathe. Everything is going to be okay.

"What if this is a trap?" I said aloud, contradicting the lame mantra I'd been tossing around in my head.

The men turned on me at the same time, both with a mix of annoyance and frustration on their faces. Saying what everyone else was thinking didn't serve the situation, I knew that, but that didn't stop me. I held up my hands, carrot dangling. "I know, I know, this is what you've both been saying. I'm just ... okay. Maybe you're right; maybe we should turn back."

Not my strong suit, admitting I *might* be wrong. But, whatever, too late for that now.

"You're unbelievable." Mastin shot me a knowing look.

Tristan nodded slowly, his eyes drawn in as they studied me like I was some kind of unsolvable puzzle.

Inwardly, some small part of me ... okay, maybe a large part of me, stirred. These two ganging up on me was not cool, even *if* I was wrong. Weren't they supposed to hate each other or something? But no, the last couple of days they'd gotten along splendidly while I'd suffered with a chip on my shoulder.

"Let's go over everything again," Tristan said, leaning back on his elbows and looking up into the blue expanse of sky. I studied his profile, taking in his thick lashes and smooth tan skin. Why did he have to be so pretty? Why did they *both* have to be so pretty? It was annoying.

"You say Branson can be trusted? He was friendly with you back at the palace, but you never officially knew him to be part of the Resistance. Jasmine was careful to keep all her secrets to herself in the interest of protecting her people, so that part checks out."

"That's all true." I nodded.

Tristan continued, "And I had heard of his name at basecamp. That makes me think he's Resistance. And if he's really Resistance, then we shouldn't be surprised he gave you that email address. He probably knew he could trust you with it."

Mastin scoffed. "The address you were supposed to turn in to my father." He rolled his eyes.

"We can *still* give it to him. I'm sure *you* will," I countered. "I just, I don't know, I wanted to be sure ... "

I didn't add the rest of my thought, that I wanted to be sure West America wasn't going to continue to treat Alchemists like violent criminals. It was true I wanted New Colony to be defeated, or at least, I wanted to dethrone King Richard. Did that mean I *also* wanted West America to take over the kingdom?

Not if it meant the end of magic. And the verdict was still out on that.

"And now all we have to show for that email exchange are a set of coordinates and a time," Mastin replied. "It's vague. It could be a trap."

Yes, it very well could be. And that was exactly why I was beginning to feel sick to my stomach.

"Which is why we're going over everything again," Tristan said calmly. "One final time before we go through with it."

I bit my lip and brushed a wayward strand of hair out of my face. Yesterday morning we'd used Mastin's slatebook to send an email to the address Branson had supplied. All we'd said was that there were two soldiers and one Alchemist on this side of the border, who wanted to help in exchange for safe passage back to West America. I'd expected Branson to give us directions, a mission, something. When we'd replied with questions, reasonable questions, we never got an answer. And now we were almost to those coordinates, the time was almost upon us, and we still hadn't gotten a response.

What were we supposed to do?

"Coordinates and a time isn't a lot to go off of," Tristan continued. "But I do think Branson can be trusted, even if it is risky."

"We should've just crossed the border on foot," Mastin pressed, his closely cropped blond hair shining in the sunlight. He narrowed his green eyes as he rubbed at the dirt on his black boot. "Our Nashville base isn't even that far."

That had been his opinion from the start. It had quickly become clear that Mastin wasn't willing to risk any more of his men to come extract us, and neither was his father. When Mastin had contacted his father about what had happened to us, we'd been horrified to learn the newest update.

The helicopter that left us had been shot down at the border.

The pilot, dead.

This was the second time American soldiers had died trying to get me out of New Colony. It would be the last. Guilt had gripped me at the news; I'd fallen to the floor, dry heaving and sick to my stomach. Mastin had punched the wall and broken his hand in two places, something I'd fixed up for him later with green alchemy. And Tristan had gone silent for hours. All very reasonable reactions.

I glanced over at Mastin, not wanting to let the guilt rip me open once more. He rubbed his bruised knuckles, the frown still deep on his face. The bruises were still there since he hadn't let me entirely heal the broken bones he'd caused after punching the wall; those actions all watched over silently by Tristan.

General Nathan Scott's livid yells still echoed in my mind, so loud he may as well have been here and not on the other end of a phone call with Mastin. What was worse, I had agreed with him. Mastin should never have come with me and we'd been in NC too long. The whole call I waited for Mastin to blame me, say it was all my fault. He hadn't though. He only listened, never implicating anyone else for the damage done. Talk about laying some more guilt on my shoulders.

But worrying about that now wouldn't change a thing. Open countryside, farmland, marshes, all stretched for miles around us. No matter which way we traveled, danger awaited.

We were stranded.

"We can't just walk across the border of two warring nations without expecting to get shot," Tristan said. "We couldn't stay hidden at the farmer's place either. We weren't welcome there. So as risky as it is—"

"Branson is our best chance at getting out of here," I finished.

Mastin closed his eyes, face grim, but nodded. "Give me one of those damn carrots." Tristan tossed him one, and Mastin bit into it like it had personally offended him. "I'm going to case the area. I'll be back in ten." He jumped to his feet and stomped away, back straight, dark camo clothes blending perfectly into the scenery and disappearing before anyone could protest.

Tristan and I fell into silence.

We'd never talked again about our earlier argument. I forced my eyes to look anywhere but at him as it festered between us like an undressed wound. Shame pressed down on me every time I thought of his words, of how quickly he'd pushed me on Mastin. And now we had only a few more hours until we had to be at our destination, facing whatever surprises waited. If there were things we needed to say, now was the time.

I glanced at him, only to find him staring. His black, unreadable eyes quickly flicked away. He reached for the canteen and took a long swallow. A tangle of confused emotions rose in me.

"I'm sorry," I blurted.

"About what?"

"Everything. This." I motioned to the cropping we were hanging out in, the backpack between us. "This situation. And ... everything."

His jaw tensed, and he licked the water from his lips. I took a deep breath. "I'm sorry, too. I don't think you understood what I meant by what I said."

My cheeks ignited in a warm blush, and I couldn't help but look away. "No, it's okay. I got what you meant. We're better off as friends."

His hand found mine and squeezed, his thumb sliding up my wrist.

An echoing boom exploded from behind us. We both jumped, panic bursting through my veins like dynamite. I pushed that away and replaced it with action.

"What was that?" Not waiting for an answer, I sprinted through the brush to get a better look, Tristan right behind me, his breath heavy on the back of my head. Branches and twigs scratched at me, but I barely noticed, intent on finding the source to the sound that now careened through the once-silent afternoon.

Mastin crouched behind a large oak, motioning for us to join him. Up ahead, on the edge of the horizon, a fire raged.

"What is it?" I asked, though the question seemed ridiculous the second it left my mouth. I already knew. I could see what looked like an outpost caught on the offensive. A row of buildings burned, and people ran to and fro, some getting into position, others trying to stifle the flames. Black smoke billowed upward, staining the crystal blue sky.

"That must be the frontline," Tristan said, voice eerily calm against the backdrop of chaos.

Mastin nodded, a slight smile pulling on the hard lines of his usually stoic mouth. "They are under attack."

My chest burned. My legs ached. My throat tightened with nagging thirst. But that didn't matter. I hardly noticed any pain as I focused my attention straight ahead on our target. We ran together, at an all-out sprint, toward the mayhem. On the horizon, it appeared that several bombs had been dropped and at least one of New America's fighter jets had been shot down in the attack. The wreckage was spilled across an open field as it burned. Rows of uniform brick and metal buildings were engulfed in angry-red flames that reached into the sky recklessly.

The New Colony soldiers didn't notice the three of us as we approached, we were coming from the wrong direction. Several of them held massive hoses as they sprayed the flames, to little success. Others loaded their injured comrades on stretchers, running around a corner and disappearing toward more of the buildings that hadn't been hit. But the majority of the soldiers seemed to be running toward the airfield. Among the gunshots, the screams and shouts, the crackling of fire, was the sound of them calling out to each other, getting into position.

As we neared the area, it was evident that we couldn't just stay out in the open. We needed to take cover. Mastin led us to refuge behind a large dumpster. The three of us caught our breath and my brain ran through all the possibilities on our next move.

"Now what?" Tristan asked, looking up to the two of us from where he had his hands resting on his knees. Sweat lined his forehead and adrenaline sparked in his eyes. Tristan was the kind of person who could easily take charge when needed, but also knew when to back down and let someone else be the leader. That came in handy in times like these.

"Let's go to the meeting spot," I offered. "Maybe Branson will still be there."

Mastin pursed his lips but he nodded anyway.

"Hold on," I said, reaching toward the men. "Stay close and I can help us." I felt the magic from my stone necklace begin to work its way into my body, like heat being poured through me. I sent out the blue as a protective noise bubble.

Gunfire, short pops followed by a series of successive clatters, punctured the afternoon just ahead of us. My heart rose up into my throat and I knew that I could do more for these men under my protection. It was my fault they were here; I needed to see they made it out of this alive. I glanced down to the necklace, taking in the sight of the stones. The colors were fading. After today, I'd need to refresh most of these, including the amber stone that glinted like solid honey in the sunlight. I prayed there'd be enough to get us through tonight.

"Okay, we weren't ever really supposed to do this," I said. "I don't even know if I can, not everyone is able to, but I should try … "

More gunshots, this time closer.

"Sasha, we've got to get out of here." Tristan tugged on my hand, but I held him back.

"What are you talking about?" Mastin questioned. "Let's go. Now!"

I turned and looked at the men, trying to get them to understand with a single expression. "If this works …" I said. "Don't be mad at me, okay?"

Mastin was distracted, already in battle mode. His hand rested on his gun, his body was crouched into position, and his eyes were narrowed in singular focus. But Tristan had turned toward me, his eyes flashing in a slight accusation. He knew me too well for his own good.

"Why would I be mad?" The question came out of his mouth slow and testy. "What aren't you telling me?"

There was no use in hiding it. "Okay," I sputtered. "I might be able to give you some of this yellow magic. I'm not sure it will work, but if it does, we'll have a much better chance at making it to these coordinates without being shot dead."

Mastin swung his head around. "I don't want it," he growled.

I wasn't about to give him a choice. There wasn't time to hash out an argument with the man.

The yellow already spun in tendrils of magic around us, already making its way toward the intended targets. In a flash, the tendrils caressed the men's exposed arms and sank into their bodies like water through paper.

This is okay. This is going to work just fine.

Alchemists used magic on others for green alchemy. The King used it for his own persuasion, something I'd seen Reed do on more than one occasion. But some of the more volatile magics were kept to ourselves. We were trained to handle them, true, but more than that, we'd been *born* for the task.

"Just trust me. I don't have a lot of this color left on me, so we need to get moving now. Mastin, do you want to take point?"

He stared at me like I'd completely lost my mind. I shrugged. I hated giving him the lead, but it would keep his mind occupied from the magic.

Another round of shots echoed, once again, closer.

"We don't have time," I reminded them and raised my eyebrows.

We took off together, first rounding the dumpster, sprinting for the closest building, and running along the back. As we moved, our speed at least five times a normal human's, I kept my head down. I couldn't bring myself to look at Mastin, or Tristan, for that matter. Tristan hadn't put up a fight at the magic, but that didn't mean I wouldn't pay for this later.

I'd kept this ability to myself for years. Would he judge me for it now? Would he think I'd been selfish? Would he understand that I'd been protecting him?

Mastin stopped abruptly, falling flat on his face in the process. Tristan jumped over him, only to skid and land on his butt with a heavy thud. They both groaned as they stood. I quickly checked to make sure the blue magic was still surrounding us. It was an inner knowing within me that called to the blue, since the magic was different than all the others. They were all unique in their own ways, each feeling slightly different from the last. But the blue? It was beginning to fade. And I didn't have much color left in the stone.

"Are you two okay?" I asked. "Anything feel broken?"

"I'm fine." Mastin jumped up, brushing himself off. There was a tear in his uniform, a small trickle of blood bubbled up on his exposed knee. I frowned and reached toward it.

"I said I'm fine," he snapped, moving out of my reach. I tried not to be offended that he wouldn't let me help him, but I had to grit my teeth to do it.

Tristan was also standing now, a teasing smile lifting his face. "You could have warned us."

"I did," I replied sharply.

He lifted an eyebrow.

"Kind of."

He laughed, two perfect rows of teeth shining. I rolled my eyes, took a deep breath, and noticed the smoke was beginning to fade. The sounds of shouting had also faded out. The battle had progressed further ahead.

Mastin shook his head, clearly unimpressed by the two of us. "The meeting point from the coordinates is just around this corner and two hundred feet ahead."

"I'll go first," I said. "You two watch for me here and jump in if I need you. Branson knows me. This is best."

Before they could argue, I took off. It was a narrow alleyway, and deserted. *For now.*

Didn't mean we were safe.

Please be there, Branson. We need you. My gut twisted. He was probably too busy to make the meeting, that was assuming he'd made it out of the battle alive.

The two buildings were about to come to an end, a tank sat right in the center, pointed outward. The relative safety of the alley was all I had left. An open road up ahead filled with smoke, a few soldiers dashing past, shouts and gunshots continuing to pierce further ahead. Not about to step out into the open, I stopped and crouched low next to the army tank. It was parked at the opening, probably ready to join the battle if needed. Where was Branson?

"Over here," a deep male voice called softly from behind, as if he'd heard my thought. I turned, tensing when I didn't spot anyone. But a moment later, Branson stepped into view from the other side of the tank. Blood mixed with dirt and sweat ran down his temple, and his mouth was set in a grim line. I stilled and clenched my fists, ready to fight if this turned out to be a trap.

He held up his hands. "I was hoping you wouldn't show. You should go," he said, voice low and tired. "This is a bad time."

"I kind of figured that part out." I glared. "You should have emailed us back."

He folded his arms over his chest, glancing around. I could sense his worry in the tense set of his shoulders and the way his eyes kept glancing about, never quite landing in one place for more than a few seconds.

"It's okay." I motioned to my necklace. "I have shielding blue around us right now. No one can hear."

Hopefully that wouldn't turn out to be a mistake, considering Tristan and Mastin were now out of earshot too.

Branson's eyes finally landed on me, impressed, and he nodded. "Then I'll make this quick. I was going to have you take a couple of people with you to the other side. Faulk is closing in on them, and I wanted them gone before she figured out that they're Resistance."

"Who?"

"Doesn't matter." He shook his head. "They're caught up in the fight."

"Who?" I shifted closer and pressed the question again.

"They're safer if you don't know," he snapped. "You'll have to come back another time. Go hide and I'll email when I can. Things are getting tense around here. Be patient. It might take some time."

Disappointment washed through me in tiny pinpricks down my spine, but what else could I do? What else could *he* do? From the looks of things, no one had expected this attack today. Maybe if Mastin had communicated with his father better, we could have avoided this. *No use fretting about it now.* Branson stepped back as I turned to go.

"Look who I found," a sinister voice called out from the other end of the alley. I whipped around and gasped with recognition. Reed. He stood behind Tristan and Mastin. Both of their hands were behind their heads as the group shuffled forward. Tristan's expression remained steady, but Mastin snarled, his teeth bared in disgust. My eyes darted to Reed, a smug smile and raised eyebrows drawing out all my anger. Reed caught my expression and pressed back with a cackle. Like pouring salt into the wound, he held their guns in both of his meaty hands and used his magic to break them in half. A flash of yellow sparked as the broken pieces clattered to the pavement. He laughed, gleeful and sadistic.

Behind him, two more alchemists were walking with a confident swagger in their step, fists up as if ready for a fight. Their black war uniforms gleamed with stones, the visors on their helmets pulled down so I couldn't recognize them, like I could Reed. They moved like a pack of lions, confident and out for blood. We were outnumbered, and worse, I was the only alchemist on our side of the fight.

Branson's hand reached around me, scrunching my shirt and ramming me back against the tank. I caught his low spoken words. "Still using blue?" His quick and violent movement caught me so off guard.

"Don't touch her!" Mastin yelled.

"Yes, I'm still using blue," I mumbled, between gritted teeth. "They can't hear us."

"This tank is unlocked. It's ready for you to go. I was going to have you take my friends in there, but it looks like the three of you will be going at it alone." I stilled as he wrenched my arms behind my back. "Now drop the blue before he catches on," he whispered again, sending another shove into my gut.

When I did, I think we both felt the magic fade away, because the moment it was gone, Branson immediately called out to Reed. "I got her!"

A few seconds later the lot of them closed in, boots clomping on the ground and angry curses and shoves between them. Branson shoved me in front of him, his beefy hands holding me in place. Reed's visor was pulled up. He strode over and sneered in my face. I could smell the sweat on him, the blood from battle, and the eagerness to prove himself.

I glanced at my boys and shook my head slightly, hoping they'd catch what I wanted. *Play along, follow my lead, I have a plan.*

"What were you thinking coming here?" Reed scoffed. "You really are the stupidest person I have ever met. You know that? We're going to torture you and your friends, Traitor. And then do you know what we're going to do?"

I glared, refusing to answer him. He leaned in so close, our noses were nearly touching. I fought the urge to spit in his face.

"I said, do you know what we're going to do?" he yelled, spittle flying.

"You spit when you talk," I replied with a growl. "And your breath is seriously rancid. Might want to rein that in, buddy."

He moved faster than I could react, his magic igniting him, as he backhanded me across the face. I jerked back into Branson's hard chest. Pain burned across my face, and I spat blood into the dirt. Anger rose in me tenfold, hot and ready to burst.

"Touch her again and you're dead!" Tristan tore out of his captor's grip as he went for Reed, but one of the alchemists tackled him to the ground before he'd made it a few steps.

"As I was saying before I was so rudely interrupted..." Reed moved back into my personal space. "After we torture and interrogate you, we will kill your friends. I'll do it myself. You can watch. And then? We'll execute you. I think the King will make that one public."

How had this guy gone from the friendly kid at the palace to this sadistic monster?

Dread gripped me and I lost my breath. My eyes flicked to Tristan and Mastin. Tristan was still sprawled out on the ground, an alchemist sat on his back, pushing his face into the ground. Regardless, he looked up at me with utter determination in his eyes. Mastin was no different, the fire rolled off him in waves. Reed inched back, turning to the other alchemists as he began barking orders.

Branson's grip on my arms went slack.

"Go for the tank!" I yelled.

Immediately, they went into attack mode. The superhuman strength and speed of yellow was still in their systems, something Reed and his little friends hadn't been expecting. Shock rang on the alchemists' faces as they shrieked and pounced. But Tristan and Mastin were both trained fighters, and with this newfound strength pulsing through them, they were quick to knock their captors down and sprint for the tank.

I pushed Branson off me with ease and ripped open the door to the tank. Adrenaline ignited the yellow alchemy and for a moment I thought I'd torn the door right off. I jumped inside, seconds later Tristan and Mastin's bodies rolled in after me.

"I got this." Mastin pulled the door shut and locked it. "Make sure all the other escapes are locked. Go, now!"

I dove for the door on the other end of the cab and Tristan leaned up to check the one on the roof. We were secured inside in seconds, Mastin already taking point behind the wheel. It roared to life with a loud rumble that vibrated up my bones. A panel of lights ignited on the dash, reminding me of a helicopter. Reed and his cronies were trying to get inside, banging on the windows and doors, but even with magic, the monstrosity was airtight and couldn't be infiltrated.

"You know how to drive this thing?" I asked Mastin, finally catching my breath.

He nodded, face grim. "Never had to use it in battle, though."

We jerked forward. A faint burning rubber smell made me cough.

"These things aren't always the fastest, but they're sturdy. If we can get out of here before someone catches on that we're in it, we might be able to get over the frontline and back into America."

"Won't your people just blow us up?" Tristan questioned.

"Good point. Here, call my father and let him know we're coming." He pulled out the slatebook and tossed it to me. I fumbled with the device for a moment before finding Nathan Scott's contact. Pressing send, it only took one ring before the General's face filled the screen.

"I'm a little busy at the moment, son!" he shouted. "We're trying to win a war here!" Then he looked down at the screen and saw me, his lips pinching, reminding me that he and Mastin shared the same blood. His face was ashen, eyes weary.

"Sasha." His voice clipped.

I quickly explained the situation, and he nodded.

"Fine," he said. "I'll relay the message. Ping me your exact location every few minutes until you get here."

Mastin took the lead, navigating the land with expert precision. There was a steering wheel, like any land vehicle, but all the buttons he pushed left my head reeling. I watched, fascinated, as he saved our lives. It was surprisingly easy for us to get out of the New Colony basecamp. Every inch we put between us and them, allowed me to relax a millimeter more.

"With the battle waging, what's one more tank, huh?" Tristan said.

I turned to smile at my friend, only to notice that his skin had taken on a pallid tone. A slight sheen of sweat had covered his face and his eyes were clouded and beginning to droop shut.

"Are you okay?" My eyes searched his body.

He pulled up his shirt with a stifled groan. A trickle of blood oozed from a round cut in his abdomen. I leaned in closer.

"You've been shot!"

He smiled. "Actually, I was stabbed, and I might need you to fix that up for me." Then he had the audacity to wink before the rest of the color drained from his face and he slumped over in his seat.

FOUR

JESSA

I needed to get north. The sooner I could connect to Lucas, the better. I was running out of time. Correction, I was already out of time because he might be dead. But that wasn't going to stop me from at least trying to help. Everything in the world might be conspiring to slow me down and keep us apart, but one way or another, I would discover the truth. I would find Lucas.

I leaned back against the wall and sighed, ignoring the rumble of my stomach. It matched the rumble of the thin wall behind me. I was still here, still riding the train north. Part of me hated myself for doing it; I was putting others at risk. I'd spent the better part of the day justifying my actions. Nobody knew I was here. Nobody would be implicated if I was caught. And even though Madame Silver had prepared me a pack, I was planning to save most of it for when I really needed it again. At the moment, I was safe…

Relatively speaking.

Earlier this morning, when the train had made a stop, I'd left. I'd asked Madame Silver to relay the message to the others, something I was sure she would do. She wanted me away from her company just as I did. What she didn't know, and what nobody knew, was that I'd immediately circled back and stowed away in one of the prop cars. I was currently hiding behind a row of hanging costume bags. The space was stuffy, squished, hot, and miserable. But what other option did I have? If I'd actually run off into that unknown town, in broad daylight, someone would have recognized me. And even if I'd been lucky enough to make it out of there, then what? Walk all the way to The Capitol?

No. This was the only way. I would hide here as long as possible. I would be grateful that every minute I was traveling closer to my love.

My love.

When had things gotten so complicated? First, I'd hated Lucas. Then I'd fallen in love with him. Then I'd hated him again, and now I was back to loving him, this time more deeply than ever. After our wedding, I'd seen him for who he really was, for the selfless person, not just the prince doing his father's bidding. He'd saved me. Not only me, but my father and my older sister. When that farmer had said Lucas was dead, it was like I'd been buried right along with him. I knew it then, knew I'd forgiven Lucas, that I loved him, and that I wasn't ready to leave him behind.

My heart had been softened and now it was too late.

Don't say that...

I closed my eyes, squeezing them against the turmoil. My fingers traveled to the necklace that rested around my neck, relaxing against the comfort the stones provided. I stopped on one and looked down with a frown. I was almost out of purple. I'd been using what little I had far too often lately. The Resistance had been able to help me replenish some of my crystals, but amethyst wasn't easy to come by. It didn't just pop up in people's gardens.

My precious stone had turned completely gray all but for one small speck of purple.

That meant one more chance to use telepathy. Over the last couple of days, I'd questioned whether I should connect with Dad again. But Lucas needed me; I had to save the color for him.

Fatigue simmered just under my eyelids, and I stifled a yawn. Tiredness overwhelmed me, the hard floor was beginning to make my lower back ache, and there was barely enough room to spread my cramping legs out. But who was I to complain? Instead of focusing on my physical discomfort, I needed to focus on using my magic to help Lucas.

I glanced up at the clear bags hanging on the rail beside me. Maybe I could use one as a pillow, or drape it over my body to stay hidden as I slept. The closest bag contained a forest green dress, sequins glistening in the shards of light slicing up through the gaps in the floorboard. A stunning color. If only I could...

Wait! That was it. Adrenaline coursed through my limbs and I shimmied up the wall. I rummaged through the bags, searching through the rainbow of fabrics. There, a purple silk leotard.

Most of my colors had to be pulled from natural elements, but purple was one I was especially talented in when it came to alchemy. The synthetic material would work beautifully. Ignoring a little stab of guilt for ruining something so fine, I ripped a large chunk from the costume. I winced at the sound of tearing fabric, then quickly zipped up the bag and slid back to my hiding spot.

I ran a thumb over the smooth fabric. There was enough color here between my fingers for several more telepathic conversations. Telepathy was finicky magic. I had to be close to my target, but the stronger I got, the further and further away I could be to do it. I also had to make a physical connection with the person first. Okay, not always; there had been that time during the initiation trails where I'd been able to hear a young girl. But our connection had been terrible. I'd tested it with Madame Silver and figured out it was best to touch someone first. They didn't even have to know about it right away. Once the connection was there, it could be called upon again and again.

I stilled my mind, relaxed my body, and focused on my task. I thought of Lucas, thought of everything we'd been through together. And that centered me. I touched my lip as I remembered our first kiss, pictured the way he'd looked at me. I heard the low timbre of his voice when he'd told me he'd loved me, and the way his gray eyes had flashed silver when I'd said it back. I could see it all so clearly, could practically feel him, smell his spicy scent and touch his warm skin, as if he were in the little room sitting right in front of me.

Lucas, I called out. *Can you hear me? It's me. It's Jessa.*

I waited, sure that there was something on the other end, like a slight crackle when the slatebooks connected to each other, and I just needed to listen harder.

Lucas, I tried again. *Are you okay? Please, Lucas, if you can just give me a sign. Just say anything so I know you're all right.*

Still, nothing.

Frustration clawed at me. The purple magic pulsed through my body, ready to make a connection, like it too was beginning to panic. It buzzed around, filling me with anxiety.

Lucas, please!

This time, I already knew there wouldn't be a response to my pleading words. But even so, something was there, lingering, some faint energy on the other end. Surely, it wasn't all in my mind. I shoved the thick wad of fabric into the pocket of my jeans and dropped my face into sweaty palms, nearly ready to give up. Maybe all of it was in my mind, just wishful thinking, just a heart trying not to be broken. Silly. Hopeless.

Definitely foolish.

I stayed like that for hours, trying again and again to make a connection. Failing.

Failing so miserably I barely noticed when my cheeks became wet and sore. I didn't know when I'd begun to cry, silent anguish dripping down my face. It lasted for longer than I'd care to admit. And when the tears could no longer flow, when there was simply nothing left inside to pour out, my mind drifted away.

It was the angry kind of sleep that found me. Not restful or a way to forget the world; there was no peace in it. Rather, it consumed me with heady nightmares, the kind laced with sinking horrors and twisted fears. Worst of all, it held me under and pinned me down with no way to wake myself, no way to escape.

The train had stopped, the low rumble gone.

"There she is," a sharp voice split through the fog.

My eyes popped open. Before I could react, hands grabbed me. I reached for my stones, but more hands beat me to it and ripped them away. Lights flickered on, illuminating the small area and momentarily blinding me. Yanked from my spot on the floor, my body, heavy from sleep, knocked over the long row of black garment bags.

I blinked, my heart racing, as the white Royal Officer uniforms took over my vision, their badges glistening silver, their ominous weapons inches from my face.

Unmistakable black boots stepped forward. I looked up to find Faulk glowering in my face, her tall, wiry frame stiff, her smile triumphant, her eyes narrowed in pure hatred. She tossed a handful of gray clothes at me and pointed her gun. "Change. Now."

I debated going for the color since it was all around me. But most of it was synthetic and wouldn't grant me any favors.

"Now!" she yelled again, voice sharp as a knife.

I turned and stripped as fast as possible, shame and anger in every movement. Without color, I would be hopeless. But I had no way out of this situation, no other choice, but to comply with Faulk. Dressed in only a white bra and panties, I took a risk and slipped the ripped piece of purple fabric inside the cup of my bra. Then I threw on the gray top and shimmied into the thin pants.

Purple wouldn't get me out of this mess, but it was better than nothing.

"Jessa Heart, you are under arrest." Faulk grabbed me and pushed me against the doorframe, locking handcuffs around my wrists.

"For what?" I growled, automatically tugging against the grip of metal. She tightened the cuffs even more, the pain biting into my wrists.

"I think you already know," she snapped, voice right in my ear.

Oh, I did. For attempting to manipulate the King by going for what I thought was his red blood? Yeah, that had been a huge error on my part and arrest-worthy. But I'd never hurt Lucas, and I prayed I wasn't about to be blamed for whatever had happened to him.

"Is Lucas really dead?" The urge to have answers made me sound desperate, but I didn't care. I craned my neck to get a better look at her, to see if her reaction gave anything away, but she only shoved my face back into the doorframe. "Please, just tell me the truth. Is he okay?"

"If you know what's good for you, you'll shut up. If you don't, I'll shut you up." Her voice grew louder. "You're in a lot of trouble. I wouldn't be surprised if King Richard orders your execution the moment he sees you."

My gut twisted. I wouldn't be surprised either, especially if Lucas really was dead and the King had no leads. I was an easy target. He'd probably kill me himself.

She pulled me from the room, deliberately shoving me into the doorframe before pushing me into the small hallway. On either end of the passenger train, faces stared back, and I ran my eyes over wrinkled foreheads, hands over mouths, and huddles of my old friends.

"Why are you arresting her?" Kenny said, breaking from the crowd and moving in close. His eyebrows arched in concern, but guilt lit his expression. "I thought you said she was in trouble. You were supposed to help her!"

Faulk eyed him with disdain. "You got what you wanted, boy. You got your reward. Don't ask questions. We know what we're doing."

A dark cloud enveloped me, and I sighed heavily. Kenny. Kenny had turned me in. He'd seemed so trustworthy, helped me when I'd saved Toby. When would I learn that I could trust no one? Madame Silver stood behind him, her eyes wide with anguish. I couldn't blame her, she'd known this would happen. She'd been smart enough to get me out, but I'd been the one to go back on my word.

"You're sure nobody else knew she was in there?" Faulk asked Kenny.

"I'm sure," he sputtered.

"You know we have ways to detect if you're lying."

Dread crashed through me. If he told the truth, it would implicate the entire company. They would be punished. Severely. But, in retrospect, I had gone into that storage car alone. Kenny wasn't lying, he just wasn't telling the entire truth.

"I'm sure," he went on. "I went in there to get something and found her, so I called the hotline right away."

Faulk nodded. "My colleagues will be conducting interviews."

A wave of dizziness fell over me.

"And if everything checks out, you will be rewarded, as promised."

Kenny's mouth twisted but his eyes widened, and the dizziness running through my mind doubled. Of course, I couldn't trust these people not to turn me in. Money was money. Who was I to them when a fortune was on the line?

Faulk yanked me down the thin hall to the exit, down the steps, and out toward a waiting car. I'd spent enough time in black, shiny cars over the last six months, and just the sight of it made tears spring to my eyes. My stomach turned and before I could stop myself, I bent at the waist and lost what little I had in my stomach. It spread across the pavement and splattered Faulk's shoes. "Sorry," I muttered, not that I really cared. A small laugh escaped me.

"Oh, you've got to be kidding," she growled, spinning me around so quick the dizziness came back with a vengeance. She backhanded me across the face, hard enough for my breath to catch and my vision to blur.

Everything fell to darkness.

★

I caught the faint sandalwood scent of Lucas; it crashed me from the tip of weightlessness back into reality. My heart, so closed until now, fluttered open—my eyes, too. My surroundings took form, from hazy to solid—I was in his surroundings, too. I shot up, a mix of fear and longing clenching me so tight I could hardly breathe.

I was lying in the center of a large bed, in the bedroom we'd been meant to share together. The fireplace, the furniture, the long, sheer curtains—everything appeared as we'd left it, as if waiting for my return. Part of me wished I'd never left it that night. If I'd stayed here with Lucas, we might not be in this mess. Maybe I could have protected him from whatever happened, and maybe he could have done the same for me. Maybe he would still be in here with me now, instead of the wispy traces of his scent, a pale comparison to the real thing.

I buried my head into his pillow, tears filling my eyes. I'd gone and ruined everything and now that I was back, I was more of a prisoner than ever. And

I didn't have Lucas. I didn't have anyone. But at least I was here. At least now I had a chance to find him. Somehow. Someway.

Maybe this was not only the better way, but also the only way. Maybe this was what needed to happen all along. It was the only hope I had, and it still didn't change the fact that I was once again in my gilded prison.

I sat up and peered around, noticing there was something a little off about the room. There was no usable color. I wasn't surprised. The furniture was dark oak, the linens were all white, and the floors the same polished alabaster marble found in most of the palace. Even the rug and wall hangings had been removed, and after checking the dresser drawers and the closet, I only found black, gray, or white, but nothing usable.

Deep in my gut, I knew that the doors would be locked, the windows, too. Still, ever the naïve optimist, I rolled from the bed and checked them anyway. The silver door handle didn't budge, and the window was firmly shut in place. I ran a finger along the line of fresh nails buried along the painted windowsill and sighed.

At least I wasn't expected to wear prison clothes. That had to mean something. I went back to the closet to study the casual outfits and formal gowns, finding a group of pressed Guardian uniforms hanging in the back. Breath catching in my throat, I ran my fingers along the material of my old uniform and felt my heart kick in protest. I had been so close to getting away from this outfit and everything it meant. The idea of wearing them hardly seemed appropriate, but I could take a hint when I saw one.

Besides, I needed to get cleaned up while I still had the chance.

I hurried to the shower and got myself ready as quickly as I could, partly from the anticipation of what the day would hold for someone under arrest, but partly from curiosity as to why I was locked up in here instead of downstairs with all the other criminals. If I had to guess, I'd say I was going to find out what was going on sooner rather than later. Surely I wasn't just going to be accepted back into the fold as a Guardian? But according to the latest broadcast, I was still the princess. But that didn't make sense either, given the circumstances of my disappearance.

Dressing in the bathroom, I found the strip of purple fabric I'd stolen and returned it to the spot inside of my bra, tucking it against my skin. I felt a little silly hiding something there, because what would happen if they made me strip? I couldn't worry about that. It was all the color I had left, and it was coming with me, just in case. Freshened up and waiting for whatever came next, I sat back on the bed, foot tapping restlessly on the floor. Breakfast, perhaps? My stomach pinched at the thought.

I closed my eyes and relaxed, thinking of Lucas, wondering if he was near, hoping he was okay. I was no stranger to pain and sadness lately, but even imagining him no longer being alive tore a giant hole inside me. I was nervous to try the purple magic again for that very reason. What if it didn't work? What if it failed so miserably I had no choice but to accept Lucas's death? I touched my side, close to the purple fabric. If it didn't work, if he didn't respond now that I was back in our home, I swore my heart would crumble.

I swallowed and took several deep breaths, my chest rising and falling with effort. Whatever the case, whatever happened, I had to be strong. There wasn't any more time to question things. I was back in the palace, and if Lucas was hiding somewhere, he was probably close. I could do this.

Mind made up, the purple came to me instantly, quickening my pulse. With steady thoughts, I reached out for him. At first, there was nothing, but then a small flicker of familiar energy rose on the other end.

Lucas! I called out. *Lucas, are you okay? Is that you? Can you hear me?*

The door flew open. I blinked several times, instantly losing the telepathic magic. With the color safely tucked away, nobody would know what had just happened. I cleared the magic from my body and turned to face my intruder.

King Richard.

"You," he spat, striding into the room with clenched fists. A few guards shuffled in after him, and the door slammed with a thud.

I held up my hands in surrender, mouth falling open, unable to utter a word. He loomed over me, looking taller than I remembered. Bigger. And angrier than I'd ever seen him, the clarity in his steel eyes was startling. His hair was slicked back and his suit was pressed to perfection, the polished exterior did little to hide the animal within.

"You have a lot of explaining to do," he growled low, a thick vein in his forehead bulging, his sunken cheeks making his facial bones extra severe. "Unfortunately, Reed is still on the frontline. He's been rather useful to me there, but I'm starting to regret that decision." He eyed me with contempt as his presence overtook the room. "I'm going to give you one chance to tell me the truth, and if you don't, I swear on my wife's grave, I will drag you by that pretty hair of yours all the way to the frontline to beg at Reed's feet."

My stomach flipped. Reed was the most powerful blue alchemist in the kingdom and I had too much to hide. I should have been more careful than to end up here! With all the suspicion cast in my direction, and Reed to interrogate me about everything, I'd have to fight harder than ever to overcome him. But I'd done it before. I could do it again. Still, I needed that to be the last resort.

"Okay," I squeaked. I cleared my throat, grasping for confidence. "Okay, I'll tell you." How was I going to pull this off?

I gripped the edge of the bed sheet, wishing I could manipulate white and get out of here. I tried to clear my mind, noticing instead that my whole body had grown cold.

He leaned in front of me, eyes narrowed into angry slits. "Are you with the Resistance?"

There was no point in lying. I'd already tried and failed to manipulate the man's blood. He hated me, would never trust me again.

"Yes."

Slam! He slapped me across the face. It was so unexpected, so shocking, I didn't brace myself. I fell back onto the bed and cowered. He didn't seem to care either way. His face was beet red as he towered over me.

"How long?" he demanded.

"Since not long after I got here. Sasha and Jasmine recruited me."

"Who else?"

"What?" I sputtered, the terror multiplying.

"You know what!" he yelled, voice booming through the room.

How was I going to keep others out of this one? Lucas had been part of the Resistance for a time, and I couldn't possibly tell his father. Madame Silver had helped me, and she could be so easily implicated. That sweet old woman, Ruth, the farmer Taysom Greene and his family, and so many others ... even the couple at the palace. I couldn't turn these people in. They had helped me. Any suspicion on them would ultimately mean their deaths. I'd seen for myself how Richard had twisted things to punish anyone he wanted. There were no consequences for a king.

"Who else is Resistance?" he demanded again.

"I don't know," I lied. If it came to the point that Reed got the truth from me using his persuasive magic, then so be it. Right now, I was all about lying through my teeth for as long as I could manage.

"I don't believe you," he said slowly, once again clenching his fists.

"No, it was only those two. When Jasmine died, the Resistance died too," I pleaded.

Died... I gritted my death. Murder was the appropriate word for what had happened to Jasmine. I longed to say it, but given my vulnerable position, I needed to appear as cooperative as possible, but without revealing too much. I needed to appear chastised, apologetic.

"If that's true, then who has been trying to assassinate my family?" He began to pace the room, arms flying about as he spoke. His guards stood back, expressions placid. But they followed him with their careful eyes, as if they knew to watch out, as if they understood the viper was about to strike.

"I don't know, honestly, I don't," I said.

"Again, Jessa, I don't believe you. You're a liar."

He should know...

"Is Lucas really dead?" I asked, changing the subject to what I really longed to be discussing. Richard didn't take the bait.

"Where did you go? The night you attacked me, tried to ruin me, where did you disappear to?"

There was no way around this one. But I could bend the truth. If I stuck close enough to what happened, then maybe he would believe the lies I was weaving.

"Your son, he got me out."

He spun toward me, face growing pale, jaw slacking in shock.

"Lucas said you'd never forgive me," I continued, holding up my hands in surrender. "He thought you were going to have me executed for treason after what I did. He snuck me out of the palace. I've been traveling by myself ever since."

"My son snuck you out?" His eyes narrowed, realization dawning in them.

"So you don't know what happened to him."

I shook my head. "I don't."

"Isn't it interesting that when we found you, you were stowed away on a train heading North. If you were really so eager to get away from me, then it seems your story doesn't add up."

I scooted back and crawled to the top of the bed, pressing my back against the headboard.

"I came back to see if Lucas was really dead," I croaked.

He silently strode to the window, peering out with his hands clasped behind his back. Outside, winter was nearing its end, but the earth was still in hibernation. I wondered if it reflected the rage simmering under King Richard's exterior.

He glared back at me and stalked forward, finger pointed. "Tell me the full truth. Who else helped you?"

I bit my lip as I shook my head. "No one."

Silence and thick hatred spread between us.

"So be it," he finally said, voice calmer than ever. "First thing tomorrow, you and I are going on a little trip."

I gulped. I didn't need to ask what that meant.

Once Reed got ahold of me, there was no telling what secrets would be revealed. I'd hidden so many in the dark for so long, the idea of them being exposed left me reeling.

He studied me for a minute more, then turned for the door.

"What about my husband?" I called after him. Saying the word husband felt like admitting just how much I loved Lucas.

But Lucas's father, his own flesh and blood, didn't bother to reply or even glance back. He slammed the door with finality, rattling the doorframe, leaving me to my imagination.

✱

Lucas! I called out, homing in on our telepathic connection. *Lucas, are you there? Is that you?* I felt it, felt someone hovering on the other side of my thoughts. Tears pricked at my eyes. Hope flooded my heart. Hope and excitement.

Lucas, I continued, *it's me, Jessa.*

Jessa?

His voice hit me like a gasp for air. I couldn't breathe. My trembling hand slapped against my mouth, holding back the choking sobs. It was him. It was muffled, far off, but it was him. Hearing him was like coming up for air when I didn't even know I was drowning.

Oh, thank God. Are you okay?

There was a long pause.

This is Jessa? he asked, this time sounding somewhat confused.

And that confused me. I blinked, unease settling in.

Yes, of course, where are you? Are you okay?

Another long pause was followed by a sharp reply. *Go away. Get out of my head.*

I sputtered. *What? What do you mean?*

Do I have to spell it out for you? I said, get out of my head! The connection slammed at me, as if he was forcing me out. But why? Why wouldn't he want to talk to me? It made no sense. We hadn't left on the best of terms, but we were closer than we'd been in weeks. He suddenly didn't want anything to do with me? No. This wasn't how this was supposed to go. It didn't make sense.

I won't leave you alone until you tell me you're all right! I challenged. *You have no idea what I just went through, and what I am going to go through. Everyone thinks you're dead, Lucas. I thought you were dead. Do you have any idea what that did to me? I came back to find out the truth!*

Finally, his voice replied. This time not angry, not calm, not confused, but also, not anything. He was completely devoid of any emotion at all. *I'm sorry you had to suffer because of me, but you need to get out of my head right now.*

What? Why? What's going on, Lucas?

I don't know you, okay! he shot back. *This head injury has been tough enough as it is, and now I don't need to start hearing voices. So, I would kindly ask you to leave me alone.*

I momentarily froze. Then I jolted from the bed. What was he talking about? He didn't know me? What was that supposed to mean?

Lucas, you're scaring me.

The feeling is mutual, Jessa. Whoever you are. Now get out! He slammed once again on the connection, this time severing it completely.

I fell back onto the bed. Bile rose into the back of my throat. I rolled to my side, drew my knees in, and clenched my stomach.

Lucas didn't remember me.

The realization of it crashed down, taking all my hopes for our future and turning them to dust. The room spun, and I closed my eyes. My body sank down into the bed, weightless and empty. The man I loved didn't even know who I was. All of this, all I went through, was for nothing. How could that be?

Except all wasn't lost because Lucas wasn't dead. I thanked whatever God was in heaven for that.

Lucas wasn't dead. But he had a head injury.

Lucas wasn't dead. But he also didn't remember me.

Not even a little bit.

And if he'd forgotten me, what else had Prince Lucas forgotten?

FIVE

LUCAS

"This is getting ridiculous." I tugged at the IV in my arm. The nurse, Cathy, raised an eyebrow but injected something into my vein anyway. It burned all the way up my arm. "Come on, Cathy, you could have warned me." I gritted my teeth but winked at her anyway.

"I thought I did," she mused, checking my vitals.

"I need to get out of here. I need to talk to my parents. Where are they?"

Three days. Three days of lying here in this bed. I was a prince and I felt fine, yet I was being treated like a child. And now my patience was wearing thin. Upon waking, I'd recognized the room as one not belonging to the palace or even a hospital, but to the orphanage Mom and I had organized a few years back. Once upon a time it was one of our royal estates, but now it belonged to orphaned children, which was better use in my opinion.

But none of that answered the question: what in the world was I doing here?

Doctor Lawson strolled in, white lab coat flowing behind him, a warm smile on his face. His calculating eyes looked me up and down from behind shiny glasses perched on the tip of his nose. "How's my favorite patient doing today?"

I rolled my eyes. "I'm your only patient."

It was true. It didn't take a genius to gather that something had happened to me and this was where my parents had decided to whisk me away. What it apparently did take a genius to gather was the reason why? Why hide me like this? I had spent the last two days conjuring up every possible explanation for what could be going on back home and I was about ready to burst.

"But why am I here?" I asked the doctor, noticing how he looked away.

It was one of many questions I'd been asking lately. I never got any answers. "Where are my parents?" I continued, lowering my voice and trying to sound reasonable. "Look, I just need to talk to someone who knows what's going on. The way I see it, I should've been placed in a real hospital, right? My parents have hidden me away and I want to know why."

Lawson and Cathy shared a pained look.

The alchemist strolled into the room at that moment, a small smile on her round face. She was cute, with curly blonde hair and thick black glasses. Cute, in a nerdy kind of way. I usually went for the more polished type, but I could bend my rules for this one.

"In a real hospital, you wouldn't have me," she said. "So count yourself lucky your father sent you up here to heal."

I rolled my eyes again.

"Thanks for listening in," I smirked at her, even though, that part was true. Her name was Callie, and she'd apparently been a huge part in my healing since alchemy wasn't something we did in hospitals. But that still didn't explain why I was here. She could have just helped me at the palace. Or broken protocol and healed me at the hospital anyway.

She shrugged, but I caught the pity in her eyes and as much as it killed me, decided to go with it.

"I need answers," I pressed, nodding toward her as if she were my only shot. "I'm not just going to sit around this place in the middle of nowhere while my parents are missing, maybe even hurt." My voice trailed off and I cleared my throat. As much as I was trying to reach them through the heartstrings, it didn't mean I wasn't telling the truth. I was worried.

The doctor fumbled with some paperwork, looking through his pages and pages of notes. I strained my eyes to get a peek, but his handwriting was atrocious. I fell back against the pillows and sighed heavily. Apparently, Doctor Lawson had decided to ignore me. Great.

"Let's go through these questions again, shall we?" he asked, voice clinical and never once looking up at me.

Oh, here we go again.

We'd gone through these questions every day since I'd woken, and my answers weren't just suddenly going to change. This was getting weirder and weirder. I sucked in a breath of the stale air and counted backwards from three, trying to relax into this. Maybe if I answered his questions, he'd finally answer a few of mine.

"What's your name?" he asked.

"Lucas Heart."

"What's the last thing you remember before waking up?"

I sighed. "I remember eating dinner with my parents and going to bed. That's it, nothing exciting."

"You don't remember any kind of accident or maybe an attack?"

Nurse Cathy, busy checking the heart rate monitor, stilled.

Doctor Lawson was no longer studying his notes, but studying me. I eyed him scrupulously. This was a new question and the whole room buzzed with that fact. "I've told you, I have no idea how this happened to me. What do you mean an attack?"

"And how old are you?" He returned back to his list.

I sunk back into the bed, frustrated. "I just turned eighteen." But that didn't stop me from watching him intently, and when his nose quirked, I narrowed my eyes. "What?" I questioned. "Why did you make that face?"

"I didn't make a face."

I spun on the nurse. "You saw it, right? Did he make a face?"

She shrugged and turned away.

"See! You totally did. What is going on, Doc?"

"I am not permitted to say anything until your father gets here."

"And where is my father?" I growled, finally losing my cool. "I woke up here, of all places. I've been sitting around for days with a constant pain in my head. And you keep telling me he's coming but I don't see anyone pulling up that drive, do you?" I motioned to the driveway outside the window, and the white-washed landscape beyond that. We were utterly alone out here.

"And anyway," I continued, "he can just call, can't he? I want my slatebook." I reached my hand out. "Or I can take yours. I'm sure *you* have one; it will have to do."

He bristled. "I'm sorry but I can't do that."

"Trust me," the alchemist girl, Callie, stepped forward. "You don't want to see the newsfeeds right now."

"And why not?" I snapped. Her eyes widened, clearly caught in the crossfire.

I threw my head back against the soft pillow, sighing loudly. "Sorry." I rubbed my eyes, a dull ache forming behind them. "I feel like I'm going crazy. I just want to know why I can't leave this room, why no one will tell me why I'm here."

The doctor shook his head, returning to his paperwork. "We have our orders."

"Can you at least tell me who Jessa is?"

His head popped up, eyes turning into round orbs as he strode forward, shining a light in my pupil.

I waved him off, only to find Callie's smiling face and nurse Cathy sighing a huge breath of relief.

"You remember Jessa?" doctor Lawson asked, a twinge of excitement in his tone.

"I hate to break it to you, but no. That's why I'm asking you guys who she is." I gulped, rubbing my temples. Were these people even listening to me? "She's been in my head or something ... I don't know."

"What do you mean she's been in your head?" the doctor asked, his expression still hopeful. His eyes searched my face, no longer interested in the pages of notes he'd been using for cover earlier.

But as much as I wanted to make progress, I wasn't about to tell the man I'd been hearing voices. I shrugged. "I don't know how to explain it, just that I know that name is important somehow. So, who is she?"

My eyes hopped between the three of them as they shared glances. A tension had gathered in the room; I'd hit a nerve.

"I'm calling your father," the doctor finally replied, breaking the tension and heading for the door. "This is a huge development. He needs to advise me on our next step."

Annoyance pulled at me like a string, tugging on my father and his unknown destination, ever the puppet master.

"Tell my *father* to come visit his *son!*" I called after the doctor. The man didn't pause as he left the room, didn't even seem to hear me. I turned to the nurse. She stood by the window, her arms crossed and her head cocked, studying me with pitying eyes.

"What?" I challenged.

She shrugged, shaking her head. She knew she couldn't say anything. We all knew it. But that didn't make it right

"How are you feeling today?" Callie held up her hands, a green stone centered in her palm. "Need another boost?"

I grimaced. "You know what I really need."

Answers.

Callie bit her lip, consideration flashing in her eyes. "You really don't remember her?" When I shook my head she frowned, her honey eyes filling with deep concern, like she was somehow invested in all of this, too. "Poor Jessa," she whispered.

What was that supposed to mean? Poor Jessa? What about poor Lucas? I let out a frustrated laugh and a sharp pain reverberated from the back of my head. I winced, rubbing the spot as it returned to a dull ache.

"You need to calm down." The nurse motioned to the heart rate monitor, which had begun to speed up. "You're aggravating the wound."

"What do you expect, given my situation? Am I just supposed to sleep and pretend I don't have a whole lot of questions?"

"The pain medicine will kick in any moment," she talked over me. "And yes, I would like for you to get some rest and put the worry out of your mind for now. It's important for your recovery."

She spun on her heel and hustled from the room.

"You sure you don't want some green alchemy before I go?" Callie asked.

I didn't answer. I just looked up to meet her stare. She had that same twisted expression from before, the one that told me she knew much more than she was letting on. I raised a hopeful eyebrow, wishing more than anything that I knew what she was thinking. Her eyes flashed once again. She felt sorry for me.

This was my chance.

"Please..."

"I can't say anything," she whispered. "It's my orders. If I break them I will get in so much trouble. So much. You don't even know."

"I swear I won't tell a soul. I just want to know what happened to me."

"I don't know how it happened, only that you hit your head really hard. Lucas, you have some sort of amnesia. The doctor thinks it's temporary, but it might be permanent."

I shook my head. Amnesia? But I remembered who I was. That didn't make sense.

"Are you messing with me?" I laughed, disbelieving.

"You've forgotten practically a year of your life," she finally relented.

My body sank into the bed like it was made out of quicksand. I didn't fight it, didn't even know how to move. A year of my life? How was that possible?

When I didn't reply, she continued on, wringing her hands, regretful eyes trained on me. "It's supposed to be temporary. I don't know. I haven't been able to reverse it with magic." Her eyes filled with tears. "What if it's not temporary? What will Jessa do?"

I squinted, breathing in the scent of antiseptic. "Who is Jessa?"

She twisted her lip between her teeth, studying me, searching for words.

"Who is she?" I pressed.

"I'm not supposed to say." Her voice came out, barely a squeak.

"Isn't it a little late for that? Besides, I'm your prince. Consider it an order."

That was total crap, and my father pulled rank, but she needed an excuse to tell me the truth. From the torn expression on her face, she wanted me to know.

"Just tell me."

She let out a slow breath. "Lucas, you're married. Jessa is your wife."

I laughed. Now, *that* was ridiculous. Was I honestly supposed to believe I was married? Even if I had forgotten a year, I certainly wouldn't have agreed to a marriage.

"It's true," she whispered. "You're madly in love with her. I've never seen anything like it, the way you look at her."

Confusion traveled through me, starting in my center and spreading to every inch of my body, of my memory, and of my life. "How is that possible? If I love her so much, then why can't I remember her?"

Her eyebrows drew in, and she glared. "Because you hit your head and forgot!" She strode to the door, locking it, then whipped out a slatebook from her back pocket. After few swipes, she turned the screen on me. "See!"

A picture shone back, leaving me grasping at the truth. It was a photo of me. Wearing a tuxedo, I had a massive grin plastered on my face as I looked adoringly at the woman next to me. My arm was wrapped around her, and she was dressed in a white gown so beautiful, it was obvious she had to be a bride. My bride. Her dark hair was curled loosely down and around her shoulders, and she leaned into me, beaming at the camera, bright blue eyes shining like a clear sky. It was most definitely a wedding photograph, but one I had absolutely no recollection of, nor of the woman.

I studied my expression, looking for a crack in the exterior, something to indicate this wasn't real, but all I could see was a man very much in love.

Heat poured over me. I finally let out a breath. Questions danced through my mind. What in the world was going on?

"That's my wife?" I asked. "Seriously?"

"Yes," Callie said, slipping the slatebook back into her pocket.

"I love her?"

"Yes."

"I'm assuming she loves me, too?"

"I always thought so."

I squinted. "What's that supposed to mean?"

She moved to the door faster than humanly possible, yellow alchemy at play. "I've said too much."

Before I could question her further, her small body, dressed head to toe in alchemist black, slid through the door. I debated going after her, demanding more answers and especially demanding she hand over that slatebook. But the IV was busy pumping fluids into my body and as much as I hated it, I couldn't rip it out. I needed it. I didn't really want to roll the thing around with me. My head pounded harder than ever and a sleepy fog was rolling into my mind, clouding all my thoughts.

I knew what came next. Every single time I thought I felt better, thought I could leave this stupid mansion and go back to the palace, more pain would crash over me. Next thing, I'd be laid out in bed within the hour and fighting the pain, drifting into the drug-laced sleep.

I needed to heal, to remember.

If I'd forgotten my wife, what else might I have forgotten?

I needed answers. But something tugged at me, a nagging fear that had wormed its way into my mind. What if I found out the truth, and I didn't like it? What if it was worse than being left in the dark?

I groaned and dropped my head into my hands. My parents had better get here and explain what happened to me before I officially lost it.

★

For the first time since waking up in the estate, I was allowed out of my room. I enjoyed dinner with the children, chatting idly over a hot stew, I realized it was the first moment of peace I'd had since waking into this nightmare. Apparently, the kids had been instructed not to talk about my injury or my past, because the subject stayed out of the conversation.

That was until my favorite little boy, Joey, looped skinny arms around my neck and whispered into my ear. "I really hope Jessa is okay. We miss her."

Then he scampered off, leaving me, once again, feeling like everyone was in on the secret but me.

"Are you finished with that?" a staff member asked over my shoulder, motioning to my empty bowl. I licked my lips, the warm broth settling comfortably in my stomach, and nodded.

She reached to take it, and when I stopped her, her busied expression flushed. "It's okay," I said. "I can help clean up."

"Oh, we couldn't ask that," she replied, brushing a long strand of gray hair out of her face.

I stared into her weary blue eyes for a moment and smiled. "Really, it's okay. I've been bedridden for days and need to move my legs anyway. You'd be doing me a favor."

"Are you sure?" Her mouth set as she frowned, brushing sturdy hands on her apron. This woman, no matter her age, was used to doing her job well and keeping out of trouble.

"You see that doctor over there?" I pointed to the man seated with the nurse on the other end of the table. They were also finishing their meals, leaning close and whispering—probably about me.

She nodded.

"He's going to make me go back to bed at the first opportunity. This is my first time out of that stuffy room and I want to make it last as long as I can." I stood from my chair, picking up the mess and stacking it with the other bowls around me. "Please, let me help."

She chuckled low and shrugged. "You did this last time you were here, you know? Always such a chivalrous boy."

I paused. "Last time?" I wracked my brain, trying to remember the exact moment she was talking about. It had been a while since I'd shared a meal with the orphans. But then Joey had made it sound like he knew Jessa personally…

She clammed up. "Oh shoot, I messed that one up."

I eyed her with interest as her round face turned as red as a tomato. "Wait, last time? Was I here recently?"

She eyed the doctor for a moment and muttered under her breath. "You were here with your lovely fiancé not less than a month ago."

I stilled. "You've met Jessa? Tell me, what's she like?"

She smiled softly. "Kind."

I took in the room, trying to imagine us here, trying to make the connection. The furnishings were solid oak, made to handle years of use. The walls had landscape paintings on each, except for the far wall where children's artwork was featured, rows upon rows of imagination brought to life. But the aroma of hearty broth, the laughter and chatter, and the clinking sound of spoon-scraped bowls being stacked atop each other, didn't spark memories of Jessa. She was like a ghost that everyone else had seen, but I only knew the story.

"Oh, you two were so adorable. I really hope they find her soon," she whispered, eyes hopeful but mouth carefully relaxed.

I gulped, letting out a defeated sigh. "I'm sorry, but I don't remember her."

"Dearest me, I've said too much." She scampered off to take care of cleaning up the younger children.

A sense of disorientation whipped through me, unsettling any comfort I had previously felt. Apparently, my wife was missing?

As I moved about the room, helping with the clean-up, my mind tried fruitlessly to remember Jessa. Who was she, really? And how had she gotten into my head like that? The way she had just spoken in my mind, was I going crazy? Or was it the kind of rare and powerful alchemy, the kind I knew was possible, but that I had never experienced? An offshoot of purple, telepathic magic was something some people would kill to have, and others would do anything to keep hidden. If that was what Jessa was doing, if that was how she got in my mind, then which kind of alchemist was she? The kind who boasted her ability, or the kind who hid it among her deepest secrets?

As I considered the questions, I found my body growing tired. Irritated, I returned to my bedroom and plopped down on the comforter, resigned to end one of the most confusing days of my life. Maybe the doctor was right. Maybe if I got some rest, all of this would heal faster, the memories would return, and with it, the answers.

One knock boomed off the door before it swung open and my father strolled into the room. I sat upright, relief washing through me the moment our eyes met.

"Son!" he exclaimed, rushing forward and wrapping his arms around me in a tight grip. His familiar smell of soap and spice calmed me further. "I'm so glad to hear you've had some of your memories return. I came as soon as the doctor called."

I hugged him back, though the question bothered me. "Why didn't you come when I first woke up?"

He stepped back. "I'm sorry. Things are … complicated."

I raised a brow. "I've been awake for days, living in this bizarre stupor and nobody will tell me anything. I can't take it. What happened to me?"

His face stilled, and I stood to meet his expression. A long moment stretched between us.

He finally relaxed, jaw releasing, shoulders drooping, and energy falling. "Why don't you tell me everything you think happened and I can fill in the gaps?"

I ran a hand through my hair, stopping at the back of my head where the headache persisted. If only it were that easy. His steel eyes zeroed in on me, more intense than I ever remembered, and something deep within me faltered. "I don't know; that's the problem. I don't remember anything from the last year of my life."

He squinted. "Are you sure? They said you asked about Jessa."

I shook my head. I didn't want to get into it. If he knew I'd been hearing voices, it was likely I'd be stuck out here in no-man's land even longer. Which brought me to my next question. "Why am I here? Why aren't I in the palace or at least in the capital city? This isn't exactly the height of civilization."

He sighed and found the chair by the window. I sat on the edge of the bed and watched him carefully, waiting for the truth. He ran his hands through his hair, and I noticed how he'd aged considerably. His hair had become grayer, his wrinkles deeper, his eyes more sunken in, and he'd lost weight. Was he okay?

"A lot has happened, Son. I don't even know where to start."

"I guess, start with Mom. Where is she?" Even as I asked the question, a bubble of fear welled up inside me.

His eyes shot to mine, anguish filling his features instantly. "Your mother is dead. She was murdered. It happened five months ago."

I blinked, my body made of ice. "What?" I sputtered in disbelief.

He nodded solemnly. "It's a long story, but we believe she was murdered by West America. And by the way, we are currently at war with them."

I shook my head. War? We weren't a kingdom of war. New Colony had spent the better part of a century avoiding it at all costs.

"West America also tried to take you out," my father continued. "That's why you're here. We're hiding you. As of right now, the world believes you to be dead."

"That's how I got my injury? They did this to me?" Again, I reached to the back of my head, fingers running over my skull.

"I wish I knew all the details. I do know that someone has been trying to assassinate you ever since your mother's death. This time, they very nearly succeeded. We found you on the edge of death. Luckily our alchemists could heal the wounds, but nobody could help your brain. You were in a coma for a few weeks before you woke up; even still, your memories of the last year may be permanently erased."

I shook my head. "That's not a good thing."

Something in his face twitched. Did he agree? Finally, he nodded and cleared his throat. "Which brings me to my next point."

"Jessa?" I needed to know more about this mystery woman who had infiltrated my thoughts.

He nodded. "We need to talk about your wife. It's time you learned the truth about why that girl really married you."

★

My legs ached to run. I longed to feel the endorphins rush through my body, longed to hear my heartbeat instead of the million questions that rolled in my head. But everything else in my body told me to take it easy; I wasn't fully healed yet. Sure, on the outside I looked as healthy as ever, but the headaches still plagued me, a constant reminder of my lost memories.

I groaned and continued on my walk around the orphanage grounds. The snow had melted, leaving pools of mud. It caked my shoes, but I wasn't bothered. At least I was outside, where the air was crisp and refreshing, where I could breathe, where the sun could warm my face and I could try to piece my life back together without Richard standing over my shoulder.

He hadn't left my side in three days, constantly quizzing me on my past. This behavior was exactly why he and I were usually at odds. He was just so demanding, his presence so consuming that it took away from everyone else. If anything was going to help my headaches, it was getting away from him.

Lucas? The voice shot through my mind.

Her voice.

Lucas, are you there? It's me.

I stopped midstride and put my hands on my waist, huffing into the blue sky above. My breath spread before me, like smoke billowing into the cold air. If only I could see this girl too, then maybe I could decide for myself what she really meant to me.

Jessa, I replied. *Yeah, I'm here.* It was strange, that I didn't have to audibly talk and yet we could have a whole conversation. But then again, maybe it shouldn't have been strange, considering who she was.

625

You're using magic to do this, right? I continued. *My father told me you're an alchemist, which explains how you're able to get into my head. But he never mentioned that you had this particular talent.*

Did you tell him about this? Lucas, he can't know! Her voice came through the connection, sharp and fearful.

I paused, considering the implications. *You're afraid of him, aren't you?*

As I should be! she rushed, her words all jumbling together. *He hasn't followed through on his threat to take me to the frontline, but I know it's only a matter of time.*

That's probably because he's here checking up on me.

Where's here? Lucas, where are you?

I'm somewhere where I hopefully won't be assassinated. You ask a lot of questions.

And you aren't really answering any of them. She quieted for a while, long enough that I wondered if she'd severed the connection. Finally, her voice came through as a soft surrender. *Do you remember me yet?*

I squinted into the horizon, studying the empty landscape but for a few trees.

I sighed. *That is a question I can answer. No, I don't remember you. Not even a little bit.*

There was a long silence before a simple, *Oh,* filtered through my head.

Sorry. I squeezed my hands into fists, exasperated. *I don't know what happened to me, how I got this head injury, but I think maybe you can enlighten me.*

What is that supposed to mean? she bit back.

The pain was returning to the back of my head, but I pressed on.

You were the last one to see me before whatever happened to me. Richard thinks it's possible that you were the one who did this to me. That you tried to kill me.

I would never! I love you.

I scoffed. *Really? If that's true, then why are you with the Resistance?*

Yes, Richard had told me all about this Resistance group trying to undermine everything he was doing, making it harder for us to win this war against West America. It was bad enough to have one major enemy, but to have another one working within our very borders? They needed to be stopped. Even I knew that!

Your dad is trying to turn you against me. Don't let him, she begged.

Are you denying it?

Another long pause. Finally, she let out a sharp, *No.*

I huffed. *So why would a Resistance spy marry the prince to the kingdom she's trying to take down? Sounds a whole lot like treason if you ask me.* I laughed again. *And I'm supposed to believe you love me? Pick a story.*

If you could remember the last year, you'd know I'm telling the truth.

It's all very convenient for you, Jessa. And tell me again where you were when I hit my head?

You got me out of the palace before that ever happened! You sent me away to protect me!

I couldn't believe this woman. Her story was so twisted, and Richard's was a clear, logical line. Who did she expect me to believe? He was my father, and yes, he was intense and incredibly persistent when he wanted to get his way. He wasn't the best dad or husband, and at times he drove me mad with frustration. He could be cold-hearted, and he could be oblivious to people who weren't on his radar. But was he evil? Was he the tyrant Jessa thought he was? I didn't think so.

I'm almost healed, I continued. *And when I can convince my father to let me out of hiding, I'm going to come with him to interrogate you. You're part of the Resistance, you've already admitted it. You were with me the night I hit my head. They found me in the Guardian wing, Jessa! You're an alchemist! What do you expect me to think? If anyone knows what happened to me, it's probably you.*

You're making a huge mistake!

And I intend to find out whatever dirty little secrets you've been keeping from my family, I finished with an angry sneer.

Maybe you should look in the mirror! You were Resistance before I ever was.

I froze, caught off guard, but only for a moment. *I highly doubt that.*

It's true, she snapped. *You were the one who convinced me to keep my red alchemy a secret from your father for as long as I could. You were the one who wanted us to get married in the first place. You made a bargain with your father, so he would allow it. And in the end, it was you who snuck me out of the palace after our wedding. You knew your father was about to figure everything out and wanted to protect me.*

Why would I be Resistance? I'm the prince!

Because you found out the truth about your father. He's a bad man, Lucas. He's done terrible things and you didn't want anything to do with his legacy.

Bad how? What aren't you telling me?

You say you can't trust me, but how can I know if I can trust you? Apparently, you're right back in his pocket.

I took a deep breath and let it out with an angry growl. *You can't trust me,* I finally said. It was the truth. I didn't know anything about this girl, had no memory of ever meeting her, let alone wanting to marry her or doing the things she'd claimed.

Perfect. Her tone was angry now. *I get captured coming back to try and help you and now I have nobody I can trust. Not even you.*

Something deep inside tugged at me but I refused to let her manipulations sway my opinion. I also wouldn't let my father do the same. I needed to figure out the truth all on my own.

Maybe you should stop talking to me like this.

Fine by me. And by the way, maybe you should check yourself before you blab all your secrets to your father. You might not be able to remember it, but there are good reasons why you hate him.

I'd never been best friends with my dad or anything like that, but hate? That was a big word.

I'll figure it out on my own.

Good. I also hope you figure out if you love me or not while you're at it. It'd be nice to know if I still have a husband.

I didn't reply. What was there left to say? I pushed the connection away. Screw it! I ran. The pain in my head exploded with the effort but I ignored it, instead clinging to the exhilarating feel of movement in my body. This was freedom.

Jessa and I were married. So what? I didn't remember making any vows. She was Resistance, a traitor, and had no place in my life, at least not while I figured things out. If it came down to it, if I learned the truth and it didn't include real love, I would find a way to end our marriage. My father had already suggested the idea; he said we could play it either way, though his preference was a quick annulment. I wasn't convinced either way.

First, I needed to persuade him to let me go back into society. Right now, the world thought I was a dead man. Maybe it was better that way. I didn't know. But I figured if I was going to get answers, we probably needed to start with the truth.

No more hiding.

SIX

SASHA

"**C**ome back with me," Christopher said for what was probably the fifth time in the last few days.

"You know I can't do that."

Dad frowned, tugging awkwardly on the sleeves of his smudged white shirt, but nodding. He did know. In fact, he understood better than most. I actually thought, given the opportunity, he would've chosen to stay and fight, too. But Lacey and Mom were safe on the other side of the country and he needed to be with them. They'd been separated for too long.

"Promise me, if given the chance, you'll help Jessa?" His expression was torn with regret. This had to be an impossible choice for him, having his family spread out and one of his daughters missing.

"You don't even have to ask," I said. "If the girl wasn't so stubborn she'd be the one you'd want going back with you, not me."

His face fell, the shadows under his eyes appearing darker. "Don't say that."

"I know," I replied. But did I?

I'd forgiven my parents for abandoning me all those years ago. The truth was, they didn't know what they were agreeing to when they gave me up. They didn't realize they'd never see me again. At least, that was what my father told me. He'd said he knew I would be raised with the alchemists, but not that the officers who'd taken me would completely cut my family from my life.

I sighed. No matter what happened, or what my parents had believed, it was in the past. It was over and done and there wasn't anything anyone could do about it anymore. And truthfully, it wasn't their fault. It was King Richard who was to blame—it was the result of a failed system.

He leveled his head with mine. "I mean it, don't say that. Your mother and I love you just as much as your sisters."

"Okay." I smiled, the feel of it on my cheeks was tight and forced.

He meant what he said, but that didn't mean I wasn't still hurt. His kind words didn't take away the feelings of abandonment that lingered within me. Maybe only time would heal that, or maybe it would never heal.

"How's your friend doing?" He dropped his gaze, digging a line along the dirt with his boot. "The one you came back with who was hurt?"

I smiled wide, thinking of Tristan. "He's fine. I healed him as soon as I could."

"He's lucky to have you." Christopher winked. He put an arm on my shoulder, squeezing once. "And you're lucky to have him. Take care of each other out there."

I nodded, biting my lip, fighting the urge to hug him. It was stupid. I should just hug him.

"Are you sure you can't come with me?" he asked one more time.

We stood together outside the barracks where I'd spent the last three days anxiously awaiting orders for another mission. People rushed around us; it seemed everyone had a job to do but me. They paid us little attention. Dad watched me, and as if sensing what I needed, he pulled me into a hug.

I breathed him in, gazing out at the distance, trying to focus on something other than the torn emotions inside. The sun was rapidly setting over the horizon, the orange semi-circle dipping low and sending out shards of golden light in its wake. With it, a biting chill had settled into my bones.

"I'm sure," I replied. Something came bursting from me in that moment. Love, maybe? I hugged him back as hard as I could, letting myself sink into him like I had when I was a child. It was unexpected. From his quick intake of breath, I gathered he hadn't been expecting it either. This was new for both of us.

"Take care of yourself," he mumbled into my hair. "When all of this is over, we will be a family again." Then he released me and, giving me one final nod, walked away.

I hoped he was right.

But at the end of the day, my mission wasn't to my family; it wasn't even to West America. It was to take care of the alchemists. When this was over, someone needed to make sure alchemy wasn't treated like a weapon anymore. Magic wasn't something to be feared, but rather, something to be celebrated and used for good.

I chuckled at the madness of the idea. When had I become such an idealist? As long as those in charge had control over alchemy, our freedom wasn't a likely scenario. It was too tempting of a power, and too ... different.

But I had to try.

I walked around the base camp for over an hour, ignoring the biting air, trying to survive the torrent of emotions that burned me. Night fell, and still, I continued, arms tight around myself, coat doing little to keep out the cold, boots clomping on the crisp earth. Under the icy air was the faint smell of gasoline and gunpowder. The camp was a mix of metal buildings and thick canvas tents, with clear roads between the buildings. It was sparse but had everything we needed.

Everything I needed was here.

What if I really do want to be part of my family? Should I have left with Dad? I shook the fool-hearted thought away. This was my place. I needed to fight, and I couldn't do it from anywhere else. Still, why did I feel so broken inside? I'd just given up the opportunity to get out of this mess and let someone else deal with it. Why did I have to be so determined and passionate about protecting the alchemists, when it was my own heart that needed tending?

I groaned and dug my boot into the dirt, leaning forlornly against the nearest building. The cold metal bit into my back, not that I cared. A hot tear fell down my cheek, and I hurried to wipe it away.

"Ugh, get a grip," I said, slapping my cheeks. I'd turn into Jessa by morning at this rate! I hated acknowledging my emotions. And I especially hated to cry. It was too ... exposing. And weak.

"Are you okay?" Mastin's voice split through the darkness like a bullet.

I closed my eyes for a second, shame burning, before turning to meet his worried gaze.

"You've been avoiding me," I stated.

He nodded once and then moved to rest against the building next to me.

"Why?" I asked, though I was pretty sure I already knew. He was angry with me for nearly getting us killed back in New Colony. It didn't take a genius to know that. Truth was, I didn't blame him.

"You confuse me," he finally said.

I glowered at his profile, the darkness broken only by the security lights and the sounds of distant soldiers. "What about me is so confusing?"

"It's not you, exactly. It's not even what you do because your actions are rather predictable." He seemed to be weighed down by his statement.

"Wow, thanks," I grumbled.

"It's how I am when I'm with you that confuses me." The light caught the planes of his face, eyes piercing.

I let out a breath. "So actually, it's you who confuses you. Not me."

He laughed, an addictive sound I wasn't used to hearing from him. It unnerved me, setting me off my axis, as if everything I saw in him was magnified by that one single laugh.

"What is Tristan to you?"

I stilled. His question threw me off guard. "He's my best friend."

"Is he more?"

"No." But even as I said it, I wondered if that was the truth. Lately, even I didn't know what Tristan was to me.

"He's a good man," Mastin stated.

I nodded. "He's a good friend." I emphasized the word friend.

"Nothing more?"

I stared at the ground, dragging my foot along the dirt in a line. "There was a time when I thought maybe Tristan and I would become more." My voice caught in my throat. "But no, we're friends and that's all. That's what is best for both of us."

"I don't think he agrees." His voice was low and questioning.

I laughed, the feel of it bitter in my lying mouth. If he'd overheard the conversation Tristan and I had back at the farm, the conversation where Tristan had told me to date Mastin, I don't think he'd be so argumentative. "Trust me," I said.

He leaned in closer, shifting so we were only inches apart. I studied his green eyes, now shadowed in the darkness. His boyish scent washed over me, making me almost hungry. I fought the urge to roll my eyes at the thought. "Still, I don't think I can compete with that." He said as he held me in his intense eyes and then they flicked to my lips. A sense of urgency welled up inside me, the hunger begging for a taste.

"Who says it's a competition?" I whispered.

His eyes shot back to mine. "Isn't it?"

Never breaking eye-contact, I slowly shook my head.

Then I closed the distance between us, pressing my lips to his. He stilled for a moment, holding me at arm's length, but then pulled me against him. My mind emptied as he deepened the kiss. For once in our relationship, I was happy to let him take the lead. He was relief and danger all in one, safety and risk. He was everything I wanted. As my lips muffled his inner groan, I wondered if maybe I was everything he wanted, too.

★

My legs burned. My breath raced in and out as my heart rate climbed. I pushed on, one foot in front of the next, careening forward. It did little to quiet the thoughts tumbling in my head. Normally running was my escape, the best way to work through my problems—or better yet, to forget them entirely.

Today was not that day.

I careened to a stop, panting for breath, shoulders heaving up and down, waiting for my body to adjust. The morning sun pressed down, the unseasonably warm day reaching into my core. A smile swelled on my salty lips. A bead of sweat trickled down my temple, and I wiped it away with the back of my forearm. The nerves anchored like a rock in my stomach, I stood, taking in my surroundings.

People bustled between the rudimentary steel buildings. The smells of ozone, packed dirt, and rain on its way circled me like a shiny-eyed crow, reminding me of where I was, of what I was, and what I needed to do.

Today I had to tell Tristan about Mastin.

It wasn't as if Tristan hadn't seen this coming—he clearly had. Tristan knew me better than anybody. And he and I were just friends, had always been just friends, so it wouldn't be a big deal that I was dating someone. He would probably be happy for me and that would be the end of it.

Still, I hated how much I was bothered by the thought of telling him.

I walked down the gravel path that led to the main gym. Although Tristan liked to run, the man had always been into boxing, and that's where I'd likely find him. I pushed the nerves down, opened the heavy door, and strolled inside.

The first thing that hit me was the heat, so stuffy and thick, it was like walking into a wall of air. That could be blamed on the multiple bodies lifting weights and boxing in a small building without air conditioning. But it was the smell that hit me next, an odor truly assaulting, like an onion that had been left to rot in the sun all day. I wrinkled my nose, held my breath, ignored the grunts of testosterone-infused men, and scanned the room.

It didn't take long to find him. My heart dropped.

His dark hair shined with sweat, his expression set in determination. He landed a punch on his opponent with so much force the other guy fell onto his butt. Unfortunately, the other guy was Mastin.

"What the hell?" I ran forward. "Are you two fighting?"

Mastin sprang back up, barely fazed by the blow. But I could tell he was frazzled, not only by the line of his mouth but by the swiftness of his rebound. Frazzled *and* angry. The pair didn't glance my way, instead matching each other blow for blow and kick for kick. Relief washed through me to see they had gloves covering their fists, considering their punches seemed to be fueled by more than the need for exercise. Tristan's eyes blazed as he took a punch. Mastin jumped out of the way, a goading smirk curving his hardened mouth.

"Seriously!" I yelled at them. "This is not normal."

Another round of punches flew, blood and spit spraying from both men's bruising faces. The gloves were making little difference. Couple of idiots! They needed to be focused on the common enemy, not each other.

"We're just sparring," Tristan growled. "Nothing to worry about. Isn't that right, Mastin?"

"Right," Mastin grunted, and then he dove for Tristan, who used the sharp jut of his knee in retaliation.

Most of the other soldiers had stopped to gawk at the show. I sent the group a pleading look, knowing they could stop this. But they only cheered the fighters on further with their hollers and bets. I rolled my eyes, annoyed, but also angry. This spectacle was ridiculous and embarrassing. I put my hands on my head as Mastin took a right hook to the chin, spittle and blood arcing from his face. I grimaced, sharing the pain. I should walk away, let them get this immaturity out of their systems. But my feet were rooted to the floor of packed dirt. My fingers itched to use my magic and intervene, but that might make things worse.

Mastin rounded a kick right into Tristan's kneecap, and he fell with a pained yelp. Mastin used the momentum to attack, jumping on Tristan's back.

Oh, screw it!

Luckily, my necklace was refreshed with new stones, and I connected with the yellow. It spun out in little strings before settling into me. I jumped between the guys and used my strength to separate them. It was easy, as if they were children and not grown men practically twice my size.

"Sasha, don't!" Mastin growled.

"I got this," Tristan snapped, pushing back at me. I didn't budge.

"If you two aren't going to act like civilized adults then I'll have to do it for you," I said.

I stood my ground, keeping them apart with outstretched arms. For a moment, they pressed against my palms, each flailing to get at the other. Mastin stood back first, arms crossed over his chest as he huffed the air from his lungs. He studied Tristan, then me, pained calculation lighting his jade eyes as they flicked back and forward between us.

I turned back and switched to the green magic, letting it pour into Tristan, who was now unfocused and giving in to the pain. He was bleeding in a few places, and I was certain his knee was broken after that kick. His face scrunched in agony as he held his leg slightly off the ground, finally sinking to the earth, a low groan emitting between gritted teeth. The green magic wormed its way into all the broken parts, healing him in a matter of moments and clearing the pain from his face.

But only momentarily.

He jumped up, brushing himself off and leveling me with a steady gaze. "We were fine."

"That's right," Mastin added, voice deadpan. "We were sparring, a little fun between friends."

Tristan scoffed. "Yeah."

"You two are so full of it." I threw my hands in the air. "But fine, if you want to beat the crap out of each other, so be it." I pointed east and glared. "Forget that our actual enemies are out there, right now, planning ways to kill us all. Sorry if I think your time would be better served doing other things than injuring yourselves!"

"You're right," Tristan said, backing away. "Forget it."

He stormed from the gym, anger rolling in his wake. I ran after him, catching him just outside the gym.

"What's wrong with you?"

He spun to face me, squinting against the sun. "Shouldn't you be back there helping your boyfriend?" All the venom had left his voice now, only defeat remained. Any anger I'd been harboring was lost in an instant.

I stopped, lost for words. Was Mastin my *boyfriend*? Part of me bristled at the word. Such a needy little word it was. But another part of me lurched forward. We hadn't technically defined it as such, we were busy with the war, after all. But we were definitely something. And we had agreed to see where that something went, at least when we weren't busy kicking enemy butts and saving the world from evil dictators.

Last night had been amazing. But it had also been private.

"How do you know?" I asked. And here was the real question. "Why do you care? We're friends, you and I. You were the one who told me I should date Mastin in the first place."

He looked up to the sky and closed his eyes, jaw clenched tight.

"Are you counting backwards from ten right now?" I challenged.

It was one of his ways to cope when he was angry. Tristan hated to be angry, said it made him feel like his father. I'd never met the man, but Tristan had confided in me long ago that his father had been abusive toward him and his mother. He still felt guilt for getting out because he'd had to leave her behind in the process. That had been years ago, but the pain of it still lived on.

He snapped his eyes open, raking his hands through his hair. "Yes, I know about it. The guy told me."

"I was supposed to be the one to tell you. I'm sorry." Embarrassment washed over me and I shifted squeamishly on my feet.

He shrugged, his face softening. "It's okay. Really, I just want you to be happy." He paused, holding my gaze. "If he's who you want then that's okay with me. I won't fight him again or anything."

"I thought you said it wasn't fighting, just good-natured sparring?" I rolled my eyes.

He laughed. "It started off that way, if that's any consolation."

I nodded, though I wasn't sure it was.

"Anyway, I've got to go." Tristan backed away. "I'll see you around." He turned and jogged away.

I stormed back to the gym in search of Mastin. He was lifting dumbbells and smiled broadly when he saw me, the earlier pain in his expression now vanished. And that was fine by me. I didn't want to deal with jealousy; I had already picked him!

It appeared he'd already wiped away the blood by the look of his dirtied shirt. His biceps pulsed as he lifted, eyes squinting through the bruising that was purpling his cheeks. I placed my hand over my necklace with the intention to take care of him, but he brushed me away with the shake of his head.

"I'm fine."

I wasn't sure if it was on principle or because so many of his friends were watching, soldiers who were still uneasy about my magic. Now they'd seen it in action again, they were staring at me like I was contagious. A few were standing with arms folded over their chests, eyes glaring in attempts at intimidation. And still, others seemed to pay me no attention at all, going about their business.

But they all had one thing in common. They all kept their distance.

"All right," I replied to Mastin. "Let's get out of here."

Mastin's smile curved and he dropped the dumbbells to the earth with a thud and a small cloud of dust. We strode out together, a few whistles in our wake.

The moment we left the gym and had a moment of privacy, he ran his hand down my arm and laced our fingers together. We walked down the path between the buildings. Quiet for a while.

"Why did you tell Tristan?" I asked. "We agreed I was going to do that."

"He asked." Mastin shrugged. "I wasn't going to lie to him. And besides, you don't need that guy."

I tugged on his arm. "Don't say that. You know he's my best friend."

He pulled me close, wrapping his arms around me, a knowing smile lifting his lips. "Yeah, I know. But he doesn't get to do this." He widened his stance, dropping closer to my level, eyes flicking to my lips.

He softly kissed the side of my face, trailing the tip of his nose down my jaw until his mouth found mine. I sunk into him, losing myself in the feel of it. We stayed like that for a few minutes, caught up in each other, when someone cleared their throat loudly, breaking us apart.

Mortified, I jumped back, wiping my lips and staring a hole into the gravel.

"Hello father," Mastin said calmly over my shoulder.

Blood rushed to my cheeks, and I turned to face General Nathan Scott. As usual, he was flanked by men dressed in tan army fatigues. They watched us carefully, like we'd committed a crime and had been caught in the act.

Or something like that ...

After a long, tense minute, Nathan laughed. It bellowed out of him freely.

"I wondered when you two were going to get together." He eyed us, face growing serious again. "This better not get in the way of our mission here, neither of you need the distraction."

"It won't," Mastin said and I nodded. But was that even possible? At that moment, I was most definitely distracted by Mastin.

"All right then." Nathan nodded. "Sasha, I'd like you to spend the day with me. We have a new prisoner, an alchemist. And I'd like your help with this one."

"I'm coming, too." Mastin inched forward.

"Very well." Nathan strode away purposefully, motioning over his back for us to follow.

Mastin slipped his hand into mine again, and despite my better judgment, I warmed at the attention. I ought to be annoyed with myself. This thing with Mastin, whatever this was, needed to stay second to what mattered most: protecting the alchemists.

As our group neared the area of the prison, the very one I'd helped to set up, a sense of foreboding fell over me, and also, a trickling of guilt. How many more alchemists was West America going to catch? And how many more times would I be forced to watch my own kind be beaten and tortured, treated like animals and punished for their magic?

I gathered determination within me like the magic that pulsed through my veins and followed the group inside.

SEVEN

LUCAS

"**A**re you really going to try to conduct your business from here?" I said, leaning against the doorframe of my father's, apparently new, office. He'd set up shop in one of the guest rooms of the orphanage. Hunched over a small desk in the middle of the makeshift office, he looked completely out of place and utterly uncomfortable.

"Until I decide what steps to take next, this is my new office." He sighed and reclined back in his chair, folding his arms over his broad chest, shirt stretching with the movement. He wore casual clothing. Well, about as casual as he got, anyway. The first two buttons on his starched white shirt were undone.

"Lucas, I don't know what to do with you. That's the truth."

"What do you mean?" I stepped into the room and slumped into a red velvet armchair, body relaxing like butter left to melt in the sun. The back of my head pounded, the persistent throb ebbing with wave after wave of dizziness. At least it wasn't the sharp knife it had been yesterday. At least the churning nausea had subsided.

Richard leveled me with a sparkling gaze. "I announced to the entire kingdom that you were dead."

I raised an eyebrow and smirked. "Why?"

"What else was I supposed to do? Once again, someone made an attempt on your life, and this time they very nearly succeeded. You were in a coma for over a week and even our best alchemists couldn't pull you out of it."

"And that's how I ended up here," I moaned. It wasn't that I disliked the orphanage. I loved the people here. But I had nothing to do here, and I still hadn't been given a new slatebook. The doctor said if I got misinformed it was possible I wouldn't regain my memories. I wasn't sure I bought it.

"Yes," Richard continued. "I decided to move you to an unknown location and wait until you woke up to take further action. It was easier to tell the world that you were dead—still is." He rested his elbows on the collage of papers and open journals on the desktop, linking long uncalloused fingers. "This way, whatever assassin West America sent, Jessa or someone else, will back off. Once we have more answers, we can tell the truth about what really happened."

I still hadn't told anyone about mine and Jessa's telepathic connection. It seemed nobody knew to ask, and from her reaction, I had to guess it was a secret. Now that I knew what it was, that I wasn't crazy, I should've said something. But I didn't. I had too many suspicions to let go of my secrets just yet.

"It makes sense." I nodded, rubbing my stubbly chin with my palm. "But you also have to consider the fact that I did wake up and I'm fine now. Am I just supposed to stay hidden until the war is over?"

"That's not a bad idea."

The very idea of being stuck here sent dread sweeping through my body. Growing up, I'd often thought of the palace in the same way. Always trapped within its stone walls usually left me itching to get out, but at least that had been my home. At least that had space to breathe and answers instead of secrets.

I bristled. "But I want to help, *and* I want my memories back. I'm not going to remember anything stuck here. Besides, don't you want me to remember who killed me?" I pointed to my head. "The answer could be unlocked if I was taken to the scene of the crime."

"You're not going to the palace," Richard snapped. "It's too dangerous. We already discussed this. That wife of yours is the number one suspect; we just need to confirm it and find out who her contacts are."

I watched him carefully, noticing the way he broke eye-contact, and for a moment, I wasn't so sure he was being honest about Jessa. The way she talked to me wasn't the way a person talked to someone they'd just tried to murder. No, she'd seemed completely horrified at the accusation. But as I studied my father, I knew he was set in his assessment of the situation. Which meant I wasn't going back home. Not yet.

"Okay, fine. Why don't we work from here, together? I want to avenge Mother's death just as much as you do. How can I help?"

He stared at me for a long moment something in his gaze shifted. "Okay, Lucas, that's something I can agree to."

"Great, where do we start?"

"One of my most trusted advisors is en route as we speak. I'd planned to keep you hidden while he and I discussed the latest reports. You can join in on our meeting."

I nodded, a little surprised with myself. I wasn't normally the type to care about politics. But then again, I *did* have a head injury. I chuckled to myself, the little bit of comic relief going a long way to ease my inner turmoil.

Richard stood and sidestepped around the desk, placing a heavy hand on my shoulder. "You're missing a lot of information, but I will do my best to fill you in. You are going to be the king one day and you're right, I should let you help."

I peered up, meeting his steely gaze. His eyes softened with pride.

"I have to admit, I like this new Lucas."

I cocked my head at the comment.

New Lucas? What was that supposed to mean? Had I really changed so much in the last year? A warning bell rang inside my head, and I held my tongue, tucking the questions away for a later day. It wasn't like I didn't already have secrets from my father, secrets I'd kept hidden for years.

My curse of alchemy being the number one culprit.

But I didn't use it much, not since I'd found a way to keep it locked away. What else had I locked away over the last year? From the way he was looking at me, the relief in his eyes, it almost seemed like we'd hated each other. Jessa made it sound like that. But had it really come to that?

While we had always had a rift between us, I'd never hated him.

"Anything else?" he asked, a question in his eyes. "Is there something you would like to tell me?"

I shook my head.

I'd learned at a young age that he believed magic was a blasphemy to be controlled. He already had enough hold on me. I didn't want to add another.

"Are you sure?" he pressed. "Son, you can trust me. If we're going to get through this, we have to be honest with each other."

I smiled, guilt tugging deep inside. "I know." I stood and walked to the door, running my hands down my jeans. I'd be expected to dress up for dinner. "I'll see you tonight."

The weight of his stare bored holes in my already aching head, but I refused to turn back.

Jessa claimed that I'd worked for the Resistance, too. If that was true, it meant I'd wanted to see my own father dethroned. But that couldn't be. The idea of it twisted and caused my headache to return with a vengeance. Still, the question remained: who was telling the truth and who was the liar?

Maybe they were both being dishonest. Maybe I was simply a pawn on their shared chessboard and not the one playing the game.

✸

I placed a stack of gravy-stained plates on the counter. They clanked together as one of the kitchen staff patted my arm and took them to the sink. The scent of dish soap and hot steam filled the room. The playful sounds of giggling and pattering footsteps on the floor above made me smile. It felt good to be up and moving. I went back to the dining room and leaned against the doorframe, watching as the staff expertly reset the table.

When the orphans had finished their meal, helping with the clean-up had made me feel useful, even if I hadn't dined with them tonight. Instead, I would be eating dinner with my father and his guest. The table was quickly finished and ready for us. Crystal wine flutes, silver cutlery, and white porcelain plates all gleamed under the low lights. The staff scampered off, and still, I waited beside the oak door, eager for whatever came next. It wasn't like me to care so much about this kind of thing, but with my memory—and my life—on the

639

line, things had changed.

On the other side of the space was another door and my eyes flicked to it the second I heard them. Voices, murmuring conversation, the low rustle of my father's voice, filtered through the door. He talked fast, urgent, and without thinking of the consequences, I rushed forward, pressing my ear to the door, straining to eavesdrop.

A woman's velvety soft voice joined the men.

"I hope you don't mind that we came along," she purred. "I simply had to apologize for my husband in person."

A male voice interjected. "Yes, truly, Your Highness, I'm so sorry. I deeply regret my insensitive and unwarranted actions toward you."

"It bordered on treason," Richard replied in an unreadable tone.

"You're absolutely right. I let my role as a father get in the way of what was best for this kingdom."

"And he had too much alcohol," the woman added. "It was foolish."

There was a long pause. Finally, Richard replied with a relaxed tone. "It's forgiven. And forgotten…for now. I am known for my strength, but I am not without mercy."

The last part didn't ring true, and I wondered if the people on the other side of the door agreed.

Another pause, and then the woman spoke. "Thank you, your Royal Highness. You are too gracious."

"Yes, thank you," the man added, voice as washed with relief as a summer rainstorm.

"And I think you're right," Richard continued. "I do think we all had a little bit too much to drink that night."

The group laughed together. The woman's high cackle and the man's low guffaw sounded a touch too forced. Something intense had certainly happened between this couple and my father, and I wanted to know what it was.

Add it to the list of questions.

"Speaking of family, mine is here as well," Richard said smoothly. "Or, what little there is left of it, I should say."

"What?" The woman's question came out sharp.

"Lucas!" Richard's voice boomed through the door I skulked behind. "Please come in now, Son."

Finally! I flung open the door and strolled into the dining room. Not two, but three new faces gaped back at me. They were vaguely familiar, but I couldn't quite place the family. I assumed they were part of the royal court and I'd dined with them before, but not recently. Well, not in recent *memory*. They stared at me as if I was stark naked or brandishing a butcher knife or something equally unsettling.

"Um, hi." I cleared my throat. "Thanks for letting me join you. I've been getting bored up here, hidden away like this. It will be nice to have a change in pace for the evening."

"You're alive?" a new voice breathed in a soft cry. I frowned at the girl who was so striking in resemblance to the couple, that I knew she had to be their daughter. She brought her dainty hand to her painted lips as she gawked at me like I was the stuff made of nightmares and redemption. Her auburn hair fell in soft waves around her shoulders and her pale cheeks filled with color.

"Uh, yeah." I shrugged.

Richard's laugh boomed good-naturedly, as if to break the tension. It didn't work. Nobody took their eyes off me.

"There was another assassination attempt on my son the night of his wedding," Richard said. "You already know Jessa disappeared, that much was true. But Faulk and I made the call to twist the truth on my son's behalf."

I raised my hand sheepishly. "Not dead."

"He's been in hiding. I'm still trying to decide what to do about him."

The family was still ogling me like I had risen from the dead. The man's eyes were wild and slowly, so slowly, he inched himself back toward the door.

"Unfortunately, Lucas has suffered quite a bit of memory loss," my father continued. "He hasn't been able to identify his attacker yet, but I'm confident, given time, it will all come back to him."

Richard was still convinced Jessa had been the one to harm me. He'd gone into great detail about how she'd tried to get to him first, and how she wasn't to be trusted because of her red alchemy. I had taken everything on face value, but the more I mulled it over, the more I questioned it. And now this man, with his face so clearly terrified to see me alive? What part of the story was I missing? And what did it have to do with him?

"You really don't remember anything?" The older woman glided forward with complete assuredness and ran inquisitive milky-blue eyes up and down me, inspecting.

I shrugged. "I know who I am. I remember plenty. But the brain injury made it so that I've forgotten the last year."

Her eyes widened. "Remarkable."

"More like annoying."

"You don't remember Jessa?" the quiet member of the family asked. When I caught her eyes she quickly looked down at the floor, as if ashamed, pink burning the edges of her cheekbones. But then a small smile formed on her rouge lips and I wasn't so sure. "And you probably don't remember me?" Her head popped back up, eyes sparkling under long, dark lashes.

"No." The back of my head was starting to throb again. "I think that my memory-impaired status has been sufficiently established. There's nothing more to say about it, really." I cleared my throat, sheepishly. I hoped I didn't sound rude. "We're here for dinner and a debriefing, correct?"

"That's correct," Richard motioned to the table and swept his hand toward his guests. "Lucas, this is Mark, Sabine, and Celia Addington."

An air of civility fell upon the group as they shook my hand before we all approached the fine white tablecloth and the array of place settings on top. The rich smell of expertly prepared food wafted through the air, warm and welcoming. I pulled out a chair for Celia, the legs scraping the polished oak floor. Her eyebrows drew in as she sat, puzzlement returned to her face as she peered up at me. There wasn't anything I could do to unveil her reasoning, so I found my own chair, resolved to pay attention to every word, said and unsaid.

Richard pulled off the gleaming silver dome covering his plate, leaned over his roasted chicken and vegetables, and inhaled. "Let's eat."

The early tension dissipated over dinner, replaced with a new sense of urgency as we discussed the status of the war and the recent battle. New Colony wasn't faring as well as we'd like. We had taken more ground, only to be pushed back again. The battles were a mix of weaponry, magic, and even hand-to-hand combat. Our losses were nearing two hundred casualties, but West America's were far higher, reaching into the thousands.

Sometime during the discussion, I stopped eating and pushed vegetables from one side of my plate to the other. I dropped my head into one palm, fighting the growing throb, gritting my teeth against the distraction.

Occasionally, I would meet Celia's gaze, simply because she was constantly watching me. I could feel those eyes on me like a shadow. She never said a word, just stared as if she knew all my secrets, as if she were the greatest one of all.

We wrapped up by indulging in a rich chocolate cake. I took a couple of bites and instantly regretted it, the dessert sitting in a pained lump low in my stomach. The conversation continued on around me as the party said their goodnights. I could hardly hear a word over being so focused on the ice in my head and the heat in my stomach.

I did catch one thing. They would be sleeping in the guest rooms before heading out in the morning to return to their post. With the new status of things, my father was itching to leave, as well. He wanted to be in the action— not that I blamed him. If only I could convince him to let me come along, maybe we'd both get what we wanted.

✦

Warm air tickled my ear, an exhalation of breath that woke me moments before a soft voice whispered into the darkness.

"You really don't remember?"

I blinked the sleep away and rolled to face Celia.

"What are you doing in here?" I hissed, sitting up, shoulders knocking into her thin frame. The night fell heavy through the gap in the curtains, only the light of the moon to see by. "What time is it?"

She pulled her legs under her and crawled up onto the bed, knees tucked under exposed thighs, sleep dress riding up. Heat burned through me and I forced myself to look up.

"It's just after 2AM." She blinked through thick lashes, the moonlight lighting her features just enough for me to see the gentle sweep of her neck, the soft angles of her face, and the parting of two full lips.

I cleared my throat and looked away, trying to take in the darkened room, but really a little bit uncomfortable with the situation. A warning bell was alarming in my head, coupling with the persistent ache.

"It was a two-part question," I continued. "What are you doing here?"

She reached out and gently ran her palm down my arm, ending at my hand. Her fingers were cool and held onto mine for a moment before she tugged, as if to pull me closer. "Isn't it obvious?"

I eyed her smile and the way her earlier sweet expression had turned far from innocent. She was right. She was being obvious.

"Besides, we used to date. This isn't anything new."

I stilled, and for a moment I was tempted by the proposition. It would be so easy. She would make me feel better, if even for a few minutes. Didn't I deserve that?

But I couldn't, not with all the questions circling me like hungry ravens.

I pulled away, inwardly groaning.

I hate myself right now. Because really, what did I have to lose? She was gorgeous and willing. Heaven knew I needed the distraction. But the simple fact that I couldn't remember having dated her was enough to give me pause; that and the fact I was still a married man, something that *had* been confirmed to me, even if I didn't remember that either.

In the end, my mother had raised me to be respectful, to view marriage as sacred. I couldn't dishonor her, not when I didn't even get to say goodbye.

"I'm sorry." Confusion laced my tone and I bristled. It made me sound too vulnerable—and I didn't like that. I added more firmly, "I don't remember you."

I expected some kind of retaliation, hurt or shock or something. She only smiled again, dropping my hand to run hers through her long, loose hair.

"Lucas, I already knew that when I came here." Her lips quirked into a demure smile. "But doesn't that make it more exciting? We can erase the past and start afresh." She crawled closer to me as she talked, sitting in my lap. The scent of citrus and sugar surrounded me. Her breath was hot, minty, and ran along my lips. I gulped, trying to ignore my own mixed feelings, most of which leaned toward giving in to this beautiful creature. My breath sped, and I pressed myself back against my headboard, trying to find space in my brain to tell her no.

Because she was a beautiful, all right. But sometimes the most beautiful things were the deadliest.

I didn't know for sure if I could trust her. Just like I didn't know if Jessa could be trusted. Or really, anyone...

I needed to remember!

If only I could get my memories back, then I would know what to do with this girl and this whole thing would be so much easier to say no to—or yes to.

"You should go," I said, my voice more solid than my decision.

Her lips parted in a silent protest, but she scrambled off the bed.

"Seriously, Lucas? I don't know what has gotten into you. You and I used to be close, and now we're not even friends. What we had was unique and special. You don't even care."

I held up my hands in protest. "I do care, but I just don't know if what you're saying is true."

She folded her arms over her chest, dejected. "Are you calling me a liar?"

I rubbed my temples. "I can't act on a past I can't remember. I'm sorry."

"Tell me one thing." She glowered at me. "If it were Jessa, would you have acted any differently?"

I shrugged. "Probably not. I don't know. I don't remember her, either."

But according to this girl, I was cheating on my wife. As much as I enjoyed spending time with beautiful women, that kind of behavior didn't sound like me. But how was I to know? Maybe it was true. I dropped my head into my hands and ran them through my messy hair as I considered the possibility.

The bed dipped, and I looked up to find Celia kneeling beside it, her wide eyes once again innocent and careful. "I'm sorry this happened to you, Lucas. It's not fair," she whispered, a long curl cascading around her exposed neck. "I'm being insensitive. Of course, I can't expect you to act the way things used to be." She paused and closed her eyes, as if considering something. "I want to show you something."

She reached to the nightstand, to a slatebook, and after a moment of fiddling with the screen, turned it around to reveal a photograph. My mind flashed to the last time this happened, when Callie had shown me my wedding photograph with Jessa. This time, however, it wasn't a wedding photo. It was a picture of this red-headed girl and me, arms wrapped around each other and kissing.

She powered down the device and smiled sadly. "We were engaged, Lucas. Our wedding was only a few weeks away when your father decided it would be a better fit if you married an alchemist. He flung Jessa on you, didn't even give us a choice. And then he showed her off all over the kingdom in the weeks leading up to the wedding, boasting about how it was time to celebrate alchemy publicly, and wasn't it so great that the royal family was marrying into magic."

"How was I supposed to compete with that?"

Without thinking, I cupped her cheek in my palm, hoping to comfort her, but finding it was wet with tears. Guilt rolled through me, sharp and disarming.

Something clicked within and I froze, uncovering a small piece of the puzzle.

"Is that why I overheard our parents apologizing to each other. Was it over our broken engagement?"

She nodded and then stood, backing up toward the center of the room. "My father and your father got into a bit of a scrimmage at your wedding. It got out of hand. It was childish, really," her voice trailed off.

I didn't know what to say to that. This whole thing was getting more and more complicated, unraveling like a ball of string, only to run into new tangles every time I thought I'd figured it out. If her father really had accosted mine, there was no way King Richard would be so forgiving unless he knew he was in the wrong. Jessa was technically my wife. That much was confirmed. But could it be Celia who truly had my heart?

As she stood there, curling her bare toes against the rug, body deflating like a wilted flower, an overwhelming desire to discover the truth pulsed through me. There was one way to find out ...

I flung back the bedcovers and strode to her in two long steps. Taking her into my arms, I pulled her to me and pressed my lips to hers. Soft and eager to please, she responded with fevered movements and a deep moan from the back of her throat. I pressed my eyes tight, focusing on our kiss, listening to my heart, to my body. It felt good, pleasant. But not perfect. Sparks didn't fly, and my mind was easily distracted.

We didn't have chemistry. It was just a kiss.

Maybe because I couldn't remember her. Or maybe because she wasn't mine after all. Could this whole spectacle tonight be a ruse?

I explored our connection for another minute, just to be sure. More of the same. Mind relieved, body disappointed, I released our embrace and stepped back. She smiled, lipstick smudged and teeth gleaming in the darkness. When she leaned in for more, I shook my head. Her face fell, eyes sparking and a soft gasp escaping from her swollen lips.

"I'm sorry," I said. "I'm not the one for you. I can't be who you want me to be."

Hand flying to her mouth, she spun and fled the room.

My feet edged forward across the plush rug. I shouldn't have been so mean, so abrupt. She clearly cared for me, but I wavered... What if that only made things worse? I didn't want to give the woman false hope. Not to mention how coming into my room like she had wasn't allowed. I wasn't at fault here; she shouldn't have done it in the first place.

That seemed off to me, too.

How had she been allowed in? That had never happened before. Sure, I wasn't at home surrounded by my normal guard, but when I'd been whisked off to this place, Richard had still brought a security team along. It was a small one, only a few of our most trusted men, but they knew better than to allow someone into my room while I was sleeping.

Deciding to investigate, I found one of the team members in the hallway. The lights were low, and the long row of doors were closed, tucking away whoever was inside for the night. He stood directly across from my door, hand resting on the gun at his hip.

He bowed, the shadow lengthening on his stony face. "Your Grace, how can I help you?"

"Why did you let Celia enter my room?" I questioned.

He paled, eyes shifting. "I thought you would have wanted her. I'm sorry if I misunderstood the situation."

I cocked my head, noticing the way his voice sped as he explained. Was he lying or just embarrassed at his mistake?

"Did she pay you off or something?" I pressed. "You can tell me the truth, I won't turn you in for it."

"Of course not," he replied. He bowed again. "I'm so sorry. Truly. It won't happen again."

I looked at the back of his lowered head, annoyed. Had he bowed simply to avoid eye contact, or was it because he was truly apologetic?

"It's the middle of the night. I was sleeping and completely unaware and vulnerable, and you let her into my room unannounced," I stated. "I don't care what your reasons are, don't do it again."

"No, Sir." I turned back and closed the door, making sure to lock it this time.

It was possible Celia had paid him off or blackmailed him. If not Celia, maybe her parents. Perhaps she wasn't the one to keep an eye on. The Duke and Duchess had seemed rather alarmed when I'd first walked into that dining room tonight.

Why weren't they more excited to see me alive and well?

I blew out a shaky breath and approached my bed. A glossy surface caught my eye, shining in the darkness like a beacon. Celia had left her slatebook on my nightstand. I smiled, relief soaring through me. It might be the middle of the night, but I wasn't going to stay in the dark for long.

EIGHT

JESSA

The door opened, sending my heart into a flutter. Was it Richard? Or Faulk? Would I be taken away? I pressed myself against the far wall, standing tall, trying to appear strong, fear rippling under the surface.

A maid scudded inside, dropping off my evening meal. Eyes downcast, she placed the silver tray on the dresser right next to the door and rushed away, the lock clicking into place behind her. I let out a deep sigh, allowing my muscles to relax. Never in my life had I been so grateful to be kept waiting. The longer I had to wait, the better it was for not only myself, but countless others. So, despite the boredom and the worry, I didn't ask for anything and I kept quiet.

The day Richard had informed me he'd be taking me to see Reed the next morning, I'd spent the night in utter turmoil. Since then, I'd imagined countless scenarios where something happened that changed the course of my fate. Maybe there was an attack and I wasn't the priority. Maybe Lucas remembered me and had stepped in to help. Or perhaps there was something I said or done during our meeting that made the King drop his plans, after all.

Never had I considered he wouldn't show up.

Eventually, I wouldn't be able to avoid the interrogation. I was here, prisoner, and it would happen sooner or later. People were counting on me to keep their secrets and their identities hidden. Lily and Jose, Madame Silver, the others who'd helped me to flee New Colony. What would happen to them if Reed got me to tell the truth?

They would probably be executed.

I skipped over to the food, drinking a sip from the tall glass of creamy milk as I surveyed the items: soft white bread with a swath of butter, thin slices of flaxen cheese, white crackers stacked atop each other, a handful of pale nuts, and my favorite, a diced pear. As expected, there wasn't any usable color.

I crunched on a cracker, relishing the way the salt melted over my tongue, and then popped a cube of pear in as well.

Maybe I was worrying for nothing. It was yet another day that Richard hadn't come for me. I'd spent the last week holed up in this room, twiddling my thumbs with nothing to do and nobody to talk to. It was better than the alternative. Twice a day, one of the palace maids dropped off a meal. They were quick, and they never spoke to me. No, I was stuck in here, and I was on my own.

I returned to the plate of food, feeding not only hunger and boredom, but depression, too.

The first thing I'd done in this place was search for color, but of course, I'd come up short. And with guards stationed outside of my door at all times, I wasn't going anywhere. All I'd ever wanted was to be free, to follow my heart and my passions, and yet, I'd ended up here.

The worst part of it all was Lucas. He wasn't here with me, wasn't mine anymore. Not only that, but Lucas wasn't even the same man anymore. He'd forgotten me, forgotten us, something I couldn't wrap my mind around. It dug at me, made me desperate with heartache.

There was nothing I could do.

I stood at the window, staring into the bitter landscape behind the fog of my breath on the glass. There were several problems with it being early February. The first was that it was freezing out. The second was that the grass was brown from winter, hibernating until the sun returned and the earth thawed, and it could return to full glory once again. Even if I could break the window and jump out like I had months before, I didn't have the summer grass to help me heal any resulting breaks. It was at least a twenty-foot drop, and I couldn't get away while hobbling on a broken leg. No, jumping wasn't the solution.

The only other thing I could think of was the telepathy, but that was also turning out to be a dead end. I had tried to use what little I had left of the purple material hidden in my bra to reach out to Lily. She was one ally here that might be able to do something. And since we already had a telepathic connection, it should have worked, I should have been able to talk to her.

But I got nothing. And that probably meant she wasn't at the palace or anywhere near it.

Lucas was close enough that I could talk to him. Maybe he was hiding somewhere in the city, or possibly on the outskirts of town. But he wasn't going to be the solution. It seemed he wanted nothing to do with me, that his father had turned him against me. Our love was one-sided at the moment, at least until he got his memories back.

What if he never gets his memories back?

I shook the thought away. I needed to think of something else—and quick.

I returned to the bed and clutched the white bedding in my fists. I willed the magic to work for me, to ignite in my veins and do what it did for Lucas. Invisibility would be the perfect escape. I was desperate, and I needed it. If only sheer willpower alone could make it work. I sat there for what felt like ages, desperate, pleading, but nothing happened. Nothing at all. Exasperated, I gave up.

Angry tears rolled down my cheeks. I was seriously going to go crazy in this room. I needed out!

I leapt back up and returned to the window. Maybe it would be fine, maybe I wouldn't break anything if I jumped. It wasn't *that* high. And the glass? That was nothing. Even without my yellow magic I was sure I could break it. I would have to be quick to jump before the guards heard the glass and came to investigate.

A flash of movement caught my eye and I froze, icy foreboding dripping down my spine. My window faced the main drive and a line of sleek black town cars were pulling up. I gripped the window frame, fingers digging against the wood, and stared down at the scene below.

Faulk strode from the palace, quick on her heels, surrounded by her officers in gleaming uniforms, as white as sharpened teeth. They fussed over the people exiting cars. I immediately recognized Celia's parents, and then Celia herself. I released a stilted breath. Maybe it was only the Addington family.

Another door opened, revealing a new pair of legs sliding from the car.

King Richard.

I stilled, the fear threatening to rip me apart. He was here for me. I knew it. Deep in my gut, in the marrow of my bones, in every cell that was me, I knew...

He glanced up toward my window, squinting against the sun. Something dark flashed across his expression. I dove from the window and ran for the door.

I need to get out of here. I may not have my magic at the moment, but I still know how to fight!

I flung open the door and attacked the first guard I saw, determined to make this quick, shock and adrenaline powering through me. He barely knew what was happening, barely had a chance to respond, as I ripped my fingernails across his face, drawing blood. It only took a second, but the liquid pooled under my fingers, slick with salvation. Red alchemy spun into the air and then settled into the man, his face going slack.

"Give me your gun," I roared, my growling voice not sounding like my own.

He immediately reached into his holster and handed over his gun. It was heavy in my hand, anchoring me into the moment.

"Stand back," I commanded. He did, but he wasn't the only guard I needed to deal with. Two more had their guns trained on me, fingers hovering over the triggers. They watched me, equal parts caution and rage in their careful movements and wild eyes.

"Drop the gun." One of them scrunched up his nose and motioned to me with large well-trained hands.

"No," I said, lifting it to point right back at him. "You're not going to shoot me." Because if that was allowed, no doubt they would've already done it.

I had limited training with guns. It wasn't exactly the GC's number one skill. But I knew how to point the thing and I certainly knew how to pull the trigger. "Just let me go and nobody will get hurt."

"I can't let you do that." Richard's deep voice boomed from behind me and a prickle of fear overran my senses, my grip weakened. The thud of approaching boots, the black guns cocking in aim, and then at last, the man himself, filled my vision.

"Put the gun down. Right now, Jessa." Richard strode forward, his eyes angry slits.

Defeat fell over me like a shadow. There was no way I could fight off this many people by myself. I was outnumbered and didn't have enough color close by.

I dropped the gun. It scattered across the floor and a guard scooped it up before I had a chance to reconsider.

Faulk snaked through the crowd, shoving people twice her size out of her way. Her white uniform gleamed pristine. Venom poisoned her eyes, pure and unfiltered hatred, as she moved toward me. "That's enough out of you, Miss Loxely."

Defiance roared up inside like an untamed lion. The lion and the snake. Who would win? I had little power in this situation, but at least I had my wit, at least I had my voice. "Actually, it's Mrs. Heart now, remember?"

She shoved me to the ground, my face slamming against the smooth marble. Pain ripped across my jaw, blood filling my mouth. I spat it across the floor in an arc of spilled rubies. If only I could use my own blood on someone else, then I could get out of this situation in seconds; but unfortunately, it didn't work that way.

"We are taking you to see Reed now."

She wrenched my hands behind my back, and once again, I felt the cold sharp grip of metal handcuffs snapping around my wrists. "It's about time you answered for your sins."

★

I shivered on my cot and pressed my back against the wall. Three days of interrogation and my resolve was breaking to pieces. Weak, tired, and hungry, my emotions fought my determination. A lone bulb shone light from the middle of the room, illuminating the concrete floor, lighting the gray box. Even smaller than the palace prison cells, the place was beginning to eat away at me. No windows and one door. No way out. I pressed the heels of my palms into my eyes, wishing I could relieve the anxiety long enough to sleep. At least sleep was a temporary out.

So far, only Reed had used his magic on me. His influence was strong, stronger than I remembered. But it wasn't foolproof, and my willpower was even stronger. I'd revealed most of my incriminating past, but I had yet to give up any actual names. Maybe I could make it out of this place.

Maybe no one else had to die because of me.

The door opened and Faulk stomped in. She looked down on me with disdain as she curled her lip and glared.

"Back so soon?" Antagonizing her wasn't going to do me any favors, but I couldn't resist.

"It's my job to get answers out of you, and now that I know you're Resistance, I will not stop until I do. You have names. One way or another, you will give them to me."

She spoke with absolute certainty, but we'd been at this for days, and as far as I could tell, she wasn't getting anywhere. Blue meant influence, it meant suggestion and persuasion, but it wasn't control. It wasn't red.

"I don't know what else you expect." I shrugged. "You already brought me all the way down here and that didn't change anything."

Her eyes narrowed in challenge.

The suite in the palace had been a much cushier jail cell than this. Now that I was on the frontline where the bulk of the alchemists and real officers were, things had gotten more serious. They'd thrown me into this dark and slightly humid room as if suffocating me would get me to talk. Reed had been so smug at first, but as the interrogations continued and he failed to extract any names from me, he'd become frustrated—right along with Faulk.

Proof that there was a silver lining to everything—even this.

"Where's Reed?" I tilted my head.

"He won't be coming today," Faulk replied.

I chuckled. "Oh, scared him off, did I?"

She smiled. "I thought it was time we changed tactics."

I'd expected this, but still a shiver of dread mocked me.

"Come to beat it out of me, have you?" I stood from the cot, yanking my gray oversized t-shirt over my squared shoulders. "Try your best."

Since my handcuffs had been removed shortly after my arrival, I could fight back. Color or not, I did remember what Branson had taught me. I should attack her. That might make me feel a little better, might change my fate. I would scratch at her, use my fingernails to shred her skin and blood, use it to fuel my power, use it to end her.

But that was only a fantasy. It wouldn't matter; there was a barrage of people outside waiting to step in if needed. But it would throw her off and that alone would make my day. I glanced up at the camera blinking down on us from the ceiling. Indicating that somewhere, behind the safety of another wall, the King was watching. He'd attended a few of the interrogations in person but then this thing had replaced him, with its blinking, watchful red eye.

The urge for action ticked through me like a countdown clock.

If Faulk sensed it, she wasn't fazed. She studied me, looked me up and down with a sneer, and then ushered in three Guardians of Color. They strode forward with complete confidence, each one of them glowering. They hated me. In their opinion, I was the worst kind of human. Maybe they didn't even see me as human at all, but an animal, a traitor, a beast deserving death at the hands of its master.

"Hey guys." I raised a defiant eyebrow.

I knew them, not personally, but enough to hate them doubly for participating in my interrogation. They had been some of the most difficult students in the class I'd taught on red alchemy. All three men were close in age to my seventeen. They were also the same guys who had competed at the first exhibition, expert fighters. I caught the eye of the one I liked the very least, Dax. He and I had bad blood. As he stalked in front of his friends, he glowered down at me, excitement flaring in his dangerous eyes.

Oh, great.

"Dax is one of our expert telepathics," Faulk said. "We have a handful of them in our organization. It really is quite a useful skill. Would you like to try it?"

My face burned. Did they know? As the boy strode toward me with clenched fists and a determined swagger, I questioned everything.

Purple alchemy twirled from his palm before shooting at me, connecting.

Well, hello Jessa. Just so you know, I won't be calling you Your Highness or anything like that, so don't pull that rank crap on me again.

I rolled me eyes, trying to fend off the worry building. I didn't want to connect back. I didn't want to talk to him. But it happened as if by accident, my magic leaping out to join his.

Can you hear my thoughts?

Fire lit his eyes, and he nodded to Faulk.

Close enough. His voice cut sharply through my mind.

I crossed my arms over my chest and glared. *Get out!* I slammed back on the magic. It didn't waver. He was too strong.

I will, once you tell me who you've been working with.

"You think it's going to be this easy?" I cut the question back toward Faulk. "Your alchemists are full of tricks, Faulk. They're all show and no substance."

She leaned back against the wall and flicked her wrist. The other two alchemists dove at me so fast I didn't have time to react and pummeled me with large, bony fists. Pain broke out across my jaw, my ribs, my sides, everywhere. I screamed. The agony rose, spilling over.

I'll ask my question again, Dax said. *Who are you working with? Names! Now!*

No, I won't.

"Hit her harder," he called out.

A heavy boot slammed into my stomach, and I went down hard, landing directly on my right elbow. Bone cracked, and agony soared through me. It was rawer, more direct, than anything I'd ever experienced. It burned up and down my arm, like liquid fire. I cried out, losing sense of time and space. My vision began to blur, and I was sure I'd pass out.

Tell us. Give us names and we'll heal you. If you don't, this will continue, and it will only get worse. Don't be so stubborn!

"Get out of my head!" I screamed.

There was no use. He kept asking his questions over and over while his friends beat me. All they needed was a slip up and they'd win. My blood spattered across the floor like spilled berries, filling my mouth to the point of gagging.

Faulk's voice filtered through the room, saying something I couldn't even begin to make out. The alchemists stilled, and Faulk walked over, leaning in with a jovial, sickening grin.

"Are you ready to cooperate?"

She had me.

And yet…

I shook my head, coughing up blood. The attack resumed, and I screamed, losing myself kick by kick, feeling my body break.

Tell me! Tell me now! Jessa, give me a name! Dax screamed into my mind. *Who else have you worked with in the Resistance? Who else is a traitor? Tell me. Start with one name. One name! Who is it?*

I didn't mean for it to happen.

It was the worst possible thing I could have done, but I did it. In the midst of all the pain, the barrage of questions and the suffocating fear that I was about to lose everything, my thoughts drifted to my love. To Lucas.

And somehow, I replied with his name.

The alchemist stopped and held up a hand. He stepped back with an odd expression. The pain still raked through me as I watched, horror ripping me up.

"I can't believe it." He shook his head slowly, but realization lit his face, drawing out a sly smile.

"Who?" Faulk yelled. "Did she give you a name? What did she say?"

"When I asked her who she's worked with, I wasn't expecting her to say his name."

"Out with it!" Faulk snapped.

He turned, glancing up at the camera then over to Faulk, almost apologetically. And the name dropped from his mouth.

"Prince Lucas."

★

As the prison cell door swung open, I braced myself for another interrogation. They'd healed me after the last one, so at least I'd had a break. But the mere thought of more pain sent me reeling. I scrambled back on my cot. I couldn't take any more! My heart kicked into overdrive and my breathing sped.

But it wasn't Faulk or Reed or any alchemist who walked inside. The fear deflated, and I relaxed. It was the people I'd least expected. But I couldn't help but smile at the royal hair and makeup team: Lars and Lainey. The way the pair looked at me, faces scrunched, huddled in the corner of the room, mouths agape, was nothing short of pathetic.

"I don't need your pity," I grumbled, peeling myself off the cot.

"Come along." Lainey tossed the command over her shoulder. She didn't need to tell me twice! The very thought of getting out of the cell had me practically giddy, my heart leaping for the first time in ages. Along with the guards, they escorted me down the nondescript hallway, into a sparse but clean bedroom with a large white-tiled bathroom attached. After giving me space for a quick shower, the two got to work.

"Am I going on camera?" I asked Lars, eyeing him through the mirror, noticing how his amber eyes didn't have the same spark they'd had on my wedding day. The lines in his tanned face deepened as he tugged at my wet hair with his hairbrush. I winced.

"Shh!" he warned me. "We're not allowed to talk to you this time."

"That's dumb." I watched them suspiciously until they spun me away from the mirror. Biting my lower lip, I looked around for a chair. Sitting down would be amazing, but I wasn't that lucky. Not that it mattered.

I could always try to use my red magic on them, get them to talk, but I decided against it. They were innocent in all this, two people doing their jobs, trying to stay alive like the rest of us.

After an hour or so of primping and prodding, they turned me back to face the mirror.

"And they call me magical." I sighed, taking in my transformed reflection. I'd gone from a dirty, bloody, sweat-covered mess, back to a princess, perfectly styled to adorn Lucas's arm. My hair was curled gently around my shoulders, my lips painted a soft coral and my eyes bright.

"Put this on and someone will be here to escort you to see the King," Lars said, passing me a white cocktail dress and matching high heels. From the way Lainey glowered at him, I guessed Lars wasn't supposed to add the last part about King Richard.

"Thank you," I croaked, fighting back the anxiety that was bubbling in my chest.

"Sorry about this," Lars continued, pulling out handcuffs. "We've been ordered."

Lainey stepped back, steeling herself. But I wasn't going to fight them on this.

"I understand." I held out my wrists, looking away as he slipped the cool metal into place.

"Remember who you are. You're a fighter," Lars whispered under his breath.

My eyes popped back to meet his, and he nodded, eyes alight with brilliant fire.

Sure enough, a couple of minutes later, I found myself following a barrage of silent, watchful guards, and entering a cozy dining room. So far, I hadn't gotten too many glimpses of the operation here. It was some kind of military stronghold, and nothing like the lavish accommodations of the palace. Still, the room King Richard was to dine in had been artfully decorated, as if we were still in the palace.

The moment I sat down, he entered the room. He was dressed, not in the royal regalia, but in a crisp business suit and tie. His presence filled the room, thick as smoke and just as toxic.

"I'm going to get right to the point," he said, sliding into the chair across from me. "I need to be able to trust my son, and as such, I need you to tell me everything."

His magnitude was enough to intimidate anyone, myself included. Everything about him made me want to crawl out of my skin. It wasn't that he was outwardly evil. It was his incredible skill for manipulation, his way of twisting every little thing to his advantage—that bothered me most.

"I don't know what you mean," I said carefully.

"Don't lie." He held my gaze. I was struck by how similar his eyes were to Lucas's, the gray so penetrating, it drew me in. "I know what happened in your interrogation this morning. You claimed the prince was Resistance, and given the nature of said interrogation, I'm inclined to believe it."

Oh, no. That was not what I was hoping for. It would have been better for Lucas if they'd thought I was raving mad!

I sank into my white padded chair, having no clue how to fix this. Lucas had been Resistance, but he wasn't anymore. What good would it be to turn his father against him? It would only put the man I loved in more danger, something I'd vowed not to do ever again. Lucas had enough on his plate, the last thing he needed was to be thrown in a prison cell and put through the same kind of interrogations I'd endured. If that happened, it wouldn't be long until he accidently revealed his biggest secret.

His alchemy.

"You're a smart girl," Richard continued, leaning over the polished oak table. "I never gave you enough credit; I see my error now. You really do know how to play politics with the best of them. Maybe you deserve the crown, after all. Too bad after everything you've done, you'll never get another chance to ruin my family. Even if I let you live, you will learn to get in line, I can promise you that."

His perfectly preened eyebrows pulled together and lowered over unblinking eyes as he delivered his monologue.

"I'm going to give you two options, so listen carefully. Option one, you tell me everything, you surrender yourself to my will, and I'll graciously let you live. With that comes the agreement to adhere to my story, my way, and always, my version of the truth."

My stomach hardened to stone. His version of the truth. My hands turned to fists, pulling at the cuffs in my lap. His version was whatever version gave him the most power, and with the war in full swing, what would happen if he managed to win?

"My son has no memory of the last year, and as much as I'm eager to learn who tried to kill him..." He paused midsentence, looking me over with knowing eyes. "I'm more eager to make sure he never realigns himself with this traitorous Resistance group ever again. So that means you will feed him whatever information I tell you. You will help me help him. Because can't we both agree that it is in Lucas's best interest to support his father, to uphold the tenants of his role of crowned prince?"

It wasn't a question. He kept going, caught in his own delusion.

"It is either that or option two. Do I need to continue? I assume by now you know what option two is. It is rather obvious."

I lifted my chin. "Enlighten me."

"You take the fall for everything."

I flinched.

He smiled. "And that means you'll be publicly shamed and executed."

I sucked in a breath, letting everything settle over me. The world stilled. I didn't want to die, but I also couldn't tell Richard everything he wanted, and I certainly couldn't help him turn Lucas into his prodigy. If I revealed the names of the other Resistance members, I would be trading their lives for mine. How could I possibly value my life above theirs? Especially when they'd trusted me?

"Hurry and make your choice," he said, nonchalantly. "I really must be getting to my dinner soon."

I stood and pushed back my chair, placing my palms flat on the table, despite the pull of the metal cuffs.

"Thank you for the offer; it's an easy choice."

He grinned, triumphant. "I knew it would be."

"I choose option number two."

NINE

SASHA

"I so don't want to do this." I sighed, leaning into Mastin's warm shoulder. He didn't respond, but did reach down to squeeze my hand. Maybe he understood.

Since the second alchemist prisoner had arrived a little over a week ago, I'd been called back in four times to work with the new arrivals. That's what they called them. Really, they were prisoners of war. I understood the magnitude of winning this thing and how important it was to the future of not only both countries, but the world at large. Still, I absolutely *hated* doing it like this.

"Are you ready?" Mastin asked, nodding toward the door. On the other side was another prisoner about to get the "Sasha Welcome Party." That's what I'd termed the pathetic attempts I made to bring these people to my way of thinking. So far, I was zero and four.

There had been small battles nearly every day, and with that meant casualties and prisoners. I'd been forced to stay back after our botched mission to save Jessa, the General's way of making me pay my dues and prove myself.

Again.

At least he saw the value in allowing me to tend to the wounded. That was one area where my alchemy was making a huge difference. But if only I could be in the middle of the battle, I could save more lives. I'd tried to argue the fact, and even added the idea of letting me join the fight so I could lend others my yellow alchemy.

Nathan Scott had shot that down immediately.

He said it was too untested and should only be used as a last resort. He also made me promise not to tell any others about the ability. His failure to see the advantage was totally foolish, but I could argue with him all day and he wouldn't see my point. I wasn't desperate enough to use magical means of persuasion.

"Sasha." Mastin nudged me. "Are you ready?"

I groaned. "As ready as I'll ever be," I replied with a huff, blowing a wayward strand of hair out of my face. I ran my hands down my black clothing, stretchy jeans and cotton top with a zip-up. My necklace of stones rested underneath it all, steady against my skin. It was nothing compared to the combat gear the Guardians wore, but considering West America didn't have black uniforms, I was happy to make my own.

Making my own way in life was kind of my thing, anyway.

Mastin turned the deadbolt, opened the steel door, and ushered me inside. My eyes lingered on an older gentleman, pegging him to be in his mid-fifties. Of course he had been stripped of his alchemy gear, now wearing the light gray prison suit. He looked up at me with challenging hazel eyes, the overhead light reflecting off his bald scalp.

I hate this part.

The business of interrogation made me wonder if I was any better than King Richard, Faulk, and all the minions who'd tortured me. The roles were reversed now, but did that make it okay?

Probably not. I knew how this went. I would try my best; he wouldn't budge, his loyalty steadfast in the King. So, I'd go and the American interrogators would get to work, a work much more effective than mine. And also, much more brutish.

"I'm here to help you." I smiled softly at the man as I strode into the room, taking position a few feet away from him. Mastin stood with crossed arms and a lethal expression at the door, my protector should I need him.

The man's focus returned to the floor, mouth twisted in something like defeat. He stayed hunched in the corner of the room, on top of the threadbare mattress on the floor. His elbows rested on his knees, not seeming to care one bit that I was attempting to start a conversation.

If only I could use magic and somehow make him talk. But no, that would be a huge mistake. Nobody here needed to know about that ability. Once they found out about red, they would turn from tolerating me to locking me up.

I held up my hands and slowly inched into the room. "I don't know if you recognize me—"

"I recognize you." His face shot up, eyebrows drawn in. "I know exactly who you are, should have known it when you came back but you'd changed so much."

"What are you talking about?" I narrowed my eyes, trying to place him.

"I remember you as a child, had you in my class back then."

I raked my memory, searching through all the teachers I'd had back then, but came up short. Trying to sort through the past was like trying to sort through the rubble of a burned down building. There wasn't much left, and what was there, was tainted.

"Sorry," I said, trying to sound as friendly and kind as possible. "It was a tough time for me, I actually blocked a lot of those memories, I think."

"And I know what you can do," he continued, grumbly voice growing sharp with every accusatory word. "So I know there's no use in fighting you."

Anxiety rolled through me. If this man had been one of my teachers, that meant he knew about the red alchemy. Magic I'd suppressed when I was still a kid, leaving it far in my past, underneath all that burned rubble. I hadn't dug it up, and I wasn't planning to now.

But if this man told interrogators about my secret, what would they do with that information? What would happen to me?

"Go ahead, just get it over with," the man said sharply.

I retreated, pressing my back against the cool wall, blinking rapidly, and pushing down my memories. But it was no use. They flooded me, drowned me with what I'd done.

I was so young then, and the King was testing the boundaries of magic—namely, my boundaries. I'd been used to interrogate people, to control people, and ultimately, to kill them.

I shook my head. "No," I muttered, clearing my throat. "No," I said louder. "That's not why I'm here. I come in peace, as a friend."

The man's eyes bulged with contempt as he slowly stood to full height. He towered over me, yellow teeth bared, and cracked his knuckles. "You're no friend of mine."

Mastin came to stand behind me, anger rolling off him, but I held up my hand to stop him from intervening any more than he had to. This was my fight, and if I could pull it off, there wouldn't be a fight whatsoever.

"Really," I said, turning back to the captured alchemist. "This is your chance to cooperate. You should. If you don't, they're going to use whatever means possible to get what information they can from you. This way, you won't have to suffer."

His eyes narrowed, the lines of his face lifting and stretching with the move. "And help them?" He spat on the floor, right at my feet. "Never."

"But don't you see? King Richard will stop at nothing until he has ultimate power. He doesn't care who he hurts in the process, he's—"

"Foolish, traitorous child!" he yelled. "King Richard is a visionary. He is taking back what is rightfully ours, restoring alchemy to full power across the world. I will never betray him."

And then he lunged, knocking me to the floor. I landed on my back, the wind rushing from my lungs. I pushed back, a frenzied scramble to get him off. Thin, tight hands gripped at my throat, and at first I thought he was trying to choke me, but then I realized he was looking for my stones. I beat him to it, connecting with the yellow. It pulsed through me and I threw the man off, slamming him against the far wall.

Mastin was there in an instant, throwing him onto his stomach and wrestling him so that his arms were wrenched behind his back. Then Mastin cocked his gun and aimed it at the man's sweat-shined head.

"She was just trying to help you," Mastin growled. "Move an inch and I'll kill you myself."

The man lay frozen, eyes facing me, burning as they glowered at me like I was the lowest form of filth he'd ever seen.

Mastin looked up at me, running panicked eyes up and down my body. "Are you alright? Did he hurt you?"

"I'm fine," I replied as I stood.

I wasn't upset about being attacked so much as I was upset that these alchemists coming in were so blinded by their adoration of Richard and New Colony. How could they not see what was plainly before them?

"When I get back," Mastin spat toward the man, "you will pay for daring to *touch* her."

Then he tucked me under his arm and led me from the room.

✦

"**Didn't go so** well, did it?" The general strode down the hallway, eyeing the room we'd just exited with the raise of a thick eyebrow. "Sasha, why don't you go back to your bunk and take a rest? You've been through a lot with these people over the last week. I'm sure you're exhausted."

His "these people" comment bothered me, but I bit my tongue and let it slide. "I'd like to stay and help. Maybe I can try again after the interrogators see him." What I didn't add was that I also wanted to make sure this man didn't tell the others about my red alchemy. The very idea of diving back into that sordid magic made my skin crawl.

Nathan Scott frowned, studying me for a long minute. "You really do need to take a break. I'm sorry, but this isn't a suggestion, it's an order."

He was used to giving orders. And he was used to people following them. But I, on the other hand, wasn't.

I opened my mouth to challenge him, no longer caring about holding back, but Mastin stepped in between us, resting his hand on my shoulder.

"I'll come find you soon as I can and debrief you on everything. Will that work?" He held my elbow and stared earnestly into my eyes, pleading with me to back down.

"Fine," I grumbled, spinning on my heel. As I did, the exhaustion overpowered me, making my eyes burn. Maybe they saw something in me before I did, and Nathan Scott really was just looking out for me. Maybe I was reading too much into things because of the lack of sleep and I shouldn't be so annoyed.

The prison was in its own building, separate from the others. It was small, with a series of rooms on either side of a long hallway that turned at a 90-degree angle down the middle. At the far end was the exit, where I was headed. I turned the corner, out of sight from the men, and a tingling of suspicion caused me to slow. Before long, that tingling grew, forcing me to stop.

Don't be foolish. Why would they be so eager to send you away? You've been tired plenty of times and they didn't say a word. Maybe there really is something going on here, something they don't want you to know about.

I bristled, hating the idea that Mastin was keeping something from me. But despite my desire to trust him, I had to know. There wasn't time to stand around and debate it. I had to take action.

I drew the blue alchemy around me, knowing it would quiet any sound I made. Nobody would hear my breathing or footsteps. I wasn't as lucky as Lucas to have white alchemy to become invisible, but this was the next best thing, and I needed to take it. I needed to be smart, to be brave, and stop being so naïve.

The blue magic swirled around my body, then settled over me like a glove.

I relaxed and listened to a conversation happening just around the corner.

"What happened in there?" Nathan Scott asked his son.

"The man isn't willing to cooperate with us. Big surprise." Mastin's reply dripped in sarcasm.

"How dangerous do you think he is? Did he tell her anything?"

"No, he didn't. But aren't they all dangerous?"

Nathan let out a sharp laugh. "That's true."

I ground my teeth, trying not to be bothered by the flash of annoyance. Because really, they were right. We were dangerous. Case in point, I was listening in on their private conversation, and they had no idea I was there. *Thank you, alchemy!*

I pressed myself harder against the wall, not that it would really help anything if someone saw me, but it made me feel a little bit better than standing right in the open.

"How many more rooms do we have?" Mastin asked. "These alchemists that are filling up our prison are not exactly easy to keep under lock and key."

"We have enough for now. And if we need to make more, then we will. But keeping them in does worry me. Because what happens if they break out?"

It was a question I'd been afraid to ask myself.

"Are we going to bring in Weapon X?" Mastin lowered his voice.

The conversation paused, silence filling the hall for a long moment. "I think we are going to have to, and probably soon. I already got permission from Madam President."

"Sasha won't like it."

My body prickled at the sound of my name, senses kicking in.

"What did we talk about, son?" Nathan Scott was gentle in his scolding. But nonetheless, even I knew the sound of a scolding father when I heard it. "You cannot let this girl, no matter your feelings for her, get in the way of what we're doing here."

"I'm not. I won't."

"You are a soldier first."

"I know," he replied boldly. "I'm saying that we're going to have to find a way to tell her about it, at least prep her for the blow."

The blow? What the hell was Weapon X?

Nathan's voice came out firm and commanding, "Under no circumstances are you to tell her anything about it. It's a State secret, and something above your rank, need I remind you?"

There was another long pause. I waited for Mastin to argue, but I also questioned if he would. He wasn't the type to argue with his father, not only because he was his parent, but because he was his ranking General. And this wasn't about fathers and sons anymore, not to a man like Mastin.

General Scott was right. Mastin Scott was first and foremost, and would always be, a loyal soldier.

"Yes, Sir," Mastin replied in a steady voice.

"Maybe you need to take a break too." General Scott sighed. "This has been a lot for you, too."

Another "Yes, Sir" quickly followed.

Mastin's boots clapping on the concrete floor echoed through the hall, heading right toward the corner where I was hiding. Any second, he would round it and see me standing here like a lunatic.

That wasn't going to happen.

The yellow magic zapped through me like electricity, the blue still there, an undercurrent of silence. I ran from the building at lightning speed, bursting out the door before Mastin even turned the corner. Immediately, I released the magic and slowed to a steady pace toward the barracks where my bunk waited for me; where those men had sent me away!

Clenching and unclenching my fists, I fumed at this new revelation. They were hiding secrets from me! Secrets that had to do with alchemy, I was sure of that. And I was also sure Mastin wasn't going to clue me in. As close as we'd become, and as much as we cared for each other, those secrets between us weren't going anywhere.

It's not as if you don't have your own secrets. You have your red alchemy!

Yes, and he had knowledge of this mystery weapon.

As I continued down the path, dodging the soldiers in my way, glaring at the shanty buildings of the base, ignoring the cold biting at my cheeks, I found myself not heading back to my room, but to Tristan's quarters. I missed him.

He was allowed to participate in the battles, and because of that he'd quickly become one with the military men. He was trained, he was smart, and he was able-bodied. Not to mention loyal to a fault. Of course, they loved him. I hated that I wasn't able to go along, but I checked up on him after each and every battle. He was always okay.

But I wanted more than okay. Tristan was still my friend, he always would be. But he was colder toward me now that he knew Mastin and I were an item, less likely to joke around or even smile in my direction, but I realized I couldn't expect to have it both ways, and at least he still talked to me, still let me care about him.

I stood outside the building where he was likely hanging out and took a steadying breath. I was bunked with the women across the way, and every time I went into the men's area, I had to be on my guard. There were still plenty of soldiers who didn't like me, some who even wished me dead. I saw the way they watched me with their calculating eyes, felt their whispers behind my back. They put up with me because of Nathan Scott's strict orders, but for most of them, that was the only reason.

The men's barracks were practically overflowing the last time I was here, but as I walked in this time, there were fewer occupied bunks.

That wasn't a good sign during wartime.

I found him on his lower bunk; one in a long row of rudimentary metal and plywood structures, complete with thin mattresses and canvas sleeping bags. His nose was deep into a novel and he didn't seem to notice me standing over him.

I smiled and spoke low, "Tristan, I need to talk to you in private."

He dropped the novel to his chest and gave me an exasperated look, mouth downturned and eyes twinkling, but the second he caught the seriousness in my expression, he threw the book aside and nodded once.

"Let's go on a walk." He stood and led the way from the room.

A military base in wartime wasn't exactly open for anyone to walk anywhere they pleased, but despite that obstacle, we'd figured out where we were and weren't allowed to roam. As we maneuvered through the metal buildings and the gravel and dirt pathways, we walked close together, shoulders brushing, and kept quiet. There was so much unsaid between us, and the air was thick with untold confessions.

"Have you ever heard of Weapon X?" I asked, peering up at him.

He shook his head.

"I hadn't either, until today. I overheard Mastin and his father talking about it in regards to the alchemists imprisoned here."

Tristan laughed, a low rumble that made me feel nostalgic. "You overheard them or you eavesdropped?"

"Shut up!" I shoved my elbow into his ribcage.

He smirked. "That's what I thought." He didn't say more, and for that I was grateful. It would've been the perfect opportunity to question my relationship with Mastin. Girlfriends were supposed to trust their boyfriends, not spy on them.

"What do you think it is?" he asked. Our boots crunched against the gravel as we dodged passersby. One particularly ugly guy gave us a deadly glare, his lip curled in disgust, hand perched on the gun in his belt, before continuing on his way up the path. I glared at his retreating form.

"I don't know but I don't like the sound of it," I whispered, turning back to Tristan. "Mastin seemed to think that it would not make me happy. He wanted me to know about it and his father told him that I was not to be told anything."

Tristan folded his arms and nodded. "Poor guy."

"What is that supposed to mean?"

"He is stuck between you and everything else he cares about." He shrugged, looking away. "That can't be easy."

I hadn't thought of it that way and I certainly hadn't expected Tristan to defend my new boyfriend. Well, maybe he was my boyfriend. It was stupid to define it when we all had better things to worry about. Despite that, I found myself fighting a mix of annoyed frustration and clawing jealousy, and then mentally kicking myself for being such an idiotic girl when who I dated should be the least of my worries.

"Whatever," I grumbled as we turned a new corner and kept walking up the path wedged between two silver buildings. "We need to figure out what the weapon is and why they're bringing it here. That's the other thing. General Scott said something about the president giving him permission to move the weapon here."

We mulled it over, neither one of us all too happy about it.

An idea popped into my brain, painfully obvious. "Do you think Hank knows anything?"

"I actually talked to him yesterday. He's doing really good. Loves his new job training the baby alchemists." He winked at me. "But he didn't mention anything about a weapon. If it's some big secret, I doubt he would know."

"I need to call him," I said, hand absently resting against the mostly unused slatebook currently resting in my pants pocket.

"You need to call him *and* call your family. Why do you always do this?"

I bristled. "Do what?"

"You push away the people who love you the most."

Like I pushed you away for Mastin? I didn't voice my thought. Didn't want to go there. We kept walking as I burned with frustration at his accusation. Was Tristan right? Did I push people away?

"You have to give me some credit." I kicked a pebble, watching it clatter ahead. "Lately, I've been trying to connect with people. I went back for Jessa, didn't I? Even though it was totally stupid." I gulped, pushing the fear at being vulnerable deep into my chest. "And I did what you said, I am seeing if I can make things work with Mastin."

We stopped, gazing at each other. I couldn't read the expression in his eyes as they peered back at me. "Relationships aren't always easy for me," I whispered, letting out a long-held breath.

"You're right." He smiled softly and pulled me into a tight hug, our tense bodies relaxing together in their familiar way. "I'm sorry. You're doing great, kid. I'm just upset about something else," his voice trailed off.

There were so many more questions left to be asked, so much I longed to know. I could feel those same questions rising and falling in him with the rise and fall of his chest against mine.

But in the end, I didn't ask. And neither did he.

Sasha, a voice shot through my mind like an arrow. *Can you hear me?*

I stilled, frozen.

"What's wrong?" Tristan asked, pulling back.

"Hold on," I whispered. "Something's happening."

I closed my eyes and concentrated.

Jessa, I thought the words back at her, aware the telepathic connection was weak. But the fact it was there at all meant she had to be close. *Where are you? I've been worried sick about you. Are you okay? Can I help you?*

They caught me, she replied and my heart dropped.

Okay, where are you?

I'm in holding somewhere along the frontlines—or something, a military stronghold. I think. I don't really know. I'm scared. Lucas doesn't even remember

664

me!

Wait, Lucas is alive? That was good news, at least.

Yes.

Are you okay? Have they hurt you? My mind flashed to my own interrogations, and my stomach flipped. Jessa wasn't strong enough to handle that kind of thing. If she broke, there'd be many people caught in the crossfire.

I need help. Her voice was laced with panic. *I don't have much purple left. I had a little hidden that they still haven't found.*

Okay, calm down. Tell me what you know.

I don't know anything. They had me in the palace for a while and then they moved me south, but I don't know where to exactly. I've been in a cell without windows.

It's okay. I think I might have an idea of your proximity. We'll get you out. It wasn't going to be easy, might even be impossible. I wanted to promise it to her, but I couldn't. *If you see Branson, you can trust him. I think he's there, too. I saw him not long ago.*

I haven't seen him. But either way, I need you to hurry.

I'll see what I can do. I shook, and Tristan reached out and grasped my hand, steadying me.

There's more. Jessa's voice broke through the darkness, shrill as it faded, the connection wavering. *King Richard just informed me that I'm to be executed.*

Our connection severed. My knees gave out and I crumpled to the ground.

TEN

LUCAS

I pressed my hand to the back of my head for no reason other than habit. The pain had subsided, but the day the doctor, nurse, and the alchemist left the orphanage was the day I knew I was in more trouble than I'd first realized. The memories hadn't returned. Those people had done all they could, but ultimately they'd given up, and I was more confused than ever.

Now it was just me, the guards, the orphans, and the staff left to occupy the estate. They were busy with classes and projects, and I was completely bored out of my mind. I moseyed about the different rooms, reading books, people-watching, and when things got particularly bad, staring holes into walls. At the moment, I was doing just that. My thoughts rolled around in my head like an unwanted companion.

I still didn't have a slatebook. Unfortunately, Celia had come back for hers the next morning after our…little conversation. I'd given it to her without question, and she'd agreed not to tell anyone I'd used it if I kept her secret. She didn't want anyone to know she'd entered my room like that. Shaking on the agreement had felt like making a deal with a viper. By then, I'd seen the footage of her attacking Jessa.

Didn't matter. I had more important things to worry about. Namely, getting my memories back, or at the very least, getting my life back, but I'd barely had a chance to talk to my father. He hadn't stuck it out in this new office for more than a couple days; no surprises there. He'd said there were only so many things he could oversee remotely, but he would come to visit as soon as he could.

I wasn't counting on it.

And he still kept my slatebook from me, kept *all* technology from me. It was all based on some medical advice from the doctor about not putting too much information into my head while I was still suffering from the memory loss. Considering I'd already secretly read everything I could that night using Celia's slatebook, I wasn't holding my breath. Even with all that, all the news stories about Mom, all the twists and turns with my two engagements, the public alchemy exhibitions, I still had amnesia. And I was still without answers.

"How are you doing?" One of my favorite workers, Martha, smiled pityingly at me as she approached me in the main family area. Since the kids were in classes, I was alone. My hips ached from sitting here like a lump. I rolled my eyes congenially at her and patted the armrest of the seat beside mine.

"You already know I'm going crazy with boredom," I said as she sat in the plump velvet chair. "How do you do it out here? I mean, don't get me wrong. I have always loved a short visit. But to stay? The isolation is awful."

We leaned back in our chairs, strategically placed next to the large window. The room was cozy, with wood-paneled walls and floors, plush rugs, and chairs throughout. A few wooden block toys had been left outside of a toy chest tucked away in the corner. My gaze flashed to the outside world, one blank as a canvas. We'd had another snow storm last night, and everything was once again covered in the stuff. A shiver ran over my arms, despite the fire crackling in the fireplace nearby.

The older woman laughed, her plump body bouncing jovially. "It's not so bad. I'm used to it. It's lovely in the summer. And besides, some people prefer the country to the city." She smiled, mossy eyes lighting in amusement, gray bun pulling at her ruddy cheeks.

I guess I could understand that. There were times in my life where I would have agreed with her, but then again, I wasn't much of a country boy, especially in the middle of winter.

"You really won't let me use your slatebook?" I asked, already knowing her answer. It was the same she'd given me day in and day out since my arrival. Still, I kept asking; I might eventually wear her down.

She shook her head, eyes crinkling. Her round cheeks balled as she smiled at me, clearly finding my persistence amusing. That wasn't going to get me very far.

I needed to find a way to convince my father to reintroduce me to society again. Whoever tried to kill me could face my guards, if needed; I wasn't going to live my life in hiding, especially over an incident I couldn't even remember. The war had started a few months ago and, for all anyone knew, it could last for years. I wasn't about to spend years hidden away in this place, no matter how much I loved the people.

"What about this." I flashed Martha my best smile, turning on the charm. "I won't go onto any of the feeds or check the news or anything like that. I only want to use the slatebook to call my father."

She eyed me warily. "Lucas, I don't know."

"Just one call, that's all I'm asking for. Let me talk to him one time. Let me lay out my case. Whatever he says, I'll take it. And I'll stop pestering you about the no tech rule."

"I really shouldn't—" Her voice faltered—I had her.

I leaned in, wrapping her round shoulders in a side hug and looked down on her with big, sad eyes. "Please, Martha. I really need this."

She sighed, resigned. "Fine." Weathered hands shaking, she pulled her device from the pocket of her floral housedress. The slatebook wasn't nearly as advanced as mine, but it would do just fine. "You better mean it, Lucas. One call. And you're doing it right here. I can't afford to have you run off with this. Your guards were in the hallway when I came in here."

My guards could shove it.

Okay, truth was, I didn't really want anyone to hear this conversation, Martha included, but I wasn't about to argue with her logic. The slatebook was in my hands now, I couldn't waste this.

It only took two minutes to get what I needed.

Two minutes. One phone call.

And just like that, I'd conjured up the exact words to convince my father that he absolutely had to have me with him.

I shut the device down and smiled gleefully at Martha, who stared back at me with worried eyes. The poor woman probably wasn't expecting to hear that. Oh, well. I was leaving this place—that's what mattered.

And I wasn't going home. The palace would have to wait.

No. I'd be joining King Richard on the frontline. That was fine by me; I wanted to be a part of the action. Who better to question Jessa before her execution than the man she supposedly claimed to love? I stood, patted Martha on the shoulder, and strode from the room. I had to get ready to leave since I'd be on the road within the hour.

I had a few pressing questions for my wife.

★

Gravel rumbled underneath gargantuan tires as we pulled up to the military stronghold. Rain pelted the metal siding, drowning out any sound from the outside world. The black armored vehicle had tinted windows, presumably so that the soldiers here couldn't get a peek at me inside. From my vantage though, I could see everything. The setup was much more established than I'd been expecting. The brick and metal buildings weren't hastily done or makeshift. How long ago had Richard built this place? With freezing rain pelting down in a torrential downpour, there wasn't much else to see. Aside from the stationed guards and patrols, nobody was out here.

What would they make of it if they could see me here? According to Richard, he'd already had a small, closed casket funeral for me. He wasn't ready to let all that hard work go to waste and reveal me to unsuspecting soldiers.

If only he knew about my white alchemy, this could make things so much easier. I could just go about my business, here, at the palace, wherever, and nobody would be any the wiser. But no, I had to keep that to myself. And maybe I could use a little bit to get around this base while I was here. I just hoped that in the last year, I'd still managed to keep my secrets my own.

I leaned back in my heated leather seat, rubbing the side of my stubbly cheek. The driver was a bulky, quiet man, known for being discreet—one of our regulars. He carefully maneuvered the vehicle into a large storage shed. Soldiers slid large metal doors closed behind us, and he cut the engine. He slid from his seat, pacing the space of the small garage. Burly shoulders relaxing in satisfaction, he trotted to my door and swung it open.

"Your Highness, you're requested to enter through there." He pointed to a heavy steel door on the far end of the garage, a lone guard stationed in front. "Your father has accommodations below ground for his safety."

"Makes sense." I slid from the car, feet dropping to the concrete floor, and shook the driver's cold hand. Then I steeled myself and strode to the door.

The guard in front stood tall, eyes forward, as if ordered not to acknowledge me. I shrugged and reached for the door, swinging it open with ease. A wide set of concrete stairs led to another door several stories underground. The long staircase was lit by low-hanging light bulbs, reminding me of our unused bunker back at the palace. I'd never liked that place.

"Here goes nothing," I mumbled to myself, and took the first step.

As I descended, the already-cold air grew colder, goose bumps rose like pinpricks on my skin, and a gnawing sense of importance gripped me like a fist.

I couldn't screw this up.

The door at the bottom waited. I tried the handle, but it didn't budge. Locked. It appeared to be as thick as a bank vault door, metal and cold as ice. I pounded on it, not sure what else to do. A slight jab of pain ignited in my wrist, but I ignored it, pounding harder.

A crack echoed through the hallway, the lock unhinging. The door pulled open, my father standing on the other side, lips lifted in a bemused smile.

I sighed and stepped inside, warming instantly as heat blasted, vision adjusting to the change in light.

"Well, it's not the palace, but it will have to do," I said jokingly, taking in the vast room sprawled out in front of me.

Truthfully, it was more impressive than I'd been expecting, and much bigger than the bunker below the palace. The two of us stood side by side, studying the family room and kitchen suite. Gleaming stone countertops, dark wood accents, leather sofas and patterned rugs, complete with framed oil-painted landscapes hung artfully on the off-white walls. Along the main wall was a series of oak doors, leading to what I assumed had to be equally elegant bedrooms and bathrooms.

The place looked like Mom could have decorated it, and my heart pinged painfully at the mere thought. She should be here with us.

"Welcome to your new home." Richard smiled, narrowing his eyes. "Since you couldn't sit still at the last place, you'll just have to make do here."

I stifled a breath, already feeling enclosed by the four walls.

"I brought her to you." Richard motioned to one of the closed doors with the quick flick of his wrist, and I froze.

"You brought her to me?" The question sounded strained and confused as it left my mouth.

669

"Jessa. Yes, she's here. Locked in one of the bedrooms, all the color removed ahead of time. I can't have you walking around the prison quite yet, that's where she has been staying up until now."

He looked up at the ceiling, eyes growing thoughtful. "I haven't decided how I'm going to reintroduce you to the world…or when."

"Great," I mumbled, spinning in a slow circle, my gaze traveling high and low as I picked up on smaller details of the space. There weren't any windows. I sighed; at least at the orphanage, I'd had windows.

"Aren't you going a little overboard?" I questioned.

Richard glowered at me from across the room, arms folded over his broad chest. "No. You've almost died multiple times. You're my only heir, Lucas. We have to be more careful."

"If you say so," I grumbled. I eyed the door to Jessa's newest prison cell as I toed my way toward it. "I guess now is as good a time as any."

"I'll wait out here. At least, for your *first* meeting together." He grinned, eyes far-off, as if remembering something funny. "But be quick, and don't let her manipulate you."

"What do you mean?" I stopped to study him, something about his tone causing me to falter.

"Remember what I told you, Lucas. It's the truth." He nodded toward the door. "That girl is Resistance. You can't trust her. You should only try to get names out of her."

"Obviously." I smiled. I already knew all that, he'd explained it to me when I'd first asked about my supposed wife.

"Don't get smart with me," he snapped back, but there was a playful glint to his eyes. "And don't make me regret letting you go in there alone."

I shrugged. "It's probably better if you're not there. I assume you and her don't have the best relationship?"

He barked a laugh. "You could say that. But I mean it, Lucas. You can't trust everything she says."

"I don't have to trust her. She just has to trust me."

I pulled open the door without a second glance in his direction.

The light was on, but she was asleep, her lanky body curled up in the corner of the bed, arms tucked against her chest. A wad of white sheets gathered between her legs, her body wrapped up in them, leaning on them for support. Her unruly, dark hair spread out around her like a halo, a stark contrast against the white pillow.

I stepped closer, searching her face. A purple bruise had blossomed across her chin, creeping up toward her eye. I sucked in a breath. Why hadn't they healed her? She'd obviously endured some beatings. I shouldn't have been surprised, or even upset, she was an enemy of New Colony. She'd gotten less than she'd deserved. But still, seeing someone so young and innocent, sporting bruising like that, made my protective instincts flare. The urge to punch a wall, to scream, to do something, *anything*, rocked through me. It caught me so off-guard, the visceral reaction so stunningly intense, that I had to catch my breath.

I kneeled next to the bed to get a better look, careful not to jostle her. The girl laying before me had tender, full lips softly parted as she slept. Her eyelids had a soft purple hue, framed by dark lashes. They fluttered as if she were dreaming. She smelled of soap and something floral. Lilac? Her smooth and pale skin had a slight pink flush just on her cheeks. Oh yeah, she was beautiful.

And a longing deep within me tugged hard at my heart.

So why didn't I recognize her? And why weren't the memories of us rushing back to me?

Beyond the photographs, I'd hoped seeing her in person would spark something in the hidden parts of my brain, but so far, there wasn't anything new. Suddenly, she began to turn in her sleep, a frightened moan escaping her lips. I sat back on my heels.

"Stop," she breathed, panic ringing in her high voice. "Please." Long strands of her unruly hair wrapped around her face, and a faint sheen of sweat along her brow glistened. My heart pounded, the heat rising within, as my body reacted to her.

I didn't think, didn't question my instincts. I just reached out and gently shook her. "Wake up, Jessa. You're dreaming."

She blinked rapidly, eyes only inches from mine and delirious with sleep.

"Lucas?" The pain on her face was replaced with relief. She flung her arms around me, pulling me toward her and closing the distance between us. Shock burned within me as her lips melded perfectly to mine. Shock, and then something else, something much more primal.

My eyes slammed shut and I deepened the kiss. She smelled of lilac and soap and warm summer nights. She felt like coming home and the inertia of free fall. And although my mind may have forgotten her, my body remembered. The way her face fit perfectly in my palm, the angle at which her jaw jutted upward to me, the gentle tilt of her cheek, the soft flutter of eyelashes against my skin. It all poured over me like salve to a wound.

Of one thing, she hadn't been lying.

I rocketed back to standing, ashamed. I didn't remember her! I couldn't be kissing her, not like that. Her eyes opened wide, following me as they blinked away the previous moment. Embarrassment crept across her cheeks in deep red strokes as she sat up, stretching her body out like a kitten. The hem of her shirt rose above the hemline of her gray cotton pants, briefly exposing a line of pale stomach.

I imagined roots extending from my feet and into the floor, grounding me in place. It was either that, or pick up where we left off. But I couldn't let myself, not with so many unanswered questions. Not with how dangerous she could be.

I glanced down at my clothing, relaxing at the all-black ensemble.

"I'm sorry," her voice chirped. "I wasn't fully awake. I was just so happy to see you. I didn't think." Her bright ocean eyes shone with such intensity, and I couldn't turn away.

I cleared my throat. "It's okay. Let's just forget about it."

She shook her head. "If only you knew how long it took you to get me to forgive you…" Her voice trailed off.

"What do you mean?"

She glanced around the room. Even though we were underground, no expense had been spared. The bedding had been stripped save for the white sheets, and there wasn't a rug, but there was a black couch along one wall, a black dresser and furniture set, smooth white walls adorned by black and white landscape photography, and a small crystal chandelier hanging above the bed.

I noticed her eyes lingering on the oak door, painted black on this side. It matched the black trim lining the room.

"It's okay," I said. "Those things are thick. Nobody can hear us."

I wasn't sure if that was actually true, not if my father had a certain kind of alchemist with him.

She looked skeptical but nodded anyway. "Are you okay?" she said. "I assume you still don't remember anything?"

"I don't."

"But, they haven't punished you? Have you talked to Richard yet? What did he do to you?" Concern knit her brow, eyes pleading. One hand was fisting the sheet anxiously. What on earth was she talking about?

I shrugged, relaxing onto the couch. "I'm fine. My father is fine. I just talked to him."

Her eyes flashed skeptical. "He didn't say *anything*?"

I cocked my head at her, trying to figure her out. "About what?"

She took a deep breath. "Lucas, they've been torturing me."

I sunk into the couch, guilt pulling me down. "I know."

"No, I mean, they want names. I didn't mean to give them yours."

"*My* name?" That didn't make sense.

"Yes, Lucas. They know you were with the Resistance. Or well, they don't know any of the details, but that you've been involved somehow."

I shrugged and shook my head. "I don't remember. Guess it doesn't matter. Everything is fine." Even as I said it, I didn't believe it. I needed answers, but I also needed her to be on my side—to trust me.

She frowned, jumping from the bed and coming to join me on the couch. Her gray cotton outfit was rumpled from sleep. She looked at me so earnestly, I almost felt sorry for her. This was too easy. She slid in close, leg pressed to mine, heat intermingling, and I stilled. Discomfort and longing warred within me, each fueling off the other.

"Don't you want to know what happened?" she asked.

"I do. It's hard to know who's telling me the truth and who isn't. Richard thinks you tried to kill me."

I gave her a knowing look, knitting my eyebrows together. Then I chuckled when she sat back, eyes wide and appalled.

"I would never hurt you, Lucas!" she challenged. "Someone needs to tell you everything that happened." She chewed her lower lip, nodding once to herself. "I'm the only one who knows everything. It needs to be me."

"It's against my doctor's wishes." I sighed. "He wants me to remember on my own without anyone else putting their versions inside my head."

Too bad it was already too late for that! The image of Celia's slatebook popped into my mind.

"But aren't I allowed to defend myself?"

I smiled. "You're right. Tell me your version of events."

Over the next hour, she did.

By the end, I sat motionless, bile rolling in my stomach. Jessa's hand was in mine, caressing my palm as she cried silent tears, as I was held captive by her rendition of events. Was it true? It was all so detailed, and hard not to believe it. But if she was telling the truth, it meant I was on her side. And she on mine. It meant my father had secrets beyond what I'd ever imagined, secrets so dark, there was no way to shine light on them without revealing the man he really was.

That he was manipulative beyond anything I already knew.

It also meant I needed to convince him to keep her around a little while longer. Last thing I wanted was to wake up one day with all my memories and emotions returned, only to realize my wife had been executed for protecting my sins.

I had to verify her story, and if it checked out, to keep her from being killed for it. I just didn't know how that was ever going to be possible. Because there was one place her story and my father's coincided.

Jessa was a traitor to the royal family and her actions were punishable by death. When it came to that, Richard was in the right. What could I do to convince him otherwise?

And I also wondered just how much of this conversation was really between Jessa and I. Richard had sent me in here on the pretense that I get names, that one-on-one time with her would soften my wife up to helping me, but what if all of that had been another game?

Fear unsettled me as I considered why I was in here alone with her. It was very possible that my father had found a way to hear every last word of Jessa's confession to me. If that was the case, she had dug herself in even further than before. And I'd helped her do it.

ELEVEN

JESSA

"I've struck a deal with my father on your behalf," Lucas said with triumph as he slipped into the room. He'd spent a lot of time in my new prison cell over the last couple of days, mostly to ask me questions. Each time he came through that door, I was reminded of how much I loved him, but also, of how worried I was for him. And for us.

I eyed him wearily. Any deal with Richard wasn't a good one—not for me.

"He agreed to put the Resistance names behind him for now, if you'll help him win the war. Then, when this whole thing is over, we can go back to normal."

I stared at him, not really believing the insane words escaping his mouth. "Are you serious?" I sputtered, catapulting from where I'd been lounging on the couch. "You really think things can ever go back to normal? Haven't you listened to anything I've been saying? And forget the fact that you still don't remember me!"

He frowned, running a hand through his hair and closing his eyes briefly. "I can't help that," he said, voice low and gravelly. "It's called compromise, Jessa. If you don't want it, if you'd rather die, then so be it."

I stilled, returning his challenge with a glare of my own. Did he really mean that? His eyes were set, his mouth a flat line, as our gazes battled. Frustration tightened, pulling me to him like a string.

"So we're helping your father now? That's the plan." I stalked the length of the room until we were inches apart, the space between us charged with electricity. "I won't do it."

He glowered down at me, any semblance of sincerity in his expression now lost. "You will do it," he barked between gritted teeth. "You will help us. You will do as my father asks. You will do whatever is needed to stay alive, Jessa. *You will.*"

Silence stretched between us. I jutted my chin. "No, Lucas, I won't."

He growled, lips pinching, eyes darkening. Folding his arms over his chest, his biceps bulged against the black fabric of his t-shirt. "Are you trying to get yourself killed? Do you want to die? You're being unreasonable."

"I can't," I said low. "You don't know what you're asking of me."

"And I don't think you know what's going to happen to you!"

His voice reverberated off the walls, hardening the thick tension that was now suffocating the room. I knew what I was doing. I'd rather die than see Richard take over West America. I wasn't going to step in line. There was no going back for me. Either way, I figured I was dead. If that's how I was going, I was going out with dignity.

Lucas and I stood toe-to-toe as I held my ground.

An alarm erupted through the room, shrill and persistent. We flew apart, looking around wildly for the source of the noise.

Woop! Woop! Woop! It assaulted my ears, bringing me to my knees. I pressed my hands into my ears, scrunching up my face and squeezing my eyes shut. A wave of sheer panic overtook me.

"What does that mean?" I yelled, looking up to Lucas.

"Enemy on base!" He replied, his voice barely audible over the screaming siren. Panic transformed into hope and my heart slammed into overdrive. I needed to get out there!

A red light popped out of the ceiling, flashing in blinding intervals. A second, deeper alarm echoed along with the first.

"And that?" I pointed to the light, squinting hard.

"I don't know. I think it's best if we stay put."

Yeah, that wasn't going to happen. I sprinted for the door. Adrenaline propelled me forward, my legs aching at the sudden movement.

"Don't!" Lucas called, but it was too late. I tore out into the main room of the underground bunker, looking for threats. Except for one lone guard, standing by the door and fiddling with his slatebook, everyone else had left, probably to aid the fight above.

The guard was distracted, not looking at me when I jumped him. My training with Branson all those weeks ago kicked in, returning in an instant. I disarmed him in one kick to the stomach, sending him sprawling. Then I took off for the stairs, Lucas right behind me.

"You can't go up there! *I* can't go up there!" Lucas shouted, but it didn't matter what he said now. His influence over me had vanished minutes earlier. He wasn't on my side; he was on Richard's now.

Through all the changes, nobody had thought to check inside my bra. Thank God! I connected with the only color I had—the purple—and reached out.

Sasha, I screamed through the connection. *Is that you? Are you guys here to get me out?*

Jessa! Where are you? This isn't going well, we're going to have to retreat soon.

I don't know! Some warehouse. A bunker is below it, they've put me with Richard and Lucas.

Richard is with you?

My legs pumped up the stairs, and I sprinted into the empty space above. It wasn't more than a fifteen by fifteen foot room with a garage door on one end, next to that, a closed steel door.

He's not. It's just me, Lucas, and one guard right now for all I can tell.

Gunfire pummeled outside, bullets hitting the garage door, bending it. I dropped to my knees, crawling to the door, needing to escape.

Lucas grabbed my ankle, but I kicked at him as I strained for the door handle. Thankfully, I gripped the metal and turned, swinging it open.

I caught the flash of a blonde ponytail, recognizing Sasha at the other end of the alleyway. Hope blossomed and tears sprang to my eyes.

"I'm here!" I called out, desperate and relieved all at once.

Lucas's hard body jumped on my back and flattened me to the floor with a crack. Pain burst through my ribcage and I gagged, the breath knocked out of me.

I don't see you, Sasha's voice shot through my mind.

I peeked up, spotting her as she sped closer, her eyes zeroed in right where I was lying with Lucas. One hand pressed over my mouth, the other pinning me to the floor, his body covered mine.

I'm here! I pushed back. The magic began to fade. I needed more purple. *I'm almost out of purple. I'm right in front of you. I'm with Lucas. He's covering my mouth!*

I bit at his hand, but he only gripped harder. He stayed silent as I writhed under him.

I don't see you. She turned and sprinted further away.

"Hey!" The guard from downstairs was in the garage now, Lucas rolled us out of the way just before the man stepped into our path. He looked around for a moment, then took off out the opened door, gun raised.

My magic faded, and I knew the strip of color hidden inside my bra had too.

I wriggled, trying to break free of Lucas. But there was nothing I could do; he had total control over me, his dominance overpowering. I craned my neck around to shoot him a nasty look, realizing he'd made us invisible. There was nothing to see here, no sign of our struggle, nothing but an empty room.

No wonder Sasha hadn't seen me.

I continued to fight, but he held strong, keeping me detained in that god-forsaken building, watching a small slice of the action unfold outside, completely unable to take part.

From our vantage point, it appeared that the fight was moving out as West American soldiers retreated. New Colony soldiers and alchemists charged after them, war cries, weapons brandished, and strands of brilliant color weaving and darting from the hands of alchemists that followed.

All at once, the area fell into silence.

"Come on," Lucas said, letting go of my mouth.

"Get off me!" I screamed, hot tears streaming down my face. "Sasha! Sasha, I'm here!"

It was no use. We both knew that. We were alone. I crawled to my knees, overwhelmed by the heavy disappointment that buried me.

He stood, leaned over, and he had the audacity to pick me up.

"Get your hands off me! You don't know what you're doing."

"I know exactly what I'm doing," he said, charging toward the staircase. His hands gripped me under my legs and around my shoulders, holding me tight against his chest. His heart pounded so loudly, I could feel it against my side. "I'm saving your life! You think people know you're here? Very few do and even less know about me. We have to be careful, Jessa."

"I was getting out of here! What did you think? That West America was going to kill me? They came for me!"

His body tensed, step faltering. "Either way," he supplied, "it's too risky."

"Oh, and staying here and getting executed is a better plan?" I shoved at him as we moved down the stairs, wriggling and jolting with each step. "I mean it, Lucas, put me down!"

"You're not going to get executed because, like I said, I already worked out a deal with my father on your behalf. A deal that you're going to graciously accept."

"We already had this conversation. I said no."

"And now any hope you have of getting out of here is gone," he snapped. "You're going to do it, Jessa. I need you alive."

He carried me into the main room then back to my prison cell, dropping me on the bed with a huff.

I bounced, then hurried to standing, hands fisted at my sides. "Why do you care if I'm alive?"

"Because," he replied, exasperated. "I don't know if I believe everything you've told me, but I do believe one thing."

"And what's that?" I asked sarcastically.

"I believe we were in love." He glared, pain burdened behind his gray eyes. "I believe I wouldn't want you executed, nor would I want you running off to West America."

What a joke! He was the one who snuck me out of the palace in the first place.

"What makes you think that? You're crazy. You're selfish and so—"

He didn't let me finish. His hungry lips crashed into mine, devouring me, possessive. I shoved him away. Hard. At first he didn't budge, but on the second shove, he stumbled back, hands flying into the air. He let out a groan and stormed from the room, slamming the door behind him so forcefully that a picture frame fell from the wall.

I picked up the broken shards, smoothing out the black and white image of a beach scene. There wasn't any glass. Nothing to get at someone's blood.

★

He left me there for hours, locked in that room without a clue to what was

677

happening above. The alarms had long since stopped and I was left to stew. I slept on and off, despite attempts to stay awake. I'd decided that the moment the door opened, I'd be ready to pounce, to make my case, to fight, anything would be better than sitting here. But when the door finally did open, it wasn't Lucas on the other side.

King Richard's tall frame took up most of the doorway, his long shadow falling into the darkness of the bedroom.

"Let's go," he said gruffly. "I have something to show you." He stalked away.

Despite an undercurrent of trepidation, I rolled from the bed and took off after him. Any chance I had to get out of this room was one I was going to take.

Flanked by a half a dozen guards, we ascended the staircase. Save for the sound of their boots clomping up the stairs, everyone was silent. Barefoot, I ignored the cold that gripped my vulnerable feet. There was no time to delay. Whatever Richard had in mind to show me, I was going to go along with it, and maybe if I was lucky, formulate a plan.

I glanced around for Lucas, but he was nowhere to be found. I breathed a small sigh of relief. The feeling was one I'd never expected to have when it came to that boy, but after today, I didn't know how we'd ever get back to the way things used to be. The Lucas I knew never would have done that to me.

We left the warehouse, out onto the tarmac, the cold air ten times worse. Sunrise peeked over the horizon. I told myself that it was refreshing and breathed in a deep breath of the cool air. A thin sheen of moisture covered the ground, which immediately soaked into the hems of my gray cotton pants as we marched down the street. Small pebbles stuck to the bottom of my feet. The base was orderly, brick buildings in neat little lines, soldiers and the occasional guardian crisscrossing the path, the faint smell of gunpowder and smoke, the low hum of vehicles in the distance.

Turning a corner, a large military helicopter waited in the distance.

I skidded to a halt and turned to Richard. "Where are we going?" The chopper was not a welcomed sight. Just thinking about the last time I'd been in one, when I'd nearly crashed to my death, sent me reeling.

Richard didn't reply as we approached the machine, its black surface shiny and gleaming. He climbed inside, reaching his hand out to help me. I eyed it suspiciously, refusing to touch him, and hoisted myself inside without help. Being unencumbered by handcuffs certainly made things easier, but I wondered how long that would last. His guards climbed in after me, passing massive black semi-automatic rifles between them and facing toward the two exits.

"Sit by me." Richard patted the seat next to him. I hesitated, but did as he said.

As we lifted into the air, a thundering roar surrounded us. Three jets zoomed out into the sky ahead. I gripped the sides of my small seat, stomach dropping with the inertia.

"They're added protection," Richard yelled, smiling gleefully as his eyes followed the fighter jets.

"Where are we going?" I called back, pushing down the sense of foreboding.

Why was he talking to me like this? Like he and I were on the same side now that Lucas had convinced him not to execute me? I would never be sided with this man. Never.

His answer was filled with triumph, like a little kid who'd won a playground game. "We had a lot of success last night. We're setting up the occupation of Nashville."

Success? What did that mean? Success at killing innocent people, most likely. I watched the scenery fly by outside the window, green and brown landscapes mixing into a blur of color.

"What's Nashville?"

Richard smiled. "One of their largest cities near the border. More than a million West American citizens live there. Only a small amount evacuated before we set up occupation."

"Okay…" My voice trailed off. I didn't get what this had to do with me.

"Alchemy is treated like a crime in West America. Did you know that?"

I eyed him, biting my lip. "I've heard that."

But I also knew my sister was there, my family, and so far they seemed okay about their situation. At least, I thought so. I hadn't exactly been able to talk to them whenever I'd wanted.

"At least with me, you stand a chance," he said.

I laughed low. "Oh, really? Is that why I'm scheduled for execution? By the way, when is that? Because I'm assuming it's still on. Even if Lucas did cut a deal for me, I don't expect you to honor your end of the bargain."

He turned a dark look on me, eyes pointed, shining like razor blades. "Don't test me," he snapped. "I'm giving you one more chance to come to our side and abandon this Resistance nonsense, and I'm only doing that for my son's sake."

"It has nothing to do with my red alchemy?"

This time, he laughed. "Of course that's an added benefit, but not if it means having a traitor living in my own home."

I rolled my eyes, lost for words.

"Before you give me your final decision, I need to show you what costs are involved."

I grit my teeth and nodded. I already knew the costs involved.

As we flew further away from our base and toward the warzone, I noticed several fields of stark gray against the otherwise normal land. I knew about the Shadow Lands up north, but not about these. The desolate earth sprawled out for miles, everything dead.

I turned on Richard. "Are you crazy? Why would you do that?"

He smirked at me like I was a complete idiot. "It was a show of strength," he replied with a reptilian smile that made my skin crawl. "It wasn't the first spot we did this, and it won't be the last."

I shook my head.

"You need to realize that West America is going to lose and the Resistance will go down with it."

I held my tongue.

We continued until we flew over the city itself, a city that appeared to be recovering from a devastating fight. Thick smoke billowed from several buildings, and a few small fires were still burning bright as sunrise. But from this height, I couldn't make out any people. My heart ached for them.

How many were dead?

"Soldiers are rounding up anything that could be used against us," he said. "Most of the people are taking this better than we'd expected. Then again, we're not holding back anything. I've ordered an excessive show of force. No mercy."

"You're sick," I whispered low.

"What was that?" He shot me a dangerous look, a challenge in his eyes that sent a shiver of fear down my spine.

Once again, I held my tongue. I needed to be smart if I was going to make it out of this alive. A possibility that seemed further and further from reach.

"I wanted to show you this so you would understand how important it is that you use your red alchemy to help us."

I held up a hand, not quite understanding his meaning, but also not wanting to fully understand this man. "I'll stop you right there. If your son can't convince me, what makes you think you can?"

He smiled softly, turning back to the window. We hovered over the city, and up ahead, I could make out the jets flying low. Beyond that, something in the distance burned. I squinted, trying to make it out, but all I could see was flames and smoke.

The jets approached the area, and a black speck fell from one, landing with an explosion. It billowed out in an all-consuming flame, the noise penetrating the entire landscape with a screaming boom.

My mouth fell open, tears springing to my eyes. "What are they bombing?"

Richard sent a conspiratorial grin at me. "That's the West America military base." A dark laugh fell from his lips as he leaned forward to get a better look. "Or at least, what's left of it."

Terror overtook me, pressing on my chest, confusing all my thoughts. My sister was there. Her friends! Maybe Dad? So many others. This couldn't be happening.

"Why are you showing this to me?" I gasped, the fear cutting me like a razor.

"I already told you, Jessa. I am going to win this war. And you're going to help me do it. This isn't the first bombing; some have been on the city."

"On all those innocent people?" As I stared wide-eyed at this monster, blood drained from my face, heartbeat thudding in my ears.

"If you don't have the decency to make this easier for me, *for everyone*, then I will use whatever means necessary."

"You can't blame me for a bombing!"

He tilted his head, eyes two pinpoints of rage. "Can't I? You have undermined me at every turn and I will no longer allow it. Lucky for you, my son convinced me that we do need to keep you. Your execution is postponed until further notice."

"This doesn't change anything!"

He motioned toward the pilot and we spun around. Even though everyone was strapped in, our bodies veered with the movement. I slammed up against him and the need to vomit rose up, clawing at my throat. I began gasping for air, unable to get enough.

The chopper righted itself and flew closer to the city.

"See that?" He pointed toward the wreckage of a building. "That was a hospital."

Tears burned my eyes and I choked out a sob.

"And see that?" His finger moved toward an intact building. It stood tall and regal, like it was important to the city. "It's currently filled with dissenters. You can either help me control these people, or you can watch them die."

"No," I said with the quick shake of my head. "You're bluffing."

"Am I?" He slid a slatebook from his pocket and pressed a number. A moment later he held it to his ear. "Do it," he said to whoever was on the other end. "I'm making the order."

I faintly made out the reply of a woman's voice. Faulk?

A jet flew over the capitol building. As the small speck fell, screaming filled my ears. My screams. "No!"

But it was too late.

The bomb exploded, sending chunks of the building flying, practically shaking the entire thing off its foundation. A ball of fire plumed up from its center, black smoke at the edges.

"It's no big loss, really," Richard shrugged with nonchalance. "Casualties are expected and those fools were asking for death. Plus, we'll be destroying any state buildings once we take over anyway."

My heart thudded. My breath caught.

He turned his evil eyes on me, talking slow, making sure I heard each and every word, "You could have prevented that. If you had agreed to help me with those people, I wouldn't have killed them."

I shuddered.

"There are more. There are others."

Dark understanding crawled over me. My vision dimmed. My mouth opened and closed repeatedly as I realized the truth. I was stuck. I had no choice but to help him, to become another weapon in his arsenal. If I didn't, he would end up killing even more people.

I nodded. "Fine." A hot tear fell down my cheek. "You win."

TWELVE

SASHA

The early morning sun glared down on us, the sunrise washing the carnage and destruction in a strange yellow light. Overnight, the world turned to chaos. What was supposed to be a quick extraction mission had quickly transformed into an all-out battle to the death. Not that anyone should've been surprised—least of all me.

"Go!" Mastin yelled over the deafening roar of gunfire.

He pointed toward the armory on base. My necklace was running low on everything. I needed to get over there to replenish it with what Nathan Scott had supplied for me. And my gun's ammunition had long since been depleted—making it to the armory was the next best move.

"You're coming with me." I pulled on his arm.

"I can't," he replied, scanning the battle ahead, the battle that had unfortunately followed us back to the base. "You go. I'll catch up."

I closed my eyes briefly, the ratcheting sounds of combat caving in on me. The smell, equally jarring with its mix of smoke and blood, sweat and metal, gunpowder and rain.

I didn't want to leave Mastin. Something told me that if I left him now, we'd be separated for good. Perhaps it was foolish or short-sighted, but my heart just couldn't do it. We needed to stick together.

The New Colony forces had moved in quickly. Swift as an axe, they'd unleashed their fury. We'd poked at them one too many times, and now had woken the beast. The moment we'd retreated from their base after things had taken a sour turn last night, they'd used the opportunity to attack. They'd started with several bombs that had thrown everyone to the ground, left us scrambling, and then their alchemists had moved in, crossing into our territory in droves.

The Guardians of Color were the worst.

Lethal, they moved like panthers, quick and cunning. They all had yellow and green power at their disposal, though some were better than others. Some were better than none—which was our biggest problem. Using the strength alchemy to their advantage, they cut down our soldiers like weeds. Whenever one of their own or a nearby New Colonial soldier was injured, they were quick to administer healing magic. But it wasn't just the green and yellow that was the problem. Other magics were at play, too.

"What's he doing?" Mastin questioned, terror rising in his voice. It was a new sound for him, something so foreign, I stepped back, his wave of panic sweeping over me, too.

I peered over his shoulder at a group of our soldiers. They had their guns trained on a male alchemist, but one by one, they dropped their weapons. Our men were surrendering!

When the alchemist turned, and I caught a glimpse of Reed, I froze.

"It's blue alchemy," I whispered in Mastin's ear. "He's using it to persuade them to stand down."

"We have to stop him."

"It's not that simple."

The moment the last of the soldiers had dropped their weapons, Reed lifted a handgun and began firing. Arcs of blood shot out of the defenseless soldiers' bodies as they crumpled in on themselves, dropping to the mud with sickening thuds.

Mastin tensed, a growl escaping his throat, hand lifting his gun, and clearly ready to run from our hiding spot and intervene. I surged yellow magic through my veins, holding Mastin back with my strength, rooting us in place.

"You can't," I gasped. "He's too powerful. He'll kill you."

"I'd like to see him try," Mastin snarled, yanking at his arm, trying to free himself. "Let me go."

"Please, come back with me," I begged, running my hand up his arm, willing him to look at me, to listen to reason. But he wouldn't. He craned his neck back to get a better look, craned it away from me, fire still burning through him, fire that I needed to extinguish if I was going to keep him from running in there and getting himself killed.

By this point, several more Guardians had joined Reed. They moved up the alleyway in a determined line, taking out anyone in their way. Swirls of color magic swung around them, mostly yellow, with a mix of Reed's deadly blue. The men in their way didn't stand a chance. They fell, landing on their knees, bloodied, faces scrunched up in confusion, before flopping to the earth. Before dying.

"We need to move," I whispered. "They're going to see us."

"I have to stop him," Mastin challenged again.

"You can't if you're dead!"

Why couldn't he see reason? His bloodlust had taken a firm hold, the desire for revenge overpowering all sense of reason. If he didn't snap out of it, I'd lose him.

A thin trail of blood ran down his forearm where some shrapnel had launched itself into his bicep earlier in the night.

I could use red alchemy… The thought pulsed, taking root in my mind. *It's been years, but what if it still works?* It would be so easy to make him come back with me.

But no, that would reveal my secret. And he would hate it.

But if it saves his life, wouldn't it be worth it?

"I was wondering when I'd find you again!" Reed's cackle echoed down the alleyway, making my decision for me. His gaze zeroed in on us as he ran. I might've been able to resist him, but I couldn't risk Mastin. Reed had made the mistake of going easy on us once and we'd gotten away. From the shine of excitement lighting his eyes, from the way he and his gang stalked toward us across the gravel, that wouldn't be the case a second time.

He was far away still, but he was the predator and we were the prey. And he loved it.

I glanced around, desperate for escape. There was only one way I saw this going. I didn't let myself debate for another second. I grabbed Mastin's bloody bicep and thought only of red. The magic came back in an instant, as if it had never left, just waiting for me to accept its presence. The electric power surged through me. Red strings of shining magic danced through the air, and I immediately pushed them into Mastin. Eyes still on Reed, he never looked my way, never saw the alchemy.

"Come on, we have to save ourselves. Follow me," I said, pushing what little I had of the yellow in with the red. It was our only shot at outrunning Reed. "We have to get to the armory. Now!"

Mastin didn't argue. I knew that he wouldn't, that he couldn't, not with my power reigning over him. I caught a glimpse of his eyes, glazed over with a singular focus on my command, and refused to feel guilt. I'd have time to beat myself up later. Boots kicking gravel behind us, we sprinted around the corner and toward a heavily fortified steel building. The wall of soldiers lining the front, guns trained, let us through without a flinch of hesitation. They barely looked our way as they shouted to each other, taking shots at the incoming enemy. The thick burn of smoke still hung in the air, paired with low moans and arresting shrieks of the injured.

We stumbled into the room, packed with bodies. Apparently, we weren't the only ones who needed more ammunition.

"Load up!" the deep voice of General Scott echoed through the large room, basically a small scantily-built warehouse with shelves upon shelves of weapons along the sides. "We're retreating. We've lost too much ground here. We're going west. Head for the airfield. Now!"

Men and women gathered supplies at lightning speed, carrying boxes of ammunition and slinging guns over their shoulders. Some worked together to carry large crates. They streamed for the exits in crushed lines. Mastin followed me, ever the faithful servant with the red magic running through him.

I crossed my arms over my stomach, trying not to be sick. This was why

I hated red alchemy so much. I never wanted this kind of power. It was too much, too much for one person to have this kind of control.

"Snap out of it." I turned on him. "Do whatever you want."

He blinked, confusion running over his face, as he looked around wildly. "What just happened?" His eyes narrowed on me. "Did you do that?"

"I'll explain later," I rushed the excuse out, breaking his intense eye contact just as I'd broken his trust. Now was not the time for this conversation—would there ever be a time for it?

"There you are!" Tristan's frenzied voice jerked me out of my thoughts. "I've been looking everywhere for you." A trace of anger rung heavy in his tone as he pushed his way around the crowd of retreating soldiers. "You disappeared! We were supposed to stick together."

"We took cover." I shrugged, biting my lip as more guilt ripped through me. "It's fine, we're here now."

He held my eyes, mouth in a thin line. "You heard the General, we need to get out of here. Get what you need. We're leaving." He hooked his weapon over his shoulder, drawing his eyebrows together.

I nodded, and the three of us sped off to replenish our supplies. Luckily, all of us had been trained to understand the layout. My stones were in a box in the corner of the room, resting high on the farthest shelf. I sprinted toward it, relieved to find the box waiting for me. Just the sight made it easier to breathe.

But when I heaved it down from the shelf, it jostled into my hands like nothing, as light as if it were empty.

I flung it open, furious. Empty.

I cussed and threw the box against the floor, splintering it along one edge.

"What's wrong?" Tristan jogged over, an added gun slung over his shoulder.

"Someone took my stones! And I'm pretty much out of everything useful."

Pulling it from under the hem of my black shirt, I studied my necklace in my fingers. The stones hung in a line along the leather strap. There was hardly a trace of yellow left and the green was completely gone, the stone a sickly shadow of itself.

"It's okay." Tristan tugged me after him. "We'll worry about it later."

He was right. As much as I wanted to scream and punch something, there wasn't time. We took off, finding Mastin who was busy loading ammunition into his current handgun and slinging another, much larger one, onto his back.

"You ready?" I asked him.

He nodded once, looking me over with a trace of suspicion in his green eyes. His jaw clenched for a moment and then he spoke, "Yeah, let's go."

We hauled it for the building's one exit, Mastin taking point as usual as we moved from the relative safety of the place. Gunfire rained down on us the moment we slipped out the door and sprinted for the airfield. We dodged the bullets as they ripped at the ground around us, sending dirt and gravel flying. The airfield stretched out next to the armory, so we didn't have to run far, but with death all around us, it felt like miles extended between us and the nearest machine.

Soldiers were climbing into the opened doors of jets and choppers. The second one filled, the doors slammed shut and the machine rose into the air. I eyed the nasty New Colony jets circling the base, white demons that roared through the sky, hungry for more death.

So far, they hadn't dropped any more bombs.

Probably because so many of the New Colonials were on the base now. Richard wouldn't care about his civilian soldiers, but he wouldn't want his alchemists to be blown up. No, those Guardians were the difference between winning and losing.

Our feet slammed against the pavement, puddles of rainwater splashing in our wake. At last, we made it to one of the mammoth helicopters just as it was getting ready to lift off. Mastin jumped in first, reaching out to pull me in after him. As I was hoisted inside by his steady arm, I landed on my butt. A prickle of relief ran down my entire being, settling in. I closed my eyes, catching my breath, running hands down my legs to wash off the mud. I spun around to make sure Tristan had plenty room as well.

He was gone.

I blinked, disbelieving. "Tristan!" I jumped up and screamed out the door. "Where are you?" My voice was a mere squeak compared to the onslaught of battle raging outside. I frantically scanned ahead, taking in the last of the soldiers, watching as the enemy approached, but Tristan wasn't anywhere to be seen. Had he gone to another chopper? No, he wouldn't have left me. Not on purpose.

Someone pulled the door shut with a sharp clang. The chopper lifted and climbed, and my panic climbed with it. No, I couldn't leave him!

I wrenched the door open, calling on the last bit of yellow magic I had, and dived down to the pavement ten feet below. I tucked and rolled on my landing, ignoring the pain as I popped up to full standing.

"Sasha! What are you doing?" Mastin screamed down but it was too late. He was too high to jump down after me.

I held up a hand. "Don't worry!"

Looking around the airfield, there were still several choppers that hadn't taken off. There was still time. All the jets had left, but all I needed was one chopper. Just one. I would have to be quick. Find Tristan, then get back before it's too late.

You can do this. Everything will be all right. I repeated the words over and over again as I took off running.

Gunfire blew bits of the dirt right next to me, and I dove for the ground in the opposite direction. I crawled to my knees and searched for cover.

That's when I saw him.

Leaning against the metal siding of the backside of the armory, Tristan hunched over, clutching at his stomach. His face shone with anguish, his mouth pinched.

I ran for him at breakneck speed, dodging bullets and crying out in both terror and relief. I was well aware that there wasn't green near me, so if I got shot, I wouldn't be able to heal myself. But more than myself, it was Tristan who I worried for. He needed my healing alchemy. I had nothing to offer. The entire area was a tangle of metal and pavement, dirt and gravel, shrapnel and wreckage, but no greenery in sight.

I skidded to a stop in front of him. "Are you okay?"

He blinked up at me, a mix of relief and fear drowning his features. "What are you doing here?" He coughed, thick globs of blood spilling out of his mouth.

"I came back for you. What else?"

He didn't seem to hear me, head shaking, his eyes rolled into the back of their sockets. The remaining color drained from his face, black hair flopping across his sweat-covered forehead.

I had a little bit of yellow left, the barest amount. I prayed it would be enough to get us to safety. Quickly, I called on what was left of the amber stone that lay, mostly gray, against the hollow of my neck. The second the surge of strength ran through me, I reached around Tristan and picked him up. His arms fell on either side, his head rolled against my collarbone as I stood.

"Hang in there!" I demanded. "You are not allowed to die!"

Magic bursting through my legs, I took off for the chopper. It was the last remaining one but the propellers were already spinning. A man with a smoke-smeared face leaned out to slam the door shut.

"Wait!" I screamed, my voice shriller than I'd ever heard it before. The man caught my eye, looking to me and then to whoever was advancing behind us. I didn't look back. It was now or never.

Mercifully, the man waited with the door opened, someone at his side leaning out and firing at whoever was chasing us.

My heart pounded, catching up to the chopper just as it was lifting off. I threw Tristan in first and jumped inside. As I turned to close the door, a sharpness tore through my upper arm. The pain was so searing that it was almost unbelievable. I cried out, panic surging alongside the agony.

"You've been shot!" A gruff voice called as I stumbled further into the chopper.

"I'll be okay." I winced, holding my arm. The pain crawled into my bone, deep and reaching. "Any chance one of you has some green on you?"

Nobody answered. I turned, absorbing the looks of a dozen astonished and weary expressions. Honestly, they didn't look much better than I did. Their uniforms were filthy with matted soot and blood, faces bruising. But at least they didn't have gunshot wounds!

"I didn't think so," I muttered, straining on the words.

I looked down to the blood pouring out of my arm. It was bad, but it was nothing compared to what Tristan was enduring. His entire shirt was soaked crimson, and he was still passed out, body slumped awkwardly beside me. If we didn't get him help right away, he would die.

The chopper flew over the blurred landscape, gaining speed.

"Land!" I yelled, lumbering to the front of the chopper.

The pilot didn't seem to notice me. Or if he did, he didn't care enough to glance back in my direction.

"We need to get to land," I said again, gritting my teeth against the pain. "Somewhere green." My breath caught. "Please."

No response. I could overtake him. I could fly this thing. But that wouldn't happen with all these soldiers here; they'd stop me.

"We need land!" I chocked back a sob. "Please, just really quick so I can save my friend and anyone else on here who needs help." I pointed to a field of sprawling green grass in the distance. "There. Land there!"

"Are you trying to get us all killed? Get out of here!" the pilot replied. "I have orders."

I turned back to the men behind me, eyeing three more injured bodies crumpled in on themselves.

"I can save people if you land this thing. I can heal them. Please!"

Should I use red alchemy on him? I don't know if I can with so many witnesses, but Tristan needs me. I'll do anything to save him. No question, I'm desperate.

Resolved, I reached toward the man.

"Fine!" The pilot relented, just before I touched him. "But you'd better make it quick."

"I will. I promise!" Pure relief cascaded through my breath as I exhaled.

We descended quickly, landing in the middle of the glorious green.

Using my good arm, I swung the door open. Landing on both feet, I reached down and tore at the grass, fistfuls of it.

"Come on!" someone called out to me. "We need to go!"

In the distance, several jets circled the base, much lower than they were earlier. A black speck fell from one of them. I stilled as I watched it, knowing what it meant. A bomb. It landed on the armory, the structure exploding and erupting into flame.

I sprinted back to the chopper, scrambling to get to Tristan as quickly as possible. The other injured would have to wait, myself included. Tristan came first.

We jolted into the air, flying low over the ground. I worked the green magic, the color twisting into the air. Saving my very best friend, my favorite person, wasn't what I'd planned for today, but I was certainly grateful for the chance.

After a few minutes, he woke, blinking up at me.

"Thank God," I breathed.

He smiled, eyes dark as storm clouds, searching mine. "Yes. Thank God for you, Frankie."

Who was I? Was I the Frankie from years ago, in love with my unavailable best friend? Or was I Sasha, the warrior destined to start a new life? So many things had changed, starting with the introduction of my family. I didn't feel like the same girl from all those years ago, but sometimes, I wondered if maybe I still wanted to be her. Maybe it was possible to meet in the middle, to be both.

I looked away, sitting back on my heels, and tended to the wound in my arm.

"I owe you. This is at least the second time you've saved my butt, you know?" Tristan teased, brushing the sweat from his brow.

Shaking my head, I laughed. "It probably won't be the last, either."

★

"I can't believe we lost Nashville." I ground out the words as I sat down next to Mastin. The dirt and rocks mixed uncomfortably with sparse grass, but I paid them no attention. I would endure much worse to spend time with this man. "And Jessa, I don't know what's going to happen to her." I sighed, defeated, an emotion I didn't know how to handle.

Mastin sat on the crest of the hill that overlooked the endless horizon when I found him, his knees bent, elbows resting on top, and his hands cradling his face. Tense, he didn't say anything in response. Frustration rolled off of him and I bristled. Was this all my fault? I'd convinced his father of the importance of rescuing Jessa, and when we'd failed the mission, everything had gone to hell. So there was that. There was also the fact that for the first time in years, I'd used red alchemy, and it just so happened to be on him.

I stared out into the sunset, blinking back the tears. I was not going to cry! I was not that girl.

I craned back to get another look at our newest home. We'd taken up occupation in a tiny town a few hundred miles west of Nashville. The residents had already evacuated, so we were able to start reorganizing ourselves in the homes and businesses. The place was quaint, a jewel in a field of vast grasslands.

My head ached, a throb that pulsed in my forehead. The entire day had been terrible as we'd realized just how many people we'd lost back in Nashville.

Guilt ripped through me. How was it that the sky could be so beautiful, a wash of bright pink and royal purple, and yet I could feel so hollow inside?

"Are you in love with him?" I froze, Mastin's question catching me off guard. He leaned back on his palms, staring off into the distance.

I took in the firm set of his profile, turning the question over in my mind. I could pretend I didn't know who he was talking about, but of course I did. "I love Tristan. I've loved him for years. But I don't know if I'm in love with him."

He winced, eyebrows drawn. "You don't know? How can you not know?"

I shrugged. "But I do know how I feel about you."

"And what's that?"

Was it love? I hadn't gotten to there yet, but I was close. "I feel like you and I are the same, like we get each other. I feel like we're supposed to see where this goes." I reached out and placed my palm on top of his, intertwining our fingers. This level of vulnerability was hard for me. I wanted to jump up and run away, but I forced myself to stay.

My heart, usually so guarded, was opening for him, and quite honestly, it hurt. But wasn't love supposed to hurt?

He sighed, closing his eyes and breathing in deeply. "How are we going to do that if you're more concerned about your friendship with Tristan than you are with your relationship with me?"

I started pulling away from him. "That's not fair."

"Isn't it?"

"Is this because I went back for him? I couldn't leave him there to die. You can't get mad about that."

He twisted his lip, nodding slowly. "It's not that you went back for him. I understand that and I would have done the same. Even though it bothered me, I know that's a selfish reaction and I don't want to be that guy."

I laughed coolly. "What? The jealous boyfriend? It's kind of too late for that, don't you think?"

It was a mean thing to say. But I was too stubborn to take it back. And actually, he wasn't my boyfriend, was he? We'd never defined it that way.

"I'm serious." He looked me up and down with his piercing green eyes. They traveled slow, landing on my lips. I tensed in anticipation. "And it's not because you went back for him that we're having this conversation." He paused, twisting the words around in his mouth before speaking, "It's the way you look at him. It's the way you *are* around him. I didn't want to see it at first; it was easy when you were staying at my house out west and he wasn't there, but I can't help it now we're all on this base. He's always around."

"No he's not. He's been avoiding me ever since you and I got together." I sat back, folding my arms over my chest. Why was I being so defensive? I could just tell Mastin that I had zero feelings for Tristan and this conversation would be over.

"And the fact that he's been avoiding you hurts you. I can tell."

"Because he's my best friend."

"Nothing more?"

I bit my lip. We'd circled back to the burning question. The truth was, even if somewhere deep inside I still wanted Tristan, he didn't want me. He'd told me to date Mastin. And that was fine. Mastin and I were the same, we belonged. I'd chosen him and wanted to keep choosing him, if he'd let me.

"Nothing more," I said.

He watched me carefully, guardedly.

"Please, don't do this," I said, letting out a stilted breath. "I can't choose between my best friend and you. I want you both in my life. I need you both."

He sighed, anger leaving his expression only to be replaced with sadness.

"Fine," he relented. "I guess it's better than the alternative."

I stilled. What did he see as the alternative?

"If it's not you and me," he continued, "it's going to be you and him. And I'm selfish, I guess, but I want it to be you and me. I–I really care about you, Sasha."

I leaned in, scooting closer. "I feel the same way about you."

Tentatively, our lips met. The argument was quickly lost to the passion that overtook us. As he held my face in his rough palms, I knew I'd meant what I'd said. I did care about him. I wanted this moment to go on forever, to live in this place where we could save each other.

THIRTEEN

LUCAS

"Start with the inner circle." I leaned against the wall, looking down at my father. We'd been arguing his reasons as to why I wasn't allowed out of the bunker. They all made sense, but that didn't make it any easier for me. My hope in coming here had been to get Richard to let me go back to the way things were. If I'd known that helping him with Jessa would result in being confined underground, I wasn't sure if I'd have done it.

Of course you would have. You wanted to meet Jessa.

"You said you got Jessa to agree to help with red alchemy." I crossed to join him on the chestnut leather couch. "So let's start with the inner circle. Let's find out who's been trying to kill me and then we can remove them and I can get out of here."

"What makes you think it's someone in my inner circle?" His jaw clenched, disbelief in his eyes.

I scoffed. "Come on, it's the only thing that makes sense."

"Plenty of people were in the palace that night."

"Yes, but what about the plane explosion, or the fire, or even the funeral?" I pressed. It was obvious to me.

He let out a breath. "You've been doing some research. You weren't supposed to look into your past until your memories returned. We talked about this—the doctor agreed."

I couldn't meet his gaze, ashamed at lying, and also, in getting caught. *Yeah, so what? Anyone in my position would have done the same.*

"Where did you get a slatebook?"

"I stole one," I deadpanned. "Did you really think I wouldn't look into my past? If it were you in my position, you'd have done the same."

He hummed, thumb running along his jaw. "True enough. I'm wondering how you can learn all of that and you *still* don't have your memories back."

I shook my head. "I don't know if I ever will."

He smiled. Why the smile? If he wanted me to remember who'd tried to kill me, I needed those memories. But at the same time, I wasn't even sure I *wanted* the memories anymore. What if Jessa was telling the truth about everything? What if I was Resistance and had turned on my own family?

"Answers," I pressed. "I need answers, as do you. Let's start with using Jessa's red alchemy."

Richard's smile spread even wider. "I never thought I'd see the day that you'd put our family's interests before Jessa."

I bristled. What was that supposed to mean?

"Luckily for you, I have to agree," he continued. "We'll do as you suggested. Let's start with our inner circle and work out from there."

"Let's start with Faulk." I'd hardly seen the woman lately. She was busier than ever, doing my father's dirty work, no doubt.

The silence between us stretched as we studied each other. Faulk and I had never seen eye to eye, Richard knew that as well as anyone. It made sense; she hated me. She could be the one behind the attempts on my life. Why not the woman who'd felt the need to point out my weaknesses all throughout my childhood?

"She has no reason to betray us." Richard's voice was smooth as ice.

"That you know of."

He grumbled. "She won't like it."

"Only if she has something to hide."

He leaned back into the couch, looking up at the ceiling, considering. I waited, anticipation creeping up me. As far as I was concerned, Faulk was the perfect candidate to start interrogations on. And we had to start somewhere, right?

"We'll get started right away," he relented, looking back to me with a pained nod.

"Do it here," I said. "Faulk already knows about me. I want to see this." Was it wrong that I wanted to see her squirm? Maybe. I didn't care.

"I'm proud of you, son. You've become more cunning than ever since your accident. You're turning into the prodigy I'd always hoped for. I'm just sorry your mother isn't here to see it." He stood, patted my shoulder, and then strode from the room.

Pride swelled like a balloon within the deepest part of me, but there was something dark there, too, something that twisted my insides and pricked my skin. I realized with a start that the feeling was shame. It was guilt and disgust and a mix of so many things and it left me reeling. What did I have to be ashamed of? My mind flitted back to all the claims Jessa had made about the last year, about my father. Even though my mind disbelieved, maybe the rest of me was trying to tell me something, trying to prove once and for all that Jessa was right.

★

She came willingly. Maybe it was like I had said; maybe Faulk didn't have anything to hide. As she walked into our bunker, I eyed her up and down, taking in her pressed white uniform, gleaming silver buttons and flashing adornments.

"Nice to see you're doing well." She said it in a way that felt much the opposite. I raised a mocking eyebrow.

"Let's get this over with." She sneered and marched across the room, arms folded defensively over her chest. She crossed to Jessa's door, unlatched the lock, and threw it open with a clang.

"Get out here, traitor," she taunted. "You should be thanking God for that red alchemy trick. You should know you'd be dead otherwise."

My fingers itched to wring her neck. She shouldn't be talking to Jessa that way. Her hate was so all-consuming, it turned her from agitating to downright obnoxious, but I kept my mouth shut and pushed down the white-hot anger that had flared within.

Richard leaned against the wall of the bunker's family room. He watched the whole exchange with unrestrained amusement playing at his lips. Guards stood at attention in the four corners of the space, hands resting on their holsters, eyes assessing for threats.

Jessa gingerly shuffled from her doorway, reluctance etched into every line of her body. Her complexion had paled but she held herself solid, shoulders back, chin up, a look of sheer defiance lighting her eyes. Her unruly hair was gathered in a knot on top of her head, one small piece loose and bouncing against her long neck. I grew jealous of that lock of hair, longing to run my fingers along that tender spot of milky skin. As if sensing my lascivious thoughts, she turned a savage glare in my direction; I couldn't help myself, I stared back.

She was gorgeous, reminding me of a wild animal, a mare that needed to be broken, but the very idea of breaking her untamed spirit left me reeling.

"What's this about?" she demanded, peeking about the room. We'd already cleared out any color that could be detrimental to us, but I could tell she was checking. Just in case. Smart girl.

I didn't blame her.

"You work for me—you already agreed. Don't look so put-off," Richard said, peeling himself off the wall and stalking toward her. In his fine suit, with his tall frame and broad shoulders, she looked positively weak, but I knew better than to underestimate her. "We're going to start with a few interrogations. You'll be using your red to get answers from our leaders, and so on down the pipeline."

Her eyes popped. "W-what?"

"Let's just get on with this." Faulk stepped forward. "I don't have anything to hide." She slid a bony hand into her pocket, pulling out a shiny pocket-knife. Flipping open the small blade, she cut a thin line into the flesh of her forearm. Blood surfaced, little crimson beads that she held out to Jessa.

The mood shifted. Jessa visibly relaxed, as if accepting the inevitable, and then reached out to Faulk. The small bubble of blood that dripped from Faulk's arm changed color as Jessa touched it. It pulsed through the air, a red swirl, before running back into the woman.

"You will answer anything we ask with 100% accuracy," Jessa said, and Faulk nodded, her normal spark of personality now extinguished.

"Do you know who's been trying to kill me?" I asked, moving to stand next to the pair. Jessa looked up at me from under her dark lashes, eyes fixed with animosity. She was still angry at me for stopping her escape; probably always would be. Didn't matter, I needed her here.

"I don't know, yet," Faulk said, voice as even as slate. "Jessa is the best explanation for the night of your wedding but not the other attempts. We're still working on it."

Jessa glared, mouth pinched.

"Don't you have any leads?" I continued.

"No living ones."

Richard strolled over, power shining in his hungry eyes as he leaned down to stare directly into Faulk's placid eyes. "Are you loyal to me and my family?"

"Yes."

"Have you always been loyal?"

"Yes."

He nodded, straightening. "Is there anything you've been hiding from me? Anything at all that I should know?"

"I wasn't upset to see Natasha die. I should have been; it was my job to protect her."

Hot pinpricks clouded my vision. Next to me, Richard's temper snapped like a whip. He struck out and backhanded Faulk without a second's pause.

She flew back with the force of it, thudding against the wall and sliding down onto her butt, knees bent awkwardly. She sat there like a lump of clay; nothing in her eyes. Nothing but focus on her task, waiting for the next question that she could answer, a puppet on a string.

"Why?" I asked. Queen Natasha had been loved throughout the kingdom, and especially by anyone she worked with. She'd been kind and beautiful, smart and strong. She was the perfect queen, and even when her headaches had stolen her daily life, she'd still fought to be the best queen she could be.

"Natasha wasn't good enough for you," she said, voice even as she glanced up at Richard. "She never did anything to help you expand your reach, never really saw your vision. She held you back. Look how far you've come since her death."

His chest rose and fell haughtily as he took it all in.

"Did you know she was going to die?" His question bellowed through the small space, causing everyone to jump in alarm. Everyone but Faulk who'd lost all emotion the moment she'd offered her blood.

"No," the woman replied evenly. "But I suspected the alchemy, as you know, we talked about that on more than one occasion."

"Thomas," Richard growled. "He got what he deserved."

"Yes." Faulk's voice rang in affirmation.

The two watched each other over the long, drawn-out, pause. I wrinkled my nose, unable to stomach what was likely to come next. If we kept at it, Faulk would probably confess some unrequited love for my father. It made me ill just thinking about those words coming out of that snake.

I turned on him. "Can we be done here? I think we got all we needed from her. Let's move on to the next person."

Richard nodded once, and after eyeing Faulk one last time, stormed from the room. Faulk hadn't exactly done anything wrong, but since she was his number one advisor, the fact she didn't mourn the Queen's death was big news. I glowered down at the woman. "Get up!"

She didn't move.

"Get up," Jessa repeated, and Faulk stood. "This is over. Go back to your normal self. If you could try not to be such a cold-hearted witch, the rest of us would really appreciate it." A small smirk lifted the corner of Jessa's lips and the desire to feel those lips again crashed through me. As if sensing my thoughts, her eyes shot to mine in warning.

"Not happening." Jessa pointed at me, jaw clenching tight. Then she spun on her heel and charged toward her room, slamming the door behind her.

Faulk took several heavy breaths as her cognition returned to her. Her mouth pinched as if she'd just tasted something sour. Her gaze drifted toward Jessa's closed door and she sneered. Then she, too, escaped from the room.

I dropped to the couch, relaxing into the cool leather and rubbing my hands along the sides of my nose, warding off a headache. That had been an interesting reveal. So, it turned out that Faulk really did have something to hide. She idolized Richard for more than just her boss and king. Maybe I shouldn't have been surprised. Maybe deep in our cores, in the places we thought were hidden from the rest of the world, we were all harboring a secret or two.

✸

I paced the length of the room, the book in my hand bouncing uselessly against my leg. If I didn't get out of here soon, I swore I was going to lose my mind. Over the last couple of days, Jessa's red alchemy interviews had continued. Unfortunately for me, they rarely happened in our bunker, since only those who knew about me were permitted down here. Of course, I had argued incessantly to go upstairs but still couldn't make any headway with Richard on the issue. He thought I was being unreasonable, but what was so crazy about wanting to get out of this god-forsaken dungeon? Deep in my bones, I ached to get out, almost as much as I ached for the whole truth of my past.

Footsteps clattered down the hallway and the bunker's door swung open. Jessa and Richard entered the room, glowering at each other and barely glancing in my direction. The tension between them was thicker than anything I'd witnessed previously. Something had shifted.

Richard threw his coat on the kitchen table and strode for the refrigerator, rooting around through the drawers. Jessa, she didn't move. She was a changed woman. I saw it the second I met her stormy eyes, looking for the familiar charge between us. But it was gone. It was all gone. She was no longer the wild mare I'd likened to her energy. She'd been broken. My hands clenched into fists, the desire to punch something strong.

"What happened?" I demanded, striding around the couch to where Jessa stood aimlessly by the door.

She shook her head. "You wouldn't care." Slowly, she peeled off her white jacket, revealing the usual gray cottons underneath. Carefully, she hung it on the rack and padded to her room, the door closing silently behind her.

One of my father's guards locked her inside before returning to his post, a silent statute in the corner of the room.

My gaze shot to Richard. "What was that about?"

He bit into a yellow pear, juices running down his chin as he beamed. "Just that things are going well for me. Nothing for you to worry about, son."

I narrowed my eyes and he shrugged, wiping the back of his face with his arm and moseying off to his bedroom. Anger and desperation surged through me at having been left in the dark once again. Letting out a breath, I knocked on Jessa's door, wanting nothing more than to talk to her about whatever the hell was going on. She didn't say a word and I didn't let myself in. Too many lines had been crossed already.

Something huge has happened and you missed it! I chastised myself. *You can't let this continue, not if you're serious about figuring everything out.*

I threw myself back on the couch, staring dully at my surroundings. The white walls, the oak trim and doors, the plush rugs in dark reds and blues. The kitchen had more of a modern look, the bare glass dining table gleaming in the middle of it all.

I squinted, the idea rushing to me. Not just an idea, a solution.

Jumping up, I pounded on my father's door this time.

"What is it?" he called through the metal, voice muffled. Then he swung it open. His face was tired, worn down, but also, happier than I'd seen him in ages. It made my stomach churn to know Jessa felt the opposite.

I cleared my throat. "You know Mom's favorite flowers are, or were, white roses?"

His eyes flashed indignantly. "So?"

"We always had several vases back in the palace. I was thinking maybe we could get some for down here. To liven up the place and to remember Mom."

The request sounded utterly stupid now that I said it out loud, but I held my ground, trying to look as earnest as possible. I sighed. "I'm just, missing her, is all."

And that was the truth.

Richard's expression softened. "That's a great idea."

Relief overtook me, and I nodded, a wide smile taking over my face.

"I'll make a call right away. Is that all? I'm exhausted, Lucas. We've had a lot of success in Nashville and in our interrogations as of late, but it's been a lot of work."

I wanted to know more. But I couldn't let him forget about the roses. "That's all. Get some sleep. Do you want me to make the call?"

I raised a playful eyebrow.

He laughed. "Nice try," he said, and then reached into his pocket, pulling out his slatebook and flashing it at me as he closed the door.

I stepped back, smiling for an entirely different reason, and reveling in the knowledge that, as far as I knew, I still had my secret. Before long, I'd have access to the white roses. It was the kind of organic material I needed. I had used a sheet when I'd worked alchemy on Jessa upstairs, but this was different. It was best to use something natural, regardless of the length of time. The white roses had always been perfect. They would be again. I had tried doing things Richard's way, and it hadn't gotten me any closer to the truth. It was time I stopped complaining about my situation and did something to change it.

★

The guards weren't in the bunker with us very often; they were usually outside the door and upstairs. That helped. My father was still asleep in his room, which also helped. And Jessa was locked away. It meant I didn't have anyone checking up on me, which was perfectly okay with me.

I woke the next morning before the bedside alarm, hastily dressed myself and padded into the main living space. Confirming that there weren't any guards, I smiled. The place was empty and my plan was working.

Case in point, in the center of the glass tabletop stood a tall crystal vase overflowing with white roses.

I snagged one, ripping the stem off an inch below the rose. I tossed the stem into the trash, and taking one last look to make sure I was in the clear, I used the white rose to make myself invisible. As far as I knew, it had been a while since I'd done it, and I was a little worried it would exhaust me quickly, or worse, not even work at all. But true to form, the white magic did its job. My body and anything touching me faded into nothingness, like sand lost to the wind.

I waited. It didn't take long.

Richard, dressed for the day, exited his bedroom and moved toward the exit, swinging the door open wide to let in a stream of guards. Then he stomped across the living room to pound on Jessa's door. She didn't fight it. She opened up almost immediately, body slumping from the room with a detached, stony expression lining her pale, forlorn face.

"We'll continue where we left off yesterday," he said.

She nodded and followed him from the bunker. I peeled myself off the wall and crept as close as I could without bumping into one of them and giving myself away. Painfully aware of the insane risk I was taking, the rush of adrenaline and magic surged through me, pushing me forward. Once I knew what Richard was doing with my wife, it would be worth all this trouble.

My wife. Why did I keep calling her that?

It was a different me that had married her. A different time. Now, she obviously hated me, barely looking at me and recoiled from my touch. She probably didn't see me as her husband. I was the enemy. I was the predator and she was the prey, the bird in the cage.

I didn't even know if we were on the same side.

Just because I'd convinced my father not to execute her didn't mean it wouldn't happen eventually. But then again, Richard had invested so much time and money into getting the public to accept her during the alchemy trials. As far as they knew, she was still missing. She was still the beloved princess, stolen from her bedroom the night her husband was murdered.

When all of this was over, would he reintroduce us together? I tried to imagine what that would mean, but came up short. Would we become partners again? Doubtful. I shook the questions away as we stepped out onto the military base. The fresh morning air blasted my skin, smelling of ozone and smoke and rain, but I didn't care. I breathed it in, filling my lungs to the brim, relishing in it.

As a group, we navigated along the brick buildings until we approached a massive helicopter. It was the kind that could hold a bunch of soldiers all at once. Everyone climbed inside and I quickly scrambled in after them before someone slid the door shut. I assessed the space, worry pinning me in place. How was I going to pull this off? They were strapping themselves into seats, not something I could do in my current state. What if I sat down and someone else sat on me? The chopper was being boarded by a stream of soldiers. I jumped out of their way and eventually settled into the farthest corner, sitting with my back against the wall, fingers gripping at the smooth metal wall. I'd have to hold on for dear life if this chopper did anything out of the ordinary. This had better be worth it.

My heartbeat pumped wildly in my ears as I waited, eyes lingering on Jessa, on her sadness. A minute later the chopper purred to life and we took off, cutting through the brilliant red sunrise. The machine's vibrations soothed me and I relaxed. *No, don't let your guard down.* I gripped the rose in my hand, the petals soft against my clammy fingers. What if this was a huge mistake? As far as I knew, I couldn't go long as invisible before the magic would become too much and I'd succumb to sleep. If that happened, I would become visible and my secret would be revealed.

But ... I should have been feeling the effects of that by now, and I wasn't, not even a little bit. How much had I practiced with white alchemy over the last year? The question burned me up, bringing more curiosities to my mind.

I studied Jessa's profile, wondering if maybe she really was telling the truth about everything that had happened to us. Had I turned against my father?

Before long, we landed in a sprawling parking lot. I heaved a sigh of relief to have made it this far and jumped out after the rest of the group. Long cracks had split fissures into the gray pavement, tall weeds growing between the divides. For early February, it was surprisingly warm out, the sun now higher in the sky and pressing down. Or maybe it was just my adrenaline kicking in that made heat rise in my cheeks. I longed to remove my jacket, knowing that was a terrible idea. I had to keep my hands as free as possible. I ignored the sweat gathering along my spine, left hand gripping the rose in my pocket harder than necessary, and trudged after Richard and Jessa.

They entered a one-story red-brick building, so old it looked like it should have been demolished decades ago. Leyland Elementary School was written in boxy script across the entrance, the Y crooked and hanging awkwardly by a single bolt. The brick had crumbled in several places and the railing that lined the steps was so rusted entire parts were missing. What was someone as regal as my father doing in a place like this?

"How many today?" Jessa's question echoed down the steps as they disappeared behind a pair of double doors. The doors swung shut before I could follow.

I inwardly cursed and scrambled up the steps, waiting for someone new to open the door again so I could follow. I didn't have to wait long. Faulk ascended the steps with no less than ten alchemists in her wake. I was so used to seeing her with Royal Officers that the sight of Guardians sent a shockwave through me. They were dressed in their specialized military uniforms, not just the black outfits I remembered from the palace. They had a rainbow of glittering stones embedded into their gear and helmets with shiny visors. Some had their visors pulled down, covering their faces. They looked nothing short of extraordinary and terrifying.

I followed, figuring that where Jessa and Richard had gone, Faulk would soon be joining them. I was right. We entered a large room with scuffed white tile and children's drawings perched on the walls. From the looks of it, it had probably been the school's cafeteria. Sitting along the edges were people grouped together. Families. West American citizens, I had no doubt. Had they taken refuge here during the attack? They huddled together, wide-eyed and afraid.

My ears buzzed as I took it all in. Richard's voice boomed, finishing up some kind of speech that I'd hardly paid attention to. Boots echoed as Faulk marched into the room.

Jessa got to work.

I stood off to the side, both fascinated and horrified as I watched Richard's plan unfold in front of me.

"Hold out your hand," a guard barked, nodding toward a man in threadbare clothing. Taking heavy breaths, the man did as he was told. Knife gleaming, Faulk cut a thin line into the man's palm. Jessa touched the blood with the tip of her finger. The red twirled into the space between them, and the man's eyes bulged. A few nearby observers gasped as Jessa sent the red alchemy back into the man.

"Repeat after me," she said, voice cracking. "I hereby swear my total allegiance and devotion to New Colony and His Royal Highness, King Richard."

The man repeated the words and Jessa moved on to the next person. One by one, Jessa secured loyalty to my father. With her power, these prisoners of war did exactly as she asked. The second they repeated after her, they physically changed. They transformed from reluctant, afraid, or defiant, to malleable and agreeable; the kind of citizens a king could only dream of. They gazed at my father like he was their savior.

Some of the adults waiting their turn held on tight to their crying children. Others resisted.

The guardians used their brute strength to force those people forward. Jessa worked quickly, Richard at her side the entire time. As she moved from family to family, I could make out the anguish in her eyes. It killed her to control them like this. Someone who was part of the Resistance would hate to comply with such a task. The Resistance...if Richard was willing to do this to West Americans, eventually he'd be doing the same thing to his own citizens. What better way to cut the Resistance down than right where they grew?

It was genius.

I doubled over, clutching my knees and fighting the rush of blood prickling in my brain. It was too much. These people were no longer free, and they didn't even have a choice. Was it worth it to be in power if it meant controlling people's choices like this? How could my father think this was okay? This wasn't the kind of king I wanted to be.

And yet this will be your legacy.

I twisted the angry thought around in my mind, unsure of what to do with it. I couldn't just forget it, couldn't push it away. Did I file it under "necessary evil" or just plain "evil"? A bead of sweat trickled down my spine.

"Don't touch us!" A woman screamed shrilly, clutching a toddler to her chest. She stood against the wall. Her son, wrapped around her waist, erupted into tears. She ran a trembling hand down his matted hair, shushing him gently.

Jessa, only feet away from the pair, held out a dejected hand. "If you don't fight it, it will make it easier for him."

"You're sick!" The woman stumbled to the side, shaking her head, her eyes round circles of fear. They flicked toward the exit, right near where I was standing. She didn't see me, looked right past me, but something inside reached out to her, longing to be able to help, and I took a step forward.

"You don't want to do that," Jessa begged. "Please, don't run. You know what will happen if you do."

"How can you do this to people?" the woman replied. "I won't let you touch my son. He's innocent. You'll hurt him; you'll scramble his brain. You scrambled my husband's brain yesterday! You saw what it did to him; not everyone can handle your sick blood magic."

"I'm so sorry," Jessa said low, shoulders caving in. "More than you know."

But the woman didn't respond. She took off for the door, feet slapping the tiles, her son still clutched to her middle.

"Don't!" Jessa yelled after her, but it was too late.

A single bullet ripped through the cafeteria, shattering the silence and sending the inhabitants into frightened hysterics. The woman fell, her body crumpling to the ground. Her son flew from her arms, bawling hysterically.

Blood pooled around her as she held her stomach.

Faulk stood just beyond, her gun raised and a sick smile on her lips.

"Let me heal her." Jessa pushed past Faulk but she didn't get far. Richard ripped her back toward him, holding her in place with a grim expression.

"No," he said, voice booming. "She made her choice."

Jessa let out a sob as the entire room watched the woman on the floor. She

700

bled out in less than a minute. The child that had fallen from her arms continued to wail as he climbed back onto his mother's body, her blood soaking him. He couldn't have been older than two. His face was a red ball of tears and snot, his blonde hair disheveled, the blood turning it pink. His chubby fingers clutched her vacant face, body shaking.

I stepped closer, the urge to comfort him overwhelming. Someone needed to do something! One of the alchemists, a tall man with the visor covering his face, pried the child off his mother without an ounce of sympathy, dumping the boy onto a nearby family.

"Shut him up before I have to do it for you," the man barked.

The family scrambled to calm the traumatized boy, but it was no use; the boy only grew louder, reaching toward the body. "Mamma!"

"Let me calm him," Jessa begged, tears streaking down her face.

"He's of little importance," Richard replied, not even bothering to look at the boy. He pointed to the next family in the row. "We have work to do."

And so they continued on, turning person after person into loyal fans of New Colony and the royal family. Anyone who resisted, anyone who tried to run, was murdered by Faulk without a second thought or a shred of mercy. If she had any remorse over taking innocent lives with such brutally, she certainly didn't show it, but seemed to revel in it, victorious.

Her glee-filled eyes mirrored her King's.

Exhaustion wore me down, starting as a trickle, but soon becoming a downpour. It tugged at my eyes and fell heavy through my limbs. I squeezed the velvety rose in my pocket, knowing I couldn't take any more. I couldn't do this. I slipped from the room, rushing for the nearest empty classroom. Crawling into a dusty closet and closing the door, I dropped the invisibility and fell into a mind-numbing sleep.

Thud, thud, thud, the whirling sound of rudders woke me with a start. I scrambled for the white rose, grateful it wasn't all gray, yet. In the dim light of the closet, I could barely make out the white stands of magic as they swirled out of the flower. The magic seeped into my skin and the invisibility washed over me, covering me like a blanket. I jumped from my spot, ignoring the pulsing ache in my body, and sprinted from the room, sped through the dank hallway, and outside onto the pavement. The blinding sun was setting over the horizon, a wash of citrus hues painting the sky. Squinting, I could make out the huge chopper my father used had already lifted into the sky. Terror ripped through me like razor blades and I sunk to my knees, gritting my teeth.

What would happen when they got back to base and I was missing? Better yet, how was I supposed to survive out here, defenseless and hungry? It was a warzone, after all, and no way everyone here had been turned.

Boots clomped in the distance, but I couldn't see anyone. Figuring they were on the other side of the building, I took off. Relief poured over me when I spotted Faulk and her people climbing into a second chopper. I sped forward, barely making it inside in time. I barely dodged the soldier who was in charge of closing the door, and then not seeing a better place to hide, I pressed myself against the door and prayed it would be an easy flight.

The occupants seemed tired, all buckled-in and closed-lipped. Holding my breath, I slid down to sit on the metal floor. I just needed to get my breath under control, my heart to stop beating in rapid-fire succession. After a few minutes, we lifted and I let out a long slow breath, studying the men and women surrounding me.

Were they traumatized by what they were doing? Did they agree with it? Or had they been changed by Jessa already and didn't care either way?

Their faces were unreadable, some even still covered by black, shiny visors. Maybe it didn't matter, maybe they were as loyal as anyone in this army.

My muscles ached and I longed to stretch my legs as I counted down the minutes. Finally, mercifully, we landed back at base camp without any problems. The red brick buildings, lined in neat little rows, both beckoned me and frightened me.

I slipped out of the helicopter. The second soldier opened the door and moved out of the way as the people in the chopper streamed from it, boots clomping in succession as they headed in different directions. I needed to get back to the bunker before my father realized I was gone. And even that seemed like a feat. Sucking in a breath of chilled air and helicopter exhaust, I sprinted toward the garage with our bunker beneath.

Just as I was about to enter, something in the corner of my eye caught my attention. Two familiar people were arguing, their voices rising above each other. They stood only twenty feet from the garage, their body language tight and angry.

Curiosity got the better of me and I made the detour, creeping forward on the balls of my feet, hand still gripping the rose in my pocket. I needed to be quick.

"I saw you go into his room." Callie's normally sugary voice had turned sour, arms folded over her chest as she stared at her companion. "I saw you do it that night at the orphanage, so don't even try to lie to me." Her Guardian armor gleamed with crystals in the setting sun, giving her an even fiercer appearance.

My body prickled, realizing they were arguing about me.

Celia glared down at the girl, nose turned up in disgust. She wore a white fur-lined coat, her red hair styled in loose curls around her face. Her tongue clicked as she thought of what to say. "It doesn't matter what you saw, whatever your name is. Nobody cares. It's really none of your business."

"The hell it isn't!" Callie stepped forward, pointing a finger at Celia and pressing into Celia's coat. "Jessa is my friend and she's *married* to Lucas, not you."

"So what?" Celia laughed, turning away as if bored by the accusation. "He doesn't remember her."

"When they find her, you'd better believe they're going to get back together. They love each other. Stop trying to get between them."

Celia smiled, eyes gleaming in victory. "You really are out of the loop, aren't you?"

"What are you talking about?" Callie glared.

"I take it you aren't one of the alchemists going over the border this week?"

"I haven't yet," Callie replied suspiciously.

"Maybe you should ask your friends who's been helping them over there." Celia rolled her eyes and turned around, hair whipping in the wind like a raging fire as she stormed away.

"Everyone knows you're a dirty gold digger!" Callie yelled after her, voice furious. She huffed, dropped the visor on her helmet, and ran in the opposite direction.

My body still tingled with what I'd heard. Making sense of everything hadn't been easy, but that argument had certainly helped. Callie was Jessa's friend, but she could also vouch for her, too. That had to count for something.

Richard and Jessa appeared from around the corner, tired gazes set on the bunker. I balked and ran full force to beat them to the door. Rushing inside, I dodged the guard, waiting with the door opened, and hurried down the staircase. The door at the bottom was closed, so I had to wait. Nervous energy pulsed through me, my hand tight on the rose as Richard and Jessa descended the stairs. The guard opened the door for them, and I slipped in right after they did. Then, I went straight to my room, where I'd mercifully had the foresight to leave my door open this morning. I didn't give myself time to think it through or to debate it. I just jumped into the bathroom, closed the door, and turned on the shower.

Nobody came knocking.

I breathed in deep shuddering breaths, letting the stress wash off of me as I undressed and ducked into the respite of hot water. I washed away the adrenaline of the day, sorting though everything I'd witnessed, muscles relaxing, breath slowing to a steady cadence. But even as I relaxed, I knew, no matter how hot the water was or how long I stayed under the pelting stream, I'd never be able to clean the images from my mind.

The crying toddler, his plump body frantic for his mother.

Her bloodied, broken body.

And all the people with their glossy-eyed allegiance.

These were the images that clawed at me, that poured through me like the water poured over me. Now, more than ever, I believed Jessa's outrageous story of our past together. Memories of it or not, there was something rotten about this war, and as much as I hated to admit it, it was my father who lay at the center of the decay.

FOURTEEN

JESSA

The interrogations, the manipulations, the forcing people to bow down to Richard against their will, it all continued. *I let it continue.*

It was either that, or they'd kill more innocent people.

I'd become the thing I'd always feared. I was the puppet, the weapon, and the right hand doing the bidding of an evil family. And yes, I had decided to start thinking of Lucas as evil, as well. After he'd held me down, silencing and hiding me from my sister, forcing me to stay in New Colony, I couldn't think of him as anything but evil. He'd ruined my chance to break free.

The Lucas I knew, the one I loved, the one I'd been through so much with, would have never done that.

I finally accepted that Lucas was gone.

I was living with a different Lucas now, one who was in league with his father. One who may not be as bad as Richard now, but that was only because he was in hiding. I feared the inevitable. One day, he would not only catch up to Richard, but he would surpass him in the amount of destruction he would cause. The Heart Family wouldn't stop at West America. This was only the beginning.

I shivered, my heart breaking deeper than I'd ever thought possible. How had the sweet man I'd fallen for turned into this? I closed my eyes, pushing back the tears.

"Focus!" Faulk snapped, ripping me from my downward spiral.

I blinked up at her. "Can't we be done?" I begged. "We've been at this all day. I can hardly keep my eyes open."

She smirked, folding her arms over her chest and rocking back on her heels. "I thought you'd have enjoyed this respite from our mission in Nashville."

I looked up at the plain white ceiling and sighed. "Fine. One more and then I need to get some food and sleep."

She clucked her tongue and motioned toward the steel door to our right. We waited in Richard's specially-appointed interrogation room, the same gray box I'd spent time in before being transferred to the bunker. I still didn't fully understand that move, but knew it had something to do with Lucas, with his memory, and with my loyalties. Didn't matter.

I focused on the task at hand. Between these walls, it was my job to sort through the minds of the New Colony operatives. One by one, with Faulk at my side, we searched for a spy. Each time some unsuspecting victim entered that door, I held my breath, praying it wasn't a fellow Resistance member, or even someone who could be misinterpreted to be Resistance. Because as much as I wanted to know who'd hurt Lucas, I was more worried about hurting *my people*, or harming more innocents.

The door opened, and Branson walked in, eyes focused and clear as they settled on me. He nodded once, confirming he knew what was about to happen. For all the unsuspecting people who'd walked through that door, he wasn't one of them.

No. My mind reeled and my body tensed. There had to be another way.

"Take a seat," Faulk said, nodding at the metal folding chair across from where I sat, waiting to ruin his life. He followed the directions, relaxed. He was dressed casually in black cottons and scuffed boots. His broad shoulders pulled at his shirt as he rolled out his shoulders, breathing deep.

"No problem," he said, smiling conspiratorially up at the woman. "I understand this is a formality and everyone will get their turn. Now is as good as any time."

Did he have a plan? A way to get out of this? A gnawing pain rolled through my stomach, and I imagined asking Faulk for a break, but it would be no use. I eyed the three guards standing by the wall behind Branson, eyes narrowed, backs straight, hands resting on the guns in their holsters.

How long will it take before they fire those guns?

Sasha had said I could trust Branson, that he was on our side. Branson's ties to the Resistance had been my suspicion since the first moment I'd met him. He was a good man, through and through. Good men wouldn't condone the crimes we were committing on West American citizens. Good men would stand up and fight. Was that what he was about to do here?

I gulped. Faulk split an inch of his tanned skin with a small blade. Branson didn't even flinch. Our eyes met in solidarity as I reached out to his wounded arm and tapped a drop of his warm blood with the tip of my finger. The red danced between us and with a single thought, I sent it back into him. His eyes grew hazy, arms settling at his sides, blood falling in long drops, splashing on the concrete floor.

I knew how this worked. I'd done it enough times. I would have about ten minutes before the numbing magic would wear off, that assuming I wasn't forced to alter his mind permanently with some kind of blood oath like what I was doing to the people of Nashville. But no, these were interrogations, through and through. I would ask questions, get answers, and that would be all.

And we wouldn't even need five minutes to get the job done. Heck, in this case, we may not even need one.

"You will happily answer all of Faulk's questions with 100% accuracy and truth," I said, my voice foreign in my ears. Then I sat back, fists clenched and heart quickening, as Faulk began her questions.

"Are you loyal to King Richard and his mission?"

Branson didn't hesitate. "No." The word hung in the air, final.

Faulk sucked in a breath, anger rocketing through her. She slapped him across the face. "How dare you!"

He was calm as he looked back to her, expression pleasant, simply waiting for more questions.

She kneeled in front of him, arms folding behind her back, teeth bared in disgust. "Are you Resistance?"

"Yes."

She stiffened, and then slowly, she smiled, her face smoothing, her eyes sparkling with delight. Goosebumps prickled up my arms and I stepped back against the wall, trying to catch my breath. *Click*, the guards readied their weapons.

"And who else is Resistance?"

He pointed to me. "Jessa."

"I know. And who else?"

"Jasmine was. I don't know any other names."

Her scream pierced the room and she leaned into his face. "How is that possible?"

"We kept everything separate, all of us in the palace answering to Jasmine."

"But there were others in the palace who were Resistance? How many?"

"There are, but I don't know who or how many."

"Guess," she spat, the reflection of the florescent light above shining off her immaculate blonde bun, lighting her head like a halo.

"If I had to guess, I would say anywhere from five to ten."

She stood, cracking her neck and knuckles, mouth grim, the anger rolling off of her in waves. "The traitors," she whispered. "I will find them and I will kill them all."

She continued on for a while, asking question after incessant question, the need to needle out every small piece of information from his mind driving her. I stood back motionless, silent tears running down my face. She would kill him. And even though he didn't know much, he would somehow reveal too much. She would find a way to root more information from him. More people would die. And if she didn't get to them today, eventually, I would. Eventually, they'd walk through that door, just as Branson had.

His eyes flickered over to me for the briefest of moments, a flutter so quick, I barely caught it. Heart racing, palms growing sweaty, I realized with sudden and absolute clarity that Branson's red alchemy had just worn off. The timeline made sense. Faulk had so many questions. Ten minutes had slipped by unnoticed.

She froze, tilting her head, eyes squinting. "Jessa." She turned to me. "Get him again. I'm not finished here."

"Too late." The words fell from my mouth, barely audible, lost in the sudden crash. Branson was out of his metal folding chair in an instant, picking it up and throwing it at Faulk. It hit her with a crack and fell to the floor with a clatter. She staggered, falling to her knees. He was quick to move on to the guards. He attacked them faster than lightening and with the force of a bulldozer, his years of skill and practice kicking in.

"Catch!" he called to me, tossing a gun into my outstretched hands. It was heavy and detached, but I steadied it.

"Shoot him!" Faulk yelled at me. I looked at her with a sneer. Why didn't *she* shoot him? And then it dawned on me that in the middle of all the commotion, he'd managed to disarm her, as well. The sight of her gun missing from its belt sent a wave of triumph over me. Maybe I should shoot her instead?

I hesitated. Branson didn't.

He grabbed me, pulling me close and aiming a gun at Faulk and her guards, all now lying injured on the floor.

"I'm sorry about this," he whispered low in my ear. "Just go along with it. I'm getting us out of here."

He then wrenched me against him, turning his gun on me.

"Come closer and I'll kill her," he said. "You wouldn't want to lose your precious red alchemist now that you know how powerful she is."

Faulk's face drained of color—he was right.

Days ago I'd been facing the execution block, but now everything had changed. Richard had gotten a taste of what he could do with me, and he wouldn't be very happy to kill me and lose his greatest weapon yet.

"You wouldn't dare!"

"Oh yes, I most certainly would." He cocked the gun and even though I knew what he was doing, my body automatically reacted, trying to fight him off. It was no use; he was way too strong, pinning me to his massive body with ease.

"Hide your gun," he whispered as we moved for the exit. "You might need it soon."

He shoved us out the door and into the hallway.

Chaos swept through the area in a cacophony of angry shouts as he shuffled us down the narrow space. The entire time, the cool barrel of his gun pressed against my temple. My heart beat so loudly, I heard the blood whooshing through me, a reminder that I might not make it out of this. I held my breath and forced myself to stay calm.

I could use the red alchemy. His wound wasn't healed. It would be easy.

No.

I had always liked Branson. He was one of the only good ones left. Besides, I hadn't seen Lily or Jose since arriving here, not once. Branson might be my only chance. I had to trust that he knew what he was doing.

Faulk and her people circled us with guns raised as Branson led us to the exit, using his hip to push it open. Pelting rain assaulted the earth, some of it splashing my face, spreading cold everywhere. Night had fallen, and freezing air filtered into the hallway fog.

"Let her go!" Faulk barked. "She doesn't belong to you."

He laughed. "She doesn't belong to *anyone*."

"Actually, she's the property of New Colony." Faulk's eyes were bright, her mouth set in a thin line. She stepped closer. "You're going to get her killed."

"She'd rather that than be your slave."

He said the words as if he knew it were true, as if he knew me better than I knew myself. And I realized, he might be right. The thought of losing my life settled over me, and a strange sense of peace rose inside. I didn't want to die, but faced with it now, I'd rather die than continue on the path of harming others.

Branson shoved me out into the rain behind him, still using me as a human shield. Rain slid down my face and arms in rivulets of ice, making the world seem muffled. I sucked in several sharp breaths, blinking away the water.

"It's going to be okay. They won't kill you," he said against my hair.

More and more soldiers from all over the base stomped in, weapons trained on us, as Branson and I trudged through the mud and toward the airfield. Faulk followed closer than anyone else, drenched by the rain, gaze fixed and determined.

"What do you think you're going to do?" she cackled.

"Yeah, what's your plan here," I said low, meeting Branson's eyes. He squinted against the water that ran down his face, breathing deep.

"Just trust me," he replied.

"You're going to give us a pilot and a way off this base," Branson yelled back, his voice sure as anything.

"I don't think so," she replied coolly.

He pushed the gun harder against my face, and I yelped.

"I *do* think so!" he screamed.

We shuffled through the puddles and mud, inching closer to our destination. Worry found its way to my core with each step. But also, a flickering hope rose inside me; what if he pulled this off? What if he got us out of here?

Maybe, I didn't have to die. Maybe, I was minutes away from freedom. The idea was so sweet I could taste it.

A chopper came into view and my heart leapt. This was it.

"Stop right there!" King Richard's voice bellowed through the stormy night, slicing through me like a knife. The crowd of armed soldiers parted as the King ran forward, water sloshing out around his black shoes. He was dressed in nothing but a white button-up shirt, and slacks. The clothing stuck to his body like a second skin.

"We're leaving," Branson said. "If you don't let us out of here, I'll shoot her."

Richard shook his head. "What makes you think I'll agree to this?" He laughed, his teeth flashing white in the darkness. "You should know me better than that, Branson."

"I know she's nothing to you if she's dead."

"That's true," he replied. Rain dripped down his chiseled face, but he hardly seemed to notice or care. He stared at us with a strange intensity. "But I would rather she die than work for my enemy."

The air knocked out of me so fast that my knees became weak.

Of course, it was true. Richard didn't care about me as a human; he cared about me as a red alchemist, as a weapon. He would never allow his most powerful weapon to end up in the wrong hands. Never.

Branson cursed and his body instantly tensed against mine, perhaps realizing the gravity of his mistake.

"It's okay," I said to him. We could figure this out.

"Stay strong," he growled into my ear as he raised his gun.

Then he shoved me down into the gravel. I landed on my hands and knees, mud and rocks and water flying. Guns shots blared, and Branson fell to the earth next to me, already dead. His blood splattered against the splotches of mud, mixing with the earth. I screamed, crawling back, my cries garbled in the sound of rain and shouting.

"Help the King first!" a voice pounded through the chaos, and an alchemist kneeled down next to Richard.

My mind tried to make sense of what I was seeing. The King had fallen? When? Everything seemed to be in slow motion and happening all at once.

Richard clutched his arm, crimson blood blooming against his white shirt. An alchemist was quick to use healing magic, the green ribbons twirling around Richard's injury. His face relaxed, and I knew he would be just fine. Branson wouldn't be so lucky. I looked away, hot tears burning my cheeks. They were quickly lost to the rain, like so much else on this awful night.

My eyes scanned the ground, noticing a few more bodies that had been caught in the crossfire. Blonde hair stained red shone from one of them, an arm awkwardly bent beneath. My entire body stilled, burning with a prickly sense of understanding.

Faulk.

I tilted my head, so overcome by the surreal sensation of seeing her dead body right in front of me. It wasn't the Faulk I knew, the determined woman with the flawless appearance and cruel center. It was a shell of her, only a shell, entirely broken in the end. A small red dot was centered on her forehead, a trickling of blood falling into unblinking eyes. They glowed like two full moons. Blood moons.

I squeezed my eyes shut and rolled to the side, fingers clutching at clumps of cold mud, and violently lost the contents of my stomach.

✱

I thought sleep would never come, but somehow it did. It wasn't a blessing but another curse, accompanied by tormented dreams, darkness so thick and heavy it threatened to destroy everything, to stifle the breath in my lungs. It left me sweaty and panicked, gripping at thin white sheets.

"Shush," a deep voice whispered against my neck. "It's okay. You're okay."

My body stiffened as awareness surfaced. Two arms wrapped around my body, a hard chest pressed against my back, and hot breath tangled in my hair.

"Lucas?" I croaked. My voice burned, and I swallowed hard. The tears came again, salty and thick. I couldn't hold back the sobs, and wondered if they'd ever stop. The wound was too deep. They wet my face, reminding me of being outside in that rain, of the blood, and the death, and just how much death would still come because of my *life*.

"It's okay. I've got you," he said. "Go back to sleep."

I wanted to fight him, shove him off, tell him to get away, but my body betrayed me and the comfort was far too good to pass up. I relaxed, eyes shutting as if my eyelids were weighted down. I sighed, breath steadying, and before I could process any more thoughts, I fell back into the darkness.

Later, I woke with a start, reaching around the bed.

I was alone.

Had I dreamed him? Had Lucas really come in here and held me in the middle of the night? My brain filtered through the thoughts, sleep giving way to lucidity, and I knew that he had. It wasn't a dream. But, why? He wasn't supposed to do things like that. He was supposed to be the enemy. No. He wouldn't have come in—it must have been a dream. That was the logical answer.

I rolled over on my pillow and breathed in, the scent of sandalwood and grass and something else, something so entirely Lucas, filled me up, soothing and heart-breaking. I held it there for several long minutes despite my better judgment. He *had* been here. Maybe he'd changed…

Enough.

I jumped from the warm sheets, tossing them to the floor. I couldn't be weak. I needed to be stronger than this. Stepping into the scalding hot shower, I allowed the water to wash away any lingering scent of Lucas as quickly as possible.

"Let me guess," I said, sliding into the chair of the ghastly interrogation room. I looked up at a man I hardly knew, but his was a face I would recognize anywhere. He had the same features as his daughter, Celia. "You're the new Faulk?"

He raised an eyebrow. "I'm taking over where she left off."

"Because she's dead," I supplied. "Don't need to tip-toe around it. I was there."

"Yes." His expression turned sour, two red eyebrows arching over amber eyes. "She's dead." He straightened in his black suit and tie, oozing confidence.

"How very convenient for you." I cocked my head, satisfied when his cheeks grew red.

"Let's just focus on the task at hand," he replied. "We have orders to go through all the alchemists and continue from there."

I barked out a quick laugh. "And what about the thousands more in Nashville that haven't been brainwashed yet? There's only one of me, you know."

"We'll get to them in time. The King thinks it's more important to make sure we don't have any more situations like Branson's. We're spending a few more days here, conducting more interviews."

My stomach fell. There would be more. The second Lily or Jose walked in that door, I would be facing my worst horror all over again.

"Interviews. That's one way to put it."

I eyed him, up and down, thrilled to be taking my anger out on him.

"What's your name?" I pressed, the question coming out like an accusation.

"I'm a Duke," he replied shortly. "Mark Addington. And I don't answer to the likes of you. I'm in charge here. No more attitude."

I grinned slyly. "Okay, Duke, why don't we start this interrogation with you and your precious little family? Your daughter did attack me, in case you've already forgotten. I think that's reason enough to question her, don't you think?"

He blanched, thrown off. Something murderous flashed in his eyes. I held his gaze for a long moment before turning to smile nonchalantly at the three Royal Officers standing watch. Not one made eye contact.

"You have something to hide," I said, leaning back in my chair and smirking. "It's painfully obvious. I'm surprised you showed your weakness so quickly. Faulk always knew better than that."

"I don't know what you're talking about," he snapped. "You'd be smart to watch your mouth. Faulk was a lot of things, but I won't be as kind to you as Faulk was."

"You call that kind?" I raised an eyebrow. "I'm not afraid of you."

"You should be."

"Why? In case you couldn't tell, I no longer have anything to lose."

He stood, pointing a finger in my face. "I'll be bringing in our first appointment shortly. Behave!" Then he stormed from the room, slamming the metal door with a clang. I crossed my arms and tapped my black boot against the smooth floor, replaying the scene.

Curious.

What was Mark Addington hiding?

FIFTEEN

SASHA

Enough was enough. I still couldn't find my array of stones, the color so precious to me it was like water to a fish or air to a bird. They'd never shown up after the evacuation, which didn't make sense. Someone had gotten them before I'd had a chance, so where did they go? I'd been patient, had listened when Nathan Scott advised me to hold off jumping to conclusions, but I couldn't hold my tongue any longer. Most of the soldiers tolerated me, some even liked me, but enough sent me hateful looks and muttered obscenities whenever I was near, that I couldn't go on pretending.

Someone had tried to sabotage me.

I stalked across the mess hall, hands fisted at my sides, eyes zeroed on a group of soldiers who'd glowered at me and whispered among themselves the second I'd walked in the door. They were also the idiots who'd cornered me that day while jogging, threatening me because of their prejudice against my magic. I refused to put up with their intolerance any longer.

I slammed my palms down on their table, rattling their bowls of stew. All three of them stood, glaring down at me. The youngest of the group, an ordinary-looking guy with buzzed hair and muddy brown eyes, also happened to be the mouthiest. He stepped into my space, sneering.

"What makes you think you can come over here, huh?"

I scowled at him. "Was it you?"

Realization dawned in his eyes and he smirked, stepping back and nodding to his friends. "Was what me?" His voice came out innocent, and his friends laughed.

"Which one of you fools tried to sabotage me? Who took my crystals?"

The oldest of the group closed in on me, breath reeking of alcohol. I didn't know where he got it and why he was drinking it in the middle of the day, but it sent a shiver down my spine. He flexed, tanned and tattooed muscles popping.

"You missing your little rocks, ya? Is that what this is about?" He cackled. "I also notice you're missing your two body guards. Not very smart of you, Sasha, to come over here all alone."

I tensed my jaw, ready to fight if it came to that. It was true, Mastin was meeting me any minute for lunch and I didn't know where Tristan was at the moment. Actually, I didn't know what he was up to most of the time, these days. But there were men and women all over this dining hall who could step in, and more importantly, the stew had a colorful array of vegetables. I'd be fine.

"I want my crystals." I sent each of the men my most menacing look. "Return them to me, or pay the price."

This sent them into a fit of laughter and hoots. The younger of the group put a sweaty hand on my bicep and I froze, itching to rip his filthy hand off of me.

"All I can say is you're not going to see those crystals again."

"Is that a confession?" I challenged.

He tilted his head, leaning in to whisper in my ear. "I'm pretty sure I saw someone throw them into the fire, but damn it, I can't remember who it was."

He patted me once and turned back to his meal. The other two men smirked, the older one chewing on his lip and traveling his eyes up and down my body in a way that made me want to either punch him or hurl, probably both.

"Sasha!" Mastin called out, striding through the mess hall. "There you are. Are you ready to get something to eat?" He stopped short when he saw the men, now returned to their table, but who were still peering up at me with distain in their eyes. The energy between the four of us was charged with such animosity, it didn't take a genius to pick up on it.

"You okay?" Mastin gently touched my elbow.

I exhaled, trying to relax. So, these men had destroyed my crystals? I wouldn't let that stop me. And I wouldn't let them get to me any longer. Nathan Scott said more crystals were coming. Next time, I'd keep them with me instead of in the armory.

I sent the group one final glare and then plastered a sickly sweet smile on my face, turning to Mastin.

"I'm great. Let's eat."

I stared down at the sidewalk, watching my shadow move beneath me, as my thoughts spun. I was upset about what had happened at lunch, sure, but it was thoughts of Tristan that were really bothering me.

I was losing my best friend.

He'd distanced himself from me, whether he acknowledged it or not. I felt the ache in my gut, like something was missing. I would turn to smirk at him over one thing or another, but lately, he wasn't smirking back. He barely even looked in my direction anymore. The truth of our crumbling foundation lingered in the subtle movements of his body, in the way his expression closed down whenever Mastin was around. I told myself that this was only natural, friends grew apart all the time. And anyway, we had already been apart for ages after I'd left to be an undercover operative, so it wasn't like I should be so upset. I should be used to the distance. Maybe Tristan didn't really see me as his friend anymore, maybe he hadn't for a long time and I'd stupidly assumed we could get back to the way we used to be.

I ran my hand through my hair, huffing in annoyance.

"What's going on in that brain of yours?" Mastin asked, squeezing my hand gently.

It felt like there was a rock in my stomach, the stew I'd just scarfed down curdling. Our boots slapped the cracked sidewalk as we walked back from what had become our new mess hall. The mess hall that was basically an old abandoned grocery store, cleared of the shelves. Tables had been set up in neat rows down the middle and the building had quickly become the gathering place for the crew out here. A crew that still shot me withering glances every so often.

"What do you mean?" I returned lamely.

"There's something going on with you." Mastin shrugged. "I keep trying to figure you out, but just when I think I do, you change."

I winked. "Doesn't that just mean I'm mysterious? Don't guys like that?" I was avoiding the question, and quite brilliantly. Maybe.

"Mysterious is definitely a good word to describe you." He sighed, unrelenting. "But I also want to make sure you're okay."

"I'm okay."

He frowned. "It's just that ever since you and I started dating, and believe me, it's been great on my end…"

"What?"

"Well, ever since we started dating, you've seemed, I dunno, distant? Sad? Something just isn't right."

I held my breath for a moment, trying to think of the right thing to say. "I'm fine." The words fell flat. "I'm just really worried about my family. Jessa's stuck over there." I pointed east. "And this war is crazy. I guess it's a lot to take in."

Liar. It's not just about family unless Tristan is also the family you're referring to.

The thunderous sound of a military aircraft pierced the sky, and tension at its arrival ran through the camp like a tidal wave. I reached up, instinctively running my fingers along the stone necklace, even though most were sickly gray. I would be able to replenish everything as soon as the next arrival came and I couldn't wait.

I vowed to never be without my tools again.

Mastin automatically rested his hand on the gun in his holster. And as the aircraft flew closer, he relaxed. It was only an airplane, not an enemy jet.

"It's one of ours," he yelled, voice booming over the area. "Stand down!"

I smiled, knowing more of my stones might be on board!

He ordered the men around him, many much older than his twenty years, with complete ease. His voice rang out with confidence, naturally drawing attention. It was one of the most attractive things about him. Appreciation purred through me as I watched the man take action. The more I got to see him in his element, the more I understood why he was one of the youngest ranking officers. He had been bred for this life. Literally.

He marched off, and not wanting to be left out, I caught up to him quickly. "What are they doing here?" I asked, pointing to the airplane.

"No," he muttered under his breath. "They weren't supposed to get here until tonight. I wanted more time…"

My eyes narrowed on his sheepish expression, on the way his hands were fisted at his sides and his gaze didn't meet my own. "Who are you talking about?"

His face hardened, looking over at me. "Please don't shoot the messenger."

I glowered. I wasn't shooting anyone, but it didn't mean I wasn't about to open up the full force on my magic if he didn't open his stupidly handsome mouth and start talking! "What? What aren't you telling me?"

"I wanted to tell you, but I was ordered to keep it to myself."

The realization sunk deep. "This is about Weapon X, isn't it?"

His eyes flashed, mouth dropping open. "How do you know about that?"

Yeah, I wasn't going to answer that one. I didn't want him to know I'd been eavesdropping on his private conversation. But then again, it involved me, didn't it? We were supposed to be a team.

I shifted my weight onto one leg, defiance rolling through me. "What *is* it? And why are you keeping it from me?"

"I have my orders." He ground his teeth.

This was where we disagreed. "Screw your orders."

He reached out and grasped my hand. "Come on then." He sighed. "I can't say anything, but that doesn't mean you can't figure it out. You're going to want to see this."

We jogged for the highway. It stretched out into the flat horizon like a never-ending runway. And that's essentially what it had become to us. It was used as a makeshift tarmac for any planes that needed to land in the area.

As we approached the airplane, its exterior gleaming black, a sense of foreboding washed over me.

"Like I said, please don't shoot the messenger. I wasn't supposed to tell you that they were coming, but now that they're here, you're going to find out soon…" His voice trailed off.

"Just out with it, Mastin!" I challenged.

"See for yourself." He pointed to the mammoth airplane.

The bottom opened, a set of stairs rolling down to the pavement. I watched, horrified, as one by one, alchemists descended from the belly of the beast. They had to be alchemists. I knew immediately, from the gray clothing they were wearing, but also, from the man who was leading the group.

Hank.

My beloved Hank, with his grizzly appearance, quick mind, and ruddy smile. As much as I loved to see him, I didn't want it to be like this!

"What are they doing here?" I growled.

Mastin rocked back on his heels. "It's been decided that they are needed. And so…here they are."

"Weapon X." I spat the name like it was a dirty word.

He narrowed his eyes slightly and shook his head.

Okay?

Then, dropping my hand, he ran ahead to greet our guests.

Anger stirred within as I slowly walked forward to join the newcomers. My eyes landed on Hank, who was talking privately with Tristan. They stood off to one side, talking in low voices, probably as upset by this as I was. Just as I was about to join their twosome, my eyes caught a flash of familiar hair.

Smooth, blonde, and glossy in the afternoon sun.

Lacey.

I balked, feeling as if my entire body was sinking into the pavement. No! This couldn't be!

But it was. And my parents were at her side. Bile rose, so nauseating I doubled over. She was a child! She had no place in a war zone!

I sprinted over to Hank. "What are you doing here? And why are *children* here?"

He held up a hand, the lines around his eyes deep as he grimaced. "We got orders. There wasn't a negotiation."

I poked my finger into his chest, needing someone to blame. "You should've refused. You're better than this!"

"Like I said, we got orders," he replied, dejected. "What was I supposed to do? They were coming either way, so I had to come too."

I shook my head, feeling like my body was sinking into the group, swallowing me up before I could get a grip on things. This couldn't be happening!

Tristan stepped in, resting his steady hand on my lower back. "It seems that the American leadership is getting nervous about this war and decided they needed to fight fire with fire."

I gulped.

"Or in this case," Hank added, "alchemy with alchemy."

I ground my foot into the pavement. How could anyone think this was a good idea? I couldn't picture the president I had met agreeing to such a thing. But then, there'd been that man, the general so convinced on doing this very thing. Maybe he had been the one behind it. Either way, it was wrong.

I spun back to study the newcomers. Most were young, some children, and I doubted any of them had much training beyond what Hank had provided. His couple of months with them wasn't enough. Bringing them here was foolish. No, not just foolish—selfish. Someone had essentially sent these innocent people to the slaughter!

This was not okay.

My mind returned to the incident in the mess hall, to the protestors outside the airport, to all the nasty comments and opinions about alchemy. Maybe someone had known they were sending innocents to die, and that's exactly why they'd done it. Anger pulsed through me once again, red hot and ready to burst.

I searched the crowd until I found General Nathan Scott. When he caught me staring, I glared. If looks could kill, he'd be so dead right now! He pinched his lips and shrugged, as if to say, what else did you expect? Then he walked away, vanishing amongst his soldiers. The coward!

Mastin, who was also in the crowd, kept sending me chastised and sorrowful looks whenever he had the chance. I put my hands on my hips and raised my eyebrows.

We'll be having a discussion about this later, buddy.

"There she is!" My mother's voice carried across the tarmac like a kite on the end of a string. My three family members beamed at me, and I tried to find a smile, I really did. But it just wouldn't come.

They ran forward, pulling me into tight hugs. Tears burned my eyes, and I breathed them in. It felt so good to be with them again, but I was breaking inside for the circumstances. I couldn't stop looking at Lacey's young face, the sweetness that was still bright in her eyes, and imagining those eyes cold and dead. "What happened?" I said as we broke apart. "What are you doing here?"

Dad looked around before speaking low, his voice gravelly with worry, "We didn't have a choice. All the alchemists were suddenly ordered to come here. Even the kids."

"This is dangerous," I replied, stating the utterly obvious.

"We know," Mom replied. "Thank God they let us come with Lacey."

I shook my head. "None of you should be here. This is a war zone."

They shared a knowing look. Christopher tucked Lacey against his leg but she resisted, side-stepping to get into the middle of our little circle. She placed her hands on her hips and cocked her chin up, looking so much older in that moment. Too much. Too soon.

I squatted, placing both of my hands on her shoulders.

"Are you doing okay?" I asked.

Her eyes were smaller mirrors of my own, a blue that shone back at me, no longer innocent and sweet from moments before. They sparked with the same kind of defiance I saw in not only myself, but in Jessa.

Oh, she was a Loxely, all right.

"I'm great," Lacey replied. "I've been practicing my magic every day. I'm really good now. I can't wait to show you."

I smiled weakly. "I would like that."

And in any other place and time, I would have.

I smiled despite myself. Nearly all my loves were seated around one table, and I couldn't help the happiness warming me. This was what I'd wanted for so long, if only we'd come together under different circumstances. I'd learned to push the "if onlys" of life away a long time ago, and yet here I was, foolishly wrapping myself up in one of the most dangerous ones of all: family.

I didn't run from it.

Because I'd also learned over the last year that the more courageous thing was to let them in.

We'd found each other in the dining hall—Lacey and my parents, Tristan and Hank, and of course, Mastin. All of us had never talked about sharing a meal together, it just happened. As we began to settle into our spots on the long benches and dug into the array of fresh-cooked food, an unspoken rule had fallen over the group. Nobody talked about the war. For that, I was incredibly grateful.

"Can you pass the butter, dear?" my mother asked me shyly.

Things with Dad and me were going okay, probably because we'd shared so much during our time in the New Colony prison. Mom and I, on the other hand, hadn't had a lot of time to talk, and the energy between us was still strained. I couldn't avoid her. We'd have to air everything out eventually, but as I'd watched her from the corner of my eye, saw the way she'd doted on Lacey, it stirred old resentment inside my chest — and I knew I wasn't ready.

Another time.

I passed her the butter with a guarded smile and turned back to Mastin, who was busy shoveling food into his mouth at my side. The man could *eat*. I'd learned that living with his family. The Scott men worked hard and practically worshipped their mealtimes. Not that I blamed Mastin; the food spread out in front of us was better than anything we'd had since leaving the west coast. The plane that had brought the alchemists had also brought provisions, and General Scott had decided to treat everyone to a feast of steak and potatoes, fresh dinner rolls, green salad, and rich creamed corn.

"Here, try it like this." Mastin lifted a chunk of potato he'd stabbed with a fork. He'd slathered it in creamy salad dressing, so much it was dripping. I wrinkled my nose.

"I like to keep all my food separated," I teased.

"What? It all ends up in the same place."

"But it tastes better if it doesn't start out in the same place." I leaned into his side, his familiar warmth surrounding me.

"Don't be a baby." He chuckled, and I elbowed him in the ribs. Not willing to let him get the upper hand, I dove in and bit the potato off his fork. The hot food mixed in my mouth, savory and sweet, and I swallowed, licking my lips.

"Okay, fine, you win."

His bright green eyes stared intently at my lips and I became immediately and unbearably aware of how we weren't alone. I sighed and looked away.

Across the table, Tristan joked with my father, his voice ringing out like a church bell. Dad doubled over in laughter, nearly choking on his food. Tristan always did have a way of making people laugh until they cried. I'd lost count of how many times he'd done it to me. A small part of me was jealous of my father; I'd love to be the one on the receiving end of one of Tristan's jokes. It had been a while since he'd treated me that way.

"Look what I found." Lacey's sweet voice tickled my ear and I smiled down

718

at my sister.

She held up a jug of some kind of frothy orange punch or juice, her eyes twinkling in delight. The citrus scent wafted through the air and my mouth watered. I glanced around, noticing that over the chatter of the room, the other alchemists, all dressed in simple gray uniforms, were enjoying the meal. Before they'd seemed nervous, but now that had melted away. Good food could do that to just about anyone.

"Can I pour you some?" she asked, nodding at the jug of juice.

"Of course. Do you need any help with that?" I reached out to steady the jug that looked a tad too heavy for her small arms.

Determination filled her normally timid expression and she shook her head. "No, I don't need help. I got it."

I sat back, impressed, as she filled my cup to the brim. She was growing up so fast, and just thinking that made me feel like an old maid. I laughed to myself.

She continued around the table, charming each and every person along the way.

"She's cute," Mastin whispered in my ear. We watched her, both of us clearly enamored. I let out a laugh and elbowed him in the ribs.

"She *is* cute," I agreed, joy rising up. Tears gathered in my eyes—I was so happy.

Wait a minute…

I caught Lacey's eye and raised my eyebrows. She nodded once, giggling, before moving on to the next person.

Holy crap! She'd become incredibly adept at orange alchemy! We'd had some lessons on it back at the Resistance basecamp, but I had no idea she'd come this far.

Everyone at the table fell under her spell. They were alive with happiness. She'd made a connection with each person, giving them this gift. And quite honestly, with everything going on, it was an amazing gift to be had. I tried to get my mind to focus on something else, but I couldn't. I was simply *happy*. The orange had taken what I was feeling and enhanced it, and it would continue to enhance whatever I felt until it wore off. I eyed the orange bubbly drink in front of me and smiled from ear to ear.

Talented little stinker!

"I've been wondering where you went." A female voice cut through the chatter, voice flirty. I looked over to find the source, noticing a woman had come to chat up Tristan. "You still owe me a rematch."

Tristan turned to converse with one of the soldiers…one of the *female* soldiers. Envy riled up in me. She was beautiful—exotic, sweeping dark hair and hooded eyes, gorgeous caramel complexion, curvy in all the right places. What the hell was she doing talking to Tristan?

She slid in next to him, straddling the bench, facing him, body leaning in with a knowing smile, laughing in a low, throaty voice.

Rage burned through me, closing in on my clenched fists and my tense jaw.

"Are you okay?" Mastin's question lingered on the outside of the haze, yet not strong enough to penetrate it. I ignored him, glaring darkly at the woman. The intruder!

Why was she so openly flirting with Tristan? He wasn't interested, couldn't she see the way he was treating her like anyone else? She needed to back off!

But then he reached out and tucked a strand of hair behind her ear, smiling intently, and I lost it.

I sprung from the table, my plate clattering.

"Sasha!" Mastin jumped up with me. "What's going on?"

A handful of nearby faces swiveled, chatter growing silent, as the joyous mood flipped to something much more curious and invasive.

I sucked in a breath, realizing what had just happened.

Damn that orange alchemy, always getting me into trouble.

"You've got to be kidding me," I spat, annoyed with myself. The magic flitted away into nothingness, and my emotions settled back to normal.

I'd gotten jealous, insanely jealous, of Tristan flirting with that girl. It was so stupid! Where had that even come from?

It had to be because I cared about Tristan. *As a friend, my best friend.* And surely, if it had been Mastin the girl had touched and flirted with, I'd have gotten even more angry. I probably would have punched her.

Right.

Okay.

Breathe in. Breathe out. Everything is fine.

"I'm good." I laughed awkwardly, belly flopping, and grinned at the people who were still staring at me like I'd just picked my nose or something. I couldn't meet Tristan's eyes—nor Mastin's. "I'm fine. It's nothing."

I sat back down, gripping the seat. My cheeks burned. That was so weird. And so embarrassing. And everyone was still gaping at me! Oh, heavens, I needed to get out of here. I needed to go for a run *alone* to clear my head.

"Thank you all for your service." Nathan Scott's deep baritone voice rang out over the mess hall. Five hundred voices quieted as every pair of eyes turned to watch their leader at the front of the room.

"We have *three thousand* more forces moving into the area at this moment," he continued. "They'll arrive shortly, ready to fight."

The room grew even quieter. Mastin shifted next to me, stiffening and transitioning into his usual soldier-self.

"I hope you all enjoyed your meal. You deserve that much." General Scott cleared his throat, steadying his gaze and sweeping it across the crowd. "Please prepare yourselves tonight. Tomorrow is a new day, a day to stride forward in our valiant efforts. Tomorrow we join our comrades in battle. We leave at first light."

SIXTEEN

JESSA

Nashville was a fallen city. As we landed in its center, my heart sank. Fewer buildings were on fire, the rubble was beginning to get cleaned up, and many more people were out on the streets. It was starting to resemble a normal city, and all that meant that Richard was gaining control faster than anyone had anticipated.

After another long day of conducting interrogations on his own people, Richard had announced it was time to head back into Nashville. I didn't know how many lived here, or how long it would take, but I knew that eventually, I would get to everyone. Richard would make certain of that.

First, he'd secured the borders, trapping everyone inside. Then, he had alchemists enforcing the rule of law, rounding people up in hordes. And finally, he had his secret weapon to finish the job.

Me.

And so we continued, taking over the city like a swarm of deadly wasps. Our job was to go from shelter to shelter where the soldiers had rounded up innocent people and forced them inside while they awaited my arrival. We would tell the West Americans what to expect and what would happen to them if they didn't do as we asked. Then, I got to work. It was usually over quick, people didn't have anything to fight with and most were trying to keep their families together, but it was still exhausting and emotionally draining work.

Mark Addington and his wife Sabine had taken over so Richard could do whatever kings did during wartime. It didn't take long to confirm why I disliked the couple for reasons that had nothing to do with Celia and the broken engagement. They were pushy, self-important, and constantly leered at me. I was beginning to think they either saw me as their enemy or as their salvation, I couldn't tell which. And I didn't know which I'd prefer.

Our boots clomped across the pavement, the soldiers leading us into yet another school turned into an internment camp. It was our first of the day and already my body ached for rest. I hadn't been getting much sleep; I was too haunted by the faces of those who'd died, not to mention the countless people who'd been turned because of my interference. It felt like a spindly pit was twisting in my stomach and I groaned, squinting as the morning sun shone off the reflective surface of the glass building. This one was bigger than any of the others and a pool of dread welled within me.

"Chop, chop!" Sabine Addington barked, her arm motioning for me to hurry through the door she'd propped open. She was a classic beauty with delicate features, a slender face that had aged well, and vibrant ruby hair perfectly coifed in a twist at her neck. I'd learned that sometimes the most beautiful people on the outside were the most ugly on the inside. The Addington family was proof.

"Can't we go easier on them today?" I said, eyeing the door wearily.

Mark laughed, smoothing a wrinkle in his pressed dress shirt. "Whatever do you mean?" He matched his wife in style, almost like they'd grown to resemble each other over the years. He motioned to some of the guards and alchemists at his disposal, urging them to take position.

"I've been thinking about it and I have a question," I continued, trying to sound as persuasive as I could. "Why do we immediately kill them if they won't willingly participate with this? I mean, if we can restrain them, then I can use alchemy on them and bring them to our side either way. This way, we don't have to kill so many people."

They both glowered at me like I was a total and complete idiot, their expressions dripping in utter disdain.

"You really don't understand social pressure, do you?" Sabine finally replied coolly, looking down her nose.

I shrugged, because actually, I didn't know what she was even talking about. Social pressure?

"Those who are killed are used as an example," Mark supplied with exasperation. "They keep everyone else from rising up. If we show leniency then we also show weakness."

I glared, stepping back. "You call it weakness. I call it mercy."

They shared a knowing look, smirking in unison.

"We give them a crystal clear understanding of what will happen if they fight us. They know what they are doing and they know there are no second chances. Period." Sabine explained it simply, as if she were rattling off a recipe. She spun around and strolled through the door with her husband in tow. I followed closely, drilling holes through their backs with my eyes. Inside this building were innocent people whose entire way of life was about to be changed, all with little force and a lot of manipulation.

I could relate to these poor people more than they knew.

I had lost count long ago of how many of them had been shot and killed in front of me. If the King had no qualms about murdering people right in front of me, then how many more had been killed when I wasn't there to witness it?

I had no idea what the death count was, but I couldn't imagine it was anything short of staggering.

It wasn't totally my fault, but still, I was ravaged by guilt. Truth was, at the forefront of everything happening here was *my* red alchemy. I was working for the King now, plain and simple. Now that his threats to kill more people if I didn't help him had become plainly evident, I didn't see what other choice I had. So, I worked.

I did exactly what was asked of me, taking away people's freedom to the point that they didn't even realize it. Deep inside, I kept hoping my magic would wear off and the people would return to normal, but so far, nobody had changed. Even if the magic was gone, their minds had been twisted by my power. They now saw Richard as their savior come to deliver them from their terrible democracy, rather than the other way around. Apparently, many of them had even enlisted in our army. He'd boasted last night about how they'd willingly joined up. It seemed I'd swayed these people to Richard's plans because they accepted my words as absolute truth. It was brainwashing at its finest.

And I hated myself for it.

"Don't you look chipper this morning," a sly voice echoed down the long glass hallway. I looked up to find not only one unwelcomed man leering at me, but two. Reed stood next to Dax, the intense broody kid with purple telepathy who made my skin crawl. Dax sneered darkly, and Reed ran his eyes up and down me, exuding sheer creepiness.

"Come on, boys," Mark called to the pair. "Remember what we talked about."

I folded my arms over my chest and glared right back at them. If I ever had the chance to get at either of their blood, I would take it. I would make them pay for the way they so clearly enjoyed their roles in this war. They had probably become murderers ten times over at this point, and not a lick of remorse showed in either of their cold expressions.

Hello Jessa, Dax's scratchy voice pilfered through my mind, like nails on a chalkboard. *Nice to see you again, Princess.*

I refused to reply through the telepathic link that he'd opened between us. The very idea this psychopath could talk to me anytime he wanted, assuming I was in close enough proximity, made me sick with anger.

I know you can hear me, he pressed.

I didn't say anything. Didn't react in any way. If I was lucky, I'd make him paranoid I couldn't hear him. If I could make him sweat, that would at least be a silver lining to this awful morning.

Reed and I have made a little bargain with Mark, in case you're wondering why we're here. In fact, if things go as planned, you'll probably be seeing a lot more of us over the coming months. I can't say I'm happy with your presence here. I've never liked you and I never will. You're an entitled little bitch. But oh well, he cooed. *Once this is all over, it will be so worth it.*

My eyes flickered to him, giving me away.

His grin was slow and wide. *As they say, the ends justify the means.*

I continued to refuse a reaction or a reply, but curiosity was getting the better of me. I held my breath, the questions bubbling over. These two had made a deal with Mark and Sabine? What kind of deal? For what reason? And what did I have to do with it?

Frustrated, I kept my mouth shut, my eyes forward, and followed the couple into the gymnasium. Reed and Dax peeled off the wall as we entered, the pair bounding in after us like excitable puppies with a new chew toy. I could feel Reed staring at me from behind. I clenched my fists so tight my fingernails razored into my palms. I wanted nothing more than to turn and punch him square on the nose.

How had I ever been friends with him? My first impression of the guy had been so good. He'd come across as funny and charming, a friend. I knew now that it was his blue alchemy at work. He had charisma in spades because of it, but that didn't make him a good person. Reed had shown his true colors, and those colors were ugly as sin.

There wasn't a minute off-script about our time in the gymnasium. One by one, I used my magic on at least a hundred people's blood, turning horrified faces into ones eager to please their new King. Two fought back. They were shot. Even though it wasn't unexpected, wasn't a surprise, I was still a shaky mess. Tears burned my eyes and blurred my vision through the whole thing.

Was this my life now? We'd go from city to city, rounding up everyone we could get our hands on, turning them into Richard's puppets. He wouldn't stop, not until every last citizen bowed down to his rule. And then what? Would we move north to Canada? South? Would this continue, on and on, until the Heart family ruled the entire planet? I couldn't do it all in my lifetime, there was no way, but somehow I wondered if Richard expected me to try.

We finished with the gym in record time. Our group exited the building with haste, soldiers swarming around us in a wall of protection, and we marched back to an armored vehicle that waited to take us to the next location. The grass was brown and squishy under our boots as we crossed the sweeping lawn to the parking lot. The muggy smell of distant rain wafted through my nose, the humid air filling up lungs. I stared up into the gray sky, wishing my power away. I'd give anything to not have this burden anymore. If that was taken out of the equation, then none of this would be so easy for them. Or just take me out. If I wasn't here…

Thwomp thwomp thwomp.

Helicopters pilfered the sky. Jet engines intermixed, loud as blow horns. I peered up at them, little black specks growing larger by the second.

"Red alert!" Mark shouted, holding up his shiny black slatebook. "We're under attack."

A swell of hope rose inside me like a brilliant sunrise. This could be my chance. I didn't stop to think about it. I took off running, my feet powering me forward. Without access to yellow, there was nothing that could save me from the other alchemists. But I had to try.

A body slammed into me, pounding me to the ground. Dax.

"Not so fast, pretty princess," he growled, twisting his hand into my ponytail and yanking me to standing. I gasped, straining against him. He tugged again and I stilled; it was the only way to get him to stop. Our eyes met and his flared with desire.

I like you in this position, he purred through my mind. *You should learn to be submissive to men all the time. It makes you even prettier.*

I wrenched my body around to face him, kneeing him directly in the groin, hoping for a direct hit. Success! He fell like a log. I didn't stop and gloat. I exploded into a run, legs pumping me forward. My eyes roamed the horizon, neck twisting side to side as I frantically searched for help. I had to get away from these people, take cover, and find usable color. With purple alchemy I would be able to tell Sasha where I was. She'd be able to get me out of here. Maybe.

It was all I had.

Angry shouts exploded behind me, my pursuers gaining ground. Scratch that. I needed to get yellow first so I could fight, but more than that, so I could stay ahead. I'd have to worry about purple later.

"Get back here!" Reed shouted, voice way too close for comfort.

My eyes continued to scan the area, looking for anything. Anything! It was February, and had been raining like crazy, but there had to be color somewhere. I'd even settle for nonorganic material—it was better than nothing!

And yet, I saw nothing.

The buildings in this area were all glass and steel. The grass was dead for the season. The trees and bushes were mostly barren, and any green they did have wouldn't be helpful. Not now. I didn't need healing!

Come on! Yellow. Anything yellow.

Reed caught up to me, only a footstep behind. His panting breath warmed the back of my neck. "Don't make me shoot you," he warned. The sounds of more footsteps in his tracks echoed through the air.

"You wouldn't dare!" I shot back. We neared the corner of a block, and I prayed I'd find what I needed once we rounded it. "I'm too valuable."

How many pursuers did I have now? I mentally tried to count the guards from today but my mind was too unfocused.

"Not if you're playing for the other side," he growled. "Remember?"

I careened around the corner, skidding so fast that I began to fall forward. Panic ripped through me as the ground rose up.

Reed took care of the problem for both of us.

He tackled me, and we rolled several feet before landing in a decaying flowerbed, arms and legs flying. Weeds scratched at my exposed skin, and I screamed. Not for the pain, but for the fact I'd been caught. Tears prickled my eyes.

I blinked them away furiously. I needed to think, to keep moving, not to start crying, and definitely not to feel sorry for myself.

Gunshots exploded on the other side of the street. People yelled, some cried out in agony. The battle had begun. If I was going to get any help, I'd have to create it myself. I had to use the battle's distraction to my advantage, and fast!

I focused on what was right in front of me. Underneath the brush, a small sprinkling of purple flowers grew. Salvation!

Reed ground my face into them as he straddled me, wrestling my hands into cuffs. I let him, not fighting. Instead, I focused on the purple smashed against my cheek, connecting with the magic instantly.

Sasha, I called out. *Are you there?*

Jessa! she returned instantly, her tone frantic. *Where are you?*

A wave of comfort crashed over me, tears springing to my eyes. Her take-charge voice was exactly what I needed.

I'm with Reed and some others. They've got me detained over by Imperial High School.

Okay, hold on, we're coming!

We're not in the high school, though. Don't go in there! There's a ton of people loyal to Richard in there. I don't know what they'd do to you if they saw you. The words rushed our connection, horrified to think what the West American soldiers were about to face. We hadn't made it through the entire city, yet. Not even close. But still, there were many who most likely fight their own countrymen.

What do you mean? Sasha's question pulsed through me, the guilt inside raising its ugly head again.

I had to use my red. Richard made me. Don't trust anyone and I'll explain the rest later. Just please, come get me out of here!

Reed wrenched me up from the ground, pushing me forward, oblivious to the purple magic I'd deployed. I smiled faintly, quickly replacing it with a frown, glaring savagely at Reed.

I don't know how long this purple will last, I continued. *I don't have the flower on me anymore. But I'll describe my location as long as I'm able to reach out to you.*

Okay. Just do your best. I'm in the middle of something here, but I'll come get you as soon as I can. We're coming to save you, Jessa. My sister's determined voice warmed me from the inside out. If anyone could get me out of this mess, it was Sasha. I'd never met anyone quite like her.

In fact, she continued confidently, *we're coming to take back Nashville!*

Reed kicked in the door and we swept into the little house. Dax ran ahead to check the rooms. "All clear," he called down after a moment and the four of us shuffled inside.

"This battle won't last long," Mark said, steering me into the living room. He peered out the window before drawing the burgundy curtains. The hems sat heavy against the scratched wooden floor, blocking the bulk of the mid-morning light.

Dax ambled into the room, running a slow finger over the stones in his uniform as he leered at me.

"Sit," he pointed to a brown, threadbare recliner.

I dropped into the chair with a huff. "You should be out there fighting," I challenged, glaring at the group of four people who'd basically taken me hostage. They'd sent the rest of the guards out to fight. "You're all cowards."

"Shut up!" Dax hissed at me, fire in his eyes.

A guy like that? Oh, I was sure he wanted nothing more than to be out there fighting. It probably killed him to be locked up, hidden away from all the action. Reed only laughed, leaning against the far wall.

"We can't afford to lose Jessa," Sabine purred, manicured fingers dancing against her chin, eyes thoughtful, as she walked the perimeter of the small room. "She's far too valuable. So, we will wait this out and make our move once it's over."

The family wasn't here, luckily. I could only imagine how Dax would have treated them if he'd discovered someone on his search. Whoever the people that lived here were, they were probably in the gymnasium, waiting for further instructions, or maybe they were out fighting their own people, brainwashed by my alchemy. Considering their home was across the street from the school, it made sense. It was either those explanations, or they were already dead.

The home had a cozy, well-loved energy that made me think of my home, the place where I'd lived a beautiful childhood, but could never return to. My heart squeezed, the truth clearer to me than ever. I studied the home, seeing the similarities. Even though the wooden floors were heavily scratched, the homeowners had centered beautiful rugs throughout. Pictures lined the walls with clean glass frames. Some held images of family, smiling faces shining back at the camera, and others were of beautiful landscapes. A fireplace with a massive wood mantle centered the room, leftover charred wood giving the room a faint smoky scent.

I'll never get to go home, but maybe I'll get to see my family again. That was most important, a thought I needed to hold onto, no matter what.

Sabine and Mark stood in the farthest corner from everyone else, whispering quietly between each other.

"I don't think that's a good idea," Reed interjected from across the room, a twinkle of blue light moving between two fingers. "She will have to agree to it *willingly* for it to work." His eyes flashed to me. "She's strong. She needs to come by things in her own time. It's either that, or you'll need really good blackmail. Might I suggest the prince as collateral? She still loves the guy, and yes, I know he's alive." He laughed. "People always underestimate my gift."

The couple glared back at Reed, Sabine's eyes were sharp ice and Mark's were incredulous. Yeah, so he invaded their privacy. What did they expect? I stifled a laugh. *Serves them right!*

But considering they were talking about a plan that included my consent, it was about time they stopped all their whispering.

"What the hell is going on? What aren't you telling me?" I asked with a sneer.

You had better agree to this, Dax's snarky voice infiltrated my mind. *If you don't, I will get you alone and I will strangle you with my bare hands. Don't think I haven't been daydreaming of it since the moment I laid my eyes on you. You're a spoiled brat and you need to be taught a lesson.*

Panic rose in the back of my throat and fear prickled up my spine. I pushed away the clear mental image he'd conjured in my mind. All these people were messed up, but Dax was truly sick. One look was all I needed to know I never, ever wanted to be alone with the kid.

Not willing to back down, I shot a heated glare in his direction. "Say that out loud so everyone here can listen to your disgusting thoughts," I snapped.

He looked away, greasy black hair flopping, heat creeping to his cheeks.

"I didn't think so." I leaned back in the chair, annoyed at the cuffs still pinching my wrists, restraining my arms behind me.

"Whatever," he growled, charging toward the door in a few short stomps. "I'm going to go find something to eat. If you need me, I'll be in the kitchen."

"Get me something, too!" Reed yelled.

"I'm not your maid. Get your own damn food," Dax called back.

Reed laughed, throwing his head back as if it were the funniest thing ever. Like it was really hard to focus on something other than food at a time like this? Breakfast wasn't that long ago. They were both idiots.

I returned my attention to Mark and Sabine, who were both looking disdainfully in the direction of the boys. They didn't find it funny either.

"You might as well tell me your big secret," I said. "I already know there's something strange about you two. You're hiding something."

"I'm not sure." Mark leaned against his wife.

"You can tell me now, or you can tell me eventually in the interrogation room." Because sooner or later, it would be *their* turn.

"She's right! We're running out of time," Sabine replied, reaching down to grip her husband's hand and losing a bit of her usual cool. "We can't have the whole country aligned with Richard, let alone all of Nashville. Not if this is going to work."

Wait a second...

I sputtered, my entire body growing sickly warm.

"You're not loyal!" I perked up in my chair, a bead of hope growing in my chest. "Are you Resistance?"

Mark spat. "We're not part of that damned Resistance!"

Sabine held up a hand, poised once again. "Please, dear. It should hardly come as a surprise that we're not loyal to the Hearts. Richard, foolish man that he is, has many enemies. We are only one of them."

"But you work for him!" I challenged. "You seem so besotted. How am I to believe you're telling me the truth?"

She smiled. "Yes. It's all very convenient, don't you think? I certainly do. Thank you for getting rid of Faulk for us, by the way. That woman was getting on my last nerve. Things will be so much easier now that she's dead."

A million questions pummeled my brain, but the biggest came out first. "Is it you? Are you the ones who hurt Lucas?"

They shared a guarded look, something dark flashing between them.

"No," Sabine said. "That wasn't us."

Mark eyed her as he nodded fervently.

"Though the boy probably deserved it, after what he did to Celia," she continued. "It's not really him we're concerned with at the moment. Lucas has always been harmless. The boy has no spine. No. It's Richard that needs to be removed."

They were lying to me. I couldn't know for sure, but I felt it in my gut.

If I could get at their blood, I could find out the truth. I foolishly yanked on my cuffs, which they'd neatly rearranged through the slats in the chair where I currently sat. I groaned. For now, I wasn't moving.

"And what does this have to do with me?" I asked.

It was a stupid question. Of course I knew. But I had to buy time. Sasha was on her way...

Sabine cackled. "Don't be daft. We want you to help us. Align with us. Use your red to end Richard. You can stay married to your little love. We'll help Lucas run things. He needs our guidance. Our families will unite."

I glared. "Am I really supposed to believe you won't somehow end up on the throne yourselves? You'll probably annul my marriage and have your daughter married to him within the week."

Her eyes widened—I had her. It didn't matter what she said next, I saw it written all over her face. I'd thought their family was after the crown when their daughter had been engaged to Lucas, but this confirmed something far worse. It wasn't just their daughter they wanted to see in power, it was themselves. It was Sabine and Mark Addington behind the whole thing.

"But why? Why not be loyal and reap the rewards of your high position?"

Sabine sneered, "Our family has been through hell for the Hearts, especially our daughter. We've been so close, for generations, really. And that's how we're repaid? A broken engagement? A never-ending war? No, it simply won't do." She strolled closer as she spoke, eyes boring into me as if it all made perfect sense. "Besides, we'll do a better job at ruling. You do see Richard's foolishness, don't you? He thinks he can take over the world by ripping it to shreds. We will create diplomacy and peace, give our society better advantages, and use alchemy to create abundance for those most deserving."

Off to the side, Reed stood with his arms crossed, nodding along to the whole thing. No doubt he would get some sort of leg-up for helping them.

"And *you* will help us," Mark pressed. "I know you hate Richard as much as we do. This is the right thing to do."

I scoffed. "Never."

"Like I said," Reed sighed, "you'll need to blackmail her."

Boots scuffled, someone groaned, and two forms appeared from around the doorframe. Dax's teeth were bared, eyes wild, as he held a steady gun pressed to the back of a woman's head. She turned, blonde ponytail swooshing, and grimaced at me. Sasha.

I jumped up trying fruitless to bring the chair with me. Reed strode across the room, pushing me back down. Mouth opening and closing, unable to speak a word, I held Sasha's eye contact. She squirmed against Dax, mouth pinched, regret and anger burning in her gaze. Nothing needed to be said, we both knew we were on the losing end of the situation.

"Look who I found," Dax sneered. "It's your precious sister. What should I do with her, huh? Should I kill her?"

"Careful with that one," Reed interjected. "Cuff her. She's a tease just like Jessa here. Not to mention more dangerous than you."

Dax scowled at Reed and then tossed Sasha to the floor, the force of his magic ripping through his sinewy muscles. Her stone necklace dangled in his free hand. He shoved it in a pocket and then set to work cuffing her arms behind her back.

Reed flicked a wrist toward Sasha, "There's your blackmail."

Mark smiled, crouching down to stare into my eyes. "And what about now? Now will you help us?"

I opened my mouth but was unable to answer. What was I supposed to say? Reed was right. Sasha was the perfect blackmail. She was the key, the bait, someone I would do anything to protect.

I was out of choices.

SEVENTEEN

LUCAS

"You have to take me with you." I followed my father up the stairs, taking two at a time, trying to catch up. We'd just received news that a battle was waging in Nashville. From the initial report he'd gotten downstairs, West America was on the losing end. Again. Of course, my father's pride had reared its head and the man had wanted to see it for himself.

"Absolutely not," he barked over his shoulder. "You're still supposed to be dead, remember? Besides, it's too dangerous for you out there."

The lights in the stairway sent his long shadow pressing down on me. "That's pretty hypocritical coming from you, don't you think? Seeing as you're going out there."

"I will have an entire team to protect me. At the first sign of trouble, I'll be back. But for now, I need to steer the ship."

He was serious with that analogy which only made me chuckle in disbelief at the size of his ego. Steer the ship? Really?

"So? Your team can protect me, too."

He turned on me then, face cast in shadow. I could only make out his silhouette, but I knew from his heavy breaths that he was done with this conversation. Didn't stop me. "Very few members of my team know you're even here, Lucas. Need we have this conversation again? My answer is no."

He whipped back around and slammed his wide shoulders through the door. I sped up but the door closed in my face, the sound of a lock clicking in place. I bristled and stepped back, my jaw dropping.

Since when had he installed a lock on the *outside* of the door? There was a huge lever on the inside of this door and the one below, which made sense, considering it was a bunker. But to purposely make a way to lock me in? All my bugging him about being down here must have finally gotten the best of him.

Either that, or he's suspicious.

I sighed and rested my head against the cool metal, momentarily lost for a solution. Jessa was over there. She was stuck in the middle, and I needed to make sure she was okay. As much as she hated me, I couldn't pretend there wasn't something there between us. I'd felt it from the moment I'd met her. I needed to see that something through and that wasn't going to happen if she was dead. Besides, I wanted to join in the battle if it came to that and help where I could. After I witnessed what she was being forced into and how broken she'd become, I wanted to offer help.

I slammed my fist against the door, cussing. *Stubborn man!* I tested the handle, just in case. It was still locked.

Running back down the stairs, I jumped over the last four in one swoop, and flew through the door at the bottom. I needed yellow. If I could just get my hands on some yellow, I could break that lock myself. But it had to be organic yellow like a stone or a plant or something.

Why hadn't I stocked up?

I tore through all the bedrooms, rummaging through cabinets and drawers. I even lifted up the couch cushions.

But there was nothing.

I plopped back onto the misshapen couch, tossing the book laying next to me across the room. It hit the wall and clattered to the floor, pages flying open. Breathing fast, I ran my shaky hands through my hair and stared up at the stark white ceiling. White was in abundance down here, even the flowers on the kitchen table were fresh. But what good would invisibility do if I couldn't get through the door?

At that thought, I heard the click of the door handle.

"Hey you," a silky voice chimed behind me. "Are you doing okay? I heard you were stuck down here."

I stood and spun around—Celia Addington. She sauntered into the room, casually removing black gloves and unraveling a long cream scarf. She unwrapped the soft fabric from her neck several times, eyeing me with interest. She tossed the items onto the table like she owned the place and sashayed toward me.

"How did you get in here?" I asked. And more importantly, was the door upstairs still open?

"Leo let me in."

I stared at her. "Leo?"

She giggled, the sound forced. "Your guard, silly."

Okay, why was she acting so weird? If she thought this was flirting, she was trying way too hard to pull it off. She was attractive, but this was not. And why were my guards so easily paid off? It didn't make sense. What did Celia have on them?

"Umm, okay," I replied, clearing my throat and focusing all of my attention on her. "And what are you doing here?"

"I came to keep you company." She smiled seductively, walking her fingers across the back of the couch as she worked her way around it, finally standing right in front of me. She tugged on the collar of my shirt, biting her bottom lip and looking up at me through a set of dark lashes. "I bet you have a lot on your mind, hmm?"

"Uh, yeah," I sputtered. "You could say that."

A lot of *Jessa* on my mind. Or maybe the problem was that I didn't have *enough* on my mind, namely my memories that still hadn't come back, and the full truth. Even though, I was beginning to piece that together on my own.

"I can help you take your mind off those troubles for a while." She ran her hands down my chest. "Nobody has to know," she whispered.

I narrowed my eyes and stepped back. Hadn't we already had this conversation?

"I'm not interested."

She pouted. "Don't pretend you haven't been thinking about our kiss."

"I haven't."

She put her hands on her hips, attitude flaring. "I don't believe you."

I shook my head, annoyed. "Believe it. I haven't thought about it once since that night."

Hurt flashed across her face, breaking her smooth exterior. "Why are you fighting this, Lucas?" She stomped her foot like a spoiled child. "You know, I've never had a guy turn me away before you. I'm sick of your prudishness. And by the way? Things will be a lot easier for you in the future if you don't fight this."

Umm, okay?

She turned, her hair flipping as she stormed toward the door.

"Wait!" I called out. I didn't want her here, but I also didn't want her to leave and lock me up again. Her arrival had marked the only opportunity I had to get out. If that door upstairs was still unlocked…

She spun back around, raising her eyebrows. "What, Lucas?"

"I'm sorry." I cleared my throat and looked down. "I didn't mean to be rude. You can stay. We can hang out for a bit…as friends."

She laughed, her cold anger thawing quickly. "Sure." She winked. "*As friends.*"

"Sit," I said, motioning to the couch. "I still don't have a slatebook. But, uh, we could read or something? That's pretty much all I've been doing lately."

That, and sneaking out a few times under the guise of white alchemy.

That, and obsessing about Jessa and what she really meant to me.

Jessa, who spent her nights sleeping on the other side of my wall.

"You're an interesting character." Celia relaxed into the couch. "We could talk, ya know? We don't have to *read.*"

"Yeah," I returned. I jogged over to the roses, sliding two out from the massive arrangement. I strode back and dropped one into her lap.

"Uh, thanks?" She giggled.

"One for you and one for me," I said, feeling and sounding like a total idiot. It was a necessary evil. I needed to play this whole thing off as nice, as funny, as anything other than what it really was.

"You're sweet." She buried her nose in the rose.

My eyes caught on a flash of metal sticking out of her pocket. I frowned. "Is that a knife?"

Her eyes popped to mine, red brightening her cheeks. Slowly, she nodded, pulling the long, thin blade from her pocket. She twisted it around in her hand, a smirk playing on her lips.

"A girl can never be too safe," she purred.

It didn't ring true. Something about this whole situation was off. A small alarm bell went off in my head, a warning to play it cool.

"Don't worry, Lucas," she grinned at me, pressing the tip of her finger to the knife. A tiny bead of blood swelled on the end. She placed in her mouth, sucking it for a moment. "When all is said and done, you and I are going to have a great life together. And if you can't see that, well, I think you know what that means."

The threat prickled over me, pins and needles covering my skin.

I narrowed my eyes. "Are you saying if I don't agree to a relationship with you, you'll what? Slit my throat?"

A smile played on her lips as she feigned innocence. "I never said that. Of course I would never hurt someone I care about so deeply, especially because I know how strongly you feel about me. Besides, it's best for Jessa this way, too. She's too busy with alchemy to be a good wife to you."

I nodded once and she slipped the knife back into her pocket. The message was clear. She was threatening me. And not just me, Jessa! I didn't think I'd ever have the urge to punch a woman, but I did right then.

"I told them you'd come around," she leaned into me, cuddling into my side.

"Who?" I stilled.

"My parents, silly. They wanted this match from the beginning. They're with Jessa right now, did you know? She's their little puppet." She laughed lightly, sighing, a craze to her eyes that I'd never noticed before. This woman was truly delusional if she thought I was in love with her, that I would dump someone as sweet as Jessa to be with her.

Taking a long breath, I ran a hand down her arm. My other still held the white rose and with a quick squeeze, I remembered my plan.

"I'll be right back," I peeled her off of me and strolled to my bedroom. "Stay right there, I have a present for you."

She bounced in her seat, beaming.

The second I rounded the corner, sure I was out of her eye-line I worked the white magic into my veins. I popped off the head of the rose and squeezed it between my fingers, the silky texture releasing a sweet scent into the air. As the white seeped from the rose, my form also seeped from view.

Entirely invisible, I carefully walked out of the room, past where Celia sat primping on the couch, and through the open door into the stairwell. Then I hurried up, my legs burning.

"Lucas? Are you okay? I'm ready for my present now!" I heard her voice call from below as I slipped through the door above. I thanked God it was unlocked.

The guard, Leo, leaned lazily against the wall, completely unsuspecting. It wasn't the same guy from the first time Celia had snuck in. She must have bribed a second guard to get to me yet again. *Gee, some guards you got there, Dad.*

To throw the guard off his game, I slammed the door shut with a loud clang. He jumped up, eyes wide and hand reaching to his rifle. The second he rushed forward to inspect, I took off in the opposite direction. It wouldn't be long until I'd be on board some helicopter, speeding away from the base. But I did wonder how long it would take to actually find Jessa. It didn't matter to me if New Colony was winning the battle at the moment. The soldiers of West America would kill Jessa on sight if they knew what she was doing to the people of Nashville.

If there was anyone I wanted to be stuck in a bunker with, it was definitely that mysterious wife of mine. In order to do that, I had to find her and get us both out of Nashville alive. And then maybe I could work on figuring out how to get my father to stop hurting so many innocent people. Because one thing was starting to become clear, one thing Jessa had revealed that I couldn't believe at first. Richard had lost his mind, and it was up to me to stop him.

✦

I dove from the chopper, rolling across the pavement. Gunshots rang out, pilfering the city street. I trailed behind the line of soldiers as they jumped from the machine and took their positions. Ducking into an empty alleyway, squeezing the white rose in my left hand, my breath came out fast. Shaking racked through my body, taking in the sounds of battle. I needed to calm down, to make a plan. My ambition, my need to be part of the action, had gotten the better of me, and that realization stared me straight in the face now.

I'd overlooked getting a gun.

How could I have been so stupid as to not bring a weapon? To make matters worse, I didn't have any other colors on me besides the white rose. And I still had no idea where Jessa was. This was a huge city, and she could be anywhere.

Searching eyes darted in every direction as I thought through my options. Weapons. Those needed to come first. I slowed my breathing as I scanned the area. No luck.

I ran to the opposite end of the alley, peeking out. The street was in ruins—an all-out battle waged in front of me. My belly churned as men and woman destroyed each other, blood and bullets flying. Our alchemists wore their gear, the advantage obvious: a rainbow of stones embedded into their uniforms. The shiny black helmets made it impossible to tell who was who, creating a menacing uniformity. They fought alongside our soldiers, and to my astonishment, what appeared to be West American civilians also putting up a fight.

Most of the civilians were on our side. It didn't surprise me, but it didn't feel right. I doubled over as I watched one kill his own countryman.

On the other side of the battle, some fighting in hand-to-hand combat, others using guns and even hand grenades, were the West Americans. They moved lithely in their khaki uniforms, skills just as impressive as any of our soldiers. They had a trained synchronicity to their attacks, a lethalness not to be underestimated.

I squinted, making out the occasional West American alchemist, head to toe in black with a ropy gemstone necklace wrapped around each of their necks. The news of West American alchemists left me staring, hands fisting and aching to help. Many of them were young. Too young. They were novices, quick to succumb to the battle. What was going on in West America that they'd send untrained alchemists into battle?

A young teen West American alchemist fell into the mud, gasping out a curdled scream, blood gushing from his right side. A West American soldier sprinted forward to help. Hunching, he hitched his gun over his shoulder and stretched out his arms. A masked Guardian jumped in between the two, shooting the soldier down, his body landing inches from the boy. Then the Guardian quickly tended to the wounds of the fallen alchemist with streams of green magic, all the while restraining the kid with a zip tie. He hauled the lanky boy into his arms and ran. I squinted, eyes following them, questions burning.

"Remember, orders are to keep as many alchemists alive as possible," someone shouted from down the street. Their barking orders barely carried over the roar of battle. The Guardian carrying the kid ducked around the fighters, disappearing into the distance.

Keep the alchemists alive? It had to mean one thing: Richard didn't want to waste magic. He saw no problem with everyday soldiers and civilians losing their lives, but the alchemists were too valuable. He would keep them, like pets.

The carnage continued and revulsion boiled up inside. Bodies littered the streets, streams of alchemy shot alongside the bullets. It tore me up, seeing something that could be used for such good, twisted in this horrific way. How much longer could this continue?

A West American alchemist stumbled into the alleyway. I threw myself against the brick building before the woman careened into me. Was she hurt? I held my rose to my chest, blood rushing through my ears, as I looked her up and down. I didn't see any wounds. Dressed in black, her wrinkled hands ran along her gleaming necklace as she gasped in short breaths. She dropped her hands to her sides and a second necklace appeared, one full of black stones. They were stacked in neat rows, shiny orbs that blended with her clothing. My breath caught, confusion bubbling inside.

Was she a black alchemist? What did black magic even do?

I forced myself to remain against the wall as I studied her. She was older, maybe in her sixties, and something about her was incredibly familiar. She had silvery blonde bobbed hair and light knowing eyes. Sweat soaked her skin in the sunlight, as if she'd exerted herself more than usual. She was powerful beyond imagination, dressed like that in a place like this.

A slatebook pinged at her belt. She fumbled, pulling it close to her mouth, talking low. "I'm here," she said. "I made it this far. Now what?"

"You're only five blocks east from Imperial High School," an authoritative male voice replied, booming from the speakers. She must have turned the sound all the way up because of the noisy battle. "That's where we have reason to believe King Richard just landed and many of his troops are there to guard him. Get there and use your weapon."

She nodded, a little reluctantly, squinting up into the sun. She slid her slatebook back into place and squared her shoulders. "Here we go," she muttered. And then she took off, jogging as fast as her body would take her.

Imperial High School?

Use your weapon?

Confusion interlaced with sinking dread filled me, making my feet feel like anchors, pinning me to the concrete. If my father was near that area, then I had to assume Jessa was near as well. I took a resolute breath and ran back down to the other side of the alley, deciding it would be better to travel in the areas that weren't currently a bloody battleground. My boots pounded against the pavement, dodging rubble and the occasional fallen body.

I tried not to look too closely at the dead, tried not to picture the way their lives should have gone, with family and friends, with happiness and living into old age. But I couldn't help it. The guilt flashed the images through my mind anyway.

Before long, I rounded the final corner of the fifth block, the school's patchy green and brown lawn sprawling out in front of me, a field of death. The entire area swarmed with soldiers, their magic and bodies and guns clashing in a cacophony of cries and smoke and blood. The sun arched high, making the air as hot as the battle.

Or maybe it was nerves that made me feel like I was boiling from the inside out.

I lunged forward. The gratitude for my invisibility pulsed through my veins as my boots tore through the field, escaping notice. After a minute that felt like an hour, I approached the high school, fully unscathed. Taking the front steps two at a time, I rushed through the doors and skidded to a stop in the large lobby.

I eyed the glass partition, looking into what appeared to be a large office on the other side. Inside stood my father, his advisor Mark and Mark's wife, Sabine, a few alchemists and soldiers, a blonde girl dressed in black who was apparently under arrest, sulking in the corner with guns trained on her, and in the center of it all, Jessa. My heart burned when I saw her, saw the way she was standing, saw the pain etched in her every line and curve. She had her arms crossed over her chest, lips turned down in a frown, and eyes so full of fear I thought they might spill over.

I crept across the lobby and waited for someone to open the door. A couple of soldiers with determined gazes careened into the lobby, going right for the door and giving me the very opportunity I needed. I followed easily, pressing myself against the far wall the moment I entered the office.

"Your Royal Highness," one of the soldiers said, dipping low in a quick bow. "Something is happening outside. They have some kind of…unknown weapon. I think you need to see this."

Richard's mouth fell into a flat line, and he trudged past me and out the door. "I'll be right back," he called after him, the door swinging shut as he went.

Perhaps I should have followed, but something held me rooted in place, my back against the wall.

"You should have done it then," Sabine turned on Jessa, her eyes two angry slits. "You were standing right next to him!"

"You don't understand," Jessa sputtered. "I tried to do this once before and I failed. It's not that simple. He'll kill me if I mess up again."

"Don't be so afraid to do your duty."

"It's *not* my duty."

The woman slapped Jessa across the face, the sound a sharp crack. Jessa stumbled back. Hate shot through every cell in my body. Who was this woman that she thought she could touch Jessa?

Mark held up a hand, eyes drawn in understanding. "Sabine, none of that. She'll do it; she just needs the perfect opportunity. She knows her sister will die if she doesn't."

My breath caught. In the corner, the blonde girl in black laughed, blue eyes shining. The same eyes as Jessa. "You think you're going to be able to use me as leverage forever?"

Her sister. It clicked into place. Jessa had told me about all of this. Why hadn't I believed her when I still had the chance to help?

"Shut up," one of the alchemist guardians ground out the insult, hitting her with the butt of his rifle so hard she slumped down against the wall, head awkwardly tilting to one side.

"Don't you touch her!" Jessa yelled, angrily charging the guy. "What did you do?"

He spun, pointing his gun at her. "Careful, Princess."

"Don't you dare point that at her!" Mark shot out, and the boy dropped his gun, a sheepish expression rising on his lips.

"Jessa, you need to relax," Sabine said, touching her auburn hair gently as if a strand were out of place. "Sasha has only been knocked out. She'll be fine."

Untapped rage built as I watched these people treat Jessa like some kind of prisoner, like a tool to use however they saw fit. What did they have on her? Was my father part of this? I considered Sasha, a girl Jessa would do anything to protect. A sister.

"You will order the King to kill himself," Sabine said, finger pointing at Jessa. "Next time he's near, you will do it. It will be easy. You will scratch him and use your red or I swear we'll kill your sister. The world would be free of one less alchemist pest, but I have a feeling she'd rather live."

Jessa nodded, face ashen, fat tears breaking loose and streaming down her face. I ground my teeth.

"And then, as we discussed, you will get to Lucas. We'll have to talk to Celia again, see if Lucas still deserves a place in this," Mark continued. "But for now, let's head outside and see what this West American weapon is all about."

The group moved toward the exit, one Guardian gripping Jessa's upper arm, shoving her forward. The other standing watch over Sasha, kicking at her boot. He let out a huff and reached down to haul her over his shoulder. Her arms and head flopped against his back as he strode forward.

I was still pressed against the wall. The rage that had been building came to an all-out eruption.

They were going to blackmail her to kill my father and then me? They were using my wife to take control of New Colony for themselves? Or maybe they were West American spies.

I didn't think so.

I dove forward, tackling Mark around his middle and slamming him to the ground.

Someone screamed, but I didn't pay that any attention as I pummeled the traitor's face. Blood sprayed in all directions. His eyes shone full of terror, probably because I was still invisible!

Realization dawned and he fought back. He kicked out at me, arms flying. He connected with my nose and blood pooled in my mouth as his meaty fist crashed against my teeth.

The sick bastard. I would kill him.

At some point, it was not only his arms that I could see flying, but mine as well.

I had dropped the rose.

His gaze leveled with mine, first widening in surprise before transforming into mocking enjoyment.

"Oh, Lucas, have you been hiding a dirty little secret?" He cackled.

Over his shoulder, I caught the sight of the others fighting as well. The girl who'd supposedly passed out was alive and well, kicking the ever-loving crap out of the two alchemist dudes who'd been guarding her. Jessa was attacking Sabine, quick to overtake the polished woman who didn't have magic or a gun.

"I should have done a better job the first time I tried to kill you," Mark ground out. My gaze returned to the man pinned beneath me, confusion peaking. I reached out my fist again, ready to strike, when he slammed me back, shifting the balance of power. I fell to the ground, landing hard on my back, elbows scraping against the rough carpet. He jumped up, kicking me with his steel-toed boots. Pain overpowered the thoughts in my brain, sweeping over my body.

"Does this look familiar?" he continued.

Outside, muffled screams and bullets and chaos echoed faintly. If anyone saw what was happening in this office, they didn't come. They couldn't. They were too busy with whatever New Colony's new weapon was to come inside here. I had to get myself out of this mess, but I could barely push past the agony as Mark pummeled me again and again.

I blinked up at the man, seeing red. Something flashed through my mind, taking in his words. *Does this look familiar?* It did. Was it a memory? Déjà vu?

I had been in this position before.

My brain sent flashes of images, electric pulses of memory. The night he'd tried to kill me overtook my vision. I saw it all. The look on Jessa's face when

I'd told her we had to get her out of the palace. The same look when I'd said goodbye to her at the safe house and when she'd dropped my mother's ring back into my shaking hand. My deep sadness as I'd wandered around the palace that night. Mark hiding out in that darkened nursery. His rage when he realized it was me who found him, me who'd shamed his family, his name. And the way he'd ruthlessly attacked me, had so clearly tried to kill me.

"It was you," I coughed, copper filling my mouth. My arms and legs didn't seem to know how to fight back anymore. They lay useless at my sides, paralyzed by pain. I was succumbing to the agony. It covered me like a thick blanket.

"It was, and it has been," Mark continued. "We've been trying to get rid of your nasty family for months now."

Another boot connected with my face.

"Your mother's funeral."

A crack broke my rib.

"The jet explosion."

Something crushed against my skull.

Fight back.

I willed every ounce of strength I had, wanting to live. I couldn't give up now. I couldn't let him win.

"You should have married my Celia," he continued.

He jumped on top of me, blood dripping as he leered close to my face. My eyes were so swollen that he blurred above me.

"This time I'm going to finish the job."

And I believed him.

More memories flashed through my mind. Meeting Jessa, the way she'd hated me at first, the way she'd used alchemy on me by accident with the fire. Sharing a meal with her out on the grass, a picnic under the stars. How much I had wanted to kiss her, despite my better judgment. And the moment I *had* finally kissed her, how amazing she had felt wrapped up in my arms. And then that helicopter had come, spinning the wind around us, pulling us apart.

And Sasha. Her sister.

The Resistance and everything that had happened with them.

I squinted up, trying to focus on something else. Jessa's sister, Sasha, was finishing off her fight with the blonde guy. He collapsed and she turned, staring down at me with wide eyes.

"Sasha!" I called, my voice sounding gargled and far away. "Help Jessa."

She darted forward, gripping at Mark's shoulders with a shrill war-cry.

Jessa appeared, on the other side of Mark, also screaming.

"No," I tried to tell her, but the word was swallowed by blood. I didn't want her in this fight, he was crazy. And she, she was everything...

Out of everything I remembered, what came through with absolute clarity was how many times I'd failed Jessa. I'd hurt her, the one I loved most. I couldn't do it again. I would die if it meant she could be free of the destruction I always seemed to bring down on her world.

Mark's rage burned down on me as he hit me one last time.

The two sisters wrenched him back and connected with the blood that coated Mark. He screamed in retaliation. But he had no chance.

The blood between us faded to gray.

Hope surged.

And then my consciousness fell, lost to the gray, faded to black, before I could even catch my breath.

EIGHTEEN

JESSA

Fury poured through me, white hot and cutting. My vision blurred and narrowed in on Mark Addington's body. I pulled and pulled at his blood, draining the color, leaching it until it was nothing but a mess of lifeless gray liquid. Too angry to direct the red magic to go anywhere or do anything productive, it swirled around Sasha and myself in a tornado of unused energy. She didn't care. Her hands also pushed against Mark. Her anger was just as thick.

I blinked at her, realizing the truth. My sister had my same power. She was doing this, too. We smiled at each other. We couldn't stop, wouldn't stop. The masses of gray blood were our salvation. We knew what it meant. Death. The power of it thundered through us, strengthening our bond, and building the magic of the moment into a frenzied, lustful, never-ending storm.

"No!" Sabine screamed. I turned the magic on her, reaching out a second hand to snatch her bloodied arm.

"Go!" I commanded. "Don't tell anyone we're here. Get away from us!"

She ran.

I turned back to the horrible man at my feet. He deserved it. More than anyone, it was Mark I wanted to hurt. And I was almost there. If I went on longer, he would die and that would be justice. His body would become nothing but a dead mass lying on top of Lucas.

Lucas...

I stopped. I didn't want to be a murderer, no matter how much Mark deserved to die. That wasn't who I was. That wasn't why I was doing this. And Lucas was the one who needed attention right now, not Mark.

I lifted my hands and sat back. My eyes connected with my sister as she did the same. "I didn't know you could do that, too," I said lamely.

"I never wanted you to know." She shook her head, sadness seeping over her deflated body. "I never want anyone to know. I put that kind of magic behind me a long time ago."

I nodded. "I get it. If I could wish it away, I would."

We were alone in the office with all of these injured men, two powerful girls who wanted nothing more than normalcy. Sasha crawled over to the two passed-out Guardians. She touched their bloodied forms, whispering for them to sleep, to sleep until tomorrow, to dream of nothing but darkness.

Outside, the battle continued.

I frowned down at Lucas, mind finally cleared enough to help him. He was passed out, but once I healed him, I was sure he'd be fine. He had to be fine. My heart couldn't bear it otherwise. Wrenching Mark's huge body out of the way, I kneeled before my prince, ready to assess the wounds. My breath caught.

Wait–No...

Lucas was white as a sheet, unblinking eyes lifeless. He didn't move. Not even his chest rose or fell. Panic swept through me as I ran my hands over his body. The once vibrant blood that had covered his face was now completely gray, dripping off him in streams of iron.

I shook him, gently at first. "Lucas?"

He didn't respond.

I shook him harder, tears springing to my eyes. "Lucas, are you okay? Wake up!"

"Lucas, please!" My voice came out cracked and hoarse. I found Sasha's gaze. She would know what to do. But she sputtered, horror struck.

"We took too much," she whispered, a lone tear rolling down her cheek.

"No." I frowned. "No. We were using it on Mark, not Lucas."

Sasha's eyes mirrored back at me, brimming with pity. "It was an accident," she said, voice even. "You have to remember that this was an accident, Jessa. We would have never done this on purpose."

"What are you even talking about?" I growled. I looked away and leaned over Lucas, shaking him once again. But he was gone.

No...

What happened? We'd gone after Mark. It was never supposed to be Lucas. I looked around horrified, everything sinking in as I realized that both of their blood had been all over each other. When we'd stepped in to stop Mark, we must have somehow also pulled alchemy from Lucas.

Lucas, who had already lost so much blood.

Lucas, who'd been on the edge of death.

No!

"He's dead," my sister confirmed. "They both are. I'm so sorry."

I screamed, a high-pitched eruption that transformed into a guttural moan.

"Go find some green," I begged. "Please."

She didn't question me, didn't tell me it was too late. She sprinted to the desk behind us, fumbling with the mess sprawled across it, papers falling to the floor.

"Here!" She tossed a small bamboo shoot growing out of a little yellow pot. I caught it, staring down dumbly at the sparkly trinket wrapped around the green shoot: a tiny golden elephant.

Refocusing, I grappled at the green, shooting the magic through Lucas.

Nothing

This couldn't be happening!

Sasha stood above me, her body trembling. "This is why I never wanted to do it again," her voice croaked. "This was why I ran in the first place. I never should've done it again. I knew better." Her head dropped into her hands. "I am so sorry."

I couldn't deal with her. I couldn't do this. I couldn't believe it.

I pulled Lucas's head to me and tenderly laid it into my lap, brushing the strands of dark hair out of his face. We'd been through so much together. Had it really come to this? Had I just murdered my own husband?

I'd been so afraid he was turning into his father but it was me who'd been overcome with power. I was the one who'd used my magic to kill, the one who'd relished in the feel of it. If anyone was like King Richard, it was me. I was nothing but a destructive force of nature.

My mouth fell open in a silent scream and hot tears rolled down my cheeks, the salt sinking into the corners around my mouth. I gasped, my heart ripping out of my chest, this day sinking in deep.

I'd been so worried about Lucas, and yet, I'd turned away from him. I'd been so frustrated with his memory loss, so annoyed, when none of that was even his fault. He didn't choose that. Mark had done it to him!

And in the middle of what had happened over the last few weeks, I'd forgotten just how much I loved him.

But I did. I loved him.

I knew it the moment we'd first kissed. I knew it again when that farmer told me Lucas's death had been announced. But here I was, with him lying before me, really dead this time, and the pain was more unbearable than anything I'd ever experienced before. It was too much.

And it wasn't enough.

"We have to get out of here," Sasha said. "There's something going on outside. I think West America's gaining ground right now. We need to take this chance while we can."

I was numb. I couldn't move, could barely hear Sasha.

"Come on, Jessa," Sasha pressed. "We need to go."

"No," I snapped. I wasn't giving up on Lucas; there had to be a way. This couldn't be over. This couldn't be the end. I couldn't accept that.

"You need to come." She reached out, tugging on my arm.

I slapped her away, my voice turning dark. "I said no. Leave me alone."

More gunshots ricocheted outside. An even louder bang shook the floor. Or maybe that was just my body shaking?

She groaned. "I'll be back." Then she ran for the door. I didn't watch to see where she went after that. I didn't care.

I took in the room, blinking.

Dazed.

744

Mystified.

Mark was dead. Sabine was long gone. The two alchemists were still asleep. But it was Lucas who needed me. I couldn't leave him.

I brushed his swollen face with the back of my hand, my tears still falling in droves. One dropped and landed on his forehead, splashing and then rolling off the side. Another fell and hit his eyelid. If I squinted, I could almost believe it was his tear.

No, there has to be another way. I can't give up. I just need more color.

Even as the thoughts came into my head, I knew they were foolish. I didn't care about that, either.

Carefully placing his head on the floor, I pried myself off the floor and looked around the office. Anything, any color would have to do. I would try it all, push everything into him and maybe something would work.

I grabbed a flag first from where it was tacked to the wall: red, white and blue. I pulled over a chair, an ugly burnt orange color. I grabbed a blue book off of the desk, tugged at the purple sweater left on the back of the desk's rolling chair.

I gathered the items around me and unleashed the colors. The magic came from synthetic materials so they were mostly weak, but I no longer cared. I had to try. It was all I had left.

And I was determined, more determined than I'd ever been in my life.

The color swirled, a weaving, dancing, pulsing messy rainbow. What color would possibly help him now? I had no idea, but I pushed them, one by one, at Lucas.

Nothing took.

Frustration left me gasping, the tears falling again. But I was not ready to give up. I kept going. And kept failing.

I doubled over, gathering the scratchy purple sweater into my hands and burying my face in it, sobbing.

"Please don't leave me, Lucas," I begged. I inched my hand away from the sweater and grabbed at him, shook him. "Please don't leave me here alone. I can't do this by myself. I need you."

The color from the purple sweater swirled in the air, a physical representation of the passion currently roiling inside me. I knew what I wanted in this life and it was him. As much as I'd always loved to dance, as much as I'd always loved my family, as much as I had loved anything, *I loved Lucas.*

I loved him more.

More than anything.

He was my reason. He was my reason for living and I couldn't go on without him. I couldn't imagine my life without him in it.

"Please," I whispered again, pulling my face from the sweater.

The purple alchemy swirling around the office separated, the color changing to red and blue. I had done this before. This wasn't new. On several occasions, I separated a color down into its two primary sources. But all it had ever done was exhaust me. It was useless! I hadn't ever been able figure out what these primary colors could do. What was different today?

At first, I was annoyed. Angry. This was the last thing I needed. It would only exhaust me and I didn't want to fall asleep in this moment. I wanted to be here with Lucas, to keep trying.

A startling thought popped into my mind.

Why not? Why not try this new magic on Lucas?

"Come back to me," I whispered to him, one last time, a new kind of power taking hold, running through me like wildfire.

Instinct as my guide, I pushed the color, the blue and the red, down into Lucas's body. The blue bounced away, became frenetic, almost electric, and bounded through the room.

The red, however, was quick to take. It swirled into him like a loving caress.

I gasped, a jolt of adrenaline shooting through me. Hope swelled, my eyes hardly believing what I saw. The colorless gray blood that covered him from head to toe was changing.

Slowly, it transformed back into its original red.

The shine of steel gray blood disappeared, vibrant red taking its place.

I shrieked, pushing green alchemy at Lucas once again. His pale face began to brighten, blood flowing.

The tears in my eyes streamed down my face as I stared, mystified, at everything. At Lucas, and at the colors still whirling through the room. The purple I had separated had created a rare kind of red magic, not the kind that destroyed, but rather the kind that *restored*. It had started that night of the ballet, and for months and months I had been wondering what this separation magic meant. Now I knew. Once separated, a color could return what had been lost. My mind raced to the Shadow Lands, to all this could do for our world. But that only lasted for a moment as I stared at Lucas, he was all I could see. I collapsed on top of him, sobbing with relief and awe.

"You okay?" Lucas asked in a scratchy voice. "Why are you crying? Are you hurt?"

I hugged him tighter. "I'm fine," I mumbled between the sobs. He winced against the pressure of my body. I reached out behind me until I found the bamboo shoot and pushed what little green I could into him, healing the last of his wounds. Then I sat back and looked at him, running a gentle palm down the side of his face, staring into his sparkling gray eyes, my breath catching, my heart filled.

"Seriously, Jessa, are you okay?" he asked again.

"Am I okay?" I shifted off of him, giving him space and studying his eyes. "Lucas, you died."

He sat up slowly, rubbing his head, looking me up and down like a man returned after years away from home. He smiled. "Well, whatever happened, I'm not dead now."

I crawled over, sitting on his lap and gripping his face between my fingers, kissing him as hard as I could. He met me with equal passion, and my tears once again broke free. To be here, in this moment with him, it meant everything. I never wanted it to end. I'd lost him once, maybe more than once. I couldn't lose him again. After a moment, he gently pried me off him, eyes gleaming with mischief and passion.

"What was that for?" he asked.

"I love you," I said. "I love you so much."

He smiled as his eyes darkened. "I love you, too. And Jessa?"

"Yes," I breathed.

"I remember everything." He wrapped his warm arms around me and kissed me all over again. He tasted of everything I'd ever longed for, his lips the comfort I'd been longing to find.

Another blast of sound followed by a violent shake of the earth pulled us apart. "We'd better get out there," I said.

He held me back. "I'm not supposed to be alive, remember?"

I frowned at him.

"What I mean is, my father has been hiding me. I had to use invisibility to get out here in the first place. I'm supposed to be back in the bunker right now. I can't just walk out there like this." He motioned to himself.

I scrunched my nose as I looked around the mess of objects and the splattering of blood. Under a pile of fallen papers, I located the edge of the rose. I pulled it out with a smile and held it out to Lucas. "There's still some white left," I said. "We can't stay here."

He took it in his hands and I wondered if he had enough strength after dying and all, but that question was answered as he instantly turned himself invisible. He grasped my hand in his free one and changed me, too.

"Come on," he said. "Let's see what's going on outside and take it from there."

I sucked in a breath, knowing I had to ask the question. "Umm, Lucas? Whose side are we on?" Now that he had his memories back, how did he feel about this war? He had to know Richard was evil. If I told him about what his father had been making me do with my red alchemy, he'd be livid, but I felt so much shame in admitting the truth.

"Not my father's," he answered quickly. "But also, I don't know how I feel about the other side, either. Mostly I just want things to go back to the way they were. I want to step up and do a better job with what we have, to make the best of it instead of trying to change everything."

I laughed. "I don't think that's going to happen."

I felt his gaze looking fruitlessly for mine. "Don't say that. We can still try."

I nodded, even though I knew he couldn't see me. Together we stood, hand in hand, and left the office. The double doors to the outside world loomed ahead. This was the beginning, or maybe it was the end, but at least this time we had each other.

"What will we find out there?" I whispered.

"I honestly don't know," he replied, his voice catching in defeat.

I squeezed his hand in reassurance. If he could be strong for me, I could be strong for him. "Don't worry. Whatever is next, we'll figure it out together."

We burst through the doors, confronted with chaos. On the front lawn and out into the streets, soldiers and citizens fought in a clash of hand-to-hand combat. Occasional bullets streaked through the air. A small bomb detonated, crumbling the side of a building. A window broke, the sound crashing through the moment of stillness.

And the alchemists? They were retreating. All of them.

I froze, not quite sure what I was seeing. Most of those left were New Colony's super-soldiers, proud Guardians, suits embedded with stones making them nearly impossible to fight. From the yellow that made them strong and fast, to the green that allowed them to heal instantly, to the more unique situations, like the persuasive blue, or the telepathic purple, or even the emotional driving force that was orange. All of that should've meant The Guardians of Color ought to be running into the fight, not away from it.

"Come on." Lucas hauled me forward, talking low into my ear, "Nobody can see us. I have the rose, remember? We need to figure out what is really going on here and make a plan."

I nodded, realizing too late that he couldn't see me. Not that it mattered. We ran down the steps together, solid in our agreement.

I caught sight of Sasha sprinting across the lawn toward us and faltered.

"Sasha!" I screamed, not even thinking.

She must have heard because she stopped, looking around with confusion and panic lighting up her glacial blue eyes. Lucas and I ran over and I spoke normally when we were a couple feet away from her.

"I'm with Lucas. He's alive. What's happening?"

She blinked. "Jessa?"

"Yes, we're here. White alchemy. Remember?"

Her confusion cleared and she spoke, words rushing out, "We have to get out of here. Our powers, they're not working. If she gets close enough to you."

"What are you talking about?"

Sasha didn't answer me. Her head swung side to side, taking in the sight of more retreating alchemists.

"There!" Lucas called out, tugging me back against his warm body. He very well could have been pointing to something off in the distance but I couldn't see it. It didn't matter. I saw exactly what he was concerned about. Fear welled up inside of me, fear, and the realization that nothing would ever be the same.

An older woman dressed in the black garb of alchemy strode up the lawn. Around her, West American soldiers held out their guns, as if protecting her. In the center of the mass of soldiers, was a familiar face. I knew him! I knew that closely cropped white-blonde hair and those intense brooding green eyes. I knew that confident swagger, the way he looked at the world as if he were in charge of keeping it. He was Sasha's friend! One of the two guys who'd come to get me out of the cellar the night I'd run away. He looked different in full daylight, younger somehow, but just as intense as before. Actually, way more intense than before. He looked deadly.

"What are they doing? Who is she?" I turned to Sasha.

Sasha growled. "She is the American President! And Apparently *she* is Weapon X!"

"Weapon X?"

"I'll explain later..." Sasha's voice trailed off.

She didn't have to explain because I saw it. A dark cloud of black billowed at Weapon X's feet, like a supernatural mist. The president was an alchemist? The news was both shocking and completely reasonable. No wonder she'd been rumored to be such an advocate for alchemy.

"See that? It's black alchemy," Lucas said.

"I didn't know such a thing even existed. What does it do?" I asked.

As if in answer, a string of the black snaked out from the woman, swirling around one of the fleeing alchemists. The speed at which the man had been running slowed to almost nothing. He stumbled and fell, and the West American soldiers swarmed him, placing him under arrest.

"It's rather obvious, don't you think?" Sasha replied, but not in a mean way, but a defeated one. "It makes it so we can't use our powers. We need to go. One lick of that black over here and you two will be visible again."

The president jogged up the lawn, her eyes darting around as she looked for her next victim. Suddenly, she closed her eyes, intense focus lining her features. The cloud of black multiplied, billowing out across the lawn, moving in all directions.

"What the hell are you still doing here?" A guy ran out in front of us, arms waving at Sasha. He turned back toward the group of West Americas, yelling over the chaos at the woman. "Stop! She's one of us! Remember?"

She froze, black magic pausing.

I also recognized the guy as another of Sasha's friends. Wasn't his name Tristan? I'd met him the first time I'd dropped my parents off at the Resistance camp, and then again later. He was the other soldier who'd accompanied Sasha to the farm to get me.

"Don't go after her!" Tristan yelled, standing in front of Sasha. "She's one of us."

"Stand down," the blonde soldier called out. "Our orders are to collect all of the alchemists, on either side."

"So that's why you brought all those untrained alchemists out here!" Sasha yelled angrily. "Most haven't even fought, you know. They all ran and hid the second we landed, my sister included."

"We have your sister," the guy replied, voice carrying over the lawn. "She's fine. I made sure of it myself."

Sasha shook her head and crossed her arms over her chest, eyes roaming the field as if she were trying to decide whether to give in to the order, or to make a run for it. The soldiers surrounding the president were much closer now, moving in succession and ready to strike. Lucas and I crept back but my sister seemed to be totally transfixed on the men in front of her.

"Sasha, come on!" I called out as loud as I dared.

She didn't budge.

"What does that stuff do to them long-term?" Tristan yelled at the group, staying put in front of Sasha. His black hair gleamed in the sunlight, so sweaty it stuck to his face and neck. His arms were folded, a rifle slung over his back. "Does it wear off?"

Nobody replied. The black magic had snapped out again, catching another alchemist, and the soldiers were at work detaining the screaming woman. Again and again, it went on. A piece would reach out from the small billowing cloud, travel across the ground like a snake, and wrap itself around an alchemist from as far as a hundred feet away.

Sasha, Lucas, and I? We were much closer than a hundred feet away. All it took was that woman deciding she was going to send her magic at us and that would be it. We'd be caught.

"Sasha, let's go," I ground out again. "We're going to leave your butt here if you don't get moving."

"They won't stop," Sasha replied angrily. "This was never part of the deal. I can't believe she kept this secret for so long! Well, the military must have known…"

She gasped and pointed. I caught sight of someone I knew. Someone I loved! "Callie!"

She fell to her knees, helmet popping off her head and glasses flying. In an instant, West American soldiers surrounded her.

"Please!" she screamed. "I didn't want to help Richard, I never wanted this."

I held back a scream, remembering the time she'd questioned me out on the terrace about the Resistance. She hadn't been one of Faulk's spies. She'd been honest, wanting to help, to join up, and I'd lied to her. Guilt swept low in my belly and I turned away. I couldn't help her, not without magic.

"Mastin!" Sasha called. "What is this? Why didn't you tell me ahead of time about this?"

The crowd parted and he stared from across the lawn. His face faltered as he met Sasha's angry expression. He broke from his group and ran forward.

"I'm sorry," he replied, coming to stop in front of her. Tristan stood to the side, glaring. Both men were dirty and bloody, both looking at Sasha like she meant the world. "We'll sort it all out later. Right now, we need to finish this thing. Where's Richard? He was just here."

She shook her head, hands clenching into fists. "I can't believe you would do this to me, after everything. I really want to punch you right now, Mastin."

His head dropped and he stepped back.

"Whatever, I'm out of here," she grumbled, and took off running. Lucas and I followed, footsteps light on the grass, heartbeat loud in my ears. Tristan caught up quickly, bringing in the rear.

"It's the only way!" The president called out, apologetic. "Please forgive me."

The black magic shot out across the grass, lightning fast. It swirled around us like a tidal wave. A dull aching pain burned through me, creeping up my bones, coupled with overwhelming exhaustion. I stumbled, losing Lucas's hand.

It didn't matter. The magic wrapped around him, too.

Visible now, we fell to our knees.

Just ahead Sasha laid on her side, face pinched in frustration. Tristan tried to lift her into his arms, but he was too slow. Soldiers swarmed. My mind was too tired to notice much of what else was happening. I pushed through the fog anyway, trying to find coherent thought or a way out.

Zip-ties cinched my arms behind my back. I was under arrest. Lucas, too.

"Don't you dare touch him!" Richard's voice bellowed over the landscape. I blinked up against the grass, the black mercifully gone, to see the King's beet-red face.

My exhaustion was beginning to weigh on me, and now it was stronger than ever. But it was my magic that concerned me. My magic, a faint humming sensation, a flowing presence in my body that I didn't even know existed before, was gone.

The King ran, guards and officers flanking him. A group of three shuffling just behind them. Immediately, I recognized Jose and Lily. I had wondered where they'd been, but had been grateful not to see them until now. Had I interviewed them like I had Branson, they'd be dead, too. They were Resistance, but as I saw them now, a tug of confusion pulled at me. Jose had a gun pressed to a man's head. A man dressed in the kind of West American regalia that meant he was important.

"Dad!" Someone called out in a horrified tone. It was blonde soldier from before that Sasha had called Mastin. My heart dropped for him. I knew what felt like to see your own father in that kind of situation.

Richard cackled, eyes angry. "It really is a family affair."

Jose, sparkling in his white Royal Officer uniform, pressed the gun closer to the man's head. "Don't come any closer or he's dead," he snapped, nodding at Mastin and the others.

"Everybody put your hands up," Richard spat. He glared at the group of enemy soldiers. "Do it, or watch your General die." The group froze, nobody wanting to relent.

Richard walked forward, "Who's the highest ranking here?"

"Me," Mastin replied coolly with the jut of his chin.

I craned my neck, looking for the president. She was the highest ranking! But in all the chaos, she'd disappeared.

Very convenient.

"Give me my son and I'll give you your father," Richard replied. He was splattered with blood and dirt, soot smeared across his cheek. But even with all of that, he was the same commanding man he'd always been.

Silence filled the area as if everyone had forgotten to breathe, and maybe they had. I forced the air from my lungs, taking it all in. The West American soldiers on one side, weapons drawn. Richard on the other, his loyalist people surrounding him. Lucas, Sasha and I, kneeling in the dirt. Jose, Lily, and the General, the gun pressed to his head.

It was too charged, too intense. My heart pounded, my palms grew sweaty, my heart racing ahead of my thoughts. Before this was over, someone was going to die.

Finally, Mastin nodded.

Jose pushed the general forward, spinning his gun on Richard.

I gasped, hope spreading. Richard balked, stepping back, confusion flashing across his face, followed by a wave of pure fury.

"You!" he growled. "You will die for this, you traitor."

"Shut up," Jose replied, shoving the gun closer. "I'd like nothing more in this moment than to kill you."

"You'll die too," Richard snapped. He nodded toward his people who'd also raised their guns. "They'll kill you the second you pull that trigger."

"It would be my pleasure to die if it meant taking you with me," Jose growled. "Unfortunately, we made a deal to turn you over to West America alive."

Richard glared. "A deal?"

"That's right. As soon as the battle started we reached out to General Scott." He pointed toward Sasha, who had now walked over to join the group. "Sasha was able to set everything up for us and make the proper introductions. It was her idea, you know. You always did underestimate the young ones."

"You're under arrest," Scott snapped at Richard as he stood. He brushed himself off and glared triumphantly at the crowd. Sasha sidled up next to him, her arms crossed, as she sneered at Richard.

"That's right, old man. The Resistance and West America joined forces. Bet you didn't see that one coming, did you?"

Richard barked a laugh. "You're pathetic."

Sasha cocked her head. "And you're the one under arrest."

There were still plenty of guns pointed in all directions, but it was clear West America now had the upper hand. And they also had Richard right where they needed him. I met Lucas's gaze and saw a flash of peace there.

"You okay?" I whispered.

"It needed to happen," he whispered back.

"Please, if you don't surrender this very minute," Lily stepped forward, her voice as sweet as chimes blowing in the wind, "you will die. I've seen it myself."

Lily was the King's personal oracle, and he was used to taking her word as gold. His eyes flitted up to her, resignation filling them. He still didn't know she was Resistance too, though he probably had his suspicions now.

"You saw it?"

She nodded, her ethereal voice high as she continued to speak, "If you don't surrender, you won't make it off this field alive. Please, Your Highness."

He fumed, but ever so slowly, he sank to his knees, raising his hands in surrender.

"Give me those," Sasha said to one of the Royal Officers. The man handed her a pair of gleaming silver handcuffs.

Satisfied, she slapped them over the King's wrists, squeezing them as tight as possible.

NINETEEN

SASHA

During my early teenage years, whenever I'd gotten extra grumpy, Hank had always told me to count my blessings. I'd found that notion ridiculously annoying and immature. But now, I didn't think so. Here I was, rattling off blessings one by one, trying desperately to feel better. Because tonight? Oh, tonight I was extra grumpy and surrounded with blessings.

Blessing number one: my family was reunited again. Or at least, we would be soon. I was assured Jessa would be released within the hour. Lacey had been returned the moment we'd come back to our base, because what did they have to question a six-year-old for, anyway?

Blessing number two: after Mastin had found out I'd been keeping Branson's email address from the General, he'd made me turn it in. I hadn't thought much about it until the morning we'd left for battle. I had gone straight to General Scott and told him my plan. I didn't know every member of the Resistance but he was able to fill in the gaps. And it was how he'd been able to join forces with Lily and Jose, pulling off the incredible stunt that had led to Richard's capture. I found Lily's role in it particularly amusing.

Which led me to blessing number three: the capture itself. That was enough to keep me happy for the rest of my life. Richard would be behind bars for war crimes and I would never have to deal with his level of evil again. It's what all of this had been for in the first place.

So why did I still feel so angry?

I trudged across the hill overlooking the little town that had become our base, my favorite spot so far out of all the places I'd stayed since joining the West American cause. The town was quaint and secluded, the sweeping views calming. But I didn't find myself calm today. Not in the slightest.

I'd been pacing back and forth along the top of the hill for nearly an hour, thinking of all the things I was going to say to Mastin. Like, how dare he keep

Weapon X from me like that. And where did he get off allowing her to use that blasted black magic on me? It wasn't what friends did to each other, let alone what you did to someone you cared about on a deeper level.

The betrayal burned deeper than I cared to admit.

"I thought I might find you up here," his voice called out gruffly. He stalked up the hill, boots smacking against the dewy grass. He had his tough-guy attitude on but his face said it all; the man knew he was in big trouble.

The second our eyes met, my anger drained away.

And was replaced by hurt.

And sadness so much bigger than I'd expected. How could he?

I dropped my head, tears prickling. Maybe I didn't want to talk to him, after all. I wasn't ready for this.

"Look," he said, sighing, stopping in front of me. "I'm really sorry about what happened. I was ordered not to say a word to you."

I turned on him, studying him, looking for a crack in his story. He was as beautiful as ever, with his flaxen hair and striking green eyes, with his high cheekbones and perfect bow lips. None of those things pulled me in as they usually did. They were a lie, an elaborate set-up to break my heart and win his war.

"Let me ask you this," I said. "Did you fight your father on those orders?"

His face fell. "No."

Because he probably agreed with it. The betrayal multiplied, but I held it in. "And if you hadn't gotten those orders, if you'd been allowed to tell me the truth ahead of time, would you have told me about her?"

Her. The wonderful, thoughtful, spit-fire president who'd gained my trust only to turn it against me. Her. The weapon who'd come between us.

He glanced away, face grim as he took in the sunset. "Probably not," he finally relented. "You wouldn't have understood. We had to do it; it needed to be perfect. This has been a military secret for so long, we couldn't just tell anyone."

"Why the kids though?" I challenged. "That doesn't make sense to me."

"That part I was never okay with," he said. "But we never actually expected them to fight and we knew Richard's people would try to keep them for him. So that's why they were ordered as soon as we landed. The idea was that Madame President needed to subdue as much alchemy as possible. She needed to get everyone in one swoop before the surprise was lost. It was the best advantage we could think of to win this war in the long run."

I huffed, disbelieving the level of their secrecy and awed at the brilliance of their plan. Had I not stayed in their home? Shared their meals? Is this what they thought of me? I was just a flame in need of snuffing out.

"How long does it last?" I asked.

"Not forever," he said. "But…a while."

"How long?"

His eyes shot back toward mine. "Sometimes a few days, sometimes a few months. Or…years."

My jaw dropped, and for once I was speechless.

"Look, if we were going to win this war, we needed to take alchemy out of the equation."

That was so backwards from everything I believed! I'd been fighting for alchemist rights from day one and he knew it. "And what else can you tell me about black alchemy?"

"That's classified," he said, visibly shutting down, mouth flattening to a thin line and eyes growing vague.

I struck out, shoving him in the chest and pushing him to the ground. He didn't fight me. "Just tell me!" I shouted. I had wanted to punch him before, and now that feeling was back ten-fold!

"We've had her for a while, okay? Why do you think we didn't really need alchemist prisons before we got out here? There was no need for all that gray nonsense when we had *her*."

I stomped my foot and stalked across the hill for a minute, catching my breath and glaring out at the happy fuchsia sky. Then I hiked back, plopping down on the ground beside him. So many emotions spun within that I was dizzy with them. I couldn't keep up. My fingers dug into the grass.

"I still can't believe you did that to me," I said, defeated.

"I'm sorry," he whispered. "It was the only way. I did it for your own good. I did it because I care about you and I want you to be safe."

He didn't get it, but there was nothing I could do. What was done was done.

"We have to break up," he said, tormented. I glowered back. "I mean, if we're even together, if that's what you think we are, we can't be *that* anymore."

"After everything you did behind my back, you have the nerve to break up with me? Oh, no, buddy." I laughed, my own voice bitter in my mouth. "It's the other way around. I'm breaking up with you. And also, we weren't ever officially anything. So whatever."

He winced. "I'm not breaking up with you because of what happened out there. I'm breaking up with you because you're in love with Tristan."

I stilled, blood rushing to my cheeks.

He sighed and laid back on his elbows, gazing up into the darkening sky. "I always knew it, but I thought maybe you could get over him once we were together. Clearly, that never happened."

I chewed my lip, wanting to disagree. I couldn't. I'd said it to myself a thousand times, hadn't I? Tristan was home. What was love, if not that?

He sat up. "Truth time. You need to stop lying to yourself about Tristan. What you and I have, or had, it was special too. Don't get me wrong. But I think it was physical attraction more than anything else. And with the war, we never really could get it off the ground. You and Tristan however…" He trailed off. "Are you really going to make me do this?"

I frowned at him. The words wouldn't come to my lips, they were caught in my throat with all the emotions. I dropped my head into my hands, breathing in the smell of grass and sunset and life-changing realizations.

"There's love between you two," he relented, "Real love. I don't know what all of it means or if it's physical, or attraction, or really just an incredible friendship. But it's more than we ever had and there's no use in competing with it anymore."

"You're chatty all of a sudden," I sighed. "I don't think I've ever heard so many words come out of you before tonight."

He was right. I knew it. But I wasn't ready to do anything about it.

I stood, brushing off my pants. "Good luck with your life, Mastin," I said, the anger lost from my voice. "I mean it."

I did want him to have a good life, even if I was no longer willing to be a part of it. I turned away and walked down the hill.

Mastin was a soldier, through and through. His first love, his only love, it wasn't me. It never had been. It had always been war, the strategy, the thrill of the fight and impressing his General of a father. And he'd gotten his dream, after all.

But Tristan? What did he love?

Me.

And it went both ways. He was my comfort. I loved him, too, more than I could ever put into words. But did that mean Tristan and I were suddenly supposed to fall into each other's arms and ride off into that stupid pink sunset?

I wasn't ready for that.

I needed to lick my wounds.

Because the truth was, Mastin had hurt me. Deeply. What he'd done had stung more than I cared to admit. I wasn't sure how long it would take to heal that. And what if, in the end, Tristan did the same thing?

I couldn't take that kind of pain. Not when it came to him.

Besides, Tristan deserved better than to heal my wounds, the way he always did. He deserved better than to be a rebound or second choice. Maybe one day it would be him and I together, but for now, we needed to stay friends.

Best friends.

So why did that thought make me cry?

I wiped away the tears, growling at myself. I would focus on lobbying for alchemists' rights. With Richard and Lucas in custody, there was about to be a lot of change for everyone, and I wanted nothing but positive change for my people. That was more important than a boyfriend. My heart could wait.

I strode toward the small town hall building, more determined than I'd ever been. Inside, General Scott was meeting with his advisors and the president. After the stunt these people had pulled today, after what they'd done to alchemists—my alchemists—security had better let me in. West America had better be prepared to give in to my demands.

I wasn't in the mood to negotiate.

★

I strode into the building with all the confidence I could muster, every step echoing determination. Holding tight to the knowledge that if I wasn't going to stand up for alchemists, maybe nobody was, kept me moving forward.

I never expected to be let right in, but I was.

I glanced around, hungrily seeking out someone important to yell at, or I don't know, something…

"They're just through here," one of the stoic soliders said, pointing to a set of closed doors. "They're expecting you."

"Oh-kay," I said, drawing it out.

I straightened my rumpled black outfit and ran my fingers through my limp hair, then took a deep breath and opened the door. The room fell into silence, everyone turning in my direction.

"There she is," the president's calm voice sparked through the space. "I've been wanting to talk to you, specifically, Sasha."

I raised an eyebrow, because if that were the case, why wait until now? Taking a deep breath, I considered the room. We were in some kind of city office building, with thick maroon carpet, wood trim, and cream walls. This room had a large round table in the middle, with leather chairs and couches strategically placed throughout. Everyone sat around the table, the seating giving the appearance of equal footing. But given who was here, equality probably wasn't first on their minds.

Next to the president sat General Scott, and next to him another man, the one from my time on the base out West. The guy who'd wanted to make the children go to war. I glared at him. The sicko had gotten his way, after all.

Beside him were a few faces I didn't recognize. I scanned the group, coming around the other side of the table until I found Hank and Tristan, and next to him was that Royal Officer, Jose. A woman smiled up at him, the purple alchemist teacher, Lily. And then my eyes landed on Jessa.

And Prince Lucas.

And a very perturbed-looking King Richard!

I doubled back.

"What in the blazes is *he* doing here?" The question fell from my mouth. "He should be locked up!"

"Have a seat." The president motioned to the empty chair in front of me.

Okay, this was beyond weird. But I kept my mouth shut and sat down in the closest chair, which happened to be on the other side of my sister. There wasn't a mess of papers littering the table, maps on the walls, or anything about this meeting that resembled the many I'd attended over the last couple of months. The war was over. Richard surrendered. West America should be making their demands, and maybe that's what this was about.

"I always thought if we could all just sit down and have a conversation together, we could talk this whole mess out and nobody would have to die," the president said, eyes running across the group and landing firmly on Richard. "Of course, that is assuming we are all reasonable people. After everything I've seen over the last few months, I know now that's not the case."

Richard glared. "After what your people did to my alchemists, I would hardly call you reasonable, either."

The president paused, her expression soft. "In any event, blood has been spilled, and we need to talk about what's next."

As Richard leaned forward, I noticed that his arms and legs were restrained in his chair. The sight of him this way sent a thrill down my body. Everything I'd been through had been worth it to get to see this.

"Death is a necessary evil of war," he spat.

General Scott's face turned red and he glowered. "A war that you started for no good reason!"

Richard growled. "You sent someone to kill my wife."

"Father, you know that isn't true," Lucas interjected.

Richard rounded on his son. "How dare you interrupt me!"

The president cleared her throat. "That's enough of that. It's time we talk about what's next."

Richard's laugh was crazed, the result of the world's most egotistical man not getting his way. Or maybe it was something more delusional. "Like you aren't going to execute my family the second this farce is over? I'd rather not play games with the likes of you."

She raised her eyebrows and the white bob framing her diplomatic face twitched with a hint of annoyance. "If it comes to that, have no doubt, we will execute you. The way I see it, Richard Heart, you now have two choices. You can die by lethal injection, or you can live in one of our maximum security prisons, that is assuming you'll even cooperate with me, which would be a requirement to your survival."

"I'd rather die," he spat out.

"Can't say I didn't try." She peered at Lucas. "And what of you? Are you going to join your father?"

"Lucas had nothing to do with this!" Richard ground out. "He is innocent."

"It's true," Jessa's small voice squeaked. Steeling her shoulders, she looked at each person in the room, courage growing. "He's only ever tried to do the right thing. He's a good man."

"He's an alchemist," the other General interrupted.

"What?" Richard sputtered, "That's a lie!"

"It's true," Lucas relented, sinking down into his chair. "I hardly use magic and have kept it a secret for years."

Richard turned on his son with a look like he was seeing him for the first time. Perhaps he was.

"But why?" Richard asked, voice cracking in a way I'd never heard out of him. The two stared at each other for a long moment, the weight of truth and lies too much for their already tumultuous relationship.

Lucas took a deep breath and explained, "I grew up hearing the way you talked about alchemists when they weren't around, how you and Mom thought it was unnatural. So I learned how to hide what I was from a young age and always kept it that way."

"I didn't know." Richard's voice was low, tormented. "If I had known, it would have changed everything."

Lucas sighed. "No, I don't think it would have."

Richard's nostrils flared, anger sparking in his cold eyes. I thought back to everything he'd done, knowing deep in my gut that Lucas was right.

"While this little confession session is fun and all," I piped in, "I can also attest to Lucas's true loyalties. He saved me on more than one occasion. He helped the Resistance when he believed we were doing good, but he didn't when he thought we weren't acting in his kingdom's best interest. I can truly say, having known him since he first aligned with the Resistance, he shouldn't be punished for his father's crimes. He is nothing like Richard. He's a *good* man."

As I spoke, Richard's silver eyes became dark holes, glaring openly at his son. But he didn't say another word.

"Well then," Madame President said, leaning back in her chair, "where do we go from here? What's next?"

"Once the magic is returned to the alchemists, we can heal as much as possible and reestablish the borders," Lucas supplied, breaking his father's eye-contact and letting his shoulders relax.

Nathan Scott laughed. "And just pretend this never happened? I say we take over New Colony and ensure this never happens again."

"I agree!" the other general added sharply.

The president shook her head, calm as ever. "Let's not get too greedy. We don't want to become like our enemy, do we?"

Richard sneered.

"I believe I can heal the land," Jessa's voice rang out, excitement growing in her tone as she leaned forward in her seat. Her curly, dark hair glowed under the florescent light. "And I even think I can help your people who had their minds turned in support of New Colony."

I whirled on her. This must have something to do with Lucas being alive. I still hadn't gotten to ask Jessa about it, but one thing I did know: Lucas had been dead. Something miraculous happened in that room, and I had to know what it was.

"Explain," Madame President instructed, curiosity burning in her intelligent eyes.

Jessa gulped. "Well, it turns out I have this *other* power, this ability to separate colors. I discovered that it's restoration magic," she said. "I can turn back the effects of other magic with it. And umm…I saved Lucas's life with it."

My eyes grew huge. "It's true," I attested, everything clicking into place. "He was dead. I was there. And then the next time I saw him, he was alive and well."

Well was relatively speaking, of course. Technically, the next time I saw him we were all attacked by the President's black alchemy, but something told me to bring those questions up later.

Jessa beamed, shooting a look of pure adoration at Lucas. "I figured it out just in time!"

Madame President nodded. "There will still be retributions to be paid to our country, but I think for now, Lucas and his bride should return to the throne in exchange for your help restoring our land and people, paying for all damages rendered, and signing a border agreement so this doesn't happen again."

Jessa nodded eagerly.

A cacophony of voices rang out, some angry, some pleased, and everyone deciding now was time to state their differing opinion. Tristan caught my eye from across the table and winked. I smiled back, warming at his gaze. Maybe everything was going to be okay after all.

"What about the alchemists?" Tristan's steady voice rose over the arguments and everyone quieted, listening.

"What about them?" the other general in the room snapped back.

"I think they should have rights, too," he said confidently, his voice smooth and commanding. "They've also been victims in this, maybe more than anyone."

The silence stretched between the group.

"And from both sides," he added.

"What do you propose?" the president asked.

"Don't ask me." He shrugged. "Isn't that why she's here?" He pointed to me.

I sat up taller in my chair. "Yes, ever since alchemists were discovered, we've been treated as heathens and criminals, or we've been used to serve other people's interests, and not always the good people."

My eyes darted to Richard and narrowed.

"I propose all alchemists be properly trained, given a code of ethics to live by, and given the freedom to choose their own paths in life. If some of them would like to serve the royal family or their country, then so be it. But they shouldn't be forced into servitude, nor should they be unfairly imprisoned."

A few people shifted uncomfortably.

"It should be illegal to harm them without cause." My fingers stabbed at the tabletop, adrenaline kicking in. "And if they break the laws, they should be treated just like anyone else and given a fair trial. At the end of the day, alchemists are as human as anybody else, and so they should be treated as such. With dignity and respect, with rights and equality, and as assets to our society."

The president beamed. "I whole-heartedly agree."

Pride swelled, and I smiled so wide that I could feel it in my entire face.

"And since my election, I've found most of my people agree, as well. Change is in the air, for all of us. It may take lifetimes to end the bigotry. As long as we have differences, there will be people who twist those differences into justifications for hate and greed. But that doesn't mean we'll ever give up on fostering what really matters." She paused. "And that's love."

A huge weight lifted off me and for the first time in my life, a sense of hope bloomed square in my chest that maybe I would actually get to taste true freedom. Maybe with someone like her in world leadership and Richard behind bars, I would get to live life on my terms. I could find myself instead of always looking out for everybody else.

"That's preposterous," Richard spat. "What a waste of resources. Alchemy has its place in serving King and country."

Everyone glared at him but he held himself strong.

"Why else would God create magic, if not to use it to strengthen those in power?"

"You will be quiet," General Scott snapped. "You've had your say. Don't forget, your time in power is over."

We discussed everything for a little while longer until it became clear that Richard wasn't going to stop interrupting. He hated everything, literally everything, proposed. Of course he did. He was a narcissist who hadn't gotten his way.

Finally, the president had had enough.

"All right, get him out of here," she called to the soldiers standing on the back wall.

Four of them ambled forward, carefully unlatching him from where he was restrained in the chair, though he still had shackles and was cuffed. He began to move from the room, chains clinking, hatred rolling off him.

Then he dove.

Not toward the president.

Not toward his son or anybody else.

But toward Jessa.

"This is your fault!" he yelled, voice dripping in venom. "You turned my son against me. Did you use red to do it?" He was quick, wrapping the cuffs around her neck and yanking hard. Her eyes welled, blood pooling.

A brief pause was followed by an explosion of action.

"Don't touch her!" Lucas jumped on his father, clawing at the man's arms. Others charged, grabbing. I went for Jessa, trying to pry her loose. But the man had just the right angle and just the right madness to keep his hold on Jessa. Her eyes rolled back into her head, her body slumping. He sneered, pulling even tighter, resilient to our attempts to rip him away.

"You're going to kill her!" I screamed, my voice joining everybody else's, lost in the panic of the moment. Fear and anger doubled with the knowledge that I was weak without my magic.

"You're pathetic!" Richard screamed. "All of you." But his eyes were zeroed in on Lucas. He spat in his son's face.

"Drop her now, or you will die," General Scott said, gun clicking into place and trained on the back of Richard's head.

"As long as she dies with me," Richard replied, yanking infinitely harder on the cuffs choking Jessa.

She wasn't going to make it. Lucas jumped up, pushing away from his father and yelling at Scott, "Do it!"

Scott hesitated as he looked at Lucas. The two men shared a quick look of understanding.

"If you don't do it," Lucas continued. "Give it to me and I'll do it."

Everything in his voice was smooth resolve. He meant every word.

Boom!

The bullet blasted through Richard's head, blood and tissue flying, his body slumping, cuffs relaxing instantly. Blood pooled and I choked back a mix of horror and relief, hardly believing the truth of what had just happened.

King Richard was dead.

The room fell to silence once again. Finally, General Scott spoke to Lucas, "Nobody should have to kill their own father, but you're a brave man for being willing to do what had to be done. I'm glad it was me; you don't deserve to live with this on your shoulders."

Lucas nodded once, his face devoid of color, his eyes hazy.

"Let me see her." I pried Jessa's limp body from Richard's dead grip, smoothing her hair and searching her swollen face for signs of life. I needed to heal her. I needed green. A little green was all it would take.

Realization sunk me to my knees.

I didn't have magic anymore—it hadn't returned.

None of us had it back *yet*.

"How long?" I growled at the president. "How long until the magic is back?"

She stood at the head of the table, hands pressed into the wood, staring down at us with a broken expression. "Months."

The room quieted, everyone watching as Lucas pulled Jessa from my lap into his own. He kissed her face, tears dropping from his eyes. She was still, limp as a doll, her hair awkwardly strewn across her face, Richard's blood splattered across one cheek.

"Please," he whispered. "Now it's your turn to come back."

Time slowed. Ever so slightly, her chest rose, her lips parted, and then suddenly, she inhaled a gasping breath.

Her eyes fluttered open, arms flailing toward her neck, and she coughed, choking for a long minute.

"Am I alive?" she asked between coughs, blood-red eyes blinking in rapid succession as she looked up at her husband.

Lucas laughed once. "Yes." He kissed her on the forehead. "Yes, we're both alive. Everything is going to be okay."

EPILOGUE

EIGHTEEN MONTHS LATER - LUCAS

I love watching her dance. Quite honestly, it's one of my favorite pastimes. The way she moves, it makes me forget myself and remember at the same time. Of all her magics, this one is my favorite.

"I wish I had passion like that," I say, pushing myself off the wall of the private dressing room and wrapping her in a tight hug. I bury my face in her warm neck and inhale her floral scent.

"Ew! I'm all sweaty." She laughs, but lets me hold her anyway. "It's the nerves. I don't know why I'm so worried."

"You look perfect," I say, because it's the truth, but also because I don't want her to be afraid. In her white flowery costume, she reminds me of how she looked on our wedding day, and that is a look I'll never forget again. "You're going to be amazing out there."

"Thanks." She smiles, excitement flashing in her eyes.

She's been preparing for this performance for months, adding extra practice time on top of the rehearsals at the theatre. Her private studio back at the palace has quickly become her favorite place, of which I take full advantage— always popping in to say hi, maybe sneaking in a kiss if I'm lucky, but mostly I watch her in her element.

"Actually, on second thought," I muse, "I do think I have your kind of passion about one thing."

She peers up at me from under long, fake lashes, nodding. They make her blue eyes stand out more than usual and I lose my breath. "Rebuilding the kingdom," she says.

I shake my head. "Well, that too, I guess. But I'm talking about you."

And I mean it. I thought losing my parents would break me, and while I was still sad about everything that happened to them, I found solace in my marriage. Jessa had helped to make me a better man and a better leader. I was starting to believe I was growing into the kind of king I always wanted to be. A king who put his people first, no matter their station, and no matter their utility.

One of the first things I did was create a parliament system where the people could vote in representatives, and those representatives help me run things. I saw too much of my father in myself that year when everything went down. I hurt innocent people. It wasn't something I could risk again. Our royal family had ruled New Colony for generations, but what had once been an idealistic leadership had turned into a greedy dictatorship. I feared if I was the sole person in charge, I might one day turn into that, too.

Never again.

Jessa trembles under my touch. Her mind is racing.

"What are you thinking about? Are you still feeling nervous?"

"Yeah, a little."

I kiss the top of her head. "Don't be. I have a surprise for you after the performance. So don't be nervous. Be excited. You're going to look back on this night with only fondness."

Little does she know I've flown her older sister in for the performance. They haven't seen each other in over six months.

And okay, the fondness line is cheesy, but it instantly calms her.

She gives me a quick kiss and then breaks free of my arms, moving back to double check her makeup in the mirror. "If it's a surprise from you, then I'm sure I will love it."

A knock sounds on the door. "Sir, it's time to take your seat."

I wish Jessa good luck one last time and then find my place in the crowd. I won't be sitting up in a box like my family had done all those years. No, I'm in a plush velvet seat, front row center. A jolt of my own nerves rips through me. Not because I think anything might go wrong, but because I know how much this means to Jessa.

She'd given up dance for most of the last eighteen months. We had to focus on rebuilding, and dance had taken the backseat. We started with the government. West America followed through with their promise to change laws and enough states voted to add a constitutional amendment ensuring alchemists' rights. There is still a heavy prejudice against magic that runs deep, but for now, things are improving, people are beginning to accept it as part of the world.

Unwinding what happened in the Shadow Lands and freeing the minds of those harmed in Nashville was a painstakingly long and brutal process, but we finally finished the job two months ago. It didn't help that the effects of black alchemy took most alchemists months to wear off. Jessa hadn't gotten her magic back for seven months. Mine had taken a full year.

"There he is!" Christopher, Jessa's dad, walks down the space between the row and the orchestra pit, arms outstretched in greeting. "How are you doing, son?"

I jump up to offer him, Lara, and Lacey tight hugs. Christopher has taken to calling me son, and I can't say I mind. They all look great, smiles beaming from ear to ear. Both of her parents look much younger than I've ever seen them before, the lines around their eyes less pronounced, their skin warmer, eyes brighter. But it's the peace that has settled over them that makes the biggest difference. The family is dressed in their best outfits, matching in bright blue dress clothes. The color reminds me of Jessa. Lacey skips and twirls, taking in the beautiful theatre with adoring, round eyes.

"Where's your other daughter?" I ask, looking over the crowd, trying to spot that telltale blonde hair among the sea of people.

"Thank you for flying her out." Christopher pats me on the back. "They've been traveling all day. She just called and said they're in the city. They should be here any minute."

I relax down into my padded seat, glad Jessa would get to spend time with her whole family over the next few days. Sasha, who we now call Frankie, has changed the most over the last eighteen months since the war ended. Or maybe it's not that she ever really changed, but just remembered who she was in the first place. If anyone can understand that, it's me.

About a year ago, she officially dropped her alias Sasha, happily returning to Francesca, the name her parents had chosen for her. And she hasn't come back to New Colony, except to visit family. She's chosen to spend her time working with the alchemists in America instead.

I still think of it as West America. But that was another thing that has changed. I created a campaign to right any misinformation about our kingdom's history, not to mention, the state of the world. It was never West America; it was always just called America. We need to stand by the truth, not propaganda.

"Hi, there! How's my favorite brother-in-law, doing?" Frankie plops down into the empty chair on my left, giving me a strong side-hug. Her blonde hair is pulled up into a sleek knot on top of her head and she's wearing her signature cut and color—a black form-fitting dress.

"I'm your only brother-in-law," I deadpan.

"And you're still my favorite," she teases.

"I'm doing well," I say, giving her my full attention. She has a relaxed air about her tonight, something I haven't seen in her. Ever. "And how are you?" I question with a raised eyebrow.

"I'm good. We're good." She motions to Tristan beside her. The two are inseparable, so I'm not surprised to see him here.

I say hello to him and he to me.

I have really grown to respect the man. Apparently, he and Frankie have been best friends for years. She credits him for saving her from my father the first time, when she was still a kid. Jessa keeps hoping they will get together and make it official, but they never do. As I watch them together now, I wonder if they are only putting off the inevitable, or if it simply isn't meant to be.

"How are things in America?" I ask.

She sighs, a small smile playing on her lips. "Better than ever."

"Do tell."

"Well, you know how the president is also the infamous black alchemist? She's been able to change some of the prejudices against her by agreeing to subdue powers for any alchemist who wants it, but they have to be at least sixteen to legally make that choice. And our training has been going better than I ever thought it would. Taking away the magic from everyone during the battle meant that it slowly returned. That ended up being a blessing in disguise."

"How so?" I question, interest piqued. Maybe the American President can make the same offer to our people. I would hate to see people give up their alchemy, but I also want them to have choices.

"Well, if you think about how hard it is to train someone, imagine how much it helps not to have brand new people who were too powerful for their own good."

My mind flashes to Jessa's first few months at the palace. I laugh to myself as I think of how she'd accidently knocked me out the first time we met. If only I had known then just how much everything was about to change, maybe I wouldn't have made so many mistakes along the way.

"It was almost as if we got to teach them from the ground up."

"And you're okay with some of them choosing out of magic?"

She nods. "Absolutely. I would never do it, and I don't advise it. I think we should accept and embrace who we are. All of us, alchemist or not. But I also believe in choice. This gives them a choice. I've learned that some people truly don't want magic. Who am I to judge that?"

"It makes perfect sense to me."

My mind settles. I'll reach out to the President first thing in the morning and find a way to get this offer available for our alchemists, even if I have to fly them out to America myself. Since I've made our own Guardians of Color optional and children are no longer being taken from their homes, there might be people who want this kind of option. As things stand right now, the GC is still housed at the palace, and people can board there if they desire. We also relocate families to the capitol and help them get new jobs so that their children can attend classes during the day at the palace, and be home in time for dinner.

It is still illegal to hide alchemy. Everyone has to train since it's far too dangerous to keep magic inside. But no one is forced into servitude anymore.

And as for those whose alliances are still unclear, those people like Reed, Jax, and the Addington family, they're on strict probation. They know that at the first sign of trouble, they'll be questioned and likely arrested. So far, they're laying low. With things working out so well for the kingdom, I expect it to stay that way, but I'm prepared for action just in case.

I lean over to Tristan and point. "Are you keeping this one in line?"

He grins, his white teeth flashing. "It's the other way around."

"Yeah, right," Frankie laughs. "You've always been the level-headed one."

She reaches out and wraps her fingers in his, bringing his hand up and pressing a quick kiss to his palm. The intimacy of the move is anything but innocent.

From several seats down, Frankie's mother pops up, eyes wide and hands clapping as she squeals. That woman doesn't miss a thing.

"Are you two finally together?" she gushes, climbing over legs and reaching out to quickly hug them both. She pulls away and watches them with anticipation. I imagine if Jessa was here right now, her reaction would be the same.

The two share a sheepish look and then Frankie nods.

"I can't keep her away from me," Tristan teases.

Frankie slaps him in the arm. "Oh, shut up. You know you love me."

"I really do." He meets her eyes and the air between them grows as thick as the magnitude of that four-letter word.

The rest of us share looks of *I told you so* and *it's about time*. Lacey bursts out laughing, a rosy blush spreading across her round face as she stares at her oldest sister. As Lacey grows older, she resembles Frankie more and more.

The two lovers break their gaze, smiling at all of us.

"Well, Jessa will be happy about this development," I say. "She's been rooting for this ever since the war ended."

"We're really happy for you," Christopher adds.

"Does this mean you're going to get married, too?" Lacey comes to stand next to her mom. "Can I be the flower girl?"

Frankie's expression turns guarded.

Tristan just smirks, onyx eyes twinkling. "Absolutely."

"I mean, it probably won't be for a while, we just started dating," Frankie interjects, voice growing weak. "I'm barely twenty-two."

"But I'm an old man!" Tristan laughs, speaking directly to Lacey. "Don't worry. We're going to get married. I just have to convince her to say yes."

Frankie elbows him in the side. "Tristan!"

He laughs. "I'll wear her down eventually." He winks at Lacey. "You'll be dressing up for a wedding before you know it."

Lacey bounces back down into her seat and Frankie stares off into the distance, positively beaming.

Oh yes, these two are definitely in love.

The lights dim and everyone hurries to their velvety seats. The chatter falls away and the room surges with promise, the faint scent of perfume and floor polish wafting through the darkness.

The nervous excitement I felt before returns as the curtains lift. In the center of the stage, Jessa stands, eyes closed, arms outstretched, body elegantly tall with one foot pointed to the side. Blue light surrounds her, as do the other dancers. They are dressed in a rainbow of color and she is the white goddess in the center.

The orchestra music swells and she begins to move. The dancers are all incredible, but I only have eyes for her. Her every movement is perfect.

She spins over to a dancer dressed in deep navy blue and touches her gently, pulling the color from the costume and tossing it into the air. Then she prances to the other end of the stage and does the same with a woman in red. The colors swirl above them, a shimmering dance of light and magic.

And so, the dance continues.

I think back to the first time I ever saw Jessa. She was on this same stage but things were so different back then. She didn't know how to control her magic, was living in secrecy with her fears hidden inside. The accidental show of the purple alchemy that night started her on a path that would go on to change everything.

For the both of us.

And now she has come full circle.

Once again, here she is, dancing center stage where she belongs. And once again, she's using her innate talent and powerful alchemy to bring all of us in the audience to our knees. But this time is different. This time, as the magic grows around her, as the colors swirl and move, the radiant smile awash on her face is here to stay. I've never seen anything so beautiful.

THE END

ABOUT

NINA WALKER lives in Utah with her family, where she spends her time reading, writing, and helping women prioritize their health in online support groups. She also has a mild obsession with Instragram Stories.

Connect with Nina:

Facebook at fb.com/ninawalkerbooks
Instagram @ninabelievesinmagic

www.ninawalkerbooks.com